NEW YORK REVIEW BOOKS
CLASSICS

ANNIVERSARIES

UWE JOHNSON (1934–1984) grew up in the small town of Anklam
in the German state of Mecklenburg-Vorpommern. At the end of World
War II, his father, who had joined the Nazi Party in 1940, disappeared
into a Soviet camp; he was declared dead in 1948. Johnson and his mother
remained in Communist East Germany until his mother left for the
West in 1956, after which Johnson was barred from regular employment.
In 1959, shortly before the publication of his first novel, *Speculations
About Jakob*, in West Germany, he emigrated to West Berlin by streetcar,
leaving the East behind for good. Other novels, *The Third Book About
Achim*, *An Absence*, and *Two Views*, followed in quick succession. A
member of the legendary Gruppe 47, Johnson lived from 1966 until
1968 with his wife and daughter in New York, compiling a high-school
anthology of postwar German literature. On Tuesday, April 18, 1967,
at 5:30 p.m., as he later recounted the story, he saw Gesine Cresspahl,
a character from his earlier works, walking on the south side of Forty-
Second Street from Fifth to Sixth Avenue alongside Bryant Park; he
asked what she was doing in New York and eventually convinced her
to let him write his next novel about a year in her life. *Anniversaries* was
published in four installments—in 1970, 1971, 1973, and 1983—and was
quickly recognized in Germany as one of the great novels of the century.
In 1974, Johnson left Germany for the isolation of Sheerness-on-Sea,
England, where he struggled through health and personal problems to
finish his magnum opus. He died at age forty-nine, shortly after it was
published.

DAMION SEARLS grew up on Riverside Drive in New York City,
three blocks away from Gesine Cresspahl's apartment. He is the author
of three books and has translated more than thirty, including six for
NYRB Classics.

ANNIVERSARIES

From a Year in the Life of Gesine Cresspahl

Volume Two

UWE JOHNSON

Translated from the German by
DAMION SEARLS

NEW YORK REVIEW BOOKS

New York

THIS IS A NEW YORK REVIEW BOOK
PUBLISHED BY THE NEW YORK REVIEW OF BOOKS
435 Hudson Street, New York, NY 10014
www.nyrb.com

The translation of this work was supported by a grant from Goethe-Institut using funds provided by the German Ministry of Foreign Affairs. It was made possible in part by the New York State Council on the Arts with the support of Governor Andrew Cuomo and the New York State Legislature.

The translator and publisher wish to thank the John Simon Guggenheim Foundation, the Dorothy and Lewis B. Cullman Center for Scholars and Writers at the New York Public Library, and the Uwe Johnson Society's Peter Suhrkamp Stipend for their generous support.

Library of Congress Cataloging-in-Publication Data
Names: Johnson, Uwe, 1934–1984 author. | Searls, Damion translator.
Title: Anniversaries : from a year in the life of Gesine Cresspahl / by Uwe
  Johnson ; translated by Damion Searls.
Other titles: Jahrestage. English
Description: New York : New York Review Books, 2018. | Series: New York
  Review Books classics
Identifiers: LCCN 2018010220 (print) | LCCN 2018012166 (ebook) | ISBN
  9781681372044 (epub) | ISBN 9781681372037 (alk. paper)
Classification: LCC PT2670.O36 (ebook) | LCC PT2670.O36 J313 2018 (print)
  | DDC 833/.914—dc23
LC record available at https://lccn.loc.gov/2018010220

ISBN 978-1-68137-203-7 (boxed set)
Available as an electronic book; ISBN 978-1-68137-204-4

Printed in the United States of America on acid-free paper.
10 9 8 7 6 5 4 3 2 1

CONTENTS

PART THREE · 879
April 1968–June 1968

PART FOUR · 1205
June 1968–August 1968

PART THREE
April 1968–June 1968

THE WATER is black.

The overcast sky hangs low over the lake ringed in morning pinewood shadow, darkness rising from the muddy ground. The swimmer's hands push forward as if through heavy dye but are shockingly pure when they come up into the air. The shores are close on all sides; in the dim dawn an observer would think he saw two ducks moving in the middle of the lake, one with dark feathers, one light. But it's too early for anyone. The silence makes the lake gloomy. The fish, the water birds, the land birds don't want to live in this dredged-out basin, these stunted trees, this chemically treated landscape set up for paying customers. Sink two feet under the stagnant surface and you'll lose the light in a greenish blackness.

– How many lakes have you done in your life, Gesine?: says the child, says Marie, says the strange fish poking her head up after a long plunge. – This is your how-many-eth lake?: she says in her strange German.

Two voices above the water, in the murky silence—one an eleven-year-old soprano, cracked around the edges, the other a thirty-five-year-old alto, smoothly rounded, not especially big. The child doesn't let the Baltic Sea count.

It was there, in the Ostsee, that the child I was first swam: off Fischland in the Lübeck Bay near the maritime boundary of Mecklenburg, formerly a province of the German Reich, now a coastal region of the Socialist state of the German nation. I swam with children who are dead now, and with soldiers of the defeated German navy who called the great mighty Baltic "the flooded field of the seven seas." But in American geography books the Ostsee is called the Baltic Sea, and Marie says it doesn't count. It's not a lake. She's an American child.

How many lakes has her mother swum, taken in, racked up. What's the number.

Here in America, where people are starved for restrained, attentive, and well-behaved children, they call her a European child. Marie stood politely at the edge of the lake, still misty with the dawn, and patiently followed her into the bone-chilling water—Marie's mother, her partner for better or for worse ever since she was born, not yet dispensable. And she acts properly, as she's learned to from the nuns who teach at her school, carrying on a conversation during the swim. Much as she'd prefer to go underwater, she keeps her head up and tries for an interested expression on her determined, shiny wet face.

How many lakes in thirty-five years?

Gneez Lake: Fritz Reuter High School gym class after the war; the public beach on the Gneez side, where Gesine Cresspahl the child was supposed to be training for competitions. Gneez Lake again, again with others, on the south side, the kids' swimming hole in tenth grade, class A-2, eleventh grade A-1, twelfth grade A-1. At home, in the military facility's pool, forgotten by the German Air Force and the Red Army, with Lise Wollenberg, Inge Heitmann, and the boy from the Jerichow pharmacy. Never in Dassow Lake, less than eight miles from my father's back door and utterly inaccessible, its shore being the line of demarcation, the national border—the water was in the British zone, the Federal Republic of Germany, the West. With Pius Pagenkopf: in Cramon Lake, between Drieberg and Cramon, an hour's bike ride from the town where I went to school, in 1951. Alone, from Jerichow in northwest Mecklenburg to Wendisch Burg in southeast Mecklenburg: in Schwerin Lake to the island of Lieps, in Goldberg Lake, in Lake Plau, in Lake Müritz. With Klaus Niebuhr, Günter Niebuhr, Ingrid Babendererde, and Eva Mau in all seven lakes around Wendisch Burg, until 1952. In Leipzig, in Halle: lifesaving courses in indoor pools, through May 1953. The last time in Gneez Lake: end of May 1953, and Jakob held my impaled foot high off the ground like I was a young horse and the way he moved it sent a shiver up through my body with no pain at all.

Never with Jakob. Jakob would still be working in Cresspahl's house, in the villages, when we left Jerichow in the evening for six laps in the Mili, the military swimming facility that we all stubbornly called the Mili (Mariengabe air base now had a new name too: it would never be known as anything but Jerichow-North). Jakob left town to work for the railroad; a photograph was taken of him once on the Pastor's Pond ferry, in Schwerin (in the company of Sabine Beedejahn, Prot., twenty-four, married). Jakob used to go lake fishing with friends, coming back from the Mecklenburg lakes with buckets of live crabs, and I didn't know those lakes, and he went without me, with fishermen, with girls, with work friends, and I hardly knew him.

After leaving behind the East German authorities: almost every day for two weeks with Anita in Wannsee, West Berlin, as far as you could get from the border. In West Germany: public pools in Frankfurt, Düsseldorf, Krefeld, Düren. In Geneva. In America: Lake Winnipesaukee, Lake Chippewa, Lake Travis, Lake Hopatcong. Again with Anita in the Vosges, in France.

– Eighteen valid, four don't count, one unclear, and bonus for Lake Travis, Texas!: Marie says.

But the landing is now just a quarter mile away, and she immediately puts her head sideways into the water, so sure is she that the challenge to a race has been understood and accepted, and after kicking underwater for a long time she comes up into a crawl, strokes sharp and precise and almost silent. She wants to get back to the borrowed expensive house, all glass and mahogany beams, where there's a phone and news on TV and possibly *The New York Times* from the village store, and soon, as early as tomorrow afternoon, the return home to Manhattan, New York City, Riverside Drive and Broadway, the corner of Ninety-Sixth Street.

This lake is called Patton Lake, named in honorable memory of a general from this country. Here heavy tanks practiced until 1944 for the last assault on Germany, until the thick old trees were stumps and the ground so churned up by caterpillar treads that the area had to be turned into an artificial lake, with trees having nowhere else to go and high yields from vacation rentals. From here came the Sherman tanks that measured out the market squares of Mecklenburg, too.

– *And you came swimming all the way from Mecklenburg!*

Marie has been standing on the deck for a while; hand on heart she salutes the flag that's raised to honor the victor in stadiums, then welcomes the loser swimming up beneath her. She speaks the words with delight, because she can assume a teasing tone, and from the heart, because at last she has a chance to say something in English, the language of her own country, not the German she speaks so clumsily now.

Vacation in the country. Somewhere in upstate New York, but no more than three hours' drive from the city, and on the long leash of the telephone line the bank can tug at will to summon Employee Cresspahl back to work from her two-day break.

– I did, I swam the whole way here from Mecklenburg: I say in German.
– *And did the nineteenth lake in your life!*: Marie says in English.

Lots of heavy black Patton water for the afternoon.

April 21, 1968 Sunday

Vacation in the country. This time it's a chore for Marie.
– You need your *New York Times*: she said the moment we were out of the water, thereby claiming the right to the mile's walk to the country store, the right to alone time in the woods. Our borrowed summer house was a model home, full of not only Finnish furniture but all the latest gadgets; in the afternoon Marie left again, for the two lemons we could have managed dinner without. There was still a long time before we had to go back but she'd packed up the car already, then she had something else to do outside, for a map of the area she was making as a gift for the owner. She announced her walks as if suggesting them; she took on the shopping duties voluntarily; she always found a way to get out; she wanted to be alone, once in a while.

For almost eleven years we've had only each other to depend on, and she's struggled to build her defenses. In 1957, for twenty-four-year-old Gesine Cresspahl, baby Marie had been part of her—for a long time Marie had to accept that. She met her grandmother, Jakob's mother, but Mrs. Abs wanted to live alone, didn't want to die near us; if any memory of a grandmother remains, Marie never mentions it. She had to deal with the brisk forceful women at the Düsseldorf day care center, but it was always entirely up to her sole legal guardian whether she would be handed over to them or saved from them. Cresspahl made one last visit to the Rhine— "to the West"—and wheeled the child around the Hofgarten, but he was wearing his black overcoat dating from 1932, kept slipping back into Plattdeutsch with Marie, and a grandfather like that might well have scared her. And then Cresspahl went back to Jerichow. Marie spent her early years waiting among strangers for the one and only familiar person to come back at last from these incomprehensible separations—work. In the morning she tried to ask if she had to share the day with this invincible "work" or if she and Gesine could stay together until the day's last bedtime—she had a hard time making herself understood. She was given her birthday breakfast with two candles, then stayed quiet. Gesine had plans for her child, parental intentions as inadvisable as they were stubborn. First, that there be no detours on the way to standard High German. It felt funny in her throat, and approximations were accepted gladly, but still the only way to produce true maternal rejoicing would be successfully combining letters into a single word, say *M* and *i* and *l* and *ch* into *Milch*, "milk"—which might in turn be a disguise for another word, named *Dust*, "thuhsty," to which a superfluous *r* had to be added in some baffling place. *Durst*, "thirsty." Marie was eager to please this person; at first, she resorted to watching her, pointing to this or taking that. But she had no desire to start a conversation or even try to. Because she was also supposed to deliver these words in an order she was rarely free to choose. And, if she'd understood aright, this woman was also trying to turn her into someone who deliberately refused to say anything about a dry feeling in the throat: whether in fun, from tact, or out of stubbornness; three proposed mimicries, three possible agreements, all reached through no intermediary but her own face. Admittedly, this was also the start of their shared secret: that Marie spoke to this woman in a way she never spoke to anyone else—not the teachers, not the babysitters, certainly not the cohort of others learning the job of being a child in their own ways. No one else even noticed the wordless understanding between her and this woman. And there was no one else around to make things easier, to whom it was even worth running—just this one partner, both there to help and no help at all.

Not having a living father, she for a long time lacked a word for fathers, lacked even the idea of one. At two and a half she didn't understand questions about mothers either. She didn't have a mother, she spent her life with someone named Ina, Zina, G'sina, a tolerable enough protector but way too clever a peer.

This person didn't insist on being obeyed; you didn't have to carry out her wishes on the spot. You could get her to change your bedtime, could have your way about destinations for outings, and after you'd asked her to take away a tree with lit candles on it you could count on her to hide how flame bursts out of a match too. And she so insisted on pushback that you had to think things over, try to remember things that would have been much nicer if they'd stayed passing feelings or sights you could simply forget. The only thing you were helpless against was the part of this woman called "Work" (an ally? an enemy?). "Work" required a plane trip to West Berlin, "Work" required staying in strange houses with people speaking an even more mysterious language; obedience wasn't enough, but curiosity came in handy, since there was nothing to be done without this woman or against her. The child could be reconciled to a trip abroad with the promise of return after a countable number of days, so she innocently came along on a trip to France and boarded a ship to America, but after a week at sea it turned out this woman had outsmarted her. The trip was a move—this friend or foe named "Work" blocked their return to Europe, and now the habit of morning separations turned without warning into an arrangement involving a preschool on the Hudson in an entirely new language. After two years in New York Marie could still describe the room by the Rhine she'd left behind. She had long since been getting around in German as if in a first second language, but still she would point to privileges left elsewhere, to a sense of injustice. She'd accepted New York as a gift and she defended her new-won city as a right.

Even before starting school she began catching up with this woman, faster than a child on the other side of the Atlantic would have. This woman's English hadn't actually been all it was cracked up to be. Didn't the child master the swallowed vowel sounds quicker, the imperceptible onsets of aspirants, the set melodies of the sentences here? It was the woman who listened to her and had her repeat certain words as though trying to learn them from her, wasn't it? And who was the one who made the Cresspahls respected customers in Maxie's grocery store, or in Schustek's, if not the child, tasting the products first, nodding to authorize purchase? Who was the first to realize that Rebecca Ferwalter was not just any child but one who called Saturday the Sabbath? Who made sure we walked on the north side of Ninety-Fifth Street, not past the Puerto Ricans and their reason for picking a fight that the child had already noticed while the woman kept going on about "happy homes"? In the subway, which of them knew how to say the names of the lines in American English, and it was the child who could find the quickest route to the Atlantic, was it not? The fact that in this country citizens had to call their policeman "sir," no matter how urgent the accident or fire—who'd had to explain that to her elder? The younger Cresspahl, the one in the lead.

Victories. And yet, in this terrain of competition, struggle, trials of strength, how slow it was in coming—the separation, the independence. How long it took for Marie to establish her standing in the eyes of this other person, always in control! By now this woman had become, for school purposes, *"my mother"*—said objectively or in self-defense. My mother is from a small town on the Baltic. But her father was a rich man. Mrs. Cresspahl's child was expected to address her mother by first name, or jokingly as "Gee-sign," and was allowed to give her, also jokingly, motherly advice. Mrs. Cresspahl's child didn't know many other kids in school whose mothers made their own money with their own jobs, and Marie decided to be proud of that. Little Cresspahl had a mother whose topmost accent sounded foreign, if British. During the 1964–65 school year, little Cresspahl read till her eyes were sore and her fingers cramped, not as a striving teacher's pet but because she had a mother who might take a child with unsatisfactory grades back to Europe. Mary Cresspahl, fourth grade, might take it upon herself to insist that her name was pronounced "M'rie"; her braids might have been her own decision too; she didn't snitch; she'd mastered school slang—but it was from her mother that she'd gotten her attitudes toward religion, and the Jews, and promises. European values, perhaps, but foreign. In the beginning Marie had met plenty of children who would innocently say they hated their parents; maybe Marie just wouldn't let herself say it out loud.

"Life with my mother wasn't easy": Marie might well think such a sentence, even if disguised in English and stored up for a future listener whom she hasn't found yet. This mother had brought ideas from her Europe that she wanted the child to apply here. All people were endowed, or were to be provided with, equal rights. Now what was Marie supposed to do with that? She could show her mother how she gives up her bus seat for a black woman with the same alacrity as for a pink one, she could go down to our basement and console Jason for the long long hours remaining until sunset, but to take the one black girl in her class, Francine, under her European wing—how would that work out with her light-skinned friends?

She had to leave things out when she talked about this at home, and the worst of it was that her mother simply wouldn't stop believing that a truth would emerge through this lie, and through other undertakings for Francine's benefit that Marie would really have rather avoided. This mother tried to teach her that there was a difference between just and unjust wars—but how is a child supposed to connect events from the year 1811 (Shawnee uprising under Tecumseh) to the American war in Vietnam when her very first attempt cost her friendships and almost got her expelled? She could speak out against today's war in private, at home, nothing binding—perhaps hoping her mother would assume that she was equally opinionated at school. But this was a vague hope, there was a lie inherent in the answer, and the question, and the silence, and it was precisely this lie that her mother was determined to ban. Didn't she get that her code of ethics was acceptable but was valid only in the other language, untranslatable into thought or deed? Anyway, she wasn't honest herself—she pretended to prefer the Socialist cause while working in a capitalist country, for a bank! While the child can't very well suggest that if that's what her mother wants she should move to a Socialist country to be consistent, because then that child would lose the whole city of New York, and all her friends and the subway and the South Ferry and Mayor Lindsay, so she has to make do with dishonesty, which she's told shouldn't exist. And then, if her mother does follow through—unopposed by her child—and leave New York for the Socialist cause, possibly as early as this summer, young Cresspahl really will be in the soup, which she's helped to stir herself. What Marie will say someday about her mother, Gesine Cresspahl (Mrs.), is: life with her was not an easy alliance.

Two days' vacation in the country. Variable cloudiness, occasional flashes of sun on the sluggish water.

Marie has lots of things to do near school, uptown on Riverside Drive, or around Broadway on the Upper West Side—and nothing to do at Patton Lake. In the city she only has to be with her mother for a few hours—by Patton Lake she sometimes perched on the landing so askew, looking like such a wreck, that it was as if she were waiting in the desert for some army helicopter to land and save her from the uninterrupted togetherness, and from the awareness of it.

– No: she said: Not an army copter. But I'd take one from Radio Boston.

(And then loyally upholding good manners she said it was her own fault she was bored.)

She read the bundles of newspaper she'd brought back. In Brooklyn they shot and killed Charlie LoCicero, a Mafia elder, in his corner luncheonette as he sipped a strawberry malted. Eleventh Avenue and Sixty-Sixth Street—Marie would have liked to go see the crime scene, and tomorrow it'll be too late. On the Hudson, five NATO warships dropped anchor at Pier 86, and New Yorkers will line up to see the destroyers, and Marie would have enjoyed walking around them too, with a fat black marker, leaving behind a Was Here doodle or Peace sign (– A Peace sign: she says). People from the rich suburbs have paid a visit to the city's northern slums to do a little sweeping, painting, and cementing up cracks there, while leaving the insides of the buildings, with the roaches and the rats, untouched. (– It's so their conscience'll be clearer when they drive through: Marie says.) Nevertheless, she too would have happily watched these visitors from prosperity, and been in New York, not on Patton Lake.

Now and then it was international news she brought outside to her mother, not without turning her mother's deck chair a little toward the sun and tucking her blanket in tighter. She actually does act like she's dealing with an invalid, the way she passes along the scraps. In the process you can leave your hand on the other person's shoulder a little longer than strictly necessary, without seeming needy, much less affectionate.

Yesterday morning in Bonn the air force marked the fiftieth anniversary of the death of Baron von Richthofen, the "Red Baron," who shot down eighty French and British planes. In Cologne's Klingelpütz prison, apparently, mentally ill inmates were regularly beaten to death. Marie takes the page back in silence, returns her mother's nod, withdraws into the house in silence.

That's the kind of country you want to go back to, Gesine.
I haven't attained honesty yet, Marie.
Maybe it's happening here too.
Maybe we'll stay.
See!

She doesn't go near our host's TV set. Six years ago Gesine Cresspahl concluded that American TV shows were damaging to children, and there's no TV in our apartment. When Marie needs to watch something she goes over to friends' houses, or down to Jason in the basement, but here she leaves even the radio alone. As a result, she can do two things: point out how true she is to a long-ago promise and show that she doesn't want to disturb a vacation in the country by making noise.

She's recently started getting uncomfortable about the fact that a certain someone is working forty hours a week not only for herself but for another person's livelihood and tuition, her own. She has promised me that in return I'll get a house in 1982, in the part of Richmond where Staten Island is quietest.

Every time Marie left the house for a walk she changed clothes. The nearby vacation homes are still almost all empty. She might run into the young woman at the gas station, and one or two dogs, and have the retired farmer at the store to talk to. Yet she trades her pants and sweater for an elaborate dress, suitable for churchgoing; she pulls her hair back into a neat ponytail, shines her shoes for the walk around the lake. She mustn't give the locals a chance to say that a New York child doesn't know how to behave in the country.

And after the first stranger has wished her good morning, she exchanges hellos with all the rest, for New York's sake.

She came back and puzzled over people in New York who'd met Mrs. Cresspahl once at a party and promised her the keys to their summer house on Patton Lake after half an hour of conversation. (She brought that up only in passing; it was meant as a compliment to Mrs. Cresspahl. She had to be considerate—tomorrow morning her mother was going back to work.)

She brought me an article from *The New York Times* that had been overlooked on Saturday, and handed it over in businesslike fashion, officially, as something for work: We have a reliable old aunt in the city who's looking out for us.

In thirty-six lines she covers the following: the foreign minister of the Czechoslovakian Republic, Jan Masaryk, fell out of a window in March 1948. Major Augustin Schramm, a security officer at the Foreign Ministry suspected in Masaryk's death, was murdered. Now another major, Bedřich Pokorný, assigned to investigate both deaths, was found three weeks ago hanged in woods near Brno.

Did you believe that he fell out a window, in 1948? When you were fifteen?

Last night we only just got to July 1945. Do you want us to skip ahead in the story?

No. Anyway, I get it.

What do you get?

That you don't want to talk about it, Gesine.

Then she had to get through a half hour with Sergeant Ted Sokorsky, the country policeman who looks after our hosts' keys. Mr. Sokorsky sat himself down on the landing, shyly accepted a beer, and started bringing out tactful phrases about the weather. He spoke softly, which Marie took as a sign of his respect for Mrs. Cresspahl, a visitor from New York and a lady. He was young enough, and Marie would've liked to ask him to take her for a ride round the lake on his ungainly motorcycle but instead she decided to display the ladylike reserve that certain mothers raised their children to maintain. Mr. Sokorsky wasn't sparing with his *madam*s in addressing Mrs. Cresspahl, and he brought off a bow, from the neck, after locking up the house; Marie will never see him again, and for years to come when the conversation turns to the police she'll bring up one named Ted Sokorsky, not brawny, almost delicate, and the deference with which he treated my mother, here I'll show you.

But now the vacation in the country is over, we've long since reached the Palisades Parkway across from Manhattan, and Marie already thinks she can see the place in the finely sculpted apartment towers where the wet lilac-colored reflection of the evening sun comes off the five windows behind which she's about to turn on the lights, all at once.

– If it's okay with you, Gesine: she'll say. *By your gracious permission:* she'll say.

April 22, 1968 Monday

In the morning a heavy fog hung over the Hudson, astonishingly bright, and like a guest over breakfast it opened a white eye occasionally, blearily, blindly blinking.

But someone who still doesn't get New York weather, even now, will end up caught in a sudden shower on the hill of Ninety-Sixth Street leading up to Broadway; she was already running from the newsstand down into the subway, and like many others she trotted to work down Lexington Avenue with *The New York Times* folded into a roof over her head.

Peeking up from under its edge at the traffic light on Forty-Fifth Street, she saw on the inside of the roof how the war had been waged this weekend: thirty-one Vietcong dead in battles northwest of Saigon on Saturday, another fifteen yesterday morning farther north... she moved forward with the crowd, hemmed in by strangers' elbows. Not until lunchtime did she review the details in the dried-out paper, for instance that *The New York Times* would characterize the battles around the foreign capital not as an American defensive action but rather an offensive.

The paper's weather forecast for today: Mostly sunny and mild. Not this slashing rain.

Bright, sunny days, shored up by steady heat—for Marie this was not enough, as the sole memory of the first summer of the New Era in Jerichow, never mind that it's almost ninety-one seasons ago now, almost four thousand miles away too. Lazy storytelling, she calls it. Squatting in front of the fireplace in the summer house, feeding the fire until, probing carefully, she finds the kindling that can light that other fire. – I gather the Russian victors didn't behave well: she said.

> *Tell her, Gesine.*
> *I was just a child then. Twelve years old. What do I know?*
> *What you heard from us. What you saw.*
> *She'll take the wrong information and use it.*
> *She's a child, Gesine.*
> *It's easy for the dead to talk. Were you honest with me?*
> *Do better than we did.*
> *And also so she'll know where she's going with me. To whom.*
> *And for us, Gesine. Tell her.*

Jerichow, all of western Mecklenburg, was still occupied by British troops, cordoned off with lines of armed soldiers, but the Soviets had long since arrived—they were nowhere to be seen and yet there, in conversations, in suppressed fears: as rumor. They were no longer the vague subhumans that the Reich Ministry of Public Enlightenment and Propaganda had been importing into Germany since 1941; they weren't even the photos from East Prussian villages where German units had managed to beat the Soviets back and could snap their shutters in front of battered women's bodies or crosses of men nailed onto barn doors—the government had made up too many news reports with too many faked photographs as proof. There was a sick child at my father's house, Hanna Ohlerich, from Wendisch Burg, whose parents hadn't believed much from the government but they had believed this and so hanged themselves: prematurely, before they'd had a chance to see and hear the foreigners from the East with their own eyes and ears, said the survivors, including Jerichowers safe under British management. Then, by early May already, came rumors amounting almost to news reports—not from the fallen government but from friends and relatives in the rest of Mecklenburg, the part under Soviet occupation. In Waren, an enemy of the Nazis known to the very end as the "Red pharmacist" had celebrated all night long with his liberators from the Soviet Union until they'd forced themselves on all the women in the house anyway and everyone in the family killed themselves with the poisonous medicine they hadn't been saving for such a purpose at all—this news was firmly grounded in a specific name, a specific market square, a specific business on the ground floor of a specific gabled building. In Malchin, in Güstrow, in Rostock the rumored Russians had tried to wash potatoes in toilet bowls by pulling the chain, then threatened to shoot the hapless Germans for sabotage, for flushing the food away. From Wismar came the report that three Soviet soldiers had hauled a grandfather clock past British sentries one night and taken it to a clockmaker, telling him to turn it into thirteen wristwatches— much in demand in Soviet Mecklenburg due to the foreigners' habit of never winding wall clocks and then throwing them into the bushes or the water, as broken. A number of country manors had burned down because spectral looters didn't believe in electrical lights, even when the electricity still worked, and had lit spills of paper on fire to help them search. They used a microscope from the pathology division of a university clinic to buy two bottles of booze; they shot at pigeons, with live ammunition; they were reportedly incapable of singing their melancholy songs. All of this, along with the Russians' infatuation with children, was both hard to believe and widely known in Jerichow when the British withdrew, and again various locals and refugees in town hanged, drowned, and poisoned themselves, but not all of them out of fear of the new occupiers: Pahl hadn't known where to go next; Dr. Berling, MD, hadn't found a cure for depression in all his studies. The rest—an estimated three and a half thousand people in Jerichow on July 3—stayed.

– Out of curiosity?: Marie said the day before yesterday. She hadn't let herself laugh often enough; she'd kept her face hidden, near the fire, her gaze on the flames so unwaveringly that she seemed not to be listening, or maybe listening only to her thoughts.

– Out of curiosity.

– Curiosity backed by a sense of how much they'd lost?

– Not necessarily what they'd lost.

– Mr. and Mrs. Maass, 14 Market Square.

– Like them. Maybe nothing had happened to them personally, but they'd heard stories.

– So now they wanted to see if the rumors were true?

– Yes, and there was another reason.

– The children weren't curious though: Marie decided.

– Maybe not. Since I don't know the words for that curiosity, you're probably right.

– And because of your Jews. The six million.

– How can you say something like that, Marie!

– I can to you. They were waiting for payback.

– Yes. Though they didn't believe all the news reports.

– They wanted to see for themselves how the bill came due.

– Yes.

– Like always.

– Yes!

– So they *were* curious: she said.

People, whether locals or refugees, stayed in Jerichow because they had a roof over their heads, whether their own or borrowed. Besides, starting July 2 the British wouldn't let anyone with household goods cross their new border, the Trave Canal—now you had to swim without luggage.

Wulff stayed, not only because of his pub and general store but because he'd been a member of a banned party (Social Democrats), declared unfit for military service too, and if not exactly expecting a reward he still felt he could count on his business being treated fairly. (– He was curious: Marie said.) By this point it was fairly obvious what was keeping Papenbrock there. My father stayed because the British had made him mayor and he wanted to hand over his official duties properly. And the locals put their faith in Jerichow's outward appearance.

Because what could the Russians possibly see in this little town, far from the main roads, tucked away in the country near the Baltic but without even a harbor? Whichever direction they came from, they'd see nothing but a low clump of modest buildings. The bishop's-miter church tower, however tall it was, however densely surrounded by the leaves of six-hundred-year-old trees, was a sign of bygone prosperity, not current riches. They would likely have already seen the country seats of Mecklenburg, magnificent metropolitan showpieces surrounded by parks; they'd no doubt have marched down streets lined with commercial properties, tokens of imperial times, in various Mecklenburg administrative centers, the so-called fore-cities— but in Jerichow they found few buildings over two stories. Wartime economy had ripped open large holes in the stuccoed ones, exposing the bricks, while the wood in the half-timbered ones had gone far too long without paint or even Carbolineum. And what did the entitled victors come driving into town on? Not asphalt, just bumpy round cobblestones, and in Rande there wasn't even a blue basalt double line for a bike path (which went with the rumor that the victors didn't know how to ride bikes). There remained the brickworks villa, where they'd set up their headquarters. They'd retreated at once from the von Lassewitzes' town house, now the Papenbrocks', after finding all the rooms full of refugees (so maybe there was something to their alleged fear of epidemics). The English had set up their club in Lindemann's Lübeck Court Hotel, now the Soviets would put their own name on it. To the uninitiated, the market square might well have seemed a bit too big—some who owned three-story properties there could be facing confiscation. Aside from that, however, the municipality of Jerichow could only have seemed uniformly impoverished to the Soviets, with nothing to loot, at least nothing that anyone let them know about.

Up until the Sunday after the entry of the first Soviet troops—until the night of July 8—only one single rumor had become fact. A Red Army man had forced his way into the shop belonging to Otto Quade, plumbing and heating, and pointed past the low partition at a floor model dating from prewar times. – Faucet: the soldier had said to Bergie Quade in his thick, *h*-less Russian accent: *Wassergahn* instead of *Wasserhahn*. Bergie—who, following the then-current advice, was dowdily dressed, with a filthy face and a rag smeared with chicken shit under her skirt—had answered, with typical Quadish presence of mind: *Wassergehn?* I'm not going in the water. Don't need to. Are you wanting to know who from around here's gone into the water? You mean drowned in the marsh, in the Baltic...? The Red Army hadn't waited to hear her whole list and marched off, shaking his head, which to Bergie looked reproachful, she couldn't help it. This was the only unaccompanied soldier seen in Jerichow that whole first week. The commandant had shut himself up in the brickworks villa along with the whole occupying force, communicating with the Germans via orders he had Cresspahl post outside Town Hall. No Soviet airplane had yet landed at the Jerichow-North air base, that unfortunate token of the town's having taken part in the war on the wrong side; even though the area, with its razor-wire fences, would have been perfect for a prison camp, the new right side didn't use it for that either.

So, which way was the wind blowing in Jerichow that first week of July in 1945?

All them rumors, seems real overdone (B. Quade).

And even if they are not exaggerated, the Russians wouldn't dare try anything among people with experience of the British occupation (Dr. Kliefoth).

Still, they really did rape Ilse Grossjohann (Frieda Klütz).

They're not running the town, they're not using the airfield—that won't last (Mr. and Mrs. Maass).

Looks like the British'll be back, Papenbrock (Creutz Sr.).

The things Cresspahl's doing, an he's not even embarrassed (Käthe Klupsch).

Maybe we'll end up back in Sweden. 'S just two hundred years back (Mrs. Brüshaver).

Papenbrock's in the elite, you know. Businesswise, I mean (Elsa Pienagel).

They're the ones scared of us. A curfew! They're scared! (Frieda Klütz).

Maybe they're driving round the country in the middle a the night (Frieda Klütz).

In the war, gossip like that was called latrine talk (Alfred Bienmüller; Peter Wulff).

Töv man, du (Gesine Cresspahl).

April 23, 1968 Tuesday

She was still on her own for a moment. Yesterday evening's sky, painted with broad brushstrokes, had crept into the last pictures in her mind before waking; in her clearing consciousness the dream remained, like a wall she could take shelter behind. Like getting up for the first time in a long while. She was no one—a field of memory in which strange grasses grew; a stormy sky over the Baltic Sea; the smell of grass after rain. Just a few glances out at the Hudson, and with the light in her eyes the sense of time would run faster, and in it her, Gesine, Mrs. Cresspahl, employee, a four-digit number in the 753- exchange, not here, midtown. Not yet.

There were further postponements. Was for a while still I, Gesine, still I, Marie, still we, the child and I, still the voices from the dream. Gradually the felted sensation of sleep crumbled into dry powder. Although woozy, she could nonetheless show pleasure. Marie had tied her hair up in a ponytail so high and tight that it stood straight up for a while. Our roles separated us. How an eleven-year-old pours tea for her elder. How Gesine pulls herself together into Mrs. Cresspahl, mirrored in the child's scrutiny: here's my mother, thirty-five years old, she doesn't see the one gray hair in all the dark ones. Disguised for an office, equipped for a day out of the house, less recognizable now. How a child sullen about school talks as if looking forward to the essay she has to write, to make it easier for her mother to go out into the world as a working woman. Marie's worried, un-American face once more, soft with sleep, in the crack of the door. Then alone.

With time to continue to drift along for a while, though on set paths, from one square of the board to the next, punctually advancing in time—but still, on her own. It was she who promised the newspaper man a good morning, and that she would never burden him with anything more; a real connection born from acquaintance, that's him. She was almost disappointed to find herself among strangers again on the express side of the subway platform, and relieved to see yesterday's lovers come running down the scuffed stairs just in time, inexperienced, unsure of each other, separated on the train as it shot downtown. She wormed *The New York Times* out from under her arm: Good weather over North Vietnam; 151 bombing missions. It was she who let herself be shoved so close to the tips of a transit policeman's shoes that he moved aside slightly, all but saluting her. On the Grand Central Shuttle she walked to the next car through the swaying doors, not to gain three seconds but to feel herself moving in something moving. She scanned the rows of underground store windows, satisfied to see all the products she could do without. At the ticket counters, again with fantasies of running away: that was her. And yet on Lexington Avenue she relaxed in the camaraderie of all the different people around her, the small-town brick buildings between the skyscrapers, the pizza chef she always saw, holding his large round disk up to her like a greeting. The low-ceilinged retreat for men, the wooden table with the breakfast beer right by the window—she's seen it so many times, she has not tried to understand it so many times. Between the facades with their many windows she looked up in search of the sky over the city, and sure enough the bulrushes swayed as they should in the drifting clouds. A few more steps and the stroll through the city of daily surprises has come to an end. The person flushed through the marble bank lobby, sucked out of one throng into a thinner one and then into the last elevator lane, that was no longer her, that was Mrs. Cresspahl, employee here for the past four years, formerly a foreign-language secretary, fourth floor, then eleventh floor, and now transferred to the sixteenth, integrated into the firm's operations though no doubt dispensably, provisionally, temporarily. – How are you! she is repeatedly asked on her ride up in the closed cabin, and she will answer: How are you! with a drawn, thin-lipped smile, the corners of her eyes not budging. That's someone else.

That's our German, that's our Danish girl. She's single, available; married; a widow. Engaged—Wes saw her on Third Avenue with some guy from Kansas. Nah, Nebraska. Has a foster child, two, no actually the kid's hers. Gee-sign. Has a sense of humor; she might say: You wouldn't find my village on the map, I'd have to write it in myself, but she also says: I was born in Jerichow, that's in Mecklenburg. Yerry Show. Looks taller than five four.

Has a thing going with the VP's son; only took her three years to make it into the tower with all the fat cats. She's allowed to eat in the bosses' restaurant but goes down to Sam's for lunch—bad move. Good move, goes back and visits her old departments, doesn't burn any bridges. Helps a friend a hers check his letters of credit; must be cause she used to be a Communist. One of the vice president's little games, de Rosny's like that. Special assignment. Don't get memos from her, her number's not in the directory. Yesterday she took a French heir out to lunch; she's just de Rosny's left hand. She has a corner office; the bank's given her a safe. Miss Cresspahl. No, Mrs. So she is available. Personnel won't say. Who is she? A girl on the sixteenth floor where men work. Won't be long 'fore she's transferred to the Milwaukee branch. Ten thousand a year. More like eleven. Cresspahl, name sounds Jewish. Celtic. In short: No one knows her. Maybe that's just what the fat cats on the sixteenth floor want. Bottom line: Unknown. Anonymous, camouflaged. Unknowable.

The sun beating through the unprotected windows takes her back again. Here in the spacious office full of functional and residential furniture is the same hot, semi-high eastern sunlight that ignites the haze over the low settlements of Long Island City to the color of a sea seventeen years ago. She was there once—held a sextant up to the sun. That was her once.

Cresspahl's in-box is stacked no higher than usual, but today for the first time there's newspaper in it: page 12 from *The New York Times*. An article is circled in big exuberant loops; her boss has put his URGENT stamp into the ad space next to it. He's even taken the trouble to dash off initials meant to denote de Rosny, and again they look more than anything like a prince's little crown.

"Memo
From: Cp
To: de Rosny, Vice President
Re: N.Y.T., 4/23/68; Czechosl.
    With reference to the claim that subsidies in the Czechoslovak economy are distributed in accord with an 'arbitrarily set plan,' I refer to my report on the 1966–1970 Five Year Plan, memo no. deR 193-A-22.
    The declared figure for subsidies in fiscal year 1967–1968, 30 billion

crowns, is remarkably close to the actual sum, which according to my calculations amounts to slightly more than 15 percent of the net national income (deR 193-CD 48).

The Czechoslovakian ruble account in the Soviet Union, estimated by the N.Y.T. as ten billion crowns, may actually have since exceeded the nominal equivalent of sixteen billion dollars. However, in addition to the lack of USSR products worth purchasing, this also represents what may someday partially eliminate Comecon's leverage (deR 23-CF-1238).

The reform efforts are presented in exceptionally general and simplified terms. The N.Y.T. describes in detail the delegation of responsibility to the enterprises themselves and the plan for gradually withdrawing subsidies. More precise information about the leveling off of differential taxes on unprofitable businesses would have been useful (above-cited source not applicable here).

If functionaries of the Czechoslovak government are communicating with organs such as *The New York Times,* not only about personal political struggles in the background of the debates around reform but also to indicate the real possibility of the country's return into the International Monetary Fund and International Bank for Reconstruction and Development, this suggests that, more than wanting foreigners to think they are creditworthy, as previously assumed, they also want to publicize the advocates for reform in their own country. Would a further report on this topic be of interest?

Negotiations of loans from capitalist countries are here mentioned in print for the first time. I would like to assure you, for the record, that the leak did not come from this office. Still, the unofficial admission should excite more than the market (see prev. par.).

Best regards,
G. C."

What on earth did you do to my English, writer?
It wasn't yours.
It wasn't this miserable limping German you've translated it into.
Your English was as business *as it gets, Gesine.*
I wasn't insane when I wrote it!
But you were tired. Distracted too.

The employer has added delighted exclamation marks next to a paragraph in the *Times* report from Prague:

"The state of Czechoslovakia's economic health is like that of an injured man so full of morphine that he not only is likely to be permanently stupefied but he is unable even to tell the doctor where it hurts."

You can see de Rosny here, in his underlining: after such prolonged strain from peering downward a moment of refreshment has been granted him. This man full of morphine might get employee Cp. a new code number.

Later, day sinks into evening against venetian blinds tilted perpendicular to block the sun, sinks into the slow return trip to Riverside Drive, to us, where we live.

– This is what Mecklenburg looks like? Marie asks. She has stood up specially from her homework, is standing behind her mother's chair, even bringing her cheek close, to have a line of vision that's parallel at least.

It was nothing. Ragged fog drifting over the river. A gap in the always astonishing green of the leaves seems to open onto an overcast inland lake, behind which memory sees, again, and gladly, a bluish pine woods on the other bank's Palisades, sees the region of bygone times made again and again transparent and unreal by the stage-set trees.

– Hm: Marie says, reassured, reassuring, as if to a shying horse. Where would she be if her New York, river and riverbank included, were something different, or even comparable to something different! To her it's incomparable. Her time living here still stretches before her.

April 24, 1968 Wednesday

In the Czechoslovak Socialist Republic three employees of the judiciary have been dismissed—no mere bailiffs or janitors but three high-ranking deputy general prosecutors, one of them the chief military prosecutor himself. The new government's spokesmen provide no further explanation. It seems as if these guardians of the law in former times have now become guilty of crimes.

The Soviets had been occupying Jerichow for barely a week but by the second Monday in the first July after the war the locals had already decided that there was one man responsible: Cresspahl, my father. "The Russians are his fault," the verdict ran, and it covered more than just complaints about the foreigners. It really did a person good to say these words. As if without Cresspahl the Russians would never have come in the first place.

It had started with throwing Käthe Klupsch in jail, and Cresspahl hadn't done that. The British, while they were there, had threatened to punish anyone who spread rumors that they were going to leave Jerichow to their comrades-in-arms from the east. One bright June day, on the crowded sidewalk outside Klein the butcher's empty shopwindow, Käthe Klupsch, however impossible she thought such a fate was, couldn't resist giving herself a pleasant shudder by uttering the forbidden prediction. Two Tommies marched Käthe Klupsch off to Town Hall between them. The soldiers made sure not to get too close to this stout lady with the heaving bosom, and for her this was "bodily assault." The four-hour wait outside Cresspahl's office: that she'd felt was "a cynical effort to wear her down"—she'd been told only that she wasn't allowed to talk. After that, the process of determining the facts had been a "spiritual ordeal" and "brainwashing" too, since Cresspahl had been obliged to translate his British visitor's questions for her. Having admitted that she was able to read, for example typed public regulations, she was given a warning; because Cresspahl didn't have time to write out a special pass that night, the British held her in a cell under Town Hall until curfew ended. Käthe Klupsch now thought she'd "been alone in the building with Cresspahl until six in the morning," and probably got herself a bit mixed up with the two refugees in Rande who'd had to stay in jail until the Soviets took them as prisoners for the same offense. This was how Klupsch talked until the Soviets did move into Jerichow; afterward her only complaint about Cresspahl was his secret alliance with them. Cause in the end they did come, didn't they? And for that they'd turned a blameless woman into a political prisoner, didn't they?

The Russians were Cresspahl's fault.

No. It hadn't started like that.

The British had made Cresspahl mayor of Jerichow. While they could have seen him as just another German, one who'd betrayed his sometime British home even, they instead seemed to trust him, like a friend almost. The British intelligence officers hadn't found anything to worry about, they'd saluted him when they left! a military salute, too! Even Americans had come, from their area around Schwerin, and spent nights in Cresspahl's office, and if they had questioned him over his (Western) reliability there'd still been drinks and fine words. Then the Soviets had moved in and they let Cresspahl stay mayor. That was their military cunning—trying to hide their secret conflict with their Anglo-Saxon allies. Still, they hadn't exactly adopted Cresspahl, much less confirmed his official position. They'd installed him. Under the reign of the swastika, that word "install," *Einsatz,* had carried connotations of something irregular—manpower shortages, stopgaps, "emergency measures," whether putting a special unit to work "to help with" the harvest or deploying scattered troops or installing an unelected official, sometimes without even asking him first. Now Cresspahl had betrayed the British again, posting a notice on Town Hall that by order of the Soviet commandant he was henceforth a henchman of the Russians, a tool in their hands—"installed" as mayor.

In May and June it had been the American Eighteenth Airborne, as represented by the British Sixth Airborne division, under B. L. Montgomery—the people of Jerichow had gotten quite used to their old occupiers. No sooner had they left than Cresspahl was serving the new occupiers, the local commander K. A. Pontiy, the Russians.

Cresspahl had helped the Russians to an eighth of the town. Their fence around the brickworks villa had by no means been the end of it. On the fourth day after their arrival, it became clear why they'd merely run a few lines of razor wire through the golden rain bushes on the west side of the property. That morning, eight able-bodied men were ordered to report to Cresspahl's office in Town Hall, summoned by name, and Mina Köpcke had to come too, representing her husband's construction firm. And was their job to clean up the Lübeck Court, wrecked by the British, so that Jerichow would get its hotel back? No, they were to build a fence. A fence running due west from the commandant's headquarters, through the back gardens of the houses on the Bäk, then straight north to Field Road, east to the edge of the yards of the houses on Town Street, and back to the property they'd already occupied! Mina Köpcke had been managing the books and supervising repairs for her husband ever since he'd gone missing with an antiaircraft gun in Lithuania; now she was eager to show him what she could do with a project of her own, and was put in charge. Cresspahl yet again showed what a Russian stooge he was, by giving them his whole stock of wood, and when that ran out Mina was free to tear down fence boards anywhere in Jerichow she wanted and her enemies didn't. She had a requisition order with a Soviet stamp to prove it, to which she could add: It (the confiscation; the Russians' construction project) was Cresspahl's fault. Unlike him, she wanted to be patriotic, she didn't set the fenceposts as deep in their stone foundations as she would have for a fence of her own, and when she had the paint mixed thinner than it would have been for a German customer she thought she could use the harsh sea wind as an excuse. But now what did this Cresspahl do, this fellow businessman and protector of Jerichow's interests back in the day? He had one of her fence boards sent to her, as a sample; when her second paint job still turned out pale lime green, the barrel of synthetic resin was weighed on the town scales before her eyes and she had to sign a receipt. Then she came to Town Hall with her bill, and did Cresspahl file it away in good faith like a fellow victim of a foreign power? Late that night Cresspahl was seen with his buddy K. A. Pontiy pacing the length of Mina's fence, like two friends out for a stroll, one wielding a surveyor's rod and the other delighting in the wide swerving arcs the compass made. Köpcke & Co. was summoned back to Town Hall and Cresspahl calculated her chicanery out for her in square feet and cubic feet. He said nothing about fraud or even about innocent mistakes—he just asked for a revised bill. Sat hunched at his mayor's desk, elbows too close together, and however tired he was he could have looked her in the eyes more than just that once, from deep under his brows, so surprised. Mina Köpcke stuck to her numbers, signed her aggressive bill, and accepted a draft on the government bank for later payment. For now she received no money at all, and she attributed that to Cresspahl, as the Russian way of doing business and as his fault.

Not only was he betraying Jerichow to the Russians, he was taking his own cut! While Mrs. Köpcke and her seven men were fencing in a whole street, the Bäk, and a notice saying "Requisitioned" was being nailed up on one house after another, and since the construction was proceeding from both south ends, the Bäk was turning into a sack whose opening narrowed day by day. The Bäk had formerly been a residential street of respectable brick houses, less than forty years old and often with generously proportioned attics, among them Dr. Semig's practically princely villa, all with sizable gardens separating them from the narrow lots on Town Street, and now the homeowners in this prosperous area had to move out, into the overcrowded town, billeted where papers signed by Cresspahl ordered them to go. They were allowed to take only what they could carry; they had to leave every room in a condition permitting immediate occupation by the foreigners. And Cresspahl refused to let anyone come complain about the single room they now had at Quade's, or above the pharmacy, sometimes even shared with refugees! He would agree to see the refugees who themselves had been billeted in the Bäk, waiting so much more patiently now that they were on their third or fourth relocation in six months, and he allocated to them the rooms that the Jerichowers had been wanting to keep for themselves or their relatives, because he knew every building in town as well as the locals knew his. Then the north end of the fence was extended right across the Bäk, and that was the last time this street was ever seen in Jerichow, to this day. The people in houses adjoining the fence on Town Street complained about the shadows it cast on their gardens, the plants that didn't like so much shade. And whose fault was that?

Meanwhile Cresspahl's own house and property lay outside the fence, on the other side of Brickworks Road. He'd looked after his friends: Creutz's vegetable garden was within the fence and even though all its products had to be handed over to headquarters Amalie was allowed to go on using the path to Town Street running alongside the pastor's house, and the land the Creutzes leased from the church had been fenced in for them too, as though permanently theirs now. Pastor Brüshaver, once again a neighbor of Cresspahl's, could also stay in his house unmolested, though it occupied a strategic weak point that should have been fenced in to make the army enclosure a solid stronghold. And Cresspahl had secured himself, too, against looters and unwanted visitors, since the only approach to his property was on Brickworks Road but now there was a road sign, the first in its history, a board sharpened to an arrow, and it said: КОММАНДАНТУРА. Who would go down that road unless they had to? Cresspahl hadn't even arranged for a German translation. It practically looked like a call to learn Russian—they wouldn't put that past Cresspahl either.

And he'd forced Bergie Quade to come to the commandant's headquarters. The Red Army soldier she'd so glibly enlightened about "Wassergahn" came back to her store with a boy, a refugee from Pommern who was staying in Cresspahl's house. About seventeen but broad shouldered. He looked Bergie in the eye as if he'd long been a man, and a silent type too; she couldn't put him off, talk him out of the store. The Red Army soldier looked at Mrs. Quade as he talked, and she felt almost attractive under his remembering gaze. The boy didn't smile, he just translated. It sounded reliably North German, even when he had to ask the Red Army for clarification. Bergie Quade couldn't resist the urge to wash her hands again. By that point she'd decided to be cooperative, so she invited the visitors into her kitchen. She hid her satisfaction while walking down Town Street between them, as if being led away, an upstanding German housewife under arrest, she even managed the requisite look of grim determination. She followed them across the Creutz property, stopped for a minute to talk to Amalie, who was supervising the fence builders as they transplanted some gooseberry bushes, and then really and truly set foot in the occupying power's sealed compound. The Kommandatura. Over the next few hours the Red Army learned swear words that would circulate for some time, a bit garbled, in the Jerichow Soviets' vocabulary; Bergie Quade also complimented Jakob Abs for following her instructions with delicate precision, like an expert plumber. The last German owners of the brickworks villa had decided to leave the Soviets with sawn-through drainpipes rather than whole ones, and the kitchen and bathroom faucets looked to Bergie suspiciously as though they'd been pounded with hammers, and secretly she couldn't believe that people who were, after all, nobility could have treated their house in such fashion. Then Bergie Quade had the choice between submitting a bill to the government bank or receiving a half-liter bottle of unlabeled vodka, she accepted her husband's balm, and had a drink on the house, too, with Wassergahn the Red Army soldier, who'd helped with the repairs. When Jakob brought her out through the brickworks villa's front door onto the civilian Brickworks Road, she was tempted to check in at Cresspahl house, to see if he didn't need help after all, with all his refugees and the child. But Jakob shook his head and Bergie walked the length of the cemetery wall to Town Street like everything was normal—tool bag in her fist, bottle under her skirt where she'd earlier had her shit-smeared rag, deep in thought about who she could tell all this to. If she wasn't mistaken, her tactics had cost Cresspahl time as well as effort. So that at least wasn't his fault. But Mrs. Quade's unwillingness to give her neighbors a full report was enough to ensure that they had something to blame him for.

Meanwhile Cresspahl had had to post Order No. 2 from the military commandant of the town of Jerichow: All residents were to turn in their radios, batteries, typewriters, telephones, microphones, cameras, "etc." at Papenbrock's granary within three days. That night, Cresspahl explained what "etc." meant: guns, explosives, rifles, and firearms of all kinds; the following day, K. A. Pontiy's Order No. 4 demanded that all gold, silver, or platinum coins or bars, and all foreign currency, be handed in at the credit union, as well as documents pertaining to foreign assets, and again Cresspahl was seen as the Soviets' accomplice. For the townsfolk saw him going to Town Hall that morning with his telephone under his arm, and another time with two army Karabiner rifles someone had thrown onto his property overnight, even though the collection of People's Receivers and "etc." in Papenbrock's granary didn't amount to much. Then Cresspahl showed his fellow citizens that he hadn't lived among them for twelve years for nothing. He posted a reminder at Town Hall that the post office had a list of former owners of radios and telephones. Some people from that list turned up, but they were planning to throw their devices at that Russia-lover Cresspahl's feet, and they had to wait a long time at the granary gate because the mayor kept announcing every two hours that he was on his way, and never came. Finally, the commandant threatened with arrest the owner of any home where requisitioned property was found, and now the locals forced the refugees to go in and hand over what *they* had while they themselves burned what they didn't bury, including the genuine Russian rubles from prisoners of war that they'd saved to do business with after the British forces returned (or the Swedish ones arrived). At least they could still blame Cresspahl for their losses; it was his fault and they had the receipts to prove it.

Jerichow could see just how dishonorable a Soviet lackey Cresspahl was from his actions toward the Papenbrocks. He kept sending more and more homeless refugees into his very own in-laws' house, to the point where they had to spend their old age camping out in Albert's office. He'd done nothing to stop the Red Army from removing the von Lassewitzes' furniture from the Papenbrocks' house, carrying it onto Market Square, spraying it with Lysol for all to see, then driving it off to the Kommandatura. Papenbrock's yard and granary were confiscated, all the grain in them too, and they became the Red Army's supply depot, and Cresspahl could just go on living his life after robbing his own family of their property. Even if he lived to be ninety, how could he make up for such guilt?

The Soviets themselves didn't respect him. The British had had him chauffeured around in a jeep from morning till night; the Soviets let him walk, from Brickworks Road to Town Hall, from the hospital to the gasworks, from one end of Jerichow to the other, without even an escort— defenseless, alone.

– But now they weren't spitting on him anymore: Marie says.

– No. Not even shouting things after him.

– Did they take it out on young Gesine?

– It was meant for my father, wasn't it. Young Gesine didn't care.

– When you were sent to go shopping—

– Yes.

– and they shoved you out of the line. Accidentally stepped on your feet. There were parents who wouldn't let their kids play with you—

– It wasn't like that, Marie.

– They didn't see you?

– They didn't see me.

– And now I'm supposed to think about a Francine, a black girl in a white school, and in the morning when she comes over to me and says hello—

– Don't make that comparison. The child I was—

– Fine, Gesine. I dig you. You were trying to tell me a story, not teach me a lesson. Still, I can think something out for myself.

– There's no comparison, you can't think that.

– I can think what I want.

– Whatever you want, Marie.

We got home late, and heavy rain hung a flapping gray curtain of mist in front of the river and land beyond the park. Behind that curtain the world stops.

April 25, 1968 Thursday

The new prime minister of Czechoslovakia, Mr. Černík, has praised his Czechs and Slovaks for their good work since 1948, as is only proper at the start of a new economic program on the set list, and then proceeded to tell them what that good work has achieved: a per capita national income up to 40 percent lower than that of "advanced capitalist countries," delivery of manufactured goods to customers often taking three times longer, transport and housing and retailing in similarly poor shape, and he actually mentions the $400 million foreign trade deficit with capitalist countries, calling it relatively small but "very unpleasant and inconvenient" because it involves short-term loans. Employee Cresspahl has already been calculating and summarizing all that herself, since December, for the bank files; she has been useful to the company and has no reason to fear being fired on the spot when she's ordered to report to the management's floor in the middle of the workday; she can look down on two sections of Third and Lexington Avenues without too much to worry about. From such a height the people down there look not just foreshortened but distorted.

Twelve years ago the bank hadn't been here and would have been rather nervous about handling a piddling $400 million. As for a female assistant to a vice president, that was unthinkable.

It was a family bank, not only in terms of who owned it but of what it did. Its name still reveals its beginnings in small Midwestern towns, giving loans against wheat on the stalk, bribing the sheriff, and taking a man's word the same way it took a promissory note. The name—with its country ring, smacking of forefathers and filial piety—has remained.

There exists a photograph, in the brownish detail of around 1880, that purports to show a village branch of the bank in North Carolina: outside the big window with its garland of golden letters stand the justice of the peace with the blacksmith and the shopkeeper, all chatting, all befrockcoated, and the bank manager is leaning in the doorway, dressed as if for church, eyes under his hat brim ingenuous and miscalculated, and every performer in the scene is really and truly bisected by the wooden railing that actual cowboys used to tie their horses to back in those days. The picture refuses to stay fixed in the second during which the photographer ninety years ago told everyone to hold their breath; it wants to keep moving, to the rattling stagecoach pulling up in a cloud of dust, the relief driver on the box seat shot through the eye, the horses frisky, the townsfolk pouring out of the neighboring buildings, ladies looking down from the top windows of the hotel, the strongbox hanging by its last strap, brutally pried open, and a shot rings out, and fresh horses are brought over, to chase the robbers—will they be bandits or Indians?—until finally, with a booming echo, the picture fades out and zooms in to the sign at the bank entrance: CLOSED FOR FUNERAL.

Not a few people in the company insist that the photo is retouched, or that all it shows is a movie set from a Western. Some claim to have seen the movie and swear they remember the scene. Anyone who dares to suggest the opposite—that maybe the film set was based on this photograph—is immediately suspected of being un-American, of mockery even. Mrs. Cresspahl doesn't say this anymore.

Around the turn of the century the bank made it to Chicago, to a little mansion inside the Loop it could call its own—narrow but noble of chest—and after 1945 it was practically rich. But the family in charge wanted to preserve its gains and increase them too, its cake should be kept in the pantry while nonetheless being eaten, a bearish attitude toward life. And so the family council believed the rumor of 1947, about the imminent death of New York City, and kept primly distant from that infamous region known to devour both men and money. They came to New York in 1951, too late. They wanted to move into the right neighborhood and found a old building five hundred yards from the Wall Street subway station; their decision to cloak it in marble and inscribe it in gold only diminished it further. And not only its appearance refused to gain in stature. They'd missed the Bretton Woods Conference, they tackled the stock market with less than stirring boldness, they couldn't find Chad on a map, probably thought it was a detergent. Headquarters was still on Lake Michigan, watching the sick child on the Atlantic with anger and defiance, yet continuing to send the little cripple ever more money. In 1961, when Gesine Cresspahl came to New York well acquainted with empires like Morgan Guaranty Trust, she barely knew this bank's name—she might have innocently called it a brokerage house or financial firm. And now she's standing high above ground level at a window in its new building, barely visible from the sidewalk, waiting for de Rosny to have a free moment—deputy chairman of the board, deputy CEO, deputy omnipotence: de Rosny.

De Rosny, too, once laughed at the idea that he might join his good name to that of this financial institution.

In the mid-1950s, more often than chance alone could explain, news came sailing out of the Bay with the Golden Gate: de Rosny was looking for something back east. Reason: the California climate no longer agreed with his wife.

It was a typical de Rosny reason, and if it made his partners smile for a moment, taking this for a familiar leg-pull, then what were lesser mortals, whose names probably struck him as belonging to harmless characters from the great American book of fairy tales, supposed to think? Not many offers came de Rosny's way, and the few that did weren't from that building near Wall Street. De Rosny didn't need them. If he felt like moving back east he could pick up the phone and ten days later everything in his house would have been rolled across the continent and set back up on Long Island Sound in a family property, precisely the same as he'd left it in San Francisco, give or take six inches. De Rosny hadn't worked or fought his way up into money, nor had he married money—he'd been born into money, his parents had given it to him and him alone, and he'd breathed through the aromatic, nourishing, protective shell of money ever since he'd known his own name, long before he'd started to learn the banking business in Singapore, because he was bored. So the word was: de Rosny wasn't available. Sitting behind phones on the fog-covered hills, he was paid whatever he wanted over and above what others were paid, simply because of his kinship with money, his descent from money, because he and money were one. De Rosny wouldn't waste his time on such a negligible problem, even if it could be rectified on the East Coast. De Rosny was considered unpredictable. He was prepared to risk a rift with Howard Hughes and publicly criticize Howie's business (not private) investments in Hollywood; de Rosny's vacations weren't spent there, they were spent with the aristocracy in Great Britain. And he had more than enough business with airplane manufacturers already, he didn't need Howie's inventions, particularly since they didn't stay in the air long enough. Others called him unserious. They didn't mean how he handled money. No, it was that he didn't know how to live. Evening meals—the blissful reward for a day of hard-fought meetings—bored him, and visibly. De Rosny didn't drink hard liquor, and he could have offered religious reasons as an excuse but instead he admitted just not being interested.

Shared confidences? Ha! Does anyone even know his first name? He once got a friendly slap on the shoulder and sent his suit out for dry cleaning! He invited almost no one into his home, and certainly not friends, and they left with no stories to tell. At home de Rosny served imported white wines from some unremarkable region in France where there's a hill—weak stuff, hardly loosened the tongue at all. While other people were happy to have their picture in the paper at a restaurant with Eleanor Roosevelt, de Rosny was sitting at Franklin Delano's fireside ages ago, and *not* having himself photographed, and F. D. had gone so far as to disguise the business nature of these chats with exchanges of boarding school memories. In the middle of the war against the Huns. No, de Rosny was given too much, too easily, it wasn't fair. He probably knows God's address and doesn't even bother to send Him a thank-you note. And this crafty rogue, this all-too-flexible fifty-year-old, his whole body trained by something other than tennis—you think anyone's going to discuss some trivial matter in New York with him, just because he wants to move back east? (Because his wife was not doing well in the sunny Pacific climate.)

De Rosny passed through Chicago, staying not in the city's luxury hotel but at the Windermere, and unfamiliar visitors graced the Windermere's conference room, and five firms in the distant south were narrowed down to two, and two to one, and suddenly New Orleans appeared on the market with a product that sold with childish ease, and a child could have thought of it, and is that what Matthew 18 meant? (Ask those Gideons.) (And the Windermere was practically buried in reservations for the next six months.) But de Rosny did deign to listen to some little eastern thing, and was annoyingly familiar with the matter already, and pointed out the considerable cost of solving it. In Chicago they thought he meant his salary, and they were wrong. De Rosny let himself be seen in New York, ostensibly back from inspecting his mansion in Connecticut, and the visitors he received at the Waldorf Towers included some who'd had to invite themselves. De Rosny brought no notebook listing his conditions, no secretary to relay them; apparently he wanted the time this little bagatelle was costing him to be made up in amusement.

Apparently his conditions were: That the board of directors would never try to make him president.

The compensation he felt was appropriate for a Vice President de Rosny, and the percentage by which it would increase annually—those are numbers that someone like Employee Cresspahl will never learn.

Then the horrible thing with his wife happened. All the better that he was moving back east, even if he had to pay for it out of his own pocket. Which he didn't. Chicago had preemptively taken care of these costs, and once again he'd made out better than he deserved.

Except for his wife. It was only four years later that her story came out, and even then as such a vague rumor that it's simply not worth telling.

De Rosny moved into the unfortunate shack on Wall Street, and for quite a long time nothing further was seen of him. Clearly the whole thing was some kind of practical joke on de Rosny's part. He even left the problem child's rustic name unchanged, although the marketing department had welcomed him with a chic, slimmed-down pseudonym. De Rosny insisted on reinstating the old-fashioned font, and replacing the comma with an *&* in the style of a year before yesteryear. He may have realized that he needed something to show, so he opened a branch office in California with his friends. (De Rosny loans de Rosny the following sum on the following terms . . .) The financial world found the part of his behavior they knew about disappointing, old hat even; de Rosny held internal meetings, not press conferences. Internally word was getting out about what all that talk of costs in Chicago had meant. It was an enormous sum. An outrage. This time no de Rosny was offering to contribute anything. His people in San Francisco had suddenly gone deaf too. They put it to a vote in Chicago. De Rosny would have been a very, very expensive ex–vice president; his only condition had a nasty catch to it, predictably enough. It was a challenge. They didn't mind picturing de Rosny picking up his hat; they couldn't bear imagining how the scene would continue: with him putting that hat on his head, turning in the door being held open for him, and saying goodbye to all the cowards. So de Rosny stayed in the boardroom, in his deputy's chair; in northern California the air force bought a bigger rocky plateau. In New York the talk persisted of a de Rosny failure.

In those years, although the elevated rail no longer hurtled by on its stilts above Third Avenue, that artery between Fortieth and Sixtieth was still mostly lined with low, four-story brick buildings, each one a box much like the others, built for classy renting and poor living. While scholarship was busy envisioning the death of New York City, the El generated more businesses on Third, the commuters walked on roundabout paths from Grand Central to Park and Madison, and the foot traffic called forth more street-level stores—bars, tailors, hair salons, little hideaways too—and on the upper floors many of the buildings were sealed off by dirt on the windows or blinds, with only a few monuments to prosperity hulking sheepishly between them. A gang of brokers swooped down onto one such block between Lexington and Third, bidding and underbidding, and no one could put a name to the purchaser, unless it was some superbroker. When a homeowner hesitated, the wrecking balls went to work next door and the plot of land was without form and void. One owner of a corner property still had a case moving through the courts while the steel frame of a new building was going up over his head, like a child's idea absurdly enlarged, and since the scaffolding was lit up at night, all the way up to the top, *The New York Times* remarked on it and backed its opinion up with a photo. You could look in at the construction site through generous ovals in the fences, even Gesine Cresspahl walked innocently by it, and stopped, and marveled that bricks were actually being stuck into the steel girders as a testament to tradition, from top to bottom as it turned out, leaving them hanging naked and exposed. The man on the corner kept tirelessly going from court to court, complaining to the construction firm, and the world, that General Lexington (or was it Washington?) had once spent the night at his establishment, which was why he alone from the whole block had let the wood from yesteryear remain, and painted it green and white, and de Rosny relented. It wasn't literally de Rosny, but he may have leased that part of the building from the construction company and apparently it was up to him to decide to keep the historic little building on the corner, under an umbrella of concrete, and again a venerable, ambitious bank from Chicago and Wall Street snagged forty-three lines and a photograph in *The New York Times*. Two gigantic towers went up, one on each end of the block, wrapped in blue glass, and even the part connecting them was fifteen stories high, and the workmen hadn't been shy about how deep they'd dug the foundations. The construction firm's name hung above the entrances in large, if removable letters, and the bank's ground-floor windows looked for the time being like a branch office, temporarily rented. De Rosny had a lease for the whole monstrosity and he sublet it out, to lawyers, to UN delegations who'd been waiting all this time not three blocks away for office space. In the end it got to the point where the bank was paying rent to itself, and now it was time to record the building in the land registry and *The New York Times*. The bank by no means wants to occupy its whole premises on its own, but it can evict at will and when needed, to make more room for itself, and the old-fashioned agricultural name with its *&* counts this milestone of uncompromising architecture as its property. Still, even this name isn't chiseled into the marble, it too is removable. For what de Rosny is truly proud of is that this building was built to be torn down at any time, within thirty days, and the empty lot sold to the next sucker at a tidy profit.

He'd been doing occasional work the whole time. The word *Chad* was now on people's lips in the bank, painfully familiar to some people, and de Rosny spread knowledge of other parts of the world too. Headquarters has moved from Chicago, the head of the family now lives on top of one of the towers, with a roof garden and swimming pool, wearing the emperor's new clothes while de Rosny is doing the work. All day long people come up out of the subways under Lexington Avenue, are swept north from Grand Central, and de Rosny has scorned neither their savings accounts nor their direct deposits. He made the building more than a few feet taller than Union Dime Savings's on Forty-Second Street, and he must have enjoyed seeing Chemical come after him, quite a bit later, and building on Third Avenue. And ads like the young lady with her lips softly, voluptuously open:

> *when she thinks of a bank,*
> *her reaction is CHEMICAL*

—none of those for him; he only barely accepted the marketing department's new logo of five lines derived from the company's initials, and the guards in the lobby may wear it embroidered over their hearts but de Rosny doesn't let his chauffeur, whose uniform is more in the British style. Everything in the building matches, every part of the machine fits together, from the square footage allotted to every workspace to the underground garage, but the template is not visible, it exists in de Rosny's head. He is considered strict, merciless even, in his role as boss; he's referred to in the building as D. R., dee-arr, in a respectfully amused undertone. The president, the head of the family, may make announcements over the company intercom in the cafeteria, but people pay less attention than they do to the rain rebounding off the sealed double windows; de Rosny's coldhearted utterances produce laughter, and one rumor among the employees is the almost sincere wish that the damn PA system someday finally be converted to television. This, they feel, will let them get at the truth, as if a de Rosny ever lets the cat out of the bag before the deal is done. So far only three people in the whole bank know what de Rosny has planned for the ČSSR, and one of them estimates the plan's worth in the neighborhood of $400 million, based on these bloodthirsty short-term loans he's been reading about in the paper.

De Rosny seems puzzled. He rushes out his door to meet Employee Cresspahl, hastily closes the door behind her, starts marching with long strides up and down his spacious carpet. A man thinking hard. A man thunderstruck. He could be a teacher, the kind who looks around the schoolroom absentminded, thin lipped, even after ten years giving no sign of his accumulated familiarity and friendship, just moving on to the next item in the lesson plan.

De Rosny cannot understand these Communists, especially not the Czech or Slovak ones. How could they go and count their money right out in the open, in front of civilians! And then say what they plan to do with it too!

Correct behavior, in Employee Cresspahl's view.

Against the rules, in de Rosny's. Not only are the Communists behaving like Communists, they're ruining the market for the loan he wants to slip them under the table, on the sly.

So that would be playing by de Rosny's rules. By this point Employee Cresspahl is permitted such comments, in this room, harmless, knees together, gaze fixed attentively on the bridge of de Rosny's nose—the schoolgirl. De Rosny amuses himself setting a little trap. Would his faithful and hardworking Gesine Cresspahl like to take a quick trip to Prague, pretending to be a tourist, and share a bit of de Rosny's inner life with the new leaders?

Employee Cresspahl doesn't want to be de Rosny's faithful and hardworking tool, she would have to discuss such a trip with her daughter first, she has a dentist appointment tomorrow, hairdresser's too. She doesn't want to, and she has to say: Of course. I'd be happy to. Tonight?

No. The Communists wouldn't take a woman seriously enough. As someone authorized to speak for a New York bank.

Employee Cresspahl begs to differ. Women's equal rights in Socialist countries.

De Rosny, with an unexpected twitch of his eyelid, reminds her of the statistics she's prepared on this topic too. Then he has her at his mercy and he starts by evaluating her report from Tuesday. He says: But with me, in the pay of us murderous man-eating capitalists, you'll get equal rights like you've never seen! Just wait four months!

– Very good. I can wait. Sir: Employee Cresspahl says.

So this is our life. This is what we live on.

April 26, 1968 Friday

Yesterday, in the middle of Times Square, New York observed the anniversary of the Warsaw Ghetto uprising twenty-five years ago, and we missed it. More than forty thousand men, women, and children died after a forty-day fight against German soldiers, and yesterday three thousand of the living stood on the sidewalk and traffic island where Broadway and Seventh Avenue diverge, and we weren't there. Fifty-five Jewish groups united to commemorate as well the six million people whom the Germans killed elsewhere, and we didn't know. Speeches were given, telegrams read, a tenor of the Metropolitan Opera wearing a yarmulke sang Yiskor for the dead, and we wouldn't have gone to that. But that doesn't help, the place where the rally was held is now, since yesterday, called Warsaw Ghetto Square, and we'll have to keep that in mind.

Cresspahl turned his town commandant's orders into regulations and behaviors in Jerichow, and would have liked to know what he was doing, and hardly once managed to understand K. A. Pontiy.

It wasn't the language. Since early July there'd been a Soviet Military Administration for the State of Mecklenburg and Vorpommern, in Schwerin, and it issued orders in German, signed General Fedyuninsky, countersigned Major General Skossyrev, and one after another they were brought to Cresspahl in the brickworks villa ready to be posted. K. A. Pontiy's German, too, may not have been good enough to teach the language but was good enough to make himself understood, at least in terms of what he wanted from the people of Jerichow. And yet Cresspahl didn't understand him. His child was given short answers

Thats how he wants it.
But he cant just do that.
He can.
Then why are you doing it?
Cause he won.
Thats what winning means, Cresspahl?
Times have changed, Gesine. Now—

and soon stopped asking questions. (The child was busy enough with other things.)

When Cresspahl tried to understand it in military terms, he got somewhere, sometimes. If he had to build a fortified headquarters in a small town, one that wouldn't be easy to see into, he would probably have started much like the Soviet commander. The houses on the west side of Town Street stood harmlessly outside the fence, betraying nothing. The mouth of the Bäk was closed off with painted wood, no barbed wire, much less a gate, and now that street was practically a blind spot in the town. Anyone wanting to get at the Soviet fort from the west would have to trample ripe grain. To the southeast the only access was a sandy turnoff into what looked like a back road petering out between the cemetery wall and the hop kiln, not like a military headquarters with armed guards, triumphal arch, and barbed wire. Cresspahl hadn't been promoted in 1917 to a rank involving officer training, so Pontiy's camp was a hideaway strictly by the tactical book as far as he knew.

By this point he'd had two weeks to observe his town commandant— in the middle of nights and early in mornings, charged with crimes and immune from prosecution at least for the time being—and whatever it was he managed to see, he hadn't been able to put it all together. K. A. Pontiy with his mussel-colored glances, no eyebrows, blunt naturally bald head, sluggish with age or from his shoulder wound, he might have been Cresspahl's age, maybe a little younger. His constant unconscious sighs might be due to illness, or grief, it didn't make him frail. Maybe he didn't stand up with

Cresspahl because then the German would be able to look down on his bald skull, and after a while Cresspahl was ordered to sit down, officially. He would walk in the door and K. A. Pontiy would be hooking the clasp of his uniform at the neck, especially for the foreigner, possibly for military dignity. Their discussions quickly turned into questioning, practically tribunals, for K. A. Pontiy would give a stretch with his numerous papers before him, and next to him there would be a lieutenant standing stiff and straight, hand on his pistol holster sometimes, adjutant and prosecuting attorney in one. Sometimes Cresspahl thought that Pontiy didn't want to lose something again, maybe his uniform, maybe his dignity. When angered Pontiy would stand up and put his cap stiffly on his head. He was suspicious of the Germans, and that was all right with Cresspahl, but he didn't threaten Cresspahl with removal from office, he threatened him with pieces of his life story. He was quite familiar with agricultural problems: Pontiy would tell him, his voice soft, sharp, and dangerous, accompanied by an unexpected wink. You couldn't pull wool over the eyes of an engineer like him: Pontiy would warn, contemptuous, but quickly shifting into an almost brotherly tone. As a sometime graduate of the Frunse Academy he stood up for the Red Army's honor! K. A. Pontiy revealed to his mayor, in obviously blind rage, right before sentencing him to arrest and execution, but then might take Cresspahl's measure with a satisfied look and dismiss him from the audience, like a badly raised child it'd be good to put a little fear into. Cresspahl couldn't figure him out, not even superficially.

If K. A. Pontiy had been to the Red Army's military academy, and was sixty years old, why was he a major with a little row of medals and nothing more? Why did his army assign him to a tiny town like Jerichow?

He'd said his parents were farmers, and marveled at charring the ends of fenceposts before digging them into the ground, and didn't know he could have demanded Carbolineum and tar oil? (He'd wanted a fence in Jerichow, and never in the Soviet Union?)

He was an engineer, and he tried to measure his fence's square footage with a field compass, enjoying the ingenious (if imprecise) instrument, like he'd never heard of a surveyor's tripod in his life!

He wanted to defend the Red Army's honor, as head
of the military branch

of the government bank
of the Soviet occupation forces
of the town of Jerichow

and his nation's representative to the German nation, and then he demanded, not from it, but from individuals, their gold and silver, and English and Dutch stocks, and every bit of platinum that turned up in Jerichow—whether the owners had come by such property during the war or not, whether they'd followed the Nazis or shunned them—and then didn't hand over these precious objects to his country, but kept them for himself, traded them for liquor, handed them out to guests or underlings. When Cresspahl was asked about Order No. 4, he might say things like: We're in the middle of the harvest, and he himself hadn't turned over much more than his out-of-date statements from the Surrey Bank of Richmond. He discovered the Red Army soldier known as Wassergahn making a fire with them in the brickworks-villa fireplace, so the Red Army and its government bank lost one or two pounds sterling. Cresspahl didn't say anything, he didn't want to get the guy with the inexplicable name punished, but he didn't understand the thing about defending the army's honor.

When the Red Army had put Dr. Kliefoth's coin collection into circulation as valid tender in Jerichow, Cresspahl put two Lübeck thalers, dated 1672, Schwerin, in his commander's palm, and K. A. Pontiy pounced on the coins like a chicken, examined the recent bite marks, and slipped the museum pieces into his breast pocket. He was head of the military branch of the government bank. Cresspahl was informed that the German Army had done the same thing in K. A. Pontiy's fatherlands, and what could he do but nod. In doing so, he had slandered the Red Army by comparing them to the Fascists and should have been shot at once, up against the cemetery wall! Cresspahl was freed with a passing question about the names of streets in town. He went to complain when the stupid child, Gesine, had obliviously worn a piece of jewelry around her neck that a nighttime looting patrol could tear off her. It was the five-mark coin from the Kaiser's time that Lisbeth Cresspahl had had Ahlreep's Clocks make into a brooch in October 1938, in defiance of the Nazis' robbery of everyone's gold, and at two in the morning Cresspahl had to explain to Major Pontiy the difference between coins and pieces of jewelry. K. A. Pontiy gave a grave nod, whether with fatigue or satisfaction; tried once with screaming; seemed relieved when the German didn't give in. He admitted he was right. Two days later, an abashed Red Army soldier walked into Cresspahl's kitchen, beckoned the child Gesine to come out, and handed her back the brooch, knotted in a silk kerchief. *Izvini pozhaluysta* means: "please excuse me"; *ne plakat'* means: "don't cry." Cresspahl went by the Ahlreeps to thank them for not having reported the hidden property, and K. A. Pontiy reminded him, days later, with a smile as pleased as it was mischievous, that he had restored the honor of the Red Army.

There were confidences exchanged. Cresspahl had wanted to know whether the commandant wanted a temporary or permanent fence, and K. A. Pontiy refused to tell him whether he would be handing the territory back to the British soon or the Jerichowers later. (The result was that Mrs. Köpcke had to set the fenceposts more solidly in stone.) What the Russian had answered, with an almost Mecklenburgish pleasure in a trap seen through and leapt over, was: For e-v-ver, Meeyor.

If only we could ask Cresspahl! From the child's point of view, the dealings between the two men often looked like hearty friendship, lurching between plain unconditional loyalty, murderous conflict, and stubborn-yet-heartfelt reconciliation. Would Cresspahl today be able to remember that far back?

When Cresspahl went walking through town with the two mysterious Karabiner 98k rifles, he didn't get home until late. K. A. Pontiy had had him picked up at Town Hall and escorted to the brickworks villa, and it turned into a party. Cresspahl was greeted with his very first handshake, given food and drink until midnight, and on the outside stairs K. A. Pontiy missed several times before managing to clap Cresspahl's shoulder, with feeling too.

Cresspahl turned in his telephone, and his Receiver for the People, because he and his house would be more severely punished than people who had only read the order. But that was the wrong thing to do. For all that his commandant spoke of the many telephones and microscopes that Germany owed the Soviets, he'd thought Cresspahl had more brains than that. Socialism had been promised, and Socialism wasn't life without telephones and radios, was it? For some it might be, but Cresspahl needed to be able to hear Pontiy, didn't he, whether by phone or over the radio. This time there was a parting handshake because Cresspahl had nodded about Socialism, and K. A. Pontiy sent him, from his personal stock, the eight-tube superhet that the refugees in Dr. Berling's apartment had turned in out of gratitude or superstition. Now the mighty blue-and-black thing sat silently on Cresspahl's desk, together with the memories of Lisbeth's first attempt and Dr. Berling's stubborn death too. Pontiy came by to see whether his mayor had consigned to the attic this proof of his trust in a select few.

Pontiy came by to see Cresspahl. Not at Town Hall, in his bed. Whether at midnight or two hours later he had him woken up, gave him two minutes to get dressed, and sat down beside him with a sigh for a chat about those nights by the sea when everything looks so low and yet the sky is the way it is over Leningrad, if not even higher. But Cresspahl had to play the host in his house just like Pontiy in the brickworks villa, which by this point included providing the vodka. (The mayor didn't have to trade on the black market in person—the one he had threatened with punishment in his official announcements—because Jakob did it for him. Jakob had brand-name liquor in stock, believe it or not, hidden somewhere in the house that no one else ever found, and Cresspahl preferred not to ask the boy questions. Only he wished the boy would tell him its equivalent value, not say that it was part of the rent for his mother and himself.) One morning, Hanna and I were woken not by the sound of birds but by the sight of two swaying men, dim in the dawn light, one of them saying, in an odd, surprised voice: *Deti, devushki.* The other confirmed: Children, girls: in a foreign, angular voice, like a mechanical dictionary, and it was my father and he'd spent the night drinking as though with a friend.

He didn't understand him. K. A. Pontiy, major in an army in possession of the science of atheism, appeared in church on Sunday with a four-man escort, waved kindly up at the organ that had fallen silent, annoyed until it started up again, then walked benevolently up and down between the pews full of singing people, gesturing like a conductor, until Pastor Brüshaver started his sermon. He did everything but sit at the front of the congregation. The uniformed visitation was over in eight minutes. Then the delegation went on to take a look around the cemetery, and K. A. Pontiy commented on the shady cave that the trees created as shelter from the July heat. In addition, he criticized the untended condition of several graves. On Monday the town commandant forbade, per Order No. 11, any future burials in the cemetery as well as parking the corpses in the chapel on Brickworks Road. Before news of these first strikes against the State Church of Mecklenburg had even reached the other end of Town Street, Aggie Brüshaver had a dapper, practically gallant visitor to lead to her husband's desk, K. A. Pontiy, military commandant. Brüshaver expected a ban on church services, and Pontiy asked for an explanation of the liturgy. He expressed how much he was looking forward to the next such performance. He noted with regret that the Nazis had indeed melted down the zinc and copper of the new bells to make cannons. A question about burials made him surly for a moment, as if his friendship were being repaid badly. When he left, Pastor Brüshaver was of the opinion that St. Peter's Church had been promised new bells soon, from who knows where. They said around Jerichow that the Soviets treated only pastors who'd been in concentration camps like that. But K. A. Pontiy paid his respects to the Catholic rectory, too, though the priest lacked those credentials (and he asked Böhm to give Brüshaver a bell after all, at least a small one). If there was to be atheism, then it would be a type with pious song and the tolling of bells from right next to the faithless commander's villa.

– *Public relations:* Marie says. – Clever guy: she says, if that's the right translation for *smart cat.* She thinks so long and hard about K. A. Pontiy, amused almost, as if she should venture to try to be friends with him (like the Gesine Cresspahl of back then. Like me!). She's having a harder time getting to sleep, stretched out under the blanket, breathing as if counting every breath. And yet what comes to her mind is public relations work.

– No, Marie. Here you're wrong.

– Okay, Gesine. Fine. I'm talking about people and times I don't understand. Presumptuous, precocious, foreign. You tell me how it was.

– No. That's not what I think of you. Who would ever—

– *Never mind.* Tell me.

– K. A. Pontiy's official attitude toward the church wasn't from 1953; East Germany was years away from being a country.

– Was the Pontiy from 1945 part of 1953?

– He wasn't in Jerichow anymore. We hadn't heard anything about him for a long time.

– So, he mostly wasn't. So, 1945.

— Cresspahl had Leslie Danzmann write up a memo about every *Vergewaltigung* reported to him, even the ones that didn't happen in Jerichow town, or Jerichow parish, the ones in the Rande military region or on the estates. There were a lot, and Cresspahl described more than where they'd taken place. That evening he'd hand them in at headquarters, to Mr. Wassergahn, and since the commander couldn't always read them right away

— there were lots of nighttime phone calls, meetings, serious accusations among friends.

— Right. At first K. A. Pontiy would have tried to be amicable. You know, young men, away from home too long, alone too long, Cresspahl's a man, K. A. Pontiy's a man...

— Man to man. Nudges in the ribs.

— Right. But no nudges.

— Cresspahl didn't go for it.

— So then came the stories about young German men, away from home too long, alone too long...

— And he had K. A. Pontiy shot for the comparison. Red Army and marauding Fascist killers.

— Right, you see? Sometimes it's okay, other times punishable by death.

— You don't understand?

— Cresspahl didn't understand.

— And so he was shot.

— Sentenced to be shot, if he ever brought another such memo without the name, rank, unit, and serial number of the perpetrator. Slanders against the Red Army that couldn't be verified were punishable by death.

— And slanders that could be verified?

— They'd be shot. He promised Cresspahl that, and

— out came the vodka again. Everything hunky-dory.

— And Cresspahl got a big sign on his front door, and another on the back door, and all the refugees under his roof got a special ID card

— Off-limits! Off-limits!

— And for a long time K. A. Pontiy would say, over and over, almost like Avenarius Kollmorgen, head tilted, remembering: Satisfied, Meeyor? Sat is fied?

— Gesine, what kind of crime is that exactly?

– *Vergewaltigung?* Never mind.

– Another water-butt story?

– No. But I forgot to leave it out.

– Gesine, I'm ten years old. Almost eleven.

– *Very well.* A man used violence against a woman to make her—

– Oh, that.

– When have you ever heard of *Vergewaltigung?*

– You mean *rape*, right?

– *I mean rape all right.*

– Gesine, what do you think is the number-one topic of conversation among every female person in New York? Don't you listen when the ladies trade stories by the swimming pool under Hotel Marseilles? You want me to imitate Mrs. Carpenter?

– Number-one topic of conversation in your class?

– Number-one-and-a-half. So admit it, K. A. Pontiy did care about public relations.

– I hope you don't get old in New York, Marie.

– You're in Jerichow, Gesine. In Mecklenburg. In July 1945.

– Right. During the first week, Pontiy asked his mayor: Why do the Germans see us, their liberators from the yoke of Fascism, and act like we're the devil?

– A negative theist then.

– Cresspahl didn't tell him that the English had tried their hardest to convince him to go with them, the night before they'd left. (That was Käthe Klupsch's night under Town Hall.) He wouldn't have been the only one they'd tried to convince. They left with loudspeaker cars and said no one but proven Nazis had anything to fear from their brothers-in-arms, but in secret they described their ally as the devil no less than the Americans did. A bunch of—

– Subhumans.

– The word was ready to hand. *Untermenschen.* Even K. A. Pontiy used it.

– For Germans. For some Germans.

– And in his innocence, he tried to get this sorted out with another order. He ordered, twelfthly, that the war was over, civilized behavior could rear its head once more. The custom of greeting one another, for instance.

Now every member of the Red Army in Jerichow was to be greeted properly, parked vehicles too, on spec.

– And the Jerichowers realized they'd forgotten the Austrian style of greeting. Something to do with the right arm, wasn't it? Ancient Roman?

– And Cresspahl didn't understand Pontiy.

– It's because he didn't help Pontiy understand the Germans. Or at least one of them, him.

– Or only this one.

– Anyone comes to their father's defense. I'd have done the same.

– But wasn't K. A. Pontiy another crook?

– *I like crooks.* As long as they just take their cut and don't do any other damage. *Don't you like crooks?* Didn't Cresspahl like crooks?

– Cresspahl could deal with crooks. He was clueless about them, he didn't do business with them—they got along just fine, like pals.

– Well, you don't have to understand someone right off, Gesine. *G'night.*

April 27, 1968 Saturday, South Ferry day
but we decided to spend our day off differently.

For this is also the day on which the Veterans of Foreign Wars show their loyalty to the nation with parades, in dark ceremonial uniforms, white puttees, white sashes around the hips and chest, kepis with badges on their heads, rifles over their shoulders, flags of club and state in holders on their bellies. Parochial-school bands and youngsters from drum-and-bugle corps will march with them, Fourth Avenue in the Norwegian neighborhood of Brooklyn as well as Fifth Avenue in Manhattan will be nationalistically decked out, the archbishop will lead and will end the march with the mayor. This year's parade, the twentieth since 1948, is also dedicated to the memory of the late Cardinal Spellman, one of the war's first and most enthusiastic supporters, and for the last two years the Loyalty Day Parade has been a show of support for American servicemen in Vietnam and a threatening fist to those who oppose the war. We could have gone to see that.

There was another option: *The New York Times*, on her Food, Fashion, Family, and Furnishings page, gives us a picture of the Scanlons and their daughters, Rebecca, five, and Caitlin, two, because someone bought an 1894 Brooklyn brownstone for $28,500 and didn't tear it down, they renovated it, and one of their delights is the third-floor bathroom with its original bathtub on claw-and-ball feet, the marble sink, stained-glass windows, and a toilet complete with pull-chain, in New York City. John Scanlon's Irish mustache could be one of ours, his Italian wife another, and the *Times* gave us their full address, 196 Berkeley Square. Subway to Grand Army Plaza. Marie doesn't feel like going there either.

She chose the peace parade in Central Park and dressed for the occasion as deliberately as a grown-up. There'll be police there, you have to wear something you can run in. Marie insisted that her mother take her dress back off and instead wear pants and an old blue cotton shirt (that could withstand a policeman's grip. That wouldn't hurt the feelings of any of the dark-skinned demonstrators from Harlem). In the end Marie, too, stood there dressed in self-defense, in sneakers intentionally left dirty, and looked in the mirror, learning from it that she should untie her braids and hold her hair in place with just a black hairband. (Shawnee uprising under Tecumseh, 1811.) And so we walked up Ninety-Fifth Street, white squaw and half-grown, wiry, blond-haired Indian girl.

On the corner of Amsterdam Avenue, we had to stop and scan the apartment buildings, the street, the corner store. Four children used to live here, friends if not great friends, and they let themselves be taken away from New York by their parents, to a suburb where the sapphire-green lawns are no more real than the imitation village streets made of plaster and aluminum. Marie can't understand a move like that, and maybe at least the children have come back to the Upper West Side of New York. Not today.

The streets were dry after a morning rain. The pale sun up ahead gave off some warmth, enough for a holiday.

On our zigzag path through the blocks, we often passed houses like the one the Scanlons had decided to save—once proud middle-class home for a life on three stories. A whole row of them had had their stairs and windows torn off; some of their brownstone comrades had been entirely gutted. The doors from inside the dead house stood around the bare lot where it had been torn down, some of them cracked apart, kicked in, weathered into various colors—inadequate fences like those surrounding a grave.

928 · *April 27, 1968 Saturday*

Marie didn't let the scars of urban speculation bother her; she looked the passersby carefully, intently in the face, unfathomable like an Indian. But when people called out Hey, Great Chief or let out the whinnying cry of the native inhabitants of this land she didn't give them the same closed-off expression she usually showed strangers. If she didn't actually say anything back, she did smile. These were New Yorkers, and she was going the same direction. Kindred spirits, friends of peace and of the Indians.

At eleven o'clock sharp we were on the corner of Central Park West and 101st Street, like the *Times* had told us to be, and the parade wasn't there yet.

The sky was cloudy by that point, letting the sun peek through only occasionally, grayly threatening rain.

The people lining the sidewalks didn't yet make them much more crowded than the usual pedestrian traffic, though they were waiting. Assistants of the parade committee were walking back and forth, trying to sell "original" buttons as souvenirs of the morning of April 27, 1968. Marie was disappointed that commerce had joined the march. She wasn't surprised; she probably expected it; still, the party now started on a slightly false note.

She took the free sheets of paper—the flyers in support of Senator Eugene McCarthy, depicting horrors of war. The Communist Party was handing out extras, too, but *The Daily Worker* offered her a language much like the one *Neues Deutschland* once offered me, and neither of us quite understood it. Lots of those sheets fluttered to the ground. Marie kept hers under her arm, as a favor to Mayor Lindsay (*which I undertook solely to keep New York City clean*).

Then she saw children holding balloons, green and blue and yellow, painted PEACE, but the dignity of her ten and a half years didn't permit her any more than a few kindly, slightly condescending glances at the littler kids. Then came adults with black balloons bearing the peace symbol. Marie clambered down the park wall and stretched so she could reach into her pants pocket. No more vendors walked by. She kept the dime in her fist anyway.

She watched the policemen, her eyes narrowed, Indian-style, under her black hairband. These guardians of law and order stood in small groups at the crossings, along the curb, familiar with one another. Their conversations looked private. Now and then they got their hands dirty, moving wooden sawhorses from the side streets to preemptively corral the parade. There were still a few cars driving down the street but the buses were already rerouted. Marie asked how many demonstrations her mother had done in her life so far. She was readier to believe a number over fifty than that we hadn't been allowed to just watch.

– You had to march?: she asked. – That's what we want to do too!

On the third floor of a building across the street, a young shirtless man clambered out onto his rented windowsill. He hung a stenciled banner across his two grimy bay windows, opposing the military occupation of the Negro neighborhoods. The black neighborhoods in New York are not in fact under military occupation. Then the agitator appeared with a telephone receiver at his ear, said some defiant and belligerent things to his distant friends, and sat down on the ledge for good. Marie kept looking up at this unathletic person, as if he were bothering her. She refrained from making any remarks; he was acting normal for New York, she couldn't tell him not to do it; she went looking for a place for us somewhere else.

But now the edges of the parade route were packed so full that any spectators stepping up to fill the gaps seemed pushy. In the soft hum of voices, the chattering of the police and network helicopters came down from overhead—none of the copters themselves did, though.

Ten minutes to twelve, and the parade got started with a group of men on motorcycles. The drivers were wearing brown suits with yellow stripes. The Magnificent Riders of Newark. Their bikes didn't roar (though the *Times* can't resist describing it that way), they whispered. The drivers had to keep putting their toes down on the ground for support, because of the slow pace. They were followed by the van with the famous people, under the protection of fifty sturdy bodyguards. Marie recognized Pete Seeger on the platform and waved to him ("Where Have All the Flowers Gone?"; "If I Had a Hammer"; "Turn, Turn, Turn"). Pete Seeger taking part in the demonstration made everything almost perfect again for Marie, but she was too shy to enter the parade right behind Pete Seeger's bodyguards. She let a bunch of other groups go ahead, mentally comparing her knowledge of New York with the neighborhood names on the banners they carried. Everyone was in a good mood, like on an outing. Instigators shouted happily: WHAT DO WE WANT?, and the chorus answered in syncopated pleasure: PEACE, NOW. Or: WHAT? PEACE; WHEN? NOW! When she decided to step off the sidewalk and join the kindred spirits, the show started.

The show was a row of young girls in Vietnamese clothing, black smocks under pointy straw hats. Short American girls dressed up as Vietnamese women. They wanted to show who the country was killing in their place in Vietnam. It wasn't their place. As if they might be killed here and now, on the corner of Central Park West and 101st Street. And as if even so it was just a game for them.

Marie could have gone with them, we would have found each other later. What spoiled it for her?

Then we saw the senior police officers walking alongside the relatively narrow column of marchers, one with a radio, another with files. Next to Marie on the sidewalk was a ten-year-old black girl with a steno pad, wearing a PRESS badge on her blouse, earnestly paging through what she'd already noted down. Marie turned in such a way that the other girl could have asked her a question, but the other girl acted like she didn't see her. Remarkably few signs in the parade that anyone had written and nailed themselves. People wearing crash helmets; in shabby military uniforms but with their shoes polished per army regulations. The occasional women tended to be wearing sunglasses; one of them, in a Pepita houndstooth suit, could have been me (in a photograph). By then we were walking on the sidewalk, looking for a subway entrance to escape down, neither of us admitting it to the other.

We also saw a tall young man from a school with an average sports team, his face strangely red. He was holding a teeny-tiny Chinese woman by the elbow, trying to be encouraging; she was desperately unhappy. (From afar, we saw the self-promoter fidgeting around on his outside ledge again; he was, as he'd hoped, greeted and applauded by several groups of people.) On Ninety-Sixth Street we found ourselves next to the unhappy couple again, she wearing his jacket now, but she still couldn't forgive him for something he couldn't suspect, at least not until later that night.

But it wasn't over at Ninety-Sixth Street, we were supposed to keep going until Seventy-Second and then into the park, to Sheep Meadow, where the rally with the speakers was to take place that afternoon. Mrs. Martin Luther King was scheduled to speak, Pete Seeger was there, Mayor

John Vliet Lindsay would come. Supposed to sit on the grass, sing in a group while waiting, chat familiarly with people nearby, about the weather, about the city.

– John Lindsay?: Marie said, disbelieving. – He was just on the platform at the Loyalty Parade!

Then she didn't want to accept that the mayor might appear in front of both the enemies and the supporters of the foreign war, equally a friend to both, wanting all their votes equally for the period after December 31 of next year. It was the first time she said, not in heralding tones, but pleading: It's still Saturday. Let's make a South Ferry day of it.

So we rode on the IND to the IRT, boarded the ferry *John F. Kennedy* at Battery Park, and traveled across the whole harbor to Staten Island. Marie braided her hair on the way, her head turned farther aside than usual and her fingers so slow that it was as if she were braiding in her thoughts. She cut up the hairband with the Indian symbols embroidered on it, with a shard of glass she found lying on the sidewalk, so that she could tie her braids. We took the bus from Staten Island over the Verrazano Bridge to Brooklyn and from there went back to Riverside Drive underground. Now it's six thirty and a yellow stripe is hanging over the Palisades, sharply outlined against the blurry bluish upper reaches of the sky. The sun has a yellow hole. Minutes later, the yellow cell dissolves into darker colors.

Marie knows not only her mayor John Vliet Lindsay's birthday, but the names of his children and what schools they all go to, she keeps photos of him from *The New York Times,* she has adopted his line about "the fun of getting things done"—she considered him a friend. She said something, as she tore his pages out of her scrapbook, but it won't get written down here, Comrade Writer. You can say that maybe she bawled while she was alone in her room, but nothing after that.

April 28, 1968 Sunday, Start of Daylight Saving Time
Sheep Meadow in Central Park: 522,725 square feet, divided by the minimal space required for one person to sit down comfortably—9 square feet— makes room to hold 58,080 persons (not counting a remainder of 5 square feet); that's how meticulous *The New York Times* is. When Mrs. Martin

Luther King arrived, the Meadow was only half filled. She read a decalogue of ten commandments on Vietnam, said to have been on Dr. King when he was assassinated, and the tenth said: Thou shalt not kill. Long, sustained applause.

Another protest took place yesterday, on Washington Square, unauthorized but justified with "The streets belong to the people." Someone who struggled against the police was wrestled to the ground by numerous plainclothes men, kicked, kneed, hit with a leather blackjack (a "sap"), and anyone who tried to photograph police loading demonstrators into a paddy wagon was arrested along with them. That doesn't make Marie feel better—she wishes she hadn't missed anything there either.

The day before yesterday, a doctor in Czechoslovakia committed suicide—a former physician in Ruzyně prison in Prague—and the new interior minister, Josef Pavel, says he was tortured by that same doctor. And wants an official investigation too. What the Communist sister parties agree to do among themselves, the Czechoslovakian one wants to break the silence on, and a "Club for Independent Political Thought" has sprung up, and not been banned, even the Socialists are allowed, who want to bring about an unrestricted democratic life. What will become of this country?

Cresspahl was now in his third month as mayor of Jerichow and still learning on the job.

He couldn't do much with his mirror image. If he tried to demand, as mayor, that the citizens of Jerichow do what he was expected to do as a citizen, that didn't work. He remembered when he'd had to pay taxes and preemptively set the deadline well in advance: August 10 for business taxes, August 15 for property taxes, September 10 for income and corporate taxes, and so on each quarter. Leslie Danzmann helped him realize, though, that most of the May and June payments hadn't been made, various people in Jerichow hadn't paid even under the Nazis, had decided to wait out the British, and had no intention of delivering either the current or past due under the Soviets. K. A. Pontiy had no suggestions except ruthless full enforcement, relying on one of his Orders and the excuse that the nonmunicipal taxes were still "Reich taxes," even if the Reich was no more (same as "German Reich Railway," which wasn't even run for Germans anymore either). Cresspahl had no one who could collect the back taxes; Leslie Danzmann had to calculate a collection surcharge of 5 percent of past due amounts, retroactive to the Reich's March and February, on every index card. The mayor's office might post it, could in totally flagrant cases send out notices—which only put the government bank in debt to schoolboys for messenger fees—but "Hitler's taxes for Stalin" did not materialize. Since the town didn't have any money it could only be in the townsfolk's pockets, and anyway it was worthless in the age of barter, but the townsfolk insisted in stubbornly seeing themselves as subjects of the Soviets, not of the municipality of Jerichow.

People like Peter Wulff authorized the town to deduct taxes from their bank accounts, for the time being. But the bank accounts were frozen, no one was allowed to make transactions—not Cresspahl, not the account owner, not even K. A. Pontiy.

K. A. Pontiy ordered Cresspahl to charge the Jerichowers an additional 5 percent of any withheld moneys, as a penalty. Now Leslie Danzmann could do her calculations in units of ten, that was easier. It stayed on paper, and K. A. Pontiy ordered Cresspahl to "take executive action" with respect to the defaulters' property if they didn't pay cash. Cresspahl asked what he meant by "executive."

Town Commandant Pontiy meant the confiscation of tradeable objects: machines, motors, tools. And the like.

Cresspahl suspected that if the means of production were taken away, labor might drop off, taxable labor included. K. A. Pontiy, with a sigh, bowed before the almighty power of dialectical materialism, and ordered such objects to be left in the owners' hands, but not as their property.

The mayor couldn't make him understand, he could only repeat, that then the work really wouldn't get done. Pontiy agreed to order the work. Sometimes Cresspahl even laughed, it looked like a coughing jerk of the shoulders, and Pontiy sighed. Strange country, this Mecklenburg.

Well, *khoroshó.* Here's an order: confiscate the real estate. All or part. Then they won't have to pay property tax.

K. A. Pontiy stretched in his seat as if he wanted to have the problem taken out and shot. It was formerly Papenbrock's office chair, and two inlaid lions were interlocked over Pontiy's shiny head. He turned around to look sternly at his second lieutenant, signaling he should take his hand off his holster. Then he ordered Cresspahl to secure the tax debt by confiscating furniture. As punishment and to set an example. Sat is fied, Meeyor?

Cresspahl drank the liquor meant to indicate mutual understanding (Pontiy had put his Mauser down on the table so that his mayor would drink), but was unable to return to Town Hall satisfied. Many, perhaps most of the houses in Jerichow had belonged to the nobility, only a few from that class had left for the west, and they didn't pay Jerichow property tax. But anyone who had left Jerichow after May 8 had had his property temporarily confiscated for the good of the town, and permanently if he didn't return within a year. Now the municipality owned a lot of its buildings, but had to pay property taxes to itself, and didn't have the money to.

(The mayor's office could have raised the rents on the town's property. Raising the rent was strictly forbidden. And the Jerichowers put aside the lease and rent money for the owners who had fled—in accord with the law, they felt, here too—and the government bank got nothing.)

Cresspahl introduced monthly payment of wage and revenue taxes, instead of quarterly. (The commandant hereby orders that a state of emergency is in effect.)

But Jerichow had been the workshop for the surrounding countryside; tradesmen didn't get enough work from the town itself. The estates and village precincts in the area, now divided into independent "Kommandaturas," paid in kind whenever they could (or were allowed to) hire someone in Jerichow. The farmers compensated their laborers not with money but with food and drink and a roof and the promise of wheat in the winter. Was Cresspahl supposed to impose a tax on payments in kind?

Mrs. Köpcke, construction, ceded the government bank's debt to Mrs. Köpcke to the government bank, to offset against any city and Reich taxes she owed, in advance, until March 3, 1946. She wrote off these payments as made. Cresspahl signed. Receipt of one (1) fence plus cash-free tax payments, confirmed.

There was another nighttime fight with K. A. Pontiy. Pontiy placed himself on the side of the German Reich and pronounced all obligations toward the aforesaid valid past the date on which the German Reich had capitulated to him and the Western Allies. The freezing of bank accounts had no consequences of a legal or civil nature. The days of civil rights were over!

Cresspahl, then, took it that the Red Army was a force majeure that had rendered the financial institutions insolvent.

Pontiy didn't fall for that and dismissed his mayor with the order to institute dog taxes. Droll and devoted creatures, dogs. Don't you think so? Omitting to register: punishable. Per dog! Let's say: 150 reichsmarks.

Cresspahl canceled the corporate tax. There were no longer such corporations in Jerichow.

Then he seized the cash reserves of the credit union and paid the concerned parties at the hospital, the gasworks, the sanitation department the wages he owed them for the past three weeks ("since the Russians"). He partly offset the amount, though, with the remaining assets of the estate owners, whose accounts hadn't been frozen, but were now, since they'd left.

– A mayor like that always has one foot in jail.

– I know, Gesine. All ri-i-ight. But your dad wasn't a crook. Like John-Vliet-Lindsay!: Marie said. That was yesterday. She refuses to be consoled, and Cresspahl's inching toward Socialism had no effect on her.

April 29, 1968 Monday

If work awaits in midtown then you have to leave Riverside Drive at eight thirty, the same as before, but the sun is rising on a different timetable. The start of Daylight Saving Time has again moved it way over to the left so that it shines blindingly down from above as it did six weeks ago. Ninety-Sixth Street's canyon floor was still deep in shadow, though, and the lost hour gives us a real feeling of shady early mornings.

When Cresspahl's child woke up, the July sun was already surrounding the house, the shade cooling the room. It was so early, though, that she still couldn't hear any sound from the other people in the house, and everyone was really asleep in the commandant's headquarters across the road. In the silence in the shadows Gesine clambered out the window and crept through house and yard looking for traces of Jakob.

He wasn't easy to find, and suddenly he'd be standing there, where just before there'd been nothing.

Going looking for him was a bit desperate, and a twelve-year-old girl has her pride. Jakob wasn't always in Jerichow. He'd rented himself out with his horses, in a village far to the west, hours away on foot. Two open

windows by the front door were a good sign—Jakob's mother kept them
closed at night, despite the big notice proclaiming the house off-limits.
Gesine Cresspahl walks past them now, almost without a sideways glance;
she's just on her way to the pump. She is up to nothing special when she
walks out into the yard, every inch a girl out for a stroll, she can casually
turn around and check if the chimney is smoking, an even better sign.
Because nobody cooks breakfast as early as Jakob. But that wakes Cresspahl,
who pads to the kitchen in his socks (so as not to wake a sleeping child)
and joins Jakob for coffee. And now the daughter of the house could walk
through the door and sit down at the table, she too has the right to breakfast,
but it would stand out, it's too early, the children in the house get their
first meal from Jakob's mother, and the one time she did join them after
all Cresspahl spoke differently, as did Jakob. As if she weren't grown up.
Jakob's year of birth, 1928, subtracted from her own comes out to the same
annoying difference every time. Five whole years. You can sit in the shade
next to the rotted beehives and calculate the years, and suddenly there's
Jakob standing at the pump, unwinding the scarf from around his neck.
How could he walk barefoot so quietly! (There was sharp gravel on the
path from the back door, scattered there years ago by Cresspahl to discourage
his child from going out barefoot.) The wound on Jakob's neck had closed
up but it still looked red and raw, and Gesine Cresspahl felt very embarrassed.
She was hoping to stay hidden, and now he was calling her. Now she is
standing at the pump like a child and helping an eighteen-year-old grown-up
splash water over his neck and head and making a face showing how
exploited and ill-used she feels. But since Jakob nods instead of saying
thank you, the child can't say Don't thank me! Then he's off, without even
a chance to ask him about the red fox, and everything's all wrong, it would've
been better not to have seen him at all.

One weekend, late in the afternoon, almost evening, Gesine Cresspahl
was sitting high in one of the walnut trees outside the house. Not to worry,
she has things to do up there. She might be carving something into the
bark with a knife. Or maybe, if she's perched right up at the top, almost
above the branches, a girl might be counting the roof tiles. Or the ones
with too much moss on them. Or looking for broken ones. In no way shape
or form was she up in the tree because you can look west from there without
anyone seeing you. You can't trust your own eyes when there's a little mark

on the horizon, trembling before the setting sun, and a quick breath later the country road is deserted. He could also come out of the forest, at the bare spot where it's called the Rehberge. But to see that you have to climb up to the top of the tree, where it's dangerously thin, and it would sway, and betray a child, who's too clever for that. She had just decided that the figure at the corner of the Russian fence was a stranger, not Jakob, when she heard his voice. She was so startled her foot slipped and made a jagged sound. But that could easily have been a bird. Only she couldn't find Jakob. The Abses' windows were open but his voice didn't sound indoors. It was soft, but as if he were in the yard. The yard was empty. – *Devyatnadtsat':* said the voice, "nineteen," and down below she saw Wassergahn the Red Army soldier squatting by the tree trunk. He shook his head and started telling a long story: *Posledniy den' . . .* – *Ne yasno:* Jakob said pleasantly, "don't know about that," and now she saw him too. He was squatting there like Wassergahn, both of them staring over the green fence and up at the top floor of the villa, clearly not doing some kind of deal but working to improve the friendship between the German and Soviet peoples. Yet she saw a fistful of the blue-and-white Allies money, no one in Jerichow would accept it as payment, Jakob stuck it in his shirtsleeve. (In his shirtsleeve.) After too long a while Wassergahn stood up and stomped over to the gate in the green fence, where he belonged, and Jakob stayed crouching under the tree. He didn't look up, oh no, but he stayed there relaxing until Cresspahl's daughter was totally stiff from sitting without moving on one and a half branches.

That night she was back up in the tree, and someone really did come out of the house, tinkling softly. Apparently a very fat man, because he walked as if on eggshells and his pants legs were exceedingly stuffed with something. This unknown individual stopped at Gesine's tree and gripped it hard enough that the upper branches actually did shake a little, then said, in Jakob's voice, dreamily, appreciatively, in anticipation: I wonder when these walnuts'll be ripe.

Blushing is something you can feel happening to you; some people learn that as just a child, even on a dark night.

And he liked Hanna Ohlerich more, that was obvious. Probably because she was a couple months older. True, he brought Gesine an egg too, but he just put hers down, he put Hanna's right into her hand. She might say as casually as you like that Jakob was in the yard, she's known it for the last half an hour, maybe she's talked to him, and it wasn't her waiting for him, was it? And you had to sleep at night next to this Hanna Ohlerich, and it didn't matter how wide the bed was, you could never get far enough away from her. There she was, sleeping, *she* wasn't thinking about . . . people tinkling like glass in the night. Hanna sat next to him on the milk-can rack and asked him questions! Like it was nothing! True, he called her "child," and called Cresspahl's by her name. Because Hanna's parents were dead. She told him about when she'd worked as a machinist at sea, but it was only the Baltic, that flooded field, and she'd been allowed near the cutter's engine only to clean it! Another girl definitely needs to sit there too, just to make sure the bragging doesn't get out of control. Lurking there a ways off, not wanting to join the conversation or anything. So, Jakob was from Pommern? Gesine had known that for a long time, and the name of the village too, and that it had been on the Dievenow River. But some girls go on to ask about Usedom Island. So it hadn't helped Jakob in the slightest that the Poles hadn't taken it? Not at all. And so Jakob is planning to stay in Mecklenburg? And some girls hold their breath until he says: *We dunno yet*. How else is someone to hide her sinking feeling of disappointment than by asking if Jakob has ever been to Podejuch? Podejuch in Pommern. Jakob's never heard of Podejuch. If someone doesn't know what to say next she has to leave the conversation, and her whole body feels like it's lost a battle. It feels shriveled up.

And the grown-ups kept Jakob all to themselves, a child never got the chance to talk to him! If there happened to be any children who wanted to. Jakob was like the house newspaper. When Jakob said that the Germans were allowed to use electricity in Lübeck again, even if only to listen to the radio, there was no point in doubting him. Maybe he'd been across the demarcation line. Jakob said: Stettin's in ruins, and the Poles won't let more than forty thousand Germans stay—and so Stettin was rubble with only forty thousand German inhabitants; a child asking, rather slyly, about the Haken Terrace was of no use, cause look, he knew it. He sat there looking a little sleepy, friendly enough, eyes a bit veiled, too much dark hair. You hardly noticed him at all. Clearly that's how he got around so much. Or did he know all these things from the papers? He didn't, there weren't any.

Not long after that, Jakob was sitting at the table in Cresspahl's house, which was where he belonged after all, and yet the man almost never came to Jerichow. Jakob said something about nuts. When walnuts turn ripe.

It's a while before a girl can leave the kitchen without overturning the table or tearing the door off its hinges!

High up in the tree—the black market tree, not the other one—Gesine Cresspahl found a piece of paper tied to a branch. It wasn't a piece of paper. It was a newspaper! The British Military Government news sheet, published in Lübeck by the Twenty-First Army. Really and truly, a newspaper, with a price on it even.

Gesine Cresspahl would have liked to think Jakob had swum the Trave Canal or Dassow Lake to Lübeck for her sake. But that was too much. He must have had business to do there.

Still, Cresspahl's daughter now shared a secret with him, and she was the only one who knew. And that night, when Cresspahl said he wished he could read the news from Lübeck for once, she denied to his face that she'd ever heard of a Western newspaper.

And Jakob had betrayed her to the grown-ups again, because Cresspahl said: It was a secret, and can she keep a secret again, and the thing was in the right-hand walnut tree, fifth branch pointing east, top surface.

– That's what being in love is like, Gesine?
– That's what it was like for me.
– Is that something I'll inherit?
– Are you ashamed of me, Marie!
– No. Really, I'm not. It's just, I might do it differently.
– Go right ahead.
– Should I tell you when it happens?
– You won't.
– So just because that's what you were like as a child, I have to—
– No. That's not why. You are free, independent, not subject to parental directives, all of that.
– Did the British news feel wet?
– It had never been in the water.
– Good. So what was in it?
– Not much. Things I've forgotten. And also that at the end of July 1945 an airplane crashed into the Empire State Building.

– A plane? Gesine!

– A B-35 bomber, and it rammed the seventy-ninth floor of a building that was the tallest in the world at that time. Empire State Building, 350 Fifth Avenue, between Thirty-Third and Thirty-Fourth Streets. Well known to every documented New Yorker.

– You want to link Jakob to New York somehow, even if it's by newspaper.

– If I want him in New York, I always have you.

– Thank you for the information.

– About the B-35 bomber?

– That my father knew that New York State's nickname was the Empire State. And that we have a 102-story building here.

– It'd be 101 in his way of counting.

– Right. And also, I wanted to say I'm sorry.

– No.

– Yes, I've been horrible since Saturday.

– No you haven't.

– Yes I have. I've been sulking, I haven't been answering you properly, I've been horrible, just because of this elected official, Lindsay.

– Forget it.

– And if I ever forget what my father was like, let me know.

April 30, 1968 Tuesday

Now what might Employee Cresspahl be looking for in one of the top drawers of Kennedy Airport, and with a child, too? The restaurant is called To the Golden Skies, if not even higher; the management prices in the triple-filtered cool air, the tables are covered in genuine linen and laid with stainless steel pricier than silver, the berth-like booths are widely separated and to hell with the exorbitant rent per square foot, each is an island unto itself, under lamps specially made in Italy, and the built-in music is so genteelly restrained that it's almost silent in the room. It's almost not an American restaurant. Whether European tourists preparing for their return or natives getting accustomed to the strange manners people have abroad, everyone here has to pay a stiff price, and at first the waitstaff, in brightly colored livery after the fashion of forgotten royal courts, view the mother and child at window table three as a risk.

The lady, thirty or thirty-five years old, is dressed appropriately for the establishment, although people have been known to dress up in such suits who in the end are nothing but typing-pool girls from midtown. She's had her hair done by a professional but it's still not much more than a negligent skullcap reaching down to her neck, practically a man's cut, a salon in deepest Queens could have done it instead of one on Madison Avenue. She's not wearing jewelry, thinks a long bare neck is good enough. Thirty-five years old. No accent, but a European handbag. *No* white shoes. Who knows, maybe she just came from the East Side Terminal by bus, she might never have enough money for a plane flight in her life, much less dinner at the Golden Skies, and she'll pay for her dine-and-dash with a visit to the night court in southern Manhattan.

The management has nothing to do with such losses—the head waiter is responsible for them out of his own pocket. It wouldn't be the first time. Anyone in the world can book a table from Washington, through the Scandinavian Airlines system, window view, two and a half hours, calling themselves Professor Erichson. This lady's no professor.

The child, now. The young lady. Now that's a child who belongs in restaurants. She's in fourth or fifth grade, she's not scared of the money she breathes in when she's here, the money quietly watching her in the form of fine woods, sheep's wool, waiters' graceful footsteps. This is hardly the first time she has accepted a leather and vellum menu with an attentive smile and then laid it aside, as though time were not money. Orders water. But a pitcher full of water and mineral ice is standing right in front of her, so now she acts modest, lets her glass be turned right-side up and filled, like a present. Says "eh-hem," not "thankyouverymuch"; samples the free sample; nods to a waiter like a vineyard owner. Maybe a foreigner, this child. They don't wear their braids so long here, the clips might be from Tiffany instead of Woolworth's, hair that white blond with sandy shadows in it probably came to Kennedy on Scandinavian Airlines, that's for sure. The child doesn't put her elbows on the table the way children do, she keeps her hands loosely folded, and not around her glass either, supported by her forearms, like they taught her in finishing school. She keeps talking and talking to the rather silent patron, in a fun-loving soprano voice she keeps low in pitch—only occasionally does the tone rise sharply. That sounds childish. Or British. You walk past them without a glance, and your glance is drawn to them anyway, and you pour the young miss another glass of her goddamn free water and get an acknowledging look in return, a nod, downright chummy. Gray-green eyes, not like her mother's. Still, a lively face. Her lips aren't her mother's either. Doesn't let the presence of the waitstaff interrupt her in the slightest, just keeps telling her story about a suitcase full of dolls. Clearly a story about some totally different child—one that's just turned funny. She's trying to cheer the woman up without annoying her; can the corners of her eyes be laughing at the same time, at a waiter who wants to finally take their order? No, a child like that doesn't do such a thing, and when the doubtful table at last orders a bottle of Beaujolais you can give the child a discreet wink, plausibly deniable. Because only one of the pair at the table is using her glass, and the party is still doubtful, isn't it.

I was sitting that same way in the Düsseldorf airport eleven years ago, a month's saved-up money in my pocket and even so the staff kept an eye on me, as someone unlikely to be able to pay. I just wanted to look at the planes departing for points farther west, where I wasn't allowed to go. I wanted to go to England.

We were sitting that same way in early May seven years ago, at a picture window like this one, when the airport was still called Idlewild, and wishing we were in one of the planes scuttling into the air between us and the thickening ink of the sky—heading out over the Atlantic, away from here. We wanted to get out of New York, go back to Europe; Flushing, Queens, New York, 11356, had been too much for us. Marie let herself be talked into one last trip into Manhattan, since her toys were all back in the hotel. Seven years later here we are.

We've been back to Idlewild/Kennedy Airport, but when it was with luggage Marie always looked at the ticket to make sure it was good for a flight back home; since then we've picked up friends or cars or bosses here, once it was money to reinstate the constitutional rights of a certain Signor Karsch. And from year to year the child was ever more helpful, a credit to us. And now and then we come for a meal as if we'd missed our usual mealtime, but actually it's a date with D. E.

Aka Professor Erichson. Suddenly, as soon as they see him, the waiters enlarge their temporary politeness into hospitality. They think they are faced with an older gentleman, what with his gray hair—he is only turning forty this year. The fat in his face, purplish more from burst blood vessels than a cold wind, makes him look older too. He sometimes has a truly gray, distant look, and however agile he may be in moving his heavily weighed-down bones, it can still look elderly. He stops in the door as if he doesn't know what to do; he hands over his hat like a sacrifice; and yet they recognize him as someone who belongs here. It's not the money. They won't inspect his jacket—constructed especially for him, and in Dublin, and for more than three hundred; when they see his pipe they won't guess that it cost what someone else might fork over for a small car, and anyway he keeps it hidden in his hand like a small sick bird. He is dressed 100 percent like an American on a trip. It's not his habits: he doesn't carry himself like a frequent honorary guest at D'Angleterre in Copenhagen or the banquet halls of the allied Western air forces. He doesn't review the restaurant while standing in front of the maître d', neither by gentle sniffing nor visual scrutiny—maybe the subtly cool air makes him shiver slightly. We can't explain it and yet from the very first word and nod and footstep he is recognized as someone who knows his business. Restaurants such as this are run for him, and he takes it upon himself to dignify their labor, and to pay for it, with pleasure on both sides if possible. He's acts like the waiter's partner, and we believe it; we can't prove anything except that the man with the serving trolley stops and looks at the new customer in an objective, almost physicianly way, smiling to his equal. Now D. E.'s here and immediately we look like a family of three who haven't seen one another for a week or three, the type to observe one another without surprise, pleased, looking forward to later, and for now with wordless understanding. Maybe he'll offer a compliment: *Your wheat's in bloom, Gesine.*

> *Your Czechoslovakia's shedding its skin, Gesine.*
> *Are all the dead the same to you, D. E.?*
> *Not the ones from 1952. But when someone hangs himself in 1968 because he was a prison doctor in Ruzyně, Prague, in 1952, he is making a statement.*
> *But twenty-six people in the ČSSR have hung or poisoned themselves this month just for having obeyed Stalin about torture and executions back in the day.*

Were they forced to?

No. Maybe then.

They had the same choice then that they have today.

The Republic should do it.

Kill them?

Punish them.

Arrest them for their murders before they commit suicide?

Yes D. E., yes. Fair trials and all that.

For that the Communists first have to take power in Czechoslovakia.

You see. But a Stalinist, the former minister for national security, gets up and tells a Slovak newspaper: It was Stalin's orders.

It's not going quickly enough for him, Gesine.

But the Czech papers act like he'd been talking about the weather!

Your Mr. Dubček, he can't alienate his Soviet friends, even with the truth.

But the Soviets've sent shipments of wheat to Czechoslovakia for twenty years and now they're suspending delivery.

They'll pin another medal on that Stalinist for having spoken of Stalin's crimes.

These homemade dialectics.

You're going to have to learn them again, Gesine.

Okay. So we'll negotiate Canadian wheat for Prague.

It's just a detour, Gesine.

There's something I want to say about these detours. When Marie's ready.

Marie's saying something.

– John Vliet Lindsay's a ——: Marie says. She's waited until the reunion was safely underway—she's been watching her D. E. and not wanting to bother him in the brooding he's been stuck in since February, which he can refuse to discuss but can't conceal. Still, D. E. has to be notified of changes in the family situation. For her latest information about Mayor Lindsay, she really and truly sat up straight and took a deep breath and still her voice cracked.

– John Vliet Lindsay's a ——: D. E. says, overtrumping her bad word with one even worse, which not everyone knows in New York, which certainly isn't meant for the ears around this table and never, ever, for the mouth of a child. But it makes Marie feel better. She has watched D. E.'s mouth and looked into his eyes and mentally compared what D. E. used to say about her now abandoned friend, and she believes him. She laughs to herself, a little embarrassed at the unexpected word but delighted to have been answered like a grown-up. Now we can start.

– Your wheat's sure in bloom, Gesine: D. E. says: Your Canadian socialist wheat: he says.

This is how we should be, together. That's what he wants. It is too bad that he has to keep an ear out for the gently squealing sounds of the engines outside the dark window, listening for a plane that will take him away, and definitely not a commercial flight to Scandinavia. Another hour and half, maybe, and the waiter will bring him a slip of paper with a telephone number on it, or bring a telephone to the table, and it really is too bad. It would be different if we agreed to live with him. Marie would agree. He won't bring it up. All that's missing is one word, spoken out loud. Why can't I say it?

May 1, 1968 Wednesday

How's it going back in the West German homeland?

In Stuttgart, after 144 sessions and one and a half years, a court has sentenced some SS soldiers who kept the Jewish population of Lemberg (Lvov) as slaves before finally killing them in the Belzec death camp. (When someone didn't feel like shooting prisoners, his superiors did nothing to him.) In Lemberg some 160,000 people died of the Germans, in Belzec one and a half million, and now one of the guilty is going to spend life in prison. The other, according to the court, spent most of his time drunk and so he's getting just ten years, since mercy must prevail.

In Baden-Württemberg the New Nazis won 9.8 percent of the vote in the state election, which is 12 of 127 seats in the state parliament. Every tenth person on the streets of Baden-Württemberg...

The federation of West Germany has eleven states and in seven of them the New Nazis have representatives in the legislature. Chancellor Kiesinger is purportedly embarrassed, Nazi that he was himself, and Brandt, his partner the anti-Fascist, is said to regret the loss of trust. So they say.

A stiff price—that's what *The New York Times* calls what the Social Democrats are paying over there for joining the right-wing governing coalition. But she stays true to her principles, our staid aunt, and blames the restless left-wing students too. If they'd only kept their mouths shut after the shooting of their leader, the voting public wouldn't have gone over to the side of those who promise New Violence and severity. It should've been a happy Easter!

– What does that have to do with you! You only used to live there once!: Marie says.

– I only used to live there once.

– But we've got a revolution right here, twenty blocks from our front door!

– Did you see it?

– Today's the fifth afternoon! Even you should know that, from your newspaper. Your aunt must have told you something.

– She didn't say anything about a foreign child running around Columbia with the policemen and the students.

– Not running. I stood there and watched, like other people. To make sure the police wouldn't start beating people when they started arresting them.

– Then they'll beat them in their paddy wagons.

– You really are a spoilsport, Gesine.

– But at least the students saw that a girl was watching, and that she agreed with them.

– It's not much, I admit it. But maybe I'm learning how to do it.

– For when you're nineteen.

– So tell me what the problem is! You're responsible for my upbringing.

– Don't get arrested.

– Gesine, don't you agree with the students?

– Agree? Oh, sure, I agree.

– There. They're trying to make their university better, and after talking and talking they're doing something now, you can see it. You must be in favor of the university stopping construction of the gym in Morningside Park and ending its affiliation with IDA, the Institute for Defense Analyses, it does research for the Pentagon.

– Those are noble wishes.

– They didn't just write letters or carry signs around. They occupied buildings, you know that.

– And barricaded themselves in with bookshelves.

– Gesine, are you against violence? Since when?

– I'm against violence to books.

– Oh, that. They drank up the president's sherry, they slept on his green carpet, leaving only cigarette butts and empty cans.

– Almost half a million dollars in damage.

– Columbia's a capitalist enterprise, isn't it? If the capitalists won't comply they'll have to pay.

– And scare people off with the vandalism of the educated youth.

– Okay, fine. A tactical mistake.

– It didn't have to be. That's what the whites left behind, but in Hamilton Hall, where the dark-skinned students were, there was no garbage. They had their own sanitation teams cleaning the building every morning during the occupation, didn't they?

– They did. A point in favor of the Afro-American Society, and one against the SDS.

– Students for a Democratic Society.

– No?

– Definitely, Marie. And last night the police came in the middle of the night and removed them. Seven hundred arrests.

– A setback, a temporary setback. But it isn't true anymore that only success counts in this country.

– There's also the publicity.

– Gesine, you yourself would contribute ten dollars for the prisoners' bail, if anyone asked you.

– Fifteen. To be polite.

– Isn't it revolutionary to fight for something that helps other people?

– It isn't selfish, that's true. Is it revolutionary when the first demand is nothing but amnesty?

– If they want to go unpunished, maybe they think the punishment is unjust.

– They can only go to school once in their lives?

– If you insist, Gesine: Yes, they're white middle-class students. Maybe they're not exactly sure where they are. Any other objections?!

– Point 2 on your flyer there.

– Cease construction of the gymnasium in Morningside Park. Totally fine.

– Marie, the university bought the land from the city seven years ago, there've been plans drawn up since 1959, and even then Morningside Park belonged to the people from Harlem, the blacks, and a separate swimming pool for the Harlem community was part of the plan, and the spokesmen for the blacks were happy for their children. What's the difference in 1968?

– That it's harder to see.

– That the public part, for Harlem, would be at the bottom, and that the blacks could get in only from the eastern side?

– No, Gesine. Maybe the people of Harlem know who they are and what they deserve more now, maybe they don't want charity from the whites' university and don't want to have to enter through the back door.

– And that's why the university should build on its white side, Riverside Drive.

– Right.

– Out of respect for the people of Harlem.

– Right.

– And Harlem still has no swimming pool in the park. Is that the right price?

– It is, Gesine. The city should build them one. They deserve it.

– I agree.

– Are you just giving in or do you really agree with me now?

– I really agree with you.

– Anything else I can do for you, ma'am?

– Point 4 on your flyer. The IDA.

– They're working for the Joint Chiefs of Staff! They've got blood on their hands! They evaluate weapons systems, do research for the Pentagon, help the government think up ways to fight uprisings!

– They've existed since 1955 and the Massachusetts Institute of Technology helped found it. Why was it okay then? Columbia only joined it in 1960. Why was that the wrong time?

– Because now we're in a war, and they're working against Vietnam.

– Why weren't the students of 1955 and 1960 on the streets protesting the atomic bomb?

– Okay, you're right. The students were a bit late.

– And they're late again. Since March, Columbia as an institution has no longer been a member of the IDA. If Columbia professors did work for them, or consulted, they did so independently.

– How do you know that?

– Guess. From a future war criminal known in private circles around town as D. E.

– This grown-up know-it-all-ness, it's like a conspiracy you're all in on!

– Marie, why are the students demanding in late April that the university do what it did last March?

– Yeah, well. A little late.

– Is the university supposed to expel from its sacred garden any professor who refuses to give up his job with the IDA?

– Exactly.

– There's nothing about that on your flyer.

– Oh, Gesine. These tiny little inaccuracies—

– It is inaccurate.

– That's all it takes for you to be opposed?

– That's all it takes.

– It's like you're apolitical!

– Maybe I've spent too long studying politics and don't know how to put it into practice anymore.

– If I invited you to take a little walk around the Columbia campus, would you come with me?

– Yes.

– To show the students that you're on their side?

– Riverside Park, or the promenade along the river, would be fine with me too, Marie.

– And I wanted you to be lying. You're tricking me, you just want to challenge me.

– No, that's not true.

– If I didn't know that you'd had a hard day at work today...

– It's not that I'm tired from today, Marie.

– If you weren't doing something every day to try to help that Socialism of yours in another country...

– Then what.

– I don't want to insult you.

– Go ahead, say it.

– How's your business going, the Socialist wheat from Canada and all that?

– Say it.

– And it's your, what's it called, "alma mater" too, isn't it?

– It's a store where I once bought four semesters of economics. I was its customer, I paid, and I left unsatisfied.

– So how's your business going?

The Communist Party secretariat in Prague denies that their Soviet friends have stopped the shipment of wheat. A gross fabrication, they say. On the contrary, they've received from Moscow a credit of $400 million in exchange for goods that the Soviet Union normally buys from countries with hard currency. Truly. Except the wheat shipments due to arrive haven't come.

May 2, 1968 Thursday

Today *The New York Times* once again has news to report from her own family. She has visibly elevated two of her most faithful nephews in her undimmed eyes; one says that the paper has already become "lighter in appearance and more inviting to read" during his tenure to date. As if we haven't noticed? He reiterates, though, that our aunt's lofty intent remains unchanged: "To be the accurate, objective newspaper of record. To serve adult needs by being complete in our coverage. To explain, explain and explain again—not in the sense of a primer but in order to fill in the gaps for readers." We'll remember that, and not forget.

We will not forget the girl in the film strip above and to the right of the ticket counter in Grand Central, ceaselessly, perpetually, eternally combing her hair for the greater glory of a company.

The child that I was had lost her hair in the summer after the war, from typhus. She kept her distance from people; there had been a few friendly types who'd tried to cheer her up by pulling the beret off her head, as though her appearance wasn't that bad. Jakob acted like he didn't see

Maurice's gift on Gesine's head—with him she could forget it was there, remembering only from the sweat. He didn't use force to try to help, didn't even use words. He sent a stranger into the yard, head shaved like a Red Army soldier, and since he was wearing civilian pants, rolled up to the knees, and a shirt much too big for him he might have been a Red Army deserter, on the run, turning up unsuspectingly at a commandant's headquarters. This unknown individual didn't seem nervous, he just sat down on the uprights of the milk rack behind the house and waited. It was early in the morning, and even though it was during harvest time none other than Cresspahl's daughter was the first to see him. She went outside, went inside to report the beggar, he called after her. His voice was so much like Jakob's. She realized only when she came back with the mirror. He looked at himself in the mirror, its frame held firmly on his knees. She stood next to him. She saw almost no hair at all in the mirror, just a long, shiny skull with a bare face on it, vaguely familiar around the eyes. He looked into the mirror a bit grumpily, as if criticizing the work of the hairstylist who'd made him look like that. He didn't have to say anything; she understood the bet, the child that I was, and took off her beret. In the mirror she was in the lead, hairwise, although the sight was still a shock. And then my hair grew back.

May 3, 1968 Friday

Now that the Communists in Prague have their $400 million from head-quarters safe in hand, almost, they can admit that it wasn't as bad as all that with the delayed wheat shipments from the Soviet Union. On the contrary. The latest reports have it that deliveries are coming in even bigger than requested—here *The New York Times* chides herself. The US government tries a different tack and speaks openly of its interest and sympathy in recent developments in Czechoslovakia, which "seem to represent" the wishes and needs of the Czechoslovak people; it is considering the transfer of gold to a Communist country, despite its own dwindling gold reserves, and in an election year no less. At the May 1 Parade, Dubček, unmoved, sends special greetings to the Soviet Union, "whence our freedom came and from which we can expect fraternal aid"—he doesn't want to stir up trouble, he wants to smooth it down on the other side. Maybe the ČSSR can use USSR dollars to purchase manufacturing licenses in the US. And as for the US government offer, that is irresponsible and unacceptable. All right, all right, playtime's over.

The town of Jerichow was surrounded by wheat fields, with Baltic fish nearby, but was short of food. The townsfolk of an earlier time could have helped one another out, tradesmen swapping with townsman-farmers; now that refugees were being put up in rooms, attics, and barns, there wasn't enough bread. The military commandant wanted to be not only a good father and provider but a proud one, and he ordered the unclaimed harvest brought in.

The mayor went about it differently, decreeing that:
Everyone who
    (1) owned a scythe
    (2) could use a scythe
should report to Town Hall, room 4, henceforth to be called the Labor Office. As of July 12, the office had been notified of eight scythes in all of Jerichow, most of them reported not by their owners but by malicious neighbors. Ten times as many people as scythes turned up for the mowing, almost all of them women, refugees one and all, and they all claimed to know how to mow, they'd brought little children along too, to tie the sheaves, to steal the grain. It was a motley crowd, dressed in rags, some intending to tackle the stubble in the fields barefoot, all of them gaunt and weak with hunger. A bottle of clear water and the prospect of a handful of grain—that was their lunch. Cresspahl remembered how a scythe tore a heavy swing from your shoulders. He mustn't sigh in front of these people. He led this heap of workers out of town on foot to a field that had once been part of one of the landed estates, mowed one length for them, along the side of a hundred-meter square, then took off his jacket and turned around to look at them. The mower women were a long way behind him, the children running around with sheaves even farther back, and now he lost a whole morning showing them, again and again, how to plant their legs against the ground and shift their weight so the swing of the scythe wouldn't pull them off their feet. And the children, including children from town, couldn't get how you can twist a skein of stalks under your elbow into a cord that you knot on the bottom. One of them, his Gesine,

was so eager she had two left hands. By midday he had little more from his team than the promise to keep trying. "Cresspahl's bunch of cripples," the people of Jerichow called them, but on the second day there really were too many sheaves to count at a glance, even if the stubble looked a bit like a choppy sea. And the dummies who'd responded to Cresspahl's decree were paid, half in cash and half in grain from the previous year's harvest, weighed out daily in Papenbrock's granary. For a while there were Jerichow townswomen who would have been glad to turn up with scythes they'd forgotten about, or just to tie sheaves.

Then some of the women were assaulted by K. A. Pontiy's comrades and didn't return. One was found too late, in a hawthorn hedge, with a shattered jaw, and she died while being transported to the hospital. *Transported* meaning carried in a horse blanket, a heavy load for four women. K. A. Pontiy refused to be responsible for men under other Kommandaturas— he was already having a fight with the commandant of Knesebeck. A soldier had come back to quarters there with wounds from a reaping hook all down his arm and on his back, and said something about a Fascist attack, but it had just been children defending their mother against him. Pontiy started a hunt for Hitler's Werewolf resistance forces in Jerichow, and Cresspahl was ordered to be shot several times over. Then came the reconciliation, and Pontiy solemnly declared himself prepared to give the volunteers an escort from among his men. Then the women refused to go to work under such protection. K. A. Pontiy ordered the harvest brought in at once.

There were still men on Jerichow's farms, and they had harvesting machines, but Cresspahl had trouble getting them onto the nobility's fields, this time for legal reasons. The von Plessens had sowed the fields, the estates had always managed them—wasn't it theft to reap the harvest there? In Jerichow, as elsewhere in Mecklenburg, it was considered a sin to let wheat rot on the stalk; the departed owners' anger was still more frightening. Finally Cresspahl was able to talk them into saving the wheat, for its owners as it were. So now they cleared the fields outside the leased areas, and guarded the grain that wasn't theirs at night with bludgeons and dogs (for which they didn't pay the new tax). Those who stubbornly refused had their machines confiscated by Cresspahl as soon as they'd finished their own harvest. And he had an easier time finding people to operate the machines once he stopped distributing ration cards to any family in Jerichow without at least one member working. (When the mayor arranged a card for Gesine on the grounds that she was working and Mrs. Abs got one for her son, this was seen as cheating.) The machines were felt to have been taken by force, and the work was not performed with the zeal promoted by ownership, so the equipment broke down more than usual. Cresspahl could talk all he wanted about benefiting the town—people felt it was being done for the Russians. It didn't help that Red Army soldiers could be seen racing their horses up and down the roads. Worse yet, a detachment showed up in a field in the Jerichow housing development and traded their two worn-out nags for a horse that was hitched to a cart, like during the war, at gunpoint. The cart could still be moved, if twenty people leaned against the spokes, but no more work was done that day. Gesine came back to town that evening leading the Russians' sick horses, which no one had wanted to bring in, and waited for Cresspahl outside the Kommandatura door. Cresspahl was already inside, busy negotiating the return of a tractor that someone from the Red Army had "borrowed" because the commander had needed it to take him to Gneez on official business and had forgotten it there. K. A. Pontiy was somewhat uncomfortable, there was also the matter of some cans of diesel oil, and he mentioned Ukraine, just in passing. In Ukraine, you know, people carried the wheat to the threshing together, they didn't need a vehicle, and women and children pulled plows there too, and you know what else, the milk production from the cows didn't markedly decrease until after four months, cf. the lessons learned from Swiss husbandry. After listening to this instructive cultural information, Cresspahl repeated his question. – Tractor? What tractor?: K. A. Pontiy said, confused for a moment, at a loss for longer.

He saw the horses Gesine had brought back as a sign of good faith—the return of army property—and he waved her around the corner onto the Bäk. But the child wanted new ones in exchange, – *Novye*: she said, scared though she was of making a language mistake, and Pontiy kindly explained to her that these horses weren't *novye*, nothing like the fine Ukrainian breed! Cresspahl tore the reins out of the child's hand and left the trampled front garden of the brickworks villa without saying goodbye. When it was dark, K. A. Pontiy paid his mayor a visit and threatened to have him shot if he didn't ensure that the town had enough to eat.

What troubled the commandant was the idea of anyone comparing the state of things under the Russians with that under the British. At one point he asked Cresspahl point-blank. My father decided to let Pontiy stew about this for a while and called English rule over Jerichow manageable, if not benevolent. They had managed things well because they knew when they were leaving. They'd lived on the supplies at hand, which were obviously enough for eight weeks. When they left there was no more coal for the trains, which couldn't take milk to Gneez or bring back potatoes. They'd forced Jerichow to shut down the gasworks, which had damaged the furnaces; its workforce had wandered aimlessly around the fields, unskilled there, depressed. Even the bakeries were without fuel. The British had generously distributed sugar and salt and oil from their warehouses, and the villages and farms had faithfully tried to deliver their quotas of beef cattle and milk. The British had given Cresspahl access to the government bank to pay whatever he needed to—wages, past-due bills. Even school had been open under them, two days after they got here. They were trying to leave behind a good impression of Western methods to make it harder for the Soviets to do the same. Even from a distance, they won hearts and minds by supplying electricity to Jerichow from their Herrenwyk power station, and Pontiy was not happy to hear this. Cresspahl half expected an order to build an independent supply of electricity for Jerichow, but first things first: his job was to supply the people of Jerichow with food, as well as the British had done, and, within four weeks, better.

The Jerichow mayor's office contracted with the Fishermen's Association in Rande, represented by Ilse Grossjohann, for the delivery of at least two crates of fish per day. (This was the old association that the Nazis had dissolved, reestablished by the kind permission of the British.) What Grossjohann asked in return often changed: sometimes the fishermen needed sailcloth, sometimes nails, sometimes lubricating oil for the engines, and Cresspahl couldn't always manage to find these things somewhere in Jerichow to confiscate. He told the town's commandant nothing about this trade, and Pontiy didn't mention it either, but after a week had passed Pontiy's jeep appeared in Rande one morning, and the Red Army soldiers demanded the "fishes for Yerrichoff." Ilse Grossjohann had learned something about the law from her time with Kollmorgen, and moreover she'd been a prosperous fisherman's wife for three years, and she insisted on the terms of their agreement, force majeure or not. Before Cresspahl could lodge a complaint, two bundles of fish—flounder, gurnard—were delivered to his door: his cut under Pontiy's socialism. He sent the fish to the hospital; he arranged a new loading point with the Fishermen's Association, though even so Pontiy beat him to it often enough.

Cresspahl was offered deliveries of both milk and beef cattle from the administrator of the Soviet Beckhorst farm (formerly the Kleineschulte farm). The farm needed baling twine, crude oil, and leather for machine belts. Cresspahl could picture the cows—tough old bags of bones—but he agreed to take them sight unseen. It was a complicated transaction. The town had to loan Alfred Bienmüller out to Beckhorst, so that he could repair the motor and combine, which needed the oil and the leather, but by that point Bienmüller's business was the Jerichow Kommandatura's official repair shop, and K. A. Pontiy's trucks took precedence, especially the one he was planning to exchange for a convertible, to the Knesebeck commandant's advantage and disadvantage, in the interests of reconciliation. Bienmüller applied for a *propusk* to go to Beckhorst for family reasons, and Pontiy had no choice but to sign it and have it stamped. Milk was in short supply in town because both the local cows and the ones confiscated from the refugees had been herded together onto seven farms, which made deliveries to the Red Army, not the district offices and the independent municipalities, and the Jerichow Kommandatura had a reputation, even among the well disposed, for being self-sufficient. Pontiy didn't get milk from Beckhorst. One night Bienmüller took a walk along the coast and the next day he repaired the farm machines and the night after that he planned to escort the truck full of milk canisters back to Jerichow. At the edge of the woods, the mayor of the village met him and told him that he was having an argument with the Soviet administrator and needed the milk for the refugee children in his village since the farmers were now tamping butter into barrels. Cresspahl did not invoke force majeure, he recast this part of the deal into a trade of salt for butter, and he sent the twine from Papenbrock's supplies. The cows got as far as the Rande country road, then the Red Army herded them into their little hideaway on the Bäk. At least that's where Klein the butcher had to slaughter them, not in his own yard where people might have seen them; his shopwindow stayed empty. In late July it had been a long time since there'd been the hundred grams of meat per person in town. Cresspahl couldn't even get the daily half pint of milk per child that he felt was essential (as did Pontiy. But Pontiy took as much as he wanted from the dairy, each time with the comment that he too had children in his stronghold). Cresspahl would have preferred it if the foreign commander had stolen the Germans' food out of hatred, as punishment, on his own account; he couldn't come to terms with the game Pontiy made of it, with his soulful *nichevo*s and gentlemanly *shustko yedno*s.

Cresspahl ordered every poultry owner to deliver one egg per day. These eggs would be handed out only in exchange for coupons from children's ration cards. All he got were complaints about stolen chickens, especially from the buildings whose backyards adjoined the Soviets' green fence. He didn't need to go chasing down the chickens, he could hear them on the Bäk, a street that had earlier been much too fancy for poultry keeping. Because the thieves sometimes left the hens' and roosters' twisted-off heads behind in the miraculously undamaged coops, the Jerichowers began to kill their own chickens without authorization. Cresspahl could forbid it. And Cresspahl could stuff his pockets full of hard-boiled eggs at Pontiy's banquets.

It wasn't so much that he was afraid of anyone "going a bit hungry"—it wasn't a hardship yet, that would come in winter. It was that he couldn't keep the talk under control, the vague, insidious rumblings, not even malicious, just resigned: that nothing made any sense, everything was falling apart, it was all for the Russians. This talk might flower into panic, enough to make the supplying of food to town collapse.

The mayor decreed:

> The town of Jerichow has sufficient potatoes from previous years'
> harvests to meet its current needs

and forbade the harvesting of new potatoes until August 15, 1945. This was taken to mean that he clearly expected a potato shortage and was actually trying to warn the town, in his heart of hearts he was a Mecklenburger after all, on the Mecklenburgers' side—and the Jerichowers stole their own potatoes under cover of night, hid them in their cellars, and introduced them as a new currency for use with the refugees. The Jerichow Kommandatura stopped a group of workers on their way to the wheat fields one morning and made them dig up new potatoes, and it wasn't even late July yet. Of course the mayor couldn't forbid the Soviets anything; he didn't begrudge them their enjoying the taste of fresh new potatoes; but he didn't appreciate their making him look ridiculous when he was trying to keep the town fed.

And so he started doing business on his own again, something that hadn't been allowed since the victors had arrived,

the US has been holding $20 million of Czechoslovak gold bullion since the end of World War II as security for the return of confiscated American property. The folks in Prague are offering 2 million as compensation and settlement. The US is demanding 110 million. Whose turn is it to bid?

and he turned one of Alfred Bienmüller's electric motors and a set of rubber tires in Knesebeck into a business transaction, equivalent exchange values with the help of a considerable addition of window glass and motor oil, and in Rande he didn't find the harvest truck he'd planned to make drivable again but he did find maybe a pile of freshly dug potatoes, the dirt still on them, and a couple hundredweight of wheat, in factory-fresh sacks. Civilians were not allowed to accept foodstuffs or items of daily use from Soviet soldiers. But he'd given his word for the window glass, and the workers who'd dug potatoes for the Soviets had been allowed to take home from the Bäk two big pots of rich meaty stew, and he hadn't been able to get any of that for the hospital.

Meanwhile he'd managed to accomplish one thing, to the considerable consternation of the military commander. When K. A. Pontiy acted yet again like the crazed Queen of Hearts and threatened *Off with your head!*, Cresspahl could now nod pleasantly, as if in agreement, but without giving an inch. It was like with the Cheshire Cat, whose head was to be cut off because it wanted only to look at the king, not kiss his hand. But only the cat's head is visible, and the executioner refuses to cut off a head when there's no body to cut it off from. The King insists that anything that has a head can be beheaded, and don't talk nonsense, while the Queen says that if something isn't done about it *in less than no time* she'll have everybody executed all round,

> *in less than no time, Gesine!*
> *is he going to shoot you, Cresspahl?*

and the cat's head stays up in the air and the executioner comes back and the cat has disappeared, head and smile and all.

May 4, 1968 Saturday, South Ferry day

The Cheshire Cat's grin followed me into my last dream, along with the sun shower from yesterday afternoon that lit the street from the side and made it black as the sound of the car tires suddenly picked up. Minutes later the sun vanished behind a thick bluish curtain, the same way the Cheshire Cat's grin did before I woke up.

Marie has left "Saturday breakfast" on the table: hot tea, toast buried in napkins, all on a tray for easier transport, and *The New York Times* fresh from Broadway. Maybe she would learn how to live in a Prague hotel.

What the students of Paris are having for breakfast are clashes with the police because some students want control over their education and want to overthrow the institutions of capitalism, the ones along Boulevard St. Michel, for example. In Prague the students are assembling at the foot of the statue of Jan Hus and thanking the Communist Party "for the present shortages in housing and transport, for bad worker morale, for legal insecurity, for a currency without value, for a low economic standard," and will the Communists think it's contagious? First of all they deny that they ever discussed a Soviet loan of $400 million with *The New York Times*. The truth is, rather, that Mr. Dubček has just now flown to Moscow to discuss the gold ruble, as well as such matters as natural gas and crude oil, possibly as payment for the Soviet debts of 425 million. The truth is, rather... and if they call Auntie Times, to her face, crowned in glory as she is, a lady who doesn't speak the truth, then she will have to relay the message to us. Feeble. And, incidentally, she adds that Comrade Dubček arrived in Moscow last night for a weekend. The truth is, rather...

Here we have someone chasing after her child—a person, a lady, you don't know who I am. Walking north up Riverside Drive, by the buildings whose entrances are separated from the big road by hilly tree-covered islands, walking as if she grew up there, and yet she once gaped from afar at the mighty colossi of the apartment buildings with their weathered ornamentation as places she would never reach. She has friends and acquaintances here, though: Good morning, Mrs. Faure. We're fine too. We're going to see a child. The trees in the park are full of leaves now. There are no evergreens there, it's bare in the winter. Foreigners insult the trees outside our windows by calling them *Bergahorn*, sycamore maples, when really with their mottled white bark they're sycamore figs, the tree from the Bible. Now, at 100th Street, she detours all the way around the Firemen's Memorial, she just wants to read the plaque again, the one that honors the lives of the horses, for they too died *in the line of duty*. The portals of the corner buildings are fancier, built to frame grand exits and entrances; some of them stand empty, though, dusty and double locked, and people use the entrances on the side streets where no one will catch them alone. As if muggers came out of the park at night. On 113th, where the Hungarians, a freedom-loving people, have put a certain Lajos Kossuth up on a pedestal, New Yorkers are said to have mourned after the events of fall 1956. We wouldn't have gone to that. And on 116th there's an evergreen after all, a spruce tucked into a grove. Will we see it in winter? But now we've climbed uphill enough, long since reached the elevation of Columbia University, and here, by the clumps of concrete and marble, obtrusive modest shoehorned into a row of town houses, blinding in the morning light, bare and inaccessible, there stands a sepulchre from the Far East, the much-admired marvel of New York modern architecture with a six-hundred-year-old stone from a Scottish monastery reverently set into its facade: Marie's school.

The school is having its spring art fair today—all the parents are invited, together with friends, yet the double glass doors in the gloomy passageway are closed. We too have to present ourselves at the porter's lodge first, to a sister who makes sure we don't have a knife up our sleeve or a gun under our jacket. There are strict rules in this building. A man without a tie would probably be sent packing. – Are you one of the parents, Mrs. . . . ?

One of the parents. Cresspahl, class 5B. That's who I am.

The art fair is set up in the lobby and one of the adjoining classrooms around the corner—a sizable event dedicated to the higher glory of the budget, over and above the exorbitant tuition, and it will yield not one single stipend for a child of poor parents. We didn't come to buy anything, we're here to see on behalf of a child. The underage sales personnel, predominantly girls, stand behind tables and are having a hard time running the business with such a small amount of change. Here we might have some batik, there a belt made of sack string, there a chain of bone rings, and whatever else you might be missing in your life. We like this girl, the one with the green eyes, the gray eyes, with the braids, with the strong shoulders in the jacket of her uniform, watching us so strangely, as if she wanted to throw us out of the sacred building. She goes behind the counter with us, shows us the homemade goods, names a price, points at "$1.20" on a headband, and says: Twelve tickets—it's a steal, ma'am.

She brings us over to a table in the second room with a dollhouse on display, behind ropes on stanchions, do not touch. It's not a model of a city house, it's more rustic, built low under its roof painted brick red and moss green, mullioned windows carved neatly in. The child slips under the rope divider. She touches the house. She lifts off the roof, holds it upside down, looks invitingly at us. Well? The workmanship on the beams couldn't be better, we must admit. – The technical term is tongue and groove: she says, and now people come up to listen and ask questions, a real audience. Now there are rooms visible in the uncovered attic, one filled with toy firewood. Firewood in the house? – Maybe it would get stolen from outside: she says. There's a smokehouse in the building, too, but empty. In another room the bare walls suddenly have old-fashioned wallpaper on them, the floor is varnished, the room is furnished with table and bed and wardrobe. – Servant's quarters: one of the people standing around says, proud and amazed; he gets a nod in return and looks like a horse that's just had its nose stroked. On the attic floor, in the corridors, stand wooden crates that don't look like suitcases—the refugees' luggage stored at Cresspahl's—and Marie explains, like a fact from the dimmest, most distant past: Clearly the people who live here traveled a lot, I mean more than the statistical average. The grown-ups nod at this. Lifting up the attic roof reveals the compartments of the various rooms: Cresspahl's daughter's in front on the left, which the child calls a guest room, and next to that Cresspahl's sleeping office, which our tour guide describes as a reception desk. She shows the furniture around in the palm of her hand, but these have been bought elsewhere, from the Museum of the City of New York, and she has a feeling they're more Flemish-style. She lies whenever she can, turning the Frenchmen's room into a sewing room, the pantry into a workshop, all in the dry, New England tone she brought back from Orr Island; it all comes off with a *Yessir* and an *I'm sorry, ma'am*? The spectators discuss the architectural style among themselves, one is in favor of Norwegian origin, he saw the same thing in Massachusetts, another claims to recognize it as Pennsylvania Dutch, and the child shrugs her shoulders, an expert, but beyond her competence here. Finally she's managed to bring one of the onlookers to the first question: What it costs. How much you can buy it for.

– It's obviously not for sale: the child says. – Maybe it'll be auctioned off this afternoon though.

– Not a Dutch auction, an American one: she says.

We won't place any bids on a house like that, we'll let it go. The child, on the other hand—her we take, fleeing the teachers sneaking up on us, and we ride the subway straight to the harbor where the ferry is waiting.

She herself was the child who built that house, and when they asked her, she shook her head, not knowing.

– One of us did: she said.

May 5, 1968 Sunday

Time to give up, Gesine. It might as well be today as tomorrow.

Oh, please. Because of "information reaching Paris"?

Information that reached Paris and made it into Le Monde.

Who is this General Yepishev?

Aleksei A. Yepishev is head of the political administration of the Soviet armed forces.

So now he's the politburo of the CP of the USSR?

Why wouldn't the Red Army want to go on maneuvers again? They are the military, Gesine.

They won't do it.

Yepishev says that faithful Communists in Czechoslovakia need only appeal to the Soviet Union for help. If they do he'll come and safeguard their Socialism.

Old Believers like that have been in the minority for a long time.

A letter's enough, come at once. "The Soviet Army is ready to do its duty."

They won't do it.

They marched into Hungary in 1956.

That's why they'll be extra careful now.

This time they say "other" Socialist troops are coming with. To spread around the bad press.

Possibly East Germans. They recommend their version of Socialism. German uniforms back in Prague again.

They may not use only their uniforms, Gesine.

They won't send tanks to Prague. Not in 1968, twelve years after Budapest!

You've only heard rumors about it until today.

That makes sense. The rumors paint a rather different picture.

Gesine, General Yepishev said it at a meeting of his party, on April 23. A French newspaper reported it yesterday. You read it today.

I've already seen denials in print.

And pigs can fly.

No! No! I didn't see it!

"A child doesn't count for anything."

The Red Army won't do it.

Because a certain Gesine Cresspahl doesn't believe it?

Exactly. That's why.

The military commander of the town of Jerichow, K. A. Pontiy, might shoot at birds with a rifle, might kick a cat out of his way as often as pet it, he might jump down Cresspahl's daughter's throat for not sweeping the path to his villa clean enough, but he didn't entirely forfeit her respect. In fact, she was downright grateful to him. He'd removed the corpses from her sight.

The British had made dead people public in Jerichow. They were the Nazis' prisoners from Neuengamme concentration camp, twelve miles southeast of Hamburg, along with its Mecklenburg branch camps, Boizenburg and Reiherhorst in Wöbbelin. At Neuengamme the Nazis hadn't managed to do it. When the German Reich had to clear out the Majdanek, Treblinka, Belzec, and Sobibor death camps in occupied Poland, it made squads of prisoners open the mass graves, dig up the bodies, and grind up the bones. The bone meal was strewn on the fields, the gas chambers and incineration ovens were blown up, and once the prisoners had leveled the camps to a plot of land smooth as innocence they were killed for their efforts. In Austria the Germans had had to leave the Mauthausen camp standing, and at Neuengamme they didn't manage it either. The Danish government negotiated for their countrymen until, in April, they could have the famous Convoy of Ninety-Two White Buses transport them to Frøslov and Møgelkaer. More than six thousand people were left behind in Neuengamme, under German command; to keep the British from finding them, they were evacuated. First, some five hundred died in the freight cars on the way to Lübeck via Hamburg, unable to endure any further starvation, lacking medical care. Four cars' worth of sick prisoners weren't even loaded onto the ships, they were screaming with fever, they were shot, and anyone who didn't hear that in Lübeck's outer harbor might well have heard the festive sounds of the German SS in the adjacent grain silo, celebrating final victory with the finest cognac and delicacies from stolen Red Cross parcels. The prisoners, whom the people of Lübeck knew absolutely nothing about, spent almost ten days waiting at Lübeck's wharf in their freight cars, German Reich Railway cars, out in the open, or else stuffed into the *Thielbek* and the *Athen*; more dead kept being buried next to the harbor. The *Thielbek* had been bombed in 1944, and not been repaired, and was hardly seaworthy: two tugs had to tow the ship down the Trave and out into the bay. The *Athen* could move under her own steam and she brought more and more batches of prisoners from Lübeck's industrial harbor to the *Cap Arcona* in the Bay of Neustadt. The three ships carrying prisoners were easily visible from land, and known to not only the fishermen. The *Thielbek*, 2,815 gross register tons, 345 feet long, draft 21 feet, had carried freight for Knöhr & Burchardt in Hamburg. The *Athen*, somewhat smaller, was also designed to carry freight, not people. The *Cap Arcona* was built for people— a luxury ship of the Hamburg–South America Line, 27,560 GRT, 675 feet long, draft 28.5 feet. Before the war it sailed to Rio de Janeiro, thirty-five days, first class only, 1,275 reichsmarks: avoid part of the winter and relax in the mild sea air under the southern sun! The *Cap Arcona* was designed for 1,325 passengers and a crew of 380; now, however, there were 4,600 prisoners belowdecks with the sick at the very bottom (with no medicine or bandages) and the Russian prisoners in the banana storage hold (with no light, no air, and for the first three days no food); the dead were piled up on deck. The ship stank of the dead, of the disease and shit of the living— a putrid heap and not even moving. For the *Cap Arcona* was not seaworthy either, not without fuel. There was almost no food for the prisoners, they were not given water, but roll call, with counting off and tallying, was mandatory. It took longer to die here than in the gas chambers, but it wouldn't be long before they were all dead. Then came freedom. Freedom came across the bright sunny bay on May 3 in the shape of a squadron of British bombers. At around two thirty they flew over the Bay of Neustadt and started in on the *Athen*. The Germans defended their prisoners with antiaircraft fire; after the third direct hit they hoisted a white flag. The British pilots may have seen it, because they left that ship and attacked the ones in the outer bay. After twenty minutes the *Thielbek* lay down on its side and disappeared altogether under the surface of the water, since it was almost sixty feet deep there. The *Cap Arcona*, with the captain's bedsheet on the mast, took an hour, then it tipped onto its port side, slowly, faster and faster, until it was lying on its eighty-five-foot side, twenty-six feet of it above water. Meanwhile death was proceeding more quickly, and in various forms. The prisoners could die in the fire, in the smoke (the fire hoses had been cut), from the German crew's rifles (the crew had life jackets), jammed in by hoarded food supplies, crushed in the panicking crowd, from the heat of the glowing *Cap Arcona*, in the lifeboats plummeting into the water, from jumping into the water, of cold in the water, by being hit or shot at by German minesweepers, and on land from exhaustion. The saved numbered 3,100, the dead somewhere between 7,000 and 8,000. At around five in the afternoon the English took Neustadt, so it was in the British zone, same as Jerichow, and contact was permitted between the two places, and that's how we knew about it.

The dead washed up on every shore of Lübeck Bay, from Bliestorf to Pelzerhaken, from Neustadt to Timmendorf Beach, into the mouth of the Trave, from Priwall to Schwansee and Redewisch and Rande, even into Wohlenberg Cove, as far as Poel Island and the other Timmendorf. They were found almost daily.

Too many washed up on the coast near Jerichow—the finders couldn't bury them all secretly in the sand. The British occupation authorities had issued orders that all corpses from the water be reported, and they insisted that these orders be followed. The British took a truck and rounded up men who had been members of the National Socialist German Workers' Party. These men were driven along the beach, and wherever a black lump lay on the white sand the British stopped. The Germans were given no gloves for the loading, not even pitchforks or shovels. The British drank their whiskey right in front of the Germans; despite this medicine, they too had to throw up. The British created no special cemetery for the dead from this watery camp. When the truck was full, they drove the load far inland, all the way to Kalkhorst, even Gneez. When they drove into Jerichow they lowered the sides of the truck. The MPs made the Germans leave their houses to look at the cargo as it was driven down Town Street to the cemetery at a walking pace. Slower than walking. The cargo was not easy to recognize. It had been damaged by bullet wounds, charring, shrapnel, blows. It was recognizable by the faded, split, clinging, striped clothes. The individual pieces of human being were often incomplete. There were limbs missing, or there were limbs on the truck bed without a torso, one day there was nothing but a piece of head. The fish had eaten a lot of that one. The British made the people of Jerichow gather on Market Square. In the middle lay the first load of bodies. The commander handed over to the Germans the Germans' dead. He made them their property. He allowed them to place the mortal remains from the sea into coffins. Then they were permitted to close the coffins and carry them to the cemetery. After the dirt had been shoveled onto the mass grave, the British fired a salute into the air. At the cemetery gate stood a sergeant, holding a box in front of him, and on this box he stamped the ration cards. Anyone who had not accepted the dead would not eat.

– It was their dead! Those English are utter scoundrels! Marie says. – You guys let them get away with anything, and then some!

– They were the Germans'. The Germans had held them prisoner, loaded them onto ships. If they'd kept them the only difference was they would have died slower.

– The British dropped the bombs. They saw the prisoners' camp uniforms and fired at them anyway. That's the truth.

– The British didn't want that truth. You could be thrown in jail for less than that. There were German U-boats above water all around the ships, and none of them were hit—that was too dangerous even to whisper.

– But you Jerichowers knew.

– It wasn't new information. You could already see prisoners like that in striped clothing in Mecklenburg (maybe not in Lübeck)—but they weren't to exist in language. Now the British were bringing in dead bodies and decreeing the cause of their death however they wanted.

– The Mecklenburgers may have been cowards, but the English weren't.

– By 1956 they'd put out five volumes on the air offensive against Germany through the end of the war. May 3 was before the end of the war, and nowhere is the bombing in Lubeck Bay mentioned.

– Official history. Stiff upper lip.

– It is also official history that the British came before the German submarines had time to sink the prisoners themselves. The monument in the Old Cemetery in Jerichow is official history too.

– And one in the British zone?

– In Pelzerhaken, near Neustadt. And four years later the British gave permission to the owners of the *Thielbek* to salvage any articles of value. The sea hadn't quite flushed out the whole ship—there were still some bodies, and heaps of bare bones—they had the ship repaired. Let's call it the *Reinbek* and put it back out to sea until 1961, until it's worth selling. Today, if you happen to see a *Magdalena* flying the Panamanian flag, that's the *Thielbek* of May 1945. The *Cap Arcona* was worthless except for the scrap metal. The *Athen*, though, that turned into the Soviet *General Brusslov* in 1946, then the Polish *Waryński* in 1947, and the Polish Line ran her from Gdynia to Buenos Aires and Rio de Janeiro. What's left of the *Cap Arcona* is the ship's bell. You've seen it.

– At the Museum of Danish Resistance in Copenhagen!

– In Churchill Park, in Copenhagen.

– And you still wanted to swim in the Baltic?

– We ate fish from the Baltic. The Germans eat fish from the Baltic to this day. There are almost three thousand prisoners lying at the bottom of the Baltic.

– And K. A. Pontiy stopped it?

– He stopped the education of the German people by means of the overland transport of bodies. This particular flotsam had to be collected in the cemeteries of the coastal villages, outside the territory under his command. That cost—

– and he made Jerichow pay for it.

– Tell it to the judge, Marie.

– No. I would've been grateful to him too.

The military commander of the town of Jerichow didn't manage to do it on first try—to keep the dead at a distance. For a while they came at him from the other side. They were the refugees, from far outside the parish, who died in the villages and on the farms surrounding the town, in early July already. They hadn't brought coffins with them when they fled the war; now that they were dying of typhus, they wanted to stay in Jerichow. Pastor Brüshaver was still notified of the first cart, so the little bell could be rung as it pulled up. As a result, Gesine no longer went behind the house; she did keep sitting in her walnut tree, even though that was impolite to the dead. It was a panel truck, with boards running down the sides and cross-planks at the front and the back. *Kretts*, Gesine called the frontboards and backboards. But language had run off somewhere, away from her. She thought: cabbages, beets. Outside the mortuary chapel the driver and his assistant raised the back *Krett* and pulled the topmost body down until it flopped onto the stretcher. Gesine tried to think that Jakob, in his strange Pommern German, called a *Krett* a *Schott*—she could feel her mind running off somewhere, away from this. The second time, it was too onerous for the villagers to have to dig such deep holes, and they offloaded the strangers into Jerichow's mortuary without Brüshaver hearing about it in time. That time it was a harvest cart, they were lying visibly one on top of the other between the ladders that the wheat was going to be brought in on the next day. A human arm like the one hanging out past the rails between the rungs, swaying alongside the wheel, seems alive. You couldn't tell where the dead had come from; K. A. Pontiy had nowhere to send them back to. He ordered sentries to keep watch the next day.

Another cart was pushed up to Pontiy's villa in the night, by hand, quietly, on rubber wheels. Hanna Ohlerich and Gesine didn't hear that one; at one point they woke up reassured when they heard one of the commandant's cars, which jolted into reverse after lots of loud rattles and shakes, making the horses whinny. Gesine was safe from any new arrivals; that morning she went outside without a second thought. When she glanced to the right she saw both of the chapel's double doors standing open, with something that looked like a shoe on the ground right outside them. She tried to tell herself that someone must have just slipped and fallen there, but she knew that now she wanted to see the bodies.

Maybe the living had brought lanterns in the night. The dead weren't piled on one another the way they'd been in the cart. They sat in the little mortuary hall as if alive, their backs leaned against the walls, most of them with their eyes open. Their dresses, pants, and heavy jackets had been left on, out of fear of infection, or else put back on—they were a bit crooked on their bodies, too high on the neck, too high over the knee. Some were touching one another, holding their neighbor seated, otherwise they might slip. There were two together in the northwest corner, as if they'd sat down next to each other on their own. It was a young man, who seemed to Gesine twenty-two years old, with black hair and long muttonchop sideburns, in a neat black suit with shirt and tie—a city man whose shoes had come off somewhere. His head was turned to the side, as if he were looking at the wall. Then, though she was right up next to him, a girl lay half slumped down—a blond with her hair up, all freckly—and she had slid halfway into the young man's lap, and her posture was so peaceful, his hand on her shoulder seemed a little embarrassed, and not there voluntarily. They looked posed.

There was also a chicken in the hall. It had escaped from the Kommandatura. It was feisty, fully alive. It had found some grain next to the corpses' pants pockets but in its confusion it was pecking at the bare flesh too.

The mortuary had its windows in the side walls. Morning sunlight slanted in from the right side and lit up the chapel like a waiting room—lit the loving couple most of all.

Gesine had taken only a half step into the chapel, for no longer than a couple of seconds. She felt watched from every direction, and immediately stepped backward. In doing so, she tripped on the body whose shoe she had noticed earlier. The jokester had forgotten him, he was the only one lying with his face in the gravel.

She didn't need to run back to the house. Walking, she considered at leisure what she was expected to do next. Now she knew she was guilty of something—she didn't know what. She refused her breakfast, and the rest of her meals that day, but it still wasn't enough to soothe her conscience. She could have eaten without getting sick, she even had some appetite, though she wasn't exactly hungry that night. It would have seemed like a betrayal of the gathering of the dead to her.

Cresspahl saw the staged scene too, and that afternoon he had it taken away and then nailed the mortuary shut. Jerichow has had its other cemetery for some time now, the one K. A. Pontiy ordered, on the Rande country road between the town and the air base, on the left, on land expropriated from the nobility. It didn't have a fence, but Pastor Brüshaver had stood there and done the things and said the words he felt necessary for a consecration. From the countryside you reached it by going around the town, about a mile and a half; it took maybe half an hour longer with a horse and cart.

Today it's called the Central Municipal Cemetery. Surrounded by a low fieldstone wall, and within that a ring of thornbushes.

The chapel, build in 1950 and much more massive than a garage, can't be seen from the road.

The old chapel, by Cresspahl's house, has collapsed and been replaced by part of a white brick wall between the red stones from 1850. The churchyard cemetery is considered an attraction, because it has been untouched for more than twenty years.

Later it must have been an honor to be allowed into the earth by St. Peter's Church. That's how Cresspahl ended up there, in a grave next to his wife, as a former mayor of the town. While he was alive, he managed to get Jakob a place there, near him.

And it's a Schott, *Gesine, that's what it's called.*
It's a Krett.
Schott.
Krett.
You laughed first!
You did.

May 6, 1968 Monday
Yesterday, on Karl Marx's hundred-and-fiftieth birthday, *The New York Times* took part in the festivities around the house where he was born in Trier. The students shouted "Ho, Ho, Ho Chi Minh!" when the chairman of the Social Democratic Party, which owns the house, sought to enter it. The East Germans staged an event of their own. In the West German one, Ernst Bloch contended that many errors had been committed in the name of Marx. "Some people not only do not know anything about Marx but they tell lies about him."

Dramatis personae:

MONSIEUR HENRI ROCHE-FAUBOURG, part heir to a French bank-ing firm. Twenty-one years old, 136 lbs., skin color yellowish, race Caucasian, hair black with split ends and curling over his shirt collar. French, graduate of an elite school in Paris. Has begun to study law and economics. Serving one year in New York. A personage insulted by not being received at once by his father's New York colleague, instead being first handed over for a subordinate to deal with. At a meal at the Brussels two weeks ago he was capable, all the way until coffee, of refusing to believe that the lady with him really spoke French. Clings fast to his role as the sole person in New York who speaks and understands French, despite the waiter's proving the contrary. Considers his language to be his exclusive possession, and while he is unable to punish encroachments on this his property with a whip, he did make frequent use of a lack of comprehension. Then he kisses the hand of the lady paying his check, and says with a smile on his impatient red lips: What a charming remark! It was a remark on the enamel-like nature of typical American makeup and was, like all the previous remarks, made in French. He replied in the same language for the first time. Has thirty-one words of American English at his disposal, thirty of them English English. Long jackets, reaching down to the tips of his outstretched fingers, sharply tailored.

DE ROSNY. First name unknown.

The scene: A descending elevator, rear shaft. It's a normal elevator, not reserved for senior executives. Time: an hour after the close of business. The vice president is alone in the elevator with Mrs. Cresspahl. He is per-forming for her benefit the conversation he had with ROCHE-FAUBOURG, alternately as himself and as the young heir.

DE ROSNY: So what did you have in mind here?

ROCHE-FAUBOURG: Yes, well, my father left the decision up to me.

DE ROSNY: He seems to have turned into an American father. He used to be fine.

ROCHE-FAUBOURG: My father is in excellent health, thank you for asking.

DE ROSNY: I guess I'm about to behave like a German father—

ROCHE-FAUBOURG: *Pardon?*

DE ROSNY: Because there's something I want to tell you. You need to finish your studies.

ROCHE-FAUBOURG: Yes, I was planning to get an MBA.

DE ROSNY: An MBA! Please! You'll learn business administration when you take over your father's business, and if you turn out to be a dud at it, you can assign the job to someone else. And all the other jobs too.

ROCHE-FAUBOURG: I thought—

DE ROSNY: Your life is set in stone, isn't it? In a few years you're going to take over your father's business.

ROCHE-FAUBOURG: I flatter myself that—

DE ROSNY: So what you need to do is enjoy the free time you have left. Beforehand!

ROCHE-FAUBOURG: This American idea of enjoyment—

DE ROSNY: If you really want to, you can work here for a year. A forced march through every department.

ROCHE-FAUBOURG: Maybe for six months.

DE ROSNY: For that, of course, you would need to be interested in the condition of American workers.

ROCHE-FAUBOURG: Now that—

DE ROSNY: You could read a few books. But what you need to do now is live a little. How old are you?

ROCHE-FAUBOURG: Twenty-one.

DE ROSNY: You need to learn how to live a little. Get a sports car in June and drive around the country for two months. Go to a meeting of the Communist Party. Cresspahl will tell you everything you need to know about New York.

ROCHE-FAUBOURG: A couple of weeks ago she gave me the impression, in the most charming way—

DE ROSNY: There, you see? Just don't take up too much of her time, she's working for me.

ROCHE-FAUBOURG: Might I perhaps occasionally—

DE ROSNY: An MBA, what nonsense. That's all right for someone to study if they haven't got anything to take over. You are taking over the firm, aren't you?

ROCHE-FAUBOURG: If my brother—

DE ROSNY: When the year's up, you're to present yourself to me and I'll give you a test. Have a good morning.

ROCHE-FAUBOURG: Goodbye.

The vice president repeated parts of the scene as he walked, to the amusement of other subordinates walking quickly past him and trying to make their haste look like tact. The vice president is in a different kind of hurry—he has no train to miss, his black, air-conditioned limo is waiting for him. Still he keeps fidgeting with a cigarette between his fingers without ever managing to bring it to his lips, because his lips are busy saying: You have to picture it, me standing there in front of this young man, no one has ever talked to him like that in his life, and he came within a whisker of missing it. And people always think German fathers are tyrants, dictators really, and I as an American had to tell a French child: Here's your job, such and such. Get an education . . .

– Marx won't be of much help to him now, Mr. de Rosny.

– Ah, there I go again, forgetting that you have a German father. Can you forgive me, Mrs. Cresspahl?

– No. I'll never forgive you.

– You're all right, *young lady*. If only everyone who worked for me was like you. If only they were all like you.

May 7, 1968 Tuesday

So, what has Alexander Dubček brought back from occupation headquarters in Moscow? "Understanding" of the process of democratization he has initiated in his country, "full respect of mutual rights," and a loan, almost, of hard currency from the leading treasury. He said he'd been happy to explain his Socialism to the Soviet comrades.

And the city of Cologne has gotten back the Cranach painting it had been forced to give Hermann Göring's daughter for her baptism in 1938. Edda G. wanted to keep it, not as her own personal property but to give it to the Free State of Bavaria, but now Bavaria has also decided to relinquish its claims.

In Jerichow's eyes Papenbrock got off easy almost when the Soviets came to get him. Maybe it wasn't exactly fair but you'd have to call it square, after all the money Albert made from Göring's air force. Now the former business king of Jerichow was going to have to pay back taxes.

That's what it looked like. One Sunday evening in mid-July the victors drove into Market Square in a two-ton truck, with no sign of K. A. Pontiy, so that it looked like orders from his superior. Three men strode into the house, all officers, not with weapons drawn but still like an arrest party. If they spent half an hour in there, they must have been searching Albert's office for his earthly gains, and the fact that they did so silently only made the ambush more ominous, that and the recollection that Albert was far from the only one whose friendly dealings with Göring's air force might rub the Soviets the wrong way. Only one person sent for Cresspahl, Bergie Quade, but her husband, Otto, was back on Town Street much quicker than the mayor; he came walking up so slowly that he seemed to be saying he couldn't do anything to help, especially not such close relatives. Papenbrock was already being brought out of his house, in a work shirt and worn-out regular pants, shoulders bent, eyes on the ground, arms hanging emptily at his sides. It was retold many times: how the old man tried to step up onto the tailgate, slipped, raised his lame foot again, and it scraped back down the side of the truck, this time banging his other shin hard, and how the officers had watched him like a sick animal there's no point in helping. Then Louise came running out of the house, wailing and wildly swinging a bulging travel bag as if wanting to hurt herself or one of the officers. Finally a Russian gave Papenbrock a gentle push, not exactly as though wanting to hurt him, and Albert stumbled and fell onto the truck's loading bed, the officers climbed in after him and latched the tailgate shut, the truck turned around and drove back south, maybe to headquarters in Schwerin, possibly an even bigger prison. They had taken the travel bag from Louise, but they hadn't handed it to her husband, they gave it to the driver, and even if Albert had a bit longer to live in custody it didn't look like he'd be coming back.

There hadn't been many onlookers, so the stories about what happened didn't end up fragmentary. The onlookers there were had kept a proper distance, so as not to be taken along on Albert's trip by mistake, but every one of them claimed to feel a shudder when Louise, still a big woman, tugged with both hands at the front door, which was sticking—clearly she was weakened by her sobbing—until she had it back in its frame and could bolt it from the inside. That spared the witnesses the expected expressions of sympathy, but when they stepped back and turned around they found themselves face-to-face with Cresspahl, the one they called the Russian lackey, the traitor. But from this close up no one wanted to tell him that now he'd let his father-in-law get arrested. They felt trapped in his silent, challenging gaze. Cresspahl had enjoyed the Russians' flight from Louise's tearful entrance, and so he seemed almost relaxed, head tilted toward the evening sun, checking the time. – *'Ts nahyin:* he said, reminding them of the approaching curfew, that Soviet lickspittle, instead of staggering under the misfortune befalling his family. They left him alone and he walked off down Town Street. He hadn't even given them any information. But anyway, it was nine o'clock. Suddenly you could smell the time—sweet, unwholesome, slightly greasy—from the scent of the linden blossoms.

If you think of Jerichow as the center of a clock (where the Hydrographical Institute puts its compass rose on its maps of Lübeck Bay), the village and seaside resort of Rande would be at approximately one o'clock. In the eight o'clock direction, but far past the edge of the clock face, was the Old Demwies estate, still southwest of Gneez, in the former Principality of Ratzeburg, far enough from Jerichow. Even if you'd hidden your telephone instead of handing it in you still couldn't get through to another number, the post office still had nothing to deliver, and the travel ban took care of the rest; and so, for some time, Albert Papenbrock was thought to have vanished without a trace. Only around the end of 1945 did people start talking in Jerichow about someone in far-off Old Demwies, managing the estate for the Soviets, by the name of Papenbrock. If you believed the reports, he wasn't acting like an old man of seventy-seven, he was bossing the farmworkers around like an old-time overseer, talking to his Soviet superiors like someone who'd never gotten his hands dirty with the Nazis. He sure wasn't shy. And if someone's only described to you in words, can you recognize him right off? He'd supposedly made his way there from the Müritz area, maybe he wasn't the Jerichow Papenbrock. You couldn't ask Cresspahl. Papenbrock's wife said she didn't know anything. Yeah it's not him. When Soviet counterintelligence came to Jerichow the translators almost always got back the same, plausibly indignant answer: You all arrested him a while back! Doncha even keep a list of who you put away?

In early August, returning from Lübeck to Jerichow, Jakob took an inordinate detour through Old Demwies so that he could tell Gesine something about her grandfather. She'd have trouble recognizing him. He now wore mended-up clothes all week long, a torn shirt, patched pants, and a black straw hat he never took off so people wouldn't know he was bald. The commandants of Old Demwies, known as the Twins, hadn't understood his name and called him the Pope; he didn't correct them. In the village they called him the Pastor, because he spoke so gentle and mild when assigning work in the mornings, and raged so furiously when they hadn't made their quotas in the evenings. As far as Jakob could tell the farm was running on textbook lines—they'd already brought in their wheat from the fields and had started threshing. The farmworkers respected the P. for it—he took care of them with extra allowances and right of residence just like the former masters who'd fled; they wanted him to be even more on their side. He avoided getting into fights with the Twins like any other employee. At night the Soviet men would go for a stroll through the farmhands' cottages shining their flashlights at the beds, looking for grown girls, but all they found there were small children—you could complain to this overseer and he'd actually send someone to the commandants, those two young guys never seen apart, but they just laughed at the nightly disturbance. One time, the soldiers had suddenly been moved by the sight of all those sleeping children right up next to one another and they stood there a long time, shining their flashlights on them, amazed at the little tykes lying there like peas, sleeping like little peas in a pod; this family was offered a room in the manor house, because the Twins decided to interpret the story as meaning a lack of space, while the Pastor could have told them otherwise. The Pope had convinced the Twins to station some Red Army soldiers to guard the farm, so that he could get the work done; at night he locked himself inside and didn't hear anyone knocking no matter how loud it was. The Soviets had put him in the foreman's cottage—the whole house, where the former Nazi regional group leader had lived with his wife and children before hanging himself and them. The Pope didn't want the privilege or the honor and took in two refugee families, putting them into the narrow rooms, as if he preferred not to be alone at night. Jakob had seen the old man only from afar; he'd seemed jittery, and Jakob didn't want to shock him with a visitor from Jerichow. Plus Cresspahl hadn't given him any message to take to the old man.

Papenbrock had hardly bristled at the deal. He was sure he could explain to any Soviet court, even a military one, what he had been doing during the past twelve years, but given that starting in 1935 he'd trusted Cresspahl more than either of his own sons and had done so all the more ever since Lisbeth's death, he was as good as submissive when in June 1945 he realized that he was no longer up to making a decision of his own, whether it was to hole up in Jerichow or flee to the British across the demarcation line. Louise had wanted to keep the house, and if not the whole business then at least the bakery. Papenbrock hadn't stayed for that reason, or for her sake at all, it was just that he lacked the self-confidence to drag his Louise away by force. Then Cresspahl came and told them that the Soviets were looking for the father of Robert Papenbrock, who'd become well known for executing hostages in Ukraine. So, the old man let himself get sent somewhere right by the border. So, K. A. Pontiy could request certain deliveries from the administrators of the Old Demwies estate—he'd sent them an extremely skilled estate manager.

We'll be gettin this back, said the farmer, giving his pig some bacon.

May 8, 1968 Wednesday

The city government is armed and ready for racial violence this summer, and city officials can better estimate the numbers now, after the arrests at Columbia University. There are 196 detention pens in present court buildings and a special pen on Rikers Island that holds 1,600 prisoners. Altogether the police can arrest 10,000 disobedient persons a day, and if there're more they'll probably be able to handle it.

Senator Robert F. Kennedy has cleared his first hurdle on the way to the White House, winning the Indiana primary—not with as many votes as he wanted, just 42 percent. Eugene McCarthy received 27 percent and he can barely give his staff pocket money. Still, according to a poll of college students, McCarthy is a good twenty-five points ahead of Kennedy, who mentions his own money and his right to spend it on whatever he wants, such as a win in Indiana.

A young man is standing in the Cresspahls' doorway, with short hair and, fervently devoted to tradition, a button-down shirt tucked into his pants, blinding white thick-waled socks in shoes polished to a military shine. Without being pushy he takes a friendly look at the set table, at the peaceful family life by the evening windows, the darkening green park; he doesn't insist on being invited in, he can say his piece just fine while standing...

If only we understood this country where we want to live! After seven years. We heard news of the 1960 election as anecdotes that reached Germany—Nixon's heavy stubble that hurt him on-screen against John Kennedy in a once famous debate, this one not about kitchen technology; we arrived to find President Kennedy and at first wanted to give him credit for abolishing the line on the questionnaire where we had to say if we were planning to assassinate him. Then we learned. We learned what a party precinct is and what a county committee can do, how someone becomes a favorite son and how much a TV ad costs per minute until it's broadcast for free as news—the whole local folklore of capitalist parliamentarianism. Without much hope, just to know where we'd be and what we'd support if we trusted and believed in who we were for.

This time it's supposed to be Eugene McCarthy, if we listen to the new generation, now not flower children but ballot children. There hasn't been such an upswelling of student support since the 1964 civil rights march in Mississippi—the democratic process counted for nothing against the executive branch's arrangements with the Four Hundred Families—and then came the New Left, you could escape into the psychedelic embellishments and desolations of consciousness, into personal excuses, whether working for the Peace Corps in South America or another antiwar protest outside City Hall or the Pentagon, still we kept hearing the word *frustration*, the disgust at empty gestures that accomplished nothing but venting feelings so they no longer bothered you. Then, unexpectedly, in March 1968 they were back, from the posh schools and the poor schools on the East Coast—from Harvard, Radcliffe, Yale, Smith, Barnard, Columbia, as well as Dunbarton and Rivier—and a campaign following all the rules to the letter started for one Senator Eugene McCarthy. Why?

Fifty-two years old, born in the hamlet of Watkins, Minnesota, pop. 744. Is that why? Because he has Irish ancestors like Kennedy, is Catholic like Kennedy, but more reliably so on both counts? That's a reason he himself supposedly gave. Fine, they no longer set store in the fear that the pope might control the children of America, they are thinking more like Stalin, admittedly not bringing up the size of the pope's army right off;

but this prejudice is so powerful around the country that even we've heard about it. What else do they like about him? That he zipped through middle and high school in six years instead of eight, with straight A's except for in trigonometry, a hero on the hockey rink and baseball diamond? That helps a man's reputation hereabouts. Yes. He was one of the few to pick a fight over the radio with the other McCarthy, the sniffer-out of Communists, maybe they credit him with bravery for that. Still, five terms in the Senate as a Democrat and not one law bearing his name. Is it because he embraced the nickname he was given, the Maverick—the animal that doesn't run with the herd (qv. Texas rancher Samuel A. Maverick, 1803–1870)? But he worked with his party in 1960, supporting in vain one Adlai Stevenson just because he didn't like Lyndon Johnson and saw nothing but reckless spending and ruthless actions when he looked at Kennedy? In 1964 he went back to the well with LBJ after all, hoping for the vice presidency, and as a reward got mightily dunked. Is it because he was one of the first senators to come out in favor of pulling back in the war against the people of Vietnam? He hadn't said anything until January 1966. All right, well, he's more or less antiwar. He's picked fights with L. B. Johnson over everything, whether the crisis in the cities or that in agriculture. Both these things are true of Robert Kennedy too. Are they more true of McCarthy?

Why do we even want to understand the students supporting McCarthy? Is it because we secretly want to be one of them, not just in our opinions but also in age?

They first went over to him for giving long-enough speeches in a dry tone, professorial, with no tricks or appeals to emotions. Maybe they went over to him first because they were students, and only then because they agreed with him. They might have liked that here was someone demanding hard work from them, not a circus. But why do they now put on his severe, restrained airs and sobriety themselves, shutting the persistently bearded boys up in the back rooms to seal envelopes or lick stamps, wearing pencil skirts instead of minis on the streets where voters walk, forgoing men's jewelry, turning up clean-shaven, avoiding any impression of eccentricity, ringing the doorbell like a bank teller, in jacket and tie? And the press can report that they're sleeping chastely segregated by sexes, the boys in gyms, the girls in private quarters. McCarthy likes it that way, the voters like it that way, but this is the discipline and ethos of an earlier time, and one of these days the merely faked image is going to turn into the reality of "*law and order*," isn't it?

Eugene McCarthy drags his family into the campaign with him like everyone else, wife Abigail, Ellen Mary Michael Margaret, for touching appearances and intimate details; twelve-year-old Margaret, in seventh grade, is his "secret weapon"—aren't the students embarrassed? Don't they notice any problem with this national custom? Are we allowed to be embarrassed?

Are they with him because he's surrounded by stars? John Kenneth Galbraith, professor of economics at Harvard, has brought every one of his Americans for Democratic Action around to McCarthy. The poet Robert Lowell said for McCarthy that the Republicans cannot sink and they will not swim, whatever that means; McCarthy writes poetry himself. And then came Paul Newman, no less, the giant broad-boned actor oozing decorum and decency, who in his recent films plays the selfless, noble detective, or the advocate for the Indians guarding the bag of their money until he's killed, his heavy head with his blond hair tipping to one side, it's all over. Is it the people like this surrounding him? And they won in New Hampshire in March, with 42.2 percent of the Democratic vote against LBJ's 49.4,

Hey, hey, L. B. Jay!

How many kids did you kill today?

and the students said that if he'd gotten 10 percent they'd leave the country, with 20 they'd burn their draft cards, with 30 they'd go back to school, but with 40 they'd come along to the next primary in Wisconsin, and some were still with him yesterday in Indiana, though now deployed against Robert Kennedy, whom they'd earlier supported. Because of Kennedy, maybe.

Robert Francis Kennedy, Democratic senator from New York, stood up as recently as January 30 and promised his friends and supporters that he would not run against Lyndon Johnson "under any foreseeable circumstances." For the sake of party unity. Sat back and watched McCarthy proceed from state to state as the only antiwar candidate and didn't help him—inconsiderate, gutless. Then he saw the number of people in New Hampshire who were sick of the president, and Robert Francis wasn't there with them. How did he go back on his word? By suggesting that the president declare himself incapable of managing affairs involving Vietnam; the president declined to do so; the next day, Kennedy announced he was running against the president, "not out of any personal enmity or lack of respect for the president," or so he said. Stood up in the Senate Caucus Room in the old Senate office building on Capitol Hill, where his brother John had announced his candidacy eight years earlier. His tie clip a model of the PT 109 patrol torpedo boat his brother John had commanded with honor, on film, in World War II. His words were those of his brother John. With his wife, Ethel, and nine children he announced his candidacy as John's brother, to take votes away from Eugene McCarthy, for whom he'd done nothing—like a hungry dog who considers another's bone his own legitimate property. Paul Newman grumbled at the shame of Kennedy choosing to take a free ride on someone else's back; others said he was endangering the young people's new trust in democratic process, or called him a claim jumper, and one student for McCarthy concluded: Hawks are bad enough, we don't need chickens; finally, Kennedy was compared to the cowbird, which sits on grazing cattle, scans them for parasites, and lays its eggs in other birds' nests. Undaunted, three hours and twenty minutes after pulling the lever in the voting booth, Kennedy marched in the St. Patrick's Day Parade in New York with a green flower in his buttonhole, an Irishman among Irishmen, and that afternoon he declared his candidacy in Boston ("because America can do better"), the next day in Kansas. A choice between McCarthy and him would be one between fairness and underhanded tricks. So would we choose McCarthy, and why exactly?

He hasn't said what he'd do with the soldiers in Vietnam. It's possible he would handle agriculture and finance and housing construction differently from his predecessor, who now doesn't want to keep going; won't he have to accommodate himself to the Four Hundred Families, and everything they need for their money and power and more money? Why vote for this guy instead of for someone else? Why vote at all in this country?

Now there's one question we'd like to ask, concerning our personal circumstances. Two weeks ago McCarthy criticized the current administration for failing to realize that the dollar was a more important factor in world stability than military power. We have a boss, de Rosny, who understands what this means; it wasn't quite clear enough for us. Are we going to lose our job? And if it keeps us, where will it send us?

So what do we do with this young man ringing our doorbell at eight at night, holding a clipboard, asking us whether we are a registered member of the Democratic Party, and whether he could tell us a few words about McCarthy. Will we understand him?

May 9, 1968 Thursday

is the day we take Czech lessons, and at two o'clock on the dot Professor Kreslil ducks into Cresspahl's office, carefully pulls the door shut behind him, and only then adopts a more relaxed manner. Maybe the long walk through the tall building makes him uncomfortable—past the doormen, next to countless strangers—or maybe it's the opulent decor on this floor, the sixteenth, that intimidates him, and it only just now occurs to Cresspahl that she should wait for the old man on the sidewalk every week and escort him in. But there's no way she can apologize and suggest this, he would implacably refuse the help even though he wants it. *Čeština je těžká.*

Hellos, goodbyes, asking how it's going—all of this has long taken place in the foreign language; the lessons have dissolved into conversations, but the small stock of things they have in common has quickly been exhausted, and when it comes to their mutual friend Mrs. Ferwalter they can only pass on a greeting, not discuss, for instance, the source of her health problems. After that, the conversation has to be restarted using occasions that lead away from personal matters, usually stories from the day's *Times*, and once again there is not only a division into teacher and student but into a Czech Jew and a German daughter of German parents—Mr. Kreslil would, of course, deny this with his implacable politeness, were it ever to be expressed. So, the task is to retell the stories in our own words. It's just that Mr. Kreslil no longer likes hearing the latest news from Prague, ever since the police roundups that swept the country in the fifties now threaten to return, or other acts of cooperation with the USSR, we can't ask him about this part of his life story.

Truman's eighty-fourth birthday doesn't yield much. The street fighting between Parisian students and the police is unclear from where we sit. We've all but forgotten the reports from Cholon, Saigon's Chinese district, as if the war news weren't new every day. The jobless rate for the dark-skinned being more than double the rate for the pink-skinned—that too is a repetition. An ad on the front page announces Wanted: Former Professional Bank Robber to give advice on new film, call Thomas Crown, CIrcle 5-6000, ext. 514. In principle yes. But no.

So let's take the *Times* poll on the protests at Columbia University. It says that fifty-five out of one hundred adults in greater New York blame the students. Even more do in the suburbs, among those over forty, and among the non-college-educated. Fully eighty-three supported the decision to call in the police, and fifty-eight found the degree of force they used to have been absolutely correct. It's a hard article to paraphrase, full of numbers and more numbers and the temptation to duplicate phrases, and here come the first hesitations. They are what spoil the almost entirely correct sentence: there was no breakdown on whether the persons polled were Negro or white, because the polling organization presumed that most were white. "Simply because of the economic factor of having a telephone."

The sentence wasn't exactly prizewinning anyway. The student realized too late that Professor Kreslil can't afford a phone, for economic reasons and also because, in the part of the city where he lives, a phone in the apartment is often a tool for burglars. I'm still making mistakes. *Ještě dělám chyby, pane Kreslil.*

– *To nevadí. Ano, mluvíte poněkud pomalu:* says the old gentleman, for whom politeness to women takes precedence over reproach, and once again he looks at Cresspahl in a charitable if baffled way, as though wanting to put the Czech language into her mouth and brain and yet not understanding how he came to be here in this room with her, or what she wants that language for. And suddenly we're not sure either. He holds his sallow skull still, attentive; he lets nothing show in his blank face; he can't exactly be enjoying how we're trampling around in his language. That's not something you can make up for by repeatedly thanking him for his efforts, or even by bringing him out of the building onto the street. Today it didn't go well.

That was a warning, but this Cresspahl wants to try her luck again. She gives herself the afternoon off, starting that moment on Lexington Avenue— she doesn't even tell Mrs. Lazar she's leaving, she can pretend the absence is for work reasons. There's a Czech film playing at the Baronet, subtitled, not dubbed. She's been studying the language for six months, she wants to take a test.

In the Baronet, on Fifty-Ninth Street, across from Alexander's department store, in one of the three new cinemas on a New York corner persistently written off as dead, they're showing *The Fifth Horseman Is Fear*, "made in ČSSR," it starts at four o'clock, the people behind the counter are not ashamed to take two dollars per ticket, there's a seat free on the aisle in the smoking section so I can leave early if needed, all right, test me.

CARLO PONTI PRESENTS:

In Prague under the German occupation, a guy is dropped off at a Jewish lawyer's apartment. He's wounded and the Germans mustn't find him. Dr. Braun arrives in the attic room of a dusty, run-down apartment building, the prognosis is not good, he probably won't make it. He not only has this wounded man to worry about now, he also works in the bare (stripped bare) office of the Department of Confiscation of Jewish Property, where he has to say into the phone: *Ano.* Yes. Bravely, reliably, hopelessly. Everything drains out of his face as he listens to the other end of the line. Mrs. Cresspahl can occasionally understand clearly the specific things he says, but she doesn't always grasp the whole, so her gaze keeps slipping down to the annoyingly helpful subtitles. Now she's distracted by the differences between the original and the translation. Braun goes looking around the city for a place that'll take in the wounded man. The screen keeps showing furniture trucks with German on them: KIRCHENBERGER—why does the audience eventually laugh at that? Then there's the bar, the Desperation Bar, copious drinking in party clothes and dancing to pathetic jazz, probably drug use. There are Jews there too but they can't help. One shot begins with ordinary-looking shower nozzles that suddenly transport the audience to the ones in Auschwitz, the ones that the gas came out of. These ones are for water after all, because when the Nazi army operates a brothel with Jewish women it wants them clean first. They haven't been whores for long, they used to be the daughters of the middle class, the bon ton of Prague. The alternative is being sent to the gas. Another alternative is a quick slit to an artery, Dr. Braun sees someone there bent over a dead woman. Is it not just the wounded man in hiding, does he want to buy morphine for other reasons? Missed that. The crosscutting with the scenes of present-day Prague, what are they supposed to remind us of? of how locals acted under the Nazis? of forgetting? Some things stick in the mind, when there's no dialogue to hinder them: the boy on the bicycle in the suburban street who sees the Germans' car outside the door of his house. The start of the sequence at a similar point, the expectation set up for the audience and then disappointed. But is that in the original dialogue? that it's the lawyer suddenly breaking off his phone call which brings the police to search the building on the second day of the story? Does Mr. Fanta really say in the nightclub scene: "I did it, it was my duty"? Groveling Mr. Fanta with his stack of *Schulungsbrief* Nazi magazines. The caretaker protecting her bunny rabbit—of course she's hard of hearing too. The music teacher talking to the pictures on her wall, she's not very plausible. A butcher's wife who never stops humming. And then there's an ambiguous hero on the stairs with a dark, decisive look in his eye. If the German police in Prague can trace an anonymous call to a specific building, why can't they tell which apartment it's from? On the second morning, the wounded man has been removed from the attic room, by whom? At the end of the movie, there is talk of an approaching "confrontation." The subtitle says "a little talk." The long circular staircase, the tenants filing past looking at the corpse. So is the wounded man still hidden in the attic, just somewhere else, and Dr. Braun is trying to distract the police from this possibility by killing himself? Done. The End. *Konec.*

Test failed.

Cresspahl is sitting in the bar at the Hotel Marseilles, a regular for years, a member of the Mediterranean Swimming Club, a lady Mr. McIntyre will serve even without a companion. A conversation about the weather, so cloudy! in May!, wouldn't bother him a bit. But this Mrs. Cresspahl is sitting there dazed, as if something incomprehensible has happened to her, customers like that you just leave alone. And turn on the six o'clock news.

NBC's *Sixth Hour News* shows refugees in a storeroom. The sounds of gunfire. Stretchers being hauled down a hospital corridor. The bundles on them no longer look human. "The exact number of casualties is not known, since doctors are unable to reach most of them." Now Cresspahl puts down her glass, more sensitive than she usually is, and goes straight home, which she'd been trying to avoid doing.

She gets a glimpse of her second defeat when she's still on Ninety-Seventh Street, during the few steps it takes to get to overcast Riverside Drive. "The fifth horseman is fear"—what is that supposed to mean. The fifth knight, the fifth mounted soldier, fear. Aren't there four, for carriages, with the fifth coachman running alongside them? The declaration sounds like something from the people who wrote under the name of Shakespeare, but she doesn't recognize the quote. She had to buy her English from a translation school; there wasn't money for a university. But she's read her Shakespeare anyway, all twelve volumes! She may not have read her Bacon as well, or Longfellow, she doesn't even have him on her bookshelf. It's not good to be an autodidact, it always comes out eventually. She doesn't push the apartment door shut, she leaves her fate to chance, she goes straight to the books. Here's the *Oxford Dictionary of Quotations,* seventh rev. ed., 1959. Under "Horseman": one single entry, Calverley's ode to tobacco. Under "Fear," almost two columns, a gaze passing swiftly over them is held up not even the third time through, there's nothing to do with horseback riders or fifths. She is so confused that she swallows her pride and looks under that too. Nothing.

She's been living in New York City since 1961. There they are showing a Czech film titled *The Fifth Horseman Is Fear,* a phrase that is apparently so familiar in English, in American English, that Oxford's book of quotations doesn't even need to include it. Everyone knows it, except Cresspahl. She's not only failed in Czech, she's flunked English too.

Then out from the elevator comes a child with schoolbooks under her arm. She closes the door behind her, slightly surprised, and says, in her unthinking, unhesitatingly fluent English: Hey, Gesine! How was the movie?

May 10, 1968 Friday

The East German government never interferes in other countries' domestic affairs, and tomorrow it's sending a special train to Bonn on its German Reich Railway, with eight hundred seats for West Berliners wanting to protest the German Emergency Acts—round trips for foreigners costing less than standard rates. It never interferes in the internal affairs of independent states, and it publishes in the newspaper that American and West German troops are entering Czechoslovakia to take part in a war film; the embassy on Schönhauser Allee immediately denies the report, but there it was in black and white in the *Berliner Zeitung.* Now, true, it was only "informed sources" who'd heard the GDR's custodian tell his Soviet friends that this act of West German aggression demands a strengthening of the Warsaw Pact forces on the western border of Czechoslovakia. With East Germans among these new troops. Still, you can lead a horse to water but you can't make him interfere in it.

Meanwhile, for the twenty-third-annual time, the Communists in Prague are thanking the Red Army for liberating them from the Germans and once again promising friendship to the Soviet Union. Those who liberated the western part of Czechoslovakia got their wreath too, placed on the site of the destroyed monument to American soldiers in Pilsen. Plzeň. And the Soviet troop movements along the Czechoslovakian borders in Poland and East Germany, these really are supposed to be just training exercises. If you ask the Foreign Office in London, reports that they are meant to bring pressure on Czechoslovakia are "hard to believe."

The military commander of the town of Jerichow, K. A. Pontiy, had given his Jerichowers a new cemetery, and now he wanted one for his army.

Cresspahl told his commandant that he hoped none of his subordinates ever died under his command.

– A mighty race, the Russians!: Pontiy confirmed in all seriousness. Maybe that wasn't enough of a reward for the German's compliment, so he gave him a nod too, overly exaggerated as if to a child.

Cresspahl didn't respond further for now, considering this another one of Pontiy's passing whims. Admittedly he'd actually had a large flag with hammer and sickle flown on the post-office tower just because an officer was monitoring the telephone exchange there, but he'd forbidden the removal of the "German Reichpost" sign.

Pontiy cleared his throat slightly. His throat certainly wasn't sore. Maybe it was involuntary.

It was early one evening toward the end of July. Cresspahl should have been out in the fields checking the day's haul from his band of cripples, he had paperwork to do in Town Hall—and he was being ordered to take some time off, sitting down. Pontiy's office with the south-facing windows was dry and cool now. Cresspahl could see his own roof over the edge of the green fence, and one of the walnut trees too, its crown swaying a little, even though there was no wind. The chimney was dramatically lit by the western sun, its smoke turning slightly yellow as it emerged from the weathered bricks. The air was so thickly laden with a sweet flavor that it couldn't be coming from the lindens alone. Had the villa's garden ever smelled of jasmine? Had Hilde Paepcke planted jasmine here? It wasn't the golden rain. Now the top of the walnut tree twitched again. Like a cat's sitting in it.

What K. A. Pontiy wanted wasn't some ordinary cemetery but a field of honor! But he was past being able to scare his German, who shifted his shoulders a little, as if collecting his thoughts from somewhere else. – And put it where? he asked, not paying extremely close attention but coming across as obedient enough.

The Red Army, as represented by this commandant, had been thinking of Market Square.

During his first years in Jerichow, Cresspahl had been constantly struck by how big the market square was in this small town. And its spacious expanse, between the colorfully gabled buildings, had been crowded and lively even as late in the day as now. At harvest time the farm wagons would start coming in starting in the morning, to be weighed on the town scales; the waiting drivers got water for their horses from the town pump, stood talking to one another, hired a boy to watch the horses and popped off for a glass at Peter Wulff's pub. There were carriages on the square too, one- and two-horse hackneys and landaus for the ladies of the nobility when they came calling on the mayor's or pastor's wife. Once the wheat and turnips were unloaded, the carts would take a wide loop through Papenbrock's yard onto narrow Station Street, where the drivers talked to the horses since the wheels of the now-empty carts were clattering louder, and they'd reappear on the other side of the square. The fishermen's guild parked their little retail truck in the southwest corner, over the objections of Emma Senkpiel's egg shop; that was where Papenbrock liked to take what he called offense. The Lübeck Court porter would come from the midday train with his luggage cart, tired summer tourists behind him like sheep. There had been a time when a car had stood outside practically every other building on the square, even if no one in the building, or in Jerichow, owned it. When Swenson, the owner of the transportation company, was feeling lazy he would park his bus on the square overnight, where it would be seen. The east side of Market Square was too nice for shops, that was the one on the postcards, along with St. Peter's Church. Not at this time of day, but in an hour, the nobility's carriages would be pulling up outside the Lübeck Court, if the men were avoiding Schwerin or arguing with the innkeepers in Schönberg. Plenty of room on Market Square, no doubt about that. When the air force had come marching into town, you could see it would have been big enough for drills. Now it was empty, and all that space not being put to any reasonable use had an almost hypnotic effect, a person got strange ideas just from standing there.

– *Khoroshó*: the commandant said cheerfully, agreeing. It wasn't clear whether he was pleased with the once and future economic bustle of Jerichow, or the available space. Cresspahl thought he'd led this Russian away from his idea, but in fact it had him firmly in its grip. Pontiy was looking forward to putting the surveying tripod to use again, having the middle of the square measured, and possibly regretting that the dignity of his office would prevent him from marching around alongside it with the compass. So, the obelisk in the middle—marble, with a red star on top and tablets on all four sides.

Cresspahl reluctantly emerged from his dreamy recollections. Shouldn't the dead be amongst themselves, undisturbed by the gaze of foreign eyes?

On the contrary, every foreign eye only adds to the dignity and honor of the Red Army! Pontiy said it to be nice, to explain. He did not yet suspect what Cresspahl would be forced to tell him; for him this was still an enjoyable conversation, because it was going somewhere practical.

Cresspahl suggested the square outside the train station. They could remove the monument to the victors of the 1870–71 Franco-Prussian War while they were at it, and of course no one would be putting up any monuments to this war. Not as big a space as Market Square, obviously, but enough for a dozen graves. Cresspahl was in command of his thoughts again by this point, and added: Everyone in Jerichow has to go to the station sometimes, and would thus have to walk past the heroes' memorial.

This was one of the rare occasions that Pontiy did not let out a sigh. He had to give vent to his distress, and he was still rubbing his hand over his sweating bald head. Clearly he was very deeply committed to someone. It was also possible that he had not yet been notified of the official Red Army policy toward the dead of the Franco-Prussian War.

Cresspahl put forward a number of other sites—the Rifle Club grounds, a section in the new Main Cemetery, a gentle rise along the Rande country road with a view of the sea. Pontiy patiently rejected them all. Then they both realized that Cresspahl wanted to hide the dead away, Pontiy to put them on display. The question was who had more power.

Cresspahl had worked out that the Red Army dead would have to be brought in from the countryside around Jerichow, if there were to be enough of them to give their place of rest the necessary dignity. Cresspahl mentioned the cemeteries used by the nobility, and by the villages.

Now he'd made Pontiy mad, but good. He'd turned redder in the face, and his voice came from farther forward in his throat. He brought up things like craftiness, deceit. Again and again he had tried to trust this mayor of his and now he wanted single graves for *geroyam Krasnoy Armii* on the side of the road even! That was how dead Fascists were buried in Soviet Union, by stick with helmet on, like dogs!

Cresspahl gave the Russian credit for trying to convince him, not simply issuing orders. He didn't want their discussion to get to the point where Pontiy would leap to his feet, put his cap on his head, and start shouting— not in this breezeless heat. He asked when the first burial was to take place.

Pontiy ordered him, in a voice monotone with contempt, to have four workmen and a stonemason report to Market Square on the morning after next. Five would be better, since after all the cobblestones would have to be taken up before the digging could start. None of them should be forced laborers, forced to pay for their Nazi connections with more menial tasks— they should be real, genuine, honest workers.

Cresspahl thought about Pontiy's order to bring in the harvest and said nothing more. He would have to ask women to help with the burying, since there weren't any workmen who fit Pontiy's criteria; he would have to drop by Kliefoth's this very evening, and go with him to see Alwin Mecklenburg Gravestones & Ornamental Masonry (now run by his widow), and tell them how to go about building an obelisk . . . but he gave up. He'd wanted to keep this Russian from being tripped up by local customs, he'd tried often enough to give him a sense of the area he now commanded, but tonight he couldn't do it anymore. And it wasn't just weariness.

Pontiy had him read through a well-worn mimeographed copy of a memo. The memorial tablets for soldiers must be made of granite, those for officers of marble. Inscriptions in enamel, crimson red. The rear echelon had evidently caught up to their K. A. Pontiy.

The commandant felt watched, and knew that reaching for the vodka that night would not be taken amiss. The two men had often shared a wordless understanding of one another. This time Pontiy was mistaken. He ascribed to Cresspahl a hostility toward the Red Army. He invited neither the mayor nor the townspeople to take part in the ceremony.

It was a young man who was driven down Town Street in an open coffin, nineteen years old. He had died on the Rammin estate, no word as to how. His face had a vague, uncertain look above the collar of his uniform. He looked like he'd stumbled upon some secret, too much for his young brow, his totally inexperienced lips. Gesine had accidentally caught sight of him outside the commandant's villa.

When five people dig a hole on Market Square in Jerichow early in the morning, and two officers with eight men are standing there watching, a square of that size can seem pretty empty.

May 11, 1968 Saturday

From the life of D. E., aka Professor Erichson. In response to questions from Marie.

He resists giving these responses; he is almost ashamed, were he capable of it. The thing is that he considers his life an ordinary one, following the rules, a standard product die-stamped in overlapping punches by the machine known as Society. He has no stories. But he can't just sit here with us, the morning sun coming through the windows, playing at family life, and refuse to give information to a member of that family—a fact he recognizes with pained looks from under his sparse eyebrows, staring into the bowl of his pipe as if down into an abyss. At least it's only the Cresspahl child who wants a sample, the other Cresspahl has raised her newspaper in front of her face. She's reading. She's hiding her secret pleasure at the trap our crafty old fox has been caught in. Don't laugh, don't laugh.

As a child D. E. had to wear his hair in a side part.

It's not much, but Marie kneels on her chair and grabs him by the hair and divides the gray mass into a thick cloud and a tiny little narrow strip over one ear. Like that? He nods, unhappily. They both shoot quick looks at the edge of the newspaper at the other end of the table, but it hasn't moved an inch.

Here we have a child from Mecklenburg just coming into view and already he's started almost everything differently from how we did.

Born in 1928, grew up in Wendisch Burg. Yes, Wendisch Burg, who doesn't know where that is? Near Jerichow. People nod too hastily and start looking around the area near Genthin, west of Berlin, not up by the Baltic near Lübeck. Never one of Mecklenburg's fore-cities, but on the other hand not under the thumbs of the Dukes of Strelitz or other nobility—Wendisch Burg was part of the Hanseatic League from the beginning. Express trains used to stop there through the end of the war!

From your life, D. E. You can't put us off with the railway.

Northeast of Wendisch Burg the railway had torn up the countryside to make a switching yard for the freight-train connections with other countries. The cars with ore for the war from Sweden arrived to the very end and were routed west, around Berlin. International arrivals came in on the Königsberg–Stettin line, too—later it was booty from Poland and the northern Soviet Union as well as prisoners for the camps near Berlin. A high narrow bridge with a narrow walkway spanned the wide field crisscrossed with tracks. A boy used to stand on it, losing himself in the heavy clouds of coal smoke, the panting of the Doppler effect coming up from under the bridge. A lively child, his head rather thin, not easy to get a handle on. His hair in a part (blond). Light-colored sailor suit (Bleyle), dark-brown knee socks. With a special talent for squinting in family photos.

Son of a barber, scion of the established firm of Erichson, Quality Hair Salon for Gentlemen and Ladies, on Old Street in Wendisch Burg, next to the Three Ravens inn. (On Adolf-Hitler-Street.) The child didn't want to sweep up the hair on the green linoleum floor after he'd finished his homework, not even once it became material essential to the war effort—that's what a younger sister is for. Erichson senior wanted to be in charge of more than just one family and pushed to be taken into the army right away, in 1939; in 1940 they took him. The boy didn't like being told what to do. Would go up onto his railway bridge, or down to Bottom Lake.

Mother from the country, distantly related to the fisherman-Babendererdes in Wendisch Burg. They wanted to keep the child from any middle-class pretensions above his station, they cut their own hair, and the boy's too, so that Ol' Erichson could huff and puff over the blemish on his professional reputation. First escape from home, from the snooty town house: to the thatched lakeside cottages. Even as an adult D. E. is grateful to his relatives who taught him not to look down his nose at them just because he was forced to go to school; he studied his Latin by day and went fishing with them by night. Learned how to boil tar. How to coat a rowboat with the hot acrid tar. Sadness over a pike found floating in the reeds, white belly up. Freeing a finch from the fish traps left on shore to dry. A bucket of eels tipping over. Rowing into a west wind in the rain, working. But the fishermen also posed one another by the shore in the summer to have their picture taken, and the male children were given the grown-ups' brown caps, the SA caps, with the swastika, maybe because this band of robbers was going to break the shackles of high-interest loans. It was here that D. E. achieved his best squint, under the visor of the cap hanging down over his thirteen-year-old ears. The war with the Soviet Union had started already.

And the famous love affairs, D. E.?

First things first, his sister, five years younger. Heike would come with when he went ice skating with the fisher children. Hand in hand with a girl of eleven, yes, but they didn't say anything and now she's married to the head of the Wendisch Burg taxi cooperative. Nothing more than that? That was it.

But there was nothing wrong with D. E.'s eyes, and his father's fondest wish was for him to be trained in one of the Nazi Ordensburgs, as one of the Austrian's future generals or executioners. Mrs. Erichson mislaid the honorable invitation and the boy had no choice but to serve in the naval Hitler Youth, nothing more. There he learned how to row in a crew; he'd rather have been alone in his sailing canoe. That summer an H-Jolle dinghy was known to cross the two lakes, when not docked at the sluice. I never knew the Niebuhrs, Marie—never spoke a word with them. The troop leader received a report: Squad Leader Erichson seen handing out food at the Sedenbohms' (mixed marriage, no privileges, yellow stars).

Photos torn up, cut to pieces, burned. One may have been kept, in a drawer near the bottom of a small dresser in Fürstenberg. It showed the winter of 1943 and four young people standing in it, around sixteen years old, in a field north of Oranienburg with a thin copse of pine trees behind them, in the fog, in the dirty snow. Three were boys, dressed in the Air

Defense Hitler Youth uniform, blue gray. They didn't have the large swastika armband on their arms, as required by regulations, but they did have them in their breast pockets, in case crazy superiors turned up. All three have managed to get hold of air force belt buckles, now that as soldiers they are so superior to the regular Hitler Youth, and they wear the shirts of their uniforms belted over their pants, like how soldiers wear their tunics, not tucked in like children do. The fourth young person in the picture was a girl. Maybe it was she who saved the photo.

D. E., famous for his string of brilliant love affairs. It was only a week before the picture was taken that the searchlight battery had had to assemble behind a village tavern to receive instruction from their leader, a lieutenant, Iron Cross 2nd Class, suspected of sexual intercourse with a Polish forced laborer on the estate. He'd ordered the boys to "clean themselves" immediately after every such act, and this was how D. E. first heard of such diseases. He'd never gotten further than shy or overly bold letters sent via the air force postal service, Berlin office.

It certainly wasn't his steelworks he was guarding, he'd realized that much.

It's just that he'd only worked hard at two subjects in school, and he attracted attention in the antiaircraft course with his knowledge of the speed of sound at various temperatures and how machines function. He was withdrawn from his searchlight course and served during the Battle of Berlin as a flight observer at an antiaircraft telescope. Despite such perks, they hadn't forgotten the Sedenbohm affair; he was neither popular nor envied. "People from the capital of the Duchy walk like they've got a stick up their ass" (alluding to his birthplace, Neustrelitz). He sometimes forgot who he was working for—the B-24 Liberators floated in the viewfinder close enough to touch, narrow wings, thick bodies, large oval stabilizers on the tailplane, perfect machines. It had turned out that his eyes were more useful than other people's. The other people "helping" the air force were groggy when roused from sleep, despite the dim red light; he had good night vision and was quickly made "senior helper." He'd already learned how to use an RRH acoustic tracking device when he was moved to the latest "Fu-MG" short-range tracking device that Telefunken had built, the 41 T. They'd never heard the word *radar*. This device located enemy bombers from almost fifteen miles away and automatically relayed the changing altitudes to the artillery and missile launchers via a directional device—the guns adjusted with violent lurches as though operated by invisible men. The machine did the killing, there was no need to touch it. But there were some officers who had tried to kill Hitler, and since then the high-power battery had been fenced in, barricaded off, a prison camp. No matter how many men and airplanes they blasted into tiny pieces, they came down onto the field like hot hard rain. After all, Berlin was burning. In January 1945 they exchanged his red antiaircraft gunner's collar tabs for black ones and ordered him to the Oder; on the way there, he deserted.

For that girl from Fürstenberg? Sure, Marie. It's just that Ol' Erichson had gone missing back in February 1942, his mother was all alone with his sister in Wendisch Burg. He had to get there before Sokolovsky was done.

The conqueror of Berlin? Who died yesterday? That's right. General Sokolovsky, commander of the Soviet armed forces in East Germany, marshal of the Soviet Union, Hero of the Soviet Union, ran the Berlin blockade. 1897–1968. The one who thought Americans could never win in Vietnam except with atomic bombs, which would be World War III.

The deserter waited in a forest ranger's home on one of the farms by Top Lake, four miles from Wendisch Burg. The house was full of strangers. An SS tank unit was making the area unsafe, looting the last food supplies, seizing the men of fighting age. D. E. spent a lot of time up in trees there. Then, when the first Russians came to look around, in their low-slung horse-drawn carts, D. E. had to keep watch, not hide. He sat on the edge of a desk by the window and watched the road running past the woods to Wendisch Burg. As soon as he saw anyone from the Red Army he had to run through the house and warn the women so that they could escape out the back doors into the dense underbrush. He didn't continuously stare at the road, he relied on his ears too. There was a lot of luggage lying around the place, from people who had hanged themselves in the woods, and in one suitcase D. E. found a reprint of Albert Einstein's remarks in the *Proceedings of the Prussian Academy of Sciences*, 1915: Jewish physics. He read them slower than he had ever read anything in his life, while listening for hoofbeats or rattling carts. His fifth time through, he had to admit that he would never truly understand this theory of general relativity, although he could memorize it. His thought had run up against a solid wall, it was downright painful. Sometimes his efforts at understanding unexpectedly turned into a sense of flying, of effortless soaring motion. Then the autopilot crashed without any clear explanation of why. D. E. was not yet eighteen years old, and was forced to admit that there was truly a limit beyond which his thoughts could not go. That this would be his life. Talented, if you ask him, but no genius. In mid-May the rumor crossed the lake that the Red Army was going to reopen Wendisch Burg High School, with Sedenbohm as principal, and D. E. set out. And so he missed his sister, who had run away to join him.

– When you were keeping a lookout from the corner of the desk in the forest, that was because of the rapes? Marie asks. She is no longer kneeling next to D. E., she has leaned back away from him. They can watch each other as if in a contest, neither one yielding, neither one relenting. The older of the two nods glumly, now he'd probably have welcomed some assistance from the elder Cresspahl. She folds her paper, lays it aside, and now she too watches him, slightly curious. If you want to be part of our family let's see how you do at answering children's questions, D. E.

– It was: D. E. says calmly: because of the rapes.

– That was your job there.

– And in return I was given food and lodging.

– And the forestry people had relatives in Fürstenberg, and one of them was a girl who had gone into hiding in the woods near Wendisch Burg?

– Who brought up the subject of my affairs? Anyway it was hers too!

– And who did that one end up marrying?

– A surgeon in Hamburg, if you want to know.

– That was a risky trip for her if the Russians were already in Fürstenberg.

– She was shrewd for seventeen. She made it through in one piece.

– And: Marie says, as dismissively as him: did you take an oath to Hitler?

– Three times.

– Is it right to call him "the Austrian" so much, the way a certain lady of our acquaintance does?

– It is right, that's where he was from. The lady in question is probably also referring to the fact that many of his helpers came from there. She would also no doubt have preferred history to take a different course, branching off at, say, the North German Confederation, 1866–70.

– Don't bother trying, D. E. You won't trip her up. She won't fall into your trap.

– *Which I undertook solely to keep New York City clean.*

– And is she wrong?

– It wasn't an Austrian brand of insanity, if I'm to believe my doctors.

– What did you do with your steel helmet?

– Buried it.

– And when other people, farmers, found it plowing—

– the skeleton was missing.

– And your sister?

– Died in May 1945.

– How old?

– The same age as Gesine in July 1945.

– And you're not going to tell me any more than that?

– The rest, *my dear Mary*, I will hold back.

– And were there really Red Army cemeteries on market squares in Mecklenburg?

– Not in Wendisch Burg. In other places there'd be an obelisk with a red star on it, lit up at night.

– D. E.!

– The public utilities connected it by an underground cable to the street lighting.

– So, what'll we do now?

Finally D. E. can assume his other role: protector, initiator, maker of plans. – We could go to the amusement park in Palisades Park; but Marie won't spend a whole Saturday on such childish things, even if he's in the mood to. Any ideas in the paper? The *Times* has a picture of the Y Bridge in Saigon, taken from above, so that the street fighting can only be guessed at; that recalls our Triboro Bridge on the other side of Manhattan? Neither of them wants to go there. A trip to Boston is rejected as well; we've missed the train to Philadelphia; finally we decided on a trip to the Atlantic, Rockaway Beach. But not the way D. E. thinks. – On the subway! Marie says. – On the subway! Because that way his car will stay parked outside our building, that way he can't drop us off afterward on his way home, that way she has him for the rest of the evening, maybe even tomorrow.

May 12, 1968 Sunday

"QUOTATION OF THE DAY: 'We tried to go down one street three times and so far we've had 5 killed and 17 wounded in my company. I don't care whose birthday it is, we're going back to clean them out.' —S. Sgt. Herman Strader in Saigon, where the 2,512th birthday of Buddha was celebrated yesterday."

© The New York Times

"AIRLINES AND LAW ENFORCEMENT AGENCIES FOUND UNABLE TO COPE WITH FLOURISHING CRIME AT KENNEDY
By Charles Grutzner

The flood of recent thefts, including diamonds, blue-chip stocks, palladium and other high-value cargo, at Kennedy International Airport has focused attention on the activities of organized criminals at the city's airports.

One of the cases brought the sentencing last week in Federal Court of the nephew of the reputed Mafia boss, Joseph Colombo, to two and a half years in prison as a conspirator in the cashing of $407,000 in American Express travelers checks stolen at Kennedy Airport.

Twenty-three men and two women have been indicted, and all but four have pleaded guilty or have been convicted of transporting and passing the travelers, checks, which were stolen on Aug. 30, 1966. In all that time, however, no one has been arrested or indicted for the actual theft.

United States Attorney Robert M. Morgenthau has called the theft and disposal of the checks here and in Las Vegas, Dallas, Baltimore, Puerto Rico, the Virgin Islands and elsewhere the work of a gang familiar with air cargo handling at the airport.

The American Express case and the other thefts have raised serious questions about the ability of existing law agencies at the airports and the airlines' private guards to provide adequate protection of high-value cargo.

In 90 reported thefts at Kennedy Airport last year, the loot amounted to $2.2-million, two and a half times the 1966 total and nearly 50 times that of five years ago. The Port of New York Authority, which compiled the figures, did not include thefts of items valued at less than $1,000, nor did it include the $2.5-million in non-negotiable securities stolen from Trans World Airlines last Aug. 10.

Among those sent to prison in the American Express case, besides

Colombo's 34-year-old nephew, Maurice Savino, was Vincent (Jimmy Jones) Potenza, 40, who has been listed by the Federal Bureau of Investigation as a member of the Mafia 'family' headed by Carmine (Mr. Gribs) Tramunti, reputed successor to the late Thomas (Three-Finger Brown) Luchese.

Potenza and Americo Spagnuolo, who bought the stolen checks at 25 cents on the dollar and sold them for twice that to the passers, pleaded guilty to conspiracy and took maximum prison terms rather than identify the actual thieves.

One prospective Government witness, John Anthony Panarello, an ex-convict named in the indictment as a co-conspirator but not as a defendant, has been silenced by gangland guns. His body, with two bullets through his head, was found in a roadside ditch in the Catskills as his rented car burned nearby…

An official expression of concern over underworld influence at Kennedy came from S.I.C. Chairman Lane during the questioning of the hearing of Alvin C. Schweizer, regional director of Air Cargo, Inc., a corporation set up jointly by the airlines to hire trucking companies.

Mr. Schweizer had told of threats of labor troubles allegedly made by Harry Davidoff, an officer of Teamster Local 295, against National Airlines and Northwest Airlines when they were considering changing trucking companies.

BURGLAR AND EXTORTIONIST

Referring to Davidoff, a convicted burglar, extortionist and bookmaker, Mr. Lane asked Mr. Schweizer: 'It seems to me that one man could tie up the whole air freight industry in New York if he has that much control over the union—is that right?'

'Yes, sir, very definitely,' replied the witness. 'Because the drivers of the catering trucks and refueling trucks and the food processors who come onto the airport with food for the flights are either teamsters or other drivers [who] would respect any informational picket line that Local 295 or any other organization might establish.'

There was testimony also that a negotiator for the Metropolitan Import Truckmen's Association had threatened American Airlines with a shutdown of the airport if it hired a 'non-associated' trucker. Mr. Lane also charged that racketeers held key positions in both the union and the trade association.

Among underworld names that came up at the airport hearings were those of convicted labor racketeer John (Johnny Dio) Dioguardi and Antonio (Tony Ducks) Corallo, identified by law enforcement agencies as members of the Tramunti Mafia 'family'; Anthony DiLorenzo, an ex-convict described by authorities as an associate of the Vito Genovese 'family,' and John Massiello, a reputed Genovese Mafioso and convicted smuggler.

DiLorenzo, a convicted car thief, was on the payroll of the Metropolitan Import Trucking Association for $25,000 a year as a labor consultant. Massiello was also on the same payroll as a labor consultant.

Joseph Curcio, a convicted labor racketeer and strong-arm 'enforcer' who once shared the same cell in Atlanta Federal Penitentiary with Joseph M. Valachi, the Mafia member who later testified against the crime organization, was on the payroll of a trucking company as a salesman. The company's president admitted during the S.I.C. hearings that Curcio had never brought in any business.

Most of the underworld influence uncovered in the air freight industry has been at the 4,900-acre Kennedy Airport, which is as big as all of Manhattan south of 42nd Street. The airport is crowded with cargo buildings and heaps of unguarded freight are piled even on the aprons of the flying field. More than 40,000 people work on the airport...

FORGED PAPERS USED

Two men drove a panel truck on Feb. 27 into the cargo area of KLM Royal Dutch Airlines, showed forged papers marked with what resembled a United States Customs seal, loaded the $508,000 shipment of the rare metal palladium from the Soviet Union, smiled at a guard, and drove away. The airline was unaware it had been robbed until five hours later when representatives of the real consignee arrived in an armored truck to claim the shipment.

Port Authority police contend that the robbery might have been prevented if KLM, which had been robbed three times in the last two years, had notified them when the men in the panel truck picked up the metal. Lieut. John Lefsen, in charge of the authority's cargo squad, said:

'If we'd been called in to guard the loading of the shipment, we'd have known right away there was something wrong. Engelhard [the consignee] always uses an armored truck and this was just an old, battered green truck with floorboards missing.'

According to authorities, the thieves had known the flight numbers of the precious cargo, which had arrived in two shipments, and the exact number of items in each."
© The New York Times

"HAPPY MOTHER'S DAY / To Sylvia, the best mother in the world, from her children Ellen, Peter, Frank, and Amy."
(Public Notices and Commercial Notices.)

May 13, 1968 Monday

In the morning the park was so stuffed with gray light that the year seemed already to be tapering off into winter.

A senior member of the Institute of International Politics and Economics in Prague writes in a journal published by Columbia University in New York about the freedom Socialist nations have to make political decisions on the basis of their own needs, too, so why might that not include working together with capitalist nations. But the article was written before the Moscow Conference, and before the Soviet tanks entered Poland.

In Paris, on the other hand, the workers understand what the students are saying and want to help them oppose the government, by holding a general strike for one day and one night.

Employee Cresspahl is scheduled to learn something this morning, something from one of de Rosny's smaller drawers, and she obediently shows up to work in the kind of dress that a distant friend of the family might wear to a funeral. For the others at the meeting, though, it is a happy occasion—an annual stockholders' meeting of an allied company—and this time she is going to experience it up close, not see it in a movie, or guess how it is from the *Financial Times*. So that she knows how it's done. As if she would ever be allowed to take part in one herself someday.

– I'm only supposed to be managing an account for Prague: she told de Rosny over the phone. He could hear her embarrassment and resistance, but once again the boss was feeling like a benefactor and wanted to give her the gift of this experience. He started small too, you know.

The stockholders are standing in chummy groups in a windowless corridor on the twenty-eighth floor, chatting away, all in agreement that they'd as it were showed up for a dull gathering and were looking forward not to it but to when it was over. There is one man standing alone, with his back to the wall, wiry, gaze aimed inward as though memorizing something but distracted by keeping an ear out for the starting gun. Like before a gallery opening. It looks more like a class reunion around the CEO, a giant Viking who holds his blocky skull still, slightly tilted to one side, as though he were only listening, thinking about nothing but the boyish hairstyle he is reshaping with one hand, but it's precisely he who attracts a happy crowd and greetings cried from across the hall that he answers with short, salty teasing. Employee Cresspahl is supposed to get so close to this man that he'll shake her hand, but she keeps ending up at cold shoulders, blind looks. She retreats into one of the telephone booths furnished in fine wood and dials the numbers that spell NERVOUS on the dial. – The time is ten oh seven: a voice in the telephone says. But Cresspahl's assignment was to introduce herself here as a representative of the bank. Which isn't the truth, heavens above—a male executive is delegated to do that. It's just that she should secretly think: she's the host here.

For a company that buys and processes and wraps up and resells information, the meeting room is quite small. They want to make do with five chairs on the platform, only two microphones at the lectern to the left, the committee's table could hardly take a heavy turnover, and the rest of the room is full of ordinary metal folding chairs, not many. Clearly this is a frugal company. With its documents in hand Mrs. Cresspahl withdraws to a place near the back wall—that gives her the salaried-professional air she was trying to avoid, and a waiter bends down next to her holding a tray of coffee cups. She can hear the CEO talking in the corridor, relaxed, lingering over the secondary stresses of the words: How can you stand it, to have them keep taking blood out of you, they don't know what they're doing. (This to an executive who doesn't conceal his disease, he uses it.) – There is no. Way. I'll be taking questions: he says, and maybe this is a running joke because the announcement is met with laughter. Then the board enters the room, with the acting president in front, and he really and truly looks at every single person along the wall as if they'd drawn him into the room with their dutifulness. He is about to nod, and again he notices Cresspahl. But this time she can't escape out into the hall, she's trapped between the hard-lipped resolute matron and heavy, flower-patterned drapes with net curtains, meant to make you forget the view of the back lots that haven't yet been cleared.

On the agenda: Increasing the stock portfolio from three and a half million to five million shares so as to buy new companies. Hiring an accounting firm. Choosing executives for the coming fiscal year. Cresspahl listens hard to the formulaic way of speaking, tries to memorize it, maybe she will, and it's possible she'll celebrate the ritual of legalistic repetitions with more delight than the men at the directors' table, it being her first time. The CEO has now delivered his annual report like a story with more intimate family details than anyone wants to hear, and now he opens the floor to questions. He insists on getting the inquiries he'd said he wouldn't take, until a man in the bank uniform carries a hand microphone on a long cable over to a questioner. It's the anxious man from before, who has mentally rehearsed his scene so thoroughly that now he blows it. Stammering, with wide eyes, and then with words tumbling out on top of one another, he starts in on a complaint about the inadequate exploitation of a tax law that he's discovered and wants to insist on, with a look on his face that is begging for mercy, and the chair of the committee cuts him off, not impatiently, more like someone dismissing a child you can't be mad at. The questioner is referred to the section of the paragraph he'd just challenged, given the address and phone number for Allen, Burns, Elman & Carpenter, the mike has already been taken away from him. Now the unfortunate man stretches and Cresspahl could tell him that the committee is rewinding the tape with his valuable protest on it and erasing it. Now for the vote.

The committee's little men in black wind busily around and between the rows of chairs, distributing forms, to the exhausted questioner too, who'd tried to scare the gathering in the name of justice and honor but is now grateful simply to be permitted to write his name. Cresspahl has attempted an unfamiliar expression, not far from head shaking, and yet the functionary repeats his question: Are you a stockholder? Your name please?

– No: the employee says. – I'm here for the bank! With that she gets a motherly, worrying sidelong look from the matron.

The CEO is not happy with his employers' patience. He talks comfortably to himself, again as if in a family circle, at the dinner table, talking to his kids between courses. – I wish: he says: we at least had the lady here who voted against me in '67, with her five shares. I wish at least she was here today! Then he can finally put down his pencil, which he'd tried to sharpen with a Swiss Army knife in the meantime, and read the results of the vote. He shakes his head, concerned; he puts on a pair of glasses especially to be able to look reproachfully out at the people in the room over them. He says: One lone vote against me, what's that supposed to mean!

The names of the executives and employees present are again read out. The executives are obliged to stand up, the employees are allowed to merely acknowledge their presence with a nod. The disappointed boss has the last word—he has come here full of strength and fighting spirit, almost none of which he's had occasion to use, and now all he has to look forward to is yet another lunch. – So, until next year.

As they file out he waits to catch Employee Cresspahl and asks her her name. He comes across like someone painfully aware of how awkwardly he's behaving, but it simply must be done.

– You were the one vote against me, weren't you? he asks, confidentially, in gleeful anticipation. With his broad back he cuts this lady off from everyone else; only a few searching looks get through the barrier to her.

– No: Cresspahl says, and explains her status under the procedural rules. – I wasn't authorized to cast a vote: she says.

At around four o'clock she makes her report of this little gathering of de Rosny's friends to Mrs. Lazar, and ten minutes later, before de Rosny leaves for the day, she's put through to him. – I'm supposed to say hello to you too! he says, and today the connection is so clean that it's like the boss's squeaky pleased voice is right there in the room. – Apparently you were a knockout! he says. You were a seasoned pro, you're a natural!

Those are the views on human nature in this bank.

May 14, 1968 Tuesday

The new Economic Council of the ČSSR is discussing a plan to make the Czechoslovak crown exchangeable with other world currencies now, not in five years. This would be the first Eastern Bloc currency acceptable on the capitalist market; conflict seems inevitable. The country could then pay its debts or trade deficits with its own money, so it would no longer need loans in dollars, and Mrs. Cresspahl would not have to be transferred away from New York.

Cresspahl sometimes thought about moving away from Jerichow. It was he, not K. A. Pontiy, who would have to go to jail for the illegal acts by means of which he carried out the commandant's orders—from fudged bookkeeping to black-market barter while in office, sometimes to the town's advantage, sometimes not. But he couldn't imagine that Pontiy would forget himself to the point of removing his mayor from office, assuming that it still wasn't enough to get him shot. There wasn't much he needed to bring with him to the West, basically just his child and the Ohlerichs' Hanna, if she wanted to come. But before he left he should at least know where he'd be taking them.

Someone told him. It was a man my father's age but skinny like a boy of eighteen, though his hair was white, and not from the dust of the road; he was standing next to the pump on a Sunday afternoon as early as August 1945, as if he'd appeared out of thin air. He asked Cresspahl's daughter if he might have a little drink of water from the pump. She hadn't encountered such manners in a long time, and she claims she immediately took him for someone from Cresspahl's part of the world. She shook her head and went back into the cool stone house to get him a glass of water. He was standing there in the same place, and while he drank the water he looked at her as if his gaze had to jump off the end of his nose, he was crinkling it so much. For some incomprehensible reason he asked her what time it was, and when Gesine looked up at the sky he sat down on the pump stone, sighing at the aches and pains of age, which were not what he had. He was wearing his watch just above his ankle, he was clever, and he had made it, the whole long way and across the border too. Now she recognized him: Erwin Plath, not so much one of the guests at a funeral in 1938 as one of Cresspahl's wartime secrets. She brought him into Cresspahl's office without anyone seeing them and took off at a run for the fields; she couldn't bring him with her through Jerichow.

This was one of the few times that Cresspahl acted like the man of the house and told Mrs. Abs to serve him dinner in his room—he didn't want to miss even fifteen minutes of a visit like this. Then Gesine was sent for a bottle of Jakob's procurement, and when it was time for her to go to bed

Erwin Plath pulled her back onto a chair, solemnly explaining that he simply had to look at her a little longer. Cresspahl looked quizzically at his child, his eyes lost in a memory, and he didn't send her to bed, or Hanna either. The children looked at the grown-ups enjoying this reunion like children: eager, trusting, enjoying each other's company, continually happy at the prospect of more, and they kept telling each other how it had been. Then Cresspahl came out with his question.

Plath started nodding, but he pulled his lips back from his teeth as if he'd bitten into something rotten. He wasn't living in Lübeck anymore, he'd ended up in Itzehoe. He didn't get into specifics about his move, or about his new line of work along the Stör River, but was happy to do so about the British. Clearly they didn't care as much about how they behaved in occupied territory of their own as they did in places they were about to hand over to their Soviet brothers-in-arms, ideally not with a bad impression of British governance. Was Cresspahl familiar with the barracks in Itzehoe— the Gudewill, the Waldersee, the Gallwitz at Long Peter, the Hanseatic by the cemetery? Cresspahl was. The British were there and there wasn't nearly enough room for them. At the end of May they'd requisitioned the best residential neighborhood in town, the Sude, ninety-five houses, most of them mansions with modern furnishings; they gave the occupants three hours to get out, with nothing but valuables, clothes, and sheets. Now English families with one or two children were in these houses, while the Germans were crammed into every last attic, shed, even basement. And Cresspahl surely knew about Itzehoe's sewer system. That there wasn't one. He did. The Military Government had permitted one sealed room per house where the Germans could store their things; these things soon turned up on the black market, that was how much respect the British showed seals. They were in the Hammonia Hotel on Holzkamp Street, in the old covered cattle market, in both movie theaters; they'd set aside the sports grounds for themselves. A lot of the requisitioned living space was standing empty, but they held on to it anyway. Sude was off-limits to Germans unless they worked there. One morning the mayor walks into his office and sees that his desk is gone, along with all the other furniture—occupation headquarters had come and taken it away. The British went and raided German houses personally, too, taking furniture, pictures, radios, cameras, stamp collections, and other items essential to the war effort, not even bothering to hide behind orders. They drove their jeeps through Itzehoe like maniacs, they didn't care if they killed anybody. One division was called the Desert Rats, they were housed in the Hanseatic barracks, which they called the Richmond Barracks. Desert Rats.

Hanna asked about the net factory, where she had some relatives. Plath knew them, they were still living near the gasworks waiting for it to restart operation, they had no raw materials, they were producing nothing. Hanna thanked him, daunted. She was looking for somewhere else she might live besides Jerichow—now here was another one lost to her.

– Richmond Barracks?: Cresspahl said, confused, but what he was confused by was the behavior of the British.

Plath waved that off, suddenly intent on business. He hadn't come because of the British. Cresspahl had been given some kind of order to form political parties, hadn't he? The British didn't allow such things. But look, the Soviets!

– Yes and no: Cresspahl said, with a not entirely clear conscience. There had been an order from K. A. Pontiy, but he'd lost sight of it. The commandant was demanding a local branch of the Social Democrats, another of the Christian Democratic Union, and a Communist one. Cresspahl couldn't go around like God creating the world now could he? Political parties from scratch in Jerichow!

Now Plath woke the sleepy children up, by saying goodnight to them. He led them into the bedroom like sheep, so sweetly that they hardly noticed, and said something nice to each girl about her hair. When he got back to Cresspahl it was quiet for a long time, and the children fell asleep to gentle rustling sounds. It was the night creatures flying in through the open windows and hitting the globe of the kerosene lamp.

Plath reproached his old Socialist friend that he couldn't leave Jerichow without having a successor, assuming that he was planning to leave.

Cresspahl grumbled something. Maybe it meant that things would probably run better without him.

So, Cresspahl was supposed to set up a party to the commandant's liking. The Communist Party. And this Pontiy would get his next mayor from there.

Cresspahl couldn't even manage a Social Democratic Party.

– The SPD? What about it! Plath said, as if his own party left a bad taste in his mouth. Then it came out that he'd already been scouting around in Jerichow for former members. They'd all snubbed him, and one of them, Peter Wulff, apparently cited the views of none other than Cresspahl himself, who also thought that this parliamentary stuff was full of shit.

– All this shit all over again...: Cresspahl muttered, suddenly confrontational.

Plath had found only one man for the CDU, a guy named Kägebein.

Cresspahl was fine with an outsider doing his work for him. He couldn't repay him, not even with a joke.

At this Plath turned patient, and eager, and started talking indirectly. Cresspahl was reminded of his time in the SPD—the secret agreements reached before the meeting started, the prearranged interruptions or questions of order, until the results of a vote "stood" before even one hand was raised. The results had been little mice. And one battleship. Cresspahl just kept his mouth shut.

Plath ignored the reminder that he'd been Cresspahl's junior back in the artillery barracks in Güstrow. He put it to Cresspahl that the Communists only wanted a Social Democratic Party to exist so they could swallow it up in a coalition later. The stuff about acting in unity with the Communists, 1931, 1935. Erwin Plath had come to make sure that the right people got in on the ground floor with the Communists. Not just refugees hoping for new land, no, local people who wouldn't be accused of opportunism. Communists from the very beginning, but actually secret assets of Social Democracy. Alfred Bienmüller, the Jerichow blacksmith, was prepared to make the sacrifice. Why wouldn't Cresspahl do it?

It was for this that Erwin Plath had slipped over the "green border" near Ratzeburg, and Cresspahl managed to spin out the evening longer with Plath's reminiscences of bygone things and another half bottle of vodka, and he didn't even let his disappointment slip out. But it was there. He thought Plath had come to see him, not for the cause. For a moment he considered whether he could say yes, just for Plath's sake. The next morning he was relieved to discover that Plath had moved on in the night, to a new local branch. For the children, though, the visit had been wonderful, and Hanna Ohlerich asked Cresspahl to write out this friendly Itzehoe man's address for her then and there.

Meanwhile, K. A. Pontiy didn't once ask Cresspahl to become the

Communist Party chairman. His mayor was supposed to create parties for him, not join any. That's how it looked.

Rudé Právo, the party newspaper of the Czech and Slovak Communists, turns to its readers with a questionnaire, more than two-thirds of a page long:

Does the internal democratization of a Communist party provide a sufficient guarantee of democracy?

Should the Communist Party carry out its leadership role by devotedly promoting free progressive socialist development or by ruling over society?

Can you speak of a democracy as being socialist when the leading role is held only by the Communist Party?

Can you imagine that?

May 15, 1968 Wednesday

This morning the subway was even more packed than usual, and at Ninety-Sixth Street a young man kept pushing back against an old man who was trying a bit too desperately to force his way in. – Stop grabbin like that! he said, and he actually managed to get the old man back onto the platform. You could still see him cursing behind the closed door as the train pulled away. The old man tried to hide among those left behind on the platform, white in the face, avoiding all looks; from his accent, he seemed to be a Jew from Eastern Europe.

The East Germans have written a letter to the Czechoslovak Socialist Republic. In it, it says: "The victims of German fascism in Buchenwald, Majdanek and Mauthausen as well as Lidiče are a warning signal that should keep one from illusions about the possibilities of cooperation with German imperialism." Prague Radio felt handicapped by the millions of dead resting behind these names, otherwise one could describe it as downright piquant that the victims of the concentration camps are being called to mind in Berlin, of all places! That was the day before yesterday.

Today we hear from Moscow, again, that Thomas Masaryk, founder of the Czechoslovak Republic, paid an anti-Bolshevist terrorist 200,000 rubles to kill Lenin. In Prague they're wanting to rename a street after Thomas Masaryk.

Mrs. Ferwalter no longer cares about the news from Czechoslovakia. Back in March she already dismissed such matters with a gesture of throwing something away, and since she used both hands, it must have been heavy and dangerous too. Maybe it seemed that way because of the testy, disgusted look of her turned-down lips, even as she smiles. Today she catches us coming out of "her" bakery, and her face is entirely transformed in a happy grimace that's only a little rigid. – Mrs. Cresspahl! she cried. – Marie, my dear Mariechen! she cried, so pressingly did she need to share her happy news with us. She hasn't found another of her long-lost relatives, her husband hasn't been given a raise for his backbreaking job at the shoe store—she has her papers.

She has to tell us about it, we're friends of the family, and besides, we helped her. We would be sitting in the park and discussing the children's progress in school or the price of bread and suddenly she would turn her big friendly bulk to face us and say, with a sly wink: 1776? and we would confirm that that was indeed the year when the states declared their independence. We listened to her recite the amendments to the Constitution, tell us who General Grant was, and how someone becomes president, and she would keep switching to a different topic with every piece of knowledge that came back into her mind. She was often discouraged—an old woman, her brain harrowed with nervous twitching and insomnia, no longer capable of studying—and she let herself be comforted like a child. When we didn't succeed in doing so, she would leave with a protracted handshake, her face averted, walking off sadly and clumsily on the legs that the Germans and Austrians had ruined for her. But she also sometimes started in with concealed glee that broadened her lips into a smile until her whole obese face was kneaded soft with the joy of being an American citizen. Now, as of yesterday, she has been given her second, third, and fourth papers.

She was reluctant to admit her pleasure outright, so as not to jinx it; she mentioned tax benefits. But she could not hide that the prospect of an American passport was like a new protective shell, another bulwark against the past.

We were also supposed to improve her German. It wasn't easy—she may not realize herself whether any given one of her words comes from her stock of Yiddish, Czech, American English, Hebrew, or German; she rarely manages a whole sentence in one language. We have talked her out of "German Federation" to help her learn to believe in the Federal Republic of Germany; we've told her she can't say she has a *Liebelei* with her daughter Rebecca—a "flirtation"—or even a *Liebschaft*, a "love affair," even though these are actually the more precise words for the *Liebe*, or love, she feels for her last-born child. But we have let her get away with using a form of address that belongs in letters, *Meine sehr geehrte Frau Cressepfal,* which she says to express her friendship, and Marie allows herself to be called *Liebe Mariechen,* however much she despises that diminutive; Mrs. Ferwalter still makes mistakes with various other German forms of address. Hopefully the West German embassy won't demand such things.

For when our Mrs. Ferwalter becomes a US citizen she will be allowed to put in a claim for personal compensation from the West Germans; were she an Israeli citizen, as she once wanted to be, the money would bypass her on its way to the state treasury. We've gathered that much, and are reluctant to get into further details with her about offsetting murders with money. The survivor also has to prove that she once lived under German rule; apparently the American certificate of discharge from Mauthausen concentration camp is not sufficient. The corner of Ruthenia where her native village was has ended up now on this side of the border and now on that side, and were she ever to admit Hungarian sovereignty she would be directed to an as yet nonexistent consulate. That's what she says. She won't actually have to go to Park Avenue and say in German where on a map of Slovakia she was picked up. She'll have to write a letter. She came over and asked our advice about who she is. – Am I a *Hausfrau*, a house wife, Mrs. Cresspahl? she said. We agreed, although we know other words that would describe her. She so insisted on honesty that instead of taking the corrected draft of her letter back home, she copied it out at our table, perched uncomfortably on the edge of her chair, knees wide apart, awkwardly bent over the sheet of paper, writing swiftly, interrupted by sudden anxiety attacks. She considered this less fraudulent. If it was fraud, it's one we'd commit again.

Not only is she happy with her citizenship papers, she has already acquired pride in this country. – The government sends out checks all over the place! she says, not forgetting her solemn gratification that the government doesn't have to help *her* out with checks, only those whom God in truth has decreed must be poor: the Jews not deft enough to get by and the Negroes, every one alas doomed to blackness by Providence. And are we supposed to spoil her pleasure by arguing? Are we supposed to abandon her because she's gained citizenship in a country that wants to exterminate another country in Southeast Asia?

There's no choice, she has to tell us about her test after all. In the middle of Ninety-Fifth Street, next to the ominous chicken-wire schoolyard fence, she has to show us how she placed one foot in front of the other when she was finally called up to the front. It seems she tried to hold her head high, and she would deny that her chin trembled. Quaking and dignified she entered the room, unaccompanied, defenseless as a lamb, holding on to herself with two fingers on either side of her dress until her nails pushed through the fabric into her flesh. No, she didn't want it as a present, she wanted to pay for it with pain. Then the educated gentlemen in their dark suits realized that she was just an old Jewish lady, they wouldn't hurt her, and they didn't. She remembers only one question. Who becomes president if Mr. Johnson dies. – Gott ferbitt! she cried, and passed the test.

She has celebrated the occasion by going home in a taxi instead of on the subway. As she tells the story we can picture her, stretching out her arm in a way suggesting more equal rights than she'd had the day before, waiting next to the taxi until the driver reached back and opened the door for her, she's a citizen now isn't she? Leaning almost all the way back in the taxi, hanging her wrist in the looped strap just like she'd seen other people do, driven home high above the Hudson, a little sad about the waste of money, a little afraid of when the pleasure would come to an end, but entirely determined to keep it alive by telling stories about it, and now weren't the Cresspahls among the first to be told?

We are so glad, Mrs. Ferwalter, and we duly offer our congratulations.

This Czech film showing, *The Fifth Horseman Is Fear*, that's probably not right for celebrating, is it? Something about fear, that's not her thing anymore. On the other hand, if it's something from olden times, with music . . .

I don't think so, Mrs. Ferwalter. It's not from olden times, and the music is sometimes used to accentuate pangs of conscience and in most of the rest of the movie too.

– And how are you, Mrs. Cresspahl?

– *Ještě deělám chyby.* This is the sentence that's as good as my Czech gets: I still make mistakes.

– No! Never no! she insists. No friend of Mrs. Ferwalter's can be having a bad time of things on a day like this, and for the first time we are invited into her apartment, for a "shenuine jewropean" cup of coffee and a look at her citizenship papers. And would Marie like her cup of milk hot or cold?

So she has returned from her new status back to the bosom of her native land. She tells us the Jews in the western part of the Czechoslovakian Republic were assimilated, just like in Germany for instance. "Moritzes." Still, in Mrs. Ferwalter's village they lived apart, a separate group, but respected. What did they have to be afraid of under Thomas Masaryk? But that meant the Germans could avail themselves of a compartmentalized society, there was no place to hide. And she says she didn't even try to flee the Germans, believing they'd long since caught everyone they wanted. You couldn't trust the Hungarians. She will never go back to the Czechs, and never to the Slovaks, not even with an American passport.

This reminded her that she is now entitled to an American passport. Since Marie happened to be sitting closest to her, it was she who was given an extravagant hug.

– The joy: Mrs. Ferwalter said, almost in tears. – The joy!

May 16, 1968 Thursday

Last night FUCK THE JEWISH PIGS was still written on an advertising poster in the lowest walkway of the Ninety-Sixth Street subway station. Today the word JEWISH has been scratched off.

The New York Times is addressing economic need in Czechoslovakia, beginning with Moscow's attack on the memory of Thomas G. Masaryk and calling it disgraceful. She says this not as news but explicitly as her own personal opinion—after all, somebody's got to be the voice of manners and good breeding. She feels it's unlikely that the United States will play a role in helping Czechoslovakia overcome its economic woes any time soon, but she may be wrong. The old lady suggests various substitute actions the government might take, relating to tariff privileges and the Czechoslovak gold in American hands. The moral case for using the gold to put pressure on Czechoslovakia has always been weak, she says. Now there is also a political case for a reversal of attitude, in fact an overwhelming one. Is she trying to give the government in Moscow even more reason to be suspicious?

In August 1945, in the middle of the week, Dr. Kliefoth gave himself two days off. He had come to the office in Town Hall especially to do so. Cresspahl was sitting behind a mountain of paperwork, Kliefoth got his time off in passing, even Leslie Danzmann didn't really give him a good look. Later they both remembered Kliefoth's tiny moment of hesitation at the door, and then they realized what he'd wanted to say.

Dr. Kliefoth didn't have to go work in the fields. K. A. Pontiy had authorized a lifetime supply of food-ration cards, once and for all, without requiring proof of work. For Kliefoth had met the Red Army representative in the walking-out uniform of the German Army, wearing all his medals and decorations according to regulations, the same way he'd done for the British, only this time expecting to be arrested. The commandant didn't even have this headstrong man brought in, he paid him a visit himself, accompanied by a large number of soldiers. It wasn't an interrogation, more like a court of honor, and Kliefoth wouldn't call it anything else. The gentlemen discussed the First World War, in which Kliefoth had been a lieutenant, and the Second, in which he had discharged nothing less than the duties of a 1C staff officer on the eastern front. It apparently ended in a handshake. Afterward, while Pontiy didn't post an order of protection on Kliefoth's apartment—looters had already removed far more than a coin collection that was a byword in professional circles—the city was ordered to continue paying his officer's pension, and Cresspahl was not allowed to house refugees in Kliefoth's apartment, Pontiy insisted. Mrs. Kliefoth had flown the swastika flag on the days required by law, like all the citizens of Jerichow; now their hopes had been dashed and of course it reached Pontiy's ears. Pontiy threw out various anonymous letters too, and although they tried to convince him that Kliefoth had been a member of the Nazi Party, he trusted this adversary's word. Pontiy spoke of the great honorable militarist in his territory not without pride, and asked after him. He shook his head when the upstanding militarist voluntarily took in homeless refugees, into three of his four rooms, and when he went out into the fields with everyone else too K. A. Pontiy brooded darkly, emitting vengeful noises with his tongue, because this pure-carat militarist scorned to accept mercy from his gallant foe.

Dr. phil. Julius Kliefoth, high school teacher in English and geography, lieutenant colonel (retired) as well, reported to Cresspahl the third day after the scythe order. Cresspahl didn't want to dismiss him. This scholar, well traveled in the capitals of England and France, former lecturer at the University of Berlin, put forward, in his depreciatory, too-brisk way, that when it came down to it he knew how to use a rake. That was supposed to be his excuse. Cresspahl wanted to think that the scholar had come for the partial payment in kind; he had heard vague rumors that the man's wife lay sick in bed; he did need every hand he could get for the harvest. They kept the easiest work for Kliefoth, but the Malchow city boy was soon seen standing sheaves upright. Honing scythe blades with a hammer is something a person needs to learn how to do—he managed it. Then he did more than his work. The women had no idea that the use of a scythe didn't come naturally to him. He was almost sixty and they didn't call him Grandpa. After a while it was he who divided the work up. They came to him with their arguments and accepted his curt decisions, even if they came out as "Nonsense." They saw how exhausted he was lying in the shade of the sheaves, panting in the heat, they saw him struggling to force his bones to do this unaccustomed work; they let him say when their break time was over. He stalked from one end of the row to the other on his stiff legs, every now and then muttering something military to himself, it sounded encouraging, nothing to take exception to. *Go on! Go on.* Wherever Kliefoth was, work got done, and many a Red Army soldier retreated in surprise when an old man chewed him out, from above. He was a leader, and he brought up the end of the row in the evening, and he stood last in the line at the granary. He looked like a day laborer, gaunt, in baggy trousers hanging on stringy suspenders, a tatty collarless shirt stretched across his protruding shoulder blades—only his staccato stride didn't fit the picture, and his slim wrists betrayed him. Fatigue pulled his wrinkled face into a sleepy expression, but he could still make a child snap awake at the end of a long dry day, with a quick look meant to suggest renewed surprise, so that the child felt found out, watched. He didn't sweat, his whole face under his bristles of white hair was red, there was spittle drying on his thin lips—Cresspahl's daughter thought he looked brave. She liked hearing how he talked to a woman about to give up, he was so helpful and concerned, it was a deep voice, a bit like a turkey gobbling. By evening he could hardly get his voice out of his throat, but Cresspahl's daughter only showed him her water bottle, she didn't offer it; to her he remained the teacher, just as, to others, his punctiliousness made him forever the Dr. phil. She always knew where he was in the field; the rakes near him were swinging, work came easier. Now he'd taken two days off.

He must have gone from Town Hall to the Old Cemetery: Pastor Brüshaver saw him. (Cresspahl and Brüshaver had learned how to talk to each other by that point.) Kliefoth owned a grave site even though he had no one buried there—it was included with the house. He stood in the middle of the main cemetery path, to gauge the view of the gate and the commandant's villa from there. It looked like a strategic reconnaissance. Brüshaver stood at a window looking out onto Town Street, to catch him when he left; he didn't pass by there, as in fact he had never once come to the church for anything since he'd lived in Jerichow.

The next morning, before the birds started singing, he was pushing a rubber-wheeled cart out his front gate; the cart was half as long as the coffin it carried. He had a boy with him to do half the pushing so that Kliefoth could keep the load from slipping.

It was an imposing coffin, dramatically vaulted and fluted, with wrought-iron garlands, three bronze handles on each side, six feet, like a piece of furniture. He had unscrewed the crucifix figure from the lid and now the box was harder to keep control of. Miss Emma Senkpiel had wanted to pass over into another life under that cross herself, she had been very reluctant to give Kliefoth this piece from her stock. Moreover he'd had nothing to offer in return. She wouldn't take a can of oil, not even a pound of tobacco, and she didn't want Mrs. Kliefoth's clothes. So she took a couple of cooking pots and ownership of one of the cabinets with seven doors. She needed neither the cupboard nor the pots, it was only to give the appearance of an exchange, he was so timid. And the old maid was worried about suddenly standing naked before death. Her coffin was not one that Kliefoth would have chosen voluntarily.

They reached Market Square and the boy stopped pushing. Kliefoth looked south across the square. There was the Old Cemetery. The sun was much too high, he would not be able to reach the Kliefoth grave site in secret anymore. – *Go on!* Kliefoth said. He steered the coffin a little to the left, aimed it at the country road to Rande. The boy started pushing again and spit into his hands.

It took half an hour to get to the New Cemetery. Kliefoth had to wear his last intact suit, of course, even though it was a bit too light a gray, with a black armband at least, those were hardly clothes to work hard in, and soon he was gasping. The road was uphill. The boy didn't look at him when he stopped for a break. Twelve years old maybe. It was Gabriel Manfras, who never talked much, and even if he later described this morning as nothing unusual, at the time he'd almost dropped dead of fear. Kliefoth really was acting like he was out of his mind.

At that time the New Cemetery was just an open field. There were individual grave mounds here and there, most of them sprawling, not neatly defined, certainly not covered with flowers. They stopped at one such wide hole, still half open. It had been dug in advance, but for a body without a coffin. New mourners would have to extend the end of the hole with a spade. Kliefoth had forgotten his spade. The boy was happy to run back for it.

Kliefoth sat next to his coffin for a while. No one could see him from the road. He started poking around in the earth. Apparently he wanted to dig a private hole. When the boy returned with the spade he could still see the tracks of the rubber wheels. They led back to the Rande country road. There wasn't a cemetery for quite a ways on it.

The detachment of Soviets guarding the gates to the former air base stopped him and asked for his identification, *propusk*. Yesterday Kliefoth hadn't had to think about that. But now he was halfway to Rande, and this was the right place to go. Gabriel Manfras had caught up to him. To the boy, the teacher seemed feverish. Kliefoth put his hand flat on the coffin lid, right before the sentry's eyes, and feebly turned it palm up. This officer had never seen such transport on this road before and sighed at the crazy German. He pointed back to town, at the New Cemetery. Kliefoth indicated the way to Rande, toward the sea. Now the boy talked for a bit, just so they could get out of there quicker. He was afraid the Soviets would open the coffin and he didn't want to see that. The Soviets let Kliefoth go, with the comment that he should go fuck his mother, and the officer clapped him on the shoulder several times.

In Rande the boy sat next to the coffin for half the day, on a side road near the landing. They had taken the coffin down, since it wouldn't stay on the tippy cart, and put it in the shade of the hedge. It sat there in the sand like a forgotten piece of furniture.

Meanwhile Kliefoth was talking to one fisherman after the other. All he wanted was a crossing to Poel Island, to Kirchdorf, they could make it Timmendorf if necessary. He'd keep going from there. The fishermen didn't ask him about that. They wanted to know what Kliefoth could offer them.

Kliefoth had nothing he could offer them at the moment.

They knew him of course, he'd been a big fish in the army and a school principal in Gneez, sure. They knew his wife too—he'd gone for walks with her on the Rande promenade, sat with her at the outdoor tables of the Archduke Hotel. It wasn't that. But the Baltic, so smooth, just slightly ruffled, was a dangerous body of water nowadays. There were Soviet guards along the beach who wanted to see a *propusk*. Kliefoth didn't have one. What if they ran into a Soviet patrol boat on the water, with a coffin on board. With a German lieutenant colonel on board. And it could take four hours to get to Kirchdorf. And a boat would have to pass right by the Wismar harbor. Where cutters from elsewhere were being confiscated. Sorry, Mr. Kliefoth, meanwhile no hard feelings.

When Kliefoth got to the head of the Fishermen's Association, it occurred to him that he did have something to offer: the rubber-wheeled cart.

Ilse Grossjohann first let him finish his argument that a woman born in Kirchdorf on the island of Poel needed to be buried in Kirchdorf on the island of Poel. She agreed about everything. Then she offered him a cemetery plot in Rande. She could, she'd been head of the congregation since May.

She was the mayor too, but found no man willing to help Kliefoth bury his wife; ever since she'd led the work unit burying drowned bodies from the *Cap Arcona* floating concentration camp, the association hadn't been happy with her. It was two o'clock in the afternoon before they'd dug the hole. The woman and the boy were worried about lowering the coffin evenly, so Kliefoth went into the hole first. He caught the foot end, inched his back slowly along the wall below ground level. He had to tip the coffin diagonally after all, if he wanted to get out from under it. Then the woman and the boy pulled him up with the rope because he didn't want to step on the box. When the hole was covered, Ilse Grossjohann left alone; Kliefoth refused to listen to anything. Well, if he didn't want anything to eat, her children needed something. After a while, the boy left the Rande cemetery too. Again Kliefoth couldn't be seen from the gate, in his summer suit, between the bright hedgerows.

That evening Kliefoth was back in Jerichow. He didn't have his key with him; usually the refugees would have let him in. But they weren't there. Two Red Army men with their families were there. Kliefoth walked farther into his apartment so oblivious to their presence that one of them held his machine gun diagonally across his chest. Kliefoth had just realized that his wife wasn't in the apartment anymore, and walked meekly back out to the stairs.

On the street he noticed a pile of trash he hadn't seen before. These were the things from his apartment that the occupiers had no use for—an almost complete run of the *Yearbook of the Association of Mecklenburg History and Antiquities*, the *Papers of the Mecklenburg Local History League*, the seventeenth-century law books, the medieval poetry, the Merian engravings, the Homann and Laurenberg maps, the pewter. The copperplate prints and maps were punctured all over from the broken glass; the pewter plates had been gathered up by the neighbors. But they didn't come out of their houses to give him back what they'd rescued, they didn't help him gather up the debris, they let him crouch there alone in the gathering darkness, not long before curfew.

He found his wife's family *Mecklenburg Hymnal*, printed in Schwerin, 1791, His Grace the Duke's Special-Privilegio. This Example of Fine Printing with Gospels and Epistles unbound Costs 14 Schillings Courant. The Kirchdorf copy was a bound one, in shiny black leather, and the silver plates on the covers together with the corner fittings kept the book from being damaged. Only the clasps were broken. The plate on the front cover bore the initials J. L. with the year 1791; the tools of his trade were engraved on the back—a compass, a T-square, a protractor divided into degrees. On the last page his wife's ancestors had kept records one after the other. "My Son Friederich Gottsch. Johann, born on April 3 and baptized April 19, Anno 1794." "Father died on August 29, morning, 7 o'clock 1834, Buried September 3." Now Kliefoth had to add another line to the last page, and he could prove that his wife had belonged in Kirchdorf. At least he'd brought her part of the way there.

In such a hot summer, Miss Cresspahl. A person gets some crazy ideas.

I would've too, Dr. Kliefoth.

It was just an idea.

They moved her to Kirchdorf in 1950, though, didn't they, Herr Kliefoth?

You see! I would have forgotten about that.

Why do I keep picturing an apple?

That's how it is, Miss Cresspahl. She didn't look dead. When I came home from the field, she lay there as if she were alive.

Why didn't you let Cresspahl help? We would've come out to you.

Your father, my dear girl, already had his head half in a noose. I didn't want to bother him. Was I really hobbling when I talked to that woman during our agricultural activities?

Gobbling, Herr Kliefoth.

You mean I talked like a turkey?

From deep in the throat. "Oo-ah, get a hold of yourself, why wouldn't your husband be alive, we'll take a break in a minute." Wanting so much to help.

Then someone else can hear me.

Yes, Herr Kliefoth. I can hear you perfectly. Are you dead now too?

All someone needs to get into your club is a modest membership fee. And that I have.

When, Herr Kliefoth?

Sometime around evening, I should say, when it's afternoon in New York. Sometime this coming November, I should say.

The military commander received a report that the indomitable militarist took only one of his two days' vacation. K. A. Pontiy issued Order No. 23, making it punishable for any inhabitant of Jerichow to house a member of the Red Army without the commandant's written permission. He didn't try to put Kliefoth back in his apartment or restore the stolen goods. He wasn't omnipotent.

May 17, 1968 Friday

We want to tell you something, Gesine.

I don't want to hear from the dead every day.

Just listen, this will help you.

Do what?

Get back up after English ran you down.

It didn't, as far as I know.

Last Thursday, Gesine. The Fifth Horseman Is Fear.

Okay, tell me.

"And I saw when the Lamb opened one of the seals, and I heard, as it were the noise of thunder, one of the four beasts saying, Come and see. And I saw, and behold a white horse: and he that sat on him had a bow; and a crown was given unto him: and he went forth conquering, and to conquer."

The conqueror on the first horse.

Let Lisbeth do it. She has a clearer voice.

"And when he had opened the second seal, I heard the second beast say, Come and see. And there went out another horse that was red: and power was given to him that sat thereon to take peace from the earth, and that they should kill one another: and there was given unto him a great sword."

The war of all against all. But my English is just what Mary Hahn taught me, and Aggie learned hers at the Schnappauf und Sellschopp boarding school on Alexandrinen Strasse in Rostock. You go now, Aggie.

"And when he had opened the third seal, I heard the third beast say, Come and see. And I beheld, and lo a black horse; and he that sat on him had a pair of balances in his hand. And I heard a voice in the midst of the four beasts say, A measure of wheat for a penny, and three measures of barley for a penny; and see thou hurt not the oil and the wine." *The third rider, on the black horse, famine, starvation.*

Exploitation.

That's how you learned it, Gesine. Now it's Kliefoth's turn.

"And when he had opened the fourth seal, I heard the voice of the fourth beast say, Come and see. And I looked, and behold a pale horse: and his name that sat on him was Death, and Hell followed with him. And power was given unto them over the fourth part of the earth, to kill with sword, and with hunger, and with death, and with the beasts of the earth." *The fourth horseman brings death, Miss Cresspahl. That's the point.*

It's just the Apocalypse! The book with the seven seals!

Just the Apocalypse, Gesine.

Nothing but a piece of the Bible I forgot. I'd have failed a confirmation test, nothing else.

And English.

But if I'm counting correctly there are only four horsemen.

And The Fifth Horseman Is Fear.

There is no fifth.

There was for the Czechs. For them the Germans were all four plagues of the apocalypse in one, and more—more than conquest and war, hunger, pestilence, and death. The Germans brought with them a fifth horsemen of their own, especially for the Czechs, fear.

That's what they offer foreigners.

That's what they offer the Germans in New York.

The Nazis.

And the people talking about Mauthausen and Belzec. Remember? It was only Tuesday.

That's why I shouldn't go to Prague?

You can't talk there. Or work. Or live. Give it up.

May 18, 1968 Saturday

Yesterday the mayors of Moscow and New York were observed on a black leather sofa in Mr. Lindsay's office. How the other man deals with strikes by municipal employees, Lindsay wanted to know. – Strike? replied Vladimir Fedorovič Promyslov. – In fifty years of Soviet power it has not happened once.

Cresspahl had problems with his police force.

He needed someone a few years younger than him, someone who'd lived in Jerichow since before the Nazis, respected if not admired by the townsfolk, levelheaded, unbribable, and Peter Wulff had turned the job down. Cresspahl had caught up to this friend two days after the war, six and a half years after the quarrel the Social Democratic Party had ordered; they'd told each other who had smuggled flowers onto Friedrich Laabs's grave every March, in unsacred memory of the Kapp Putsch; who had watched from in hiding when the flagpole outside the Nazi headquarters was sawn almost through in the night. Cresspahl didn't mention his business with the British;

Lisbeth's death could not be discussed. As far as the SPD was concerned, they had reached a tacit agreement not to forgive them for their meddling in personal friendships. There were plenty of other things, for both of them liked spending their leisure time together, and soon it was not just for old times' sake anymore but with the joint intention of getting Jerichow back on the rails and moving it in a new direction. Wulff was glad that the British had made the other man mayor; under the Soviets he'd continued to help out with kidding and advice, but was not willing to back him up as the police. Wulff would rather turn up at the schoolyard each morning when work was being assigned and haul sacks of grain or help dig the holes for K. A. Pontiy's fence than go down into his fellow townsmen's cellars or up into their attics. He could see that Cresspahl was stuck with his job for the Russians and didn't want to risk getting caught the same way. He suggested Fritz Schenk.

Pontiy and Jerichow needed a manly figure.

Cresspahl would rather have Mrs. Bergie Quade at his side.

The war had left few of the men of Jerichow behind, and Fritz Schenk was one of them. Since 1939 he'd avoided conscription with an inexhaustible stream of attestations, petitions, and testimonials; to prevent the women of Jerichow from looking askance at him, he'd given the town numerous and thorough descriptions of all his abdominal complaints, sometimes without anyone asking. He had joined the Social Democratic Party in 1928 for his job as town clerk and registrar, was expelled (willingly) in December 1932 for conspicuous remarks criticizing a Reich government's refusal to use violence, reinstated under the Law for the Restoration of the Professional Civil Service, loud in his praise of his beloved Führer *and* Reich chancellor, coy about invitations to join that party, deaf to all such suggestions after February 2, 1943, and registered as unfit for military service all the way through to Total Surrender in 1945. Cresspahl was inclined to see all this as skillful maneuvering; he recalled some rather exaggerated congratulations he'd received upon registering the birth of a child in March 1933. He didn't trust his dislike of the man and recommended him to Pontiy. Maybe what bothered him about Fritz Schenk was his stay-at-home complexion, his long thin stick body, his smooth, affected manners, his lips too full for a man of fifty and pursed when he scented victory. Schenk was his name; Sourbeer would have suited him. And Peter Wulff suggested him mainly to watch him put his foot in it, not to mention keeping his own hands clean. Cresspahl tried to find someone else. He couldn't pick a refugee who wouldn't know the town's back alleys and back doors. He wasn't pleased— appointing Schenk as chief of police meant he had to pile more paperwork from the housing and registrar's office onto his own desk. Schenk took it as an insult, and Wulff's scheme slowly dawned on Cresspahl. Just recently a paper-pushing clerk, Schenk now faced the choice of filling in bomb craters or being Alfred Bienmüller's dogsbody. So he decided to work for the authorities, and spoke just as he had twelve years earlier of the sacrifice he was making for the new era. – I vouch for the files up until and includ- ing today! he said. Cresspahl recognized Schenk's anticipation of things finally going wrong for this carpenter turned mayor, this cobbler who hadn't stuck to his last. – You're the boss! he cried, carried away by his own obedience, taking this tack rather than responsibility for what he was go- ing to be asked to do.

At the swearing in, Pontiy asked him, playfully, enticingly: You Fasceest? Schenk was unaware of the commandant's addiction to private jokes and, breathing heavily, rejected any such suspicion. He spoke of the German People's sense that when the war was over life itself would be over, and the German People's relief upon finding that it was not in fact over. Cresspahl watched Schenk's fussing in embarrassment; that kind of patter might be all right coming from someone like Wulff, but Wulff's lips would never utter such stuff. Pontiy was merely disappointed that his chief of police had concocted such a speech; he called him You Good Example, You Go First and You Become Communist, put his cap on his head, and swore the man in. Cresspahl still didn't know what Schenk was planning to get out of a job like this. And when Schenk was asked about the Social Democratic Party he had shuddered with such palpable disgust that in the end Pontiy decided to use him to found the German Communist Party, Jerichow Branch. Again Cresspahl mistrusted his own instincts. If Schenk had hated the Nazis as much as he now exclaimed he had, maybe that had been how it really was and Jerichow just hadn't seen it.

For his subordinate Schenk picked Knever, Berthold Knever, former senior postal clerk, demoted as a result of his indefatigable altercations with the head office to working behind the counter and finally to mail carrier. Cresspahl didn't object to his choice. If Knever chose not to believe that there would be a postal service under the Soviets, that was Knever's business, and he thought the old man might keep an eye on Schenk. Knever had always been a stickler, down to the gram when manning the postal scale, also in his attire, patched though it might be, and the shopkeepers could set their clocks by Mrs. Knever back in the day, so strict was he in demanding punctual meals. If Cresspahl was right in his suspicions, Knever could dispel them and keep tabs on Schenk's every last move—glowering, observant, bristling, perfectly fitting his nickname, the Silent Parrot. So Cresspahl gave Knever a uniform too, as well as a third man, from East Prussia, Friedrich Gantlik. These were German Army uniforms stripped of insignia, with the swastika cut out of the middle of the white armbands with a pocketknife and POLICE painted on instead, the seal of the town of Jerichow stamped underneath.

They'd begun their service on July 4, and right on their very first shift they failed to carry the Karabiner 98k rifles they'd been ordered to take with them. Pontiy was probably trying to let his man Cresspahl know that he really meant it about the Red Army's chivalry toward women, and that if a black sheep ever did turn up it was up to the German police to deal with him, armed. That struck Cresspahl's policemen as rather gruesome. He could hardly blame Gantlik for wanting to avoid an exchange of gunfire with the Red Army—he had taken the job with the town mainly to acquire residence papers. He was short but tough, a farmer without land, and maybe he'd lost his harmless appearance on the long trip from the Memel to Jerichow. Cresspahl sent the three men to Pontiy, to test their marksmanship, and they came back with good results and a stern warning from the commandant that the negligent wounding of a Red Army soldier would be, in his words, unforgivable. Schenk looked blankly at his mayor, his swelling lips pursed. Cresspahl spoiled Schenk's schadenfreude by appealing to his men's manhood. After that they sometimes made their rounds armed. But when the full-scale looting of Karstadt's department store was under way, half of Town Street overrun with people, strewn with bales of fabric and cooking utensils, the police hopped around the edges of the excited crowd, almost as confused as the crowd was, like chickens, never thinking even to fire shots into the air. Schenk fired a shot into the air when Hanna Ohlerich ran away from him after coming down from a cherry tree Amalie Creutz had pressured her to climb. The police took their guns with them when they were called out to an argument between Germans; when a Soviet assault was reported, they marched tamely out of Town Hall so as not to get there in time to do anything, rifles over their shoulders instead of at the ready, and Miss Senkpiel came to complain that they'd picked *her* shop to leave their guns in, just for fifteen minutes, and sometimes it was evening before they came to get them. So the squads of harvest workers lacked protection, few infractions against Soviet chivalry were reported to the commandant, and two Red Army soldiers with their followers could put eight people out on the street from Kliefoth's apartment.

Jerichow's police were conscientious in performing their lesser duties. Anyone digging up new potatoes in defiance of the law was reported. Anyone putting up a sign offering to swap baby clothes for a work shirt on his own gate instead of on the official noticeboard at Town Hall was brought into Cresspahl for punishment—he had actually needed to forbid the posting of such signs. After Pontiy thought it over and decided not to take part in a rally of former members of the SPD, the police appeared and ordered the group to disperse. A stretch of street not swept clean enough, that made them really mad. Dogs without license tags had it rough.

What Cresspahl's police liked best, though, was going into people's homes. They had enough orders to do so from the commandant or the town government. There was cattle and poultry to be counted, so that the deliveries to start August 10 could be planned. When a sheep was put to the knife on schedule, there was still the skin to be seen to. The children had to turn in their textbooks for German (anthologies and grammar books), history, geography, and biology; everyone had to turn in the books they owned in Cyrillic script—so here came the police again, to plant themselves in front of the bookcases. The tradesmen's businesses were required to report their supplies of raw materials and fuel, so the police checked, lifted floorboards, crawled around under the roof, rummaged around in water butts, to make sure the lists were complete. The hunt was on for Köpcke's motorcycle because it hadn't been registered with the mayor's office, until one day Mina Köpcke dismounted and showed her *propusk*, signed not by the Soviet Military Administration in Schwerin but by K. A. Pontiy in person so his fence would be finished faster, and the motorcycle had been turned overnight into a little truck. On their treks through the kitchens and parlors and stables of Jerichow, Mr. Schenk, Mr.

Knever, and Mr. Gantlik saw more than enough to amuse them. Their eyes would light on beanpoles only partly concealing a barrel; they'd say nothing for the time being and then report such discoveries to Cresspahl. He couldn't object, he needed anything that was in short supply for his deals with the Soviet Beckhorst farm or the Fishermen's Association in Rande, so he'd write out his request for permission to confiscate and send it to the DA's office in Gneez and hope for a good word from Slata in district military headquarters. The district of Gneez was a large one, it was up to Slata to present reports on emergencies in Jerichow and she probably didn't want to remind people too often of her previous life there; sometimes the form came back from the courthouse too late. Sometimes Schenk seized the property before it was authorized, "to avoid any risk of suppression of evidence," as he put it, snippy because unassailable. It wasn't Schenk who was cursed out for hauling off an eighteen-month supply of artificial fertilizer—the guilt was hung around Cresspahl's neck. He was happy as long as Knever didn't report him for embezzlement. Then, in one of the townsman-farmer's houses, which hadn't been thought to have a cellar, they found coal: the house was sitting on a mine of briquettes, enough to supply Jerichow with gas for five days, and next door lived Duvenspeck, gasworks superintendent, and so a brigade of women with handcarts had to go bring back the black gold; in the end half a ton was missing from the quantity Duvenspeck was willing to admit. That was more than the two briquettes each refugee had sneaked under her apron added up to. Cresspahl's police had gone in on it with the guy who'd revealed the storage space, and the loyal and faithful Knever, upholder of the law, hadn't reported the misappropriation because he himself has built a neat tower of briquettes in his pantry, edges lined up perfectly, elegantly tapering toward the top, camouflaged as a wall. Gesine had seen it when she'd gone to bring him a message; these days she couldn't take her eyes off pantries. For Cresspahl it wasn't just about upholding the law, it was that the district commandant sometimes came to Jerichow and hauled off things Cresspahl had applied for, and it didn't go well for him if there were shortages. He preferred not to have his policemen's apartments searched on the evidence of a child, so instead he went to the commandant and suggested he give his forces of law and order a little extra training in their jobs. Pontiy would not rest until he knew the nature of the goods in question. He was delighted to hear that there was coal in the gasworks for his winter. He invented on the spot the proverb of the ox which thou shalt not muzzle when he treadeth out the corn. – Yes, the ox: Cresspahl said. Pontiy agreed with an emphatic nod.

Meanwhile, there could now be found traveling through the countryside around Jerichow a young man, Gerd Schumann he called himself, formerly in the National Committee for a Free Germany in the Soviet Union, and dispatched, after a management course in Stargard, Pommern, to this out-of-the-way spot as a canvasser for the Communist Party. Cresspahl had talked to him and found him agreeable enough, if a little too High German for around here. Twenty-three years young, stocky and already running to fat, with an aggressive but at the same time withdrawn look, invariably dressed in a military tunic that, oddly, showed no signs of wear and tear, and he squared his shoulders in military fashion too. Redhead, he was nicknamed, even though his hair was somewhere between white and gray, with a silvery sheen. – From now on

the great flag
of the freedom
of all peoples
and the peace
of all nations
shall wave over

Europe! he would shout, oblivious to his listeners' aversion to any more flags. He brought out such proclamations in a carefully calibrated tone that rose and fell in a kind of singsong, and, again like Pastor Brüshaver in church, the young man could quote chapter and verse: Generalissimo Stalin, May 9, 1945. This manner of speaking had become second nature with him; he would work his way through the KPD's whole ten-point program like that, to an audience of tired day laborers and farmers that the village commandant rounded up and brought to him after work, and because the Communist Party of Germany was demanding things like a war against hunger, unemployment, and housing shortages, a few coins would eventually drop into his collection plate, and he would hand out his leaflets and membership applications. He had far more power than Cresspahl. He carried a very visible pistol in his belt, and with that and the Russian language he could defend himself against uninformed Red Army soldiers; he had a say in the allocation of housing, he had money, he could use bedsheets and red paint to make banners with slogans that stretched across village streets, and when refugees asked him about their old East Pommern territory he would simply bang his fist on the table and calmly expound the guilt of the entire German people for the war, in singsong paragraphs, reverberating pauses, and elevated pitch. By the end of June his party had almost a thousand members in Mecklenburg-Vorpommern; it had more than three thousand by the end of July, almost eight thousand by the end of August. Cresspahl probably realized that the young man liked his unfettered movement from place to place, and his evening performances, his ever-changing overnight stays, but still he invited him to stay in Jerichow. Once this able and fearless man had a place to live in the town, he could probably be offered the post of police chief. (Secretly, Cresspahl hoped that this rival king might succeed him as mayor.) The young man refused to even hold a meeting in Jerichow. – That's your business, Cresspahl: he said, in an unexpectedly Berlin tone—so mocking, so amused around the corners of his eyes, that Cresspahl thought the man must have seen through him.

The man demanded power and didn't take it. Cresspahl was stuck with the problems he had with his police force: *like the cuckoo's stuck with his song.*

Yesterday around noon the Soviet general Aleksei A. Yepishev arrived in Prague. He was taken aback when asked whether the Red Army really did stand ready to move in response to a call from Prague for help, and perhaps because it was a young lady thrusting the microphone in his face, a brunette in a powder-blue shirt, the short, plump man wearing many medals finally answered her with a slight smile: This is a stupid thing. What stupidity.

May 19, 1968 Sunday

Today in the column for Commercial Notices, under an ad for shipping your car, the American Society for the Study of the German Democratic Republic steps up to offer a lecture this Friday on European Disarmament and the Two German States. To ship our car we should call 227-6334; to study the GDR, MOnument 6-4073. That number might live right around the corner from us.

Where we live is on the park named after the river.

For seven years we have lived across from Riverside Park, this wide expanse of meadows, gentle hills, walking paths, retaining walls, highway cuttings, tunnels to the river, old trees, hawthorn bushes, monuments, and pergolas, we have walked almost every one of its 106 hectares, and because we didn't grow up next to it—because we had no right to it, even by proximity—we tried to earn it by using it, and reading about it too, the way only newcomers, foreigners do.

A hundred years ago there was no park, only the railroad Cornelius Vanderbilt ran along the shore of the Hudson: seven long-distance trains per day in both directions, plus seven slow trains stopping at every station from Thirtieth Street to Poughkeepsie. Then the landowners—the Martins, the de Lanceys, the Stryckers—campaigned for a park on their property, and the city had to buy it off them, strip by strip, for more than $6 million. By 1879 the inner edge of the park was finished, a civic playground with paths for bicycles and horses, with little temples and secluded, restful corners. The river was still closer to the buildings than it is today; in 1910 it was pushed back with stone excavated from the Catskill Aqueduct, in the 1920s still farther with the rock that had been in the IND subway's path. Even in 1930, there was still a lot of empty land between the park and the railroad tracks; in 1937 the tracks were built over, hidden inside natural-looking hills, and by 1940 the park looked like it had a hundred years earlier—mildly civilized with angular paths and other signs of artificial construction, but thoroughly disguised as a pristine landscape. Henry Hudson's parkway, hidden by mounds and hedges, is like a miracle, looking every time as if it sprang up naturally.

In summer the park is like the site of a continuous public festival, and we are among the attendees. The banks along the shoreline promenade are packed with day-trippers from the poorer areas, the tennis courts are in use, chess players are sitting astride the benches and teaching kibbitzers lessons, people with the day before yesterday's newspaper draped over their face are asleep as if in their own apartment (which the park may well be), on the field at Seventy-Fourth Street the walkers let their dogs run free and are happy to stand and have a long conversation about their animals, picnics are spread out on the grass, half-naked children are jumping and squealing under the glittering cool fountains in the playgrounds, or chasing after the swings, or crowding around the man with the ice-cream cart. Long-distance runners are on their way, a bike parade with balloons came by around two. In the city marina on Seventy-Ninth a child can see how a boat is rigged up, on Eighty-Eighth a clientele that always looks the same is busy holding their rods and hoping for fish with robust constitutions— they catch a pathetic eel every now and then, and the sport of it is enough for them. We can see what street we're at without needing to leave or even look outside the park: there are number plates on the lampposts, PL 38310 corresponds to Eighty-Third Street, and the fact that the lights were designed by Henry Bacon, who built the Lincoln Memorial in Washington, is one that we've looked up, so that we might be more at home here.

The park is built for use, and it has found favor with the police. They drive their patrol cars there for breaks and man-to-man talks, and at warm times of year the forces of law and order rest their horses in the deep shadows of the shrubbery. You can see them, and people on the benches don't need to know one another to start a conversation. The park seems to be a picture composed of nothing but peaceful occurrences, and in fact many of the inhabitants of Riverside Drive feel a sense of solidarity. They are like one another in their level of education, their incomes are comparable, they lack pink skin only in exceptional cases, they send their children to the same schools, they all have the same housing conditions to defend, they act as a bloc in political and parental meetings. Someone around here who waits for the bus in the morning holding a child's hand can be almost sure of going to kindergarten or to school accompanied by no one she does not know, at least by sight, and the bus driver, who has escaped from the traffic crush of the city into the swiftly flowing river of Riverside Drive, speaks to the people getting on here as if to a family that's nicer than the other families.

The dark-skinned parkgoers, on the other hand, come from neighborhoods where parks are not provided, or are less in favor with the police and now destroyed, the grass withered and trampled, the few trees damaged, the ground covered with shards of glass from bottles broken there in neat, clean, steady rage. On weekdays the dark-skinned children are a minority in Riverside Park, they play in their own groups, and the Negro woman keeping an eye on a pack of kids running wild is watching her white employer's boys, not her own. The Puerto Ricans are among themselves on the baseball fields, the Negroes practicing for themselves alone on the basketball courts, and the West Indians play soccer with one another. They are borrowing the landscape that is theirs by right.

We can take the Promenade along the Hudson from the narrow paths running alongside the highway, past the magnificent paved play areas and well-tended fences under lampposts, up to the unprotected grassy roads and to 124th Street, where a stone tablet has been placed in the shadow of a large-tooth aspen to honor the efforts of the Women's League for the Protection of Riverside Park. We wouldn't have been a member of that. We have the river. The river under the unobstructed sky pulls you in toward the nearby sea, presents slowly moving ships, foghorns at night, green and gray and blue colors mixed with those of the park, a holiday view, and so poisoned is the river by industry that people aren't even allowed to swim in it. The river gathers up from the sky both its light and its dirt, which helps give the sunsets their ominous coloring. The smell of the river comes with us back to Riverside Drive. The leaves in the park are already holding the lamplight under them in glowing caves. The goods trains are rumbling through the belly of the park, bringing meat for the New York markets from Iowa and Nebraska, the Maine and Canadian woods transformed into paper for tomorrow's *New York Times*, for the diary of the world. Above the sparkling terraces of New Jersey's lights, above the tangle of colors of the amusement park in the Palisades, above the gray river, that wide gateway to the north, there are white bulbs arrayed on nearly horizontal arcs of cables; above the double-decker shelf between the two piers of the George Washington Bridge, headlights and taillights grope their way along, and Europe's tour guides recommend the view. We can't recommend more than the view ourselves.

We live here.

May 20, 1968 Monday

Charles de Gaulle has found the word he was looking for to describe the general strike in France: "Reform, yes. Shit-the-bed, no." *Chienlit.* The Grand Old Man.

Near Manhattan Avenue and 119th Street, in the vicinity of Morningside Park, the following method has been noted: The bus driver sees a pretty girl standing at the bus stop, pulls over to the right, and opens the door. In steps not the girl but three or four gang members who have crouched down and crept up along the side of the bus, unseen by the driver. They hold a knife to the driver's throat, grab the money changer, and vanish. The whole operation takes less than thirty seconds. *The New York Times* calls the scene of the crime the Upper West Side, where we live; actually it's only near here.

Shifting clouds and white bursts of sunshine, like one more snowball a child throws onto the roof so that it'll roll off, leaving a thick track, bursting apart in the hand.

In winter 1945 one of Cresspahl's daughter's troubles was over.

She didn't want the two members of the Abs family to move. Jakob should stay; Jakob's mother should stay. She cooked my meals and showed me how to do my hair, she helped me in a strange land. I still remember the evening when I was standing with my hands behind my back, – Gesine: she said, lightly and politely touching my shoulder with her rough hard hand; I still remember her fast subdued voice. I remember her face: long and bony and far advanced into old age in the narrow dry eyes. I always had a mother. Always.

Mrs. Abs felt that in Jerichow she was in the wrong place, and the wrong house there too.

Her husband couldn't find her in this small town, tucked away near the sea, tucked away in the wheat fields. He hadn't promised to find her and the boy. When he was released from the military prison in Anklam and dispatched to the East Prussian front, he'd made a secret detour across the Dievenow in order to spend two hours in the middle of the night on the Bonin estate, to give her his last will and testament verbally. She hadn't believed it. She'd promised him she would go west, cross the Oder, cross the Elbe even, but so he could find her. That was only five months ago. When the Wolin regional party leader threatened anyone who set off for the west with death, von Bonin drove off with nine heavy covered wagons; all that was left for the wife of the missing estate manager was an open potato cart, an extremely old horse, and instructions to look after the estate. Long before the regional party leader ordered the evacuation west, she'd left the island. Near Augustwalde she found herself on the autobahn to Berlin and under fire from Soviet strafers. Jakob was more scared than she was, and she had blood from his neck wound on her face. After they laid the dead to one side there was an extra horse, the sorrel. She'd wanted to take the boy to the Podejuch hospital but he didn't agree to stop now that they could hitch two horses to their cart. From then on, it was probably him in charge. He held their course through Neubrandenburg and Malchow toward the so-called gray area in western Mecklenburg, and after passing the mouth of the Elde they were forced ever more to the north, no matter how small the roads they took, as far as Wismar, and they'd come to Jerichow because the road by the sea was so empty and seemed safe from army and party patrols. She'd stayed because for the first time they were offered a place to stay; because Jakob wanted to wait out the war, and then because of the British occupation of the town, and then because of the two sick girls in Cresspahl's house, and then to wait for the British to come back. But her husband wouldn't be able to find them in Jerichow. He had taken her from a farm in the gray area, the seventh child, the unpaid maid—a dairy inspector, educated at Neukloster Seminary, and he'd wanted her for his wife. She had not left her family on good terms, she couldn't go back there for some time; still, he would look for her near Eldena, if anywhere. She'd obediently learned the job of cooking in Hamburg, thirty years old already, spending three years there while her husband was in Brazil looking around for somewhere they could move to together, until at least he was forced to return to shattered Germany. She was thirty-eight when Jakob was born in an estate manager's apartment near Crivitz; that too was where her husband might be looking for them—in Crivitz, in Hamburg, near Hagenow. Once the post office started accepting postcards again she had sent Cresspahl's address to eleven estate managers, schoolteachers, and church offices, wherever her husband might think she was; she had even made herself write to her family. No answer had come back, and she didn't believe Cresspahl when he said he'd find the man if he ever turned up in Mecklenburg. Cresspahl was trying to comfort her. She was willing to believe that his offer of hospitality was good indefinitely.

There was so much about the house that she didn't understand. This Cresspahl didn't own it—it was the property of his daughter, a twelve-year-old girl, and if you didn't believe that you could go ask Papenbrock. Papenbrock as a father-in-law, with his mighty palace of a house on Market Square:

how did that go with the remains of a woodworking shop behind the cemetery. He had one dead son he was allowed to put up a memorial plaque for at the family tomb and another that couldn't be mentioned, he'd killed children in Ukraine, set villages on fire. Yet the Papenbrocks had a Ukrainian girl living with them, at first as a maid and starting in December 1944 officially as a fiancée, and the Germans would say hello to her on the street, because of the Papenbrocks. In Pommern, on the Bonin estate, the forced laborers were treated like cattle that could talk. This Slata hadn't been deported "to Siberia" by the Red Army, she was working as an assistant in district military headquarters, she'd apparently earned her nickname the Angel of Gneez and now the people in Jerichow were denying the rumors that she'd knelt at Pontiy's feet and kissed his hands. Now rich old Papenbrock had been ordered off to a Soviet farm south of Gneez, to work as a supervisor, and refugees and Russian soldiers had taken over the house from his wife and were turning the big parlor into a dance hall at night. Cresspahl was the mayor, he could have stood by his mother-in-law; she never came to ask for anything, he always walked right past her house. Cresspahl's child hadn't been allowed to visit her grandmother for several years. People said. Every now and then Mrs. Abs heard talk about someone called Our Lisbeth. Lisbeth could've pointed the mayor in the right direction; Lisbeth had been dead seven years now. "Our Lisbeth" came up in conversations outside empty shopwindows, during breaks in the fields. For a long time Mrs. Abs thought she was someone living in Jerichow, maybe sick. Jakob discovered that she had been Cresspahl's wife, and since November 1938 could be visited only in the cemetery. She had died in a fire, possibly suicide. Her husband didn't look after the grave, and Amalie Creutz hadn't been able to do much for it since early 1945, the mound had almost fallen apart. Mrs. Abs took Cresspahl's child with her and showed her how to replant and maintain such places; the husband averted his eyes now when the child set out for the cemetery with the watering can. But when Mrs. Abs set up a kitchen garden behind the house he was almost overcome with surprise, he even thanked her. He knew what people in Jerichow had been telling her for three months—about the house, his wife's death, the Papenbrock clan. He praised her cooking, talked about the weather, asked after Jakob, whenever his duties gave him time to come home. Plus the Soviets liked having him as mayor since it had been the British who'd appointed him.

Then again he'd since had any number of risky fights with the commandant, involving shouting matches and shrewd reconciliations; he couldn't count on a salary, or gratitude, but could on a hard time for years to come, what with the nasty ideas the people in Jerichow were cultivating. He'd said something on the topic once, which made sense to Mrs. Abs. Someone had to do it, didn't they? That she understood. Someone has to do it. But there was too much about him that remained baffling.

She wanted to repay him for the food and lodging so she kept the house in order. He'd taken in more homeless refugees than he'd needed to or than K. A. Pontiy had wanted him to, and now the stovetop was crammed with pots and pans and casseroles. Mrs. Abs couldn't stand the constant bickering, everyone hiding things, she had learned how to run a large kitchen, so after a while she had taken over cooking for everyone. The people staying in Cresspahl's house, even the schoolteacher from Marienwerder, bowed to the authority of this tall gaunt woman who would look at you so silently, talk to you so evenly yet firmly. And she did have the head of the house behind her, and had been there longer than most of the others. There was no more sneaking meals in the bedrooms, in the attic; meals were served at the big tiled table in the kitchen. There were still a few hidden supplies of grain or potatoes, but the rule was introduced that everyone had to contribute something for meals, and after a while the possessions that had been such sources of conflict sat out in the open alongside one another in the pantry, behind an unlocked door. When Jakob came home with his earnings he was allowed to slip the children an egg, an apple, but the piece of bacon or the rabbit went into the common pot. Mrs. Abs got her own share to contribute, sometimes a big hunk of meat, by doing the laundry for the commandant and his two officers. There wasn't always enough to make everyone feel full,

Mrs. Abs! Theres a horse lyin in the marsh path! A dead horse, Mrs. Abs!
How longs it been there?
Just today.
Who knows about it, Gesine.
Just me. But we cant eat horse!
Youll get somethin else. Can you keep quiet?
Quiet as a tree.
Then go get me the knife.

and the children would rather there'd have been a lock on the pantry door. But there were fewer arguments in the house, the grown-ups could go out with Cresspahl's band of cripples and earn ration cards, and the teacher knew that her baby was being taken care of. The children learned from Mrs. Abs how to keep their room clean, Cresspahl's too, and they were at least shown how to wash windows. She would have been happy to make dresses for Gesine and Hanna out of the ones hanging in Lisbeth's bedroom; she asked Cresspahl for permission and the next morning they were gone. Jakob traded the patterns Cresspahl didn't want to see again for parachute silk and uniform fabric, and a sewing machine came into the house, where it stayed for five days before it had to be converted into alcohol. There was work to do in Cresspahl's house and that was enough for Mrs. Abs. She could put ointment on the children's scrapes and scratches from the wheat and rapeseed stubble, she could treat swelling boils with an Ichthyol salve and send the children off to work with an ever-so-slightly thicker slice of bread spread with sugar-beet molasses. Sometimes the children felt like a reason for her to stay. She'd won Hanna Ohlerich over immediately; Gesine remained out of reach for a while, maybe because she'd surfaced from her fever in such hesitant baby steps and was able to recognize her only afterward. Neither of them called her Mother, but also not Auntie, and though they almost always stuck to calling her Mrs. Abs they did slip into first names often enough. Hanna Ohlerich was a guest of Cresspahl's too, and she occasionally betrayed her thoughts of living elsewhere with narrowed, unfocused eyes—already it didn't really matter to her who she'd have to live with. With Gesine, Mrs. Abs felt half welcome. She would give Mrs. Abs a faraway look, ask questions in roundabout ways, stand there mute and withdrawn when Mrs. Abs ran to meet the mailman and came back disappointed. When it was possible to hear Jakob with the children, Mrs. Abs pushed the kitchen window's flap open a little. She heard Gesine's sudden urgent questions about Podejuch, noticed how Jakob was pulling her leg, saw how Gesine slunk off and came back to the kitchen crushed. And if she ever smiled at such twelve-year-old misery, it was never in front of me. By the time I'd learned not to let it show anymore, she'd helped me.

In late August, Mrs. Abs was carrying around a clipping from a newspaper in her apron pocket, folded small. When she was alone she sometimes read about what Edwin Hoernle, cofounder of the old KPD and now president of the German Agriculture and Forestry Administration, had announced about land reform: "that what matters today is to fulfill the old dream of every German farmworker and small farmer, the dream of a little farm of his own. These people are linked to the democratic Germany for as long as they live," and while she didn't understand the word *democratic* she took the rest to be a promise. She wasn't a farmworker, she had worn a white apron in the von Bonins' kitchen, but she'd worked in the countryside until her thirty-second year. This time she felt the days until Jakob came back to Jerichow were even longer. She was fifty-five, she wanted to take a farmstead with him. Jakob was almost eighteen, he could run a farm.

She had a bad conscience and talked it over with Jakob only at the end of the day; she didn't want to do it in the house, she went out onto the marsh path with him. Jakob didn't like doing that, it couldn't help but seem to Cresspahl like they had a secret.

Then he started talking to her like she was sick. He didn't want to settle the land somewhere. He wouldn't be able to farm anything with two horses, and a seventeen-year-old farmer. He admitted that the land around Jerichow grew lots of wheat; he'd seen the manor houses that were going to be torn down as emblems of feudalism, they would have to rebuild there. With the rubble? With wood? They had no plow, no harrow, no mowing machine, and there weren't any to be had on the black market either. And you didn't get the land for free, you had to pay for every hectare with the equivalent of a ton of rye, sometimes a ton and a half, and sure you could spread out the payments in installments until 1966 but did she want to start off with a debt like that? Not to mention the delivery costs: 550 liters of milk per cow, twenty eggs per chicken, and they didn't have the animals yet, there was their liveweight too. He presented this all to her cheerfully, and his mother felt patronized, and even though she was shocked to hear the difficulties in such detail she thought he had ulterior motives.

She was almost angry at him. The boy should have property. Now isn't the time for that: he explained, again in a dry, dismissive way, and she was so at a loss that she asked Cresspahl to help get her unreasonable offspring's head screwed on straight.

Cresspahl sat on the front steps with both children, even though it was already dark, and they looked at the Abs boy as if they'd been waiting for this moment. Cresspahl stood up, put his hands in his pants pocket, and looked ready to stand there for as long as it took. He himself had thought about settling the land, whether with the von Zelcks' permission or not, and he hoped Mrs. Abs would come with him. The children and Jakob made five, Jakob's father would make six, maybe enough to get by on a farm, and even the loans didn't scare him off. But he hadn't expected Mrs. Abs to agree to it, and K. A. Pontiy certainly didn't.

– Y'see? said Jakob cheerfully, although he hadn't actually won the argument. It wasn't the first time that there seemed to be some kind of arrangement between the two. She grabbed the children and took them inside. She could still see Jakob sitting down with this Cresspahl. Out of the brickworks villa's gate came Second Lieutenant Wassergahn, pulling the shirt of his uniform into pleasant pleats, rubbing his hand over his chin, smelling his hand. Mr. Wassergahn was on his way to a dance in Louise Papenbrock's parlor, and now Jakob and Cresspahl discussed the question of whether "these brothers" could be trusted. They were far from used to talking to each other, and what we could hear through the windows late into the night sounded a lot like an argument.

Mrs. Abs didn't go back outside to them and kept her bedroom windows closed. She was outraged that such a proposal had been made to her, in front of the children. She wasn't unhappy about the fact that Cresspahl wanted to settle the land only if she would come too. She figured out what lay behind all these clever arguments of Jakob's. He didn't want her to work in the fields. She should work standing up straight, or better yet sitting, not bent over; things should be made easy for her. He thought she was too old. Cresspahl, even though nothing could come of his proposal— he didn't think she was too old. She disagreed with both, and agreed with both. A week later, she showed them both that she wouldn't let herself get tied down to Cresspahl's house. She started working half days, in the hospital, as a cook.

Gesine didn't like seeing Mrs. Abs get dressed to go into town and pack her black bag. It was a leather case you could go on a trip with. Someone who could leave the house to go to work for no good reason could leave town too. How was Mrs. Abs to be kept in Jerichow?

May 21, 1968 Tuesday

First the French Communists didn't see the general strike coming, then they didn't support it, and now they want an alliance with all the forces of the Left, a veritable republican regime, which they even see as opening the way to Socialism.

The Polish ones, on the other hand, have finally figured out why the Poles keep misunderstanding them: it's the Czechoslovak ones' fault. The way they keep letting themselves get questioned in public about their plans—that can only be damaging.

The East German ones have gotten caught in Sweden with buried radio transmitters and several fake mailboxes.

The Czechoslovak ones are still playing host to Alexei N. Kosygin. After two years of negotiations, they are helping to open a branch of Pan American Airways in Prague, eighteen years after it was shut down following the coup, and the airfare to London can be paid in crowns. In Karlsbad (Karlovy Vary), the Soviet prime minister strolls openly through the streets and takes the famous healing waters.

Today we decided to no longer shop at Don Mauro's.

Don Mauro has a shop on Broadway (take the last car of the West Side express, come out of the Ninety-Sixth Street station walking east and in the opposite direction from the train), a little trap with tobacco products, candy, and cheap stationery for teeth. A row of phone booths may lure in a few customers, but he doesn't carry newspapers, he hasn't even supplied a bench where customers could linger any longer than it takes to exchange some money for merchandise. It's a shoebox of a trap, thriftily partitioned off from the business next door, and the slowly circling fan blades in the ceiling seem like luxurious furnishings. But the truth is that Don Mauro is a pillar of the Puerto Rican community on Manhattan's Upper West Side—a jewel on the church council, a man respected by the police, the head of the citizens' association, and anyone intending to win an election in this district had better not try without Don Mauro's goodwill. When Don Mauro arrived from his island eighteen years ago he could barely afford an apartment and had a hard time finding work, but he started off differently from the Negroes. The blacks still say, even today: See? That's how they treat us. From the word go, he thought: They're not going to treat us like that. From the beginning, Don Mauro had more equal rights, was more an American citizen than other people; he was helped by his family's lighter skin and the "right hair." Don Mauro started in this very shop and soon he was teaching his first son how to deal with the police and simple bookkeeping; by now he's training nephews for the stores that he is going to find, stock, and lease to them. Those other people may still have to pay protection money to the guardians of law and order, at Don Mauro's said guardians have to pay for their purchases and a proffered box of cigars is already an honor (one cigar per uniform). Don Mauro stands behind the counter in the back, chewing the same cold cigar stump from morning till night, or maybe all week. Sometimes the stump shifts around in the corner of Don Mauro's mouth, transforming his thoughtful expression, as if he's spit something out, but actually something's just popped into his head. He monitors the nephew at the register, he runs the expiring lease of the laundry next door through the calculator in his head, he chews around at the hard nut of a rental clause, nimbly, delicately, until it opens under his clever bite. Don Mauro doesn't merely look contented, the ceaseless plans and discoveries are depicted so joyfully in his face that clearly there's real happiness behind them. When he goes back every other year to check on the Estado Libre Asociado de Puerto Rico, visit his mother, attend mass in his native village, and see which younger relatives are ready for New York, he'll tell them stories about this piece of Manhattan, willingly if a little moodily. There are some places there that look like home, with the shop names, the neon signs, the bodegas. The buildings may be taller, but there are holes in the bottom with the island's music wafting and swimming up out of them. There are churches there that have service in Spanish, theaters showing only movies in their language—the homesickness isn't bad, and it doesn't get worse. The family sticks together there, just like here, and so do families; on Sundays you can see the girls in the park, respectable, dressed nicely, still Spanish looking. If your skin color's light then a lack of English isn't too big a problem. And so a new young man is standing at Don Mauro's cash register every year, acquiring the English of the Yanquis, moving on with the rank of store manager, later he might own one himself. The ones who understand this can sometimes be left alone in the store while Don Mauro climbs the narrow stairs in the side of the building—the discreet entrance to a second-floor office where he talks on the phone (no one knows what he says), keeps his money in the safe, has his secret bottle of cough syrup. The stairs lead only to this office. Who's going to know about it aside from the super? You hardly see anyone on the stairs. The door in the alley is half covered by the bins and bags with the hotel's garbage— just a crack that opens and closes again before you know it. There's a lot to think about regarding that office and the dime-store padlock on the door, the customers seem like a dream, and just a moment ago there weren't any.

Is this one? A Yanqui, a man about fifty, in a white shirt but needing a shave, with razor burn on his neck, saying something about dimes. Is he wanting to exchange his small change for bills?

It's the supplicant's lucky day. He looks, concerned and paternal, at the youth behind the counter—a sixteen-year-old with a hard narrow head, a dreamy look in his eyes, kind of friendly beneath the furrowed brow and still childlike waves of ash-blond hair. He tries to repay the cashier's favor with politeness, and is moved by his own feelings, too, to try to do something in return, so he says, a little recklessly: I'm not really a bum, you know... and he turns for support to the lady standing next to him, and she really does smile, not in pity, she's trying to encourage him.

Enter Don Mauro. He sees the apprentice's fingers in the till and no sale. The group stands paralyzed as he very quickly covers the distance from the door to them, though they've all seen him come marching in—an old man, shoulders stiff, his dignity only enhanced by the fury in his face. The youth gets a whipping from some Spanish whispered in a monotone, that won't heal before Saturday. The beggar is driven out of the shop like an infectious cow, every one of his submissive gestures intercepted by Don Mauro with a thrust of the chest and hisses of abuse; he adroitly shifts his legs to maneuver his victim until the man manages to escape out onto the sidewalk: the beggar, the failure, the parasite, – *You bum! You dirty bum!*

Barely out of breath, Don Mauro steps up to the lady customer still in the shop, not triumphantly, just a realistic businessman who came up the hard way. The youth lurches aside as if shoved with two hands. Moody, menacing, demanding, Don Mauro snarls: *Yes, ma'am?*

He knows this customer, he knows what she buys. Now she apologizes. Says she's made a mistake. She doesn't need anything in this shop.

– You're trying to give up smoking, Gesine?

– Not this way.

– You want to change the economic structure of the whole city of New York?

– Not this way.

– You want to go ten blocks farther every time, to the next Don Mauro, Don Fanto, Don Alfonso?

– No.

– You give to beggars, you said it was a personal choice.

– I know, Marie.

– You taught me it's wrong.

– No I didn't.

– Yes you did. So now you've showed your true colors, Gesine.

May 22, 1968 Wednesday

The New York Times, educated lady that she is, not only interprets for us what Charles de Gaulle might have meant with the soiled bed of his nation. She wants to give us an all-round education, and today she presents us with a key to the language of the American armed forces. Light losses are those that do not affect a unit's capability to carry out its mission. Moderate losses or damages mean that the unit's capability has been noticeably impaired, and finally heavy means that the unit can no longer perform its designated function. Decoded: If an installation in Vietnam reports light losses, a good hundred men might have been killed out of three thousand. In this language, those hundred don't count yet.

Last Tuesday East German border troops tried to fence in five hundred acres of West Germany near Wolfsburg, basing their claim on an 1873 map showing the border between Brunswick and Prussia, which was supposed to be the demarcation line in 1945. The West Germans admitted that there had been deviations in their favor, but protested that it was the Soviets of back then who'd drawn the line in the first place. – The Russians can err, too: the East German colonel said. According to the recollections of someone living on that border, his friends hadn't erred unless a gold watch or a few bottles of schnapps were part of the deal; then they would draw the fateful line in a bar with their English associates, on a beer coaster or a cigarette case. Today it's a shooting matter.

By October 1945 the people of Jerichow had long since stopped believing in the arrival of occupation troops from Sweden. They'd halfheartedly resigned themselves to the Soviets' staying, and now my father was being greeted on the streets again, when he wanted to be.

The mayor was credited with making things so bad for the refugees that most of them had left town. A man who relieved the townsfolk of the burdensome duty of hospitality couldn't be all bad.

K. A. Pontiy, commandant, had helped him do it. In the week he'd arrived, Pontiy had had his police register everyone in all of the houses, locals and refugees on the same list, the actual hard-power capacity, how many ration cards were needed—and Cresspahl thought it was only a paterfamilias's duty. He would learn more about Pontiy during the registration process. Two weeks went by and Pontiy started to doubt the security of his vouchers. He declared them invalid as of August 1 unless they bore the commandant's stamp as well as his signature. Again the people lined up outside Town Hall, up the stairs and down the hall to the room where Wassergahn was wielding his stamp. (All while the main and supreme directive from the state was to get the harvest brought in.) The sanctification of the documents went badly for the residents who'd been kicked out of the Bäk, for Wassergahn found any change in the information once he'd affixed his seal inconceivable, and the "moved parties" had to come in yet again, with Leslie Danzmann, to have their emergency lodging, the address for their ration cards, recognized. Wassergahn did not like having such cases explained to him—he looked darkly from the supplicant to the mayor's secretary, with furrowed brow; he hadn't forgotten the reason for these moves, he just thought of it as in the past, hence not open to discussion, particularly since it introduced messiness into his neat clean documents. On top of that, Wassergahn, for all his clean-cut professional appearance, kept uncertain hours. Two days' work on the harvest was lost. Pontiy was counting on 3,224 hungry subjects and on August 1 Cresspahl showed up with a request for 3,701 ration cards. Patiently, pedagogically, threateningly, Pontiy told his mayor to cease the annoying custom of letting every refugee who turned up in town make it into the registration card files with the right to a stamp from the commandant. The "illegal arrivals" were to be presented to him in lists, twenty heads each; he was stingy with his permits, shunting whole families off to the country whether they were willing to work or not.

At the same time, he tackled his population from another direction and had them register for labor duty, in a separate card file, whose data nonetheless had to be entered into the main card file. The contours of Pontiy's economic power had gradually grown blurry, given the differences between citizenship rights, residence rights, and applications for new citizenship and for repatriation, and in late August he ordered another registration of all residents. They had to bring in only two of his documents, plus identification cards and birth certificates, and this time he threatened anyone who failed to report with either arrest or expulsion from the town. That same week, he issued an order looking for every member of the former German Army with a rank of major or above, and likewise for anyone who worked in the former arms industry, whom he threatened under martial law. That was the occasion on which 1C Kliefoth, with all his service and military papers, was not arrested, though leaseholder Lindemann was, for not having registered as a hotel owner, solely because the Red Army had commandeered the whole Lübeck Court and was now running it. Leslie Danzmann and Cresspahl worked whole nights through on the general index that Pontiy wanted in the brickworks villa, and if it wasn't ready by September 1 then it would be up to the governor of the state of Mecklenburg-Vorpommern what to do—he had set that same date as the deadline for the registration of all male persons over the age of sixty, all females over fifty-five, and all university graduates of any age, on penalty this time of withholding ration cards and prison and/or a fine. Among the refugees there must have been some who didn't want anybody to be able to look up their previous life in Pontiy's safe, and others who resented the time spent on registrations instead of working or standing in line outside shops; they went looking early for a place on a Soviet-run farm, or in a village, far from Jerichow.

The indefatigable counting and recounting of heads and limbs, of elderly, sick, underage, and subject to compulsory insurance, all helped but was not enough alone to make Jerichow unsafe for many refugees. The town's supply of food was exhausted. The harvest had eventually been brought in, and faster than usual—mostly during personal nighttime trips out to the fields, and in the form of single sacks of potatoes and private bags of ears of wheat— but this was not food the townspeople would be distributing over the winter. There was absolutely no work available in town, putting at risk the right to a ration card. The displaced farmers went first. (Officially, no one could be referred to as "displaced" or "driven out" anymore—only as "evacuees" or "resettlers.") Anyone who wanted a piece of land from the stock of expropriated land needed to hop to it with the winter tilling. The papers that K. A. Pontiy and Cresspahl had collected from every refugee in only three months were a treasure trove, in the eyes of the commandants around the countryside. (The term "refugee" was no longer permitted in spoken use either.) Out there, the city people had gone back to city jobs by that point and new laborers were welcome. Near potato clamps, getting paid wages in kind, refugees might yet make it through the winter. There were lots of reasons why Leslie Danzmann had to register the departure of resettlers, but first and foremost the people of Jerichow chalked it up to Cresspahl.

It was under Cresspahl's regime that the schools were reopened. Starting October 1, the children, who'd been running wild, were finally kept busy again, and each one was given a rye bun in school too.

It might have been Cresspahl who'd pulled off a real live train at the Jerichow station, three passenger cars in tow, every day since late September. It departed for Gneez in the morning and came back in the evening. Heinz Wollenberg was glad that his daughter Lise could attend her high school again, and had suggested that his daughter be nice to Gesine Cresspahl. Cresspahl was just doing his duty. – Hi there: Lise said on the platform, for the first time since June; this cheerful nonchalance seemed a bit fishy to Gesine, but she said: Hey.

Cresspahl was given one hundred and twenty marks a month, plus twenty marks as a housing allowance, for working from morning until late at night. He couldn't supplement his income with carpentry, having neither the time nor the opportunity to get materials on the black market. He was hitched to a wagon in which sat K. A. Pontiy and the Red Army. He took no benefit from his office; let him have his losses.

He may have introduced bicycle registration to give his buddy Pontiy an overview of who had what, but still, it helped reduce thefts a little.

No, Cresspahl was still needed. It was thanks to him that Jerichow got fish from the Baltic, even if only for the hospital; on ration-card coupon No. 10 there was an unexpected allocation of salt; he would keep pestering the Gneez district office until it released some coal to run the gasworks with. And those utter scoundrels, the Englishmen, had cut Jerichow off from their Herrenwyk power station, the town had gone dark, and Cresspahl had found a generator for the hospital in exchange for Mrs. Köpcke's truck and the last spare tires Swenson had left in his hideaway, and the two victimized companies had been compensated at peacetime prices and told not to make a fuss. Because who was going to get Jerichow connected back up to an eastern power grid, them or Cresspahl?

In mid-October when all male and female persons between the ages of sixteen and fifty were ordered to report for exams for venereal diseases, "by order of the commandant," the talk in Jerichow was that Cresspahl had won one against Pontiy. Older women came too, bringing girls under sixteen. Pontiy hadn't realized the consequences, but the mayor of Jerichow had. It started to look like Cresspahl was in charge now.

The Jerichow government bank had recently started collecting taxes again. The new city bank, formerly the credit union, no longer stayed open from ten a.m. to ten p.m. just because it was ordered to: the tradesmen were depositing their earnings there daily; word had gotten round that the money wasn't disappearing, it could be used to make payments, with forms and signatures, just like before. It was a meager economy, a hungry life, a barren town—but Cresspahl had helped get it on track.

On October 22, two Soviet officers who were strangers to Jerichow paid Cresspahl a visit. It was evening, already dark, the people's movements around the jeep outside Town Hall were unclear. Leslie Danzmann was able to say that Cresspahl had left without a struggle. Not even a kerosene lamp knocked over. Then Cresspahl's secretary was arrested too. Pontiy issued his Order No. 24 through Fritz Schenk:

> In the interest
> of stabilizing
> the town's autonomy
> and increasing
> the productivity
> of the municipal economy
> and introducing
> a stricter order
> into the affairs
> of the Town of Jerichow

I hereby relieve Mr. Heinrich Cresspahl from his duties as mayor, as of this 21st day of October, 1945.

May 23, 1968 Thursday

The West German government spokesman gives the number. Czechoslovakia's Socialist neighbors will send in ten to twelve thousand special troops. The intelligence services, along with well-informed Czechoslovak and Western sources, call the information nonsense. That's true, they didn't even name a date.

– Cresspahl trusted his man Pontiy one too many times.

– And for too long, too.

– Yes, yes, grown-up psychology. Not for children.

– Cresspahl had gotten some news in September. Dr. Salomon still considered the German a client. He had found Mrs. Trowbridge and Henry Trowbridge. They'd died in an air attack on the British Midlands on November 14, 1940. Cresspahl hadn't had the slip of paper from Lübeck long before he got into a fight with K. A. Pontiy about his order to bring in the harvest, and it was a long night.

– A drunken night.

– A night in a state where things weren't blurry, where you were anchored to a particular thought that seemed to grow bigger and bigger. Toward morning they were barely drinking any more, just taking longer and longer to answer each other, half an hour sometimes. And Pontiy said forgetfully, sighing, that his son had fallen in Germany in April 1945.

– And Cresspahl told him about his son in England, that he'd lost to the Germans too.

– No. It was just two words, he never forgot them, they were his two best words in Russian: *Ne daleko.*

– That was all it took? That Pontiy's son had died *ne daleko*?

– That was enough for a while. *Ne daleko.* Not far. Near Jerichow.

May 24, 1968 Friday

Since January 1, 1961, 23,500 Americans have died in Vietnam. Which the military calls light casualties. The Vietnamese victims are not included in this number.

The presidium of the Czechoslovakian Communist Party had something to say to newspaper editors, executives, and radio commentators: Stop talking about the Soviet Union's past crimes all the time. Don't insult the Union of Soviet Socialist Republics. Don't dwell on the new KAN clubs. The party presidium isn't giving orders to the press or anything. The leaders believe that a good Communist understands the need for self-censorship when facing dangers "both from the left and from the right," and that belief is good enough for them.

KAN: *Klub Angažovaných Nestraníků*. Even in English we don't exactly understand it: Club of Committed Nonparty Members. How would that go in German? A new party founded on the principle that its members are not in any party. *Bund der engagierten Parteilosen?* "Alliance of Politically Active Independents"? It could also be the Left with nowhere else to go, under a new roof.

8 p.m.: Dr. Laszlo Pinter, Hungarian Delegate to the United Nations, will be speaking at Church Center, 777 United Nations Plaza, as a guest of the American Society for the Study of the German Democratic Republic. Topic: "European Disarmament and the Two German States."

There's a table by the door where you can donate 99 cents, more if you want. We ask for our one penny back, despite the cashier's embarrassed opposition—we want to keep the coin as a souvenir. The flyers on the chairs give the society's address as 370 Riverside Drive. That's on 109th Street. Marie has definitely babysat children there. It's a nice place to live.

Most of the audience members are old and seem to be timidly acquainted. A gathering of party members in the audience of a gathering of not the party. Strangers are exposed to surprised and searching looks, as if they were uninvited guests.

The first speaker emphasizes that visas to visit the UN have been refused to representatives of the GDR. Pithy American English. *My-self,* etc.

The second speaker proves, in a swift, soft, professorial voice, that the study of the German Democratic Republic is desirable for reasons of culture, peace, and understanding.

The guest from Hungary is a tall man with a red face and bulging flesh, maybe thirty-five years old. Narrow-framed glasses, thick black hair. His English teacher taught him not to nasalize endings: he calls certain things *promissink*! He says: Yu-RO-pean. Probably learned his English closer to Moscow. He begins with the ancient Greek myths, Crete, Europe the cradle of ideas and colonialism. Two world wars. Germany is divided. NATO. Warsaw Pact. This is not my official position, please don't quote me on that.

The effects of atomic bombs. Not the horror movie the way it appears on-screen. Very, very crucial factors. The attempted putsch of 1953, which was not successful: snippier, haughtier tone.

The fire alarm keeps going off in the hall.

The Danube Federation. The Rapacki Plan. This brings me to the German question. *What do we have in Germany?* Five NATO divisions, a leading role in the Atomic Planning Staff, the Potsdam Agreement not in effect. The fellow isn't set on cigarettes from back home, he smokes the local brands, bright red-and-white packs, Marlboro or Lux.

The Nazis. Started in 1930 with 2.2 percent. All the things the emergency laws allow. He forgets the confiscation of cars, in front of this audience of all people. The demonstrations in West Berlin: putting the laws into practice for the first time. The demonstrations in Warsaw, Paris, and New York may have been at the same time. For every one of these facts I could mention a counterfact. If this was the proof, it is not complete yet.

The matter of peace. *Vesch' mira.* This is why we need dialogue. A statesman has made a proposal. He talks in long circumlocutions about this statesman, talks in worshipful tones. When the suspense has gone on too long, he gives up the name: this statesman was Mr. Kosygin from the Soviet Union.

Applause. Q&A.

– The East German attitude toward the developments in Czechoslovakia.

– Yes, well, you know... I have to tell you something. The Czechoslovak Socialist Republic would subscribe to everything I said, nearly word for word. I don't see the connection. I don't know anything about attitudes. Congratulations to *The New York Times* on its self-proclaimed promotion to spokesman for the GDR!

– (Examples:) GDR jamming stations, lead articles in government papers, a top television commentator's trip to Bohemia.

– Yes well if you want to change the topic...: counters the comrade from circles not used to being addressed in that fashion. He doesn't shirk from his argument, here it is: I can't compete with *The New York Times,* I can only rely on my own clipping service.

An older woman, long diagonally cut white hair hanging down to her neck under a kind of bonnet. She says something mild, something overindulgent about government credits for home purchases here.

– And how do you have a dialogue over a wall?

– Well yes. Of course. (Expected question.)

The government's credits when someone wants to buy a house are . . .

– My comment on that, in a word, is this: It would be a damn good thing, if you ask me personally. ONE SHOULD ALWAYS ADDRESS A TOPIC FROM THE PROPER PERSPECTIVE. While West Germany had the Marshall Plan, East Germany started with absolutely nothing.

The mouthpiece does not have it easy among the curious, some of them readers of *The New York Times,* and he has no clippings from that source. One calls himself a genuine Communist. One is a clergyman, one is a West German immigrant worker, one

has been to the GDR. He is the president of this society, he has talked to the young officers at the Brandenburg Gate. White hair, too red in the face. Talks in a slightly complaining voice, looking sharply down to the right at the floor. The soldiers at the Wall are unarmed but people shoot at them.

Well then.

– Why did the meeting between the SPD and SED in Hanover fall through?

– Because it wasn't supposed to be a conversation between two sovereign states. The Hungarian guest has to get the right answer handed to him by the man taking the entrance money, who translates the word *Handschellengesetz,* "handcuff law," from East German propagandaspeak via American English *safe conduct* back into West German: *freies Geleit.* The East German speakers don't want a guarantee that they won't be prosecuted, they want diplomatic immunity. Bravo to the man at the entrance!

There was someone else with a question about West Berlin. Why does the East German press always refer to West Berlin as "on" GDR territory instead of "in" it, as both natural and political facts would suggest? We'd like to hear the answer to that one ourselves. How did the western sectors of Berlin find themselves on GDR territory before the GDR even existed. That question got in reply a gesture of helplessly raised arms, already weak from the flood of other questions: Hungarians can be so likeable. How dearly he'd love to answer this question, of all questions, if they'd only let him. The man with relatives in West Berlin doesn't raise his hand again. Cresspahl is afraid she'd offend him if she repeated the question. So we won't hear the answer from this man whose mind has been made up for so many years and will remain so.

The president of the Society for the Study of the GDR is, in conclusion, in favor of goodwill. Of appreciating the GDR, once it's been studied. And we're in the red to the tune of $250, which is why there's a genuine, antique, Methodist collection plate set up at the door. Thank you.

And just like on the old collection days, an assistant puts three five-dollar bills on the plate at once, to fool the later contributors. Mrs. Cresspahl unloads her cent there, wishing only it were a red one.

May 25, 1968 Saturday, South Ferry day

In the IRT subway line, the management—may they suffocate in the heat—have removed one of the pair of fans in every car! When the cars creep screeching in the tight squeeze up to the curved platforms under the ferry terminal, the passengers in the front cars first have to walk between dark tunnel walls, and inside the station there are ramps to the train doors. Only then are the doors opened, and today the sticky air intensified the fear that they wouldn't open at all.

– So both my grandfathers had criminal records: Marie said the moment we were aboard. She was trying to take this news of her forefathers like a devil-may-care desperado, but ancestors like that have always made her uncomfortable. Whatever she hears at home doesn't stand a chance against what she learns in school, which is that being arrested proves you're guilty. She wasn't supposed to learn that: white middle-class thinking. But that's how she thinks.

– Jakob's father was never put on trial, Marie.

– He was in a military prison, in Anklam, you admit that. Did he at least avoid the draft?

– You may not have liked what he did. And I don't know what he did.

– He could have been your father-in-law. It's my grandfather, Gesine.

— All I know about him is that he was born in 1889, Neukloster Seminary, Brazil in the twenties, jobs as an estate manager in Mecklenburg and Pommern, drafted into the army in 1943, and prison—what I picked up in conversation over those fifteen years with Jakob and his mother. I was in no hurry to ask questions and then Jakob died. I didn't want to press his mother and then she died. Neither liked to talk about Wilhelm Abs, and I only know his first name from the will. If I had to say his birthday, I could only say July, I'd have to look up the exact date.

— And where's he buried?

— His wife refused to believe he was dead until she was. He'll be seventy-nine in five or six weeks, if that's what you want to believe.

— In the Soviet Union. We wouldn't recognize him.

— You wouldn't mind a stranger, would you, Marie?

— Tonight I want to write down his birthday. Not to celebrate it, but so at least one of us knows it.

— And no criminal record.

— Make Cresspahl innocent, Gesine. Even if you have to lie a little.

— The officers who arrested him started off treating him like he was innocent. He wasn't pushed into the jeep, they patiently held the door open for him until he found his seat in the dark. He wasn't handcuffed. They gave him a blanket. There was a little chat about the chill in the air, winter's coming, hope the frost doesn't get the potatoes. When Cresspahl asked them to let him go to his house for five minutes, they didn't refuse rudely, it was more bemused, like he was someone new to a different world. They gave him some coarse *makhorka* for his pipe, like hosts. At Wehrlich station they locked him into a chicken coop.

— That was something he could never forget. He could never even speak of it!

— They did apologize. They didn't want to keep driving that night, one of them had a friend in the Wehrlich Kommandatura, there were no prison cells set up at the ranger station. Plus he wasn't supposed to be seen by the German staff. What else would you have done with a prisoner if you were them?

— Good, just keep on lying, Gesine. Then they brought him dinner on a tray.

— Maybe they forgot about that because they were so happy to see their friend again and the party was so fun. Cresspahl could hear their voices late into the night, singing, toasting, why would they think about a chicken coop.

– Now the escape.

– The lock was meant to protect the bygone chickens from both foxes and robbers on two legs. It was hard to pick in the dark. They'd moved the jeep in front of the door, he couldn't tip that over. There was no window, the walls were solid brick, the hatch was for chickens. He also might not have wanted to admit guilt straight off by running away. And in fact Soviet soldiers searched our rooms several times over the next few weeks, they were waiting for him in Jerichow. The chicken coop wasn't bad to sleep in; they'd left him the blanket. It's just that he banged into the low perches at first, and the stink of old droppings revived with the humidity of the night air. A sour smell, the legacy of three generations of chickens. Seeps into a person's clothes. Still, the Russians found their prisoner asleep the next morning. And now they were driving in a stinking jeep, trapped with the smell by the rain, and they all told jokes, every joke they could think of about roosters and chickens. Cresspahl got a hunk of bread, a sip of vodka, *makhorka*, like one comrade among others on a holiday trip, only he was the only one who didn't know where they were going. Where they were going was the basement under the Gneez district courthouse; his companions took their leave with encouraging if cautious claps on his shoulder. Ever since then Cresspahl thought that an arrest wasn't seen as anything to be ashamed of in the Red Army, at most it was a bit of bad luck that could happen to anyone. Good luck, they wished him. That was the start of the first phase.

– You walked to school above his head.

– The girls' high school in Gneez had been converted into a Red Army hospital. The lower grades were put in the Sacred Heart School—

– a parochial school, like me!

– a city school named after a convent and a chapel, long since burned down, commemorating the ritual persecution of the Jews in 1330. From the ruins of that pious quadrangle to the station I only had to cross two streets diagonally, and then I was right by my father though I never knew it. All I saw was the monument for the Franco-Prussian War, black and shining like a freshly polished train engine, and the two red flags like tongues sticking out of the courthouse roof. That was where the German police took the people dealing in food on the black market, gun owners, members of the German Army arrested during the July registration, young men under suspicion of being in the Werewolf resistance—it never crossed my mind that Cresspahl might be locked up under that building. Language dictated that anyone the Soviets picked up was sent "to Siberia," no one had to tell me.

– And now we have the tortures, the water chamber, the starvation diet.

– Cresspahl felt like they'd arrested him just to put him away somewhere and then they'd forgotten about him. The jailers brought food to his cell twice a day, sometimes in the evening too—bread from their field bakery, fish soup made of water and cod heads, leftovers from the soldiers' meals. At school we learned to write and speak Russian but Charlotte Pagels might have been using a book from the German Army's supply: she told us kasha was cabbage soup,

shchi i kasha
pishcha nasha

when actually it was buckwheat or semolina groats with jam or a few shreds of meat, my father in prison would have marked those days on the calendar if he'd been allowed a calendar. When the cell door was unlocked he had to stand at attention against the wall, head touching it, so that he couldn't see into the hall. When he did this according to regulations they would hand him the bowl. They didn't like it if he talked. They called him *otets* and *durak*, Father and Fool, neither meant in a bad way, and gradually he learned. Apparently they'd counted the inscriptions and drawings on the saltpeter-covered wall and he wasn't allowed to add to them, so he got himself a day with no food when he started a calendar. He found month grids from spring 1945 scratched into the wall, final remarks before transport to Bützow-Dreibergen, the notes of the British national anthem accompanied by a blasphemous text, swastikas with entreaties for luck in battle—those could all stay. It might have once been Dr. Semig's cell, but he found no sign of him. To teach him about secret possessions they ripped open his straw mattress every now and then and scattered the filling across the cell; they praised him like a child when he'd reassembled a mattress from it by nighttime. In December they noticed him shivering and stuck a thermometer in his mouth. He wasn't allowed to see what it showed, and his next meal came with a blanket. More horrible than the cold was the lack of light: it came in through a round tapered shaft terminating below a grate at the back of the building, for only a few hours a day. There were two or three voices in the next cell; he remained alone. His departure was quite a ceremony. The young men in their exquisitely spick-and-span uniforms had taken him to the washroom lots of times, with gentle nudges of his arm, because he seemed blind; this time they helped him remove his beard and gave him warm water. He was given parts of uniforms—air force on the bottom, army on the top—and for the first time in seventeen weeks he didn't smell like chicken shit. Sitting all alone on the bed of a covered truck he was driven south, and he learned to see again from the blurry spring green by Schwerin Lake. He was taken to the Soviet Military Tribunal in the capital, and now he was supposed to talk.

– The unauthorized withdrawals from the nobility's accounts.

– He'd paid those back as soon as enough taxes had come in (and as a result the Jerichow government bank stayed empty to the floorboards). Maybe he hadn't been able to bring himself to pay interest on the loans, and such transgressions were part of Phase One.

– Woken up in the middle of the night and made to recite numbers.

– In Schwerin the Soviets were working round the clock, the court calendar decided when it was his turn. For days on end they didn't need him for anything, of course, and in the heated cell, with the plentiful light from above, he almost relearned what it was like to have a place to live, then without warning they'd come get him in the middle of the night. The court ran like a machine, demanding trot and walk and gallop from a standing start from both defendants and prosecutors; Cresspahl couldn't blame the specific people in charge of his case. One of them seemed like a military man to him, the other an auditor, they traded off. They'd prepared their case, they had the Jerichow Town Hall files on the table, and at first Cresspahl only had to tell them about everything he'd done. If one of his stories pleased them, he was allowed to repeat it. They watched him uneasily; they were expecting him to defend himself, not agree to one judgment after another against himself.

– With a clear conscience, Gesine. He hadn't taken anything for himself.

– It was for someone else's benefit, not his. While K. A. Pontiy had bindingly abolished civil rights in Jerichow, he had not explained the new kinds of guilt. So now the gentlemen of the Schwerin SMT read Cresspahl Law No. 4 of the Allied Control Council, and took it to mean that the laws in force on January 30, 1933, were valid for the time being. He hadn't been able to follow them.

– What he'd done was its own defense.

– What an American! You and your truth! The truth can be used in the service of anything.

– But it's what really happened!

– Cresspahl wasn't interested in going beyond his own truth. He did find out some new information. He'd confiscated two bags of roasted coffee beans from Böhnhase, with the permission of the Gneez DA's office, but now in Schwerin the hoarded merchandise was described to him as originating in an illegal act, and it wasn't even coffee anymore, it had magically transformed into crude oil for the generator powering the hospital lights. In other words, Cresspahl was supposed to answer for the hidden hands through which the coffee had previously passed—for a past he knew nothing about. He didn't see how he could do that, so he didn't sign. The two interrogators found his rigidity amusing. They went along with his quirk of not naming any names other than those on paper in front of him—they had names, they helped him out. He was gradually led to believe that not only Leslie Danzmann but Gantlik was in jail, and Slata, and Amalie Creutz, and Peter Wulff, and Böhnhase, and the mayor of Beckhorst village. For a long time the conversations stayed friendly—he wasn't kept standing, they moved his chair from the edge of the room up to the desk, and when it came to tricky memories he stood next to the interrogator like a colleague, bent over the files, searching, turning pages. Since he was used to smoking a pipe he was allowed to go pick one out from the seized-property room and he found one of English manufacture, barely damaged, with a curved mouthpiece, like the kind Uncle Joe used to smoke; it would be taken out of a drawer at the start of each session and locked away again at the end, like a medical instrument. Sometimes he even got Krüll instead of *makhorka*.

– Uncle Joe, I should know that one.

– You should, you American. Josif Vissarionovič was shown with just such a pipe when he was introduced to the public here, back when he was still supposed to be an ally. The photograph shows him with a mischievous look in his eye, like a good uncle.

– The defendant with his resemblance to the supreme lord of the court.

– The interrogators didn't care. They were from another country, they might not ever have seen that picture.

– Did they also call Cresspahl "Little Father"?

– They addressed him in bourgeois fashion. They wanted him to feel competent, an adult who'd made mistakes while of sound mind and body. The mistakes had been established, now he needed to recognize the crimes. And to help him along they presented various bits and pieces the way they saw it: Slata had been taken to another court, in the Soviet Union. Her name had served only to prove Cresspahl's connection with a perpetrator of crimes against humanity. Amalie Creutz wasn't in jail at all. And why would she be, from Cresspahl's own statements he'd been perfectly willing to believe she was pregnant, his request to have an abortion approved had been found in the Schwerin Department of Health and countersigned by him as proof

of the goal

of the defamation

of the honor

of the Red Army,

they didn't need Mrs. Creutz as a witness anymore. And the gentlemen were certainly prepared to summon Fritz Schenk for a face-to-face confrontation, they were very interested indeed in such a thing, only Schenk was no longer in Jerichow, and the German comrades reported that he was indispensable. Even a Soviet examining magistrate has his limitations, you see. All that talk about omnipotence is greatly exaggerated.

– Whose side are you on, Gesine! You belong on Cresspahl's but you're not advocating for him.

– Why should I be on just one side? What I know has more than two sides.

– Would Cresspahl be okay with that?

– They covered everything with him all the way back to 1935. He had done carpentry work for the Jerichow-North air base, until 1938, and until 1945. He admitted it. He had, therefore, starting in 1935, with no evidence of coercion, helped German militarism up onto its feet and into the air. Although Cresspahl realized that the one implied the other, and that they were trying to cast him as someone who'd paved the way for the Nazis, he didn't want to follow them across the bridge to economic sabotage in Jerichow as a past and present Fascist. He wouldn't sign. They tried it again, this time offering something in return. When he would ask about his child in Jerichow, they would sternly refuse to say anything, shaking their heads at his denseness; after two weeks, they revealed after all that Schoolgirl Cresspahl had been transferred to the Bridge School in Gneez with a B in Russian. He thanked them for bending the rules; he didn't deviate from his own. They scolded him, not without a certain sadness; they had failed in their goal of at least moving him to somewhere between the subjective and the objective truth. By that point they had enough facts, they no longer needed him. He was sent to a camp where the Nazis had once kept their prisoners, he was supposed to help straighten it up.

– Was that his sentence?

– It was a holding camp. The gentlemen of the Schwerin SMT hadn't threatened him with any specific punishment. Only once, when they didn't know what else to say, had they asked: if he'd really rather spend thirty years in prison than fifteen, or at most twenty.

– He was clever enough. You got mail from him.

– The camp was well guarded, with dog patrols between the two rows of barbed wire, searchlights at night. He was there with other people but they were quickly taken off to sentencing and other countries, they couldn't take messages. Even in his work he couldn't smuggle out any messages—the bedframes, the window crosspieces, the barrack sections, everything stayed inside the fence. Anyway, he could only guess at the nearest town or village. He might be anywhere in southwestern Mecklenburg. Other people knew more precisely, Neustadt-Glewe they said; that didn't fit the route he'd been brought on, as far as he could tell from the night transport.

– When are we up to now?

– August 1946.

– So now I'll be your guide, through Staten Island, New York, as of May, nineteen sixty-eight.

The Czechoslovak Communists have had to pay. To avoid having eleven thousand special forces in their country and a Cominform within the Warsaw Pact they are now to permit military exercises on their soil in June. The East Germans dismiss the stationing of allied troops in Czechoslovakia as West German provocation, and have the following information about the plan to move Socialism into the present: "The wheel of history cannot be turned back." History as a winch that winds up the past, irrevocably, for eternity. Onward!

May 26, 1968 Sunday

The parts of Staten Island, borough and Richmond County, that Marie showed me yesterday. *Now you know, Gesine. I won't have to bring it up again.*

After the wasteland of single-story brick on the north coast of the island, finally some trees and landscape at Silver Lake Park—sheltering lines of trellises and windbreaks. Gentle rises and falls of the streets, uncomplaining, with the undulations of the land. Still some country houses from former times, ingenuously armed with columned porches, Greek antiquity in wood. Verandas in leafy shadow, windows dark in the heat, concealing quiet, creaking rooms. Boxes sheeted in bright Dutch brick with white frames precisely cut in. High branches stripped by the Atlantic's breath, corpulent whispering clouds of green. A gathering of gulls on the leeward shingle roofs. Electrical lines on rough-hewn poles that are often tilted, from an age of modest technology. Grass growing in the cracks between slabs of the sidewalk, weeds and shrubs high and rampant around the stairs. Lawns sloping down to the street, cool, hedges wild. Neighborhoods. What would it be like to wait here by the window, in the hazy overcast air of early summer, and later warm in bare damp November. *Here you'll have a country life. Mecklenburg, California. Stay here, Gesine. I'll buy you a house here as soon as I can.*

The trains of the SIRR crossing the island make less of a susurration than their name. They claim to be Staten Island's Rapid Transit, an offshoot of the Baltimore & Ohio Railroad—what they are is a jerky, rattling suburban line. Wobbly train cars from not long after the First World War, stopping every mile at narrow, barely roofed platforms. Nervous clanging at crossings; hollow howls when approaching stations; bravely onward drives the little train, as though heading straight to the Gulf of Mexico. A number, a year, catches the eye, engraved too formally in a concrete sill of one of the cramped little bridge houses: 1933. Ragged bushes right up next to the third rail. *Start here, Gesine; stay here.*

The Verrazano Bridge sends wide lanes of traffic shooting to New Jersey above the railroad tracks cut into the landscape. From Oude Dorp and Arrochar on, tiny airplanes hang in the sky, boarders at the aircraft field near Richmond Avenue by the creeks flowing into Arthur Kill. *You could get away here, and we could come visit you, by land, by sea, by air.*

The ferry building on the southern tip of the island is even more vacant now, the planks falling off it, walls of wooden pillars aslant in the putrid water. The water has burrowed right up next to Tottenville station, chewing on garbage, nourishing rust and sludge. Tottenville station was built to serve the ferry to Perth Amboy; that end of the station was now silent, wrapped tight in chicken wire, as though no boat had left for New Jersey in a very long time even though there'd been one since colonial days. The other shore lay there waiting, inert, with cranes, warehouses, a church, roofs flashing in the leaves, motionless in the midday heat. To the north, a bridge on stilts crossed Arthur Kill, frozen in midstride like a gouty cat. Construction rubble, oil barrels, junk on the beach, splintering posts in the water, and, farther out, backlit pleasure craft and fishing boats. Everywhere, vegetation reclaiming the sick land, covering the scars and wounds of the ground; *the externals of vacation, Gesine.*

In Tottenville, death passed by. In the white light laid out by the sun, two black-clad couples walked toward a building that looked like a fancy dairy or private school. The two women's skin was very warm beneath the transparent fabric. One man, in a business suit, shyly brought up the rear, as though embarrassed by the prospect of seeing the person lying there, or by the expectation that they would be carrying him in himself through the back door of the funeral parlor in a few years. (As though he were visiting his future home, with himself inside it, having not thought about his move at all.) *When you're dead, Gesine, I won't let the embalmers get you.*

In Tottenville, crippled houses huddled together, collapsing, draped with pieces of plastic. A little synagogue shack with a skin of asbestos shingles. Italian plaster figures on dried-out patches of lawn. A living cat, white, with deeply blackened eyes, wants to be noticed, there is something it knows. Children on porches, an old woman sitting with a book upstairs, watching. Swings and wading pools in the backyards. Hot wood smell, acacia blossom. One of D. E.'s love affairs, Wannsee, Berlin, 1949, long nights next to a girl leaning on the garden gate in the scent of acacias; by day the little white flowers stayed hidden in the green of the leaves; in 1949 what she wanted from a man with black-market connections was not chocolate or a phonograph record but a swim cap. *Or go live with the poor, Gesine.*

An unexpected wide field of high grasses, wild shrubs growing everywhere. A steam freighter so close to the shore it seems grounded. A white gable outlined against the horizon of leafage, a canting roof set in front of an almost cube-shaped wooden box. Behind the dark windows, on the long porch facing the Atlantic, not a sign of movement. A steep, overgrown path for the mailman. *Or that, if you want.*

On Raritan Bay. The Raritan Indians' name for the island was Aquehonga Manacknong, "Place of the High Sandy Bank," and they thrice succeeded in driving off, with fire, the invaders from the Delaware territories. Henry Hudson said he sighted land here on September 2, 1609, and at once named it in honor of his masters, the Dutch Staaten-General. Staaten Eylandt, lost to the British in 1664. Four years later, the Duke of York had a hankering for the islands in his bay, he wanted all of them that could be circumnavigated in twenty-four hours, and one Captain Christopher Billopp sailed around Staaten Eylandt end to end in the prescribed time, for which feat he was rewarded with 116 acres out of the roughly 37,000 he had procured for the king's brother. He did not have Dido's problem. In Billopp's house, around the corner here, General Howe met with a delegation of rebels after the Battle of Long Island for the first peace conference of the Revolutionary War, to no avail. William Howe read the Declaration of Independence here for the first time, and said: This here has been signed by rather determined men. *Your Mecklenburg was stolen land too, Gesine.*

On the sandy roads, covered with puddles of water, lonely cars drove as if cowed by field and thicket, so far from eight-lane highways and apartment buildings. Marshlands, no longer traversable due to broken bottles and rusty tin cans. A colony of summer houses falling apart. Children who stared at strangers walking by, giggled at the strange child's city airs. Near the water, a married couple sat in a car, helpless, ready to drive away. Look, real reeds. This is plantain, good for cuts. We made soup out of goosefoot. Rabbits used to like to eat this. A red maple. Chicory. Ribwort. Shepherd's purse, you could eat that. Nettles were good as spinach. Sunburn weather. *Don't forget why I showed you all this, Gesine.*

Anyone who sent Ho Chi Minh, the President and Enlightened One, many happy returns on May 19 has now gotten something from him in the mail:

At seventy-eight
I don't feel very old yet.
Steadily on my shoulders still rests
The country's burden.
Our people, in their resistance,
Are winning tremendous victories.
We march with our younger generation.
Forward!

© Viet Nam Press, Hanoi

A testimonial to Alexei Nikolayevich Kosygin. Premier of the Soviet Union. For our reading pleasure in *The New York Times.*

A quiet and retiring man of sixty-four, taking the waters in Karlovy Vary, seen going for walks with his granddaughter, cannot possibly mean the Czechs and Slovaks any harm. Hard currency from Moscow, that was the carrot. Military action, that was the stick. Both merely shown, for now.

He gained: troop maneuvers, tightened censorship, a ban on legal opposition.

If the generals continue to growl in the *Red Star* about an American finger in "internal affairs," he will have to cut short his visit to the ČSSR and go see them, and yet he is forgiven.

For what he explains to the Stalinist faction will shape Czechoslovakia's future—and the world's.

Placed on record, today's, in New York, Forty-Third Street, west of Times Square.

The Communists in Prague are taking their first steps toward a law, to be passed in July or August. Relief is planned for a hundred thousand persons who have suffered penalties à la Pontiy, such as expulsion from their homes, removal from jobs, and the like. Forty thousand prisoners from between 1948 and 1956 are to receive 20,000 Czech crowns for each year spent in prison, with 25 percent to be paid immediately and the rest over a period of ten years.

That would add up to about a billion crowns by the end of 1970. A dollar, the paper says, is worth seven crowns, or in special cases sixteen. Compare the exchange rate of the ruble. Factor in not only the $400 million from Moscow but the 20 million in overseas assets, plus the 5 million in pensions that US Social Security withholds from Czechoslovakian citizens. Will it be enough?

So that was work today. In forty minutes we'll be back on Riverside Drive, at home.

Anyone could come.

She just comes from Grand Central, lets the crowds push her toward the West Side line, finds her place where the third door of the first car stops.

As if New York functioned properly every day. The subway as sunset.

They didn't announce anything at Grand Central!

And you fell right into their trap, young lady.

No trains running here.

Even if they were, you couldn't get on.

That was always my place, where the third door stopped.

Well that's where we're standing now, you Caucasian, you pink child.

Oh, you big black man!

At least let her stay on her feet. Don't knock her down!

Me? Knock over a lady? Theres just surges here underground.

What's the problem here?

That we're stuck standing here packed tight in the heat, as if they're planning to spray water all over us. Then put the lid on.

I'd sure like to move an arm.

No electricity.

Stay! You stay in your bag! Stop climbing on the nice lady.

She brings you home and then what!

None of us is ever going to get home.

Where's the problem?

Look. She wants to know exactly too. With a diagram and everything.

So, if you move my bag between your legs a little, there, you see what I mean?

I can move my arm from the shoulder—

If you block out this fat black man—

Aha. Probably better for him too.

There's almost something you can do to help, y'know?

It's an outrage, the subway system!

We know. New York'll always be New York.

Don't look at me like that! My hand's on the outside of your bag, not the inside!

Itchy?

None of your business. I've got a job.

And the two of us together?

When the little one smiles, she means me, you foreigner.

I'm not little.

Here comes a train.

Like a hobbling horse.

A power station's on fire in Brooklyn.

Hey, they're not getting out!

This is our train. We're not giving it up.

It's my train! I need to get home!

And even if we need to take it to the Bronx, the thing does *move.*

You can escape from the Bronx. Not from here.

They're looking at us like an enemy army.

Well this is a reason for war, isn't it? They're cooped up in their train, we're in this pit of a station.

We look at them like an enemy army. And then they ride off into the darkness.

If the train stops in the dark they won't know where it is.

Anybody else ready to give up? I'd be happy to give up, but not alone.

No one here's giving up.

You'll never make it up the stairs. More new people keep pouring down the stairs.

They don't know yet.

Anyone can come.

The place where the train's broken! New York is falling apart!

The system's been bringing in money for sixty-four years, why should they fix it?

For us?

That's how they treat us.

Well, the thing is, in a taxi this time of day…

If not I'll just lie down next to the rail and be under one fan after another. It was nice being able to breathe.

I bet I have money for a taxi.

We won't let anyone not with us through to the second row.

You see the train on the opposite platform? The batteries under the cars are glowing.

That won't get far.

None of us are getting anywhere.

You've already got one foot on the edge of the platform. Next time—

Push 'er in!

Turn around! Shoulders out!

Don't move! She's lost a shoe.

She can do this barefoot.

Two upstanding citizens like us and still we can pry the subway doors open! Just stick the shoe in! Between their heads, they'll notice that.

Look, they actually put her shoe back in her hand.

Usually a train comes every two minutes and bites off a piece of the line. Now they're coming four minutes apart, and this one's been sitting here an extra thirty seconds.

We shouldn't have pushed her in after all. She's in and we're looking at empty rails.

Maybe she'll be stuck in there when she wants to get out. Or just stay like that, in the dark, somewhere under Broadway.

I don't envy her.

We don't envy you.

Have a nice trip!

Have a nice trip!

Did she thank you?

Just wrinkled her nose, like this. Wouldn't want to be pushy and actually give a smile, you know?

I know what you mean.
And there she goes. Hey, don't mention it!
See y'all tomorrow!
Sounds good. Till tomorrow.

May 28, 1968   Tuesday

This morning the train stopped in the dark, past the Fiftieth St. station. It was hard to judge how far we were from the lit platform. My memory keeps reporting that there is a bright spot next to this stretch of track, a hundred feet wide, two hundred feet wide, seen just the day before yesterday, an opening into the light, a staircase to the surface. The ever-returning search for a way out marked time, took up space, pushed thought aside. Fear of every additional minute grew and grew in the motionless silent crush of people until the train jolting into motion was unbelievable. On the stairs beneath Times Square the policemen were standing around, in a good mood, hands comfortably clasped on the billy club behind their back, and they looked at the scared passengers as if to say: Are they after you? Did they let you go this time? You're running like there's a prize at the end.

After Cresspahl disappeared, Jakob reluctantly took over his household.

His mother had tried to do it alone. The refugees in the rear of the house kept to the rules she'd introduced, both in the kitchen and taking turns to keep the halls and stairs clean; maybe they thought Cresspahl had given some last-minute instructions, but Mrs. Abs felt that this was dishonest since she hadn't been given any such authority. If Gesine and Hanna Ohlerich weren't there she would probably have packed up her things and sought refuge where Jakob was working, two hours from Jerichow, where she wasn't known as the housekeeper of a mayor the Russians had arrested. She wasn't afraid of being arrested herself, but she expected nothing good from any authorities, and she clung to that opinion until the day she died. She had difficulty dealing with the envoys from Warnemünde or Lübeck who showed up at the door in the middle of the night with business only Cresspahl could make heads or tails of. But there were the children. She had to organize Gesine's mornings and evenings like she had before her father's disappearance. She took Gesine to the Gneez train in the morning, took Hanna to school in Jerichow, and in the evening had to keep them both busy, in the kitchen, with mending clothes, with homework, and, not trusting herself as a storyteller, she relied heavily on the deeds of the famous medieval Wendish king. On one such evening, sitting around the kerosene lamp on Cresspahl's desk, the first squad that turned up to search the house came bursting through the door—two Soviets they didn't know, with Mayor Schenk and Gantlik as witnesses, a purposeful whirlwind that was soon gone again without leaving even an overturned chair in its wake. Still, she was so shaken that she spent the night on a chair next to the girls' bed. She left the chaos in Cresspahl's room alone until Jakob had been fetched. Jakob wouldn't do what she wanted. These arrests weren't only happening around his mother, he knew about some day laborers, and about the Lübeck Court. The wind was blowing the same way everywhere in Mecklenburg, and the border to the new Western Poland had been closed on November 19. His mother let him give all his reasonable arguments and he realized she needed an unreasonable one. He stabled his horses with his business partners at the border and stayed in Jerichow. For him it was the wrong arrangement. He still had a credit of grain from his wages but the sorrel and the tottery old gelding were eating it up. He got nothing but money for his work repairing the gasworks—out in the country he could have earned potatoes. It wasn't even that he owed this Cresspahl anything. He wanted to do him a favor.

It was because we couldn't get to Lower Saxony with the horses anymore, Gesine.
That's why you stayed?
What would people think.
That you two were going away and leaving me in the lurch. So you wanted those bastards to starve you slowly.
Don't forget, we were looking to grab that house of yours too, jung Fru Cresspahl.
You sure know how to make fun of me.
A younger sister like you was just what I wanted. Pure selfishness.
It was me who was selfish, Jakob.

How does a young man from the country who's landed in a strange town go about being head of a household that hasn't even been entrusted to him? This young man started by charging rent, retroactive to July 1—the coming of the New Order. He'd measured out the house in his head, and the people in it hadn't even been warned before he put a receipt book down on the kitchen table. It was no more than Mrs. Quade or the Maass family were charging but still it rubbed them the wrong way, because they weren't used to it. The teacher from Marienwerder threatened to lodge a complaint because he couldn't put a rental agreement down on the table. A light bulb went on in the others' heads when they heard "put down" and they started paying, after all it was only money. Now the Cresspahl child had an income at least, enough to cover the cost of boarding her friend Hanna. They were free to take up the matter with Town Hall if they wanted—the name Abs was known there, because when he'd applied for his ration cards he'd insisted he was someone doing heavy labor. That led to an argument over the 2,450 grams per week instead of the usual 1,700, but in the end they had to give those grams to the gasworks repairman; in the confusion, he'd accidentally been given a residence permit, and it was in the files, and irrevocable. It was also hard to dispute that he needed 0.43 reichsmarks for the 1,600 grams of bread for each of the two children too. And if that wasn't enough, young Abs had brought back forms for the latest registration of every resident's personal information, and it was his job to fill them out. "You are required to enter all persons forming part of the household as of December 1, 1945, regardless of whether they were present or temporarily absent on that cut-off date." The name Cresspahl, Heinrich, b. 1888 was staunchly put right at the top, as head of household. The Abs family put themselves down as his representatives, not as caretakers. "Do not include members of the occupation forces": young Abs might get in trouble because of course he'd included one Mr. Krijgerstam as a member of the household, since this ingenious survivor from the Baltic provinces did sometimes wear a Red Navy uniform. But he could also be found in Jakob's room wearing a dressing gown—a sallow-faced man in his forties, smelling of fruit. With a serious expression and the manners of a well-paid waiter, he would offer for sale ladies' underwear, some even silk, a private Soviet citizen. Jakob dried his hands on the same towel as the Russians did, as they say; he called them by first name and patronymic. He hadn't taken his stake off the black market when Pontiy's detachment was transferred. Even Wassergahn still came by to see him. Jakob had his own room, solely because he now and then conducted some German-Soviet meetings in it, and he hadn't hesitated to move his mother into Cresspahl's room, possibly to be a guard for the two girls' bedroom, but he had made sure that the Housing Office forgot to inspect the house he was in charge of. He might not escape punishment forever, but for now what he brought to the communal evening meals was satisfactory. By bringing little jars of milk for her baby boy he'd gotten the bewildered schoolteacher from West Prussia to the point where she said he was "a man of true sensitivity" (a doctor had prescribed it for Jakob). The two girls used to burst out giggling at such comments but he soon put a stop to that; not only did they learn to feel pity for the unfortunate teacher, they wanted to make it up to Jakob, too, and secretly kept their eyes on him when he relaxed at mealtimes. His face had turned blank; he liked to adopt a faraway look, then he'd drily swallow a smile. When he looked at Gesine she felt trapped, unable to escape; she was often reminded of his sorrel, who when drinking would always turn his eyes to look at the person holding the bucket. What the others saw in Jakob was that he'd spent ten hours mixing cement or shoveling coal in the gasworks, and for now they accepted him as the man of the house.

Jakob was dissatisfied with himself as head of the household.

He'd had to look through Cresspahl's papers with Gesine, whatever was left after the search, since she rightly viewed every decision now as one she needed to make—her own decision, to be made together with Jakob. Cresspahl's account books and drawings were left in Lisbeth's secretary, to catch future prying eyes, while the 1935 life history and two passports were tucked away down in the east corner of the basement, where there was no basement. Jakob watched his step carefully, but she still realized they'd put his papers in order like a dead man's. Her lips started quivering, because she didn't want him to see her actually crying, and he didn't know what to do. Whatever it was, his own words weren't enough and he had to go looking for his mother so that she could hug the child to her apron. That night he realized that there shouldn't be a place set where Cresspahl used to sit. She understood him in a quick glance, which immediately swung wetly over to Mrs. Abs; he could see her thinking about the chair that she used to pull out at the empty end of the table when she heard Cresspahl coming; it seemed to him that she knew another way and just couldn't tell him. Eighteen years old and not seeing what's right in front of his eyes because his mother doesn't want him to see it—and now someone like that is supposed to console people.

He was only doing his duty when he cut Amalie Creutz down from the wire around her neck; his mother had had to fetch him because old Creutz hadn't dared set foot in his dead daughter-in-law's room, after fifty years living next to a cemetery and supervising burials. Jakob lay the body on the bed, his mother washed her and changed her clothes, because Creutz refused to come away from his golden rain bushes along the Soviet fence and wouldn't come near the house until morning. That was all the Abses had in mind to do, they didn't owe this stranger anything more. That evening Cresspahl's daughter got back from the school train and acted calm. She asked about the coffin, the appointment with Brüshaver, how the body was to be transported. She also knew that there was a letter for Cresspahl, and Mrs. Abs admitted that she'd found one in the dead girl's jacket; it was put with Cresspahl's things under the floorboards. The child would have tackled the obligations of this family friendship on her own—unhesitating, oddly experienced—but here the Abses decided to help her. Jakob went to Gneez with some Schlegel brand liquor to see Kern the carpenter and came back with a coffin, Mrs. Abs wrote Gesine an excuse note for school, and together they took Amalie Creutz to the New Cemetery in Swenson's (Kliefoth's) rubber-wheeled cart. Jakob stood like a genuine mourner next to Creutz just because the old man needed a firm grip on his arm, and Pastor Brüshaver shook Jakob's hand too, then his mother's, then Gesine's. In the eyes of Jerichow, they were representing Cresspahl's house, but representing the Red Army too, and even if Cresspahl would've wanted them to, in the end it wouldn't help his cause.

Keeping Cresspahl's house safe didn't only involve knocking a broken lock back into shape and onto the door, or distracting children from their hunger or putting up shutters. Jakob could only guess whether or not Cresspahl wanted his daughter kept away from her grandmother so permanently. He would see this Mrs. Papenbrock behind the shop counter, she would look so weepy and bitter when she asked after Gesine. He had seen her in church at Amalie Creutz's funeral and noticed that her eyes were brimming with tears, though directed less at the coffin than at the left front pew, at the back of her granddaughter's neck. (Jakob couldn't know everything about Jerichow after only five months; he didn't realize that old Mrs. Papenbrock had a talent for tears until later.) She didn't send for the child, she didn't come get the child—Jakob could see her waiting, like a fat sad bird with ruffled feathers. Did Cresspahl mean times like Christmas too? His child nodded. Did Gesine? She looked at him clear-eyed, didn't stop to think, and said: Should I? She would do what he said, he had taken Cresspahl's place. Jakob shook his head, and again after Gesine left the room; he now answered Mrs. Papenbrock somewhat more curtly. He wasn't sure if that was what Cresspahl wanted.

How do they celebrate Christmas in Jerichow? In church? With everyone in the house? With just the two children? Another thing for Jakob to worry about. All he knew was the presents he'd be giving—a standing sled for Gesine and a bike lamp for Hanna Ohlerich. Then old Creutz brought his advent wreath over as he did every year, the children asked for a baked apple for their Christmas dinner, and prepared the party on their own. When they came to fetch him the table was all set and ready, and he felt he had gotten off easy.

And now what is a head of household like this supposed to do when it gets out after all that December 25 is his birthday, and everyone in the house shakes his hand and thanks him?

Cresspahl had been supposed to be shot too often, he'd gotten inured to it, he didn't think they could take him away, so he hadn't even made a plan for Hanna Ohlerich. Hanna knew that her parents were dead and buried in Wendisch Burg. She vaguely realized that she had inherited the woodworking shop, but the will was somewhere with her fishermen relatives in Warnemünde. Why didn't Hanna want to go to Gesine's school with her? Hanna was only going to go to school for as long as it was mandatory, then she'd study carpentry. With who? With Cresspahl. And if Cresspahl wasn't back by Easter 1946? With Plath. But if his trade wasn't carpentry then it didn't matter to Hanna if she went back to the fishermen. She walked next to Jakob on Brickworks Road, he thought she wasn't paying attention. He changed his stride. She took a short step, in the middle of the snow, so she'd be even with him again. She listened to him. She blew on her hands to fight off the cold, she sniffled in the cold air, she was obliviously doing her own thing. Maybe she was surprised at him. He was four years older than her, he was the head of the family. Who else was supposed to know what was to become of her!

At the corner of the cemetery, the other child came up to them, satchel on one shoulder. This Gesine walked right past them, indifferent, like she didn't know them, but it wasn't that dark on a January afternoon, in the glittering snow. She often did that when she saw him with Hanna, and Jakob didn't understand it. There were many times he thought that she wanted to show him something, then she'd cover it up again. In November she'd come to him with questions about the English. Whether the Soviets didn't want the same things as the English. Jakob granted that they used to, before. In that case would the Soviets help someone who'd helped the English? – Yes-and-no: Jakob said cautiously, he had become plenty Mecklenburgish. He no longer thought English connections were a positive in the Soviet zone but didn't want to say so too soon. The child understood perfectly and ran off; later she dismissed the question, said she was just curious. Why was she so insistent on taking it back? What was there to be scared of? And why was it enough to give her a bad conscience? Now he'd have to watch out for that child, still he couldn't figure it out.

That day he didn't need to call her back, she came back on her own, ran through the loose snow, one time she slipped onto one knee. – Jakob! she cried when he was standing right in front of her already. – Jakob! The English have made a trade!

Again these English. What did the Cresspahls have to do with the English? The child had totally forgotten to act aloof and dignified, she was beside herself with excitement. Jakob couldn't deny that the English had made a trade. It had been the talk of Jerichow for a week, again they were saying: This neck of the woods is going to end up in the West. Not in Sweden, dammit, but still, with the British. In December the British had ceded a large piece of land to the Soviets, near Ratzeburg, almost twelve thousand acres, in exchange for some four thousand acres east of the town so that the demarcation line wouldn't run so close to it and it would have some backcountry to farm. The villages of Bäk, Mechow, and Ziethen were granted to Schleswig-Holstein; Dechow, Groß Thurow, and the whole east bank of Schaal Lake along with the Stintenburg Holm now belonged to Soviet Mecklenburg. Around two thousand people were handed over to the British: the population of a small town (like Jerichow). If the border

wasn't drawn properly in one place, then it wasn't in other places either—
if territory could be found for a town like Ratzeburg, then just think how
much space the Free Hanseatic City of Lübeck needed to stretch out in!
The demarcation line at Schlutup and Eichholz hugged Lübeck a little too
close for comfort too, and then if you factor in the strategic requirements
of the British, you could probably draw a line from the north tip of Ratzeburg Lake, or from Dassow Lake, over to where Wismar Bay starts. And
then Jerichow would be in the West.

– You knew! Cresspahl's child cried, and if it made her so mad and so
miserable then Jakob wanted to make it up to her by making a guilty face.
He didn't think Jerichow would be a morsel to satisfy England's strategic
hunger. When he turned to look at Hanna, he noticed how awkwardly she
was looking down at her feet, as if she were present at a bereavement, if not
partly responsible. If Jerichow went to the West, Gesine would be separated
by one more border from Cresspahl's prison.

Jakob should have brought up the rumor himself, so he could rid her
of the idea that Jerichow was going to the West. Now Gesine firmly believed
it was and took even the most vigorous denials as nothing but efforts to
console her. Now it was for nothing that Cresspahl had been put down on
the registration form as "temporarily absent," and she'd asked to see the
form so many times, just to read that one section of it.

Jakob was not satisfied with himself as head of the family.

May 29, 1968 Wednesday

Cost of Living Index, taking 1957–1959 values as 100:

U.S.A.

	APRIL 1968	PERCENTAGE CHANGE FROM MARCH 1968
All items	119.9	+ 0.3
Food (includes restaurant meals)	118.3	+ 0.3
Housing (includes hotel rates, etc.)	117.5	+ 0.3

Apparel & upkeep	118.4	+ 0.7
Transportation	119.0	0.0
Health & recreation	128.8	+ 0.4
Medical care	143.5	+ 0.4
Personal care	119.0	+ 0.5
Reading & recreation	124.9	+ 0.6
Other goods, services	122.5	+ 0.1

NEW YORK

All items	122.5	+ 0.3
Food (includes restaurant meals)	118.8	+ 0.3
Housing (includes hotel rates, etc.)	121.1	+ 0.2
Apparel & upkeep	122.8	+ 0.5
Transportation	119.1	− 0.1
Health & recreation	133.3	+ 0.5
Medical care	145.2	+ 0.5
Personal care	115.6	+ 0.8
Reading & recreation	136.6	+ 0.7
Other goods, services	127.7	+ 0.2

This means that what cost $10.00 ten years ago is now $2.25 more expensive. Some workers lost thirteen cents a week in their purchasing power. The dollar is now worth 83.4 cents. Will we make it here?

If Jerichow had ended up in the West:

Town Street would be a ground-level canal, paved over between banks of plate glass and chrome. Even in the poorest houses the wooden window frames would have been torn out and replaced by display windows or double-glassed sealed devices that swing open both up and to the side. Two driving schools, a travel agency, a branch of Dresdner Bank. Electric lawn mowers, plastic household appliances, transistor radios, TV sets. Methfessel Jr. would have had his butcher shop tiled from top to bottom. The assistant's sports car, complete with roll cage, parked at the entrance.

Of course you would still be able to buy, maybe at Wollenberg's, wicks and globes for kerosene lamps, centrifuge filters, carriage whips, axle grease, the kind of chain laid out for the cow to step on so that it can't run away when the farmers pull up in their Gran Turismos to do the milking.

And there would still be bargaining over the counter, that would've stayed the same.

Jerichow would be part of the Lübeck Zone Border District. Representatives in the Kiel state parliament. Grousing about Kiel. The surviving nobility as CDU candidates.

Newly counted among the "good families": garage owners, drink distributors, army (Bundeswehr) officers, public works officials. Not Bienmüller—he wouldn't let his son join the Federal Navy. Though he wouldn't mind listening in on ship-to-shore phone calls via Kiel Radio. (Rügen Radio too.) Vacations in Denmark, TV from Hamburg, pop music and a TV station from Lower Saxony, Hanover Broadcasting Company. Officers of the Federal Border Guards would partake at the Lübeck Court, which would be called the Lübeck Court; enlisted men would drink at Wulff's pub. No one would set jeeps on fire here.

Jerichow would have five picture postcards for sale instead of the earlier two. The new ones: The red-brick addition to Town Hall (Hamburg-style). The rebuilt "Swan's Nest" (formerly Forest Lodge). The monument to "Divided Germany" (or to the prisoners of war) on the square outside the station.

A small town in Schleswig-Holstein. Maybe the farms would be reckoned in tons, in acres. There'd be a coastal road from Jerichow through Rande to Travemünde with room for three cars abreast.

Papenbrock would've gotten rich again by 1952, from managing the new great power: the nobility's property. He would have disposed of the von Lassewitz town house before he died. The town would renovate it, even bringing in stucco workers from Hanover for the garlands under the windows. Half the building would be a museum, the other half a cave for various offices. The sweet-tempered German Socialist Party, Gneez.

The town council would have laid sewer pipes under almost every street by that point. The brickworks would have turned into a factory for plastic household goods to keep a labor force in Jerichow. Lampposts even on the Bäk. A neon mushroom on a long stem illuminating Market Square at night. The hospital would have been turned into the gatehouse for a clinic with an operating room. In the station restaurant they'd have lowered the ceiling, the furniture that had been used for fuel would've been replaced by Gelsenkirchen Baroque, a refrigerated display case for cakes, wall-to-wall carpeting.

The old inn on the way to the Countess Woods would have been appearing in guidebooks for some time. Set on fire in the midfifties, rebuilt as a hotel and restaurant: a three-story L-shaped building. The swans wouldn't recognize the Forest Lodge, not reading its new name. A rapid turnover in the lease, with restaurateurs first surprised and then horrified by the lack of customers. Hadn't the brochure described a "pearl" of Nordic urban architecture, invoked the beauty of the countryside?

Jerichow would once again have submitted to the district capital. There'd be five buses a day on road to Gneez, to the greater glory of the Swenson family business. The front of the buses would read GNEEZ–RANDE (VIA JERICHOW), not JERICHOW. Gneez would attract and take from Jerichow: housewives, workers, civil servants, moviegoers, schoolchildren. In Gneez not only the movies would be as fresh and current as in Ratzeburg or Lübeck. In Gneez there'd be night schools offering language courses, slideshow lectures, readings from novels. In Jerichow people would be miffed at the new building for the Gneez Tax Office. Jerichow's best-known attractions: a rather old air force pool for swimming classes and a location slightly closer to the border.

Rande would have grown, with Jerichow getting little to show for it. The beachfront would've been built up to a depth of over half a mile with weekend cottages, condos, villas. Concerts in the pavilion across from the Archduke Hotel. Which might be called the Baltic. Even in Rande there would be products and entertainments unavailable in Jerichow. Rande would have a spa therapy center, a temperature-controlled seawater swimming pool, a more modern cinema than the one in the Jerichow Rifle Club, and many of the stores would stay open in the winter too. The Rande streets would have been torn up and redone two or three times. The signs on the roads approaching and leaving Gneez would say "Rande" more often than "Jerichow." Ilse Grossjohann would not have stayed mayor for long. Still, she'd have two cutters docked at the new landing, and a cozy little tourist trap dotted with shrubs and bushes, the Naiad Garden Restaurant, where the day-trip boats from Denmark dock.

The airport at Jerichow-North would be Mariengabe Airport, licensed

1078 · *May 29, 1968 Wednesday*

only for private planes, competition for Lübeck-Blankensee. The runways were already more than a mile long, solid 1936 workmanship too. Mariengabe, annual mecca for international air rallies. Sporty, noncommercial, right near the border, and entirely peaceful.

A radar-monitoring station would have been built near Rande, on the coastal cliffs not far from the border, screened from view with hedges. (The Federal Republic of Germany would still not have sovereignty; in 1960, as a military partner, it would have been allowed to take over the facility from Great Britain.) Even now, in 1968, the three old naval barracks on the east side of the little sports field. They would still look temporary. The rotating radar dish can be rapidly taken off its support, disassembled, and loaded onto the three trucks parked in such a way that they seem waiting to drive off. Flagpole on the little square outside the exit. A lost dog (German shepherd) next to the sentry box. The sound of the Baltic ruined here by the droning of engines. Signs below the barbed wire on three corners: Military Security Zone, No Trespassing, Violators Will Be Shot, Barracks Commandant, Federal Defense Minister, Liable to Prosecution under §100 Subsection 2 Par. 109g. Jerichow wouldn't have that.

Sometimes, most of the time, the people of Jerichow would act like it was a real backwater, somewhere like Klütz. Shut down Town Street for three whole days just to change a cable. Let the tourists who're just going to the sea anyway take a detour! The excavator digging out the trenches is the latest model, and its driver can cut edges with it as foursquare as Heine Klaproth used to do during his labor service. He can even make nasty asides about how idiotic the staring tourists are. Maybe Heine Klaproth's his father. The deft orange-painted monster would have been rented from a company in Lübeck, though.

Because graves in Jerichow would still be dug by hand. It would've come too late for Amalie Creutz. Families visit the cemetery at Christmas. The blue spruce wreaths they bring might have been stolen, but not from someone the deceased didn't know—that could be taken as an insult. Then they'd go home and feed the cows a second time, as a Christmas treat. But they'd all have to be there. Evening church service. Brüshaver would be under the ground, though, not up in the pulpit. They'd know where to find old Papenbrock's grave. Cresspahl wouldn't want to go on. Let someone else live.

The out-of-towner in the pharmacy asking where she might find a dry cleaner would not only be directed to the building "opposite the Shell station," she would also get a verbal assessment of the duration and quality of the treatment. That would still be the same.

Legal advice: Dr. Werner Jansen. Real estate: N. Krijgerstam, working for R. Papenbrock Co. Taxis and buses: Heinz Swenson. Information on the names of fields and meadows, and local history: O. Stoffregen. They would, perhaps, have still been there.

Friends in Wismar would have to be over sixty-five years old to visit people in Jerichow. Transfer at Bad Kleinen to the interzonal train to Hamburg via Schönberg and Lübeck. They'd have become very different people from one another.

If Jerichow had ended up in the West.

May 30, 1968 Thursday, Memorial Day

On May 30, one hundred years ago, General John A. Logan gave an order. He was commander in chief of the Grand Army of the Republic at the time, and it was well within his rights to decree that this day be set aside to decorate the graves of comrades "who died in defense of the country in the late rebellion." It has expanded, the remembering is now supposed to include the dead in foreign wars too, especially the unknown soldier.

In our neighborhood they go looking for him around the corner, at Riverside Park and Eighty-Eighth Street, where there's the Soldiers' and Sailors' Monument. Outside the noble, unused little temple, modeled on the choragic monument of Lysicrates in Athens, they went marching this morning with drums, trumpets, and glockenspiels, men and children in uniform, so that even up by us the air is filled with drum rolls and fife whistles.

We were on our way to Grand Central Station when the remains of the parade swung onto Ninety-Fifth Street—we couldn't escape. It was parts of a women's regiment, fiercely determined ladies who in no way brought to mind office work or nursing during the Korean War, so erect did they hold the flag, so stiffly did they swing their arms and plant their legs. The two buildings of poor people on the south side of the street were covered with flags. As many as three faces in each window. On our side stood the alcoholics—woozy, defenseless, patriotic. One was holding a little child's flag in his hand, unaware it was there. The parade was accompanied by boys and girls running up and down alongside it, with toy plastic machine guns and handguns: they looked similar enough to the real thing to fool you, and the sounds at least were right.

The schools, post offices, stock exchange, and banks are closed for the sacred occasion. The holiday lasts through Sunday.

Vacation in the country, on Long Island Sound.

Vacation with Amanda Williams, Naomi Prince, and Clarissa Prince. Mr. Williams is waiting back in New York, Mr. Prince has gotten a divorce, Clarissa Prince is five years old. Marie Cresspahl will have to work for her vacation.

The house belongs to Naomi's father, an accountant who's worked his whole life to pay for it. His loneliness is there in the living room and on display in the study: yearbooks of the New York Stock Exchange and the *Collected Best Plays on Broadway, 1931.* In 1931 he got married, in 1942 he went off to fight the Japanese, in 1943 Naomi's mother moved to an unknown location in New Mexico. Collections: pipes, mussel shells—both abandoned shortly before achieving real stature. Leaves outside dim the rooms.

Today and the next two days: meals together, walks, until the big cleanup on Sunday morning. On the screened porch, a boat's deck on stilts, it'll be nice to watch the rain, if it rains. On Saturday night we'll watch the presidential candidates debate on TV, McCarthy the workhorse against Kennedy the high-strung foal. Or maybe we'll forget to. At night, before we fall asleep, we'll talk, half honestly. That afternoon two young men turn up, friends of Naomi's, maybe Mrs. Williams's. They're both named Henry. They drink very moderate amounts, talk about job prospects in New York, and direct every fourth sentence to the outsider, Mrs. Cresspahl. Oh yes, this is just the kind of landscape I like. They come back in the evening and pick up Amanda to go to a barbecue in a backyard far away; Mr. Williams's call from New York misses her by minutes. Who is going to go pick up the phone and lie to him? We all talk differently than we do in the bank, our workday familiarity here broken up into caution, shyness, privacy. Amanda has suddenly turned timid and afraid, hardly speaking up at all, even though she's usually the chattiest. Naomi and Amanda know something about

Mr. Prince that they still need to talk about, but not till they're alone. It's as if Amanda is scared of the children, but a house with so many wooden rooms is supposed to be even more full of children. A cleaning lady came by and was sent away, Naomi doesn't explain. Do you like the rain? My father isn't exactly strict, but he expects you to behave a certain way. Did you have to raise a father too? I'm afraid I did try to do that too, Naomi. *Y'see?* The instant before night reaches the ground, the moment before we feel fear, we see the children coming back. They've been at the beach until now.

The beach is the shore of a bay curving out into the Sound. Hard sand. Expensive villas on the water in the bluish light. Motorboats anchored past the bathing area, a tiny sail heading northwest. Reeds, marshy meadows. Fifty acres of mixed woodland, narrow access roads. A marina on the other side of the spit of land. Not many boats out on the water. Elaborate, elegant revolving cranes, several floating decks. The water still, almost black. Fingers glow in the darkness. When you surface your face feels pulled, as if it's slid back into an earlier shape. On the middle jetty a blanket has been laid out under the open sky, there's a shower next to it—you can live here, by the water. Finally someone came walking up to us, he doesn't know any neighbors who'd go swimming at this hour. He stops next to the strangers, greets them warmly, starts a conversation about temperature and humidity. And he wishes us a restful night, a relaxing vacation. As if we'd come home.

May 31, 1968 Friday

Vacation in the country. Country rain.

A day trip in West Germany four years ago. We were on our way north from the Hamburg Airport, and in Grömitz there was a bus in our way. Marie was curious about "Holstein Switzerland," even if it came with explanations from the Holstein Swiss. We were tourists—and we bought two excursion tickets like tourists.

The bus was tightly packed with mostly women and children. We were crammed onto the seat that folds down in front of the rear door. Now that our way out was thwarted, Marie would've liked to escape. One lady, quiet, with an elegant hairdo, stepped hard on her foot and it wasn't enough to just land on the toes either—she put her full weight on Marie's instep. The child couldn't help but look long and hard at her. The lady stood next to us, pulling four rows of passengers in around us, complaining all the while about a child who wasn't grateful for a stomp on the foot, these foreigners, whatever will a spoiled girl like that do when she gets hip problems. Marie crawled so fast up over her mother's lap to the window seat that it looked like she was about to jump. But the door couldn't open, the bus drove off, we were trapped in the hostility steaming over at us from three sides. It's about respect for your elders! And what was infuriating was that this child showed no fear, merely wanted some distance.

The bus driver spoke through a microphone, selling us the region. His passengers' commentary about the new single-family houses, the lakeside property for sale, was tinged with good-natured envy: Well now! Isn't that something? Yes, but what it costs! The driver had dialed back on his dialect to accommodate his paying customers; some grammatical mistakes remained, of course, he'd learned them especially for the job. – This might interest youse. He pointed out an abandoned inn, reported the tragic death of its owner. The men used to really like to go there, there was no phone in the place. Explanations of the local economy: it was agricultural. Cultivation of grain, rapeseed, – you use 'atta make öil. And of course tourism, – it's you, ladies'n gentlemen, who're paying the bills now! After sounding the depths of tolerance in such fashion he would look expectantly into his rearview mirror and gather up the approving laughter of his cash cows. Stories about refugees from East Germany, with bedsheets as hoods, coming across the frozen Lübeck Bay into the channel, – break emselves off an ice floe n sail right over. This stuck in the mind and would turn into a dream of drifting corpses whose hands you brush with your hand while you're swimming, but he'd only been trying to show the blessings of the free market economy in the proper light. White, cheerful light, flowers in the front yards, bricks as if scrubbed clean, thatched roofs neatly mended, all as if the war had passed this place by. Before, in, and past Lensahn, the microphone explained the wealth of the Grand Dukes of Oldenburg, – but in Oldenburch now! estates, forests, whole villages all 'longin' to him! The passengers' silence briefly disturbed by respect. Views of the storks' nests must have been included in the price, the way every last one of them was pointed out. One village had won the contest for the title of Most Beautiful Village, the prize was a bronze chicken, – but the president of our district assembly lives there, he maybe helped out a bit. Obedient laughter at the human weaknesses of high officials, indication of a property far to the north of the road, – y'see that there man-see-on? a film was shot there, *Hochzeit auf Immnhof,* youse all remember it? Lots of ahhs and yeses, craned necks. We're supposed to picture a precipice in the Kasseedorf Fir Woods (actually a mixed woodland), hidden by trees: that's where Carl Maria von Weber got the idea for the Wolf's Glen! A little later, by the shore of Lake Eutin, – youse remember the four trees? That's the swimming scenes from *Hochzeit auf Immenhof.* Eutin, City of Roses, the composer's birthplace, Voß's house, no shortage of culture here. And Eutin Castle, that belonged to the Grand Duke of Oldenburg too, – but that's in Old-enburch! Coffee break between Lake Keller and Lake Uklei, announced as if giving an order, no doubt about his cut from the inn.

Marie, without a glance at the beauties of the landscape that had been paid for in advance, walked over to a jetty and lay down, pulled the sock off her foot, and put her mistreated leg in the water. She didn't complain, she did what needed doing. She was just seven that August, she'd been in New York only three years, she showed the discipline Castle Hill summer camp had taught her. She was limping visibly when she got back onto the bus. The lady, her hairdo the very picture of otherworldliness and grandmotherly elegance, turned in honest outrage to the mother of this child who had turned out so badly and wished her hip troubles in old age; she was almost weeping with rage. – *Vi forstår desværre ikke tysk*: Mrs. Cresspahl said.

As he started driving, the bus driver solicited some information. Look left, look right, is the person who was there before the break still there? He was unable to restrain his delight at the fiftieth repetition. The fact that his attention was split between chauffeuring and *conférence* sometimes sent his sentences into truly rustic pleonasms: Here in Malente there're some rilly beautiful w-walking paths, and there you can go on some rilly pretty w-walks. He announced the boat ride across five lakes and mentioned the one life preserver ring for a hundred and fifty people, – it's there for the captn! The owner'd splained it all to him: Captns are in short supply, see?, but you can always get more passengers. The passengers, instead of giving him one to the kisser, smiled thoughtfully.

There were three people who didn't want to take the boat, and the driver

took them to Plön by bus instead, continuing to explain the landscape.
– Yeah, that's where 'ey burn the straw-aw. Not done samuch these days.
They go right upta a stack of it n set it on fire. Now something about the
name Fegetasche: today it's the name of a famous restaurant, that's what it's
still called today. They rilly do clean out your pockets there, *fegen* the
Tasche, costsa lotta silver for your coffee n coke. Marie looked evenly at her
enemy, who even as the steamer was pulling into Plön was searching for her
obstinate victim on the lawn—she looked the old bag straight in the eyes as
she slipped by, but didn't finish her scrutiny, and still said nothing. She knew
that the only way we'd get back to our rental car quickly was on this bus.

On the ride back through Plön we were shown the castle and the former
cadet school: the superfamous boarding school! next year we'll be getting
some relative of an Oriental despot! The passengers were familiar with this
particular dictator and nodded understandingly. That's how it is. After
that, we got a stud farm for Trakehners, an old barn whose straw roof
reached down to the ground, more storks' nests, – for the children. This
innuendo, too, was met with a pleased noise. Satisfied and exhausted, he
slumped down and turned on a cassette of canned music—songs from
concerts by Greater German Radio and the Nazi army:

"But That Can't Rattle a Sailor" (to be sung after losses in the sea war)
"Dark Brown Is the Hazelnut" (light brown the SA)
"And That's a Sailor's Love" (...)
"In a Little Town in Poland" (lived the girl I longed-to-be holdin')
And a women-make-the-world-go-round operetta number: "Ganz ohne
Weiber geht die Chose nicht":

– *ganz ohne Gummi hält die Hose nicht!* the women in the back of the
bus sang along—wobbly, menopausal, dressed in discreet bourgeois style.
Their choirmaster took them through Neustadt, charmed them with the
funds that a bypass road would gobble up, made them meek just thinking
of the cost of building a new harbor. He did not tell them anything about
the seventy-three hundred prisoners of the Nazis who, in similarly pleasant
weather in May 1945, were killed in the sea off this city, not even of the six
hundred sailors and guards who died in the line of this kind of duty, so he
didn't need to show them the memorial on the beach near Pelzerhaken
either, even though it really is a point of interest, and quite possibly worth
the question of how much it cost and who paid for it. The passengers sang

along with the tape and were so wiped out with bliss when they got out in Grömitz that they no longer berated the foreign child, Marie, just felt sorry for her as a victim of deeply flawed child-rearing. Marie locked the car door as soon as she got in.

A day trip in West Germany. At midnight we were on the ferry to Bornholm. Marie denied she felt scared for one single second. Now we're in Connecticut across from Long Island.

June 1, 1968 Saturday
Marie was on an expedition, and she found no spare *New York Times* in the woods around the house, she would have had to steal one from the marina. It was lying open in a cockpit as if posed for a photo shoot. (Marie thought it was pretentious; since the day before yesterday she's wanted her own boat.) What she did find was a plump little duck in the general store. Since no one wanted to cook it—not Naomi, not Amanda Williams—it was time for Mrs. Cresspahl to show off her kitchen skills. The last time Naomi's father got a new stove was in 1937, a sturdy smoky thing where you have to guess the temperature. The task is to cook for five in a strange oven, and the two other women are warming up their appetites on the beach in the evening sun. There was once a girl in Cresspahl's kitchen standing next to Jakob's mother taking lessons: chop the liver, heart, and stomach very fine with an onion and mix in one egg, a pinch of pepper, salt, and a piece of white bread softened in broth. There's no broth. Luckily there's a girl standing in Mr. Gehrig's kitchen, watching the work: Then stitch the stuffed body closed at the top and bottom openings, melt two ounces of butter...

– You didn't have any duck to eat in 1946, Gesine.
– In 1946 we went hungry, strictly following the recipe.
– What were you like as a child at the New School, Gesine?
– It wasn't anywhere near finished. Even in spring we were the class from the old Girls High School. It's true, Eike Swantenius was dead, a Brit had shot her, driving by. Even Wegerecht's daughter came to class sometimes. The commuter students from Jerichow were still Wollenberg and Cresspahl,

same as before, and they still didn't sit next to each other. There was a quota of refugee children assigned to us, and they had to fit into our curriculum irrespective of theirs. Since we'd already started Latin, we and they had to continue it. The law said I wasn't supposed to leave Jerichow until I was done with eighth grade. One new thing were rye rolls in the break after second period.

– Couldn't you get your revenge on Julie Westphal now? Slapping you for forgetting your notebook, she'd been a real fascist!

– Julie Westphal had retreated before the wrath of Schoolgirl Cresspahl. She didn't even report for work at the beginning, under the Soviet occupation; since July she'd been second deputy chair of the Cultural Association in Gneez. There she held musical evenings, with seventeenth-century aphorisms; she apparently melted at the grand piano, neck held high like a gulping chicken, and because she was an artist she received the rations of a heavy laborer.

– What did they say when you transferred in Gneez?

– The same as here: Please keep clear of the platform edge. We had old ladies for teachers: Charlotte Pagels, with her sister, and Frau Dr. phil. Beese. Mrs. Beese had been given early retirement in 1938, Lottie and Fifi Pagels as the civil service law required, they all considered themselves victims of Nazi despotism and they held out their grievances to us like badly mended clothing. They felt they were doing us a favor by bothering with us, and hadn't tried to learn anything about how to deal with twelve-year-olds. What they wanted was a salon of well-behaved children, rather like Louise Papenbrock when she'd take the fine porcelain out of the glass cabinet but only to look at, not to touch. Fifi would sometimes throw up her hands in the middle of math and cry: You bad, bad children! She'd turned fragile and vulnerable under Lottie's lash, now a sketch of her in the dirt from the rain on the windowpane was more than she could take. Beese stuck to a strategy of contempt: silently averting her head when your handwriting slipped below the line, smushing her lips together and gravely stepping backward to the safest place, the lectern, the bridge of the ship.

– And Stalin on the wall behind her.

– No Stalin, no Marx. We were given objective lessons in the subjects we hadn't had to turn in our books from. The Soviet Union could never come up, so no geography. The rule of three in cross-multiplication, the ablative, Friedrich Schiller—we covered those. Not biology. The new textbooks weren't invented yet. Lottie, who we also called Charlie, learned each day's Russian lesson in advance from one Mr. Krijgerstam, in private lessons, not by taking his Cultural Association course.

– What could you get with an A in Russian?

– Nothing from these ladies. Anyone who could recite Goethe's "How gloriously gleams / all Nature upon me!" well, which meant in sparkling fashion, would get Lottie's nature gleaming upon her. Brigitte Wegerecht was taken out of school with typhus on January 3 and came back on March 6 with a cap on her head. (She was teased for her half-bald head, and Schoolgirl Cresspahl and she made plans to sit next to each other the following year.) Brigitte got a D in Russian, since she'd missed it—no crime at all in the Pagelses' eyes. Getting a D in needlework, on the other hand, was considered absolutely positively unforgivable. We were being brought up for a bourgeois household.

– Not in an anti-Fascist way?

– Not in a pro-Soviet way. One of our assignments was to research our name. This was the worst possible invitation for nicknames. Schoolgirl Cresspahl didn't want to be pegged as "cress on a pole," but she'd also prefer if the name didn't come from "Christ." Maybe from *chrest* in Wendish. When it was her turn, she said her name was put together from North German *kross* and Plattdeutsch *Pall*.

– "Pawl"?

– Yes. A sailor's term. The ratchet brace in a geared wheel that prevents it from slipping back when you turn it, and a big, crude, crass one too.

– Just like the bread rolls in Germany.

– Exactly. Mrs. Beese said: Nothing doing! Cress, from the Greek *grastis*, "green fodder," Old High German *kresso,* plus *falen,* as in "Ostfalen," Eastphalia. And now I had my nickname. Greenfodder.

– Did you put jumping jacks on her chair, or a needle, or a wet sponge . . .

– Jumping jacks! We didn't have those. A needle was a valuable property. Anyway, she herself got rid of the name for me. To help the local children and the refugee children get to know one another, we all had to share a little of our life story—

– There, you see?

– No, she still didn't have a handle on the children from Stargard,

Insterburg, Breslau—the East. For her it was about their father's job. And here's where you get your anti-Fascism: Wegerecht's father was held against her as though he were her fault personally. Beese, with her graduate degree, had been free to do nothing. Wegerecht had stayed head district court judge until 1940; in 1942 he was shot and killed by partisans in Greece. Brigitte felt that was punishment enough for her father, plus it seemed to her that he had made her, she hadn't made him. She looked at me, afraid I'd go back on our plan for next year, and I nodded, especially now. Mrs. Beese cried: You've got it coming to you, Cresspahl!

– Did you pour ink on her hair from an upstairs landing? You could've done that at least.

– We didn't have any ink to spare. Anyway other people started in on Frau Dr. Beese. Lottie Pagels felt it just wasn't right that Cresspahl's own father had been dragged off by the Russians. Fifi at her sister's side, letting her lower lip droop with grievous disapproval. From that moment on I was a favored child, nobody cared anymore about a flaw in the needlework or a crossed-out number on my math homework. No one calls a kid like that Greenfodder, they look kindly and forgivingly at her. I never forgave her.

– Wasn't that as good as an apology?

– Now the whole class knew what had happened to my father, and what might happen. Would you have liked that? I always thought about him anyway, it's not like I needed particular occasions to think of him. The thought of him thought me. Now I'd be reminded of him in school all the time, by strangers. All that was missing was for them to ask me about him every week.

– Someone must have seen him—in Gneez, in Schwerin, somewhere.

– Marie, when the Soviets arrested someone he really and truly disappeared. Jakob didn't know the countryside and even Cresspahl's friends from Neustrelitz to Wendisch Burg to Neustadt-Glewe couldn't tell him anything. Jakob kept his Russian business partners as secret as he could—I wasn't supposed to notice anything at all about Krijgerstam's or Vassarion's visits. I knew he was looking. They were nice to him, but questions about Cresspahl made their faces go stiff. Too dangerous. Contagious. They didn't want to end up arrested by the Red Army. Comfort was one thing, pity was fine. Where he was stayed a secret. As if he was dead.

– You recently told me your Easter water story. You heard his voice. But he wasn't there, Gesine.

– He'd told me I wasn't allowed to leave the house in a dress. But if I wanted to get some Easter water and wash in it to make myself beautiful I had to go out in my best dress, the green velvet one. When I got back I heard his prohibition again. He wasn't there, and he was speaking as though through the door.

– In your head.

– Now you'll think your mother's crazy.

– I hear voices too, Gesine. Now don't you have to sprinkle some water on this nice bird here?

– You can take off his string.

– And may I stay up late to watch the battle between McCarthy and Robert Kennedy?

– You usually don't even ask.

– Naomi! Clarissa! Mrs. Williams! It's ready!

June 2, 1968 Sunday

We must have looked like a crumbling chunk of family, rough around the edges, on the Stamford platform—two children shivering from the rain, three aunts or mothers, with luggage as though snatched up in a quick getaway. Whether the adults in the group were relatives or trapped in some other kind of fight with one another, the passengers already on board the train made room in the nearby seats—maybe they were curious, maybe it was just because the new arrivals were dry, but they were rewarded with neither a continuation of the argument nor a reconciliation. They could see Naomi's thin face, pinched into the shape of a lovely svelte owl mask, pointed severely and joylessly at the wet scenery outside. The train swung back and forth, she remained stiffly at the window, even when the Sound disappeared in the fog, or behind the backs of houses. Amanda, our Amanda Williams, the delight and eye candy and terror of men traveling alone, still hid behind dark reflective sunglasses after it was half-dark in the train, brooding over what hadn't been said, lips pouting, as if imitating a sulking child. The children took no part in this game their elders were playing, withdrawing to a double seat at the far end of the car with their backs to them. The girl with the braids held up a newspaper page with comics for the smaller one, explaining to her some of the final acts. She didn't really take much pleasure in the latest news of Bugs Bunny or Li'l Abner, she clearly had trouble getting the point, and Clarissa kept her impish face impassive and mad, like in school, no resemblance now to the hopping olive from earlier today. And it wasn't only from the rain still hanging in her curly hair. Mrs. Cresspahl read, in many sections of *The New York Times,* what she'd missed on vacation, but her ears too were still ringing with the sound of three voices—Amanda's aggressive alto, Naomi's careful girl's voice, and the flat tones that had sounded so halfhearted in the bones of her own skull. It had been a painful session, over the rest of their breakfasts, cozily tucked away from the heavy country rain that pelted the roof and the lush greenery outside the windows. It was supposed to be a game. How all three of us could live in this house by the sea,

your Marie with Clarissa, Amanda, yours truly Naomi, and you, Gesign.

For the children?

Us too, we've never had such a fun weekend in the country. Couldn't we have a piece of vacation every day?

Would there be room for us?

One room for each of us, and for the girls. And one common room.

And we'll pack the husbands away in the bunkbeds in the garage.

Mr. Prince is banned from the house. I'll go by Gehrig again.

Mr. Williams can go jump in a lake, and not one near here either. Yeah, it's been in the air for a while.

Anyway, we'll need the garage for our cars.

Gesine, don't you have someone? Wouldn't he come?

He'd be glad to, Naomi. Just the man for you, Amanda.

The guy from Nebraska?

Not exactly . . . German, at least he used to be.

You won't have to tell us what he's like in bed. We know you don't like that sort of thing.

Okay, that helps.

Right. So that we wouldn't be a family, more like a club.

All the laundry together, all the dishes in one dishwasher, making one meal a day instead of three.

And someone to watch the children during the day.

And after work you drive to the station and pick us up from the New York train.

So who'd be the head of household?

You, Naomi, and the former Mrs. Williams.

Who'd be the housewife?

Whoever wants to. Do you want to, Mrs. Cresspahl?

She can't. She has something going on with de Rosny, she doesn't have to say what it is. You, Naomi.

I'd try it, for two months to start—if your Marie agrees to it.

You'd be perfect, Miss Gehrig.

Yeah but you know I could never make duck like you did.

So the kids would go to school here.

Where I went to school. Half the way runs through the woods, then on Main Street to the golf course.

Tell us more. Traditions. Curriculum.

Gesine, I'm another one of those children who was supposed to have it better. Your Marie will lack for nothing. Educationally speaking it's almost New England. With a ticket to Vassar College included.

What do you pay for Marie in New York?

$890 for tuition, 200 for meals, 150 for school uniforms, 300 for after-school activities. It comes to $1,600.00 a year.

You see. You see?

Now it's also true that Marie wants her own boat.

I can teach her to sail.

She knows how to sail.

You see. You see?

It's just, she won't give up the apartment in New York.

So keep it. We'll have a pied-à-terre. You'll have a pied-à-terre.

How long'll we do it for?

We'll try it and see. As long as it works out.

And the cost?

What do you mean the cost.

We'll open a pot. We'll set up a budget. We'll sign a contract.

The house.

I'll get the house, Gehrig Sr. would rather give it to me before he dies anyway. I'll contribute the house.

And if your father wants to come back, or when he comes for a visit, we'll stick him in a hotel?

Oh, Gesine!

We'll have to tell him.

Okay, Amanda, Cresspahl's right. We'll tell him.

Because of the neighbors.

They've known me since before I could walk.

I meant buying.

What do you mean, buying?

He'll give it to you. But we're not his daughters.

I wouldn't take advantage of him!

Okay. We buy it. If he puts the money in his will, I'll get even more.

Naomi, we're not going to talk about your inheritance. You started with the house.

Let him sell us his house. He'll have one more story to tell. I have six thousand. Your turn, Gesine.

We could get our hands on four. Amanda?

Does it matter if...I don't really want to take anything from Mr. Williams...two thousand, to start. My folks in Minnesota...

Twelve thousand in cash, that's enough. Henry'll get us the rest. Yeah, the guy from Thursday, who couldn't take his eyes off a certain Mrs. Cresspahl! His father runs the First National branch in the village.

In the village. In the village...

You see. You see?

Okay, how many shares. Five?

Three, Gesine.

But what about Amanda? She'd have to pay more than she should for just one person.

Amanda, say something!

It won't happen.

Because of money, Amanda? Mrs. Williams! Either you're over him or you're not ready to do business.

It's over. I'm done with him. Just, sorry.

Amanda pays one part, you pay one and a half, I pay two.

You pay two? Marie's not even twelve. I want to pay two if you do.

For the price of the house? For the household expenses? For the sailboat? For the two cars?

Stop it. Don't be so German, Gesine.

Should we stop talking about it?

What a ditz you are, Naomi.

That's right, I'm an idiot. A real pig. A ... Can I stop now if I say sorry?

Okay. Forget it.

You two would have to keep things a bit cleaner. How else are we supposed to live here.

Fair enough. Look, Gesine, I'm not Jewish. My grandparents were, and not all of them either. In my father the Austrian side is much more pronounced than the tribe of Israel. I'm no more related to the Jewish ones than I am to the other ones, Gesine. I don't have any personal thing against the Germans. And if your father was in a Nazi camp, on the wrong side—

No. No. Not that.

I'm talking about you. We'd want to do this thing with you.

Because you liked my duck.

Enough already!

Okay.

Be honest, du. I still remember that from high school, in German you can call someone by their first name but you have to not think the second-person singularis pronoun, it also goes with the second ... the third pluralis. Thou ... be honest, you!

I think of you in the second singularis. "Du," and "Naomi."

Now you two have to tell me everything.

See!

The housewife. Amanda, you start.

We'll need a schedule. Like on a bulletin board.

Like in the office. But we're trying to get away from the office!

I think work schedules are appropriate.

Okay, make us one, Amanda. But yesterday she wanted to watch something other than channel seven. You didn't care what McCarthy and Kennedy had to say, you just stayed to be polite.

Still, we agreed about Kennedy.

Still, we'll need a second TV. If you know what I mean. Gesine.

I'm trying to keep Marie off TV.

And that will be fully respected. No, I mean for what you don't like.

We've known each other since, what, 1963, 1964? If I were—

Gesine, don't be so . . . Okay. I saw you. And this morning you set the table again, I'm sorry. The milk in the carton would have been good enough for me but you wanted it in a little pitcher, and not a plastic one, porcelain. Am I right?

Well, if we have pitchers.

We'll have them. What else?

What about vacations.

Here it'll be vacation every night, every weekend!

She means vacations from us.

No! Amanda! It's just, I need to go to Europe in August.

Yeah, well, relatives.

Maybe you'd rather stay with us than visit them.

No, it's not that. A tourist trip, to Czechoslovakia.

You have to . . . ?

She can't get around it.

You don't need to explain.

You won't have to pay your household fee and Marie will stay with us.

If you convince her to.

You don't want her to, do you, Gesine.

On the contrary, this trip—

Something's going on here. If you don't trust us, get a separate lawyer. Are you afraid we'll steal your guy from Nebr—your guy from your bed? Or have you lost your mind after all, just because you're a few stories higher up than us now? You think you're better than us?

Amanda. It was supposed to be a game. Leave her alone.

If anyone's ruining this game, it's her!

Do you want to leave New York, Gesine?

No. No.

You don't know exactly what's going to happen come fall, right?

Right.

You know that, Amanda.

Right. And we'll need a room to cry in too.

until all three of us were sitting around the table as if we'd lost our language, moved to tears in the corners of our eyes by friendship, goaded into rage by disappointment. We were rescued by the children, who'd had enough of *East Side Kids* on TV—the merry adventures of gangsters back in the thirties, which Marie wasn't supposed to be watching though. She hesitated in the doorway, as if walking into an awkward mood like a headwind. The adults were duly ashamed of themselves, and so that Clarissa wouldn't get upset too we silently finished the big cleanup and took the village taxi to the 1:50 train from Stamford, although we actually could've stayed till tomorrow morning. Since then we haven't really spoken.

The New York Times describes again what we saw last night on channel 7: Robert F. Kennedy's right-handed gestures quoting his brother, his striped tie, his indefatigable smile. The *Times* reveals that he'd refused a public debate against McCarthy for many weeks, until he was too upset by the latter's win in the Oregon primary. The *Times* has heard Kennedy's wife say that she can't ever think of him except as having won, and the *Times* also prints as tentative ellipses what we didn't understand in the broadcast either, for the sake of accuracy. And what does she have to report from the home country?

In one Germany, the Communists blew up the Leipzig University church on Thursday, at four in the morning our time. First-semester student Cresspahl had been struck by the building for not being made of brick and for having been built to stand between other buildings, the Augusteum and the town house containing Café Felsche that had been totally bombed away. Completed in 1518, consecrated by Martin Luther in 1545, used since 1945 by both Catholics and Protestants—the child from elsewhere had learned these things about Leipzig, too, she was planning to stay awhile. Stud. phil. Cresspahl (first semester) was inside the church only once, for a concert, in a space divided into neither galleries nor naves, a bourgeois, almost domestic space from which the piety had been removed, and very bright, even though the rounded dormer windows scurrying all around the roof let in no light that made it down to the ground level. And now it hadn't been enough to, say, remove the ridge turret from the roof, or the top of the globe with the cross on it, the Wendish Cross; some students had to be arrested, other people protesting behind police cordons threatened with arrest if they "whipped up emotions against the authorities." That sounds like a bad translation. There were architects who sought to preserve the Leipzig church and include it in the university building project, but the "East German leader" said something about old teeth that had to be extracted by Socialism. *Mr. U. is a native of Leipzig.* Even a tiny piece of common sense like this has to be taught to people against their will; they need to be made—by threats, with force—to revise the picture they want their city to show the world. "Citizens, disperse or else you will be arrested": that's probably more like what the loudspeaker cars actually hurled at the people.

On the same page, p. 7, adjacent as if related, we are told something about the other Germany's lower house, no, Bundestag: 384 representatives cast their votes for the Seventeenth Amendment to the German Constitution. Now anywhere the government detects a state of emergency it can snoop into people's letters, packages, and telephone conversations, force them to do government work, at gunpoint too—all achievements that aren't exactly making West Germany less like East Germany. Then the Social Democrats promise not to permit any misuse of the law, as if there were guaranteed to be a Social Democratic Party for all eternity and as long as this state exists. The workers have understood that strikes under such states of emergency can be broken by armed forces; the middle-class citizens seem not to have realized that a state of emergency can confiscate their cars. The government wants gratitude—they claim they've extracted a little more West German sovereignty from the General Treaty between Germany and the Allied victors; the Allies have given up some of their dirty deals, a couple of ungrateful brushes with West German nationals, but in their barracks they remain rulers under their own laws, and it is they who decide about Berlin and about Germany as a whole, even if the Soviet Union has a word or two to say about it. This is what the Federal Republic calls sovereignty.

Explain this to us, please, Mrs. Cresspahl. You're German too. Explain to us what the Germans are doing.

And now it's homework time. On May 4 the Czechoslovakian defense minister announced a visit from Warsaw Pact troops for maneuvers. This General Dzúr let people believe that the maneuvers would come in, maybe, the fall. Last week he corrected himself and stated the time as June. And it was still just May 31 when the Soviet troops moved in anyway, across this most casual of borders.

Others wanting to join in the fun are expected from Hungary and Poland. But the East German Communists aren't sending their troops yet, for now they're just mad at their Prague comrades.

As the train pulls into the tunnel under the East River, Mrs. Cresspahl has disappeared from her taciturn group. As the light above the bare factory roofs of Queens returns to the train car she does too, unsuspiciously, from the buffet car, for in her hands she is holding three paper cups full of a brownish fluid. What's surprising about this tea is only that there are ice cubes floating in it. At this point Marie turns around after all and takes her mother's measure with a cool, instructional look. Because if a lady goes off to get double bourbons, however demurely disguised, Marie is sure that she could've learned such behavior only from long-lasting contact with Soviet military personnel.

What's left of the rain is sitting on the flat roofs outside. Again the train needs to duck into the ground and under the river, and then we'll be home.

– Have some tea: Mrs. Cresspahl says, and the friends accept their portions. Amanda W. can do so only by raising her head a little too impetuously, still ready to take offense. Naomi smiles a little off to one side and closes her eyes for a moment, as if wanting to indicate a secret that Amanda is now excluded from. The other passengers miss what they've been waiting for, because they have to stand up long before it's time and pull together their coats, bags, umbrellas, newspapers. The three women sit next to one another, comfortably unhurried, and one says once that this is some good tea, and another one answers, not bad as tea goes.

Then, in Pennsylvania Station, the other two don't want to take the subway with the Cresspahls, they go upstairs to Seventh Avenue with the disappointed screaming Clarissa to hunt down a taxi. What will the driver talk about? The murder of his colleague Leroy Wright, the demonstration crossing Brooklyn Bridge to City Hall, joined by no police presence except a new taxi partition made of bulletproof glass . . .

Outside the Ninety-Sixth Street station exit the air is heavy with humidity. Those who can sweat release pearls of it from their foreheads as involuntarily as breathing—Marie, on the other hand, promptly turns very red in the face. As soon as she can, right inside the Riverside Drive door, she's going to ask. She will say she approves of what happened: even a secret with de Rosny needs to be kept, Indian-style. She will say she doesn't approve of what happened, because someone who starts an extended family on Long Island Sound lives only an hour from New York, not nine with transfers on the other side of the Atlantic. She'll say: This dialectic of yours, Gesine, you could've left it behind in Europe you know!

June 3, 1968 Monday

Yesterday the mayor of Saigon went to inspect the main battle line in his city, along with other friends of Vice President Ky's, mainly police officers but also relatives. They entered a school, now converted to a command center. At which point the house was blown to bits, as if by a missile from an American military copter. Now the army says it wasn't using any helicopters in that area. Before, the US embassy prematurely apologized to the South Vietnamese government, and the victims' families, "with deepest regrets and condolences." His Excellency, President Nguyen Van Thieu, friends with still other Americans, suddenly has seven sinecures available for his underlings, and if he ever writes his memoirs in the West he will have a thing or two to teach us about the nature of the home front.

The new Communists in Prague both do and don't want to take the old ones to court over the murders they committed for Stalin. Removal from office, yes; investigative committees, definitely; "settling accounts within the party in public," no. Alexander Dubček is less eager to have a reputation for vindictiveness than his predecessors were, and is urging his comrades to protect their friends by not exposing Soviet involvement in the crimes of the 1950s, and his comrades are complying. As for those outside the party, what business is it of theirs, even if they do demand public probity? They are not being governed against their will, not yet, but this wish is refused to them. They were just bystanders, you might say, on the inside but not inside the party.

Hanna Ohlerich had wanted to wait until Easter 1946. By that time Cresspahl should have been released and back in the workshop and she an apprentice in his trade. She took his release for granted, and afterward had to find something else to do. She started writing letters—not even secretly, Jakob's mother was supposed to see even though she didn't let her read them.

She had turned to Mrs. Abs right away, but only as a mother-like person from whom she expected comfort, help. (You could more or less tell what kind of parents the Ohlerichs had been. The father dealt with whatever came their way; any outward steps to be taken were decided by him. The mother was allowed to run the kitchen, the cellar, and the home, albeit under his supervision. He had the last word, interpreted by his will alone, right up to the rope he gave her and the other one he took for himself. Strict, also affectionate, easy for a child to look up to. Just as Hanna's father had exerted authority in the home, he'd been a bulwark against the outside world.) She pinned her faith on Cresspahl for all this, not on a woman.

She still counted on Jakob and on many evenings followed him out into the yard so that he'd postpone his business deals and go off to the marsh with her, two leisurely saunterers in the damp May twilight, strolling along like a long-established and permanent couple (on which occasions Cresspahl's child didn't want to be seen as abandoned, bereft of the appropriate companionship she deserved, so she withdrew to the walnut tree, making very sure not to look west where the pair could just be made out in the haze with the setting sun behind it). Jakob was allowed to read the letters, which in fact were intended more for him than their addressees, the Warnemünde relatives. To him they seemed pleading, desperate, as if Hanna needed to be saved from a den of thieves growing more and more dangerous by the day. Cresspahl didn't return. "Get me out," she'd written. Jakob acted the big brother and merely explained the difference between Hanna's actual situation and her description of it; he talked her out of her mistrust for the Warnemünders and into a mistrust of Erwin Plath; eventually she pretended she'd only wanted reassurance. He was not satisfied with himself as head of the household.

He told Gesine she needed to be more considerate of her friend. Gesine wasn't aware that anyone had been inconsiderate to Hanna! They shared everything, didn't they? They shared a bed, neither wanting to go to sleep without the other; they did their homework together at Cresspahl's desk; they waited in the long line for soggy Papenbrock bread, in silent solidarity; people not from town thought they were sisters. Whenever Gesine asked

Jakob for some money over and above her weekly allowance, she held out her hand again for Hanna's share and they went to the market together, to buy a packet of grass seed each from Wollenberg, just to buy something, because Wollenberg wanted to make a sale for once, and then they watered each other's test plots. She treated her friend like a welcome guest, didn't she? Took Lisbeth's box camera, which Jakob had bought back from Vassarion and given her for her birthday, and gave Hanna a half share in it? She paid the forty-pfennig fee for Hanna's ration card herself, that was only right, and she didn't mind doing it. They shared their hunger, their pimples, once even a CARE package. Jakob knew that, what could he be thinking?

The package wasn't full by the time it reached them, it was just a lump of American lard, two cans of American corned beef, a pair of stockings, and a Waterman fountain pen, all packed together in an old flour sack and dropped off by a man from Berlin ("West Berlin") on a motorcycle, who also left behind an uneaten sandwich on unbelievably white bread as though it were nothing. Gesine couldn't think who might have sent it; only later did she realize that the photograph of three strapping German shepherds was news from Grunewald, from Dr. Semig's dog Rex. Anyway, it came for Cresspahl's daughter, but after contributing the foodstuffs to the pantry they cut the sandwich neatly in half and ate it together, and Hanna could choose whether she wanted the pen or the nylon stockings that suggested shimmering shadows of night on her legs. Hanna was free to give Jakob the stockings after trying them on, and Gesine couldn't think of anything more worth doing with the Waterman—were they not united?

Didn't they see, hear, think the same things? We witnessed the liberation of Leslie Danzmann's boots in such unity that ten years later she could still tell the story in detail and I could still recall every single still or moving picture of it. It was in early June 1946, Hanna had come to the Gneez train with me that day, and a procession caught up to us on Station Street. In the front strode Leslie, chin held stiffly high, eyes pointed straight ahead, which didn't help her on the cobblestones. She had worn out her presentable shoes during the war, and her one pair of "indestructible" shoes from 1937 may have survived her walks to the mayor's office but not her arrest by the Russians, so now she'd brought her husband Fritz's lace-up boots up from her hiding place, padded them, and was wearing them to work hidden under long pants. Would've said something about self-respect. Since she'd been arrested the Gneez Labor Office hadn't taken her back, but she had found a job in the Housing Office department whose mission was to protect the resettlers from the wrath of the locals, and she wanted to look like a properly dressed civil servant there—Hanna and Gesine saw this as vanity. Now this lissom lady having trouble walking was being followed by a young Red Army man, excited by the unfeminine heels he'd glimpsed under the masculine cuffs, and he was offering her a trade, making himself perfectly well understood despite using only personal pronouns and nouns, and doing so relentlessly, so that a pack of jeering children was running along after them, little brats who'd just reached school age, eager to see how the show would turn out. Leslie Danzmann made a beeline through the station and clambered up into the train, hand over hand, as if into a lifeboat, and thought she was safe. Her business partner in uniform was so merrily drunk that morning that the door hit him when it swung shut, he fell flat on his face, into the train car, not discouraged in the least, for now he had an even better view of the object of his quest. Both hands fervently clinging to Leslie's legs, he crawled on his belly like a crab back down the footboard onto firm ground. Our Leslie, stunned by the exclusively blank looks she was getting from the other passengers, slipped and landed on the floor of the train car, unladylike, legs sticking straight out, boots exposed. By that point the Soviet had unhooked the crisscrossed laces, neatly and not unskillfully, under a barrage of pleading remarks too. The Cresspahl and Ohlerich girls had had plenty of chances to squeal with pain at the gravel sticking into their own bare feet but they stayed in the shadows of the rotted bicycle stand, watching wordlessly. The man in the army uniform dyed to another color stayed where he was at the window of the station shop (which was the post he'd been assigned); he was not as out of view as he might have liked, and, with a gun in his holster, he was the very image of the "Volkspolizei" as depicted in the new newspaper, *New Germany*, that both Gesine's and Hanna's schools had gone over in detail. We saw the stationmaster in the train engine, far enough away from the scene; we heard him swear about the train car's door that was still open, in which we could see that Leslie Danzmann had sat up, her mouth in a tortured smile. We saw the Russian carefully wrap his foot bindings back around his feet and pull the former Danzmann boots up over them, not without difficulty, and as the departure whistle blew he pushed the door open wider, into Leslie's legs (knocking her over), threw his own felt rags in after her (in faithful observance of their agreement), and marched in elation over to the station exit with the band of little children timidly, excitedly dancing around him. That day we both cut school, fully understanding one another from the tiny wink that slipped from our eyes and tugged at the corners of our mouths—we were united. United against the adults, united in our pitiless suspicion of them (with Cresspahl secretly and Jakob's mother more vaguely excluded). Is that not unity?

But on June 30 the Soviet Military Administration shut the borders between their zone and the Allies'. Too many people had run away from their New Life (not Leslie Danzmann)—one and a half million going over to the British alone. Hanna might have recognized in this a law of political economy, but all she saw was that yet another possibility had been taken from her. Again she felt trapped with us. How could Jakob have talked her into staying in Jerichow?

For the harvest he loaned us out to the Schlegels. She went uncomplainingly. We'd had enough of waking up every morning with shriveled stomachs, walking around all day bent almost double with hunger, having to leave the table bravely every evening while the Marienwerder schoolteacher was still feeding her baby son. Besides, Jakob had promised to visit us on the weekends.

At the Schlegel farm we were greeted as "Jakob's girls" and put to work that same afternoon, but our only job was to eat thickened milk with sugar. We were allowed to accompany Inge on all her chores around the farm, but not help with any. She'd have let us pluck strawberries, but only as many as we could eat. From the outside the house looked like an ordinary half-timbered building under a thatched roof, standard Lower Saxony style that textbooks would call classic; nothing inside it was to be hidden from us. We could climb into the space under the living room and examine the still, we were shown the tobacco field disguised by the sunflowers planted throughout (more than two hundred of them), we even got to take a look at the collection of Karabiners in the bench next to the stove that looked so solid to the uninitiated. That's how good an introduction Jakob had given us. But we never did find out where he slept here. It wasn't a farmhouse anymore. Where the wings of a farmhouse would usually have open stalls for horses and cows and sheep and pigs, these had been partitioned off with walls between the roof beams, a carpenter had laid wooden floors over the beaten earth inside, and the stall hatches had been neatly enlarged into double-leaf casement windows, so now there were three nearly square rooms on either side of the hall and six doors opening onto the big dining table that reached almost from the front door to the kitchen. A sea breeze came in from the northeast, it smelled of warm clean wood everywhere, the walls were intact as well as the doors and the windows, as if the war hadn't passed through these parts. And Inge Schlegel wasn't nervous at all about being alone on the farm with one polite Doberman and two half-grown girls. The agricultural work all took place on the other side of the farm, in a brick building that looked like a factory only at first glance, before you noticed the moss-free thatched roof. Inside it, the ten-year-old Schütte-Lanz thresh-ing machine looked more like two years old, all oiled and polished; there was a smithy neat enough to be in a museum; the shelves in the storerooms were fully stocked with boxes, kegs, and other containers; the stalls smelled occupied and active; the pigs were running free in their wallow; and again the girls couldn't shake their sense of peace, a false sense, for all this couldn't be explained by the semicircle of forest ringing the farmstead to the east and toward the sea. That evening, with the return of the mowing machines and harvest wagons, they realized that the war had passed through here after all, and settled down to stay. The rooms along the hall, once apart-ments for workers and sometimes summer visitors, were now occupied by refugees. But these weren't like the refugees in Jerichow—they had come to Schlegel's farm with their eyes open, they didn't immediately lie down and wait for pity but wanted to earn their keep with work. Even though it was work on someone else's property, not on their own which they'd lost in the East, most of them had nonetheless been here for more than a year and few of them wanted to move on. Johnny Schlegel had laid down rules for his farm; newcomers were given a share of the profits according to how many horses they'd brought and how much work they'd done, the same as when he'd been starting out before the war, going by the books about land resettlement until the National Socialists had outlawed it. Still, except for the estates left behind by the local nobility who had fled, there was only one large farm like this in 1946—not even Kleineschulte had left anything comparable behind—and the girls from Jerichow remained mystified. Later, as time went on, they started to understand what was going on, but on that first night Johnny treated them differently. They were happy to keep their heads bent over their plates, for once not because they were hungry but because they were almost frightened of the man who would be their employer for the next few weeks—a little worried about where Jakob had sent them. They noticed that no one said prayers at this table. From fleeting glances they got the impression of an older man (he was fifty-eight) who had worked outside his whole life: one-armed, ridiculously tall (in the evenings he was six foot three), oxycephalic, bald (though a little tuft of curly blond hair had sat high atop his turret-shaped head for many years), an educated man because he sometimes raised a pair of fabulously tiny oval-lensed glasses to his eyes. While the rest of the group, all equals, chatted harmlessly across the table, especially with their children, Dr. Schlegel said nothing; he looked like he was grimly calculating things in his mind, and the girls from Jerichow were scared of him. Nor did they see a chair for Jakob. Then they heard Johnny's booming bass voice, without any throat clearing or other warning, and they nearly jumped out of their skins. Because he was talking about them, and by name. They almost stood up out of sheer obedience. They learned that they were the children of *my friend Cresspahl* and of Gustav Ohlerich, *a good man, from Wendisch Burch.* They were *good Meeklnburg chilren our Jååkob's entrusted to us.* They *long to uur farm now.* That was all. It transformed their tablemates' friendly looks into something like encouragement, and now they felt welcome. Inge Schlegel was still wearing her engagement ring from Alwin Paap, she probably had quite a lot she could say about Cresspahl, and about where he no longer was, and Johnny most definitely knew more than he said about how Hanna's parents had died. In spite of their relief, they still felt their wages of hundredweights of wheat were in danger, and they asked what their jobs would be. – *Jobs'll turn up*: Johnny said in an offhand way. What jobs? they shyly asked. Johnny'd imagined them as a kind of fire department maybe, or kitchen help when necessary, maybe pick some apples, churn some butter (nothing about tending geese). And didn't we protest together, practically as one, probably proud of our ages of thirteen and fourteen? We hadn't come here for a vacation! We'd come to do serious work in the harvest! We were instinctively of one mind, right?

Full work in a harvest. That's what we wanted? No mercy? Out to the fields we went. Johnny Schlegel's commune had wheat as far as the eye could see, fifty or sixty feet above sea level, gently rolling hills that at first we thought would make for a nice change. The previous summer we'd distributed the wheat sheaves across the whole field; here the latest science sent us to the edges, out of the dips, and we were constantly running, pursued by the magically returning machines and carrying sheaves not much smaller than ourselves. The days went by fast. Where we'd been the day before, the stubble was already being plowed over, deep for the seed and fertilizer drills, shallow for the sugar beets, because a day in July's worth as much as a week in August: as Johnny taught us on his frequent visits out to see if "Jakob's girls" were ready to give up. We would have been ashamed to look Jakob in the face if we gave up; what he'd brought back from Schlegel's farm were earnings, not presents. Sometimes Hanna was older than me—she said about the thirst: It's worse at sea. When the sheaf-binding harvesters had to be run without twine, those were bad days, because the straw rope didn't easily reach around the sheaves the machine could tie, and also because it was harder to tell when our work would be over. It gradually dawned on us that Schlegel might not have just cut some pages out of the land registry to save his nearly four hundred acres from confiscation; probably the Soviet officers from the Beckhorst farm had helped him out, the ones who often came by at dusk, greeted casually and without fear, like ordinary visitors. Maybe. But why was Johnny's missing arm inevitably the cause of such laughter, even from Johnny himself? We were equipped with pieces of truck tires that we tied onto our feet with gas-mask straps, as sandals, but still the ankle-high stubble found its way in, and at night Hanna would put balm and bandages on my feet, and I on hers. We dreamed gray and white and yellow, the massive clouds in the sky, the ears of wheat, the stubble, the firm sandy paths. Over breakfast there was a BBC program in which, again and again, the Austrian was made to scream out his thing about the last battalion on earth. We learned how to pack cartloads of wheat. Our skin hardened, much too slowly. Awns of wheat in our face continued to startle us. Grain is what the earth bears and everywhere in the world what's most important is called corn, *Korn*: maize in America, rye in Germany, wheat in France and Mecklenburg. *Triticum vulgare*: Johnny said. When the carts drove in, Hanna took the spot up on top of the wheat, I liked walking next to Jakob's sorrel and wanted the horse to recognize me. I meant it as affection when I took hold of the harness as if to lead him, but it was more like hanging on for support. When the thresher started up with its flapping belt it looked ingenious yet cruder than the simple trick nature might still have up her sleeve for exploiting the corn. The wheat. The other children spent the harvesttime in the orchard, or cleaning out the stables, or helping in the kitchen—Hanna and I were taught to operate the Schütte-Lanz. She was allowed to go onto the threshing floor before me, to cut the ropes around the sheaves and pass the wheat, fanned out in a flat sheet over her arm, to Mrs. von Alvensleben. The names on the farm were: Inge, Johnny, *Johnny sin Olsch* (his missus), Mr. Sünderhauf, Mrs. Sünderhauf, Mrs. von Alvensleben, Mr. Leutnant, Mrs. Lakenmacher, Mrs. Schurig, Mrs. Bliemeister, Mrs. Winse, Anne-Dörte, Jesus, Axel Ohr, Hen and Chickee, *the Englishmin*, Epi, and then the children under thirteen; there was an old strip of film in the drawer, but it was for a box camera, and that had been left behind in Jerichow and couldn't be fetched, so all but four of the faces are now forgotten. Anne-Dörte had stuck close to us out in the fields; back at the farm she pretended to be Johnny's goddaughter. We suspected her, if only vaguely, of having had something to do with our new clogs: newly carved, with an arched sole, padded with cloth under the leather, held together with real tacks and wire, they were hanging from our ladder one morning, and they fit, once our feet had healed up. Cresspahl's daughter reigned behind the threshing machine, leaning on the handle of a pitchfork, and every couple of minutes she would fork a load of the long straw onto a box wagon. If there was twine for the baler, though, the other children had to help out, the ones stationed by the chaff, the sack openings, the short straw. The whirling hum of the machine slowly peeled your brain away from the inside of your skull. Every hour Hanna and Gesine would trade places so that we could keep working, as a team. Anne-Dörte was nineteen and we'd never in our lives seen anyone so pretty—we would never be like that. The clogs couldn't be from her. Johnny crouched under the machine with us and taught us, there in the dark, the path that the precleaned wheat took through the bucket elevator. He was so pleased. When August 20 arrived he had actually done what he'd planned, forty double-centners of wheat had been driven off to the Soviet Beckhorst farm and he'd been given his receipts, bilingual, with stamps, and now the gentlemen there owed him twine and crude oil and a good reputation. When weren't Hanna and I together? We always sat together at the table, at the same places, a flask of barley coffee would be sent out to the fields for us and us alone, we were occasionally addressed as a single person, we slept next to each other in the hay in the apple loft above the living room. Of course we didn't tell each other everything. I was now sure that Cresspahl had slept like this, next to pears and apples arrayed on slats, at Schmoog's farm when *Our Little Granny* had died; I wasn't going to bring up relatives dying with Hanna. Though by this point she knew about her resemblance to Alexandra, and asked about her. Where Alexandra might be now, if. Whether Alexandra would've been strong enough to handle the wheat harvest, if. On other nights we would decide—shyly, cautiously—that some other adults might be exceptions. Mrs. von Alvensleben, definitely. Johnny, with reservations. Hanna would fall asleep with a great sigh, as if sinking down deep into something. Not a word about Anne-Dörte.

Yes, Jakob kept his promise and visited. Before long we could tell when he was near the farm: Anne-Dörte's chair would remain empty at dinner, and at around our bedtime she would reemerge from the woods and come into the hall, her hair more carefully combed than usual, in her one, gray knit dress. A few minutes more and there would be Jakob in the doorway, relaxed, cheerful, not like he'd just been walking for two hours. Maybe it was the wind off the sea that had tousled his hair like that. Then, before disappearing into the living room for his business with Johnny, he would talk to us. Have a little chat. Concern himself with the children. Like a legal guardian. He'd never promised us any more than that. We never followed Anne-Dörte, even though we'd see her on the footpath leading to the sea between the pines. Sometimes her hair would be wet when she came back, Jakob's too. Now we knew why we'd never found Jakob's bed. On the nights of Jakob's visits we would lie in the moonlight shining from over the sea, silently pretending to each other that we were asleep; neither of us would be woken by the other one's tears, and we were too tired to talk in our sleep.

That was also how we lay there the night of the rain that destroyed the rest of the harvest across the whole region. It was on August 27, 1946, and people said there'd never been a storm like it in living memory. The clouds poured down with a violence that Johnny decided to describe as tropical,

like the torrents of rain a little while ago, at 2:45 p.m., filling the space between the buildings on Third Avenue with such deep darkness. When brightness flashed up, the racing drops seemed sharp. New darkness, now accompanied by thunderclaps, made the riverbed of the street look wintry, the slick pavement full of reflected light from the shopwindows, like at night. The thick panes rattled under the blows of a normal New York rainstorm

and people were assigned only work that could be done indoors. A thick sack folded into a hood would be wringing wet after the fifty feet to the farm building. Not even the animals calmly endured what was darkening their stall doors for so long. There were places in the farmyard that looked like deep lakes. Johnny taught us the average August precipitation in the region: 2.6 inches. That evening he said he estimated there'd been 7.5 inches of rain that day alone. The forced inactivity, the creeping damp soon emptied the hall; we couldn't stick it out any longer with Johnny either and lay down on our tarps in the apple loft. The thatch roof crackled and smelled more and more like a crushing weight. It was already dark, because of night, but we couldn't close our eyes. Worse than during our dreary monotonous motions in the wheat, a single thought kept turning around and around in our heads, returning again unchanged every time: It was not our fate to be a countess like Anne-Dörte. But someday we too would be nineteen, with faces as lively as hers, with visible breasts, firm bodies, aware too of our legs—just not at the right time. It would be too late. In our cave under the pelting rain it was so quiet that maybe Hanna thought I was asleep. The empty blackness woke to her furious voice: I'm not a child anymore! It sounded determined, unrepentant, and I hated her, because she wasn't suffering enough under the calamity I'd thought was as huge for her as it was for me. Again she was older than me.

"When the young fellows talk to you don't you answer them and don't look at them and don't turn around. If they still won't stop then get rid of them nice and quick: Yes. No. Might be. Don't know. I see.

When a young fellow's peeled an apple or pear and wants to give it to you, just let it be, don't eat it.

When the young fellows sit next to you and want to talk to you and want to hold your hand, just pull your hand right back and stick it in your apron, and then if they won't stop turn your back on them and don't give them any answer at all.

Then when the young fellows bring some musicians in the night or act crazy some other way, like they'll probably do, and right outside your room too, say: You think I'm here for you? I don't think so. You don't look the type to me. Boys from next door are always the worst."

On the way back home, honorably discharged, thanked man-to-man, we couldn't believe our eyes. In the forest one of us always walked ahead of the other with her hand behind her back, ready to give the sign: Someone's coming (on the right or on the left); no one came, we thought we'd just been lucky. The people in the village, who'd always given Schlegel's people such grumpy answers or better yet none at all, looked angrily right past us as usual—but we saw an open farm gate, and a box on undamaged rubber wheels in the yard, with a long bar that you could attach to a jeep, it was new, in five hops we could have had it and been long gone. It was eerie seeing the gate open like that, unguarded. On the long walk down the shoreline cliffs, the wind from the sea hid the smell of the motorcycle that shot out of the Countess Woods and was right in front of us before we could even start running; the Red Army men drove right past us, not looking at us, looking mad, all officers, one huddling in the sidecar as if sick. We were positive we recognized the uniforms. We couldn't believe it. In Jerichow, though, by the time we got to the Rande road, the Germans were truly taking it too far. We saw a girl in a skirt and a white blouse, right there on the street, well within sight of the Soviets guarding the airfield; from a distance she looked a bit like Lise Wollenberg, who knew better. Then a woman passed us riding a bicycle in broad daylight, through this area, and she had an honest-to-God canister of milk hanging on the handlebars. Walking down Town Street we realized how many women there were in Jerichow now, because suddenly they were wearing dresses again, and we could see who was poor because they were still wearing pants. Bergie Quade walked by as we were scouting out Brickworks Road, and she had buttons open at her neck, her stocky arms were bare and immodest, and Bergie told us. We'd been in the country, we weren't up to speed on Jerichow. No! The Russians were gone.

But we saw some on the Rehberge too. Are the Swedes coming? Children. No. The Russians aren't allowed out anymore.

Like a kinda curfew?

No, seriously. Sokolovsky worked it out on his own with the party. "My dad is in the party / My mom is in the party . . ."

Marshal Sokolovsky? The commander in chief?

He's confined em all to barracks. They're living in their rooms. No more going out alone. Almost makes you feel sorry for em, locked up like that.

Is the commandant still here?

Yeah, not exactly, Gesine. But otherwise the last few days have been like living at peace.

Oh. Peace.

You two might wanna go pritty yourselfs up a little too. And they're going to be holding elections soon.

We're not pritty enough how we are?

You are. You both are. So its all working out. Everything in life comes in fits and starts

like when you're milking a bull.

What depraved little girls you've turned into!

Hanna promised us again that she'd stay. If Vassily Danilovič Sokolovsky could impose such order, then surely the next thing he'd do would be send Cresspahl back. Hanna could have her apprenticeship.

Meanwhile the Soviet Military Administration had increased the rationing. With our Card 5, Hanna and I could get three hundred grams of bread instead of a quarter pound. And we had our fat bags of wheat on top of that. We would definitely survive the winter.

Cresspahl's front door, previously sealed shut with the board of the protection order, now stood open late into the evenings. The Russians in the Kommandatura were ones we didn't know. This was apparently the third crowd since K. A. Pontiy.

– It's the Twins: Jakob said. We were sitting with his mother, telling her about the farm. We were back from a long trip. She'd kept us close to her while we talked, one arm around each of us, and she exclaimed in the pleading tone that she otherwise used to express disappointment at naughty children: Girls, what a sight you are! She was so quiet and hollow-eyed that she would have looked dead if she weren't moving. It felt totally and completely like Sunday evening in the house. We bragged about how much food we'd had and refused our dinner. Hanna politely asked who was looking out for Gesine's grandfather now that the Demwics Twins were in charge in Jerichow. Jakob, the psychologist, the appointed guardian, the expert on girls, let slip: Papenbrock's been . . . transferred. They've transferred him.

Hanna finished it for him: – Arrested. Gesine was more shocked, but merely blinked. This house was a magnet for danger. It wasn't safe here.

And she wasn't given time to reflect. On September 8, the NKVD worked on Sunday. The following people were hauled away from their breakfasts in Jerichow: Mrs. Ahlreep of Ahlreep's Clocks, Leslie Danzmann, Peter Wulff, Brüshaver, Kliefoth. The rumors that wouldn't stop going around Jerichow were quite sure that a carrier pigeon had been sighted over the town. By this point Hanna had lived in Jerichow long enough and was more inclined to notice that all these names had a connection to Cresspahl than to think that the Red Army had gotten worked up over some unsurrendered pigeons or a banned club. That evening the arrested people were released, to avoid attracting notice in their places of work. Rumor had already put them in Neubrandenburg concentration camp, to keep Papenbrock company; in fact they'd been held in the basement under Town Hall. All had been strictly sworn to silence. Having started with Leslie Danzman, Jakob wasted an hour—she lied from fear. Wulff, Kliefoth, and Brüshaver assured him: during their questioning, there'd been maybe two questions about Cresspahl. One poking into Cresspahl's service on the eastern front in 1917, the other trying to link him to a certain privy councilor in Malchow named Hähn. Kliefoth had heard that name only once before, in connection with some arms deal back in the early twenties.

Hanna thanked Jakob when he came back from Warnemünde, but only as if he'd done his job. (In our new mode, we only talked to this person in the most cursory way.) Her fishermen relatives had gotten into trouble with the Volkspolizei during the municipal elections. Apparently they'd already sent for Hanna. Hanna was to board the boat in Rande, so that her departure for the British zone wouldn't attract attention.

Jakob wasn't to bring her there. While Hanna said goodbye to him in the house, Gesine stood outside the door, not wanting to see how Hanna and Jakob were going to leave things. In Rande, Hanna didn't want to board Ilse Grossjohann's cutter alone. Around midnight we were at the spot known as de Huuk, 11° 7' East, 54° 2' 4" North. Later Gesine realized that Hanna had hugged her as she would a boy.

For days she could still feel in her arms the sensation of pushing Hanna onto the other boat. She also found it easy to think that Hanna should have stayed with her after all.

When Gesine came back to the empty bed at sunrise, she found Hanna's wooden clogs next to hers, all four placed neatly in a row.

June 4, 1968 Tuesday

This country now has more than three and a half million men in its armed forces, almost as many as it had in 1953 during the Korean War; today the voters in California will tell Robert F. Kennedy something preliminary about his suitability for the presidency; today's armed robbery happened at 71 West Thirty-Fifth Street; the citizens of Czechoslovakia, with the permission of the new Communists there, can now know officially as well that the great and good Antonín Novotný was dishonest about political activities not only in 1952 but also in 1954, 1955, 1957, and 1963;

the East German Communists have released a Columbia University art historian even though "forbidden" buildings may have ended up in front of his camera during his dissertation research on Berlin architecture, and without the Americans having to give anything in return. "You could say it was done with mirrors."

That was something that Cresspahl the certified translator, living in New York for the past seven years, had to go look up—just to make sure she wouldn't feel too at home in the language: "done with a trick." Nine months in jail and then returned to the outside world without a trial. Sleight of hand. Magic.

Cresspahl hadn't been in jail twenty months yet and he wanted a trial. Wherever things led, he had to get beyond waiting for nothing but the next day.

Through the wet March of 1946 he'd been busy, which at least felt like movement. The camp on the western border of Soviet Mecklenburg had been meant as a holding camp, but a prisoner was allowed to volunteer for work without risk of punishment. The commandant didn't thank you if you went through a barracks from floor to ceiling until it was waterproof and draftproof as a house, so the other German prisoners wouldn't have anything to hold against Cresspahl either. But meanwhile he had his skill to set him apart from the future prospects that made the others crazy with rumors, arguments, bragging. So if he wanted to keep such a facility in good shape it wasn't to get thanks in return. When he carved himself a birchwood spoon, why not carve another for his bunkmate—though he would have preferred to teach that intellectual's two left hands how to do it themselves. If a thank-you wasn't enough, he might accept two pinches of tobacco, but he didn't let himself get talked into manufacture or trade. And since he divulged almost nothing beyond his name and, more or less, Jerichow, he thought he was simply being ignored in his bunkhouse, at best tolerated. Then, without warning, a sentry came to take him to the guardroom; he didn't get back until around midnight, and found that not a few people had waited up for him. This was a story he could tell. A wooden trunk was sitting in front of the commandant—Cresspahl had made several. This one had been confiscated direct from the woodshop, not yet bearing the initials of the person who'd ordered it. When challenged he confessed to having built this item of evidence. Questioned over its false bottom, he misunderstood even the second translation before finally admitting the possibility. Then came the order. It earned Cresspahl more sympathy than suspicion from his fellow prisoners—commiseration for forced labor. He spent almost a month over the birthday present for the commandant's granddaughter: a little chest eight inches high with three divided drawers, a rolltop, a wooden bolt, and, at your command sir, a secret compartment. This thorny assignment had, for once, let him think about something different, his own children: how he would someday build them an even more ingenious miniature dresser, and with real tools. His fee was two packets of Krüll, which he shared with anyone who asked—he knew all about how to act in the slammer by that point. But he needn't have bothered. The others had started acting like good neighbors; they were more worked up about the lower ranks of their guards ordering trunks too, for what could that mean if not that the Russians would be leaving soon, possibly as early as next week? Cresspahl, though, had to produce even more such containers for Germans, for their trips back to Röbel or Lauenburg, and so was protected from the masses' preposterous spiritual crises. He had been told: You, wait. That's how he managed.

He did not end up spending the winter in the barracks from which, despite the nearby Elde River, he'd hoped for some warmth at least in the morning hours. Starting in December 1946, he was kept beneath a solid house that he imagined was the arsenal in Schwerin. The basement was damp, but not from Pastor's Pond. His task was to write his life story again. He didn't produce much, for if running water froze in the cell overnight how were his fingers supposed to relearn how to manage a pencil? Also, the light from the yard, chopped into gray pieces by a grate in the ground overhead, made him go somewhat blind again. The first version of his second autobiography came out in basically tabular form, and so he was severely beaten; he counted himself lucky that the blows hardly ever broke his skin. He'd survived and starved too long on soup to trust his body to heal open wounds. He grasped that his invisible masters were interested in a complete delivery, not a quick one; and thus he was deprived of his childhood years. Born in 1888, son of the wheelwright Heinrich Cresspahl and his wife, Berta née Niemann, a day laborer's daughter, I was apprenticed to master carpenter Redebrecht in Malchow, Mecklenburg, in 1900, at Easter. They were all dead but there might still be some von Haases, whom Cresspahl remembered not only from when he was a five-year-old shepherd boy but from when he was a thirty-one-year-old member of the Waren Workers Council who'd dug up weapons on their family estate to be used in the agriculturalist Wolfgang Kapp's putsch. He knew all too well how that family treated sick estate laborers, even before his mother's death. He was very glad to have such people chased out of Mecklenburg to the other side of the Elbe, even if it went against the grain for him to denounce them personally. This produced such gaps in his chronological account that he got blows in the kidneys from a rifle butt when a year was graded as Poor in the interrogation room, in the neck if it came out Unsatisfactory. The young guys working for the MGB knew the approximate extent of treatment requested but not the daily reason for it, so in the underground corridors they seemed to be merely urging their charges on. They hardly ever seemed to care too passionately. No hatred was required to keep a prisoner awake, the truck engines making music outside in the yard during the interrogations took care of that, and for four nights straight a circular saw too. During the days he had to continue work on his writing assignment. Cresspahl earned himself a lonely week by taking the genealogical aspect of the question a little too seriously and detouring to his grandparents and the years after 1875. Solitary seemed fair. He was free to choose, after all. His new superiors, the expert from *Kontrrazvedka* and the auditor from the SMT, had handed him an analysis of his class position and his personal role in the wrong turns of world history, *i*'s dotted and *t*'s crossed, and it was his choice not to sign it. He didn't resist out of stubbornness, since he must have been wanting to go back home to his girls. It couldn't have been solely in service of the truth, since he was soon describing himself as a man who had been in this world for fifty-eight years and had never once made deals or spoken or cooperated with anyone. Possibly he was trying to come clean with the New Justice only to the extent that he could keep others out of it. Sometimes the men evaluating his learning process put an idea or two into his head, for instance an essay on the year 1922, and the name Hähn, privy councilor and arms dealer. Whenever the pupil failed a lesson he could almost perfectly picture the beating he'd be getting the next morning at daybreak, but even so he would sometimes escape from his life into blithe carefree daydreams of a different one, which could equally really have been his: not parting from Gesine Redebrecht in 1904, spending a while with her, with Mrs. Trowbridge starting in 1930, in Bristol, consistently avoiding Richmond, with a thirteen-year-old son Henry, or killed with them both by a bomb, being with Mina Goudelier starting in 1920, but not for long on Kostverlorenvaart behind the Great Market in Amsterdam, better on the Fella River, in Chiusaforte, where he could have not only learned fine inlay work but practiced it too, no not there, not where the Germans would occupy, so ... Australia, if Goudelier's daughter would have gone that far with him, across other seas than Papenbrock's Lisbeth, who in this case would have survived November 1938, or else with all four women together, remembering other High Streets, lakeshores, Broadways, sunrises, picnics in the grass. He didn't take it personally that he was marginal to those lazily unspooling pictures, or hardly present at all. But when the Red Army gave him a pill it was nothing but aspirin. These didn't have to be dreams. Nor did his conscience bother him at being confined with food and lodging and a job he had a very poor understanding of while all around the prison people were helping each other get back to normal life through hard work (that was how he imagined it). Responsibility for his actions had been handed to the Ministerstvo Gosudarstvennoy Bezopasnosti, let

them answer for his useless sitting around. With such abundant encouragement he had, by January 1947, written his way through his military service
in Güstrow (which his idiot daughter never asked about), in February to his
touchy feud with the SPD (and his idiot daughter thought she'd hold off
on her questions), which added up to 260 pages of his life story but still
only two pages typed up and signed, the first version. He persisted in
considering himself his judges' partner, known by name and number,
possessing the right to a trial and verdict, moving along a more or less
agreed-on path, not only moving in time. In late February they canceled
the agreement. He was ordered to report "with all his belongings" for
transport.

"Belongings" were something he'd not had since his last move, and he
joined the group in the barracks yard like someone just out for an evening
stroll. The transport was on foot, in columns of unkempt men who'd been
arrested just days before and carried out their guards' orders with downright
Prussian ceremony. They took the doddering old man along out of curiosity,
holding his arm as he groggily put one foot in front of the other, but they
soon gave up on him, since all he could say when asked about his "case"
was: I-I d-d-unno... He spoke haltingly, his sentences broke apart, there
seemed to be something the matter with his throat too. – 'm fittyeight! he
said, maybe because they'd called him Grandpa, but really more to himself,
and they all chipped in to give the strange ragtag fellow a cigarette. It was
his first tobacco in eleven weeks, it made him feel like his Australian dreams
did, to the point where he later wasn't sure that their march hadn't actually
started in Schwerin. Anyway his eyes weren't working too well either. Near
Rabensteinfeld he realized which way they were moving, and when they
reached various crossroads and the others cursed at their steadily eastward
direction he thought the whole thing might be for his benefit. For the way
through Crivitz should have reminded him of something, maybe a promise,
he couldn't put his finger on it. At Mestlin there was something else he
needed to think of, it nagged at him for the next six miles, then he remembered:
the turnoff to Sternberg and Wismar and Jerichow, so now he'd missed it.
Past Karow it was distressing not to see the rails that should have been off
to the left of the road, it was like he was going the wrong way. He reluctantly
believed it when he caught sight of Old Schwerin—something was missing
at the train station, Krebs Lake confused him, but finally he saw the compass

rose on the vane-less old windmill outside of town and stopped resisting: they were giving him one more look at Malchow. Only it was all high, high above him. Knowingly in disguise, as in a dream, he stepped back into the summer of 1904, with wavering songs from the lakeside boulevard wafting over the water of a Friday evening, he walked into the children's playground for the fair that lasted the whole next day, the Parchim dragoon band was playing, wearing their colorful fairy-tale uniforms, and three horsemen rode out through the town gate, and right in the middle of the leisurely crowd of the dead stood a young man with the master's daughter between Linden Alley and the big canvas tents, seen by all, discovered by no one, *Oh you're my darling but you've got no money, no clogs, no shoes,* in 1920 the workers seized the town of Waren and Baron Stephan le Fort of Boek shelled Town Hall with a cannon and the Strikers Council delegates couldn't get any farther with the people of Malchow, *those fellows're shootin at us now,* and a forester on a count's estate who'd refused to supply the estate owners with wagons for collecting wood and tried to bamboozle them was the only one to be driven out of his house. *Never hit man nor beast with a stick stripped of bark, whenever you do they're bound to die.* And that was Olden Malchow on the island, it was, the Gierathschen water between the island and the new town lined with lawns and landings and gables, Mill Hill—the one small bit of the mainland that hadn't let churches on—a storm a hundred fifty years ago'd helped—the subterranean folk needed somewhere for their Midsummers. A hole had been blasted in the embankment on the other side and sloppily filled in like the soil there couldn't bear it anymore, you could just about swim over to Wenches Hill, the old Wendish castle mound that a six-year-old had herded geese past, nowadays the subterranean folk were invisible when they walked out on Laschendorf farm in the daytime but a shepherd had once heard them cry *Give a hat, give a hat!* and he called for his hat and put it on and saw them standing in front of him, *Teeny little men with their three-corner hats, they jumped at him and scratched his eyes out and took his magic cap. The little folk in Wenches Hill made such lovely music, they say.*

Here lies Fünfeichen, the sanatorium! A long, brown, rectilinear building with its barracks and guardhouse, set in a spacious barren field abundantly equipped with muddy wooden walkways, barbed-wire passages, and squat watchtowers; behind its tar-paper roofs the mountains of Lindental and

Tollense Lake tower heavenwards—evergreen, massy, cleft with wooded ravines—and prominent signs on the fence inform the nature lover in Russian and German and English: OFF-LIMITS. ENTRY FORBIDDEN. VIOLATORS WILL BE SHOT!

Now as then the Red Army directs the establishment. Dressed in a belted tunic studded with medals and hanging far down over his baggy breeches, his head held high under the clay-colored cap, automatic rifle at the ready, the soldier herds the prisoner across the camp road; he is a man whom knowledge has hardened, holding his patients in his spell in his curt, reserved, preoccupied way, in amused amazement: all those individuals who, too weak to give and to follow laws unto themselves, put themselves into his hands, body and mind, that his severity may be a shield unto them.

It took till early summer for Cresspahl to come to; he was furiously intent on concealing this. In all seriousness he considered himself mushy, gamey, plucked out of the world and set to one side somewhere else.

For one thing, he couldn't find in his memory how he might have gotten from Malchow Abbey to Fünfeichen. He knew the Red Army from the first postwar autumn—they would have shot him on Wenches Hill if he'd slipped and fallen. He could hardly believe that the people in the transport—strangers—would have dragged him to Waren, Penzlin, Tollense Lake. He'd woken up on a lower bunk in Fünfeichen Camp without any idea how he'd gotten there, as if from nowhere, too weak to eat and too tired to open his eyes and weary of life. For another thing, he kept hearing talk of Neubrandenburg Camp in the tightly packed barracks. But this was Fünfeichen, two and a half miles from the Stargard Gate—as recently as 1944 the British had told him to take a look around this area, both at the Trollenhagen air base and at how the Germans were treating their prisoners of war at Fünfeichen. If he could believe his eyes he was in Fünfeichen's old south camp, barrack 9S or 10S, next to the barbed wire around the vegetable garden, facing Burg Stargard, and the fenced-in compound of rooms and workshops lay to the north just as it had in his old drawing. He couldn't be this wrong, could he? Why did everyone else think this was Neubrandenburg, and only he thought Fünfeichen? For a third thing, why, even now, could he not stop hoping for a trial, to get closure? Ending up here was his closure.

He tried to find the prisoners he'd come from Rabensteinfeld with. He barely knew any of their faces, and it's hard to find someone out of twelve thousand. The workforce was herded out of the barracks only when the camp command's Operations group and the German kapos working for them turned up to search the bunks. From this last piece of his past he found no one, for they'd all had more of their journey ahead of them, while he'd been parked here, disposed of for good. The kapos not only rummaged through the rags when they searched the bunks, they tipped over the bedframes too; the prisoners argued for hours about confiscated or mistakenly switched property. Cresspahl just watched. When the soup was doled out he had to wait until someone shoved him their own bowl, contemptuously, like he was a sick dog, and by that time the tureen was often empty, and still he had to pay for the loan of the bowl by washing it. He would have had his own dish soon enough, except that you also had to pay for permission to work. What he had on his body no longer fell into the category of barterable goods. He volunteered at once when the German kapos needed replacements for latrine duty; he had to march in goose step for ten yards in front of well-nourished representatives of the Soviets, barking in snappy military fashion: I am an old Nazi pig and I want to carry shit! He didn't get the job though. He tried to look on the bright side—he'd been spared the stink—but soon realized that the other prisoners tended to move away from him, despite there not being much room to move, because he stank. He had lain too long in his own filth, unconscious or asleep or whatever it was. And now he was defenseless against fleas and lice. Hot water had a price, too, he could have paid it by informing on his bunkmates but he had no information. The kapos fetched him from the barracks at night and handed him over to the Soviets for leaving the barracks at night. He'd expected solitary but was only penned up closer to the others than he'd been in the barracks, except now in the dark, and with no food. Because a scarecrow's clothes were in better shape than his, a kapo reported him (for neglecting his appearance) to the Soviets, from whom he was instantly told to take five steps back. In the clothesroom the kapos had no witnesses and were free to torment him with beatings until he recited what they wanted: As an old Nazi piece of shit / I walk on a cripple's stave / My pants are full of shit / As I head for a shitty grave. The German personnel also had in mind that they were allowed to hand out clothes only from dead men. But he kept his old shirt and managed to wash the caked pus from the new one and after the third washing he could trade it for the bottom half of a fish can, rusty but with no holes. When the kapos went after a prisoner the others moved aside, uneasily, but it still looked cooperative, as if wanting to let the beaters move comfortably. Whatever he was supposed to learn from the whole process, Cresspahl probably got it wrong.

So many Mecklenburgers (though hardly any among the kapos), and it was so easy to set them against one another. Was that supposed to be the lesson? The kapos paid in bread, in half cigarettes, and very rarely with a job in the barbershop team: that was enough to break up any solidarity. Cresspahl saw one man (he refused to name him) that the others harassed just to pass the time, or because his scared, weepy carrying-on invited it. They won his confidence with wild stories from the eastern front and appeals to his comradeship, proved their friendship with gifts of soup and promises of a pipeful of tobacco, until finally he trusted them, made them promise not to tell, and told them about his background, being given leave to play the violin at Reich Governor Hildebrandt's state dinners and other occasions; before long the kapos were making him reenact his ceremonial postures and way of walking, the way you train an animal. Then he did cry, out of exhaustion or lost pride, but his pals didn't let him run off into the electrified outer fence, they gloomily kept an eye on him, hardly out of guilt or shame but because the Operations Detachment knew all about such deaths and took out their inconvenience on anyone involved in them. The men seemed relieved when the Soviets took their violinist away like a rabid beast; would they have been right if this had gotten them released? Not a single rumor involving release went around. Cresspahl listened in on one of the banned cultural discussion groups, this one about the Hague Convention with respect to War on Land and the illegal incarceration of civilians in a prisoner-of-war camp; he kept close to the speaker until the speaker's arrest, to avoid any suspicion of having denounced him; he refrained from commenting that Fünfeichen had been a Soviet "special camp" since 1945 under international law. One seventeen-year-old deserter, "also here by mistake," had confronted his elders, somewhat vehemently, over their shooting of hostages in the Soviet Union; they'd beaten him up for it that night and accidentally strangled him. An orderly who'd studied medicine for three years lectured on the soggy camp bread's actual caloric content vis-à-vis the calories in the camp administration's calculations, arriving at the absolutely unintended conclusion that the Soviets must have adopted SS concentration camp calorie charts; this was a student for whom no time of day was too early or too late to clean out a prisoner's festering sore or give him medical advice, they all listened to him talk, a single word would have been enough to save him from the insulator prisons, and Cresspahl too said nothing. What kind of virtues had he renounced? Or were these new ones? In March new people were still being brought in who didn't grasp the distance between civilian life and camp life; they blithely rattled off their slogans from Socialist Unity Party election posters, with which they'd opposed the lower allocation of paper to the bourgeois parties, and before you could blink they were in lockup and they wouldn't be coming back out. This process was referred to as "moving on," a kind of substitute for dying. Cresspahl's thoughts kept running in circles around the news that the Soviets couldn't get by without elections, and that paper was used for such things. One new admit called it a war crime that the Soviets had fired on the city of Neubrandenburg until it went up in flames, leaving the whole area ringed by the old walls cleaned out except for Great Woolweavers' Street, then he moved on; Cresspahl said nothing about the city's refusal to surrender and tried to mentally sketch out the wiped-out town hall, a cute little boxy building with a ridge turret perched up in the middle of the roof, *built like it'd been plucked out of a box of Christmas toys many long years ago and set right down in the fore-city of Neubrandenburg's marketplace for the magistrate and townspeople to play with a little.* Now admittedly he'd grown stupid from exhaustion, from sitting in the stench and chatter of the barracks day in and day out; he might be confused, seeing as his thoughts so often slipped right past the others'; can he really have failed to notice that he'd just lost heart? that he no longer did anything from the heart? So how did he act when a new guy was brought to the barracks; only yesterday he'd been sitting down to dinner at his own table in Penzlin and now he was being shoved from bunk to bunk before finding a place on the drafty floor—why did Cresspahl let him discover all by himself that he was in prison, that he would never ever be able to get word to his family, that this rotten dishwater was the very best that morning soup could be, and that the path through the hospital led not to comfort but to a filthy and miserable death? He knew what help the man needed; he hadn't been given it himself. Was it indifference? What had he chosen to do?

He occasionally did something for friends. In August 1947 Heinz Mootsaak appeared in the barracks door, in pants and shirtsleeves as if brought in straight from the fields. He looked completely idiotic—after the silence between the barbed-wire fences and the wooden shacks he probably hadn't expected such a loud group in such close quarters; he was still the shy country boy who's polite when he enters a room full of other people. For him Cresspahl stood up and turned his back on him, not to betray mutual recognition, but so that they could meet later on by chance without arousing suspicion. Here he miscalculated, exaggerated. Heinz Mootsaak hadn't had the slightest idea who that decrepit bag of bones in tattered rags of mismatched uniforms might be, and by the next morning he'd already moved on to lockup.

In October—it was already pretty cold—Cresspahl was drawn into an escape scenario by two prisoners who may have taken his new concept of sociability the wrong way. They could hardly recruit him as a full partner; they were acting charitably. The old Cresspahl wouldn't have hesitated for a second, he'd have answered clear as day with the look on his face and said out loud just for the record: *Nonsense. Don't be idiots.* The one from 1947 did hesitate, to keep up good relations, and then answered helpfully with a Mecklenburg saying: *The nobility wont stand for that.* He evaded by asking for time to think it over and that was enough to catch him. Meanwhile it had gotten around the room that the glum old sourpuss had finally nibbled the bait, or else that a new trio was up to something. There was positively nothing to deliberate about in the plan. It would take months to pry three adjacent floorboards loose and reattach them so that no accidental footstep would make them pop up and yet so that they could be taken up within a few minutes during the night. They wanted to go under barracks 10S and 11S to the south edge of the camp, then right along the wire and past the middle watchtower, then under the whole length of 18S to the inner ring of barbed wire, under that to the auxiliary power unit, where they'd turn off the power and finally force their way out over the last fence, more or less exactly toward the Soviet staff barracks, behind which ran a road. One of them said he was an electrician. He tried to talk them out of it, out of neither pity nor concern, he just didn't want to be responsible for anything. He mentioned the Soviet guards' swivel-mounted searchlights, the quarter mile of crawling and tunneling in a single night, the open space for miles around. To be polite he at least praised the escape route for leading away from the kilometer-long eastern edge of the camp. He warned them of armed patrols in the Forst Rowa woods, the waterlogged fields of Nonnenhof, the Red Army's large off-limit areas north of Neustrelitz. One of the men pretended to be insulted, maybe he'd been the one who'd come up with the plan. They both thanked him, loud enough to be heard three bunks away, extra noticeable after all the whispering.

After the second twenty-four hours had passed Cresspahl thought he was out of danger—that's how long it took for him to be brought before the Soviet administration. At the staff barracks a signed and sworn statement was sitting on the desk: Prisoner C., Incitement to escape, Unscrupulous plot against Soviet People's property, Slanderous comparison between Red Army and feudal aristocratic caste. Supplemental attachments: sketches of the south camp and the escape route continuation via Nonnenhof and the Lieps Canal, reconstructed on the basis of the accused's suggestions. Cresspahl now enjoyed another opportunity to appreciate the Soviets more than the German kapos. The Soviets' Operations Detachment went unarmed down the camp road or into the barracks; they ordered no punishments worse than standing at attention for up to three hours, and if one of them did lash out it was clearly out of a desperation that had once been good-naturedness, which could now no longer put up with a prisoner's doing whatever it was he was now doing wrong. The worse punishment was the German camp officials accentuating their interrogations by keeping sausage and bread within the prisoner's reach, pouring coffee into cups before his eyes, ersatz coffee but hot, and with milk; the Soviets treated their interrogation rooms as offices. And it was true, they didn't beat him. For the Mecklenburg saying about the nobility he had to stand against the stove for an hour and a half, spine pushed back by it, hands firmly on imaginary pants seams. When, even after that, he could only explain the defamatory phrase in terms of the nobility's dominance in the 1896 Mecklenburg-Schwerin parliament and the remoteness of the Malchow railway station, the gentlemen presented him with a statement to sign. In it he was permitted to deny every accusation except for that first and last conversation, which had been seen by too many people, and he signed. By this point, around four in the morning, the officers were in a convivial mood, though not without contempt for this wreck of a human being. They thanked him for his love of the truth, regretted disturbing his night's rest, expressed the hope that he might fall back asleep soon. Then they handed him over to the German kapos.

The kapos held him in a detention cell in the north camp until noon the following day, taking turns in groups of four, using whips. Can someone refuse to speak simply because he's decided he doesn't want to speak? How can he know for sure that even shortly after losing consciousness he's kept silent? Did his lapse warrant them hurting him so badly right away that there was nothing he had to care about anymore but the pain? Can someone refuse to speak a word to others just because he doesn't understand them?

When the Soviets had had ample time to observe what Germans are capable of doing to one another, they ordered an end to the questioning. The last shift of kapos resented having to drag the copiously bleeding heap across the camp road themselves. The Soviets didn't let the regular prisoners help, but they did let them watch. They needed the kapos as sturdy hunting dogs, not gone soft or anything from being liked. Since the Russian guards supervised the whole transport, Cresspahl was laid almost gently on a bunk in the barbers' quarters in the north camp.

The wounds took until the following summer to heal; he could walk by early December. At which point he started all over again: food dish, hot water, foot wraps. He was immediately known among the north camp inmates as a crazy man, for when asked why he'd told the kapos nothing he actually had an answer, and it sounded credibly deranged:

– *Ididn likem*: he said. He hadn't liked them.

They tried again around Christmas and offered him a job in the burial squad,

> a chance
> to demonstrate
> a change of heart and
> atonement as well as
> the forgiveness
> of the community

with additional rations and a change of clothing. Since it was work, which involved physical movement, the prospect nagged at him. Why shouldn't he be able to do what other people could do? The bodies looked bloated, they no longer weighed much. Most often there were only a few to pick up each week, always two bearers per stretcher. It came down to the fact that he'd survive the day when they had to clear out the corpses from the storage cellar and lug them onto the truck; he'd have time to recover during the drive to the cemetery on the Fuchsberg. He didn't dread the task of undressing the bodies before dumping them into the mass graves, if anything he doubted he'd be able to dig the graves, at first. He didn't want to do it for the dead, nor to get a couple of extra potatoes in his soup, nor to survive—he wanted to have something to do. Some career military men who had appointed themselves the illegal German leadership of the camp around that time talked him out of accepting, making mild threats. They couldn't rely on him to remember the correct numbers, and for a while they firmly held on to him in the back row during roll call until the kapos gave up. The job went to a prisoner considered worthier of the extra rations and the drives outside the camp, and who wanted to be transferred to Sachsenhausen just because it was closer to Berlin. For the men in the burial squads were suspected of keeping count, and so were often replaced or sent off to other camps, that way the lists of the dead could only be put together out of approximate fragments. The number for Fünfeichen was 8,500, not always documented by names. And so Cresspahl lost a chance to escape before he even knew it, the kapos didn't get him out of the camp and still had to remove the two conspirators from the old bunkhouse; Cresspahl was compensated with a month's priority in getting a shave and owed thanks to nobody. Was this one of the things he was supposed to learn?

It had been a long time since he'd even thought about escape. He'd seen one though. The march to Fünfeichen had passed through the town of Goldberg, and as the column rounded a corner one of the prisoners stepped out of it onto the sidewalk, grabbed a thoroughly startled housewife by the elbow, and made her keep walking with him, loudly marveling at their reunion: – Elli, my goodness! he cried in excitement. The scene had apparently looked plausible enough for the Soviet guards; as they left town they replaced the runaway with a civilian who happened to be digging in his garden. For a while Cresspahl had held on to this example of Red Army principles of order, as something to tell Gesine; then the yarn had been told a few too many times in Fünfeichen and the gardener ended up getting shot for his unreasonably horrified reaction two miles past Goldberg, or else he was still in N22 today without any idea, sometimes the woman was named Herta and sometimes the man leaving the column had shouted: Hey, Aunt Frieda! Eventually Cresspahl himself doubted he'd ever seen it happen.

Flight, revolt, liberation—he was no longer susceptible to these things. The piece of land near Ratzeburg that the Soviets had traded to the British had grown in the Fünfeichen rumors to the whole strip west of a line from Dassow through Schönberg to Schaal Lake, and if American paratroopers weren't expected outside the Fünfeichen gates the next day then it would at least be the Red Cross from Sweden. Cresspahl recognized in others the feverish, frenzied effects of latrine gossip and feared them for himself, for he was in such a state often enough already, when his thoughts ran at such an unnerving distance from the talk around him. He had never read the warning sign on the camp fence from the front but he was perfectly certain that Western military commissions, even in Burg Stargard and Neubrandenburg, were being kept at a distance by multilingual prohibitions. He couldn't understand what the other prisoners expected from their former enemies. The camp workforce was shoveled in and out so regularly that informers were not immediately detected, however thickly larded with them the barracks were—any plot with more than one person involved was as good as blown. For himself he couldn't even envision an escape. Once he'd made it to the other shore of Tollense Lake he might be able to get to the fabled new border of Mecklenburg in nine days, but the Soviets would be waiting for him where he'd need to go to fetch the children, and as soon as his escape became known they'd arrest them. That meant he was less separated from them in Fünfeichen. And anyway escape from Fünfeichen was impossible.

Fünfeichen had become the world. Life outside the camp never entered it.

There were a few possible changes. These were: Deportation to the Mühlberg, Buchenwald, Sachsenhausen, or Bautzen concentration camps, all well known from new arrivals' reports. These were eternities like Fünfeichen—time did not pass there. You could also decide to die, voluntarily by starvation, voluntarily at the fence.

Fünfeichen offered any number of ontologies.

Still, Cresspahl would have preferred a trial and sentence.

– Where *were* you, Marie? Tell me where you were!

– It's a quarter to six p.m. and I'm here at home. Those are your rules.

– Where were you all day?

– What about you, Mrs. Cresspahl, you're not home a minute earlier than usual either.

– Should I have come home? Is that an accusation?

– You have a job, you're not allowed to leave work. Maybe if it's raining, or if there's a subway strike, but not for private matters.

– Marie. How did you hear?

– In the park.

– That's not your usual walk to school.

– Okay.

– We'd agreed—

– on West End Avenue. Like the police are lining the streets there! People have come up and talked to me there, again and again. I can take care of myself in Riverside Park too, on bright sunny mornings. I'm not a child anymore, Gesine!

– You're not understanding me.

– I'm *not* understanding you!

– When I got to Broadway they were sold out of *The New York Times*.

– I went to school through the park because on Wednesdays I have first-period gym. At the playground. In Riverside Park, on the corner of 107th Street and—

– Right.

– When I left for school it was like I was wearing an invisibility cloak. Eagle-Eye Robinson was up and about on the stairs with his back to me. The elevator door was open, Esmeralda's swanky purse was on the stool, totally unguarded, she was nowhere in sight. No neighbors, no bus drivers on the street. So the news would hit me without warning. There was a guy sitting on the bench by the memorial fountain for the firemen, all alone.

Young guy, nineteen. Not a college student, more like an off-duty shift worker. Baseball sweatshirt, long pants, thick white wool socks, not a tourist. Crew cut. He was leaning back on the bench, all comfortable, arms stretched out, not a care in the world. Radio next to him, steamer trunk, flustered voices. That's where I heard. Kennedy'd been killed.

– *Angeschossen*, not *erschossen*, Marie. *Erschossen* is more final than "shot."

– It's because I have to talk your damn German with you! *He was shot. He wasn't dead.*

– You don't have to use German if you don't want to.

– The guy was sitting there doing nothing, so relaxed, nothing to do, he was perfectly happy to let me listen without looking at me. Like everything had gone as planned. Like he was glad.

– What did you know at that point?

– The senator from New York had won the California primary. He was giving a victory speech at the Hotel Ambassador in Los Angeles. On the way to the press conference, in a kitchen corridor, he was shot in the head from behind. 1:17 California daylight saving time. When it was quarter past three here. I know, I know, you say *viertel fünf* in German, not *viertel vier*! He was lying on the ground, his wife kneeling by his side. The thing with the rosary. The last rites. Unconscious in the hospital. Then again, from the top: Robert Francis Kennedy, the senator from New York—

– You could tell in the subway that something had happened, but maybe not. Maybe the reason everyone was so gloomy, not looking at anyone, not saying anything, was because it was the hottest day of the year we've had so far. There wasn't necessarily anything worse going on than the usual tragedy that life sometimes is for some New Yorkers. Then, at Grand Central, I saw a TV in a window, something filling the screen, nothing from the loudspeakers. There was just one word on the screen the whole time, crooked, like it was written in dust with a finger: *Shame.*

– *Schande* in German, "a scandal"?

– Also that they felt shame.

– Yes.

– I tried calling the school as soon as I got to the bank.

– Gesine, would you have gone to school on a day like this?

– You'll get your note for Sister Magdalena.

– For tomorrow too.

– Do you want the rest of the week off?

– You're not a bad mother, Gesine.

– Am too. I was probably being ridiculous. I thought I had to talk to you.

– You were right, you did. I needed to talk to you. First I got super mad at the bank, for not allowing private phone calls, then at you because you follow their rules. Now I feel better. You tried.

– I tried calling home too.

– I was already in Times Square. There were so many people there, craning their necks, reading the line of news running around the building. Whenever anyone left he pushed his way out past the others, so depressed, so angry. One time I was almost knocked off my feet.

– You know, I saw so much politeness underneath Times Square that it must have thrown everything off schedule. A young black man, black leather jacket, Afro, wanted to let a fat white accountant go first. – After you, go ahead! he said to the befuddled white, who was expecting to be cursed at. – *After you, brother*: the black man said. In the subway! "Brother"!

– I didn't see any of that. In Central Park the middle class were out playing holiday. I heard: nice weather, Tonya's varicose veins she's so young!, summer clearance sale at Macy's, the intrigues on New York's baseball teams. It was the same on Broadway. Music playing in the supermarket like any other day. My cashier was griping about the customers without small change.

– I'd have been mad too.

– I was mad at you, Gesine! Because you told me that this was normal for America—John F. Kennedy, Martin Luther King—and now you were right again. Robert Francis Kennedy.

– The Ferwalters didn't know where you were either.

– I was walking around, alone in the city.

– Buying newspapers, one after the other.

– Not as classy as you, though. I also got New York's Picture Newspaper, *The Daily News.*

– Can I give you the money for them?

– I used my pocket money. Pocket money's for personal needs, right?

– I didn't stay in the bank at lunch, I went across the street. Two more times in the afternoon. I kept going downstairs, I was sure you were standing outside the building, waiting.

– I was!

– Mrs. Lazar just looks so strict, doesn't she. That doesn't work with children. She'd have brought you upstairs to me.

– I wasn't embarrassed! I was mad at you, because you'd expect me to do that too! I spent ten minutes admiring your beautiful lobby and then I left, so that you and your ideas wouldn't get me.

– Ideas about myself?

– Ideas about yourself! Who can possibly console me except Mother! And that I needed consoling at all! What if I wanted to be alone? As if you know me inside and out!

– I don't even know what you've decided on for dinner.

– Nothing! Not for me. There's a T-bone steak for you. And green beans.

– I'm not hungry.

– Gesine, you've been working, you need to eat. Tomorrow you need to go back to the bank. Eat. Or can you stay home tomorrow?

– I have to go to work.

In the end there wasn't much left standing of that knowledge inside and out. Where Mother wanted to make up, Marie wanted a deal. She showed signs of strain, the same as when she has to make herself speak nice about purchases, or doing the dishes; she would have been happy to go off into her room behind the curtained double doors. But she needed her mother for one more thing. She listened for the clicking of the elevator cable and was standing at the door at the first ring or the bell. And what were two furniture movers bringing this late at night into the Cresspahl apartment, which for seven years had been immunized against American television? What now overrode all educational, economic, and maternal considerations? The muscular men rolled a TV set over the threshold, and a mother was needed to sign the rental contract. Marie had the TV moved to her room and paid the $19.50 herself. Pocket money is for personal needs.

She must be embarrassed at having broken another agreement—she makes a point of turning the volume down whenever the ads interrupt the news. It'll be a long time before she believes me when I tell her that her love for a politician is starting to look from the outside a lot like how I fall in love.

"Marie H. Cresspahl, Class 6B
Teacher: Sister Magdalena
Subject: Science? History? Social Studies?

Preliminary Notes for Optional Essay
                    ROBERT FRANCIS KENNEDY
Outline? Later as Table of Contents

Biography
1925 born November 20. Father a banker, shipping executive, speculator. 1 million for each child. Isolationist.
      Education: Catholic, in Rhode Island. Private prep school near Boston. Classmates' impression: K bad at small talk, bad at parties. Marines training program while at Harvard University. Served on a destroyer. Back to college without making contact with the enemy. Liked football but too small to play
1946 $1,000.00 from his father as a reward: No smoking, no drinking, not much going with girls
1948 B.A. from Harvard. Correspondent for The Boston Post in the Arab-Jewish War. Studies law in Virginia
1950 marries Ethel Skakel: a Great Lakes coal company, Manhattanville College of the Sacred Heart. Children: Kathleen Hartington, Joseph Patrick, Robert Francis, David Anthony, Mary Courtney, Michael L., Mary K., Christopher, Matthew, Douglas. Dog: Freckles
1951 Bachelor of Laws degree. Job in the Department of Justice. Internal Security division. $4,200.00 a year. Roots out homosexuals, then learns all about corruption in the Criminal division (under the Truman administration)
1952 Campaign manager for John F., wins him the job of senator. Then

in McCarthy's House Unamerican Activities Committee. And so what if Gesine was right about that. Joe McCarthy godfather of his oldest child

1955   Supreme Court attorney. Trip through the Soviet Union. If a Russian doctor saves his life, Communism can't be that bad

1957   Fights crime in the unions, using investigations and interrogations. Said he'd jump off the Capitol Building if he couldn't get Hoffa (Teamsters). Hoffa is acquitted. Kennedy doesn't jump. Refuses offered parachute.

Guest at Joe McCarthy's funeral

1960   Campaign manager for John F., wins him the presidency. "Jack works as hard as any mortal man can, Bobby goes a little further." Votes bought in West Virginia? Bobby is Attorney General and starting in

1961   Adviser to the president. Civil rights for Negroes. Attack on the Republic of Cuba

1962   Travels all over the world. Bali, Tokyo. Stood at Checkpoint Charlie in Berlin with just the tips of his toes on the white line, flowers in one hand and waving at the East German guards with the other

1963   John F. shot. Bobby head of the family. Fights with Lyndon Johnson. But gets Hoffa, eight years prison

1964   Resigns as Attorney General. Elected senator for New York. We'd been here three years. I was seven years old

1967   Calls for negotiations with the South Vietnamese Liberation Front. Role model for draft dodgers

1968   January 30: "I will not oppose Lyndon Johnson under any foreseeable circumstances."

March 17: "I am announcing today my candidacy for the presidency of the United States." Takes advantage of (Eugene) McCarthy's campaign

June 5: Wins the California primary, wounded by two bullets

June 6: Dies in Los Angeles, 4:44 AM Eastern Daylight Time.

Don't mention time of death. Looks too private.

Shorten the biography. Unfortunately this is the length Sister M. wants. Fill it out with other material.

Honorary doctorates from: Assumption College, 1957

Mount St. Mary's College, 1958

Tufts University, 1958
Fordham University, 1961
Nihon University, 1962
Manhattan College, 1962
Philippines, 1964
Marquette University, 1964
Berlin Free University, 1964

Books written: 2. <u>The Enemy Within</u>
                4. "How I Would End the War"
                   (DER SPIEGEL, April 8, 1968)
                1. ?
                3. ?

Justification for the importance of the topic:
    The news announcers sometimes say "President Kennedy" by mistake.
Possible future and all that
    Death in America (Gesine)
    Presence at a historical event via television. Historic
    Senator from New York

SIRHAN BISHARA SIRHAN

1944 born March 19 in the Armenian quarter of the Old City of Jerusalem,
under the British Mandate. Father Greek Orthodox, waterworks
supervisor

1948 Arab-Jewish War. Sirhan watches as Israeli soldiers kill relatives and
family friends. The Sirhans move many times in the Arab Quarter.
After the British withdrawal East Jerusalem comes under Jordanian
rule, father working as a plumber for the new government

Education: Lutheran Evangelical school. "Did well in school," the best of
the five Sirhan sons. Father wants to make sure that something will
come of this one; beats him. Parents fight

1956 Suez War. Sirhan 12 years old

1957 U.N. and World Council of Churches pay for the family to come to
the US under a refugee-admission program. They receive visas from

a limited quota; can immigrate on January 12. Come to New York City

1957–1964 (?). Sirhan at John Muir High School in Pasadena, did well enough to gain admission to Pasadena City College but dropped out
Mother had a steady job; Sirhan often unemployed. Liked to hoard his money
Doesn't smoke, doesn't drink. Can't stand being told what to do
Tends the garden, the neighbors like him, plays Chinese checkers with elderly neighbors, one of them a Jewish lady
Wanted to be a jockey but was only allowed to walk horses around after a run to cool them down

1965 Applies for work at a state racetrack. Has to have his fingerprints taken
After the Negro riots in Watts a man named Albert Herz in Alhambra fears for his life and buys a snub-nosed Iver Johnson eight-shot revolver for $31.95

1966 Works at Granja Vista del Rio ranch. Moves horses. Falls off one, injures chin, stomach problems. Doesn't think he receives enough compensation. Claims vision problems

1967 Israeli war against the Arabs. Loses his homeland
Since September 24 employed at a food store in Pasadena. $2.00 per hour. Gives tirades about the Israelis who have everything but still use violence to take Jordanian land. Meanwhile Mr. Herz has given his gun to his daughter, Mrs. Westlake. She became uneasy about having a gun in the house and gives it to an eighteen-year-old neighbor in Pasadena, who sells it in December to one of Sirhan's brothers

1968 In the store Sirhan boasts often that he is not an American citizen (which is required to legally buy a gun). On March 7, his employer makes a comment about Sirhan's work. End of that job
On June 4 walks into the Ambassador Hotel in Los Angeles.
On June 5 at 12:17 (3:17) a.m. shoots the whole magazine at Kennedy and his friends

Evidence against Mrs. Cresspahl: TV is appropriate. Useful for schoolwork even. Ads don't work
Now bring Kennedy and Sirhan together. Reasons why they met.

Death in America (Eagle-Eye Robinson, Gesine C., probably D. E. too).
Evidence or counterevidence?
Violence a national characteristic?
Conflict because immigrant nation, many countries of origin?
Violent eradication of the Indians
Darwinism transferred to pursuit of gain?
Nation enriched by
    War against the Indians
                    Mexicans 1846–1848
                    Spanish 1898
(Civil War 1861–1865)
National history as a Western movie with a guaranteed murder, usually by
    shooting
Murders in labor disputes: the Molly Maguires in the coal mining districts
    of Pennsylvania, 1854–1877
    Again 1937, during River Rouge plant strike, Dearborn, Mich.
The right of an American man to carry a gun. Toy. Ernest Hemingway.
Gun clubs. Gun manufacturers and gun dealers lobby. Annual gun deaths:
21,000. Per capita of population 1 gun in the cupboard.
Recent murders (1966): Richard Speck, 25, murdered eight student nurses
    in Chicago
    Charles Whitman, 25, shot at random down from the Texas University
    tower, killing 16, wounding 31
    Robert Benjamin Smith, eighteen, forced three women and two children
    to lie down on the floor in a cosmetics salon in Mesa, Arizona, like
    spokes in a wheel, shot them as planned, two survived
1967:
1968:
Attempted and successful assassinations since the Civil War (guns only):
    ABRAHAM LINCOLN, President, † April 15, 1865
    WILLIAM SEWARD, Secretary of State, wounded, 1865
    JAMES GARFIELD, President, † Sept. 19, 1881
    WILLIAM MCKINLEY, President, † Sept. 14, 1901
    THEODORE ROOSEVELT, ex-President, wounded during campaign,
        Oct. 14, 1902
    FRANKLIN D. ROOSEVELT, President-Elect, not hit, Feb. 15, 1933

ANTON CERMAK, Mayor of Chicago, † March 6, 1933 (instead of Roosevelt)

HUEY P. LONG, Senator for Louisiana, † Sept. 10, 1935

HARRY S. TRUMAN, President, not hit, Nov. 1, 1950

JOHN F. KENNEDY, President, † Nov. 22, 1963

MALCOLM X, Negro leader, † Feb. 21, 1965 (Broadway and 166th)

JAMES MEREDITH, Negro leader, wounded, June 6, 1966

GEORGE LINCOLN ROCKWELL, Nazi boss, † Aug. 25, 1967

MARTIN LUTHER KING, Negro leader, † Apr. 4, 1968

ROBERT F. KENNEDY, Senator for New York, † June 6, 1968, 4:44 ante meridiem, Eastern Daylight Time

Did Sirhan Bishara Sirhan have enough time here to learn the American way of having a conversation? Eleven years, one hundred and forty four days

Reason (from Sirhan's notebooks, found at 696 East Howard Street, Pasadena): For June 6, 1968, the first anniversary of the last Arab-Israeli war, Robert F. Kennedy was due to give a speech, a plea for Jewish votes in this country, a favor to the Israelis who had taken Sirhan Bishara Sirhan's country away from him, or at least his part of it. Kennedy needed to die before he could give that speech?

(But why are they letting that be broadcast on the news so that no one can deny they've heard it? They won't be able to get an untainted jury anywhere in Los Angeles. Again with no trial?)

Played Chinese checkers with an old Jewish lady

For this reason

From that day on

Then the first bullet entered Kennedy's right armpit, burrowed upward through fat and muscle, and lodged just under his skin, two centimeters from his spine, in one piece.

The other bullet hit an extension of his temporal bone just behind his right ear. One centimeter farther right (viewed from the back of the head) and the small bullet would have ricocheted off. As it was the empty tip of the bullet hit the "spongy, honeycomb mastoid bone" and sent bone and metal fragments into the cerebellum, the midbrain, the right hemisphere. The brain, already damaged by lack of oxygen, was impaired in the following functions:

Balance and movement control (cerebellum)

Vision (occipital lobe)

Eye reflexes, eye and body movements, nerve connections between cerebrum and cerebellum (midbrain)

Control of heartbeat, breathing, blood pressure, digestion and muscle reflexes, emotions (the brain stem, the "old brain")

So he wouldn't have wanted to live.

He took slightly more than twenty-five hours to die. He never regained consciousness. After the three hour and forty minute operation the blood was circulating properly in the brain, twelve hours later the circulation was undetectable. He had to pump blood through his heart and breathe for seven more hours. Then he was no longer able to give his speech.

Now I just have to write it all up.

The Air Force Boeing 707 with the coffin on board left Los Angeles International Airport at 1:28 (4:28) and is expected to reach Kennedy Airport in New York in four and a half hours.

In Fremont, California, 2,400 workers left a General Motors assembly line when a supervisor prohibited them from stopping work by saying Robert F. Kennedy "got what he deserved." He allegedly explained his opinion by saying: "All these Kennedys are ——————."

Outline

Contents   ?

Sources: New York Times, Vol. CXVIII, No. 40,310 and 40,311

Webster's International Dictionary of the English Language, 1902

Columbia Broadcasting System and National Broadcasting Company, news programs, panel discussions, medical demonstrations, etc., June 6, 1968, between 8 a.m. and 6 p.m.

Telephone calls with friends

Addendum: Evening programs on the radio

WQXR (the New York Times station)

The announcer of the Seven O'Clock News had tears in his voice. The commentators used words like "tragedy" and "saddening turn of events." Mr. Apple recites in a rickety voice what he still remembers about R. F. Kennedy.

Ads turned off.

General Telephone & Electronics brings you, in consideration of the tragedy, a musical program without any interruption by commercial announcements. You are listening to music by Michael Haydn
WCBS

9:35 p.m. The coffin is off the plane
it's on the Triboro Bridge
the funeral will be organized by an expert, Mr. McNamara

9:40 p.m. eight to nine thousand people are standing at St. Patrick's
Cathedral
sirens in the air on the radio, everywhere
the reporter describes where he's standing, the people along
the street, whatever he sees. Calm voice, swinging in strong
slow acoustic waves
almost all the cars following it are government vehicles
police whistling
the close family is gathering for a private viewing. They've
really left you shaken up
they're arranging that themselves
the coffin is in its box, broadcast dead
only notes. Now I just need to write it."

June 7, 1968 Friday

On the south side of Ninety-Sixth Street, starting at West End Avenue,
workmen are painting the curb, about a hundred feet of it to the number
19 bus stop. The men are using hand brushes fastened to broomsticks with
two pieces of string. They are working away, unhurried, not without a
certain pleasure in their expertise, they're about to take a break. Dave
Brubeck, "Take Five." The yellow paint shines in the sun, fresh enough to
eat. Life must go on. But we know one child who doesn't understand that.

I wonder if Marie knows that these TV sets have a way of imploding
when someone watches them for ten straight hours with schoolbook in
hand, as she did again today?

At the newsstand the papers were again stacked up higher than in
normal times. Along the plywood fence around the burned-out building

there are additional copies, it's hard to say how many. The line stretches south from the newsstand; the people coming from the north slow-wittedly follow their usual habit and just grab the topmost paper, holding out money in their other hand. This morning the crippled fingers are already busy with other people's money, though; the papers have been divided up into those available to anyone and those for preferred customers; now line up with everyone else, fifth on line.

– You, darling! the old man says severely, as if reprimanding. Today he wants to talk to you, doesn't he. – Don't you ever stand on line with me again! Are we friends or what?

The customers on line patiently, even approvingly, hear that the old man's on special terms with this lady and is willing to say so out loud. Today it seems the display of emotions is allowed, even entirely unaccustomed emotions.

In the subway fewer passengers than usual are waiting on the platform, though it's a work day. They get onto the train with almost no pushing and crowding, and who do we have here? a heavyset old Negro with a rheumatic bent back offering some random white woman his seat. – It's not easy for you either: he says. Are we still in New York?

Beneath Times Square the city is like itself again, so thick is the stew of people. On Lexington Avenue the people are walking shoulder to shoulder, as if all in a march. The sunlight here has shriveled up. Signs hangs on some of the shop doors saying they're closed, other stores announce that they will be closed tomorrow, and thus still manage to attract customers' attention the way they want. A young West Indian girl bats her eyelashes on a side street—she is wearing an elegant shirt, from Bloomingdale's at least, and showing off her thick eyebrows and thin legs, she has business to take care of too.

From the cafeteria entrance to Sam's counter is about sixty or seventy feet, and Sam calls to the kitchen as soon as he's glanced at the door: Large black TEA! so that he can hand over the brown paper bag two minutes later. Meanwhile he wants to know how things are going. – First with me! I want to, but I can't! he says, and he means the proper emotion he is incapable of producing. – Man, Gesine, this is going to be quite a day!

For the bank is working. That is, our allegedly adored vice president can't leave it at mere instructions, he has to explain the obvious in a memo:

Today is Friday, regular payday for most wage earners in the city, and all the checks need to go out before the weekend; For All Departments, de Rosny. If he wanted to he could have added: Incidentally, I also have the support of the Chamber of Commerce in this matter. The employees on the lower floors might be obediently counting bills, weighing bags of coins, checking accounts, or clicking conceptual money through the four arithmetical operations on calculators; on the sixteenth story we find the most blatant reading of newspapers. They are hardworking, these people who allow their employer two weeks' grace in which to pay them; they have long since turned to the center page, where the articles on Kennedy are continued from page 1. Mrs. Lazar, whose job is to defend the department with life and limb, barely looks up from whipping the pages backward and forward in an irritated, schoolmarmish manner. Here we have Henri Gelliston, who regards the banking business as the pinnacle and indeed the whole extent of earthly knowledge, absorbing the headline with a look of amazement: White House Plane Flies Body From Los Angeles. He's about to find out that the hearse there was blue and that Mrs. John F. Kennedy yielded precedence to no one, even in boarding the plane. As far as Wilbur N. Wendell is concerned, the financial business of all of South America might just as well suffocate under the spread-out pages of his *Times*—he is busy studying a photo of the cemetery personnel at Arlington measuring out the grave for tomorrow. Tony, Anthony, so intent on making us all forget that he was born in a poor Italian neighborhood of New York, our man with his rigidly perfected manners, is sprawled right across the desk to make sure that he doesn't crease the newspaper; like yesterday, the first page of a paper he normally wouldn't polish his shoes with—*The Daily News*, New York's Picture Newspaper—lies neatly folded in his weekly planner. It's as quiet as a reading room in the executive lounge; apart from one minor detail the sight could serve as an ad for *The New York Times*. De Rosny may know why he shouldn't make the rounds this morning: he'd be in for a shock at his subordinates' industriousness.

The employee by the name of Cresspahl betakes herself into her office none too swiftly either. She fritters away work hours next to our elegant Tony's desk. On the front page of the Picture Newspaper, on the left, the word "Final" is printed, which probably means Last Edition. On the right is the price, eight cents, so now you know. Below that, a weather report:

sunny and warm. You could put it that way. The letters in RFK DEAD are almost two inches tall. Why not five? Below that, in a thin black border, the dead man is looking the newspaper buyer trustingly in the eyes, somewhat concerned about the bad state of the world, his lips suspiciously loose, his face a little bloated. His hair is shaped into artificial dishevelment as ever, his left shoulder juts forward a little, dependably warm and attentive. His wife has been able to tug his tie closer to the top shirt button than he usually wore it. Cresspahl would be happy to buy this scruffy paper from Tony, she's not sure whether Marie has it, but she doesn't have the courage to suggest it. It would be for Marie, right? Who else would it be for.

All the papers now have to eat their words like old hats. *Ruthless*: it turns out he wasn't that. He may have fought more recklessly than wisely in his younger years, but the *Times* is willing to forgive him for that now, since he hadn't done so for a low or merely personal triumph. It still doesn't grant him a full regard for the legal process, it sees him as a warrior, and also as a big man who at his death was still growing. What is de Rosny to do now with his countless stories about Bugs Bunny, the crazy cartoon inventor who robbed his neighbors of health and property with, say, a motorized hammock—he will have to come up with a new victim, de Rosny that is. Want to bet it's Richard Milhous Nixon, who cries so nicely?

As if there were no homework in the newspaper. Not all the Czechoslovaks smiled and waved at the Soviet convoy rolling through the countryside, probably in greater than expected numbers, and with heavy equipment; the weight limit had to be raised specially from thirty to seventy tons, not a problem among dear friends. Such mutable bridges might have given the interior minister something to ponder, except he had his own secret police to worry about, which were acting like they were still answerable to Stalin. Write that down. Recently there've been up to thirty thousand cases in which internal security officers provided trumped-up charges for the prosecution of innocent citizens.

The person who, by three o'clock, can no longer stand such preparations for a trip to Europe is Employee Cresspahl. Marie doesn't answer the phone in the apartment. That may be a good sign. If she can't hear the phone she is far from the tube, the newscasters, doing homework at Pamela's, or in the park with Rebecca listening for the ice-cream man's bell instead. If you can't believe that, you'll think the child is at St. Patrick's Cathedral. But what's the point, after all the coffin is closed. She wouldn't care, she might still want to walk past it and brush the flag on the casket with her fingers. She shouldn't be standing there alone. Someone should be there to get her. Cresspahl decides to leave early, and can't tell anyone, even Mrs. Lazar has already left.

The line now ends on Lexington Avenue, at Forty-Seventh Street. It's so wide that walking next to it on the sidewalk is like walking on a balance beam. Too early to find Marie outside the angular plate-glass cookie of Chemical Bank—she must have joined the end of the line a long time ago. She's not in front of the Barclay Hotel, nor the Waldorf-Astoria. How yellow the General Electric building is: crazy Gothic with a crown full of holes that has a water pot in it. All the people standing still make you feel like you're walking faster—irrational but true. Business is merrily going on all around, hawking pins that say "In Memory of a Great American. Robert F. Kennedy. 1925–1968." Maybe buy one for Marie. Fifty cents each. Probably 100 percent profit. Here's another entrance to the IRT, Fifty-First Street, the next stop is Grand Central, from there it's twenty minutes to get home. The people are hardly dressed in mourning—this man could board a sailboat in those clothes, you'd expect to find that lady working in her backyard. Here we have a mailman who's gotten stuck in the procession once too often, and now even the phone booth is occupied. – I'm forty-five minutes behind schedule! he says to the people standing near him, who smile and nod back. That's how things go in New York when something's happened; anyway, he was only looking for sympathy, and found it. Where's this line going? Now it's winding around the Seagram Building block and turning south down Park Avenue. Seagram's is handing out plastic cups, though not with whiskey, water is good enough advertising. Nobody's visibly in tears—the conversations may not be happy but a certain good humor prevails. Here there are more commemorative buttons, now they're a whole dollar, maybe due to the fancier surroundings of the Embassy Club and the back of Chemical Bank. How much percent profit there? Here a garbage can is being stormed by two teachers intending to make paper hats for their whole class of boys. Such stately towers of business and at their feet the people are strewing plastic, paper, tin cans. Whenever someone collapses the line bulges out toward the curb; here two girls in too-tight pants are leaning against the pillars of Union Carbide, tired out. People faint not so much from the muggy heat as from the car exhaust fumes. For other New Yorkers are driving on Park Avenue, out to the country, or the beaches, even if many have their automobile lights on as a gesture of mourning. Here it takes an hour to move a single block, if you stay with the line. The police have set up gray barricades to protect those waiting against line cutters. There are a lot of children here, almost every third person looks underage; but this must be about number five thousand, it'd be easy to miss Marie. No one is talking about the reason they're all there, not even about Thursday's amendment to the gun laws. Previously, mail-order businesses were free to send out pistols, revolvers, hand grenades, and mortars; now they are limited to rifles and shotguns. Including the kind of rifle used for the other Kennedy. Bankers Trust, the Colgate-Palmolive command center, the headquarters of International Telephone & Telegraph. Looking back from the corner, before the line turns west onto Fifty-First Street, you could still see the Pan Am Building, where the Kennedy fortune is managed. At Madison Avenue the police actually did form two rows, to let the line cross the street. On this corner, one cold winter, Cresspahl too once walked up and down, carrying a sign, outside the New York Archdiocese, the palace of Cardinal Spellman, who so loved the war. Here the last stage begins, and the soft-drink vendors are becoming aggressive. One vendor feels stared at by an extremely ragged beggar in the line—he'll teach that beggar to envy him, for a while he holds out the brightly colored cans so that they invariably pass under the thirsty man's nose, until he turns away. Again and again there is a Puerto Rican, a Negro, among the whites—about every fifth person has dark skin. They were the ones who felt spoken to when this millionaire spoke of them. What could they have believed he would do? Among them most of the women are not carrying their shoes in their hands, the men have only slightly loosened their ties. At the church the police are in a holiday mood, moving nimbly between the elephantine TV broadcast vans, chatting comfortably over their walkie-talkies, waving up at the helicopters. The true lord of the scene is a cameraman, hanging with his equipment high overhead in a seat shaped to his buttocks. This close to the goal, people now begin to resist when someone tries to cut the line, though not as viciously as on normal, unsacred days—with comments referring to the dignity of the occasion, in a preachy tone where possible. At the northwest church entrance, uniformed men lop off five or six heads at a time from the front of the line, with wordless gestures. Inside there is something golden, brilliantly lit, to see. If Marie did go in she'd have wanted someone Catholic with her. She'd have wanted to do everything right: the genuflecting, the sign of the cross. She isn't here either, and for the next fifteen minutes, the length of time it can take to walk past the coffin, she doesn't come out the south entrance, and yet her mother has seen her many times and sees her again while walking away past the gray wall of Fiftieth Street and the weeping women in the hot western light.

Marie hasn't left the building. When the telephone rang she had just gone down to the basement to ask Jason for advice adjusting her TV antenna. She watched the whole route, starting at Lexington Avenue, up and down Park Avenue, all the way to the cathedral and past the coffin. She didn't need to go in person. She wasn't there, and yet she's even learned the basics about how to make a sign of the cross. She was there with the TV. Of course we couldn't find her today either.

June 8, 1968 Saturday

A day in front of the TV. But we won't spend it unsupervised. When Mrs. Cresspahl called D. E., Mrs. Erichson had to go get him from the car, he was just about to drive off, as Marie had called and asked him to, in fact. The child wants a referee too.

Bring her back to me, D. E.
To you?
Away from the Kennedys.
Didn't she get this obsessive joy in grief from you?
If it's from me get it out from her. Bring her out of it.
You're giving me free hand?
Get her back, D. E.

By eight thirty a.m. he's arranged his long bones in our apartment, on one of the Salvation Army chairs, with his back to the luminous park so he can't be suspected of paying insufficient attention. Next to him he's set out a tin with eight ounces of tobacco, three pipes, all kinds of implements, and now he requests a liter of tea—he's ready for a lengthy undertaking. He is dressed more for the weekend in the garden in New Jersey to which he invited us, down to his sneakers; with his expression of somewhat sleepy gravity he is giving a good imitation of a professor who's up to the task of one more long exam. The language is American English.

His preparations managed to put Marie off balance; his role forces her to be the organizer. She moves the TV set back and forth in front of him, apologizing for the distorted picture; he nods gravely. He may be an authorized professor of physics and chemistry but he doesn't know how to improve the technology of this kind of machine. – The tube is overworked: he determines, his objectivity an unanswerable reproach; Marie nods meekly. She can't prove he said it pointedly, but her pious feeling slips a little. Now she's sitting next to him and he can touch her consolingly on the neck, the arm, it's allowed. He strictly refrains, out of respect for her grief, and by reflecting her behavior he forces her to question it. Having expected nothing less from him than proper silence during the programs, she soon can't stand it anymore.

Around nine she sucks in air through her teeth, as if in sudden pain, for there on-screen a staticky distorted picture appears, sliced up into its own shadows, of the widow of the day in the moment of crossing herself. Her face shines out bright and clear in its jinxed surroundings. D. E. looks at Marie in surprise and perfunctorily explains: The raster, you know. She nods, innocent and teachable. The raster. I see.

Mrs. Cresspahl would have long since burst out, against her will but needing to score a point: This Robert Kennedy of yours, he had Martin Luther King's phone tapped! That's the kind of attorney general he was, just so you know! But now she's unable to make these further pedagogical mistakes, and is moreover amused by her sidelong glances at the pair sitting stiffly in front of the TV. She gets carried away by sudden mirth, she smiles, whether from gratitude or elation. She gets in return an indignant sidelong look from D. E., as if there's nothing to laugh about here, and obediently withdraws with the radio into the one room whose door can be firmly closed.

WQXR, the voice of *The New York Times*, broadcast on 96.3 MHz, is now going to show her educated readership how a Grand Old Lady of the World behaves upon the death of a murdered adversary. Cheerfully, respectfully, she describes a well-respected banking firm and recommends its services to the public. Worthy Auntie Times not only earns a little pin money by advertising for friends, she launches into the ether with plugs for her own in-depth features she'll be selling tomorrow. It's her station, after all, she refers to herself by name, she is it. She's not prepared to accord her fallen foe an iota of indulgence: she honors the dollar undeterred, no one's giving her anything for free.

In the other room, D. E. hasn't yet invited the child to visit a funeral parlor in New York where dead people are lying with their sharp noses pointed upward too, equally Catholic but with no prospect of a burial in the most chic cathedral on Fifth Avenue, but he is playing a game with Marie. Each player gets a point if they're the first to identify by title the dignitary being conducted through the checkpoint and into the cathedral before their eyes. They were tied on the secretary general of the UN, the head of the United Auto Workers union, the president of the United States, and the former head of the CIA; Marie scored wins on almost all the others, from poet Robert Lowell to Senator Eugene McCarthy—only with Lauren Bacall does D. E. say he got her first; Marie doesn't notice anything. Then they start guessing the colors in the procession since the TV set doesn't supply them: they sense the white of the seminary students, mistake the brown of the monks, the olive green of the army chaplains, the purple of the monsignori, and the violet of the bishops, but agree on the scarlet of the cardinals; by this point, Marie, simply by being forced to imagine a colored picture, has gained insight into the finer details of the staging. D. E. is able to compare one meaning of "service" to another, and she lets herself go along with him in estimating the costs.

She won't yet crack or laugh at jokes with him, but every now and then they give each other one of their old looks, sly and conspiratorial, like for instance when the surviving Kennedy brother's voice cracks near the end of his eulogy. She is still trying to honor his teary tone, but D. E. expresses some of her own suspicion with his remarks about the dead man's motto,

"Some men see things as they are and say: Why?

I dream things that never were and say: Why not?"

Once he's cited the source of the tearful quote (George Bernard Shaw), complete with a short history of Fabianism, he is able to add: Even when they borrow they take the best.

After that she looks a bit more suspiciously at the eight half-orphans carrying bread and wine in golden vessels up to the high altar; she is not moved to defend the water sprinkled on the coffin, meant to call down from Heaven God's purifying mercy, nor the swinging of thurible filled with incense, meant to carry the prayers of the faithful up to God. She's had to recite such things all too often in school, against her will. She gradually comes to see what's happening in the cathedral as a private ceremony, which is taking her Kennedy away from her, and during the playing of the slow movement from Mahler's Fifth by thirty members of the New York Philharmonic she can't yet put into words how the Kennedys look when they're borrowing, but she reveals the thought, with a painfully amused sidelong glance. The cheerfully galumphing "Battle Hymn of the Republic" unnerves her again; she can't defend herself against D. E.'s reminder that the tune was stolen from another song,

John Brown's Body Lies a-Mouldering in the Grave
about the abolitionist's attack at Harpers Ferry, West Virginia. The theft bothers her, as does the suggestion of a rotting body, plus there's the sense that this is educational material she will never hear from Sister Magdalena, and all the thinking she has to do about that dries the corners of her eyes. Before long she's arguing with D. E. over the placing of dead Catholics vis-à-vis the altar—feet toward the altar and head under the stars of the flag, she points out to him, so that eventually she cries out: But they're carrying him out of the cathedral head down!

At first the only joking she permits D. E. is at the expense of the other Mrs. Kennedy, the president's widow, who stood rigid and unmoving on the top step outside for almost four minutes, *you can all see me, right?*, never mind if the motorcade gets hopelessly delayed, she wants her share of the limelight, and finally Marie does say, half embarrassed, half annoyed: That's just what she'd like. She's practically inviting someone to shoot!

Her store of reverence took a serious hit with the news from London inserted into the program. The fact that a man suspected of the murder of Martin Luther King had been arrested at Heathrow Airport, that they finally caught him after such a long time but on this very morning, today of all days, a perfect link to the spectacle of the senator's burial—it's too pat, too calculated, it feels to her like a trick played by grown-ups who think kids are dumber than they really are. The precision work bothers her, and even if she doesn't quite doubt the truth of the report it still seems damaged somehow by its placement. – They're trying to distract us! she says angrily. She's been distracted.

She is also being unscrupulously unjust, heaping criticism on the president's widow for her desire for yet another bullet and further fame; the current president, Johnson, has long since finished his journey from the New York cathedral back to Washington; the train with her senator's coffin is still in Pennsylvania Station. The commentators on-screen are so at a loss that they allude to the train that carried the assassinated Abe Lincoln, tell stories from the history of the station, one mentions the renaming of Idlewild Airport.

– *Which I undertook solely to keep New York clean:* D. E. says incautiously, and immediately worried; she nods pensively, lips pursed. Her dead Kennedy cannot be separated from the staging of his last journey; his family represents him; this is how he would have wanted it. – No: Marie says. She would vote against renaming it Kennedy Station.

Her stubbornness persists for a while yet, the TV set stays on, but she's lost her agitation and excitement. The course of events has become predictable. She will see the old-fashioned observation platform of the last car many more times, and the coffin placed on six chairs there; the camera in the helicopter will show her both trains many more times; but she still has to face the American character of the drama. There are three trains—the first to intercept any explosives (one reporter quickly corrects his mistake, "dummy train," into the correct official term: "pilot train"); the third consisting of two diesel engines, for repairs and the consequences of any new assassination attempt. But it is none of the thousand famous friends of the Kennedys on the funeral train who are struck down, it is two onlookers in Elizabeth, New Jersey, hit and killed by an express train going the other direction on the opposite tracks. This interjection of the everyday disappoints Marie, but D. E. doesn't take advantage of the first sign of boredom, it's only at nearly two o'clock that he uses Annie's bath thermometer (prewarmed) plus some demented science to demonstrate that an implosion of the TV tube is imminent. It's Marie who presses the button, and as a favor to D. E. she takes him to the Mediterranean Swimming Club in the Hotel Marseilles. She keeps her eye on him as they leave the apartment. He says goodbye to Mrs. Cresspahl with a casual air, not a triumphant one.

It's hot on Broadway, as if the street is being roasted from below as well as above. A predictable crowd is dawdling busily along, with only the heat sweeping the east sidewalks sparklingly clear of people. With no fear of TV cameras, the Upper West Side goes about its business—women in curlers out shopping, young men in undershirts discussing the day in the shade of the awning outside the Strand Bar or carrying bags of laundry into the laundromats. Whatever the TV stations may have shown of the flags at half-mast on Fifth Avenue and the solemn crowds along the coffin's route, here it's a normal Saturday. Only a few stores cover their displays with black-framed photographs of the senator, or funeral ribbons, and hardly any are closed; Mrs. Cresspahl can get her four bottles of spring water (the tap water is disgustingly brown from deposits in the main pipes that have washed up from the changing water pressure, since children throughout the city have been turning the fire hydrants into street showers and the adults are sitting at home in front of their TVs for the third day in a row); she has no trouble finding the extras to go with the proper lunch D. E. has graced us with. And Marie eats up much of her sorrow with herring from Denmark on black bread from West Germany. She would have felt that it was indecent to be hungry, but she doesn't notice, because D. E. finishes not one second ahead of her. We'll hand the child over to you yet, D. E., you know how to be a legal guardian after all.

By around three the TV is repeating segments of the morning's broadcasts, since the train doesn't pass before the cameras often enough and the crowds on the platforms along the route to Washington can only produce the same waving, shouting, and swinging of signs yet again. Marie has the younger brother's eulogy practically memorized by now and knows in advance the place where his voice starts to break. Meanwhile the train has been driven at reduced speed for the onlookers so many times, and has been plagued by so many mechanical difficulties, that it's hours behind schedule, and one more of D. E.'s calculations works out: tired from swimming, Marie nods off, right in the middle of the discussion of whether the broken brake shoe on the last coach would be called a *tormoznoy bashmak* or *tormoznaya kolodka*. She is so fast asleep that she slides down until she's lying against the back of the sofa; she doesn't hear the hollow sound of the engine's bell on TV coming to an end, nor the closing door.

Riverside Park seems no emptier than usual, and maybe *The New York*

Times tomorrow will have counted for us to prove it. Mrs. Cresspahl isn't hoping to run into anyone on the steps, dried out in the heat—she's looking for secluded nooks and finds one just before the underpass to the Hudson River promenade, a staircase well sheltered by trees where she can put her head against Prof. Dr. Erichson's chest and cry uninterrupted, never mind propriety or pride. In such situations, some people administer regular strokes, down over the other person's shoulder blade, like you do for a disconsolate horse; this one here just holds tight, doesn't try to touch you more than you want, doesn't talk.

It's infection by mass hysteria.
You're not infected, Gesine. You're not hysterical.
Because I've been divided from my own child for three days.
You'll get her back, Gesine.
Because maybe she got her sentimentality from me.
You think so? Don't you realize you're not sentimental. She's fallen into being a bit American.
I am not raising that child right.
Jakob wouldn't have minded. I wouldn't.
You could say it now, D. E., if you want. But not out of pity.
Just believe me when I say it.
I believe you.

By evening, faithful to the four-hour delay, TV has arrived in Washington too. The coffin's location is indicated by the flashbulbs the spectators are firing at it; the darkness is all-powerful. The family's stage manager has decided that the dead man should pass every Senate building in which he'd had offices. Welcoming cheers that die away shyly. Sharpshooters on the roofs, plainclothes police everywhere. The body has to spend four minutes saying goodbye to the softly lit figure of Abraham Lincoln—to the two of them next to each other on their two chairs, the TV picture is so distorted. And again: the Battle Hymn. President Johnson in the first car behind his felled opponent, with Secret Service scurrying all around him. The moon draws veils over the milling crowd, it cannot brighten the Potomac's dark waters. At the unloading, one of the dead man's sons insists on helping to carry the coffin and so has to hold it by the head end. The bearers move off in the wrong direction at first, walking more or less toward the eternal flame, and have to veer off at an angle over the rise. After the final service, John Glenn folds the flag into snappy sharp corners and hands it to the new head of the Kennedys. A state limousine has brought a cocker spaniel from the dead man's home—it's Freckles, in person. *The* widow once again feels the need to assert herself against the senator's: she makes a point of laying small wreaths, and having her children lay wreaths, on her own nearby grave sites. The other relatives kiss the new coffin, leaving it standing on the lawn. Again and again strangers kneel by the African mahogany, brush their lips against it, pray. Marie sits on the bench with her legs drawn up, holding her hand over her mouth, merely surprised at a ceremony that her mother has described as taking place differently in Europe.

The radio says nothing about relatives not staying for the interment here. Clearly one of her nephews has taken *The New York Times* aside at some point during the day to point out the unseemliness of her behavior, as well as the possible consequences for future business; now she reassures her customers of her good taste with lugubrious classical music and announcers reading the news in properly subdued voices. A station next to hers on the dial ends its broadcast with an ad about the dangers of smoking.

The television department moves to views of the ocean, accompanied by saccharine singing, and then to a photographic portrait, presented as now the only thing left to us. The eleven o'clock news is sponsored by Savarin Coffee. Their ad shows the expert surrounded by coffee plantation workers anxiously awaiting his reaction to the drink. He approves, and anthropological joy spreads across the Indians' faces. The expert then rides off in his genuine South American railroad train. Also helping to pay for the news is the roach spray Black Flag, *Kill & Clean*. If it were up to Marie, we would not buy these products, for a while. Now music is being played at the moment it's performed, continuously, interrupted by a photo of the dead man that seems to be hung slightly crooked. He has his hand on his chin, conversationally, and looks younger than he did three days ago.

At one a.m.: *THE GREAT GREAT SHOW*, tonight with a fable from prewar Hungary: *The Baroness and the Butler* . . . Can't alienate the viewers.

D. E. has stuck it out the whole time on the chair next to Marie, having roasted about two and a half ounces of tobacco in his pipe and cracked the third bottle of red wine. It's not going to be him who gives up. Almost as soon as Marie realizes they've switched over to normal programming, she asks for permission to turn off the set. She rolls it over to the apartment door, its cord wound around it, ready for the rental company to take it away.

– D. E.: she says. What do we have to do to get you to spend tomorrow with us?

– Drive with me right now across the Hudson and all the way to the New Jersey woods where my log cabin is.

– Okay: Marie says, looking at him affectionately, amused, in anticipation. She leans against his chair, arranges his gray hair this way and that. He has earned her thanks.

In D. E.'s car, before entering the tunnel to New Jersey, she turns to the back. It's dark enough there, her mother won't be able to see her face.

– *Thank you for letting me have this:* she says.

– Who, me? Mrs. Cresspahl is startled out of her doze, she almost thinks there's someone else sitting next to her.

– Yes. You. For letting me watch TV. That's what I'm thanking you for.

June 9, 1968 Sunday

is the nation's official day of mourning, just as the City of New York decreed one yesterday. Marie wasn't interested in a trip to Arlington National Cemetery, to test the TV's representations against the fresh grave; what she wanted was an outing to Culver's Lake and Lake Owassa, to the Delaware River on the Pennsylvania border, and across Little Swartswood Lake to the country seat that D. E. calls his log cabin. They may be marching with flowers for RFK in Arlington; we saw people like ourselves out for a Sunday drive, people at the side of the road selling eggs and cherries from farms and forest paths, flaneurs strolling around the small towns, crowded coffee shops, children lining up at jingling ice-cream trucks, shores lined with people in colorful swimsuits. Marie watches us without the least disdain as we spend the whole early evening in D. E.'s shady yard, chatting idly, carefree in the green twilight; she appears more by chance than anything at the bay window of the kitchen, where she is advising Mrs. Erichson about preparing dinner, her occasional glances in our direction meant merely to reassure that she isn't going to bother us. She speaks German with D. E.'s mother, although with an American "Granny" slipping naturally over her lips. – Why are we making such a big dinner, Granny?

– How far have you gotten, Gesine?

– Yes, I need your advice. 1947. I can't get Cresspahl away from the Soviets.

– You should tell Marie more about them.

– She'll take it the wrong way, D. E.

– She gets today's Russians all wrong too.

– She's a stalwart anti-Communist. On that topic she believes what they tell her in school.

– A clueless anti-Communist, you mean. She's put a poem in her collection reprinted from the June 7 *Pravda*, by that guy, what's his name—

– Him. I know him.

– You know the one.

– I read all about him in *The New York Times*. In November of '66 he paid a visit to RFK...

– Gee, I just can't get enough of that name Kennedy.

– ...to the living RFK. It's a historical event. When they were voting on a civilian complaint review board for the New York police.

– *The vote of fear.*

– No sooner had Senator Kennedy cast his vote than who should ring the bell of his apartment on the fourteenth floor of the UN Plaza building? It's a visiting Soviet poet, he lolls around on a cream-colored sofa high above New York City and talks with this representative of American imperialism, and what do they put out as a communiqué? The poet: "I have faith only in politicians who understand the importance of poetry."

– The senator from New York: "I like poets who like politicians."

– And the poet, comforted, set off for home, reduced to a scarecrow but breast swelling with pride.

– Oh, I've just thought of the name. Eugene.

– Yevgeny Yevtushenko. Right.

– He's struck again. Maybe he meant it as an act of friendship for the dead man, not even Marie's quite sure.

– Tell me.

– "The price of revolver lubricant rises."

– You anti-Communist!

– That's what it says. And:

Perhaps the only help is shame.

History cannot be cleansed in a laundry.

There are no such washing machines.

Blood can never be washed away!

And:

Lincoln basks in his marble chair,

wounded.

But what does Abe like to do in the evening? Wasn't he at a play? Listen to the Yevtushenkos' Eugene:

But without wiping the splashes of blood from your forehead

You, Statue of Liberty, have raised up

Your green, drowned woman's face,

Appealing to the heavens against being trodden underfoot.

– Do you believe that?

– Marie even wonders if he believes it himself.

– I'm telling her things that don't fit her views, D. E. Things about the Twins, who ruled in Jerichow longer than any other Soviet commandants before or after them. They acted like gentleman: aristocratic. Refined. Superfine. They would have made perfect von Plessens. Estate owners from the nobility, and running Jerichow the way the von Plessens once had. Breakfast together, not before nine, each with his own server to wait on him, white linen, silver, punishment for the slightest spot of dirt. Departure for Town Hall at ten, to rule. They kept the mayor in a filing room where he was allowed to sign things; they were in his room, together even behind the desk, and the Germans had to keep a distance of three paces, the same as the hirelings from the nobility back in the day. Even tempered, never got mad, never drank, never went a single step in the town on foot. They weren't brothers—that was the one and only private fact about them the Jerichowers knew; they didn't even look alike—and rumor gnawed away at their nickname and could never figure it out. When they caught a subordinate fraternizing with Germans they'd have him hauled off like a mass murderer, and the beating would start only behind the fence. Terrible beatings. If a German came to them with a complaint, say Mina Ahlreep, and she didn't know the first name and patronymic of the Russian who'd shot the fake clock off her gable, the slanderer would find herself in the basement under Town Hall for the night, without trial, to give her time to remember the Soviet man's name, and no one would bother to explain this to her, and she'd be let out onto the street the next morning without a word. That was how disgusted the Twins were by Germans. Their arrival put an end to the all-night parties in Louise's front parlor, and while she did request compensation for her broken furniture and ruined parquet floor she didn't know Mr. Wassergahn's serial number. Pontiy had sometimes kept bonbons in his pocket for the *devushki*, these two didn't even say *idi syuda*, they shooed children away like chickens. They'd had the fence around the Kommandatura raised by two feet and even though they received no visitors in the villa they had a triumphal arch built in front of it, on which Loerbrocks the painter had to paint fresh slogans for Soviet holidays and anniversaries of great military victories. And if Loerbrocks isn't dead yet he can still crank out a portrait of Josif Vissarionovič Stalin from memory, although only in three colors and in size DIN A2 per German Industrial Standards, this being how he had to repaint him every Christmas. Stalin got his place at the top of the arch; the army and the army alone was the constant topic of the changing slogans below him, which meant that I knew the four case endings for *Krasnaya Armiya* better than for any other words. After work, still in unwrinkled uniforms and crisply ironed caps, the two Wendennych gentlemen would go riding out to the Rehberge Hill, now without adjutants. From ten to eleven we could hear their phonograph records: Tchaikovsky, Mussorgsky, Glinka, Brahms. These are not the Soviets Marie learns about in school, and she doesn't like it.

– Cresspahl wasn't kept in Fünfeichen forever.

– She pictures it like a cell in Sing Sing.

– If she had a more precise picture she wouldn't let you go to Prague.

– That reason has only existed for six months.

– Still, it's a reason.

– You, on the other hand, never once told a lie, even as a boy.

– But whenever I could since then. And liked doing it too.

– Marie should see the Russians of today.

– Who were eighteen in 1947.

– I am not going to help her school! Didn't I tell Marie how the Soviets got their hands on Cresspahl? That was bad enough. If I tell her the food they got in Fünfeichen, never mind anything else, she'll never trust Socialism for the rest of her life.

– You wouldn't be backing up Sister Magdalena, you'd be preparing Marie better.

– She's too young for that!

– She already knows all about the rapes in New York.

– That's what we get for letting you study physics and chemistry. You think truth has absolute value.

– Marie would know more about you too. She'd understand why you want to take one more trip to the other side. No, not that. But she might have some idea.

– I know what's in fashion in things aside from ladies' clothes, D. E. It's not chic to disparage the Soviets. But those aren't my reasons.

– So approximately when is Marie supposed to get this lesson?

– I don't know, at fifteen . . .

– In that case she'll hear about 1953 when she's an adult. We'll be allowed to tell her about your death when she's on her own deathbed.

– Fine. Cresspahl concedes. Erichson wins on points. Your solicitude for the little miss is just ridiculous!

– I owe her that much. She's about to get me a beer. The stories you know!

– You tell her about the camps. You'd somehow do it so that all she gets is justice, the rule of law, and humane treatment.

– Then you do it.

– School in 1947. Josif Vissarionovič was hanging on the walls of the seventh-grade rooms by then, much higher than the Austrian's pictures used to. Which made a faded rectangle very noticeable. But no one could expect the new leader to be short. His title had been expanded too: Wise Leader of the Peoples, Benevolent Father of the Nations, Generalissimo, Preserver of World Peace, Creator of Socialism, Guardian of Justice, "There Is Still Light in the Kremlin," Guarantor of a Truly Humane Future. Something's wrong with that last one, "Guarantor," we'd heard that word a bit too often.

– All correct.

– I have never once seen a portrait of him looking straight at the viewer, he's always squinting down to one side, as if someone there had stepped out of line, or sneezed. We were never allowed to talk about him that way at school—as having a physiognomy, as being human in any way. Someone ratted on Lise Wollenberg, who couldn't help laughing at the parting the *Vozhd'* had put in his plump mustache: the scare was punishment enough, plus she got an F in Russian and an F in conduct. She had reason to watch out. Schoolgirl Cresspahl also wanted the followers of this Leader of Peoples to give her her father back—that made two strikes against her. Was she just being scatterbrained? She dutifully learned the new history of technological inventions, a bit like how Marie learns what they teach her in religion: knowledge to regurgitate when needed. It hadn't been that feudalist jerk Karl Drais, Baron von Sauerbronn, who'd thought up the velocipede after seeing some Chinese drawings—it was a Russian serf, freed for biking from the Urals to Moscow, fifteen hundred miles. Russian feudal lords were more benevolent too, apparently. It wasn't Marconi who'd been the first to send wireless signals, we had a Russian to thank for that too. The demise of the Kunze-Knorr compressed-air brake at the hands of a Russian was taught in literary style: As the venerable Moscow scholar demonstrates braking tests to his German colleagues in a tunnel, and his system gently and firmly brings the train to a halt, one of the foreign bumblers lets out a groan: Awwf, Kunze-Knorr, eet iss feenished! The first car drove in Russia, the party didn't invent the airplane but a tailor from Minsk or Tula did, the pharmacy was Russian in origin, and the crane, and your caran d'ache, and the telephone, and every part of the railway, from *stantsiya* to *passazhirskiy* and *pochtoviy* cars. But if you learned all this you were allowed to take English classes with Mrs. Weidling, who wasn't arrested until the following fall.

– You forgot penicillin.

– An obedient little student like that writes an essay for school, "I look out my window...," and describes what she sees—the green Russian fence topped with barbed wire, the roof of the commandant's villa above it, and an American truck with a bulletproof grille over the headlights parked inside the open gate—and if she leans awkwardly far out the window she can see around the corner of the brickworks to the east, where the sun rises, as *krasniy* as the Red Army. She really liked that ending, Schoolgirl Cresspahl did; she was genuinely out to please and flatter. Mrs. Beese gave the essay back unmarked and kept her after school, and it had to be rewritten looking out the window at the schoolyard, where there was nothing at all to see. Mrs. Beese didn't tell Cresspahl the lesson she was meant to learn here, she had to find it out for herself, and two months later the girl handed in a plot summary of a Russian novel that mentioned in passing "the Russians' wild nature," "the wild nature of the Russians," thinking only about the part of the story where a Russian nobleman keeps a wild bear in a room and locks unsuspecting visitors in with it—she'd worked so hard on her summary and it got her sent to the principal. A Social Democrat, a teacher since 1925 and again since 1945, so furious at the oblivious child that he couldn't even explain her sin. He personally went to the school secretary and borrowed some nail scissors and cut out the four or six words and gave back her notebook. "This really won't do, child." Whether the slip of paper she should now stick over the hole should have corrected text or be virgin white—that decision exceeded his powers, it overwhelmed him, he flailed around like someone busy drowning and now you're asking him the time.

– That's not true.

– You see? And yet I'm supposed to tell Marie.

– Did that really happen?

– His name was Dr. Vollbrecht. The one who almost wasn't made principal. In his inaugural address he was supposed to welcome the Red Army as the bringer of true culture and humanity, and his wife had been raped at gunpoint by twenty-one Red soldiers. They kept him in the Gneez courthouse for three days, and he talked around town about a visit he'd made for family reasons, then eventually admitted he'd been arrested but only "by mistake." Then he gave the speech.

– No. You're pulling my leg. I'd do the same thing. The New Schools repudiating Pushkin? I don't believe it.

– You see. Marie would love to believe it. And she'd have another advantage over you.

– That it's true?

– That it really happened and I was there.

– *The shoe comes out the way the leather is.*

– Right, and *what can you do about it?*

– Erichson concedes. Cresspahl wins, and not just on points.

– Write to young Vollbrecht! Go ahead! He's a lawyer in Stade, the post office there can find him.

– Gesine. I wouldn't dare.

And so why the big dinner? D. E. stood up after the meat course, stuffed a napkin between his collar and neck the way all the best people do, and gave a speech for Marie. He'd originally been hoping to marry the Cresspahl family on this day too, but work had prevented him, and now he promised not to bring up the tiresome topic again until September. As a substitute might he offer an amateur theatrical production, rehearsed for two hours, with several parts, the cast of characters including a prince by the name of Dubrovsky, one bear (guaranteed untamed), . . .

– Does September work for us? Marie asked.

June 10, 1968 Monday

Marie was going back high above the Hudson, on George and Martha Washington's bridge; her mother was riding under the river, from Hoboken to Manhattan on the PATH train; Marie emerged from an unmistakable Bentley at the school entrance; Mrs. Cresspahl arrived under Times Square at almost precisely the usual minute, and already it was no longer her, she was cut off from her day of free time in the country, slotted into the way to work, already transformed, already an integral part of the day that's not hers, that's hired out. A drowning man is more reasonable—at least he struggles.

In the second of the three light boxes with which a cosmetics company frames the departures board in Grand Central Station, a photograph of the assassinated senator is still hanging, trimmed with black and purple ribbons. Clearly the arrangement had simply been forgotten.

De Rosny has hired someone to read *The New York Times* to him. And today again a confidential message is tucked in it for him. From London comes the portent that Soviet exercises on Czechoslovak soil were not meant to exert "a certain intimidation." Who would dream of such a thing. The military maneuvers had been scheduled for six months ago, i.e., an opportune January—they'd just been postponed. The Novosti press agency personally vouches that the leaders of Czechoslovakia have time and again confirmed their loyalty to the Warsaw Pact defense system. Another visitor is coming tomorrow, today—a high-level delegation for economic discussions—and they will definitely be discussing de Rosny, i.e., loans in hard currency. The usual calculations won't, of course, apply. For officials concede that the ČSSR sends to the Soviet Union manufactured goods that fall short of world market quality and are not favorable for convertible currencies, and doesn't look too deeply into why that is. In the other direction, the Soviet Union sends raw materials that are everything they should be. The equivalence between them is thus tantamount to a Soviet hard-currency credit for Czechoslovakia. This may not enlighten mathematicians or give much more than basic information for economists, but no one is trying to speak to such circles anyway.

Meanwhile, Employee Cresspahl doesn't touch a typewriter all morning, or anything else that might make noise in the office. The noise of the outside world is muffled, kept at a distance already. Without a word, almost assiduous from the silence, she is calculating numbers for a diagram based on the Czechoslovakian Five-Year Plan; behind her, lulled by the even breaths of the air conditioner, a visitor is lying on the sofa, asleep.

Amanda Williams, if she'd been at our school in Gneez, would have been given a nickname like Black Beauty. In high school. Or maybe Our Fine Filly, and not because of her curvy body but because a child like her moves quickly, stepping gracefully but nonetheless with a surge of power, whether coming out of a reverse-flip dive and plunging straight into the water or stepping on a teacher's foot; devoted without fail to her girlfriends, innocently out for her own advantage, surprised by some of her successes, in short far advanced in her training as woman and without much realization of the fact. A girl that the boys in the class are still proud of even if she's rejected them twice. And yet this whirlwind of a person can be found in a strangely tame state, crying and for the time being inconsolable over a lost ring, bungled homework, an avoided glance—still strong in her sobbing, defenseless against unhappy reality, like the shyest dolt in the rearmost row. This other Amanda crept, yes, slunk into Mrs. Cresspahl's office and before she could guess whether it was a sleepless night or alcohol the shirker's tears indicated another misfortune. Now nothing will come of our house on Long Island Sound, our man-free commune. Amanda needs forgiveness for this, as though it were the worst thing that could happen. She was one of the hundred and fifty million viewers who followed the massive coverage of the Kennedy ceremonies, and sounding just like *The New York Times* she calls herself emotionally exhausted but ready to make one more mistake. One that she again can't discuss with Naomi. She has reconciled with Mr. Williams, psychological counselor to New York's police; she is quite sure she's pregnant. She slept till noon, in the bank where she belonged but sheltered in an office that not even our vice president sets foot in without announcing himself first. She lay on the three-seat visitor's sofa for a very long time, her back trustingly to the wall, hands cupped and folded over her eyes, an overgrown child.

Strangers noticed nothing as they went down to lunch, even though she could check her makeup in no other mirror but Mrs. Cresspahl's eyes; she was talking in her usual galloping, easily overheard way too, and the other customers in Gustafsson's sandwich shop might well have taken the sharp rage in her voice for mimicry, for clever exaggeration:

– You don't watch TV, Gesine. You don't know this country. We used to have a TV show here, very popular, showing terrible accidents, you know. The mother of the sweet little boy who lost his arm in a garbage disposal sitting in front of the camera, the father of a hemophiliac son, the parents of a deformed child, and they'd all tell you everything, with photos, and the invited audience voted on the various diseases and travails, awarding third, second, first prize. The studio had a phone line where viewers across the country could donate money for the sufferers, or a wheelchair from up in the attic, or a brand-new garbage disposal, *do you even have a pig at home?!*

said Amanda; in Berlin she'd have been called a *flotter Dampfer*, a sassy girl; she has long since taken in the horrified and lustful looks of the men at Gustafsson's, through her skin, through her temples; she doesn't turn her bitter gleeful face away:

– Here's a series that would be a real hit, I'd call it *Fantastic Funerals,* copyright by me. An hour a week is probably enough. Your host: the ravishing Amanda Williams. I'd show the different rituals—the Catholic one, I have no idea how that goes, oh never mind I do since two days ago; the Jewish customs, Protestant, can't forget Voodoo, the white tears, the black tears. That'd be a real contribution to national education, don't you think? Knowledge and Sympathy—that's the slogan, to bring in the viewers. I'd interview the bereaved, show the bodies, have a group of judges for the flower arrangements. The funeral parlors, can't forget those. *It is a cold April morning, our melancholy coast guard cutter chugs through the biting wind out to Potter's Island, its cargo a heavy one, that no one wants to . . .* whaddaya think? What percent do you think the advertisers' sales will go up by? You could get everything into a show like that! Grass seed, weed killers, all kinds of makeup, insurance, US Steel, umbrellas of course . . . Whaddaya think? You know what that is, that's a million-dollar idea. Six months and I'll be rich! Do you think I'll still talk to the likes of you?

– You're thinking about money again. Just go play the lottery.

– You think I don't? I'll hold my press conference in the Hotel St. Moritz, out on the lawn. I'll tell the reporter from the *Daily News* "I'm not talking to you," so that the *Post* reports on it and the *Times* gives the whole thing a veneer of seriousness. What else am I supposed to think about if not money, Gee-sign?

We were together for half the trip home, to the destination boards in Grand Central. The bottles still shone on the frosted glass, not entirely unlike a penis. – A woman belongs in bed, the men in the ads! Amanda said.

She doesn't want to borrow money for an abortion. Not from Mrs. Cresspahl. No best friend could do more for a person than Mrs. Cresspahl.

If only she understood what she's done. The fact is, she was entirely elsewhere all day, since this morning.

June 11, 1968 Tuesday

– I won't give you a *Spiegel*: the old man at our newsstand says, hardly as friendly and forthcoming as last week, and someone coming home from work with dulled senses is especially taken in by his grumpiness. In fact he's protected his stacks of paper from the dripping rain with transparent sheets of plastic, they're items to display more than to sell. Maybe he feels like keeping everything for himself today. He scrapes a smile onto his stubble and smugly says: Your daughter's already gotten herself one!

Bringing something special home for Marie is harder to do. She'd rather get her toy cars from Herald Square than Upper Broadway, and anyway she's enjoyed her collection less and less as it's approached completion. She has two Bentleys. A men's outfitter on Lexington Avenue promises to print anything you want on T-shirts, and of course they had size 12Y in stock, I just couldn't think of the text, Marie doesn't feel the need to share her first name, PARTLY SUNNY TOMORROW is not something she'd want to promise the world too often, it would be a burdensome present. An extra pork chop, a kosher bundt cake, European chocolate—if she's in the mood for any of that she'll have it at home; she's in charge of the groceries. The lively Puerto Rican who's sometimes on Ninety-Seventh and West End Avenue hawking the tastiest hottest dogs and sauerest kraut in a one-mile radius is one last possibility—but today he's moved somewhere else, whether because of the policemen collecting their money or the nasty humidity in the air. So as I finish my walk to the apartment door all I'm bringing home is the wish that I were bringing something home, *and saying something stupid like*: Hey. Marie. The East German government is sending condolences to Ethel Kennedy too.

When Marie is startled, you can see it most easily in the eyes. She can't help the lurch of her pupils, she would have liked to keep her lids from snapping down, when she manages a mask of patience it's too late. At age four she still pursed her lips at unreasonable requests—protruding them resentfully at the ice-cream man speaking a foreign language, for instance—but this person will keep her face stiff at the oblivious adult, while thinking over and over that she has to accept it, especially from this one, has to behave herself with this adult who'll just never learn. Embarrassed for her mother she shifts her shoulders back and forth, she even stands up from an inner conflict between answering sharply and being considerate. She politely says: If you could at least stop repeating the name, Gesine.

– It was for your essay: her mother lies, submissive, and prepared well enough for the admonition that not every essay is meant for the eyes of the child's legal guardian. But Marie puts the news from Germany down on the table, with the cover folded back—it must show that Kennedy in front of colors of mourning—she sees that one of these evenings when we sit trapped, as if in a snowed-in post office with no horses, is soon underway, and we talk politely to each other, like strangers, and she says:

If it's no trouble.

If you're not too tired.

For at least a week, okay?

And:

Here's your weekly rations.

How are the East Germans consoling Martin Luther King's widow?

How was work?

And:

There was a *Versammlung* against the *Notstandsgesetze* in West Germany. Translate that for me?

What does this poet, Enzensberger, mean by "backrooms"?

What kind of workers does he want to go out onto the streets with, exactly?

What are these French conditions he wants?

And:

Dmitri Weiszand wants to know whether I'm going to Prague.

Can I learn Czech too?

I'm not arguing with you! Not at all.

June 12, 1968 Wednesday

Rain. Rain. Rain.

The Soviet Union is having trouble with its Socialist brothers and sisters in Czechoslovakia. Among them it had an erstwhile confidant, a major general, who last December attempted a military putsch against the scorners of Saint Novotný, though in vain. His employers may have forgiven him his lapse, and also that he then crossed the wrong border. They will hardly hate their former friend now that it turns out he's a big thief ($20,000 worth of clover and alfalfa seed). But the fact that he got his diplomatic passport from a Soviet general! That's serious. If it were only the *Times* from New York telling the tale that might be all right—let the world know. But for people in Prague to hear about it through a reprint in the newspaper *Lidova Demokracie*, that is just too much, and the ambassador in Moscow gets a sorrowful letter. It would really be a shame about those amicable international relations you've got there. If the appropriate authorities of the Czechoslovak Socialist Republic fail to take immediate action against their own news organs then look out! Alfalfa and clover seed, hmph. It may be true, but does that mean you have to put it in the papers?

– Your Soviets weren't so funny: Marie says. I'm supposed to tell her what they were like, she's been promised, and reconciliation depends on it. It's our Professor Erichson who's promised her—he feels that there's no such thing as an abstract truth, truth is always concrete. Why was Mrs. Cresspahl so relieved at every postponement? Why did she want to table the whole thing, at least until fall, preferably for a whole year?
    – "My" Soviets.
    – In *your* Soviet Mee-klen-burg. You were there with them, in the same place. You met each other. You know them.
    – At age twelve. I turned thirteen in 1946.
    – Gesine, tell me there's one child in Mecklenburg who doesn't know about my country.
    – You can have a whole grade of schoolkids in Gneez.
    – Couldn't I tell them how things are in New York, from Harlem to the Hudson?
    – It would be just what you've seen. What you know. Just your truth.
    – My truth.
    – They'd never believe you, not from the word go.
    – Gesine, I want to believe you.
    – You think I have an ax to grind but you say you want to believe me. How is that going to work!
    – I have an ax to grind too, Gesine. Oh yes. I do too.
    – All right, I admit that things were bad for Cresspahl in Soviet prison. Sometimes. Worse than I want to tell you about.
    – Starvation?
    – Starvation too.
    – Physical abuse?
    – Injuries of all kinds.
    – It happened to him because of a mistake, Gesine.
    – It happened to him.
    – The Soviets had won. They were soldiers, foreign ones. Why couldn't a clerical error have crept in somewhere? Maybe they'd misunderstood the foreign language, a lot sometimes.

– Some of the interpreters had learned their German from Nazi occupations and had to get to Russian through Polish.

– Gesine, am I being a bad granddaughter and daughter if I don't want to hear all the details about Cresspahl?

– It's not exactly a water-butt story.

– Okay, Gesine: He wasn't there for a while.

– He wasn't there. So he couldn't help me for a while, while I'd taken in all my earlier whiles with him. With his words, but more through the information that passed through moods, glances, shifts in facial expressions. I had Jakob's mother, but she was a stranger in Jerichow and couldn't bring home much more than the hospital and its neighborhood. With Jakob there was yet another way to share things, and just like he didn't bring children along on his business deals, he didn't tell us about them either. For the other families still in Jerichow I was the daughter of the mayor who'd been arrested—they were more likely to talk to Hanna. In Gneez there was truly no one who wanted me to count on them. What I can tell you now is nothing but what a thirteen-year-old happened to be there for, along with all the confusion that later knowledge imposes. Is that all right with you?

– What else haven't you told me about?

– Slata's disappearance.

– I'd almost forgotten about her! You were avoiding her on purpose!

– Slata opened the door to the first Soviets to walk into Papenbrock's foyer as if she wanted them to take her away from that house, that family. The Gneez military commander kept her as an assistant, not just a translator; he would have let her visit the Papenbrocks. She never got around to it. Louise had treated her like a maid for too long, Albert had merely watched without helping. So in Gneez hardly anyone knew that a Nazi "special unit" commander had hauled her off to Mecklenburg as a bride, with a child, to in-laws themselves linked to the air force and the Nazi Party by profitable business dealings. Instead they knew her as "the Angel of Gneez." She'd been in the country since fall 1942, it was impossible to lie to her in standard German, fancy German, or Plattdeutsch either, and there were a lot of people who credited her with their having made it out of a Soviet interrogation in one piece, their innocence more or less proven. Still, she was a stranger, there was no one who could count on special treatment except sick women, starving children, or a refugee who'd stolen potatoes not to sell them but because he needed them. She was nastily scrupulous in helping her boss, J. J. Jenudkidse, "Triple-J," keep tabs on the Gneez business world: the mighty Johannes Knoop had had to hand over his cart for transporting wood, never mind any "import-export." In these higher circles, her former future relatives were kept in reserve as a moral failing, a snare to be used down the line if needed, but not for now, in deference to their good Jerichow business partner, Albert. When they got mad they called her a slut and, can you believe it, a traitor. But the Angel of Gneez didn't live in the military housing on Barbara Street, protected from the Germans by an eight-foot fence; she left her son Fedya with Mrs. Witte during the day, in the requisitioned City of Hamburg Hotel, and slept there on the top floor, still furnished as Alma's private apartment, behind two doors not counting the hotel's main entrance. She spent some evenings downstairs in the former dining room with various officers from the Kommandatura and functionaries of the German Communists. There Slata understood almost no German, and especially not one young man's repeated attempts to strike up a conversation; he stood five paces away, kept his scornfully baffled eyes on her, with a deliberately gloomy expression, as if he weren't the future district councilman of Gneez. No. Not even Cresspahl's requests, with which he tried to circumvent K. A. Pontiy with even-higher-ups, passed through Slata's typewriter any faster than the rest, even though he'd talked with her under the Nazis about more than just the time of day, for example about Hilde Paepcke, who used to wear her hair in a scarf just like she did—clearly a woman he liked, too. In a twelve-year-old girl's eyes the district councilman was a stupid boy, but she wouldn't have minded turning out like Slata someday.

– I like how you look in photos from then, Gesine. *If I may say so myself.*

– But she was blond, Marie. That was considered pretty in those days. She was a grown-up; she was over my problems: what to do with your breasts, how a girl gets a baby. She was tall, almost willowy, but impressive. I loved to see how she held out her arm, or bent her knees to lean down. Such harmonious, flowing movements. She had a small, voluptuous mouth; I was mad at the language for saying my lips were "protruding." Slata nodded with her eyes when she listened to you. She would pass me on the street with a closed, withdrawn expression, preferring not to acknowledge me;

still, I felt invited to look back, be playful even. I would feel like we'd exchanged smiles after all, and said: Hi. Hey, how are you? You too.

– Such an important character. And you try to keep her from me.

– Then she disappeared. She was gone from my life. Once, when the midday train to Jerichow wasn't running again, I dropped in on Mrs. Witte, not knowing, just remembering when I'd had my lunches at the City of Hamburg, I wasn't thinking about Slata at all, and Slata was all Alma could talk about although she'd lost the power to form words. She just pointed around the room she'd given Slata as a bedroom, I followed the movements of her crippled finger, wanting to reassure her, and I set a nightstand back on its feet, swept up broken glass from the rug, hung some dresses back up, tidied up Fedya's torn-apart bed, and was just about to dash off and run to Jerichow on foot to warn Cresspahl but I had to go into Alma's kitchen and put on a kettle, get tea out of the can marked "Salt," all following her helpless breathing and panting.

– It happened to Slata because of a mistake, Gesine.

– It happened very suddenly. J. J. J. had driven up to the hotel like he did every morning, whistled cheerfully up to her window, but this time he'd brought four armed men with him and whipped up his anger by stomping up the stairs. That's how much he'd changed since the night before, but she hadn't.

– Did they beat her?

– Yes, because she resisted. Her child had a fever and needed to stay in bed.

– She was the wife of a Nazi, even if not legally. One who'd set villages in Ukraine on fire.

– Triple-J knew that when he hired her and trusted her. He'd forgiven her.

– She'd had a son with this Robert Papenbrock.

– He spoke Russian better, his name wasn't Fritz anymore, he answered to Fedya.

– Her name turned up in Cresspahl's files.

– Yes. But that's not why they picked her up.

– Gesine, you didn't want to tell me this because of that ax you have to grind. You think I'll misunderstand the Soviets again. But I'm understanding them.

– As long as no one gets beaten.

– Gesine. I don't like that kind of punishment. But I don't like when someone betrays his country. You're trying to tell me it's a good thing. First Cresspahl, then Slata.

– Tell it to Slata.

– I see. She came back. We can talk to her, try to explain. Someone explained it to her a long time ago.

– She didn't come back. And Fedya survived the trip to the Soviet Union, then died in the camp.

– Gesine, rewind the tape to Alma Witte. I wish I hadn't said all that. Let me think it over first. Next time warn me. Say: "Stop."

– Here Mrs. Witte had lost something: Fedya, who'd learned to call *her* Grandma, not Louise Papenbrock. A little three-year-old boy. She could carry him in her arms. *Where are you, where are you, my little chickee?* And she'd lost the mother with the child. A mother who could've easily lorded it over her landlady but she'd been quiet, a shade too independent but occasionally daughterly. This young thing had given her the respect she was entitled to. A Mrs. Witte liked that. And when the proprietress of the City of Hamburg Hotel praises Miss Podyeraitska's politeness for no apparent reason, it cuts a wide swath through public opinion, especially when she hints at the presence of other virtues too. The Angel of Gneez. In addition to that, Alma Witte had lost what the good townsfolk call pride. It takes more than hard work in a Mecklenburg country town to keep a hotel in second place behind the Archduke, with no close third. The district court judges had dined with her, the teachers and principals, army officers from good families. At night when she walked through the dining room the men would stand up to greet her. If someone from out of town wanted to be introduced to her, he'd better have one of the old well-established guests with him. One time, she'd told the Mecklenburg Reich governor's entourage to keep it down, and hadn't waited to see that her request was obeyed, and their corner had settled back down to the usual level. Commissioner Vick—from the police, not the Gestapo, because I'm an upstanding National Socialist!—had to watch his behavior or else she'd refuse to serve him. The Soviets had turned the building into an inn for functionaries of the new administration and visiting party officials, and yet she called Mr. Jenudkidse "chivalrous"; she'd joined them for dinner like an honorary chairman; merrymaking of the kind that went on at Louise Papenbrock's was unthinkable. Whether Mrs. Witte felt affable or respectful behavior was appropriate, the behavior always was appropriate. The thing is that her whole sense of propriety depended on her being accepted, recognized, responded to. Such mutual partnership had been wiped out by the raid on her apartment. She no longer trusted in the exchange of similar manners and mutually agreed-upon forms. The Alma Witte of earlier days would have turned up at Town Hall in her best Sunday clothes and requested that the commandant clear up the incident, diplomatically assessing whether to demand an apology or if she'd ultimately have to let the faux pas go. But they hadn't even waited for her to open the door, they'd crashed through it and broken all her rare frosted glass. They'd ignored her dignified protests and dragged guests out of her home, in defiance of all morality. They'd shoved her in the chest, and certainly not held out a hand to help her get up—a lady of sixty-five! Alma Witte submitted nothing in writing to the Kommandatura, neither a request for mercy for her young friend nor a petition for compensation for damages. She couldn't even feel satisfaction at J. J. Jenudkidse now spending his evenings off at the Archduke Hotel, now known as the Dom Ofitserov—it wasn't because he felt any embarrassment in front of her. Around town she was invited to comment on Slata's departure, and declined with sad dignity, as if refusing a course at the dinner table; again she was leaving an exaggerated wake of Soviet renown behind her, but actually she'd only wanted to avoid complaining. From a child she could demand that a shameful sight be forgotten. And I didn't need to be especially obedient to do that. To me she was a very old woman, why wouldn't she have fits or bouts of something. I hoped she felt better soon.

– You liked her too, Gesine.

– I've liked lots of people in my life.

– Couldn't it have been pity, Gesine?

– Pity for what. If she'd cried it would have been contagious and I would have too. But I couldn't be a pitying child.

– Am I jealous, Gesine? Of Slata? Of a proprietress of the City of Hamburg Hotel in Gneez? Is it possible?

– "Stop."

– No. No. I need to know.

– Mrs. Witte was never the same again, except outwardly. It wasn't the Red Army's manners that were her undoing—it was about her. Once, in spring 1946, I had to ask her if I could spend the night, the evening train to Jerichow had been canceled as well. She casually gave me permission, because one didn't set foot in Alma Witte's home as an imposition or to make some request, you had to follow the formalities of a social visit. Her salon had been repaired and she made me sit down in it for a proper conversation about the canceled train, sabotage?, requisition?, about the Gneez district administration office, about Cresspahl. She hadn't become nervous or afraid. And along with all that she was educating me in the finer points of middle-class polite conversation: replies in complete sentences, clear enunciation, euphemisms where appropriate and the whole truth when proper. She seemed undamaged to me. At about nine o'clock, unhurried, every inch a lady, she went downstairs with me into the former hotel reception desk, where she'd heard some noise that she planned to put a stop to. It was nothing but a lost Red Army soldier, two girls had caught his eye at the train station, a couple of junior teachers, guests of this establishment, chicks from out of town, they were supposed to just precede the young drunk to the Kommandatura, where he'd have gotten what was coming to him and a safe place to spend the night too. Now he'd stumbled into the Hamburg Hotel lobby and was waving his gun around in the half-open door to the reception area, admittedly too drunk to shoot, totally wasted in fact, but still drawn to the company of the young ladies who'd so mysteriously vanished into a wall here. That's when I saw Alma Witte's crooked index finger again. She pointed at the flailing figure in the lobby the same way she'd once indicated wrinkles in a table-cloth, spots on a knife, cigar stubs on the rug, whatever had to be straight-ened out, cleaned up, discreetly removed. But now there was no staff to leap to do her bidding; now she could not speak. This imperious person found herself surrounded by two educational experts, a woman who had almost qualified as a People's Court judge, Comrade Schenk emerging slowly from the dining hall—a man by the look of him—but not one of them understood what Mrs. Witte's trembling finger meant. It was a young female person who crept along the wall to the lobby, pushed the banging door shut, and turned the key in the lock, reaching up from her cautious kneel.

– He could have fired!

– He took his cue from the door. It was shut. The girls were gone. He just wanted some sleep.

– Why didn't any of you report him to the Kommandatura?

– Someone would've had to go out the back of the hotel, down a swaying ladder from Mrs. Bolte's apple yard, into the courtyard, over the wall, onto the street, and maybe right into the arms of another wandering lost soldier. Comrade Schenk forbade it, for the public good. At which Mrs. Witte forbade it again, pointing her finger at him outraged that he would give orders in her house. She wasn't vindictive. The drunk kid would've gotten a terrible beating at Town Hall and then another round after Triple-J had been woken up, because he would have reminded Slata's protector of where she'd lived. No, Alma Witte hadn't become nervous or afraid, and wasn't vindictive. She'd just lost her pride. The befuddled sleeper moved off before it was light out, and Mrs. Witte scrubbed the area between the inner and outer doors twice before anyone else in the hotel woke up. That's how she was now.

– And the person who locked the door, Gesine, was that you?

– I stood there, unable to tear my eyes away from that crippled, humiliated finger. I kept telling myself, over and over and over again: Don't laugh. Whatever you do, don't laugh. Why aren't you laughing, Marie?

– You know a lot more stories like that, don't you.

– A lot more.

– And you're sure I'll take them the wrong way.

– I'm afraid you might.

– Wait and see, Gesine. Wait and see.

The East German Communists plan to demand even more money from citizens of West Germany on their way to West Berlin. Now these citizens will have to pay not only for the tracks their tires leave on the roads but also for a visa, whether they're rich or poor, retirees or trucking companies; and a passport for foreign travel will be required too. There are three obvious reasons for the stratagem: They want to intimidate the people in the foreign city; they need hard currency to buy Western machinery and equipment; they are simply stressing their sovereignty and national dignity. They do not want to be misunderstood in such ignominious terms, and so they provide a reason of their own: it's about retaliating for the West German emergency laws, which don't apply to them.

Because give them a whole basketful of Easter eggs and they'll incorruptibly stick to the rules of international diplomacy. They do not get involved.

The Czechoslovak Communists have put a new travel law before the National Assembly, all they have left to do is finalize the precise wording for the exceptions. The exceptions are citizens facing judicial proceedings, persons in active or upcoming military service, bearers of state or scientific secrets, and those who have damaged Czechoslovak interests on previous trips abroad. Everyone else is guaranteed the right to a passport valid for all countries and not requiring an exit visa, and they'll be able to go wherever they want for as long as they want and the homeland will welcome them back in friendship upon their return. Hopefully the Soviets won't be sad again when they read about this in a Prague paper, or in *Freedom*, out of Halle, East Germany.

The weather. It's supposed to be sunny, dry, and mild today, cool tonight.

– All right Gesine, can I set a trap for you? I was clumsy yesterday. Today I'll get you.

– Can I set a trap for you too, Marie?

– I know yours. You won't see mine.

– Mary Fenimore Cooper Cresspahl!

– And Henriette. Ready?

– The tape's running.

– Gesine, were the Soviets in your country more out of control than the British in India?

– They behaved like occupiers. The country was theirs, they wielded the power, and along with the glory they wanted to make sure they didn't get a raw deal.

– But the losers weren't all equally afraid of them. The ones who had something to lose. The middle class. What you call the bourgeoisie.

– If they were scared of the New Order it wasn't over their place in it. That had already been locked in.

– It was such a fat index finger, Alma Witte's. Chalk white, trembling. She was bourgeois.

– No. Take just the people in Jerichow, they weren't the Witte type. They genuinely wanted to surrender everything, starting with their sense of identity, if only they could keep their money, as a way to acquire possessions and more money. And the Soviets let them. The potatoes and wheat and milk went through their shops, just like before, and even the green Soviet fence went through their account books, they made money on others' labor same as ever. Even Papenbrock had been able to keep his granary, and his representative managed it for him, Waldemar Kägebein, who'd turned out to be right after all with his copy of Aereboe's *Handbook of Agriculture*. He charged a fee for receiving the grain, another for storing it, another for shipping it, and they weren't only written down in Papenbrock's books, they were deposited in the bank. If Louise could only charge forty-three reichpfennigs for bread, she just mixed in enough bran so that she could still make a profit. No one gives me anything for free either, she used to say, contentedly in a position to think: And no one's gotten much off me.

– They took her husband though.

– He was replaced by a trustee. Exactly as under the old laws.

– Wasn't she in danger too?

– If Albert came back and she hadn't taken good care his property, never mind if she'd let it get frittered away, then she'd really be in danger, that's what she thought. True, the Soviets might invite her on a little joyride who knows where: she thought she'd survive it, knowing she was innocent, the same way she expected Papenbrock home any day now, vindicated, pure as the driven snow. Besides, hadn't she been nice to the Red Army, hospitable even, when Mr. Wassergahn's crowd destroyed her living room parquet with their dancing? The only thing that could happen now was an accident of some kind, and for that eventuality she had Horst's widow in reserve, admittedly of inferior background, from the shoemakers' town, but still a daughter-in-law, predestined to take over managing the inheritance. Why would the chain be broken?

– Her friends in the nobility had run away from the Russians.

– That was a relief, as far as your middle class were concerned. The victors' punishment had fallen on others' heads, for now. How could your middle class keep up a friendship that had become impractical, which is to say bad for business? Pure friendship for morality's sake, without any value? There was no longer any point in imagining an alliance with the Plessens, the Upper Bülows; in fact, quite a few things came to Louise's mind that implied, if anything, a certain hostility: a greeting ignored or airily returned, failing to be invited to the von Zelck double wedding in 1942. Back then she would never have found fault, not even with a doubtful nod at the Lüsewitzes, at the fact that a member of the German landed aristocracy was keeping forced laborers locked in the farm stalls, foreign laborers but still—now she tucked her chin firmly into her collar and spoke of justice with pious severity. Another family, the von Haases, were staying in one of the Papenbrocks' attic rooms. They'd been deported from southern Mecklenburg, farther from their estate than the prescribed thirty kilometers. Louise nagged at them in the kitchen when they came to get water, and if their daughter Marga gave her the slightest bit of back talk Louise would shout after her: I bet your mother used to hit prisoners of war too! Which she had no evidence for at all, beyond her imagination. She wanted these people and the uncomfortable memories out of her house. She would have slammed the door in a fugitive von Bothmer's face.

– And denounced him.

– You don't trust me. You think I'm twisting the story around against her. Just to make her out to be bad.

– You hate her.

– There was nothing about her for a thirteen-year-old to hate, Marie. I avoided her because Cresspahl more or less told me to, and now Jakob wanted it too. Did I know why? Can you hate on command?

– That wasn't my trap, you know, Gesine.

– She would never have denounced him, it would have gotten around to the neighbors that she was being more accommodating to the Soviets than she needed to be. And besides, she still shared something else with the other Jerichow homeowners: they wanted their little entries in the nobility's good books. The situation might change again, after all.

– Back to what it had been? They'd lost!

– The Soviets were incomprehensible conquerors—they didn't introduce their own economic system in Mecklenburg. Not the big nationalized communal farms, their famous kolkhozes. They faithfully kept the agreement with their Allies, the Potsdam one, and took the land away from everyone who owned more than a hundred hectares, and of course from any Nazi leader. They did so earlier than promised, but did they do it in a Communist way? Socialist production is large scale, you'll learn that one of these days, but the Soviets handed out their stock of land in small parcels, many of them just five hectares, to farmworkers, small farmers, resettlers from the eastern territories, even old farmers got something, and the municipality of Jerichow, can you imagine? got fields to cultivate that had once been the nobility's, and a piece of the Countess Woods to boot. To approve so much property, in such quantities, both the concept and the reality, and provide the Mecklenburg world with it—that didn't look like they were planning to stay.

– They must have done it with gritted teeth at least. Just to honor their treaty?

– You don't believe they'd do such a thing, Marie.

– Aha. So that was your trap. Right, Gesine?

– That was not even the spring in the door of the trap. But they'd signed an agreement saying that the German people were not to be enslaved, and they stuck to it. They kept their version of Communism for themselves. Sometimes they acted in such a way that even the most ethical bourgeoisie couldn't help but approve. They communicated with the Germans through a newspaper of their own, and they could have called it *The Soviet Military Administration News*, *The Anti-Fascist Observer*, *The Free Red Front*, but they called it *The Daily Review—Tägliche Rundschau*, "The Frontline Newspaper for the German Population," and dropped the "Frontline" as early as June 1945. And that wasn't any random title, it had once been the name of a Christian paper with fiercely nationalistic leanings. The Soviets took that, too, from the booty they'd pocketed from the Nazis, all strictly legally. The middle-class concept of property counted for something with the Soviets.

– Maybe they needed your bourgeoisie for a while, for economic reasons. But they didn't let them into the government. That would have been like promising to cut off their own arm.

– Well, don't ask Sister Magdalena about the Potsdam Agreement.

– You're kidding me.

– The Soviets couldn't make their position with regard to their share of the conquered people any clearer than they did with their leader's prophecy, painted on bedsheets and hung on town halls or painted in red Gothic on the front walls of school auditoriums:

Hitlers

Come and Go

But

The German People, the German State,

Remains

all center-aligned the way type designers and calligraphers like. When you have that before your eyes for hours on end you can't stop trying to translate it into Latin, with *et,* or even more elegantly, *atque,* it looked so classical. Wise as the Leader of Peoples working nights in the Kremlin, a perfect example of his style and yet the voice was off a little, it wasn't one of his feats of dialectics, just the ebb and flow of history: Hitler a recurring type notwithstanding the growing power of the international working class, eternity promised to a state identified only as German but that meant it included a strand of Mecklenburg too. It was nothing less than a lesson in irony, perfect for bourgeois minds.

– They didn't believe it, Gesine.

– If the Soviets were using perfectly good sheets for it? Cotton they otherwise could have slept on? Your middle class bowed their head and accepted it, they liked showing off how clever they were. How sly, how shrewd. As promised, the Soviets didn't just hand over the administration of their conquest to Germans, to opponents of Hitler's; as expected, they sent in relatives, German Communist Party émigrés trained in Soviet schools for this German state; predictably, they sent in people with them representing the class which, according to Soviet science, was the sole source of productivity and historical strength, and which, moreover, was overdue for an equalization of both income and power; to no one's surprise, the Communist Party arrived. Now it was their turn.

– Arm in arm with the bourgeois parties. Before K. A. Pontiy's very eyes.

– This commandant left them behind in Jerichow as a memento. After Cresspahl's arrest—

– "Stop."

– In fall 1945, Pontiy was no longer the Oriental potentate. His orders

grew more detailed by the day, treating the former British Mecklenburg
in accord with the same plans that applied to the rest of it. Sighing, he gave
up his statistics. He would have liked to just issue orders. He ordered Mrs.
Bergie Quade and Köpcke's wife to come to the villa for coffee, on the last
Sunday in November, the Sunday for the Dead, and amazingly enough he
served coffee. They could sit down, too, if only in the brown leather armchairs
facing the corner of the commander's desk, but they tried to make up for
this by sitting bolt upright, knees decorously together, expecting a discussion of their idiosyncratic bookkeeping. Instead it was suggested to them
that they

> found
> a regional branch
> of a Party
> of German
> Liberalism
> (or: Liberality) and
> Democracy

while Bergie couldn't stop dreaming of filing a complaint over the removal
of the old mayor; Mina was encased in an almost new dress, let out at the
back with two gussets, acquired to be worn for the widowed Mr. Duvenspeck,
she had just started feeling like a woman again; now they missed their cues,
it didn't matter what else they said: *we're simple womanfolk*, you know, I'm
just taking my husband's place, you know, I mean in the business, that's
all, a political party's for special interests, *youve still got our men locked up*,
you know, and what will the neighbors say! Commandant!

– Liberalism. Isn't that something to do with the gold standard?

– Not in that context. There it was the idea of stimulating the economy
with the economic self-interest of the individual, unrestricted competition,
a free market that the state protected but did not interfere with, international
free trade, manage best by managing least, laissez-faire laissez-aller . . .

– Must've been a translator's mistake.

– Well, they were certainly willing. It was a gift, they weren't going to
ask why they deserved it. Whatever they thought of this party's name, it
did have a ring of the old days, of prewar times, pre-Nazi. They were clever
about it, asking for time to think it over, pleading shyness, what with the
public speaking. Bergie couldn't get it out of her head that Pontiy's adjunct

Wassergahn could be her son, she'd have no trouble pulling the wool over his eyes. Mrs. Köpcke licked her lips, she'd been chosen because she was a woman, and if the Soviets were offering tea and cakes for honest doings and dealings then she could cut herself as big a slice as any man. Each of them hoped to palm off the top spot onto the other, but that didn't yet get in the way of their friendship and trust. There was only one snag to be taken care of, and that was the neighbors' ignorant chatter about sucking up to the Soviets: they'd learned a thing or two from the reputation they themselves had created for Cresspahl. And here they both bethought themselves of K. A. Pontiy's shortest, curtest answer, which had sort of agreed to offset their political activities with the expedited return of their husbands from Soviet prison camps—wasn't that an honorable reason? It took some time to get it known among the good citizens of Jerichow. Duvenspeck, though in charge of the gasworks, was the most amenable to accepting it. Then, out of left field, Böhnhase emerged as the founder of the local LDPD (German Liberal Democratic Party)—Böhnhase the tobacconist, former DNVP (German National People's Party), sentenced to seven years in prison for the crime of bartering tobacco for bacon in 1942 and yet not recognized as a VoF (Victim of Fascism) but nonetheless ready and willing to serve as a pillar of anti-Fascist Liberalism, office hours whenever his shop was open, tobacco rationing no argument against the party, abolishing tobacco rationing an argument in its favor. Mrs. Köpcke had to admit, along with Bergie, that they'd underestimated the male appetite, and anyway Böhnhase had been too far away from the trough for too long. They both joined his party, now no longer the main offenders, just fellow travelers. They brought in others too: Plückhahn the pharmacist, Ahlreep the jeweler, Hattje from the general store, tinker tailor soldier sailor rich man poor man beggar man thief—the whole native population faced with a minimal state. A "night-watchman state," they called it. Translation from the German.

– Did Louise have to join a party too?

– She wanted to, Marie. It was voluntary. Allowed. Desirable. Louise, standing in for her husband, joined the Conservative party, which called itself a Union, and wanted to be Democratic like the liberals, but unlike them Christian. Christian Democratic Union, CDU. And that's how K. A. Pontiy achieved his public

expression
of my respect
for the cause
of the equal rights
of women

because even though Pastor Brüshaver didn't generally preach atonement for German war crimes, even in what he called "the social sphere," he did think party politics was irreconcilable with spiritual office, it was enough simply to call for an "honest self-reappraisal," and Pontiy was happy to have a woman in charge—

– Louise Papenbrock.

– Käthe Klupsch.

– She was the laughingstock of the whole town!

– Käthe Klupsch was incapable of laughing at herself, though. What she was best at was the forgiving tone in which she spoke of people who went over to the Communist Party or Farmers' Mutual Aid just to get a second residence permit or a claim to a plow or maybe a head of cattle from the stock of the land reform agency. Swenson, Otto Maass, Kägebein, whenever one of them asked another how things were going the other would say: Scared as shit, same as ever! It sounded much better in public when Käthe Klupsch announced: We have joined forces not for our personal advantage but for the cause.

– Well, whatever your trap was, Gesine, it blasted mine to pieces.

– Mine was just to show you that you're wrong sometimes with all your talk of merciless oppression by the Soviets.

– I was trying to prove I can learn a lesson. I can think the Russians are right, sometimes, at least when they punish a crowd like that. But now the old crowd's back on top.

– What do you call a double trap like that, Marie.

– You know perfectly well.

– Your English is better than mine.

– A *double cross*. Probably a *Vorspiegelung vermittels Tatsachen* in German, or something.

There once was a time when we believed Herbert H. Hayes—that time when he looked up the weather over Easter 1938 for us. Let's hope the New

York Weather Bureau never employs him anywhere but in the archives. They'd have to worry about him in the forecasting department. Today was neither sunny nor dry. It might have deserved "mild," if only for the persistent rain that wouldn't stop for hours.

June 14, 1968 Friday

The Czechoslovak government delegation is back from Moscow. Bringing gifts. The Soviet Union will increase its annual natural gas shipments to Czechoslovakia to three billion cubic meters (100 billion cubic feet). The Košice steelworks will receive two million tons of iron-ore pellets a year, though not until 1972. Do we think he's gotten the fear of God put into him, our confident Vice President de Rosny? No, the Soviets refused to provide a hard-currency loan, modest though the requested sum was, $350 million, a mere seven-eighths of their debts on the Western market. All the more quickly and happily will de Rosny provide more. We're not going to get out of our trip to Prague. Marie knows, too. She doesn't want to talk about it.

The *Times,* prim and proper Auntie Times, makes a decorous curtsy. She apologizes. She's made a mistake. In that Soviet poem on the death of the New York senator, it wasn't supposed to say that Abraham Lincoln basks in his marble chair. It should have said that the marble Lincoln "rasps." Marie could use this for her Kennedy folder. But she doesn't want to hear that name for a while.

– So, what are you not going to tell me about today?

Sometime before Christmas 1945, Erwin Plath came trotting through northwest Mecklenburg again—his home territory, and assigned to him by the Socialist Party in Hanover. You make an effort for a guest, and Plath got his meeting in Jerichow, twenty minutes standing in the brickworks drying shed, perfectly in view of the Soviet Kommandatura, so it wasn't only from the cold that he was shivering. It was a bitter enough pill to swallow that he had to admit a mistake before informing his audience of the new party line; they heckled him mercilessly, not even respecting his status as a messenger. Fourteen men and two women had come; he knew two as former card-carrying members, was willing to believe it about two more, for eight of them he could imagine neither a past nor a future in the Social Democrats, and in one case he thought he must be dreaming, hadn't he been kicked out of the party in 1938, following the full illegal procedure? What's more they refused to give their names, so we'll have to content ourselves with their initials, although we can assume that W. was Wulff, and B. was Bienmüller. P. was Plath and wrote out his name, Plath, and had come from headquarters—important delegate Erwin Plath. The others soon cured him of that. – In all my life: P. was still saying nineteen years later: I've never been through a party meeting like that!

W.   This meeting is now opened. Be it resolved: This is not a meeting. About the agenda, let it be unanimously agreed: There is no agenda. That takes care of the role of secretary. I ask that the election of the secretary be approved. Now get lost, you.

P.   The party regrets the erroneous directive of August of this year.

S.   Do we have a chairman? We don't have a chairman. Permission to speak can only be given by the chairman.

H.   You've gotten us into a fine mess, comrade. If the Soviets know any of our names now, it's your fault.

P.   Who's been found out?

L.   None of your fucking business.

P.   The party concedes that the attempt to acquire secret spheres of influence within the Communist Party has not succeeded. There are comrades who applied for admission into the Communist Party who have been asked to found their own local branch of the Social Democratic Party. It was wrong, I'm not ashamed to admit it, I'll say it again.

K.   Let's hear you say it again, mister. Like in school!

P.   There's no "mister." And who are you, anyway?

L.   None of your fucking business.

P.   We must apply all our strength to create a strong party organization as a counterweight.

W.   We're not in Krakow here. The Communist comrades in Krakow am See sent all their papers to the State Criminal Investigations Office in March '33. The Soviets probably found them there.

P.   That's beside the point.

L.   None of your fucking business.

S.   They don't know a thing about us. We didn't send any parcels to the Nazis and none to the Soviets either.

H.   But there's one man they know. And that's your stupidity, dumbass. It's your fault.

P.   Is it you, comrade?

H.   Me you can call "mister."

P.   Needless to say, the party will do everything in its power to cover for that comrade.

K.   Permit me to inquire: Do you have anything to cover him with?

S.   Because he can run away on his own. He doesn't need any chickenshit from the party for that. So that's one less of us.

P.   How many of you are then, anyway?

L.   I move that this is none of his fucking business.

W.   Since we have no meeting, no official agenda, and no procedure, there is no way to propose a motion. The motion is passed.

P.   The most important consideration, in case of unification with the Communist Party, is to create a strong counterweight within the Unity Party. If it comes to that.

S.   Feel free to come back when the party in the British zone unites with the CP.

P.   We must avoid any weakening of the party. But your case is different. You've still got to found a local branch!

H.   Register it, you mean. Inform on ourselves, that's what you mean.

P.   So you already have a local branch? And you're it?

L.   None of your fucking business.

H.   You'd like that, wouldn't you. Something to report.

P.   Children, children. I've worked my way north from Ludwigslust to Gneez. Local branches of the SPD hard at work everywhere. We hear about everything that goes on in the administrations, from the state level down to the districts!

S.   Then they can have a nice little chat with the Communist comrades about us being Socialist Fascists. What we meant by that coalition with the Nazis. What happened to the Social Democrats who emigrated to Russia.

K.   And will we have the pleasure, perchance, of hearing a word from headquarters to clear this up?

P. Maybe you won't have to unify at all. All the more reason for you to be here as a branch!

A. Anyway, it's only the Soviets who want a Unity Party. That doesn't matter.

P. Children, children. You have no idea what's happening in the world.

B. If you call us children one more time. Just one more time!

P. But you have no idea! Oh, how the Communists lost ground in Austria on November 25! And how well the Social Democrats did! In the Soviet Zone in Austria! Four seats for them, seventy-six for us!

K. Next you'll be comparing the Social Democrat wins in the local Hungarian elections with the defeat of the Communists.

P. I almost forgot about that! Yes! That's how you'll do, too!

A. Go ahead, help the Soviets.

P. Only an independent SPD in the Western Zone of Germany will be in a position to support you.

B. How on earth did Cresspahl ever come to it. A high opinion of you, I mean.

L. None of his fucking business! None of his fucking business!

W. The minutes have been read and approved. We will now proceed to the vote. For. Against. Abstain.

H. Every time someone's cover gets blown we're going to hold it against you. In twenty minutes, next year, doesn't matter.

S. You wanted something to report, didn't you. There it is.

W. It is hereby resolved that there are no minutes. This meeting is adjourned. There was no meeting.

– So, what do you have today that you don't want to tell me about?

– A casualty. "Stop"?

– You're emptying your Jerichow out. Soon no one I know'll be left.

– Paul Warning wasn't in Jerichow. Because he'd helped out on Griem's land for a while he was allowed to call himself an agricultural worker and take part in drawing slips of paper out of a hat Gerd Schumann had obtained from the von Zelck manor especially for the occasion and was passing around. Warning drew four hectares of moderately good land, an hour from town by wagon, almost uncultivated. He couldn't live on that this fall with his wife and two young sons but next year he just might. But his work in the fields hadn't taught him much more than how to follow orders. When he'd gotten back from Dreibergen prison he'd been in charge of minding the town's cows, a job he'd been given for his wife's sake. He told no more stories of any kind anymore, leaning comfortably on his pitchfork handle as a cow lowed next to him, and no one discussed their stories with him anymore either. He had turned hardworking, eager, obedient, afraid of another trip to Dreibergen. After the war his wife became set on having a plot of land of their own, but he would've done better with someone to supervise him. The Narodnyi Komissariat Vnutrennikh Del picked him up on Christmas 1945, no one paid much attention. He was still under a cloud because of that business with *Our Lisbeth*, so neither his arrest nor his release aroused much comment around town.

– If he gets shot, you're all to blame.

– Peter Wulff took the blame. He was only trying to help get the browbeaten fellow back onto his feet when he brought him along to a meeting of former Social Democrats with Erwin Plath; he regretted it right away, because Warning thanked him so effusively for the show of confidence, for taking him back into the party, he actually spoke of happiness. That was no way to talk. It hadn't been meant like that. He'd only been trying to help.

– They'd needed him as a stopgap.

– Exactly. Still, Wulff would've enrolled him in the party again, no, welcomed him as a comrade, because he'd been unobtrusive at the meeting, levelheaded, and above all kept his mouth shut. Wulff wasn't the only one to feel that way after Warning refused to say a word about his interrogation by the Soviets, neither high nor to heaven—maybe the guy really had firmed up, at least in one spot. Wulff trusted Warning, all the more when Warning assured him, with a twisted smile and a painfully solemn handshake: *Nothingll happen to you lot.* On New Year's Day, Warning went and hanged himself.

– It was a crime to expect someone like that to keep silent.

– Warning hadn't told the Soviets a thing about the mood of the Jerichow Social Democrats. He'd withstood even his own family—his wife knew not a thing about the arrest except that it'd lasted four days. He didn't even tell her, or leave her a note saying, why he could no longer face life. All she had was the slip of paper in his breast pocket, a new summons to the Gneez Kommandatura "due to a formality."

– He hanged himself where the meeting had happened. So they'd believe him.

– Right. In the brickworks shed.

– But if he didn't snitch on anyone then someone must've snitched on him!

– Right. So he did leave a legacy after all. In his way.

June 15, 1968 Saturday, South Ferry day
Public Library day

Sometimes you need to look at it scientifically, as the man says. Before a fight starts the public is given details about the boxers, weight, earlier victories, etc. So,

In the Prague corner:

ČESTMIR CISAŘ, b. 1920. Known for his very short hair and candid way of speaking. Note: wears glasses. Graduated with a degree in philosophy from Charles University in Prague. No injuries from the Soviet purges! Served in 1956 as secretary of the Czech Communist Party regional committee, Plzeň; came back to Prague in 1957 as deputy editor of its newspaper, *Rudé Právo*; and in 1961 was put in charge of its monthly journal *Nová Mysl*, well known to sports fans as *New Thought*. Joined the secretariat of the CCP in May 1963, demoted that same September for an inclination toward cultural dialogue and listening to other points of view. In his new post as minister of education and culture, he began to reform the Czechoslovakian school system while remaining fundamentally true to the Soviet-designed Education Law of 1953, yet he loosened up the curriculum, reduced instruction in party matters, and did not station a watchdog to look over every teacher's shoulder. Too popular with both students and professors, he received from St. Novotný not the highest punishment but the post of ambassador to Romania, in other words, training in Romanian cultural policies. After Novotný stepped down, he was called to be the Secretariat of the Central Committee's man in charge of education, science, and culture, was mentioned as a possible new president of the country, and has recently been entrusted with delicate missions for the party chairman, e,g,: persuading the press to deal gently with the Soviet brothers. Stated occupation: journalist and philosopher.

In the Moscow corner:

FYODOR VASSILYEVIČ KONSTANTINOV, b. 1901. In leading positions in the Communist Party of the USSR since 1952. Author of the textbook *Historical Materialism.* Allowed to celebrate the second anniversary of the Stalin's death with an article, "J. V. Stalin and Questions of Communist Superstructure," in—but not on the front page of—*Pravda,* known to sports fans as *Truth.* Author of the sentence: "The forces of production continue to develop even under the conditions of Imperialism" (*Voprossy Filosofii,* No. 2 [1955]). Since December 1955 head of the Division of Agitation and Propaganda in the Central Committee of the Communist Party of the Soviet Union, results negative. Since 1962 director of the Institute for Philosophy in the Academy of Sciences of the Union of Soviet Socialist Republics. Stated occupation: Professor. Philosopher.

A-a-a-a-nd Cisař comes out swinging in the first round with a speech at a public meeting in Prague. The occasion is the 150th anniversary of the birth of Karl Marx, and in his speech Cisař casually describes Leninism as a monopolistic interpretation of Marx's views. That was on May 5.

Konstantinov is in fine form, quick in his wit, fast on his feet, and he counters as early as June 14, raining massive blows down on his opponent, which can be gleaned from *Truth* as follows:

Cisař's criticisms put him into the ranks of a Menshevik such as Yuliy Ossipovič Martov (Tsederbaum), 1873–1923, Russian socialist, cofounder of *Iskra (The Spark).* That's right, Tsederbaum.

It has become fashionable among contemporary revisionists to attempt to give a different, non-Leninist interpretation of Marxism, Marxist philosophy, Marxist political economy, and scientific Communism.

With the industrial and economic successes of the Soviet Union, Leninism has become the banner of the world's Communist movement.

Revisionist exponents of reform seek to discredit Leninism and demagogically preach a "rebirth" of Marxism without Leninism.

Communists have always considered, and still consider, Leninism as not a purely Russian, but rather an international Marxist doctrine. And this is the reason that Marxist parties of all countries have originated and developed on its basis.

Now turn your attention to the finish, as the man says, but don't lose sight of the timing!

Because where are the first secretary of the Czechoslovak Communist Party and the prime minister during this fight? They are off in Budapest negotiating a twenty-year friendship pact. What else are they saying? They are emphasizing the enormous importance of their alliance with the Soviet Union.

Referee to the phone!

Where, in contrast, one might well ask, are the delegates to the Czech National Assembly? They, with their president, Smrkovský, are off with the head of the Soviet Communist Party, Leonid I. Brezhnev, and even if every last one of them has the *Truth* with Mr. Konstantinov in his jacket pocket, the Soviet press agency is only allowed to report a "warm and friendly talk" and everyone's confidence that the visit "will help further strengthen the fraternal friendship and cooperation between our countries."

Is there any way Fyodor Vassilyevič Konstantinov's not going to lose? That his trainer won't throw in the towel? Or on points?

They need to look at it scientifically, too.

June 16, 1968 Sunday, Father's Day

The third Sunday in June, set aside in honor of fathers.
Der dritte Sonntag im Juni, vorgesehen zur Ehrung von Vätern.
Because someone's a father.

Equipped as usual by nature, they take credit for such an exception.
Proud of their procreation.
If there's any guilt involved, it wasn't theirs.

There have to be children.
So that a father can pass himself down, even just part of himself, into a future.

That they neither know nor need fear.
They just want to be in it.

That's how much fathers love themselves.
And their possessions shouldn't be left just lying around, so they make someone to keep an eye on them.
A name should remain, a rank, a right to power.
As always: inheritance.

The hope of being looked after in old age.
Fear of being alone.
Dying with someone there to see.

Such a child, a gage of marriage.
See the Civil Code.

Hunting around in the sacrificial victims to make sure that they are truly contained in them. Being like them.
They want to be the measure, whether filled or broken: the type is to be theirs.
Children should have it better than their fathers.
What fathers do for the better.

And if the children don't want to have anything?
Not the place of consciousness that knows its end to be the goal, not even themselves?

In Europe, fathers stagger along in the gutter, wearing paper hats, tooting horns, yelling, beer in their throats, to honor themselves.
Vatertag. Father's Day.
Boys go with them who haven't yet made a baby with a girl, but they will.
Father's honor.
Nature's wisdom.
Continuation of the human race.

Fathers know why.

June 17, 1968 Monday

The US wants to release some Czechoslovakian money. No, not the gold worth $20 million that belongs to them and that the US wants counted toward the compensation owed for property nationalized in 1948. This is only $5 million—annuity payments in the form of social security, railroad retirement, and veterans' benefits to which some ten thousand Czechoslovak residents are entitled by virtue of contributions they made while here, as long as their new government gave written assurances that the sums would actually reach their recipients, at a fair rate of exchange. – We are not thieves: the Czechoslovak Communists need to say.

Once again a Soviet poet has given voice to his feelings. This one's name is Voznesensky. He does it not for the sixty-six-year-old doctor shot and killed and robbed on Friday night in Brooklyn during a house call, no, he does it on the occasion of a less mundane death:

Wild swans. Wild swans. Wild swans.

Northward. Northward. Northward!

Kennedy... Kennedy...

and he laments the loneliness of the roots of the apple trees on Kennedy's balcony on the thirtieth floor, availing himself of poetic license, in the opinion of *The New York Times*, due to his failure to remember that Mrs. Kennedy lives on the fifteenth floor. The poet had also been struck by the dead senator's resemblance to Sergei Yesenin, a Soviet poet.

– You're right, it's been a week: Marie says: But do you mind not bringing up that name for a while more?

– Sowwy. I mean, Sorry.

– You wanted to try and see. That's fine. I would've done the same thing.

– You know, in the IRT the fans are mounted in pairs, and now they've taken out one of each pair. It makes everyone start sweating as if their whole body was cr—

– I know, Gesine, I'm being silly. It'll heal. Someday it won't matter at all.

– If only you'd have a good cry!

– You also hold it against me that I got over MLK's death in a couple of days. I didn't know as much about him, you know.

– How was it on the South Ferry on Saturday? First time on your own!

– Calm, gray water. I wanted to punish you. And I did.

– You did. No you didn't. You had to do it alone for the first time someday.

– Gesine, is it because I'm from Mecklenburg that I can't make up with someone just by trying?

– Let's wait a little more.

– Okay. So tell me something that's got nothing to do with me.

– Louise Papenbrock?

– Good. She's got nothing to do with me.

– With trap or without?

– Without.

– Your great-grandmother's new political importance made her uncomfortable. Sometimes the only thing she could use as a crutch was spite against her fractious son-in-law, Cresspahl, who'd warned other people besides her off all this government nonsense. Going against that didn't turn out quite right either, and it didn't help her sleep any easier. This was the first time in her life she'd joined a party, and she suspected tricks while thinking herself too good to ask questions. How happy she'd have been to follow Pastor Brüshaver in everything! When it was precisely he who was causing her more annoyance than anyone, enough to make her shudder in secret. She'd joined this Christian Democratic Union for her husband Papenbrock's sake, following the command she imagined he'd have given; she was only trying to keep him a place in it. But Papenbrock, it seemed to her at least vaguely, had kept business and politics strictly separate, even at the office, certainly at the dinner table, and now she'd brought politics into the home! Pontiy's unit had beaten an ignominious retreat, she was rid of Wassergahn's parties (she didn't see Second Lieutenant Vassarion as a political figure); secretly she was trying to get the large ground-floor parlor back into Papenbrock's property, and might well have earned a few square feet of it once she'd spent four days on her knees scrubbing it clean. To her it seemed that the room would be easy to conceal, as unsuitable for housing refugees in, she meant, and the current Kommandatura wasn't set on amusements involving dancing. Oh how tart she could look when she had to pretend to be kindhearted, pretend to be making a sacrifice willingly! Her smile slipped off her face quite often when she had to reopen the double doors for her friends from the Union so soon. These friends had known, even children had known, about this magnificent great hall, three-foot-high oak paneling with von Lassewitz fauns and nymphs above it, the plaster-relief hunting scenes, the deep bay of plate-glass doors at the back, the green light from the garden everywhere. (One child had wondered why the grown-ups used a room like this only for special occasions.) There would be few meetings of the Jerichow CDU for long stretches, and still Louise's ego would take a hit every time. Here was that Klupsch woman, the party chair, that old biddy; Louise begrudged her not the job but the place at the front, she would have liked to bang on the table herself. That Klupsch had more fat on her bones than those bones wanted to carry, still it reminded Louise of her own fullness of form amid all these shabby, emaciated figures around her. So few people realized that you could get fat from grief and sorrow, you could! Then this Klupsch was allowed to read the newspaper, the *New Era*, to the group—every now and then a copy made it all the way from Schwerin to Jerichow. This Klupsch could decide whose turn it was to talk. Kägebein, her own employee, might think of something he had to say about the temporary allocation of town land as garden allotments for refugees, without even asking her permission first. Then Mrs. Maass, to suit her husband, would say something about the injustices that had occurred in the expropriation of large landholdings, and Louise too had felt that some compensation was called for but now she could only nod. She'd only been trying to remind everyone she was there when she cosigned the telegram that the Jerichow local branch of the CDU sent to Colonel Tulpanov in late December 1945, informing him that he couldn't simply replace the chairman of their party on a whim, and now a certain Colonel Tulpanov, Soviet Military Administration, Berlin, had had his attention called to a certain Louise Papenbrock and the fact that she was causing trouble. She couldn't lean on Brüshaver for support; he just sat there, and in the front row too, like a visitor. He did speak up sometimes, of course, but only about German mistakes, about honest efforts at improvement. Louise was inclined to forgive him, he must have come up with these ideas in the Nazi camp, but why did she keep feeling like he meant her? Would he dare? It was exactly like when he would stand in the pulpit and preach about virtues like friendship that meant nothing unless they were turned into action. Did he mean . . . Louise's reserve in her dealings with the von Haases? He couldn't know about that. He had no right to tell her that. It often happened that she wanted to shout at every last one of the seventeen people present at the party meeting: What about me?! What am I getting out of this? Are you even paying me rent?

– Was there someone writing down everything Brüshaver said again?

– Not in church. Yes in Papenbrock's parlor.

– Then all they could do was talk.

– And they'd been given the room to talk in which the Communist Party hadn't been able to fill. That group, which met at Prasemann's Rifle Club, really did see it as a game of hide-and-seek with the Soviets. It was not only Duvenspeck (German Liberal Democratic Party) who let himself be heard expressing the opinion that in Liberalism the freedom of each individual was compatible with the freedom of every other individual, hence had to be restricted by it. After the Sunday in October when the CP collected a group of people to burn down the estate manors "which were a disgrace to the landscape," even though in truth that surely applied more to the farmworkers' cottages, the local historian, Stoffregen, just released from his labors dismantling the railways, gave a subtle lecture on the influence of Italian and English architectural styles on secular buildings in Mecklenburg, "which we were permitted to see for the last time this past Sunday." In the minutes there was only something about the urgency of the potato harvest.

– And then Stoffregen was arrested. Oh, Gesine...

– No. But that's how Stoffregen got himself known. People like Duvenspeck on the other hand, and Bergie Quade, even though they claimed that as housewife or civil servant they'd been purely apolitical, were needed for positions in the Anti-Fascist Women's Committee, or as municipal advisers, and maybe they felt more important when they could apply for a permit not merely as a private individual but by starting their letter: As a member and representative of the Christian Democratic Union...

– What exactly could they apply for?

– Whatever they wanted. They could petition for the removal of Friedrich Schenk as mayor, for the construction of a power line to Jerichow...

– But what did they get? What were the limits?

– I can tell you one of them. They had banded together as private groups—they were appointed, not elected to public office—but they had one mandate, assigned to them by everybody, and there was no getting out of it. They needed more living space. An urgent mandate, you might say. Imperative. There you are, Mina Köpcke, you've been running around after your workmen six days a week and Sunday morning is wasted on bills and taxes and now you're sitting on the sofa in the evening, Duvenspeck's there too, in his shirtsleeves, you wouldn't mind taking your blouse off too, at least undoing a few buttons, Duvenspeck's a little tipsy, now that doesnt hurt, jus' top off my glass there, fill it up, fill it, Eduard, cheers Edi... and here comes the refugees' oldest child walking into the room, right on schedule, wants to warm up the pillows for her brothers and sisters by the fire, a ten-year-old girl like that sees more than you think, the kids'll lose all respect for you just because they can't find anywhere to live, the Liberal Democratic Party hereby proposes to improve the lot of the resettlers and requests that the Soviet Kommandatura approves an allocation of living quarters from the occupation power's holdings at Jerichow-North airfield.

– So that was the limit.

– Right. They thought they'd pull a fast one Pontiy's successor—surely he could see the houses for the former civilian employees standing empty on the airfield, all those broken windows. They promised to have living quarters restored by the honest tradesmen of Jerichow. They provided proof that an airport like that is too big for just one company of guards. If not a single plane is flown in or out, then the strategic value must be—let's just say it, zilch. Now don't you agree, Mr. Commandant sir?

– Now who was this commandant?

– I didn't know him, I never once saw him. Around Jerichow he was known as "Placeholder," because he left after only three weeks. But I know what he answered, and I can imagine his despair at these screwy Germans, exasperation buzzing around in his brain like a swarm of bees—no clue about territorial tactics, right on the border with the British, they say this crowd almost beat us? It was a short answer, given with his very last scrap of patience, and I can hear his tone of voice too, imploring, beseeching, rising to outright fury on the last syllable. Guess.

– "The commandant regrets to inform you—"

– No.

– "The Red Army refuses to allow any interference in matters which—"

– Nope.

– "Get out!"

– No.
– "There's no such airport"?
– There! is! no! such! airport!

June 18, 1968 Tuesday

Brezhnev had tears in his eyes. In a two-hour meeting with the Czecho-slovak parliamentary delegation on Friday, things weren't going as Profes-sor Konstantinov wanted and as the Soviet news agency knew to be true. Admittedly, a representative of the People's Party said so, which is a party with a Roman Catholic orientation, but it is part of the Czechoslovak National Front, allied with the Communists; admittedly, he said it to that tiresome *Lidova Demokracie*, but anybody in Prague could buy a copy. Brezhnev denies that his country intends to intervene in Czechoslovakia's democracy. Many things that the now uncontrolled Czechoslovak press is spreading among its citizens are making him sad and hurting the Soviet Union's feelings, but there is no thought of intervention. Leonid Ilyich was prepared to justify himself before any international tribunal! He also concedes that errors have been made, though he doesn't say what they might have be. The general secretary of the Central Committee of the Communist Party of the Soviet Union, Leonid Ilyich, cried.

– They were always going to be bringing you Socialism, Gesine. They never denied that, right from the start.
– It was going to be Socialism. But not off-the-shelf Socialism. The Germans were going to make their own.
– What does "German" mean, Gesine?
– The German version of Socialism had to be something special. Sweepingly specific. In February 1946 the Communist Anton Ackermann wrote to the Germans: In particular cases the

> pronounced characteristics
> of the historical development
> of our people,
> our political and national idiosyncrasies,
> the special features

of our economy

and culture

will find full expression.

– What did he mean by these German idiosyncrasies? The robes the judges wear? How many doors the buses have? The color of their military uniforms? Blue for the navy?

– The German military was outlawed. Weapons, buildings, literature. Everything.

– Was it that you were supposed to do it in the German language, not in Russian?

– Yes. But imagine how people like Stoffregen the local historian started drawing up a list of German things! What was German about the state, about the people . . .

– Gesine, when're you going to show me just one person who liked it. Who was sitting in the driver's seat. Who did it because he wanted to. Who was enjoying himself. Someone like that. He knew what was going on and he liked it. You must know *one*!

– I do know one. Imagine that you're twenty-three years old . . .

– Sounds great, Gesine. Sounds great.

– . . . in the summer of 1946, you're the district councilman for Gneez, you've gone over to the Communists not for a bit of bread but across the eastern front, you've founded practically every third local branch in the area around Gneez, you're allowed to carry a gun, you talk to the Russians in their own language with a Moscow accent, you've got a room in the City of Hamburg Hotel, now with breakfast, but in winter Alma Witte has to heat it for you . . .

– His name's Gerd Schumann.

– That's what you're called these days, you've been given that name and by now you're even used to it, it's missing only a few deep crannies you can crawl all the way into, where you feel it to be really yours, where it couldn't be anyone else's. You shouldn't change it again, you should keep it for now, you've gone around to too many villages with it, people wouldn't know you; but who has the forms you need for another name, and the authority to stamp them and sign them? You do. You don't exercise this power too, there are enough other kinds that you wield.

– He's got everything he wants.

– You were one of the very first, the Soviets brought you into Initiative Group North, you were not with Comrade Sobottka in Stettin on May 6, you were still studying administration in Stargard, but you were there in Waren on the Müritz when the Sobottka Unit voted itself head of the party for Mecklenburg-Vorpommern, you're not on the wrong horse, you've proven your worth. No one's given you anything for free, you worked for it. And it's thanks to you that nobody's homeless in Mecklenburg now even though the population's doubled, 52 percent are resettlers from the East but they all have roofs over their heads, you've put them to work, they can feed the occupying power, feed the friends, they have food to eat themselves, and you receive bread for your labors too. Where 2,500 estate owners used to exploit the soil now you've helped settle nearly 65,000 new farmers, it was your party that repaired 26 large bridges rather than leaving them in ruins, the waterways are open again, except for the Bolter sluice, your accomplishments include 539 drivable trucks, 243 tractors, 437 automobiles, 281 motorcycles, laid rail, 11 omnibus lines running on schedule…your party got them all moving. You did that. That's what you have to worry about.

– And he can't have had any other worries, Gesine.

– Oh yes you can. You can have trouble with the party. The Red Army deploys you to Mecklenburg and a little knowledge of the local dialect would've come in handy. No idea what the people might be saying to one another, maybe right to your face. In a rural area you would've liked to know the acreage needed to feed a family, how much milk a cow actually gives, that people here still measure the land in rods. The same kind of thing had happened with the other comrades in Initiative Group North— they came from Silesia, Bavaria, the Ruhr, they were miners and clockmakers, some of them knew nothing but the inside of the party. One had waited it out in Sweden. Sweden! The party helped you, it sent you up and down the coast from one village to the next and soon the people were no longer laughing at you, you even proved to them that five hectares was enough to feed a family, not the fifteen actually set by the party back in 1932; hopefully the other comrades did as well as you did. You know the reasons: The German émigrés in the Soviet Union could only produce cadres of activists, and not even enough of those, certainly not agricultural or technical experts; take what you can get. Those the Nazis didn't kill off in their prisons and camps are broken, sick, exhausted people; have to make do with them too. You have to talk them out of the nonsense they've dreamed up away from the party. They come to you with their thuggish Socialism—total expropriation, large-scale agricultural production—you can't be a spoilsport, you have to let them find out for themselves that we can't entrust the administration of Socialist farms to the same estate managers who served the agrarian capitalists. One of them, who'd been in a camp since 1939, objects to you that after the brown straitjacket he has no desire to put on a red one—you explain the exceptional path of the German nation to that one. They demand from the party the immediate and complete seizure of power by the working class and you gently point out to him that Socialism can only be forged with the human material at hand, with farmers, the lower and middle classes, and of course with the working class in the lead; that's precisely why the Red Army has removed the large estate owners, the military leaders, the major banks, the leading industries. Sent them away. Others can't get it through their heads why Mecklenburg would demolish its proletarian centers in Rostock and Wismar; it falls to you and none but you to itemize that the workers at Heinkel and at Arado built warplanes, at Neptun they built warships and rocket parts, at Dornier seaplanes, and you pose the question of restitution in moral terms first, only then political ones. When they ask you to intervene in Soviet arrests, you just silently shake your head and suggest that when it comes to security the Russian friends trust none but themselves, and rightly so. Yet another person understands about the demolitions but not about the Razno-Export or Techno-Export stores where the Soviets are buying up gold, precious stones, porcelain, paintings, every last valuable possession down to the wedding rings, in exchange for cigarettes at precisely the black market rates; you ask that one: Who owns such things? He wouldn't happen to have any of that himself now would he? When they ask you about the years between 1935 and 1938 in the Soviet Union, or émigrés there who never came back, you're too young for a moment and then you ask about the harvest. You have your own burden to bear. You have no choice, you have to tolerate a Social Democratic mayor in Gneez who, you personally know for a fact, from a prisoner's statement, encouraged comrades to defect during the Nazi years, that is to say volunteer for the German Army; he survived with his tobacco store and now they call him senator. And if that's not enough you have to let the bourgeoisie into the administration for the time being, as long as they weren't actual members of the Nazi Party, or if they'd been locked up for refusing to give a Hitler salute once; actually what matters more, more often than not, is that they know something about business. The head of the Mecklenburg-Vorpommern State Bank is one Dr. Wiebering, bourgeois anti-Fascist, all right, Forgbert's a Communist and he's vice president and supposedly he'll pick up the banking business but will he? As for you, you're a bit up in the air—every file comes across your desk, you sign the permit, a duplicate of every order is filed, but now this deputy of yours, Dr. Dr. Heinrich Grimm, what did he do after the Nazis kicked him out of office as a district councilman? He says he behaved properly. What does that mean? Who is this Elise Bock: almost all your files pass through her hands and typewriter but who is she going around with, why doesn't she want to join the party? Of course you'd trust her any day over all these people who come running with their applications for party membership, talking about their good will, offering up the exceptional German path to Socialism as their justification, they don't have the faintest glimmer of an idea about the party, you need to find an empty building somewhere or other in this district of Gneez where you can teach them, sound them out, prepare them for the party, since you're not allowed to refuse them membership. This language! *Kåååmen sei, so kåååmen sei nich; kåååmen sei nich, so kåååmen sei; if they come then they dont come and if they dont come they do come so its better when they dont come so they do come than when they do come so they dont come*...Once you've slowly finally learned to understand the words then what are they talking about? At least if it were a riddle, but no: it's a problem predicting the future, and what's the answer? *Duven un Arwten*. You had to get that translated for you. *Tauben und Erbsen*. Pigeons and peas. Hopes for the harvest. All right. Not that you're homesick for Mannheim, the Allies have blown it to bits anyway, but down there in Baden the people wouldn't look at you so funny just because of how you talk. There's plenty for the Communist Party to do in the Neckar region too. Now your proper place is wherever the party sends you. But you could think of another place.

– Don't make me a whiner, Gesine!

– You're twenty-three! You want everything to be perfect. The party must be pure. And all you've got is pure chaos. Hodgepodge. Odds and ends and none of it fits together.

– That I can understand. It's like in that Soviet film we just saw. Where the Red Army man loses his party book. To him that was worse than . . . than if you woke up tomorrow morning in a hotel room in Outer Mongolia and had lost your passport. I get him, I think. And if he can't handle Mecklenburgish right off then let him keep talking Russian. With his friends.

– That's what they were called. You were allowed to call them that.

– Dancing at the Dom Ofitserov! Not everyone gets to do that.

– As if you have time for that! You get to the office, for once you're going to clear your desk of the ten-day pile of leftover paperwork, and Triple-J phones you up. Mr. Schumann: he says. They'd almost gotten to first-name-basis brotherhood the night before last, hadn't they? Well, maybe he forgot. What else does he have to say? Wants to know whether you've been to the station. Have you been to the station, Mr. Schumann? That's it. End of conversation. You have someone drive you to the station, gun in your coat pocket, must be some kind of dustup going on there, what else could it be. What it is is a freight train full of resettlers, transfers, from Pommern, from Poland, and they're sick, and have lice, and now once again the city is faced with typhus. These few hundred people could infect forty thousand. Now you've got to waste three days—burying the dead, setting up a hospital in the Barracks of the Solidarity of Peoples, ordering the doctors onto night duty—while your Social Democratic mayor spends a few extra days on his official trip to Schwerin. Does Triple-J ever once show up, take a look around, intimidate the stretcher bearers a little? On the contrary, the station and the streets around it are declared off-limits to the Red Army. And what does Jenudkidse say on the fourth day? – Good boy: he says. You don't lose faith in him, you don't imagine yourself as his equal, but he could be nicer when he tells you certain things, not quite so patronizing. You get it, this unification with the Social Democratic morons can't be avoided. Tactical reasons are reasons. The whole People's Front thing has to happen. You give Triple-J reports on the problems with the bourgeois parties; you make it funny, with amusing details, you don't complain. You get the new farmers to trust their property, you remind them of the Count von Gröbern who told the Prussian parliament that he needed three oxen in his fields, two to pull the plow and one to drive it—finally the people believe that you're trying to bring them justice. In Wehrlich they invited you to the celebration after the drawing of lots. You danced. A woman put her arms around you, not out of gratitude, just because she felt so happy. You turned red, and the men helped you out of your embarrassment by slapping you on the shoulder, and for one afternoon you weren't an outsider. Then the SMA sends you men from its own Centralized Agricultural Planning Office— well-dressed well-fed gentlemen, one with a pince-nez—and at a public, authorized meeting they prove that Mecklenburg's climate and soil quality make it the best region in the country for the cultivation and propagation of seed potatoes, enough to feed half of Germany, it won't take more than, say, 1,500,000 acres of estate land staying in large, undivided plots. And there goes three weeks of agitprop. The people don't believe you anymore. They start asking each other if they're really working the land for themselves. This is the hot water the Red Army has gotten you into with its People's Front, 1936 model. All of a sudden you realize that they were just letting the bourgeoisie talk their talk, the land has been divided up and distributed and it'll stay that way. You apply yourself with a little patience and suss out the ultraclever variation being played out before your eyes and you forgive Triple-J for everything, almost everything.

– He was having his fun with the bourgeoisie.

– All you can do with the bourgeoisie is laugh at them. They're playing hide-and-seek with you and you're playing it with them. They think they're so smart when they can fill the post of building monitor with one of their own people, after the old one moves away or dies, and you just turn him, the second step is to warn him, the third is to reward him, and now the party knows everything it needs to know about what's going on in that building, or at least as much as they did before. When the elections for block monitor come up, the bourgeoisie get nowhere. Some people compare the new building monitors with the Nazi building wardens but you just don't get it, you weren't here then, those days are over; the question you maybe ask back is who they think should collect the fees for the ration cards? They think their meetings are secret; you're in stitches laughing at Stoffregen, this local historian who tallies up all the things about the new administration that are Mecklenburgish, i.e., conducive to Mecklenburg sovereignty and eventually unification with Denmark. In Rostock a Dr. Kaltenborn turns up trying to prevent the demolition of the Ernst Heinkel AG factory with the argument that the British don't consider Heinkel a war criminal; in Bützow, after a liquid-oxygen plant in the Peenemünde Center has been demolished and is being rebuilt, the owners come from the West and offer their services on the condition that you don't bother them with a second demolition later—after a while you can only shake your head at the ingenuity of these people who can't even figure out where they are. Let them think you've been Russified, that you're a helpless babe in the woods of German culture: one day you too notice how often the party slogans are inscribed centered on walls, and you put a stop to that nonsense, not mad, with a burst of laughter that takes you entirely by surprise, that expands your rib cage, they like that. Someday they'll like you too.

– The one thing he can't forgive Triple-J for. Slata?

– Yes, well, you are twenty-three...

– In that case I don't want to be that after all. She goes out with a German and he defects to the Soviets. Maybe at the same time.

– If Triple-J didn't mind, why should you?

– It's a dirty trick.

– Maybe Slata told a clean story. She hadn't run away with the British, she'd waited for her own people. What do I know?

– Exactly. What do you know.

– Now you need to take the insult with the injury. There's talk going around your own party that you'd have taken Slata if she'd have brought you Triple-J. You know what that's called: careerism. Their ideas of you don't match your idea of yourself. But you want them to.

– You have no way to know that.

– He had a photograph hanging in his room. It showed Triple-J, Jenudkidse's adjutant, his political adviser, and a random young woman standing behind the three of them, blond, sporty, the only one not smiling.

– Alma Witte. She shouldn't have showed you that.

– She did it to show me he was a brave young man. So that I wouldn't make any dumb comments when he walked past us. She too wanted to bring me up right. I was supposed to realize that even someone like that can have cares and sorrows like a normal person.

– That's why he stayed in the City of Hamburg Hotel.

– Almost directly under Slata's room.

– But he had power?

– Never before had a Gneez district councilman had so much power. It grew and grew every week, too, the more other people thought that he had all the power. He liked it.

June 19, 1968   Wednesday

This morning the blind beggar on Lexington Avenue (my days are darker than your nights) set up a yellow bucket of tasty-looking clear water for his dog. This evening the rim of the bowl is smeared and the water silted with dirt. Especially civilized passersby tossed their charity of coins into the water.

In the main hall of Grand Central Station, amid the monstrous blend of noise, footsteps, and tangles of voices, there is another, smaller sound, much better known, getting quite unreasonably louder in the ramps to the commuter trains. It comes from a man collecting the subway tokens from the turnstiles. The tokens rattle against the gray metal and the bucket scrapes against the floor when the man moves on. A wide squat bucket, the kind we had for horses to drink from.

At night, a storm stays over the river, not moving. Lightning flashes turn the park into silhouettes; sometimes, their bright white shaded, they light up only the opposite shore. Some, the very short, barely perceivable ones, etch sharp furrows into the brain.

As children, in haystacks, caught in a storm, we thought: Someone can see us. We are all seen.

PART FOUR
June 1968–August 1968

June 20, 1968 Thursday

WOKEN by a flat cracking sound in the park, like gunshots. People standing at the bus stop across the street, unafraid. Behind them, children playing war.

Our newsstand at Ninety-Sixth Street is covered. No papers today, due to a death. The old man could have at least written whether the death was his. The weeklies are covered, too, with a weathered plastic sheet. The customers come up as usual, stop a few paces from the grave-mound-like bundles, and peel off in an embarrassed arc. No one tries to steal anything. A customer still groggy with sleep expects the handwritten cardboard sign to say: Closed out of respect for...who?

In the tunnel under the subway platforms a boy in a yarmulke walks past a whiskey poster on which someone has added, in cursive, twice: Fuck The Jew Pigs. The boy holds his head as if he doesn't see it.

In Grand Central Station there was one *New York Times* left. Weather: partly sunny, partly cool. Kept: the photo of Adolf Heinz Beckerle, former German ambassador to Bulgaria, on trial for complicity in the 1943 deportation of eleven thousand Jews to the Treblinka death camp. Since he suffers from sciatica he is lying dressed in business clothes on a stretcher, between the blanket and pillow, and two Frankfurt policeman are carefully carrying him up the courthouse steps. Frankfurt am Main.

Sometimes the final stage of waking up happens only at the fountain outside the passage to the Graybar Building. Today two men are clinging to its sides, alternately bending down and raising their heads high like chickens, numbing their hangovers.

Today the beggar outside the bank has a red bucket for his dog.

Approximately thirty people can attest that Mrs. Cresspahl entered her office at 8:55 and did not leave until 4:05!

Four fifteen during this deferred lunch hour was the only appointment that Boccaletti the hair stylist could find all week for his customer Mrs. Cresspahl. The other regulars are sitting in the waiting room, including the two ladies who enjoy addressing each other with tender solicitude, each happily certain that the other is a lot worse off than she is herself. There were signs a long time ago, back when we were fleeing, in Marseilles, you remember. Mrs. Cresspahl would have liked to hear more of this spoken German but Signor Boccaletti summons her over in more of a hurry than usual. He's not trying to gain a few extra moments for the next customer, he's wanting to complain about how very very far away Bari is, where they do things differently. He flings two hands covered in lather into the air and only then can he cry: *Signora, uccidere per due dollari? Ma!*

(Giogrio Boccaletti, Madison Avenue, is requested to write to *The New York Times* advice column—discretion guaranteed—and say how much money *would* make it worth it.)

Delays on the West Side line's express track. The loudspeaker promises, in a growl that gets gruffer with each repetition: The local will be stopping at all express stations. It's impossible to imagine a human being behind that distorted voice, and anyway, local trains always stop at express stops! I didn't make it on till the third train, where there was not enough air to breathe.

For ten minutes I stood in front of a poster exhorting us to SUPPORT OUR SERVICEMEN. Below the words was an SOS in Morse code, and below that a photograph of a white soldier giving a blood transfusion to a black soldier. Support our servicemen. On the left, under a red cross: HELP US HELP. According to Amanda Williams's reliable information, this poster secretly means: The Americans are in dire peril in Vietnam.

Then two Negro women executed an almost simultaneous rotation of their bodies around their respective central axes, and moved their neighbors along with them, so I could stand facing away from the poster.

On Broadway another Negro, perhaps drunk, staggered into a deli and greeted the proprietor with a word I don't know. – And if you don't want to hear that then get lost! he shouts. He stumbles on between the glass cases and gives a revolutionary speech that no one understands a word of. The proprietor, in a slight crouch, hands on the counter by the cash register, watches the enemy from under his brows, not at all upset.

At home Marie has flowers. There were originally a dozen peonies, for six dollars, and – Then there was a Puerto Rican woman there with her little kid, nine years old, and the girl wanted some too and the mother kept saying: *But they don't last, child!* So I waited for the girl outside the door and gave her six of mine. Is that okay, Gesine? Hey, *talk to me!*

– I approve, Marie. But why were you getting flowers at all?

– It's Karsch's birthday today! Do they take out your memory too, at the bank? It's Karsch's birthday!

In the mail there's a letter from Europe, in which someone appeals to Mrs. Cresspahl's acquaintance with him and wants her to put that connection in writing, for a festschrift. A testimonial of friendship, made to order.

June 21, 1968 Friday

Military exercises on Czechoslovak soil involving the Soviet, Hungarian, East German, and Polish armies along with the Czechoslovaks officially began yesterday. According to Ivan I. Yakubovsky, marshal of the Soviet Union, only command staff and signal, transport, and auxiliary units would be involved. There was no indication of how long the exercises would last.

– Okay, Marie, what's needed to hold free and open elections?

– They had elections in Mecklenburg too? Well they could just use whatever was there, couldn't they.

– They could if they had to, Marie. So what would that be?

– First you need parties. You had those. Second, the people in the parties have to invite in people who aren't in the parties. They have to promise them something more or something different than the other parties. A party that's not in power has to have the same rights as the party that is in power. If the parties can't include all the people who aren't in parties, they have to persuade the rest with newspapers, fliers, posters. Third, when it's time to vote, they need arbiters or referees, who only care about the rules— people voting voluntarily, in secret, the votes being counted properly—and don't give a hoot about the parties. Then you need people who aren't sick of it all and actually want to vote. There are *some* people I know who don't even care anymore.

– But the borders had been closed since June 30, 1946. The Soviets had done that in their own interest, but still in the Control Council with the Western Allies. They'd also wanted everyone in Mecklenburg to stay in Mecklenburg and face the demands of the day there. The municipal elections were on the Mecklenburg calendar for September 15. Mina Köpcke, to her dying day, couldn't have said what she had in her hands except when it was Duvenspeck's soft neck; all the same, she too said: Why should we let anything slip out of them?

– I know who won. This is getting boring.

– It wasn't boring for the Socialist Unity Party's campaign manager in the Gneez district. It was dicey, downright unpleasant. In the weeks before the election he often had the creepy feeling that someone was standing behind him in the dark. He couldn't figure out who it was. It turned out splendidly for him and his friends; he would say: It's all nice and cozy! He wasn't stupid, he'd learned something from January's municipal elections in Hesse, when the Socialists had gotten eight times as many votes as his own party; the Gneez district was one of the first where the Social Democrats gave up on their party and joined him in the new one; eventually the Central Committee had no choice but to believe and obey the call for unification rising up from below. He'd talked himself blue in the face! He'd had to promise the Socialists so much: clean procedures for organizing the economy, which they were weirdly insistent on; not transposing every last thing Lenin said and wrote into the German situation; fundamentally honoring the particular German path of democracy, if only for as long as the capitalist class remained on the soil of democracy, and then, unfortunately, the path of revolution, which the Socialists seemed to see as opposed to democracy. Everything promised, signed, sealed, and transcribed. That suited him fine—he stuck to what the comrades from Kröpelin had done, having the resolution to unify the parties signed by the mayor and assistant mayor and the chief of police too. They started calling Kröpelin their *sister city*, in Platt. Oh yes, he'd learned. He'd run into Social Democrats who called unified meetings with him only when the local Soviet commandants ordered them to. Some of them didn't get it until they were ordered to resign early. There'd been a lot of evenings that were pleasant enough, even fun: he had signatures in his collection which plainly showed the exuberant zest of the vodka. These were the rogues he was sharing his party with now; it was for them that they'd abandoned the title "German People's Daily" in favor of Neues Deutschland, "New Germany"; more than half the members of the Unity Party were former Socialists; but it was also true that the votes people cast for them wouldn't be going to them alone. That reassured him. So why did he have that flickering feeling in his wrists whenever the municipal elections so much as flitted through his mind, not even settling into conscious awareness?

– He feared for his good name, this Gerd Schumann.

– You shouldn't say it like that, Marie. He didn't like hearing "Gerd," it had a falsely young ring to it, childish even. And just one syllable. When Triple-J said it there was almost nothing left. Slata had always called him "Comrade Gär-kha't" when he was there, though always as if he weren't. And she was truly speaking to him, he felt. As for "Schumann," what was memorable about that? It practically invited you to forget him. He felt detached from such a stillborn name himself. "Comrade District Councilman" was better—it at least reminded him of what he had to do. (How happy he'd have been to hear his nickname, "Redhead," if only he'd ever caught wind of it!)

– Maybe this Comrade District Councilman of yours was scared they wouldn't pick him!

– That would be enough to wake you up in the middle of the night, in sweat-soaked sheets? In August? In a building as cool, its walls as thick, as the City of Hamburg Hotel, in a room with a breeze from the west? Worries like that can ruin your sleep?

– Gesine, I was just saying. In case the voters saw Comrade District Councilman and his party as tools of the Soviets.

– Don't tell him that. You'd make his heavy eyes widen and darken with surges of blood; you'd have done much more than insult him a little. You'd have wounded him, truly ambushed him, his shoulders would crumple. You'd feel bad—a handsome young guy like that, reddish-gray stubble on his red face, innocent lips now bitterly pinched together. Almost desperately, practically paralyzed, he would ask you who, if not he and his party, was working in the national interest. No! For someone to see him, him of all people, as a stooge!

– All right then, sorry bout that. He's just friends with the Soviets.

– You can say that again. He's their ally. He knows that. He's grateful to them, and not in the bourgeois way either, where all that matters is material things. Though of course they help you that way too. When you need a car the commandant sends you one, complete with driver and as much gas as you need, vouchers too. Grimm doesn't get all that, Christian Democrat as he's unmasked himself as being—he doesn't even get time off for campaign trips, he needs to get the district administration in order first. If a bourgeois local branch in Old Demweis seems a little fishy, you can just say so and before you know it the SMA has revoked its registration. There were 2,404 municipalities in Mecklenburg and the Liberals wanted 152 local branches for them—they should be happy with 65! The Christian Democrats tried to register 707 local branches; they'll be lucky to get 237! Your party, though, gets an office everywhere, and your *New Germany* is for sale in every store, and the *Tägliche Rundschau* too, daily as promised; you think the Soviets should slog away with things like *Neue Zeit* or *Der Morgen*, which come out only twice a week anyway? At first your jaw drops when your party gets eight hundred tons of paper for marketing while the CDU and LDPD are allocated just nine tons between them—but then you see why. What do they have to say anyway. What do they know. The people have to be given the right information, you won't disappoint your friends; while the bourgeoisie are still wrangling with the local commandants for permits for their meetings or posters, you've already been sweeping through five villages. You don't need to submit your speeches for approval, and anyway you speak without a script. And if you're stuck in the deepest woods near the coast with engine trouble, who comes and gets you, in a jeep, with a spare car? The Red Army—they sacrifice time and manpower to get you to your next meeting, in Beidendorf, almost on time. And anyway, a Communist is the only man friends can know for sure is a natural-born foe of Fascism to the death; there was nothing to worry about there, that tremor, which passed through his brain as he fell asleep and sometimes half the night through, couldn't be coming from that.

– What else does he need to be grateful for, Gesine? It's like having Rockefeller help you in an election!

– What else is he grateful for? For being taught the right way to think! The Red Army doesn't just give him rent-free housing with Alma Witte, bring him food from the city's communal provisions, eventually give him a leather jacket and a pair of ankle boots, used but that's all right. No, his bodily comforts are not enough, and he would forgo those if he had to, as long as your friends go on making sure that your mouth doesn't get stuck, like the flounder's after he'd gulped down a dozen herring. The things they taught him! Let's take the word: *election*. In the beginning he used it to refer to something that actually exists. Everyone means the same thing by it, no one has more control over it than anyone else, it's a simple label for your current assignment from the party. Then J. J. Jenudkidse summons you to Town Hall, in the middle of a workday, and these are five minutes you will never forget. Triple-J, all fake unapproachability, is sitting behind an empty desk, in front of a three-foot-wide three-foot-high portrait of Goethe, next to Dr. Beese who is supplementing her income by giving German lessons in Town Hall. Both of them are giving you a silent, roguish look, as if to say that you're in for a surprise. But no one purses his lips as impishly as Jenudkidse. He asks you one single question—just one word, a German one: *Wahlkampf.* "Election." And you've grasped once and for all your special ownership over the *Wahl* or choice, the different choices, the *Kampf* or struggle, the hostilities, and of course the enemies required for there to be such a thing; you wanted to explain it to Elise Bock but she just put the folder of signatures down in front of you again, perfectly calm, not interested in your excitement. You can hardly wait the few days until the meetings, until the moment when the respective mayor introduces you as the comrade from the district and at last you can start your speech! You don't come to the office for days, you can be reached only by phone and chance in the villages around Gneez, ten meetings a day are one too few as far as you're concerned and you show up to the eleventh like a boxer, and wherever you wake up you find a slip of paper next to the bed that you've scribbled full of the ideas that've come to you, that'll help you do even better! Then you think maybe you're feeling guilty.

– Keep talking, Gesine.

– The first harvest on free soil. The Junkers' ruthless exploitation, from the twenties right through to the liberation. Three hundred thousand more acres cultivated than in 1945. The Red Army halts the dismantling of the Neptun docks in Rostock, creates jobs by setting up an SAG. The Hanseatic dockyard in Wismar is expanded around the Dornier factory, given harbor equipment from Szczecin (formerly known as Stettin). The Soviet Union is helping, as brothers, and not only today, it always has. The *Krassin,* the same Soviet icebreaker that saved the crew of the airship *Italia* in the summer of 1928 after it crashed and was trapped in the ice off Spitsbergen, also battled to rescue the icebound ships off Warnemünde in the winter of 1929, including the ferryboat to Denmark. But it wasn't about the Soviets, it wasn't about the dictatorship of the proletariat, it was about the New Beginning, the Reconstruction, in alliance with the anti-Fascist forces, including the bourgeois ones, insofar as they're honest. Neglect of the victors' anti-Fascist obligations on the part of the English and Americans, Nazis left in the government there, in the police, in the Schutzpolizei, in the Gneez gendarmerie. Swept out of power, the country cleaned up, parliamentary democracy, all democratic rights and freedoms to the people—under the protection of the Soviet Union.

– "SAG"?

– Sowjetische Aktiengesellschaft. Soviet joint-stock corporation.

– I wasn't asking for a definition, I was heckling.

– *When in Rome. . . .* Use the bourgeois economic forms at hand.

– Equal rights for women. Women get less tobacco rations on their cards than men!

– Alcohol too. Well, there it is. That's why Comrade District Councilman always carried a packet containing two cigarettes on him. He'd throw it in the general direction of the woman complaining, shouting: Take them! My last ones! And first things first: massive election turnout, victory for the Socialist Unity Party (for the name if nothing else), then we'll handle this. It looked cute, actually, him shrugging his shoulders in his leather jacket and giving a slightly pained smile—giving up his last two cigarettes!

– He wasn't a smoker himself.

– Of course not. Got his pairs of single cigarettes from the Red Army commissary.

– And then he lost the vote.

– Then he lost. In the September 15 municipal elections the LDPD and CDU received almost twenty-five percent of the votes cast. His party, along with the allied Farmers' Aid and Women's Committees, received a mere sixty-six out of a hundred. He was truly crestfallen, avoided Triple-J and everything. Only got through his first night by drinking. No matter how insistently he told himself that it had, after all, been a fight, the fact was he hadn't won it overwhelmingly. More than a quarter of the people in Mecklenburg didn't trust him. Plus he'd disappointed his friends. Now he thought he could put his finger on what he'd been feeling during the past few weeks: fear of failure, a premonition of defeat. Someone older would have felt relieved at least to know; at twenty-three, he was almost beyond help.

June 22, 1968 Saturday

In České Budějovice there's a bishop who'd been out of commission for sixteen years, i.e., expelled from his diocese and under house arrest. Last Sunday he was permitted to celebrate mass once again in his St. Nikolaus Cathedral, in the presence of three representatives of the secular authorities, who acted perfectly polite. The very next Tuesday, the police called him to tell him about a man who'd lost a large sum of money while counting it on a train at an open window. Might the custodians of law and order bring this unfortunate man over, to receive from the bishop the kind of consolation a police precinct couldn't give?

The Bishop from Budweis could only consider such a request, from the selfsame state that had deported him in March 1951 (then too using a detail of three men), as a most heartening symbol of his future in the ČSSR.

In the second autumn after the war, Cresspahl's daughter stopped giving Pastor Brüshaver the time of day. She didn't even try to pretend she hadn't noticed this man of the cloth. She saw him all right—who didn't? His thinness was not from the past year's hunger—the Nazi camp seemed to have restructured his whole body into a small-boned frugal model; the pants and coats of 1937 flapped about him, flapped from his careful, almost stiff movements too. Nor did Gesine give Brüshaver an ostentatious refusal to greet him—she showed that she recognized him, the way a person walks right by something familiar and of no further use. Just as Brüshaver had managed in the past without pride and severity, he tried for a while to nod at her—first, even though he was the elder! Then he'd just look at the child, without reproach, without seeming puzzled; so then the child could top it off by denying outright any acquaintance at all in this exchange of glances.

Jakob generally recognized soon enough when Cresspahl's daughter got such a bee in her bonnet; it's just he rarely managed to talk the bee back out. Jakob was dissatisfied with himself as head of the household.

The household had shrunk: he'd had only three people to report on the People's Census, plus Cresspahl, Heinrich, under the heading "Resident But Absent." The NKVD's Sunday labors in September had done their job, even more so the rumors trying to make all paths lead back to the mayor who'd been hauled off. By the end of September all the refugees moved out, even the teacher from Marienwerder, who'd rather live way out in the Wehrlich forester's lodge with two other families and look after her baby boy on her own than stay any longer among such dangerous enemies of the Soviets. The housing office didn't make up for these departures; even the new batch of Sudeten German resettlers were warned in time by the refugees already established in Jerichow to avoid the lonely house on Brickworks Road, right across from the Kommandatura—a place of countless house searches, a dead loss for future prospects. Living in isolation, like in a haunted house, were Gesine in her little room, Mrs. Abs in Cresspahl's big parlor, and Jakob on the other side of the hall. In the back part they used only the kitchen and, every now and then, put Mr. Krijgerstam or kindred business partners up in one of the pantries. It was a real household only in the evenings; at breakfast Mrs. Abs made lunch for the two others, then the door was locked until everyone came home from work and school, unsupervised. At that point there was sometimes a light on where Cresspahl used to do his writing: the child was doing her homework, Mrs. Abs was carding wool, and Jakob, on nights without overtime or business appointments, would furtively watch the others over the top of his Russian dictionary, head of the household, dissatisfied with himself.

His mother had handed him both the official status of head of household and the actual responsibility of running it even before Cresspahl's disappearance, as soon as he'd refused to participate in the land lottery. However much he'd disappointed her, the farm property had been intended to be his in any case. She didn't want to discuss it any further, not even attempts at explanation or apology. Her job cooking at the hospital left her just enough energy to make dinner and keep things moderately clean. It was he who'd decided that they should stay with this utterly parentless child, in a strange house, in a rural part of Mecklenburg without more than a few dozen square feet of garden—let him manage it. He was old enough. Let him be responsible. Anyway she was busy waiting for her husband. She described neither him nor Cresspahl as someone who would return as a

judge to condemn Jakob's stewardship. And as for her, Jakob thought she
was resigned, if not content. This strange child, Gesine Cresspahl, on the
other hand was unfathomable to him. She had shaken hands with Brüshaver
at Amalie Creutz's grave. Was it only because they'd been there to assist
the mourners? She had obediently accompanied her father to the first
church service this Brüshaver had held after the war—the fourth time
total she had set foot in St. Peter's Church since her christening, same as
Cresspahl. So why not since? She was only thirteen, after all; what could
a child like that know about the pros and cons of the Protestant congregation?

He did see her making distinctions. If it was in fact contempt she was
showing to various particular adults. If there was anything at all she was
trying to show. So, for instance, she would sometimes come back on the
same train as Dr. Kliefoth—they'd have shared a compartment and would
walk together down Station Street to the corner of the market square; the
old man and the child had no need to talk, they clearly belonged together.
Were allies. From earlier times? Jakob had no way of knowing. This Kliefoth was a university-educated man, like Brüshaver, someone to show respect
to—to him she practically curtseyed, while Brüshaver she left in the dust
like an empty shopwindow. Then there was Louise Papenbrock, the girl's
natural grandmother, and the girl would cross the street to avoid her. That
might go back to habits from her father's time—impossible to know, as
always. But she'd let Heinz Wollenberg stop her for a chat. Just because
she took the train to school with his Lise? With Peter Wulff she would
stop on her own; she would talk to him. Jakob could see this with his own
eyes, and she'd tell him about it. Usually it was about Cresspahl. Then
Jakob would keep his mouth shut and his eyes on the Cyrillic column in
his book—he didn't think Cresspahl was coming back. (In his view, Cresspahl was dead.) If she needed comfort, she should go get it from the man
whose job was to provide it. But to him she wouldn't give the time of day.

While well brought up children always greet their elders. Right, Jakob?
We certainly wanted you to learn such things.
Because you'd never been around people like Stoffregen.
There was something between you and the church, Gesine. After a year in
Jerichow I knew that much.

Did you go to St. Peter's Church on Sundays, or out to Johnny's?

Gesine, we weren't from your denomination. I didn't feel like going to Gneez just because there was someone there from the Old Lutheran Church in Schwerin every three months.

Didn't I go to the Old Lutheran services in Gneez with your mother? I brought her there. I stayed there. I sang along with them!

Stoffregen was with the Nazis. He'd beaten children. Brüshaver spent seven years in the camps. Lost four children of his own. And instead of giving himself a rest he goes into politics.

Exactly.

And you won't say hello on the street.

He went into politics with the Soviets. The Soviets had my father. Brüshaver didn't get Cresspahl out of Soviet hands. He didn't even try.

That's how you divided people up? Into friends and enemies? Is that what children are like?

What were you like when you were thirteen, Jakob?

Lately the incomprehensible Cresspahl child had gotten involved in the black market. Johnny Schlegel had been able to unload another two sacks of wheat flour at Brickworks Road on the wagon's way back from the town scales—all aboveboard and in good faith, though Kägebein and the Papenbrock granary would probably have to chalk up a little extra loss to the Red Army. Or to himself. Or to no one at all. Whatever these two sacks might have turned into on the highways and byways of bookkeeping, in reality: Jakob thought: they'd been standing in the back pantry for some two days. Suddenly this Gesine forbade the conversion of the wheat. Because half belonged to Hanna? Her share of the profit could be forwarded. No. Because only Gesine was entitled to make decisions about her property? He'd be happy to discuss it with her. She didn't give a damn about his discussions, she didn't want to sell. He calculated for her that she had six thousand marks sitting in those two sacks, but money that would go bad. That was 160 hundredweight of coal. She could get a winter coat out of it—thread, lining, dependable tailoring—with a fortune left over. He knew someone who would part with a pair of winter boots in her size, used of course, for 560 marks, ten percent cheaper if paid for in wheat flour. This was an evening during the winter of 1946, when he was explaining to her the ways to commercially exploit her harvest earnings: the stove was already burning coal converted from butter (four pounds per hundredweight), the lamp burning the oil he'd laid in for the winter (one mandel-dozen eggs). He hardly seemed very enthusiastic in laying out these calculations for her because such transactions would cost him a lot of time, not to mention the distances, but he was happy to do his part toward paying a real rent in this house. He was even sure that he hadn't used a didactic tone, he certainly hoped not; all of a sudden the child leapt up—you try to understand it—snatched up her school notebooks as if someone was trying to rip them out of her hands, and ran off. Jakob was left with the slam of the door; a shake of the head from his mother, whose veiled derision was aimed at him, not the girl; and two shouts from Gesine that scared him. Not because they were unjust but simply because he couldn't make heads or tails of what she was shouting. Is this how children are?

Jakob didn't understand. The next morning the child apologized to him. Breathing heavily as she chewed. Asked if he'd really meant it. What, accepting her apology? Of course, it was nothing. No, his plan for the winter. Then this child stands facing the window and resists so stubbornly as he tries to pull her by her braids that eventually the older boy lets go and promises, in a dignified, distinctly reserved manner: Whatever you want, Gesine.

Vilami na vodje?
No. Not written with a fork in the water, as you put it.

This was on the Sunday before the state elections, so they had plenty of time to draw up the plan according to which the wheat would be converted into enough supplies to last until next spring. For a long time Jakob felt uneasy in these meetings because of Gesine's submissive acquiescence to everything. He felt like he was cheating her. She approved of whatever he wanted to lay in—shoe soles, new wool, fire starters; he'd have preferred an occasional protest. He was all the more taken aback by her one and only condition, which he had blindly promised to accept: not only the list of commodities was to be agreed on between them but every trade route, every business partner had to be discussed with her.

He thought she was curious—children are like that. He agreed, with misgivings. He tried to keep some things secret; this Gesine was liable to go to a partner and start asking questions. She was Cresspahl's daughter and she got answers, since they thought she already knew in any case. There was no way around it, he had to tell her Mr. Krijgerstam's business, and from then on this skillful veteran from the Baltic fleet rarely got from the firm of Abs & Cresspahl the bacon he needed to exchange for the oil painting in his Razno-Export, however set on it his sense of art appreciation might be. The connection with Knoop the bigwig ran dry for a while too—here Gesine had heard around town in Gneez more precise information than Jakob could come by in Jerichow: Knoop had been nabbed, he'd tried to go big a bit too fast. The NEP isn't so easy to tackle for everyone, Emil had to learn that the hard way. There was no doubt that she knew more about people in Jerichow. That's how Jakob ended up with Jöche, a friend until fall 1956; that's what brought him together with Peter Wulff, a bond as lasting and irrevocable as any on this earth.

Jakob had heard that the children in both Jerichow and Gneez schools carried on a trade in the ration stamps they were meant to hand in for their school meals. But this Gesine wanted to know about every shoemaker he approached, every lawyer who turned up, and this even after they were long since past the two hundred pounds of wheat flour. She learned too much. She ended up involved in business that was dangerous, and not only for children. This isn't how you teach children by example. This isn't how you head a household.

And why wouldn't she have it any other way—who could figure it out?

Maybe his mother was right and this Cresspahl child was in need of religious instruction. Gesine had a bee in her bonnet about that, he'd certainly realized that by now. But how should he try to talk the bee out of it?

June 23, 1968 Sunday

At midnight the American war in Southeast Asia became the longest in the history of the United States, if we assume that the Revolutionary War ended with the British surrender at Yorktown on Oct. 19, 1781. This war has lasted six years, six months, and now two days.

Yesterday five Vietnamese children arrived at LaGuardia Airport in a military aircraft on their way to hospitals here. The boys are named Nguyen Bien, ten, hit by a bullet that went through his back on Jan. 8; Doan Van Yen, twelve, wounded by rocket fire on March 4; Le Sam, eleven, third-degree burns by napalm on March 31; and Nguyen Lau, nine, paralyzed below the waist by a gunshot wound in the spine about nine months ago. *The New York Times* photographed the girl, eight-year-old Le Thi Thum, who came down the staircase in white pajamas, eager and smiling. The *Times* did not get any closer. In words she adds that the girl has a scar across her face and that her nose is there but lacks a bridge. A *Nasenbrücke*? *Nasensteg*?

– No. *Nasenbein*.

For Mrs. Cresspahl is traveling with her daughter through the towns and forests north of New York, on trains, on buses, in taxis, so they share the paper and one corrects the other's language. Every child has a right to an education. The town squares are quiet, looking forward to lunchtime; in one park, a policeman is motionless on his spot like a monument to himself, an equestrian statue with a radio to his ear; in the woods the creeks running down from the mountains are so clear that you'd think you could drink from them without risk of death. It's a day trip; it's a business trip. Every year around this time we have to find somewhere for the child to spend the summer: Marie has a right to a vacation. She inspects country manors, shantytowns, campsites in New Rochelle, Mamaroneck, Peekskill; what she cares about is how long the bus ride is to New York. For we've agreed to just four weeks in Prague and she might want to stay here and wait. She pesters the foreman of one construction site with serious negotiations: paying children are apparently supposed to transform the plot into a recreation area with their own hands, since the brochure promises "creative activities." The man is genuinely tormented—clearly it gives him a headache to confront matters like sculpture . . . cardiovascular activity . . . French courses in the rain. Two hundred dollars a month. Late in the afternoon, Marie finds a camp on Long Island Sound, half an hour from Riverside Drive, with a brisk lady at the counter holding out no creative prospects at all. She rattles off in military fashion what the place offers: Size of camp (in sq. ft.), two pools, completely supervised athletics, thirty-five years of day-camp experience, regular service to and from Manhattan, insurmountable chain-link fence cordoning off the camp from life-threatening natural water. And, due to the planes taking off or landing every two minutes from LaGuardia Airport across the Sound, a discount price of thirty-five dollars a week.

For six hours we've been meeting Americans who've been acting like friends, far above and beyond the requirements of business: the teacher whose art practice involves making mobiles, the custodian, the woman driving the taxi, even the hapless man asked to market a desolate construction site as a children's paradise thanks to the presence of a few forests on steep hills nearby. On one train, the conductor not only invited Marie into his cabin but let her hold the lever and push it forward and now she knows what's it's like to be all the way in the front when you drive into the tunnel under North River. In Yonkers we were allowed into a bar even though the male clientele had just started their afternoon drinking; the owner may have wanted to offer to one and all the Italian cuisine listed on his sign, and he brought out pizza, Italian-style. Marie decided in Yonkers. The soldierly conduct had won the day. That's where it'd be. Across from LaGuardia.

– You know, huh? You think you know me? Tell me, Gesine.
– Forty-five dollars for children.
– Fifteen dollars a week saved. That makes sixty.
– This committee is acting in the name of "responsibility," Marie?
– I'm not responsible and neither are you. Does the money bother you?
– No. It's just that you're doing it out of pity.
– I'm not necessarily the kind of child you were, Gesine.
– Pity isn't genuine, Marie.
– Pity's not bad. I soothe my conscience for four weeks. It's practical, is what it is, don't you think?

June 24, 1968 Monday
The results of the Mecklenburg state election of October 20, 1946, are known. The Socialist Unity Party won forty-five seats, the Conservatives thirty-one, the Liberals eleven; Farmers' Mutual Aid were able to send

three representatives to Schwerin, and the Cultural League for a Democratic Renewal of Germany received not enough votes for even one.

In this new election as well, the campaign manager for the Gneez district had made his rounds with an uneasy feeling, perhaps due to his defeat in September; moreover, the feeling was different. True, the honor of the assignment had once again fallen to him, though this time more than just towns and villages were at stake so his failure could be all the more dire. He drove such fears out of his mind, once he'd recognized that they were selfish. A similar sensation remained, though: the certainty that something was coming that might ruin everything. He could feel it in the back of his neck, like the premonition of a blow. He could ward off a sudden attack, he knew how to deal with insubordination—he'd made his name doing such things—but what should he do in case of a real disaster? All you could see by looking at him was fatigue; on the inside he felt limp and weak. It wasn't because of the many repeat performances each and every day—those were fine, they enacted the truth. So what was it then?

When he drove into Jerichow he thought he'd caught a glimpse of at least a little piece of it. It was the last day before the election and he'd never set foot in this windy backwater that called itself a town. Perhaps he felt some pricks of conscience for having avoided this Jerichow. Slata, the intended wife of a murderous Fascist arsonist, had lived here for three years in a capitalist businessman's house; he had no desire to see the house, and especially not these in-laws of hers. The father, Papenbrock was his name wasn't it, was probably long since lining his pockets again as a middleman, under the Red Army's nose, safe and sound under its New Economic Policy; what a pleasure it would be to deal with him once they'd turned a new page. He decided not to ask about this Papenbrock. Admittedly there was a private aspect to this resolution; maybe for now, or until the votes were counted, it was enough not to admit such weaknesses to anyone but himself.

He stood with his back to the window of Papenbrock's emptied office, incognito, since without his car, driver, and leather coat he thought himself unrecognizable enough. The woman who squeezed out the door next to him was Louise Papenbrock, who used to have a maid to send on such errands. Now she had to walk down Town Street in person to alert her comrades, and the Liberals too, out of Christian duty, for the SMA had again denied them a list of candidates. Even Alfred Bienmüller learned within an hour that a stranger had come to town and had a car with driver and leather coat parked behind the freight shed.

For now, the evening's speaker was strolling down Town Street like someone who wanted to buy himself a little treat in this new place, not that he had anything definite in mind. Nothing he was secretly worried about could ever happen to him here. Plus he didn't know the object of his fear, which made the sensation inherently unscientific. The mayor here was from his own party, though his two advisers were Christian Democrats, and as a result the town hadn't received the full allotments on its ration cards in the past few weeks, though it certainly had gotten almost half the printed matter. That would help. His friends had also availed themselves of an element of bourgeois democracy in which a French Conservative would give amnesty to political enemies or a German Social Democrat would send flowers to a war criminal's daughter, assuring themselves of correct votes—here the dialectic had merely brought about a reversal: no flowers, arrest instead of amnesty. Gerd Schumann had ceased to find such rhetoric from this Ottje Stoffregen fellow witty or amusing; Ottje Stoffregen was now, today, unbolting rails on the Gneez–Herrnburg line and using his delicate teacher's hands to carry them off for transport to the Soviet Union. They certainly hadn't skimped on using the printed matter they'd received, either—almost every shopwindow, every yard gate had a poster of sufficient size stuck to it.

As soon as he read the first one, he knew for certain that his worries had turned up and reported for duty in the right place. What a godforsaken dump, this Jerichow. If only he'd never set foot in it.

The notices summoned the public to appear at tonight's political rally and were signed by Alfred Bienmüller on behalf of the Unity Party. The text opened with a personal description: Gerd Schumann, member of the German Army, admitted to the National Committee for a Free Germany after his desertion to the Red Army, twenty-three years old, district councilman. There were countless posters, all saying the same thing. At the brickworks he turned back, for there was Town Street's name visible for the first time on a sign on the cemetery wall. It was clearly the main street and did not bear the name of Generalissimo Josef Vissarionovich Stalin. An old-fashioned sign, with trim lines around the Gothic script, written white on blue, all so attractive and undamaged that it looked like it had spent a few years wrapped in wool in a drawer,

The evening's speaker hurried back to the market square. Which was called Market Square.

And he was in the right place, the location gave him an almost complete view of the train station's facade ("Most everyone in Jerichow has to go to the station at least once a day"). He could see his driver on the steps, slapping his arms for warmth, right under the bedsheets with a slogan painted in black on it:

FOR IMMEDIATE MERGER WITH THE SOVIET UNION!
VOTE SOCIALIST UNITY PARTY (SED)

and not even centered.

He got into an argument with Bienmüller almost immediately. As a district councilman, he was used to being invited into the parlor for a little bite, a little drink. As a comrade, as campaign manager, he took it for granted that people would agree with him. This Bienmüller didn't leave his muddy workshop yard, held a truck crank in his left hand as though it weighed nothing, even kept his felt hat on so his face was largely hidden, and actually bent down to continue his work.

– That business at the station—that's provocation! It's worse than in Gneez, where they sent postcards saying things like "Are you a intellectual? Vote SED! For the Latin scholars: that's BUT!"

– Huh.

– And you claim to be a comrade!

– *Innt that watcha want, m'boy? Doncha wanna join the Sooviet Union?*

– I demand that we clear this up right now with the commandant!

– *We don have one. Got two.*

– You'll explain your posters there, my friend.

– *Cant go there withiss jeep. Occapation orders.*

– Listen, comrade, you're not going to be mayor here for long!

– *Spose not. I'mma third one already.*

The evening's speaker, in the middle of his march on the double to the Kommandatura, was held up again, this time by the sign on Peter Wulff's shop. He was vaguely familiar with that name. He'd had its file card pulled from the lists of the old SPD in Gneez: member until the Socialists were banned in 1933; courier services; illegal actions (voluntary); arrested during

Mussolini's visit to Mecklenburg (Bützow-Dreibergen); KZ Sachsenhausen 1939–1940; unfit for military service; not yet unified into the SED. Sloppy recordkeeping, probably. He was close to sixty, tall but bent as if he'd been a stevedore not a bartender, pale in the face, still blond. In the hallway shadows he looked merely massive, soft, but outdoors he unexpectedly proved forceful, much more aggressive than Bienmüller. In fact Peter Wulff had immediately taken a shovel off a hook and gone to dig in the garden ("*Our Petey's a good guy he juss forgets himself a little an lashes out sometimes*"). If you keep digging you don't have a free hand to start a fight with.

– Hello, comrade.

– *Red Front yer sposed ta say.*

– Red Front, comrade.

– *Notcher comrade.*

– But you're a member of the Socialist Party, aren't you?

– *Was.*

– Your name's still in the card file. Now you just need to unify.

– *Yeah Im thinkin it over.*

– Yes, why don't we talk it over together?

– *Nope. Juss bring me Cresspahl.*

– What on earth is that?

– *Our mayor.*

– Don't you like Bienmüller then? Is he being removed?

– *Cresspahls who we wanted. Now your guys have im. Bring im back. Go ask about it inna Kommandatura.*

– I will just have to do that, Mr. Wulff.

– *Or ask yer Slata, she knows bout it too!*

The evening's speaker might have been shaken by this reference to Slata. How could he realize that Wulff's singular possessive might have been just a grammatical plural in Platt—"Slata who's with you Russians"? The district councillor probably did announce himself a bit too forcefully at the Kommandatura, since he was a district councillor, and he was perchance not quite polite enough when the gentlemen didn't choose to receive him. In the end it would have been smarter, politically, to have his dispute on the administrative level, as the Wendennych comrades suggested, who had all sorts of second-rate complaints to deal with about supplying their district with adequate food, fuel, building materials. The district councilman, a friend of Triple-J's, may have taken the wrong tone in trying to show them the errors they had committed in their political work among the people of Jerichow. In any case, that in no way justified their taking away his gun. The moment stayed in his memory as a kind of pantomime: while he was distracted by Jerichow's favorite guessing game—which twin was in charge of politics and which in charge of military matters—an orderly had twirled him around on his axis, uncoiling from his body in one smooth, dreamlike motion his belt, his holster, his firearm. They handed him the army decree about German civilians' possession of weapons, in German, while he kept insisting that he spoke Russian perfectly, comprehension, speaking, even written Russian! They had him taken back out to Brickworks Road, with the firm promise: The request to punish him would be submitted to the SMA in Russian, not to worry, but only on Monday because of the election.

Later, he seemed to remember trying to take shelter in a house diagonally across from the Kommandatura—a strangely solitary building that made him feel like it stood at a great distance from this town. All he wanted was three hours of peace and quiet before the rally started. He couldn't face people again so soon. But he was refused, by a child, a girl, thirteen years old at most, who kept answering him in two sentences, now separately, now connected, sometimes in Low German or in standard German if he wanted: *Cant do it.*

– Why not?
– *The Russiansre right over there.*
– What's that got to do with it?
– Can't do it. The Russians are right over there.

He finally gave her up as crazy, feebleminded, a figment of his imagination. A man can imagine things like that in moments of severe emotional strain. Mirages, illusions like that, do exist.

As six o'clock drew near the market square was packed. He stood on the balcony of Town Hall with Mayor Bienmüller, flanked by the Wendennych Twins. The rally started half an hour later, because these commandants had insisted on a written list of his key points, signed and dated before witnesses. How are you supposed to give a speech like that! He began faintheartedly with the harvest, industrialization; it was still with far less than his usual verve, the swelling in his breast from within, that he mentioned

the Bolshevik Leonid Borisovich Krasin, explosives expert and bank robber under the czars, representative of the new Soviet Russia in London and
Paris, who had also managed, as commander of an icebreaker in 1929, to
free a German rail ferry trapped by the ice off Warnemünde. Then he deployed the two weapons the party had put in his hands to ensure that the
embarrassing results from September would not be repeated. The market
square was quite quiet when he repeated the line from the election appeal
of October 7: Our party stands for the protection of property rightfully
acquired the workers' own labor.

Then came the ploy that experience had taught him was sure to draw
cheers and applause, prepared beforehand with volume, pacing, and into-
nation marshaled properly: in words straight from Berlin, from the party's
own mouth, manly opposition to the Soviet foreign minister and his recognition of the Oder-Neisse line: *Our* position, though, must be defined
on the basis of *German* interests—Molotov is pursuing *Russian* policy!

– More than that: cried the evening's speaker: we need not say! *Our*
party—pursues—*German* policy!

And at that point one of the Twins had to take his arm. He hadn't
noticed that some people were crying down on the market square. Someone had fallen down too.

The rally was concluded by Alfred Bienmüller, as mayor and local chairman of the Socialist Unity Party. The guest speaker from district headquarters didn't understand everything he said, since he was still somewhat
dazed; in addition, Bienmüller's variety of High German grammar left
plenty of room for slipping into Plattdeutsch cadences.

– You all hadda good laugh at me: Bienmüller said. – We told you, didn
we, that a kind and humane great power like the Sooviet Unron wouldn
ruin a people just for territorial gain, righ'? Seems to me, seein' how even
our Swede here didn . . . all right, Mr. Duvenspeck! You all laughed at us.
Wouldn believe us. Now youve all heard it for yerselves, ya numskulls. And
you know who youve heard it from! It wont just be good news for our
refugees that theyll be allowed to go home again, lets givem a little good
news ourselves. Since we havent given em much a that before. Shut yer trap,
you! Now one more thing. Theres some rumors been goin round. We know
whos been starting em too, and weve been payin the child support. Theyre
not true. Theyre sayin that if a city gets too few SED votes the people

therell get less on their ration cards, less coal, and less of everything that isnt there. As true as I'm standing here and reading that from this here piece of paper, that's how truly I'm going to rip this piece a paper to pieces right in front of you, that's how truly it isn't true! Thats not how we wanna win your votes! Look at us, look, an then vote! *Im not sayin this from the party, Im sayin it myself, as mayor. Now quiet! No one here* .... This meeting is adjourned.

And so the Gneez district councilman lost his election. In Mecklenburg as a whole, his party got 125,583 fewer votes than in the test run in September. He'd have liked to blame it on Bienmüller's closing speech but couldn't, on scientific grounds. Because, look, in Jerichow his party got a percentage of the vote equaled only in two, maybe three other Mecklenburg communities—more than seventy percent.

He never got his revolver back. That was definitely a loss, one his feelings could latch on to. Only it wasn't the real loss. What was it he'd really been afraid of?

Nowadays, when a leading member of the Czechoslovak Communist Party gets an anonymous letter in the mail, reviling him as a Jew and threatening that his days are numbered, what does his party's newspaper— *Rudé Právo,* "Red Law"—do? It prints the letter in its entirety, and he is allowed to respond to it just as openly. What is he allowed to respond? That anonymous letter writers like this only unmask themselves by adopting the tone of 1952. And what happened in 1952? That's when Rudolf Slánský was executed in the name of the people. We learned that in school.

June 25, 1968 Tuesday

The Czechoslovakian delegation to the national assembly explained to the Soviet Union, clearly and logically,

"that the conditions under which we began to build our socialist country after February, 1948, have changed and that the qualitative changes that have taken place in the economy as well as the socialist structure of our country called for rectification of mistakes, shortcomings, and deformations of the past and a modernization of the economy that has fallen shamefully behind.

But the new realities require a great deal more. They require a transition to a democratic, humanitarian and popular concept of socialism not only in the economy but also, and primarily, in public and political life, where socialism must provide new, wide-ranging concepts of rights and freedoms for the individual as well as society as a whole."

The Soviet comrades showed considerable tolerance for these explanations, perhaps placated by their choice of words. But it may also be true that one of these words got brought up too often. They listened with a certain lack of enthusiasm. Their leader—and no one denies this—had tears in his eyes.

The October 20, 1946, Mecklenburg parliamentary elections produced three results.

I.

On the night of October 21–22, the Red Army came out from behind its fence and paid some visits in Gneez. They parked large trucks so quietly at various locations around the city that the ensuing events that night went virtually unnoticed. Where the patrols entered a home they hauled off whole families. Accusations of harsh treatment are not appropriate, since the soldiers consistently helped the affected parties pack their bags and carry any item they wanted, from the kerosene lamp to the oak sideboard, down the stairs and loaded them carefully into the trucks. This took place repeatedly in some buildings, on other streets not at all. Toward morning, when the reports from eyewitnesses started overlapping and the relocators themselves were in passenger trains well on their way to the new eastern border, the conjecture was bruited about that this had been just another instance of the Soviet national character—impulsive, arbitrary. On the contrary. Comparing the eliminated addresses revealed that they all, although widely dispersed through the city, had two things in common: first, the departed residents had all had residence rights for at least five years—they were locals, by no means refugees (resettlers); second, the male heads of households had without exception been employed in the Arado factory by Gneez Bridge station. The Arado factory had been in a special category of war industries, because for one thing it had made rocket parts for the Peenemünde army testing site. As for the other thing, the prefabrication of parts for Ar 234 jet bombers, those behemoths with four BMW oo3 engines—we'll keep that to ourselves. Any conclusion to the effect that the plant's dismantling and the rounding up of its labor force had logically followed from the rules of war must be rejected as rash. There was no way these actions could have been intended as an ethical favor to Great Britain, which had been harmed by the Peenemünde rockets, since the victorious powers had each reserved its own zone of occupation for dismantling and confiscating industries by way of reparations and—we must emphasize—the British had, during their provisional administration of West Mecklenburg, confiscated blueprints of the Arado Works for their own use, as war booty; the capitalist bandits hadn't even shied away from encouraging scientifically trained workers at that factory from coming with them when they were forced to exchange their Mecklenburg territory for the British Sector of Berlin. Moreover, nothing was dismantled near Gneez Bridge on the night of October 21–22, since, under the SMA's Order No. 3 of June 25, 1945, the machinery, assembly lines, cooling facilities, etc. of the Arado factory there had already been dismantled and removed to the Soviet Union on July 5, immediately after the Red Army entered Gneez. In this regard, we cannot warn strongly enough that rehashed horror stories about piles of telephones in the courtyard of the Gneez post office being heaved onto army trucks with pitchforks, and other such tales, are to be avoided. The dismantling of Gneez-Arado took place under the supervision of a diplomaed (engineering science) high-school teacher attached to the Soviet rocket troops with the rank of colonel—that is to say, were carried out with the utmost care. Proof of which is the cataloging of the equipment: after each written entry, every machine was photographed three times: at rest; being operated by its trained worker; and finally from the rear, again attended by its operator, who was required to appear in the photograph visible from hair to toe. In this connection, one should also recall that the city's carpenters had turned their entire stock of lumber into custom-made crates, and been given orders to spend two whole days making wood chips, not as waste but as the product itself. The Arado factory in Gneez had had its power completely turned off in early August. Certain bourgeois elements bring up as a counterargument that the remaining workers didn't abandon the factory at that point and began manufacturing primitive tools from the leftover materials, supplying the population from September on with rakes, spades, stovepipes, pots, pans, metal combs, and rulers, or at least carrying out repairs on such objects. To which we must reply in the sharpest possible terms that in a great many cases the People's Police were unable to determine the origin of the material used (aluminum sheets for rabbit hutches!), and that the factory, situated in a country town as it was, carried out every imaginable kind of blacksmith work except for horses; that the man in charge of the factory, Dr. Bruchmüller of the CDU, who was elected in an illegal and arbitrary way, has not been cleared of the suspicion of having made off with whatever tools and tradable items were left in the Arado factory before the second dismantling in November of last year; that (here we come to the fourth and fifth points)... the greater part of production went to fill private orders; and that the members of the former Arado factory at Gneez Bridge were sabotaging the circulating currency organized by the SMA with contracts stipulating payment in kind. The deportation of former factory employees can be considered just punishment on that account alone, permission for families to move with them as merciful. Since there can be no question that the above is true, not to mention any alleged contempt for the Fascist capitulation terms, the word *Osavakim* circulating among the population can only be rejected as enemy propaganda seeping over the border from the Western occupation zones. Those who allowed the interpretation of this Soviet word as an acronym for "Special Authority for Carrying Out Dismantlings" to get out should have their heads chopped off. (And anyone blabbing about how it's really something quite different—Osoaviakhim, "Obshchestvo Sodeystviya Oborone, Aviatsionnomu i Khimicheskomu stroitel'stvu SSSR,"

for the Promotion
of the Defense,
Aviation,
and Chemistry Industries
in the USSR,

deserves to have more chopped off than his head.) Any and all further inquiries from the Free German Trade Union Council shall be met with the response that five-year labor contracts have been concluded with every displaced family and the Soviet trade unions will be looking after their interests henceforth. Copies of these contracts can be forwarded on request.

The narrow circle within which this discussion is taking place permits us to subject the tactical discernment of the Soviet Union and the Red Army to a well-meaning appraisal. If our friends had undertaken such a vitally necessary measure during the run-up to the parliamentary election, the results in the Soviet occupation zone would have been comparable to the vote counts in Berlin, where the SPD, under the protection of American and British bayonets, is still capable of opening its maw wide and receiving 63 seats out of 120 in total, whereas we could score only 26. By now the light must have dawned on even Comrade Schumann about why he's spent the last few weeks scared shitless. Yes, if only! The fact is, the Red Army did not invite these citizens from Gneez to the Soviet Union during the election campaign, or even one day before the vote. No, it was one day after the vote. Comrade District Councilman sure knows how to talk convincingly about a debt of gratitude to the Soviet Union, but when it's sitting right in front of his face he doesn't recognize it. In conclusion, since the call to vote placed the securing of peace and friendship with the Soviet Union above all else, it is a fact that the former employees of the factory at Gneez Bridge turned in their ballots and voted as they did.

II.

There was a kink in the October 1946 census. Osavakim affected people not only in the city and district of Gneez but also in other Mecklenburg businesses of armament-strategic significance, and still further in the other provinces of the Soviet zone—for instance, Carl Zeiss and the Jena glassworks, the Siebel airplane factory in Halle, Henschel in Stassfurt, the AEG factory in Oberspree, Askania Friedrichshagen in Berlin, etc. The census was to determine who was home on the night of October 29–30, as well as what job they claimed to have. Thus the undertaking failed to detect a type of migration undetectable by statistical means. In addition, the results implied that fewer specialists in heat-resistant glass or electrical measurement equipment (GEMA, Köpenick) resided in the Soviet occupation zone than in the zones of the Western Allies, for natural reasons. Here sciences other than sociology must be summoned to our aid. In the city and district of Gneez, Osavakim had disseminated among the peace-loving population the conviction that the Soviet Union now, at the conclusion of what was after all a whole year, considered the demilitarization of their

Germans complete and that their job census had proven that Soviet interest in military specialists was no empty delusion. Local rumor had it that anyone who volunteered for the Red Army as a mercenary in the war against Japan could count on like-new clothing, solid footgear, and regular meals. Here people's hopes for the future might be summed up with the question that itself indicated a dual result: *If I only knew where to sign up!*

III.

The Gneez district councilman spent one and a half days in a prison cell under Gneez City Hall. The cause was a quarrel initially about a gun that Triple-J's colleagues in Jerichow had taken from him. As it proceeded, Comrade Schumann unexpectedly, inexplicably even to himself, asked for Slata's address. (Just to write to her.) J. J. Jenudkidse was generally considered a placid commandant, uninclined to malicious or even impulsive behavior. He had the young man delivered to one such address. Sixteen years later, in spring 1962, he who had been that young man tried to explain to a woman that this had been the end of his education, his final renunciation of private desires, the complete submersion of his self into the party. This listener wouldn't have been a woman he was married to, but still, he would have mentioned neither Slata's name nor her whereabouts. He is married. This will have been an evening in the palace gardens in Schwerin, after a concert of serenades. He won't be going by the same name anymore. His last name would be the same as his father's, except for two letters, while for his first name he would be called exactly what his mother wanted. Two days after the parliamentary elections of 1946, seven days before the census, he would have been summoned to Schwerin. His name would have been waiting for him there. Personnel Department at the state administrative level, Security Department at the central ministry level. He never returned to Gneez. I never saw him again.

– But I, if I was coming along to Prague, I'd see him: Marie says. She'd see him. I'll recognize him.

All day long we've been waiting for the black rain that is finally hanging above the Hudson. At lunchtime the air was thick with humidity. Bone-dry people acquired a second skin of sweat as soon as they set foot outside an air-conditioned building. It was impossible to calculate in your head anymore: 89 degrees Fahrenheit minus 32 times five over nine makes something or other in Celsius. The upper edges of the buildings shimmered. After ten blocks, Lexington Avenue itself was blurry; whether the whole thing would have melted away after twenty blocks remained an open question. Now, at nine p.m., rain has come down from the north with two short lightning flashes in its midst, which stab into your eye, short-circuit something in your brain.

– The New York rain, I'd miss that: Marie says. (Children bring the rain with them when they travel.)

June 26, 1968 Wednesday

The Czechoslovak National Assembly has unanimously voted to rehabilitate those who were unjustly persecuted, jailed, and tortured since the Communist takeover in 1948. The sentences may be voided or reduced if the legal rights of the defendants were violated. Survivors are to receive monetary compensation, maybe a new party book for the dead victim. There are also provisions for compensation for physical harm suffered during imprisonment, for court costs, and for material loss. The responsible judges, policemen, prosecutors, investigators, prison wardens, and Interior Ministry employees face the loss of their posts and/or possible further legal punishment, it all depends. The party functionaries, or so-called political leaders, who ordered the purges and persecutions are exempt from the new law. Nothing is going to happen to Antonín Novotný, who was there in the Central Committee of the ČCP since 1946. That's good news for authorities of other nationalities as well.

Every last representative of that National Assembly is the same as in Novotný's days.

Bad news for Karsch. In Palermo seventeen Sicilians and Italian Americans have been acquitted of having juggled with currencies and transported narcotics to the local Mafia or the American Mafia. Terrible news for Karsch. Now there's at least half a chapter in his book he'll have to plow over. The index is toast. No way he'll finish by the end of July. Oh well. We won't be like that about it.

Today Mrs. Cresspahl laughed about Mrs. Carpenter.

Mrs. Carpenter doesn't know that. She can't imagine anyone would, since she'd never do it herself. And there's no way she could prove it.

Mrs. Carpenter ("Call me Ginny") is a young person of thirty-one, five foot four, size 4, shoe size 7 1/4, all estimated in American measurements. In appearance a tall, attractive girl with broad shoulders, pear-size breasts, narrow hips, regular features to the point where each half of her face is a mirror image of the other, framed by harmoniously wavy hair that used to be straight but was always as white-blond as it is now. What's known on the Upper West Side as a Scandinavian type. She is rarely to be seen like this since she's always in motion. When she's driving she plays with the steering wheel, if only with her little finger; in any kind of conversation she moves a foot back and forth, stretches an arm, runs her fingers through her hair; when she walks, any onlooker is faced with a whirlwind of rapid attacks—jerking of neck, clutching of pearls, twisting of or rummaging through handbag, down to legs unheedingly hammering the pavement. On the tennis court this all seems connected to some kind of performance and so becomes enjoyable. Even when she's reading the paper she'll widen the whites around her narrow gray eyes to a surprising extent, as a display of attention, of presence of mind. When she isn't paying attention to herself—when she's observing some child's nonsense, for instance, or when a first raindrop falls from a blue sky—the pretty monotony of her mask slips, revealing displeasure, what you might go so far as to call weariness of life; even that would seem only right, if not for the fact that her symmetrical features went crooked. Then the smile promptly returns. She thinks of herself as beautiful, desirable, ideal—others tell her so. Her calves might be judged flabby by a female observer; a European woman would be more likely to wrongly assume aftereffects from college hockey in Michigan. Anselm Kristlein spent half the length of a cocktail party unable to tear himself away from her long willowy neck, her deep alto voice, the earnest drollery she uses for verbal flirting; she is faithful to Mr. Carpenter in submissive fashion, almost as if incapable of doing otherwise. Once she brushes him with a smile, with girlish sympathy, with a delighted cry from across the room, it's hard for him to imagine she has any secrets.

Since the beginning, when she moved to Riverside Drive four years ago, she's insisted on us being more than just neighbors: friends. Marcia was in the same class as Marie then. Soon Marie was going over to the Carpenters' alone. She wanted to see for herself what exactly that is: a stepmother. Ginny put on a fake deep voice and accused herself of being an evil step-mother out of a fairy tale to anyone who would listen; the child listened in amazement, since this woman then quietly did whatever the child wanted anyway. (They could become partners in crime all the more easily since Mrs. Carpenter had no children of her own. Didn't want to have kids for now.) Marie went over, ostensibly to watch television; she also wanted to find out what it was like to live with a father. When Mr. Carpenter comes home from his chambers, that's when work really starts: here, beatified anew each evening, stands a young wife at the door, slightly red in the face from housewifely zeal; the furniture is waiting, comfortable, clean, more extravagant than he'd exactly wanted for a third marriage; fresh highballs at his preferred temperature are waiting by the window overlooking the Hudson. Now it's his turn. Stories from the office. How Elman was today. Whether Burns via Elman is going to foist the real estate case against the National Guard off on him. Carpenter, a colonel in the reserve, is now buried under household incidents and others that *The New York Times* has already told him about. The caresses all come off in a form it doesn't harm children to witness. He can escape as long as she hasn't planned a party, fifteen people, right before dinner, attention to be paid to acquaintances passing through town or intellectuals from Europe; but just then is when he's supposed to realize how lucky he is, for the liveliest voice is his wife's— a sound well aware of its loveliness. Indefatigably cheerful, she spins the guests around one another, speeding them up with delicate deliveries of excellent drinks, then transforms back into the ardent student she once was: philosophy major, sociology minor, cocooned in a private one-on-one conversation by the fireside, now immersed in an erudite discussion of an article in *International Affairs*, a magazine that in this living room lies out no better or worse than *Cosmopolitan*, *Newsweek*, or *Saturday Review*. The *Playboy* is not out. The household is run along strict yet generous lines—the guests reassure one another of that once they're back out on the sidewalk— but we'd never go there to borrow a pinch of salt. The Carpenters' maid, Isobel, from a village in the Alleghenies, looks a bit like the lady of the house after only two years, and not just because of her youth. A polished girl, she wants to stay not particularly for the half-orphan Marcia—she keeps Marcia rather at arm's length. Tessie, who used to help us, would never set foot in this apartment. Tessie is a subject of Her Royal Majesty the Queen of Great Britain; she likes living in the Bronx, she doesn't need to care what conclusions Mrs. Carpenter pronounces about the dark-skinned race as such.

Ginny Carpenter is without question a major power in our neighborhood, a pillar of our community. If it occurs to Governor Rockefeller that this Riverside Park is utterly useless and would suit him much better as an eight-lane highway for trucks only, Ginny will have ruined the spring of her phone dial within three days, by using it as you're supposed to for once in human history, and presto, here's is a rock-solid committee, fiercely named from the acronym for Save Our Riverside Park, and now Rocky is quaking in his wingtips. She serves as a member of almost every group concerned with the external beauty of our neighborhood, whether with respect to the large-tooth aspen on 119th Street or a trampled trash can on the river promenade. For a passably honest lawyer could hardly pay the expenses of such a wife on the East Side, a location befitting her social status, and so Mrs. Carpenter lives here among us, because of the housing and tree stock, the sunsets over the Hudson, and, not least, the incomparable mix of people here, whose sense of community she could hardly expect among the soulless apartment towers east of Fifth Avenue. – Never!: she says, stamping a little with her long foot. In fact, when she spots us walking on Riverside Drive, she backs up her Cabriolet ($6,780.00) especially for us and entertains us during the ride with the swanky sensitivities of a car like this, stopping without a trace of shame in front of our gray-painted front steps, where there's not even a carpet. – After all, we're neighbors!: she cries, beaming, a good-natured child, sincerely happy at all times.

She is certainly honest. It didn't take long before she noticed something. We don't live in a building you enter under a manned baldachin; we have just three rooms, with a view of the park from beneath the tops of the trees; no liveried doorman keeps watch over us. Our incomes are incommensurate, we can hardly repay invitations like hers in kind, so a pleasant neighborly relationship is preferable to a friendship in which one party feels bad. In circles too elevated for us, Mrs. Carpenter might express admiration for single working mothers supporting self and child year after year, like Mrs. Cresspahl for instance, she wishes she were a woman like that—if only she could get rid of the sneaking suspicion that this Mrs. Cresspahl is leading such a life for the sake of a half-baked feminist ideology, not because she wants to. She is willing to grant us our European origins—although her Europe consists of France, Spain, and Monaco; our neck of the Continent is more dubious even than Yugoslavia. No, she doesn't insist on being friends. Neighbors is just fine.

Today Mrs. Cresspahl is supposed to pick up her daughter from a birthday party at Pamela's. Marie insists on such formalities sometimes; she wants to show off her mother in her best clothes and a brooch at the neck, please. So it's change after work, out to Riverside Drive, elevator to the twelfth floor. And there was Ginny, through the half-open door to the Blumenroths' living room, doing four things nearly simultaneously.

She was savoring what she'd just strewn across the room: Utterly charming, no, dazzling; You look like a June day in the flesh; etc.

She was sitting on the edge of the sofa, eating cookies, hand cupped under her chin to protect her red silk from Lord & Taylor, her taut brow evincing a certain contemplation of how marvelously tolerant she was to be paying such an extensive visit to Jews (admittedly, rich ones); now, to whom could she say that, and from whom better keep it; finally, a gobbling curiosity: are these kosher cookies she's eating?

She was giving a lecture: In twenty years the blacks will have been driven out of Manhattan. We'll be living on a lily-white island surrounded by the black boroughs—the Bronx, Queens, Kings. Richmond County, no, that's not clear yet. It's very simple—economic factors. Our charming four-story brownstones, expensive sandstone on numbered streets, what could be their fate if not a return to being luxury houses for one family each?

She was fingering Marie's blouse, the concealed placket, the double-stitched seam along the button-down collar: it seemed un-American to her; suddenly she pulled the napkin from the child's neck, reached for the label, and spelled it out, aghast: from Geneva.

Mrs. Cresspahl doesn't recall how she waved her child out of there.

Mrs. Cresspahl will need to apologize to her surprised hostess for how she whisked past her. When the elevator doors slid shut before her, she started laughing. Twelve stories down she fell, laughing, seriously disconcerting Marie, and as soon as they got out to the sidewalk the child demanded an explanation, to keep her mother from laughing any more, in public like that. It's not so simple.

Listen, Comrade Writer. I've got something to say to you.

You laughed, Mrs. Cresspahl. Gesine. You did.

Maybe I did. But not just this once.

That may be true, Mrs. Cresspahl.

I gave you a year. That was our agreement. Describe the year.

And what came before the year.

No tricks!

How you got to this year.

And during this year we've agreed on, beginning August 20, 1967, I've seen Ginny Carpenter at Jones Beach, twice. Three times at the Philharmonic. For a meal in the city once. She loaned me her car—no, that didn't work out.

Renting a car cost less than owing her anything.

(I don't know about that.) She's a part of my daily life.

Not on Broadway: she has her meat delivered from Shustek's. Not in the subway: she's never ridden the subway in her life. When the Italian delegation invites you to the UN, you don't bring her along. You're afraid she'll say something embarrassing.

Gimme a break. It's like the thing last Thursday. When you want to show something about shopping you can't help making a drunk Negro assault me in the store and vent his sexual fantasies. I see Ginny Carpenter twice a week and you give her her moment in the spotlight exactly once in ten months: one striking, conspicuous moment.

An important moment.

I laugh every time I see her. Marie just has to mention her. It's not unfriendly laughter, there's no mockery in it at all, usually. It's just funny that someone like that exists. Almost never mocking. I'm glad she exists.

That America can be like that too.

Exactly. So write that down.

You want this to turn into a diary after all?

No. Never. I'm keeping up my end of the bargain. So write about her more often.

If I did, what was important about today's laugh might get lost.

There you go again with your quantity and quality! Add more of one if you want the other!

By accumulating more Mrs. Carpenter, all I'd get is Mrs. Carpenter. I was trying to show that you're preparing for your departure. Reassuring yourself that not everything you're leaving behind is essential. For instance, Mrs. Carpenter. You want to make it easier for yourself to leave, at least to leave this one person in New York.

My departure? For three weeks in Prague?

Business travel of this sort has a way of being extended, Mrs. Cresspahl.

I'm afraid of losing New York but I just can't say it?

Go ahead and say it, Mrs. Cresspahl.

I create my own psychology, Comrade Writer. You need to take it as you find it.

So, you've never laughed like that about Ginny Carpenter.

Agreed. You can write that. I've never laughed like that.

Mrs. Cresspahl had never laughed like that about Mrs. Carpenter. Like that? Never.

In fall 1946, the Cresspahl child moved many of her things from Jerichow to the county seat of the area, Gneez. She lived in Jerichow, she was on the official lists in the registration and housing offices there, she got her ration cards there (Group IV), it was there that she and her father had arranged to meet again, in case he came back from the Soviet prison or wherever else he might be from which return was conceivable. But she went to school in Gneez, and the railway management often combined the afternoon train to Jerichow with the evening one, and when there was no coal even for that one she would stay until the next school day with Alma Witte, in the room from which Slata had disappeared. She went back to Jerichow in the dark, as if into the dark.

Gneez was a big city. For a child born in Jerichow—who ever since then thought of such enlarged one-street villages as the way the world was supposed to be, if not the only possible world—Gneez is a city that only makes you think of bigger ones.

Back then the train needed an hour to cover the Jerichow–Gneez branch line—nineteen tariff kilometers, four regular stops and one flag stop, forty-one minutes according to the timetable. The train consisted of three third-class cars, the kind where compartments lining the corridor have a door on the left or the right alternately, plus two or three freight cars, delivering the potatoes, beets, and sacks of wheat collected in Jerichow to supply the needs of the city of Gneez. These cars drove back empty at night, as a rule, and as soon as the train got out of sight of the Soviet control officer in the engine routing center, the People's Police swung out of the empty boxcars and tumbled back along the long running boards to the passenger cars, where they might stay warm at least with card games. In the mornings, though, in rain or in frost, they would crouch along the edges of the box-cars next to their products of the country, 98k Karabiner rifles propped at an angle, implacable enemies of snipers, thieves, and black marketeers. If the district administration in Gneez had been able to meet its need for trucks by confiscations from the coast, this largely single-track rail line, too, would have been unscrewed and sent off to the Soviet Union, like all the second tracks in the Soviet occupation zone. As it was, the line was used, three times a day according to the timetable, and the Cresspahl child took it to her secondary school in Gneez, as the Educational Reform Law mandated.

The dairy train from the coast approaches Gneez along a wide bulging arc to the west, letting viewers build up a semicircular picture of the thin sharp spires of Lübeck, as in a peep box; at the Gneez Bridge station, then closed, the line heads south-southwest and the rising sun paints the windows; at Gneez station the Jerichow train rests on an almost precisely east-west line, and with only a little shunting it could be dispatched to Hamburg or Stettin, the two cities on the classic line, but now that they're both cut off by borders no train can get there from platform 4. Gneez had four platforms.

Outside the station was a plaza that took up more space than the whole market square in Jerichow, and it was surrounded by buildings like a market square too. To the right were the steel gates, more than six feet tall, to the freight loading area; next to them City Hall, in three red-brick stories, flying the Red Army flag; straight ahead the prince's mansion, converted into Knoop's storage and haulage firm, crossed hammers on the frosted-glass windows; to the left, alongside the track running onward to Bad

Kleinen, were bicycle sheds and the bay in the sidewalk that country buses used to pull into. In the middle of this incredible expanse they had laid out a genuine park, a square of grass now admittedly trampled black with bare trees here and there. The path running straight across the plaza, though, led to the showpiece of one's first impression: a four-story gray stucco building, its continuous columns and fluting rising clear up to the elegantly rounded hipped roof—a palace, the Archduke Hotel, built in 1912 and designed by an architect who'd believed in a future for Gneez as a major metropolis. Not only did the building jut into the rose garden with a restaurant and a three-story wing of rooms, it bulged out into the street in front half again as much, its ground floor enlarged into a café beneath graceful stucco garlands, a mighty portal to the reception halls, and another, more subdued one leading to the Renaissance Cinema. Only then, fifty-six yards down Railroad Street, did this colossus yield the frontage to midgets—bourgeois houses of few stories, painted white, with stores and bars at their feet. This was Railroad Street, which had been named after an Austrian for a few years and now bore the name of the place to which it led, from which it came. The name "Archduke" was still on the hotel's roof, attached to a wire frame in proud Roman letters, and just as the place had once scared off the less impressive traveling salesmen, nowadays it was kept for the better sort with a red-and-yellow tin sign on the bulging semicircular reception desk, illegible to most Germans, presumably to be translated as Officers' House but meaning only the officers who could read Cyrillic. This was Station Square in Gneez—what a rich country town had once resolved to create as a lasting monument, not ostentatiously, just humbly presenting what the city had to hand. The citizens of the new century had no desire to boast of more than that; their solidity was only to be made visible. This had been the site of political rallies since the 1914 war, and here was where the Red Army had established its civil government.

The square was guarded by a ring of streetlights, it didn't matter that they weren't on—maybe the panes of glass had been shattered by rocks or bullets—anyway, they stood so tall, making sweeping gestures, in stiff pairs, they were still candelabras, lacquered black. And between the pair, almost every one, a pole had been set up flying a red flag, or else a sheet was stretched, bearing words from the Red Army to the locals in their own language, German black-letter.

Anyone who found the Dom Ofitserov too threateningly grand might take a narrow path straight ahead, past Knoop's edifice of hereditary ownership, and might genuinely be shocked by the difference between the doorless side of the prince's mansion facing the station and the south facade with its generous balconies, statues in niches, and serenely sweeping outdoor staircase commanding the southern prospect. There had once been a park there, which had gradually been devoured by a neighborhood of new buildings that had burned down once every century since the fifteenth until the 1925 SPD planned to put up a middle-income public housing project there, with reduced-cost lots, credit assistance, and a salutary dislike of rushing things. As a result six units were finished only in 1934 and 1935, and as a result Gneez-Neustadt was depicted in photo books from then on as an example of Mecklenburg's flourishing under National Socialism. It was hardly what you'd call the city. It was a field of scattered red villas, each with its own fenced-in garden plot, organized in groups of six with frugal paved paths under the patronage of the Musicians Guild. Felix Mendelssohn-Bartholdy's name could not, it turned out, be restored on the customary enamel sign, but it could be recarved into two oak signs. This was "the new good part of town," assigned to employees of the administration and the parties, the imported brain trust, and now thickly settled with refugees, children's homes, and Soviet private quarters. Only after you'd wandered through this pattern of boxes, turning left and then left again, would you find yourself at the tail end of Station Street, at a modest square that had once held the widened city walls, the Lübeck Gate, the guardhouses Lisch the local historian had failed to mention, and a humorous image in bronze of the animal to which Gneez owed its nickname. Now all the square had to offer was the bridge over the city moat, a low-lying, nearly stagnant body of water as wide as a man is tall. Here was the start of Old Gneez.

On maps, Old Gneez resembles the attempts of early mathematicians to carve a piece of wood into a many-sided polygon approximating a circle. This crude disk, divided by thin veins, was split down the middle by Stalin Street, an artery for shopping, strolling, and through traffic big enough for two horse-drawn carriages to pass each other without moving aside. Almost everything east of this thoroughfare, down to the rose garden, was considered "the old good part of town," the collective address of people who could document ancestors there since Napoleonic times, or, when in doubt, refugees. To the west, the side streets might start off by putting isolated stuccoed buildings on display, but they betrayed their true nature with the crumbling half-timber at the sides and stood convicted by the cottages, small farms, and tradesmen's yards sloping away behind them. These were houses built not just for single families but for those who wanted a rental income too. Anyone walking through the Danish Quarter could tell by the doors. Factory-made, barely any woodwork or mottoes on the beams. Just workers. Happy with anywhere they could lay their heads. That's how it is, west side, can't be helped, right? Anyway, there were such crooked walls there that you hardly noticed the odd door handle. That's how several of those houses had avoided the looting. Gotten off easier in terms of being assigned refugees too. But even the Soviets hadn't been able to eradicate the border to the respectable part of town: Stalin Street.

Stalin Street, previously named from its orientation toward Schwerin, crept south toward the market square for a quarter mile and then vanished into the cobblestones, starting up again on the opposite corner but less grandly, and now as Schwerin Street once more. There was Bulls' Corner, Bleachers' Road, Coopers' Lane. There the child sometimes visited a building with a grand entrance and a cramped upper story of living quarters and servants' rooms. There she sometimes watched Böttcher at work. She liked that. It was across the street from the Chapel of the Holy Blood. Schwerin Street had once been a way to walk to school.

But the market square was unforgettable for a child from Jerichow. Its square footage might be comparable to the market square back home, but in Jerichow everything had been left at that; the square here was clearly the model for Gneez's modern ceremonial plaza by the station. Here the buildings often showed four rows of windows, one atop the other, each of its own dimension, in individually upward-scalloping facades, behind whose pinnacles was no mere empty air but an indisputable window to an attic room, which existed there too. They kept such a proud distance from one another; they left alleyways, *Tüschen*, between them, not from necessity but from self-respect. They had to have those. The roofs had their backs turned from the market square; like hair partings above faces, they were all supposed to be unique. There were pulleys built into the gables, on which every single gap had been upgraded to a half wheel with spokes; there were coats of arms painted there, from interlaced initials to a burning circling sun. (The south side of one building turned the long end of its roof to face the market with a mansard in masonry not to be found on any postcards from before 1932.) Here you had the Court and Council Apothecary. There you had buildings that spoke of history, and not only in their weather-beaten bricks: In this hall the citizens paid their contribution to Old Freddy's seven-year war (1756–63). In memory of the time of the French: arson and pillage under General von Vegesack. Friedrich IV, King of Denmark, spent the night here, December 19–20, 1712. The post office, formerly the palace of the counts of Harkensee, was on the market square, its Doric columns courteously retracted. On the west side a spacious building has raised its brows so high that the roof needs to keep to the horizontal for a while before bending downward in back. Its facade has double doors proportioned according to the golden ratio, with staircases to the second floor closing in on both sides. And yet it stands in a row with the other buildings, not insisting on a greater separation. This was the former City Hall. The double staircase had been meant to show respect for authority, for the man elected first among equals. The cellar below was to keep its view of the market square. But for twentieth-century views it was too modest. With all their grand ideas they still hadn't managed to wean themselves from linden trees, full and round of crown, all around the market square near the surrounding buildings; they had just kept on growing. The candelabras wouldn't grow. Station Square might suffice as a parlor for the modern era, but the market square was Gneez's good room, now as ever.

The city didn't end there—south of the market square was almost a third of it, known as the Ducal Quarter, designed by court architects somewhat more generously between the forceps formed by tree-lined avenues along the old fortress walls: police prison, district council office, district court, county court, palace theater, cathedral yard, high school converted into Soviet army hospital, and the esplanade, about a hundred yards long, between the city swimming pool and the Little Berlin housing development on Gneez Lake. At the corner of the cathedral yard there was Alma Witte's hotel, where the child from Jerichow sometimes spent the night.

The city of Gneez. First mentioned in the Ratzeburg tithe register in 1235. Approx. 25,500 inhabitants in 1944, just under 38,000 in 1946. District capital. Industries: Panzenhagen Sawmill, Möller & Co. Canning Plant (a branch of Arado). Apart from that, trades; no mercantile business to speak of except for one company. Surroundings: forest to all sides except the south; a ridge of hills to the east, 320 ft. high, forested under the gracious supervision of Duchess Anna Sophie of Mecklenburg. The last witch burning took place there in 1676, hence its second name, Smœkbarg (Smoke Hill). Along with Gneez Lake: Warnow Lake, Rexin. Train connections to Bad Kleinen, Herrnburg, Jerichow.

Ever since the Cresspahl child had been transferred to the Bridge School, she could have turned right straight from Station Square, walked down Warehouse Street, and crossed the bridge to the Bridge School in the suburb known as the Lübeck Quarter. If instead she wanted to learn more about the city of Gneez than she was assigned, perhaps that was due to the time she had to kill until the next train departed?

She had long since stopped being a stranger, someone who noticed the buildings first and the people second. She was still a commuter student, but she'd moved to Gneez with many of her things.

She would enter the houses. With the people there she'd talk business, and she had much more time to do so than Jakob. She asked Böttcher the price of a butter churn, compared his answer to what Arri Kern was hoping to spend, and Böttcher got the difference.

In "the new good part of town," the suburb around the station, she had a Russian officer's wife to visit. This was the supervisor of the district council office. Her German landlords tried to hound at least this one newcomer out of her house with grossly inadequate services—they gave Krosinskaya no bed linen, started rumors in the neighborhood that her kind could hardly be used to any. Krosinskaya didn't have a husband in the barracks on Barbara Street; hers was buried near Stettin. This meant she had to buy sheets and blankets. She bought liquor. Once, she took all her clothes off except her silk slip right in front of the Jerichow child, pushed up an invisible weight with both hands, and asked: wasn't she still beautiful? The child guessed her age to be about forty and gave her the adjective she wanted; she wasn't lying either. It's just that everything about Krosinskaya, from legs to breasts, was a little too large, too heavy. Krosinskaya always paid the exact amount. She laughed at her German hosts. They wouldn't give her any furniture, so what? So she lived in bed, spread out sheets of the army newspaper on the bare mattress and laid out her dinner every day on the *Krasnaya Armiya*: sausage and bread and onions, separately. She ate them with a knife. In other ways she was quite finicky.

Another Soviet family, employed at the station, were bringing up their little boy to hate Germans. He would kick over Granny Rehse's mop bucket and treat her like the lowest scullery maid every way he could. Granny Rehse would have enjoyed being affectionate with the seven-year-old; as it was, she didn't understand him. This was the Shachtev family, who didn't buy liquor, they bought LP records. It was supposed to be Beethoven's music and cheaper than you could get it at Krijgerstam's Razno-Export. They brought out some liquor after all, under protest; berated the German child as a Fascist brat; weren't above threatening her with denunciation once—all with the pointedly good manners that made any real familiarity impossible. Mrs. Shachtev had been a doctor before the war. Her darling child, Kolya, had had his own nanny back home.

The Jerichow child learned from Alma Witte, or from Wilhelm Böttcher, those little scraps of local history that newcomers so like to use to imagine they understand a strange place:

The cathedral burned down in the hot June of 1659. Every other building remained intact undamaged, so it was presumed to be a case of arson. (According to the calculations of the New York municipal weather bureau, June this year was unusually wet and cool.) The Church has been waiting for the city to donate money for a new spire since 1660. The city had to accept the Protestant faith at gunpoint; the cathedral received nothing but a new transept until 1880, with the city giving nothing for the tower. The city could wait. As long as the Church was annoyed, the citizens could accept that ships no longer used the blunt emergency roof of Gneez as a seamark but instead used St. Peter's Church, Jerichow.

The Lübeck Quarter's official name was Bridge Quarter, even though it was on the Lübeck side. Well, we can keep the big neighbor to the west, even its *name*, out of our city at least once, can't we! For another thing, there *had* been a bridge there, over the channel with which Johann Albrecht I of Mecklenburg, long before Wallenstein, had intended to link the Wismar Bay to the Elde and thence Asia Minor. Wallenstein had lent his name to the scheme; what remained was a putrid ditch between Arado Works I and Arado Works II.

Gneez Lake had once been named after a large farmer's village to the south, which was wiped out during the Thirty Years' War and then later in the seventeenth century came under the plow and turned into moors. Woternitz Lake was the old name. The higher Gneez rose in the world, the more urgently it wanted a city lake of its own—Gneez printed it on tourist brochures, screwed hands with a pointing finger onto the enamel signs already in the train station. True, the Reich's land surveying office hadn't budged. Gesine learned to listen to such stories without bringing up Jerichow's Town Street. The right thing to do when Gneez's "Town Lake" came up was to purse one's lips a little and give Willi Böttcher a sidelong glance. Then she almost seemed to belong.

She had to take care of things in Gneez. On September 1, 1946, when she started at the Bridge School, the signature *Abs* on the old report card had caught the eye of the homeroom teacher, Dr. Kramritz. He'd asked just out of curiosity, but her panic made her realize the truth: Mrs. Abs was not her stepmother, not her aunt, not anyone entitled to sign report cards. The Cresspahl child had no legal guardian at all.

In late October she heard about Control Council Directive 63. There were now to be "interzonal passports" for trips to the western zones. The border was open again. Whatever it was keeping Jakob at the Jerichow gasworks and Cresspahl's house was a mystery to her. He might go west any day now. Dream up a funeral to go to there, or a deal in nails, and the People's Police would give you the piece of paper you needed. Mrs. Abs wouldn't stay without him. But Cresspahl's child had to wait.

In Gneez you could see it. Brigitte Wegerecht had stopped coming to school from one day to the next, without an excuse for Dr. Kramritz or her friend. Then she sent word from Uelzen (British zone).

Rooms in Gneez would suddenly turn up empty overnight, or whole apartments. Leslie Danzmann scattered a glorious treasure of residential assignments over the refugees' heads. There were again families living all by themselves, behind their own door. When Dr. Grimm was due to take over the district council office as senior administrator, Krosinskaya energetically made certain suggestions and his family took a trip to Hamburg for a christening—no great surprise for so Protestant a family. He spent a long evening over wine in the Dom Ofitserov discussing the work Gerd Schumann had left behind after his departure; by the next morning he had swum across the lake near Ratzeburg. He knew what he was doing. Brigitte's mother, née von Oertzen, may have been complying with her husband's last wishes, or her brother's advice. Could Cresspahl's child have blamed Jakob's mother for doing likewise?

Jakob still went to visit Johnny Schlegel's often enough. He was in love with a girl there. Anne-Dörte was prettier, and smarter, than any younger girl could hope to be; she might be a countess and all that; but Gesine Cresspahl knew—she was thirteen, wasn't she?—that loves like theirs last a lifetime. There was no doubt about it. If Anne-Dörte was summoned to Schleswig-Holstein, Jakob would follow her there too. Then Cresspahl's child would be without the care to which she had a customary right and which the Abs family had temporarily given her.

Children who are alone in the world are sent to a children's home. There was no such place in Jerichow. The one that took in all the children from the area was in Gneez.

June 28, 1968 Friday

Yesterday, června 27th, in *Literární Listy*, the weekly journal of the Czechoslovak Writers' Union, published in Prague, authorized by the Ministry of Culture, price one crown twenty, was a letter to all the citizens of the country,

> *dělníkům,*
> *zemědělcům,*
> *úředníkům,*
> *vědcům,*
> *umělcům,*
> *a všem,*

signed by almost seventy workers, farmers, engineers, doctors, scientists, philosophers, athletes, and artists,

Dva tisíce slov, The Two Thousand Words:

"The first threat to our nation was from war. Then came other evil days and events that endangered the nation's moral integrity and character. Most of the nation welcomed the Socialist program with high hopes. But it fell into the hands of the wrong people. It would not have mattered so much that they lacked adequate experience in affairs of state, factual knowledge, or philosophical education, if only they had had enough common sense and decency to listen to the opinion of others and eventually agree to be gradually replaced by more capable people.

The Communist Party, after enjoying great popular confidence immediately after the war, bartered this confidence away for office piece by piece until it had all the offices and nothing else. We feel we must say this. It is known to both Communists and the others who are equally disappointed with the way things turned out. The leaders' mistaken policies transformed a political party and an alliance based on a great idea into an organization for exerting power, one that proved highly attractive to power-hungry individuals, to unscrupulous cowards, to people who had something to hide. Such people influenced the self-image and behavior of the party, whose internal arrangements made it absolutely impossible for people to attain leadership positions and adapt the party to modern conditions without performing scandalous acts. Many Communists tried to fight this decline, but they managed to prevent almost nothing of what was to come.

Conditions inside the Communist Party both epitomized and caused the corresponding conditions in the state. The party's association with the state deprived it of the asset of separation from executive power. No one was allowed to criticize political and economic decisions. Parliament forgot how to advise, the government forgot how to govern, and the leaders forgot how to lead. Elections lost their significance, and the law hardly mattered. We could no longer trust our representatives on any committee or, if we could, there was no point in asking them for anything because they were powerless. Worse still, we could scarcely trust one another anymore. Personal and collective honor collapsed. Honesty was a useless virtue, assessment by merit unheard of. Most people accordingly lost interest in public affairs, worrying only about themselves and about money, despite the fact that it was impossible to rely even on the value of money under this system. Personal relations were ruined; there was no more joy in work; in short, the nation entered a period that endangered its moral integrity and character.

We all bear responsibility for the present state of affairs. But the Communists among us bear more than others, and those who served or benefited from unchecked power bear the greatest responsibility of all. This power was that of an intractable group, spreading out from Prague into every district and community through the party apparatus, which alone decided who could or could not do what. The apparatus decided about the cooperative farms for the cooperative farmers, decided about the factories for the workers, and decided about the National Committees for the public. No organization, not even a Communist one, was truly under its members' control. The chief sin and betrayal of these rulers was casting their own whims as 'the will of the working class.' If we accepted this premise, we would have to blame the workers today for the decline of our economy, for crimes committed against the innocent, and for the censorship that hinders us from describing these things! The workers would also be to blame for the misconceived investments, the trade deficits, the housing shortage. Obviously no reasonable person can hold the working class responsible for these things. We all know, and especially every worker knows, that the working class had no say in deciding anything. Working-class functionaries were given their voting instructions by somebody else. Many workers imagined that they were in power, but it was a specially trained clique of party functionaries and state officials who actually ruled in their name. In effect these people had stepped into the shoes of the deposed ruling class and themselves became the new power.

Let us say in fairness that many of them long ago realized what a false game they were playing. Today we can recognize these individuals by the fact that they are trying to redress old wrongs, rectify mistakes, hand back decision-making power to rank-and-file party members and citizens, and set limits on the power, and size, of the administration. They share our opposition to the reactionary views held within the party. But a large number of officials have been resistant to any and all change. They still retain the instruments of power, especially outside of Prague, at the district and community levels, where they can wield them in secret and without fear of accountability.

Since the beginning of this year we have found ourselves in a process of regeneration and democratization.

It started inside the Communist Party—that much we must admit, even the non-Communists who no longer hoped for anything good to emerge from that quarter. It must also be added, of course, that the process could have started nowhere else, since for more than twenty years only the

Communists could conduct any sort of political activity; it was only the opposition inside the Communist Party that enjoyed the privilege of being heard by their antagonists. Now the efforts and initiative being shown by democratically minded Communists are only a partial repayment of the debt the entire party owes to the non-Communists hitherto refused an equal position. Accordingly, no thanks are due to the Communist Party. But perhaps we should give the party credit for making an honest eleventh-hour effort to save its own honor and the nation's.

What this process of regeneration has introduced into our lives is nothing particularly new. It includes many ideas and problems older than the errors of Socialism, and others which, having emerged from below the surface of visible events, should have found expression long ago but were instead repressed. Let us not nurse the illusion that these ideas are destined to prevail now because the power of truth is on their side. Rather, their victory will be decided purely by the weakness of the old system, obviously falling into exhaustion after twenty years of unchallenged rule. Apparently the basic defects of the system, already hidden in its ideological foundations, had to come to full fruition. So let us not overestimate the effects of the writers' and students' criticisms. The source of social change is economic. A true word makes its mark only when it is spoken under conditions that have been properly prepared—conditions that, in our context, unfortunately include the impoverishment of our whole society and the complete collapse of centralized government, which had enabled certain types of politicians to get rich quietly and at our expense. Truth does not prevail alone here—truth is merely what remains when everything else has been frittered away! So there is no occasion for a national victory celebration, merely a reason for hope.

In this moment of hope, albeit hope still threatened, we appeal to you. It took several months before many of us were able to trust that it was safe to speak up; many of us are still afraid to do so. But we have already spoken up enough, exposed ourselves enough, that now we have no choice but to continue and finish our efforts to humanize the regime. Otherwise the old forces will exact cruel revenge. We appeal above all to those who have waited on the sidelines thus far. Now is the time that will decide our future for years to come.

Now is the time for summer holidays, a time when we are inclined to let everything slip. But we must not forget that our dear adversaries will skip their summer break; they will rally everyone who is under any obligation to them, and take steps, even now, to secure themselves a quiet Christmas! Let us watch carefully how things develop; let us try to understand them and have our answers ready. Let us give up our impossible desire to have someone from on high provide the single possible explanation and the single correct conclusion. Everyone will have to draw their own conclusion, on their own responsibility. Common, agreed-upon conclusions can only be reached in discussions among all sides, and those presuppose freedom of speech—which may remain the only democratic achievement we have accomplished this year.

But in the days to come we must act on our own initiative and make our own decisions.

First and foremost, we must oppose the view, whenever it is voiced, that a democratic renewal can be achieved without the Communists, or even in opposition to them. This would be unjust, and foolish too. The Communists have a well-developed organization in place, and we must support its progressive wing. They have experienced officials, and, not least important, they still control the crucial levers of power. They have presented their Action Program to the public. This program should start to resolve the most glaring injustices, and no one else has a program worked out in such detail. We must demand that they present local Action Programs in every district, every community. Then we will suddenly face very simple decisions, to be decided the right way, as we have so long awaited. The Czechoslovak CP is preparing for its congress, where it will have to elect a new Central Committee. We demand that it be a better one. If the party says that it now plans to base its leadership position on the confidence of the public, not on force, let us believe them, but only to the extent that we can place our trust in who they are sending as delegates to the district and regional assemblies.

People have recently been worried that the progress of democratization might come to a halt. This feeling is partly a sign of fatigue after the thrilling events of the past few months, but partly it reflects the truth. The season of astonishing revelations, of removals from high office, and of heady speeches couched in language of unaccustomed daring—all this is over. But the struggle of opposing forces is merely taking place on another level, over the content and formulation of the laws, over the scope of practical measures. Besides, we must give the new people time to work: the new ministers, prosecutors, chairmen, and secretaries. They are entitled to time to prove themselves fit or unfit. Beyond this, we cannot expect much from the central political bodies, though they have, in spite of themselves, made a remarkably good showing so far.

The practical quality of our future democracy now depends on what happens to the factories and *in* the factories. Despite all our discussion, it is the ones who manage the businesses who have us in their power. Good managers must be sought out and promoted. True, we are all badly paid in comparison with people in the developed countries, some of us worse than others. We can ask for more money. But then it would just be printed, as much as we want, and devalued in the process. Let us rather ask the directors and the board chairmen to tell us what they want to produce and at what cost, to whom they want to sell it and at what price, the profit that will result, and how much of that profit will be reinvested in modernizing production, how much will be left over for distribution. Under seemingly boring headlines, our press is covering a hard battle being fought—the battle of democracy versus the feeding trough. The workers, as employers, can intervene in this battle by electing the right people to management and workers' councils. As employees, they can help themselves best by electing trade union delegates to represent their interests—honest and capable individuals irrespective of their party affiliation.

If we cannot expect much from the central political bodies at the present time, it is all the more crucial to accomplish more at the district and community levels. We demand the resignation of those who abused their power, damaged public property, and acted cruelly or dishonorably. Ways must be found to compel them to resign. To mention a few: public criticism, resolutions, demonstrations, demonstrative work brigades, collections for their retirement, strikes, and picketing their offices. But we must reject all illegal, dishonorable, or boorish methods, which they use against Alexander Dubček. We must reject so forcefully and completely the practice of writing vile anonymous letters that any such letters that are reported in the future will be known to have been written by the recipients themselves.

Let us revive the work of the National Front. Let us demand public sessions of the national committees. For questions that no one else will look into, we will set up our own citizens' committees and commissions.

There is nothing difficult about it: a few people come together, elect a chairman, keep proper minutes, publish them, and refuse to be intimidated. Let us convert the district and local newspapers, which have mostly degenerated to the level of official mouthpieces, into a platform for all the forward-looking elements in politics; let us demand that editorial boards include National Front representatives, or else let us start new papers. Let us form committees for the defense of free speech. At our meetings, let us have our own security forces. If we hear strange reports about someone, let us seek confirmation, then send a delegation to the proper authorities and publicize their findings, posting them on doors if necessary.

Let us support the police forces when they prosecute genuine wrongdoing, for it is not our goal to create anarchy or a state of general uncertainty. Let us avoid quarrels among neighbors and drunkenness on political occasions. But let us expose informers!

Summer travel throughout the republic will also make it more desirable to settle the constitutional relations between the Czech Republic and Slovakia. Let us consider federalization as one possibility for resolving the national question, but as only one of many important measures for democratizing the system. This particular measure will not in itself improve life in Slovakia. Having separate governments in the Czech lands and Slovakia doesn't solve anything. Rule by a state-and-party bureaucracy could still continue, and might even be strengthened in Slovakia by the claim that it had 'won more freedom.'

There has recently been great alarm over the possibility that foreign forces will intervene in our development. Faced with all the great powers, we can only defend our own point of view, behave decently, and not defy or challenge anyone. We must show our government that we will stand by it, with weapons if need be, as long as it does what we give it a mandate to do. And we can assure our allies that we will observe all our treaties of alliance, friendship, and trade. Exasperated reproaches and unfounded suspicions on our part can only make things harder for our government, not help it. In any case, the only way we can achieve relations on a basis of equality is to improve our domestic situation and carry the process of renewal far enough to someday elect statesmen with sufficient fortitude, prestige, and political acumen to negotiate and maintain such equality for us. But this is a problem that the governments of all small countries face.

This spring we have been given another great opportunity, as we were after the war. Once again we have the chance to seize control of our common cause, which bears the working title of SOCIALISM, and give it a form more appropriate to our reputation, once good, and the fairly high opinion we used to have of ourselves. This spring is over and will never return. By winter we will know where we stand.

So ends our call to the workers, farmers, officials, artists, scholars, scientists, engineers, and to everyone. It was written at the behest of scholars and scientists."

Employee Cresspahl got to work late today. First she played hooky and stopped by the Italian delegation of the UN—uninvited, without phoning first. Signora Sabatino couldn't quite believe that someone she knew only from the Rolodex for second-tier cocktails was standing here in person. But at the receptions she serves food and gives every guest an encouraging look, which says silently but clearly enough for everyone to feel they've heard it: Well? Another hors d'oeuvre? Just a little something? How about this one?

She had only one question. How could someone get ahold of a Prague paper from yesterday in New York today. The one, you know, that today's *Times....*

– *Ma!*: Mrs. Sabatino cried at once. – *Ma abbiamo quattro edizioni di questo manifesto!* La Práce, Zemědělské Noviny e Mladá Fronta! *Anche le Sue* Literární Listy! *Signora*, do take off your coat! Your hair's wet! You're the lady who sends letters for Signor Karresh, aren't you? I'll announce you to His Excellency Dr. Pompa, he is very busy at the moment, doing nothing whatsoever. Just two minutes, I'll go in and interrupt him with coffee. *Facciamo cosí, signora?*

But Mrs. Cresspahl left right away, through the rain, seven photocopied sheets under her coat. One has to at least pretend to be at work. And then she cheated the bank out of a whole workday; our Vice President de Rosny himself would have asked in vain what this Czech document has to do with a trip to Prague. Employee Cresspahl wouldn't just have reminded him that it was she and none other who was to take that trip in August to the land where the Socialists talk like this, on a mission from the bank. She'd likely have added how disruptive it is for bosses to interrupt one, or something like that. This was practically homework! Mrs. Cresspahl had her lunch brought up from Sam's! The radio, set to the Prague station, emitted foreign words, another country's music, it was hot to the touch when she took it home that evening. Today it looked like almost no work had been done in the office.

Komunistická strana, která měla po válce velikou důvěru lidí, postupně ji vyměňovala za úřady, až je dostala všechny a nic jiného už neměla. Musíme to tak říci. . . .

No, even closer to the beginning: *Událostmi, které ohrozily jeho duševní zdraví a charakter.* Destroyed the integrity . . . ? That's not the right word at all.

Today, too, our radio gives the good honest water levels of the Vltava, and it also offers the answers of some citizens.

Prime Minister Oldřich Černík denounces such letters before the National Assembly. He concludes by practically inciting deeds from which might arise things such as nervousness, unrest, and judicial uncertainty.

The presidium of the Central Committee of the Communist Party of Czechoslovakia believes its policy is under attack from this letter—the program of the National Front and the government itself in danger.

If you want to know what's possible for Socialism in our time, learn Czech, my friends!

June 29, 1968 Saturday, South Ferry day

The Rawehns, ff. Ladies' and Gentlemen's Apparel, had had a store on Gneez's market square since Napoleonic times. It had once been loosely affiliated with the famous Ravens of Wismar; in fall 1946 a coat for the winter should still turn out in a way that Rawehn deemed fashionable, all the more so if the customer was merely a tradesman's child from Jerichow, under the care of an old woman from even farther out, a refugee. Madame Rawehn, a short strapping woman not yet forty, in a city suit as tempting as it was unbreakable, acted by no means snooty toward this Mrs. Abs and her protégée, who promised to pay in wheat. Mustn't provoke rich customers. And it'd been a long time since she'd had such fine black worsted fabric in her hands, it had probably been lying in a drawer since 1938, a French drawer perhaps; she would have been happy to buy more than one and a half yards, double wide. Not to mention the tartan pattern lining. But how this Gesine Cresspahl looked at her! It made her check the mirror! Where she saw herself taking measurements—her whole body tight in its crouch, chestnut-brown hair done up in tight rolls, the hairdo known as the all clear: "Everybody up!" So it wasn't about how she looked. In the end it was just the defiance that girls at that age are so prone to show.

The girl was picturing a long coat, below the knee. Children wore short coats at Rawehn's. The girl wanted the buttons hidden. Brought eight large horn buttons with her, could you conceal those? The girl wanted a high collar, standing up around the neck; Peter Pan collars were in fashion for children, covering half the shoulders, with rounded corners. The girl would have preferred no belt in the back. – But that'll ruin the chic? Helene Rawehn cried. – Everyone will know this is our work, *what'll the people in Gneez think!*

She did not fail to realize that the thirteen-year-old was looking for support from her companion's face every now and then, the woman with such a hollow look about the eyes. She received glances meant to console and encourage, in which Helene noticed no sign of any knowledge of the art of tailoring. Plus the woman barely spoke. Madame Rawehn gave in about the belt in the back. She'd just fasten it with buttons at the side seams, removable at will. She could whipstitch the hem if the girl wanted to wear it Soviet-style. The coat would be big enough to grow into so she could wear it for two years. As for the visible buttons, the flared cut, and the collar, Helene refused to give an inch: she felt the art and the honor of the House of Rawehn (Raven) were at stake. In the end the child rarely balked during the fittings (on Sundays, after creeping diplomatically down the *Tüsche* and through the back door so as not to give the Soviet ladies in the waiting room with their English magazines too tempting a look at the fabric), and Madame Rawehn actually didn't cheat the child out of a single ounce of flour, even sewing the buttonholes by hand; she sincerely wished she could have put the finished piece in the display window to advertise her services, if these times had been like those of peace; she had worries of her own, about the husband missing near Kharkiv—Heini, that love-crazed skirt-chaser. Why shouldn't a child get to pout a little in times like these?

The child was unhappy with her coat. Not because it failed to serve its purpose. Slash pockets, once they tear, need crude seams; you can reattach patch pockets easily and it won't show. She didn't want a coat with a collar named after a little boy, and someone could grab her by it and the belt. She found herself in crowds so often these days, and the buttons seemed to come off by themselves; if they'd been concealed she would've kept them longer. She had planned the coat as one to do more than just live in: it had been meant as a durable shelter for the trip that the Russians might send her on, as they had her father. Now Gesine Cresspahl had a coat that was merely contemporary and elegant.

Ask Countess Seydlitz—she'll say she knows all about this subject too. She predicts that the child of a successful marriage will mature much earlier and more fully, acquiring a stronger sense of self or at least of the place from which it wants or desires, maybe also the place where it knows itself and can show that self to the world.

Marie Luise Kaschnitz, on the other hand, has seen how the perfect union of two parents can do damage to a child. They band together against the child, don't let her individuate, forestall her search for different possible avenues for loving, keep her trapped in inevitable self-denial; even at thirteen barely more than the child of her parents, almost entirely defined through them.

Both of these children can run back to their parents when the world refuses to understand them or hurts them—there is also the big-brother figure, *hes got nails on is shoes*—secure in their protection while still not lacking in self-understanding. The elders only set right what such children have not yet been able to learn to do for themselves; children learn from them how to remain undamaged even when things go wrong.

The mother had abandoned the child Gesine Cresspahl back in November 1938—at four and a half she'd already been betrayed. The father, indispensable and not only for that reason, but also as her ally in the English secret, had served as the mayor of Jerichow in a way that angered the Red Army, whether it was the business of the abortions or a certain insubordination, and now the Russians had him, unreachable, less in charge of the child every day, for he didn't see what she saw. There was a woman from the island of Wolin living in her house, whom she craved as a permanent mother, but she could hardly ask her: Take me as your very own child!

This woman helped—more than that, she accepted help, when a stove had been lit by the time she got home in the afternoon she was happy with this child who wasn't hers. Another thing I learned from her: Now you can have children of your own, Gesine.

There was Jakob Abs, Mrs. Abs's son, who treated her like a little sister. Whatever time he didn't spend working he spent thinking about his business affairs, and most of all about a girl who wasn't too young for him, a creature of unimaginable beauty, Anne-Dörte was her name. He left, not only to go see her but to get away from Jerichow. He studied his Russian from a book of zheleznodorozhnykh terminov; he was headed from the gasworks to an apprenticeship with the railway that would take him away, to Gneez, to Schwerin, and someday out of Mecklenburg altogether.

Those were who she had left.

So what is a child like this Gesine Cresspahl to do when she's about to turn fourteen on March 3, 1947, and doesn't have a single person in Jerichow or its surroundings she can count on? Will she become so blind with fear that she runs after anyone who happens to be around, from her father's friends to a teacher who for once doesn't ask where her father is? Or, another option, she could see herself as alone against the grown-ups—not in open hostility but without any chance of help from them? Can't she, too, regard herself as an "I" with desires, with prospects that just have to be kept hidden for the time being?

The child that I was, Gesine Cresspahl—half orphan, at odds with her surviving relatives in memory of her father, owner on paper of a farmhouse by the Jerichow cemetery, wrapped in a black coat—she must have decided one day to give the adults what they wanted while smuggling herself out of their reach and into a life where she'd be able to be what she would then want to be. If nobody told her, she'd just have to find out for herself. It's not about being brave.

Strangely enough, she thought of school as a way out. Her father had withdrawn her from the school in Jerichow and tucked her away in the Gneez academic middle school because the teacher in Jerichow, Stoffregen, liked to hit; also because she might accidentally betray him one day to the Sudeten German Gefeller, principal in Jerichow and regional speaker for the Nazis. The child concluded from the move that her father wanted her to pursue a higher education. That being the case, she had no choice but to take a deep breath and forward march all the way to where school ended at that fairy-tale place called Abitur, finals, graduation, and permission to make her own choice. No, she wasn't particularly brave. She was scared.

She started by lying. To enter seventh grade at the Bridge School in Gneez she'd had to turn in not only a sixth-grade transcript but also an autobiographical statement. This was a school administered by the Red Army, and her father was not on good terms with the Soviets. Or maybe vice versa. She couldn't know. But there was something else she'd learned. She put him in her statement, she described him as a master carpenter, self-employed, minimized his role in the construction of the Mariengabe Airfield, confining it to that of a construction worker, brought up the liberation by the Soviet Union, and implied that he was still living, working, and residing in Jerichow.

Anyone comparing the various autobiographical statements made by this Gesine Cresspahl over the years will be forced to conclude that there were several different people by this name. Or maybe one person who turned into a new one every year and didn't know who she was from one day to the next!

Zeal attracted attention—she decided on diligence. Just as she'd been able to supply Fontane's ballad "John Maynard" in her old school, whether as memorized recitation, answers in class, or essays, so too she delivered to her teachers in this new school the description they wanted of present-day life in Mecklenburg:

Structure of the Anti-Fascist/Democratic Constitution. I. Definition. The initial prefix, an attribute used only in compounds, expresses opposition. It is here directed against a form of government that in ancient Rome was symbolized by the bundled rods of the lictors, which oppressed the people through violence at the disposal of the few. We have no violence in Mecklenburg. Democracy, a combination of the Greek words for people and rule (*demos* + *kratein*), means the exercise of power by the people themselves. We can see in the Gneez district how the exploiters robbing the people were chased away by that same people or at least forced to find housing a minimum of thirty kilometers away from their property and forced to work. The people consists of the workers, the farmers, the petite bourgeoisie, and the middle bourgeoisie, in that order. (This was a dicey part for her, because her position in this ranking was rather unfortunate, as a tradesman's child.) All this taken together characterizes a constitution. II. Implementation. One example is the recent Educational Reform Law.

In Physics she wrote on demand: Aleksandr Stepanovič Popov, Russian physicist, born March 17, 1859, in Bogoslovsk, guberniya of Perm, died January 13, 1906, in what was then St. Petersburg, invented the telephone in 1895. (She believed it, too, taking no further interest in the origin of this story; up to age sixteen she could only think of telephones in the context of authorities and a few select bourgeois families, minions of the NEP.) Even in her final exams, in June 1952, this would still have been the right answer. One day, accidentally, certainly not looking for anything in particular, she opened the encyclopedia inherited from the Papenbrocks in 1950 to the page giving Alexander Graham Bell's life story. Even much later, she wished she didn't have to forget the year 1895 for that reason, and that she might find another reason to look forward to visiting Edinburgh.

In 1947 she was taking third-year Russian, still from Charlotte Pagels. The topic was the derivation of Mecklenburg words from the Slavic, a language group preceding Russian, well then. At the end Cresspahl raised her hand, with all the timidity this child had by then become known for, and asked permission to say something about Gneez. Maybe the name was derived from the Soviet word for "nest," *gnezdo*? An A in the roll book! (Such things hurt her standing with the other girls in the class, even Lise Wollenberg; she had to make up for it by bringing up her house's location right across from the Jerichow Kommandatura and stories about Lieutenant Wassergahn. Finally Lise came to her aid. – It's true: she said. – The Cresspahls were practically occupied territory!)

As long as you didn't take the slightest peek to either side of the lesson plan—you'd lose your balance and fall:

> *Bow your head and bend your knee,*
> *Silently think of the SED;*
> *Give us not just potatoes and cabbage,*
> *Also give what the First Secretary and also the Deputy of the Social-*
> *   ist Unity Party of Germany get to eat and take home in their*
> *   baggage!*

When a classroom full of girls is left alone just before lunch, freezing in their coats, fifty or fifty-five degrees in the room in the very best case, what crazy song-and-dance routines they put on, shrieking and hopping on the tables like madwomen!

> *Eat less sugar?*
> *Wrong, wrong, wrong!*
> *Eat more sugar!*
> *Sugar makes you strong!*

until Fifi Pagels came rushing in, entirely forgetting the price of sweeteners on the black market, remembering only her dream of well-behaved children circa 1912, wounded, crying: You wicked, wicked children!

In February 1947 Dr. Kramritz's class was studying the new Mecklenburg constitution, which the parliament resulting from the previous year's election had just adopted. All inhabitants of German nationality are citizens of the country. Civil servants are servants of the people and must at all times prove themselves worthy of the people's trust. II. Citizens' Basic Rights and Basic Obligations, Article 8: The freedom of the individual is inviolable.

Persons who have been deprived of their freedom.
Must be informed on the following day at the latest.
Which authorities have done so and for what reasons.
This curtailment of freedom was ordered.
They are to be given the opportunity without delay.
Of objecting to the curtailment of their freedom.

Herr Dr. phil. Kramritz rented two rooms in Knoop's building, the prince's mansion. When Knoop came back from his curtailment of freedom in March, that was the first his loyally worrying mother had heard of him since February 3. Knoop said nothing, even to trusted friends, about his place of detention or other events connected to his diminished freedom. What he liked to say in response, smugly, wearing a smirk no one could prove he wore, in broad High German, was: The charges were struck down. Just like Emil.

In March, Mrs. Weidling called on Student Gesine in English class even though she had long since reached the middle of the alphabet, going in fair and proper order. And for this lesson Mrs. Weidling had brought with her a young man in city civilian clothes, introducing him as a future New

Teacher whose training included sitting in on classes like this one. Dr. Weidling already had Soviet counterintelligence going after her husband pretty hard, you could scarcely blame her for not warning us. Who wanted something to be blamed for from those times. After a few grammatical questions to the *N, O,* and *P* parts of the class, the Cresspahl girl was called on and asked to recite a poem that had been distributed in parts for memorization. She always thought it was a mistake for the Soviets to allow English as a second foreign language; she was more than willing to spare Mrs. Weidling any disgrace; she started and kept going, with vile pronunciation and a childishly singsong rhythm but a perfectly automatic and acceptable sentence melody, the way she'd learned it from her father since 1943, whenever they were without earwitnesses, and which Mrs. Weidling's instruction had been unable to modify:

Recuerdo
by Edna St. Vincent Millay
born 1892

RECITED BY HEART

"We were very tired, we were very merry—
We had gone back and forth all night on the ferry.
. . . .
We hailed, 'Good morrow, mother!' to a shawl-covered head,
And bought a morning paper, which neither of us read;
And she wept, 'God bless you!' for the apples and pears,
And we gave her all our money but our subway fares."

Marie may not believe it, since we take that ferry to Manhattan and then use the subway to get to Riverside Drive. Marie is suspicious of stories where everything fits together—I've taught her that much. The truth is that in teacher conferences Mrs. Weidling had already been introduced to certain signs of the times: having us learn poems like "The Song of the Shirt," by Thomas Hood, 1799–1845, With fingers weary and worn, / With eyelids heavy and red, /A woman sat, in unwomanly rags, / Plying her needle and thread for her daily bread, the sociocritical indictment. It's just that she'd had acquired her academic rank at a university, not by marriage; she had traveled through numerous countries, thanks to the favors her husband did for the army; she may even have actually owned a copy of *A Few Figs from Thistles* (1922), and she really and truly did subject her visiting auditor from the land of the Soviets to a recitation of this ferry poem with the pernicious message that personal charity could take the place of systematic reform, if indeed it had any message at all—she did not permit herself, or her students, any sycophancy; as with Leslie Danzmann, it was important to her to think of herself as a lady. The Cresspahl child suffered a terrible defeat.

Whend you realize, Gesine?
Oh Cresspahl. You cant forgive me!
I forgive you. Tell me.
I didn see im at first. Then I realized he hadn talked the whole time. Just sat lookin mute. When I was done he said something to Weidling in English. Thats when I knew: Hes a Russian.
Wasnt too bad, Gesine.
It was for me. That was the first time I knew for sure you were still alive. But I'd betrayed us. You had to spend another year in Fünfeichen.
Please, Gesine. He was just sposed to check if I'd really spent years in Inglant.
And whether they could send you back to South London with a child who could pass for a native speaker.
That's right, Gesine. You might still have had the chance to learn Richmond English.
Would you have gone to England for the Russians?
I would've for you. That's what I wanted to ask you as soon as they let me go back to you.
We're getting to that soon. When we do, I'll say the wrong thing again.
Fer me, Gesine.

June 30, 1968 Sunday
Colonel Emil Zátopek, the man himself, who'd been held up to us as a model for the link between humanism and sports under the benevolent

Soviet aegis ever since his victory in the 5,000-meter at the International Allied Meet in Berlin's Olympic Stadium in early September 1946,

Emil Zátopek, who'd wanted to speak those two thousand words to all the people in his country, now doesn't understand why the party is angry at his hope that the guilty will finally be treated as guilty. – I see nothing counterrevolutionary in it: he says. He says: All those who signed the statement are concerned with the fast construction of democratic Socialism and human freedom. That's what he says.

And he's not alone—*Zemědělské Noviny*, the farmer's newspaper, says something similar, as does *Mladá Fronta*, the Communist youth paper for the whole ČSSRepublic. Now even the carpenter's son, winner of a gold and a silver at the 1948 Olympic Games in London, master of interval training, not only an icon for long-distance runners but a live model for the Soviets during a year spent living in Crimea, winner of three gold medals in the superfluous 1952 Olympics in Helsinki, for running

5,000 meters in	14:06.6
10,000 meters in	29:17.0
42,200 meters in	2:23:03.2;

holder of nineteen world records in total, head of Czechoslovakian military sports since 1958, chosen as athlete of the year in his country as recently as 1966, living in Prague, near the main train station, at U pujčavny (Pawn-shop) 8, the Czech Locomotive, him too: Emil Zátopek.

The Abses managed to get me into Pastor Brüshaver's confirmation class for only two hours, then he kicked me out; I had to take dancing lessons two afternoons a week at the Sun Hotel in Gneez behind the district council office—but in the spring of 1947, because in the winter there had been neither heat nor daylight enough. I had no time for my homework, came back grumpy to Jerichow on the evening train, but my grumbling didn't sway Jakob or his mother: the child had to get what was proper for her. Dancing lessons.

They could see it in Jerichow, Jakob could see it at his training courses in Gneez: some things about bourgeois ways were to be preserved. They saw me as a middle-class child, never mind that my father had disappeared and one of my uncles was guilty of unspeakable crimes; it was almost like they had taken on the job of giving me a fancy education. In Jerichow as in the district capital, they saw high society unscathed, except for those who'd been caught with weapons in the Soviet Union, or in the Nazi Party's files, or with noble titles and title deeds too and overly profitable business deals with the old Reich. Or else in anonymous notes. The others were left to believe they would still be needed, and believe it they did. Whether trading in shoe heels or weighing out twenty-gram slivers of butter for the workers, they all felt certain that the system for feeding and provisioning the population would have been running even worse without them. No one in our class at school said so out loud, but almost from the beginning we'd thought of ourselves as divided into the natives and the refugees. The grown-ups extended the distinction to long-established citizenry versus newly arrived lowlifes; in part, no doubt, because the decorative wood carvings of the Sudeten Germans and East Prussians took a little money out of their own pockets. These newcomers had had to leave practically all their possessions behind; as for the articles of gold or paintings in oil that the right people in Jerichow owned, the plundering Soviets hadn't managed to find them all, not by a long shot, and in times of greater need these could be exchanged at the Red Army's Razno-Export for cigarettes, exchangeable in turn for butter or a sailor suit (Bleyle), worn just twice, that a refugee boy had managed to hold on to. This better sort had rarely lost sight of one another—even Gneez was small enough for that—and now they congregated again, in conservative political parties for instance, where they discussed the minimal or "night-watchman" state, or a future annexation by a Scandinavian country. The revolutionary Red Army had even left them Mecklenburg as an autonomous province; the irritating addition, "-Vorpommern," had been removed by the law of March 1, 1947, so now they had less to say and really you had to chalk that up as a win for Mecklenburg. The province of Mecklenburg. *Land Mecklenburg.* Article I, §1, paragraph 3 of the new Mecklenburg constitution defined the official state colors as: blue, yellow, red. These were also the traditional colors, but what business of anyone's is that.

These people showed what they thought of one another in other ways, too. Sure, Johannes Schmidt's heirs in Jerichow eventually let the SED use its loudspeakers free of charge for election campaigns; Wauwi Schröder, likewise in the musical and electronic field, but in Gneez, had two display windows and in one of them hung, through February 1947, a calligraphed sign in a gold frame:

We consider it an honor,
now and in the future,
to put our loudspeakers at the disposal
of the Red Army and the party allied to it
in service of the anti-Fascist cause,
free and without charge,

with the addendum:

The microphone that was apparently forgotten about on September 19 we consider a token of our goodwill.

Plus two medium-sized azalea pots. After the next large rally, held in connection with the Moscow meeting of the Council of Foreign Ministers on April 24, Wauwi disconnected his microphone along with the remaining cables and also replaced the document in the display window with the latest dictum of the ranking functionary: The SED would continue, as ever, to oppose any change to the borders. These people would have been more than happy to let the refugees return to their territory beyond the Oder and Neisse—anything to have Mecklenburg to themselves again.

They found one another in the realm they considered their ancestral birthright: that of cultural functions. Proper table manners, nuanced forms of address, status-appropriate clothing—all self-explanatory. But how could one accuse a paint dealer of narrow-minded money-grubbing if he almost never missed a meeting of the Cultural League (for a Democratic Renewal of Germany), even the meetings devoted to interpreting a poem by Friedrich Hölderlin or some such? The old families of Gneez had collected Mecklenburgana, not just Lisch's five volumes or the *Yearbook* but glassware, silhouettes, chests, portraits of old-fashioned mayors, and views of the cathedral before the inexplicable incident from the summer of 1659. They had almost pulled together enough money at one point to give a commission to the sculptor Ernst Barlach—a bronze rendition of their embarrassing heraldic animal in as dignified a form as possible; nothing came of it after all, what with his disputes with the Güstrow and Berlin Nazis. Gneez was no Güstrow. They just put the Barlach books that the Nazis didn't like toward the back of their display cases; first of all, such poems had been the *dernier cri* around 1928, simply indispensable for one's self-respect; secondly, their eventual monetary value was perhaps only suffering a temporary setback. And Gneez had a writer of its own!—born as the son of a day laborer on the Old Demwies estate, true, but claimed by the good city of Gneez in Mecklenburg ever since being shipped on to the Cathedral School on a municipal scholarship in his eleventh year. He'd managed to publish a volume of poems and two novels before he had to flee the country because of the Nazis; even under the British occupation, the city council had requested to rename Wilhelm Gustloff Street after Joachim de Catt; to Triple-J, too, de Catt's emigration was credential enough. *Nu vot*, unusual legislation calls for unusual legislation. *Pochemu nyet? Mozhno. Imeyem vozmozhnost'.* Admittedly, "our poet" hadn't yet found his way back to his proud hometown, neither in person nor by letter. Were he to return from his transatlantic climes, Gneez would gladly forgive whatever had been a bit irksome in the likeness he'd captured of a Mecklenburg small town in 1931, Gneez was hardly petty; he should get his celebration, and for now Mr. Jenudkidse had already approved the second poetry recital in honor of J. de Catt. They found one another there too, not just in the lectures given by Mrs. Lindsetter, the wife of the chief justice of the district court, who publicly communicated her memories of the wartime-shortage recipes of 1916. The church was part of it—religion was clearly a component of proper decorum; the cathedral was more crowded during evening organ concerts than during religious services. Dean Marjahn's sermons were certainly edifying and innocuous; if he went on a titch too long on a major holiday, his ears were bound to be set ringing afterward by the tongue-lashings of conscientious ladies who'd been forced to take their goose out of the oven too late, apron tied over their Sunday dress, or found themselves behind on their carp. In the 1946 Hunger Winter too. Those ladies were still there. If Dr. Kliefoth had had his apartment cleaned out, that was just his bad luck. Anyway, in 1932 he'd gone and picked that backwater Jerichow to live in, not the upstanding city of Gneez, which could boast no fewer than two town chronicles over the centuries. Still, happy about it or not, one would probably have to take him back into the old fellowship—PhD, senior instructor, lieutenant colonel in the army, oddly respected by the Soviet authorities; he didn't come. *Ah never mind. Murrjahn was a stubborn dog but in the end he hadta give in.*

Cresspahl's child, though a commuter student from Jerichow and a bit of an awkward case given her father's arrest, was felt to belong—the elite families welcomed her with pleasure. The British, after all, not the Soviets had made this Cresspahl the mayor. What a chic black coat she wore. She took pride in her appearance; she didn't have refugees do her tailoring, she went to Helene Rawehn on the market square. And, just as propriety demanded at her age, she was taking dancing lessons.

They called their commandant "Mr. Jenudkidse," even to his face. They weren't going to be found lacking in proper manners. He liked it too, unfortunately. But they thought they could get him to commit to being polite as a result.

There were exceptions, characterized with the saying about the traces left on a person who's touched the devil. Leslie Danzmann, for instance: the Knoops, the Marjahns, the Lindsetters predicted a dim future for her when she too got involved with the new powers that be. Leslie Danzmann— old Mecklenburg family, English grandmother, navy lieutenant's widow, a lady. Turned up near Gneez right around the middle of the war, rented one of the most modern villas by the sea, lived absolutely comme il faut as the housekeeper of a gentleman who had something to do with the Reich Aviation Ministry in Berlin. No false moves. Classy. Then the people who still played tennis had attracted attention in Gneez; Leslie Danzmann, also, was made to work, drafted into the labor office. Force majeure. But did she have to go to the Russians and look for work in their administration? The fact that someone owns nothing but a lapsed pension and has never learned how to do any kind of respectable job—give piano lessons, be married to a doctor—what kind of excuse is that! Now she too had been arrested for a bit, part of the Cresspahl business, strange don't you think?, but did she take that as a warning? No, our fine Danzmann has gone and offered her services to the Soviets again. You tell children: Don't get too close to that. Now she's fallen right in—let go from the housing office, had to go to the fish cannery. Didn't she realize that Comrade Director of the Housing Office was inviting her to join the SED? Couldn't she think of any other answer besides: But what will the neighbors think of me, Mr. Yendretzky! She was pretty much right about that, in terms of the neighbors, but to go and blurt it out. As if you didn't teach children: Hold your tongue. Now she went to work early every day, on foot from the coast, on the dairy train to Gneez, standing at a stinking table all day cleaning flounder, boiling fish stew. No, she didn't complain. She's still one of us to that extent. How cannery women talk, a housewife with some experience of the world can easily imagine it. You know their word for a woman's private parts. A cultured woman won't put it into words. What happens when a woman, a married woman, when she voluntarily lays down with a man, they talk about that as ——. Well, working-class women, what do you expect? What a hideous word too. Speaking of which, *when you think about it its maybe not so far off really.* Such a word will never cross my lips, Frau Schürenberg! Leslie Danzmann had it coming to her. If a girl gets herself brought up all nice and proper and wants to live like that and have everything come to her just the way she likes then she shouldn't go somewhere she can be kicked out of into a cannery! And did she show any neighborly feeling, this Leslie Danzmann? She was right next to all that fish, couldn't she ever bring some by? Just as a courtesy? Not once. If she talked about her work at all it was to praise the proletarian women. So good-natured, supposedly. Always helped her, she said. There was one, Wieme Wohl from the Danish Quarter, known all around town, who'd said more than once at the end of the day, before the bag inspection: Hey, Danzmann, cmere, here's an eel. Tie it round your waist. If yer too squeamish I'll do it for you. 'S just for ten minutes, Danzmann! Don' be so proud.... Danzmann had stayed firm. It wasn't pride, she said. – It's just that it's not mine, girls! It doesn't belong to me! The women persuaded her. In the end Leslie was willing to believe that fish, especially eel, never made it to the stores, only to the private Red Army and party distributors; she had no problem with that, she could see that. But then she'd insisted: the eel wasn't hers. That's what happens to someone who lets herself drop out of morality and respect for property!

Cresspahl's child didn't like going to dancing class. She did it because Mrs. Abs told her to.

She spent those afternoons in Gneez with Lise Wollenberg. In dancing class they were known to boys from elsewhere as the blond and brunette from Jerichow. The dancing master was Franz Knaak, from a Hamburg family whose members, with a single exception, had all been dancing masters since 1847. This one was fat and liked to speak French, emphasizing the nasals; he was so proud of his mechanical gestures that he was able to console himself for his ample corporeality with languid, brown-eyed glances. First he taught them the old German dances—the Rhinelander, the Kegel— all with references to the heritage of our fathers. Instead of something Soviet.

He let himself be talked into teaching the slow dance only after universal, almost deafening requests; he showed how the movements looked in such an oily, filthy way that we would be filled with disgust for them all the rest of our lives, at least that's what he hoped. He wore something resembling a frock coat, soapy at the neck, and held up the hem on each side with two fingers, demonstrating the single steps of the mazurka with a feeble spring in his step. What an unbelievable monkey: Gesine Cresspahl thought to herself. But she saw the absorbed smile on beautiful, merry, long-legged Lise's face as she followed Herr Knaak's leaps and hops; Lise knew so much about everything. – How'll you ever get a man if you don't learn to dance! she'd said, and all down the long end of the room the mothers were draped on worn plush chairs, Mrs. Wollenberg among them, dabbing their eyes. That wasn't how the Cresspahl girl saw it. She didn't want to get a man that way. She already knew one, and he went dancing with someone else.

She'd decided her coat should be black because she wanted to wear it in mourning for her father, *not* because he was probably dead but just in memory of him. That was only proper. She knew it. But it was something inappropriate to talk about.

On the evenings after dancing class she almost always ran into Leslie Danzmann on the train platform. She greeted her, stood far away from her as they waited for the train, and never got into the same compartment as her. Leslie Danzmann may have imagined another humiliation, this time due to the smell coming off her. But it wasn't that. Cresspahl's child rather liked the smell, if anything. She wanted to punish this Danzmann woman. She'd been let free, her father hadn't. She hadn't brought any news from him. She might even have betrayed him.

July 1, 1968 Monday

Sometimes I think: That's not her. What does that mean here, "she," "me"? It can be thought; but it is unthinkable. If she were alone, I would have to think: That's Gesine Cresspahl (Mrs.), a woman around thirty-five, not a lady, in the very best posture for elegant occasions—chin high, back straight and far from the back of her chair, gaze so mobile that it can shift from moment to moment between surveying the room and an indissoluble bond with only one object, only one person; from a distance I could tell it was her from her short hair in what the stylist intended as a feathered cut, but the overlapping close layers of a bird's wing now look too loose, too ragged over the forehead. Close up there is no mistaking her for anyone else, what with the cautious movements of her overly narrow lips, whether chewing or speaking; the shallow hollows below her cheekbones, skin sometimes stretched tight over them, straining to mimic the right behavior; the little wrinkles that have hardened in the corners of her eyes, the involuntarily narrowed pupils: the first thing I'd think is that she's scared, and hiding it, skillfully. She's on her guard, she's going to defend herself—but she wants to seem polite, friendly, ladylike. It would take a lover to observe specifically how she takes a deftly apportioned bite of fish from the end of her fork and dismantles it with barely visible chewing, so that her mouth is empty again at once, ready to smile or give an answer—we don't notice anything in particular. But, she is not alone.

She is just one of many people in a long, spacious dining room with very white vertical bands of cloth blocking the sun coming in through the floor-to-ceiling windows on two walls; she is sitting surrounded by men at one of the north tables and an empty, dirty sky is behind her, with the shy tops of skyscrapers, silhouetted like cutouts, reaching up into it—airplanes there would be less unexpected. She may know how to act in restaurants, be familiar with the comportment demanded by the damask tablecloth and silver place settings with a knife rest and three drinking glasses; her nod to the waiter over her shoulder is irreproachable as he bends down to let her examine the plate with the next course—she will have learned all these things. But this is the restaurant high in the East Tower of the bank, closed to the public, to ordinary people, even to employees. The head manager for office supplies is honored to be invited up into this circle of heaven, permitted to read the menu with its French formulations that he approves every day when it comes out of the in-house printshop. While Mrs. Cresspahl is not only lower in rank—that in itself would suffice to make the waiters slightly standoffish with her—she is also the only woman there today. Oh, women are brought here sometimes, it does happen. Only then they're part of the family, one of the bank's owners; they're wives, invited along when a vice president is promoted or shoved off into retirement and his nearly paid-off house on the better or worse side of Long Island Sound; ladies sometimes come on business from allied firms, after a contract has been signed, a scam's been pulled off; when the National Bank of the People's Republic of Poland dispatches for negotiations not a man but a Mrs. Paula Ford, a meal in these well-protected heights to honor her is indispensable. Less than a year ago Mrs. Cresspahl was still a secretary for foreign languages: she used to work down on the lower floors, in a big group office, with cassette players, and the voices speaking from them didn't belong to people she needed to be introduced to; she started even farther downstairs, at an adding machine in the Finance Department; what is she doing here? And she's not at just any table—she's at the one reserved for de Rosny, the true monarch of this bank, the Vice President of all Vice Presidents, deputy chairman of the board of directors. He receives state visits from the competition here, he conducts his seminars for the heads of the foreign departments, and at noon today he turned up with Mrs. Cresspahl. Maybe she's on a secret assignment for him, something statistical probably; still, she's one of the dispensable ones, owed two weeks' notice and then basta; yet everyone summoned to the table, with nod or call across the room, has had to say hello to this Mrs. Cresspahl following all due formalities, while some of them have run into her earlier in the day, with nothing more than a normal Hi. *Hi.* Now, though, what's called for is: *It's a pleasure....*; now she's sitting at de Rosny's right hand, as if hosting the gentlemen with their grave responsibilities along with him. But it's just a woman! De Rosny can do whatever he has planned, but this isn't what he should be doing. What does she want here!

She wishes she were somewhere else. She likes to go downstairs for lunch, out of the building. It may be hot downstairs, the forecast is 95 degrees, but she could have crossed Lexington and Madison Avenues to Fifth to buy blouses like the other "coworkers" with no time for department stores after work; she could sit in Gustafsson's fish shop on Second, leaning back, with Amanda Williams, with Mr. Shuldiner, with friends, in conversations where she doesn't have to watch out like a hawk the whole time. She'd be more than happy to give up the arctic chill that the appliances here fabricate for the bosses in exchange for the relaxed hour she's guaranteed by contract. She knows it won't be forever. She's one of the other class of people in the city, who can neither buy nor pay to operate such an air conditioner. Tonight, when she gets back to the Upper West Side, there won't be many of these expensive boxes overhead sticking out of the buildings; people will be sitting on the stoops, hoping for the protection provided by the naturally occurring shadows and nothing more, all they can do is push open the windows and hope for a breeze from the air rushing down the channels of the streets. Marie will keep the apartment door open to try to get a cross-breeze between the Hudson and the stairwell, to hell with burglars. The electricity can be turned off, the gas pressure lowered, the faucets left thirsty. The firefighters will once again have neglected to outfit their hydrants with spray caps, so children will have to use force before they can hop around in the spraying streams intended for use against fires. Anyone driving by of an evening, in a sealed and air-conditioned car, will see classic New York local color and not suspect a shortage of working showers on the poor streets. After the high-pressure system that's been moving so laboriously from the Gulf of Mexico over New York since yesterday, others will come to pay a visit, and someone like Mrs. Cresspahl will never officially own a doubly and triply guaranteed air conditioner— this single hour in the climate-controlled fortress of the bank may be hazardous to her ability to survive in New York. Since de Rosny wants her to, she is sitting in the cold with her back to the north while the breeze from the blades behind her caresses her back. Her shivers often turn into shudders.

She has a sense of what de Rosny's getting at by bringing her into this company of privilege-laden men; she knows that it isn't about her. If asked by his own ilk he'd say something about women's equal rights; no less a word than *emancipation* might cross his lips, with the cheerful earnestness that even his friends from the West Coast have a hard time reading mockery into. Then it would all be taken as one of his whims, and one tiny misstep would turn Mrs. Cresspahl into someone paying the price for it. As long as she sits up straight and yet puts one foot in front of the other in exactly the right place, he can accustom his subordinates, men though they are, to the presence of a woman at business lunches, and even to her competence to speak up, so that someday they'll discuss with her a matter of business where she'll be representing de Rosny—business in a country that they know very little about ... but we won't discuss that now. De Rosny started with invitations to places like the Brussels and Quo Vadis, where his peers, friend or foe, were to help spread the rumor that he seemed to

be consoling himself after all for the nasty situation with his wife, he's
barely sixty after all, de Rosny, isn't he; here, in the boss's restaurant, the
boys'll think what they're supposed to think if he wants them to. In any
case, de Rosny has clearly forgotten how you're supposed to treat women—
he doesn't need to give advance notice, it doesn't occur to him that she
might need to prepare her schedule or wardrobe, when he calls he expects
Mrs. Cresspahl to come as she is. So now she can no longer come to work
in the older dress that's easy to clean, it's okay if she sweats in it; her small
raise is eaten up almost every month by the shopping she has to do in stores
that maybe the Kennedys' maids could afford but not a bank employee!
She got lucky today, with her sleeveless ribbed-silk number from Bergdorf
Goodman with a short jacket—formal enough, the color next to the white
hopefully works with her hair color—only she'd tried to save on tailoring,
it doesn't fit as well as it could, and up here she feels like she's freezing in
it. The women who work as news announcers on TV get supplemental pay
for their clothes, don't they? *Thats messed up.* Anyway, we hold our end up
well enough in the art of conversation.

Today it plays out once again like a kind of test, because that's what de
Rosny wants. He doesn't come across as manipulative, he seems fully at
ease—the philosophizing boss. The younger men try to catch his eye and
at the same time get their meat (grilled lamb cutlets with peas flown in
from somewhere) off their plate—worshipful as puppy dogs they are,
Wilbur N. Wendell, Henri Gelliston, Anthony Milo, despite the fact that
they'd been dictating truly imperious letters to banks on other continents
just an hour ago. They're invisible to de Rosny, who is busy recalling the
years 1899 and 1900, as though saddened by the passing of time—the Open
Door policy, the directives to expand American business abroad, the can-
onization of the faith that America must not keep its system, the best of
all possible in business as well as politics, to itself but instead bestow it on
other nations. Employee Cresspahl keeps her eyes on her plate: she has
learned all about this in school, exactly the same facts, just with other
words, along with the conceit that the thoughts of anyone ignorant of
dialectical materialism were not to be taken seriously. De Rosny has brought
his puppy dogs to the point where they want to prove themselves good
students. Anthony, poor Anthony. He probably left Brooklyn too soon,
left his recent-immigrant mother with her embarrassing peasant head scarf

whom he now rides past every day on the commuter train from Long Island. He should have scouted out the lay of the land! Instead, falling for the new nationalism, our Tonio launches into the legends—the troops sailing to the Philippines from California, Dewey's victory in Manila Bay (1898), the sinking of the *Maine* earlier that year; blind with zeal he runs right into de Rosny's knife: Not even John Jacob Astor ever talked like that, young Mr. Milo. Think of our missionaries in China!

It all has something indirectly to do with Mrs. Cresspahl's secret assignment—this dispatching of American trade and traffic to the benighted nations; she can sense de Rosny's gaze passing over her out of the corner of her eye. No thank you. It's too soon for her to triumph over these better-paid men under de Rosny's thumb. Plus she's too angry at them. Does Mrs. Cresspahl own a house on Long Island? Does she have a stock portfolio? No, thanks anyway. Tomorrow Tonio will tell James Carmody: You were lucky you weren't there!

Now de Rosny decides to use ribbed silk as an example: international credit can't do it, of course, the poor natives can acquire the goods and services of the industrialized nations only when they get jobs, purchasing licenses, trade by means of which they can send the results of their own prosperity back to the USA, let's say. Now take the ribbed silk in this exquisite dress our Mrs. Cresspahl is wearing....

Thank you. That she does say, then she talks across the table with Mr. Kennicott II, about the Long Island Rail Road strike. Was it bad? Mr. Kennicott may be the head of the Personnel Department but this was a swish of the matador's red cape that got him, he's confused, he starts complaining about the heat in the stopped trains this morning. Mrs. Cresspahl won't let herself be herded into purely feminine topics. Let our purportedly universally admired vice president hold forth on barre ribs, Ottoman ribbing, ribs ondé—the lady isn't listening, her devoted attention is turned to Kennicott II and nothing seems to matter more to her than how it was on the Montauk line with eighteen out of twenty-four trains from Babylon not in service. She nods, she can imagine, who would doubt it.

Shortly before reaching the late-Egyptian evidence for ribbed fabrics, de Rosny gets bored; he generously yields the floor to Mr. Gelliston (Harvard Business School) and Mr. Wendell, letting them pronounce on how the Open Door policy grew and prosperity resulted under McKinley,

Roosevelt, and Wilson, from the Algeciras Conference to the Webb-Pomerance and Edge Acts, the requirements as act, as law, and of American business and the White Man's Burden. But we have a lady at the table who is not only charming and beautiful but fully educated in Marxism. What do you have to say, Mrs. Cresspahl?

– It is the indispensable duty of all the nations of the earth: she says, apparently gladly, and firmly confident in the preacherly voice by the fifth word, if anything falling too deep into the orotund hollow that the *d-y-u* leaves in her throat: to know that the LORD he is God, and to offer unto him sincere and devout thanksgiving and praise. But if there is any nation under heaven, which hath more peculiar and forcible reasons than others, for joining one heart and voice in offering up to him these grateful sacrifices, the United States of America are that nation.

Laughter. Applause. She does blush a little, why try to hide it. But it does come out cute, more feminine, diminishing her success somewhat. And again she's too angry, even more than when she read in one of Marie's textbooks Levi Frisbie's sermon dated five years after the French Revolution. Now there's a bet about this date, and she forgoes the prize, adding an extra year so that de Rosny hands it out to Henri Gelliston. The boss laughed so heartily that his eyes weren't free to do anything else; she catches his small, approving nod.

Now the conversation turns to dialectics, the railroad strike, the heat, constantly if cautiously circling around politics. The plane with 214 American soldiers on board that Soviet fighters forced to land on the Kuril Islands yesterday is not even mentioned: de Rosny frowns on the current president's policies, why force him into any awkward repetitions. (On March 16, de Rosny was not received at the White House.) The cost of summer camp, coffee, vacation plans. Mr. Kennicott II is given suggestions for restaurants in Amsterdam. Someone's already told him about one, what's the name again, something about a yellow bird. De Rosny advises against. Does Mr. Kennicott want to spend his time in Holland dining with Americans or stock market people? De Rosny knows another place, dark wood paneling, solid old-fashioned furniture, fatherly waiters, the floorboards tremble—some kind of schoolroom Latin name.... – Do you mean Dorrius?: Employee Cresspahl says cautiously, like a schoolgirl; she doesn't want to overdo it. (She's only seen Dorrius from the outside, it was too expensive for her; she knows more about it from D. E., whom of course all good things are there to serve.) De Rosny is now free to either ruin her offering or visibly praise her among and before his students.

– Dorrius! That's what it's called! de Rosny cries.

– It has three exits: Mrs. Cresspahl adds meekly.

Their duet is applauded, de Rosny bows for the both of them, and the amused chitchat about dialectics lasts all the way to the elevator. She can't get free of him there either. He still does not withdraw into his distinguished chambers; he chivalrously accompanies his team down to their office foyer. Where it turned out he was accompanying Mrs. Cresspahl, and it wasn't about chivalry, it was to have a word with her behind closed doors. She is suddenly so nervous that she stays standing in the middle of the room that's set up for her work.

De Rosny doesn't want to sit down either. He leans against the door, looks around at the charts on the wall, the documents on the metal bureau, seeking an opening.

Who is this de Rosny? What on earth is her connection with him? Was he one of the men who celebrated the fall of France on June 26, 1940, with a banquet at the Waldorf-Astoria? No, not him, but maybe his parents. She feels no threat from him with regard to anti-Fascist elements—Fascism's bad for business. Should she be suspicious of him for being anti-Fascist for the wrong reasons? What does he want, here in her room, behind closed doors?

She has before her a gentleman who has taken care of his body since youth. He won't die from that. It'll be an advanced old age indeed that gets him. He's kept his brain busy, but not forcing it or letting it drift into alcohol. This guy'll be sharp as a tack when death comes for him. Barely a wrinkle in his brow. A full head of thick hair, flecked with gray but not white like an old man's. Still, his eyes, usually cool and sharp, are dull today, hardly even still blue. He'll lose that look tonight, on the golf course on the Sound. She looks at him; she'd recognize him even in disguise; she can't let her look show what else she knows, which is that he's one of the people we were warned about in school. He is Money, hateful and malevolent. It has raised him; he serves it; if he does want to extend credit to the Czechoslovak Socialist Republic it's not to improve Socialism there. He understands the aspects of politics that can harm money. He finds it useful to send the Czechs and Slovaks someone who once lived in the vicinity. It doesn't need to be her, but it is her. Why isn't that disgusting?

– Mrs. Cresspahl. So here's the opening. And she clears her throat, and already he's brought to a stop. Which isn't what she wanted to do, she was trying to help him out of his embarrassment. – Sir?

– You're willing to do all these things for us. . . . You're going to Prague for us, taking your child out of school, from her home in New York . . . it might take three months, six months: he repeats, insists, but not with any regret in his voice. It's not sympathy he has in mind. Why isn't he looking her in the eye?

– Yes. Sir: Employee Cresspahl says.

– Would you do something else, too? Something . . . I can't tell you what it is, I've already said too much! You can say no. . . . : he has sped up; in anyone else she'd be sure he felt embarrassment, timidity, shame. He just gives a little smile. I saw Cresspahl's cat look like that, holding its paw above the mouse.

It's not the bank I'm doing this for.
I realize that.
You have no idea why I am doing it, Mr. de Rosny.
Maybe not. But as long as it's useful for us.
I don't need to say a word to you.
You can refuse the assignment. This is your last chance.
And then get my two weeks' notice.
You know the terms of your contract, Mrs. Cresspahl.
After two months I couldn't afford my apartment, after six I'd have to take Marie out of her school.
And if that's worth it?
You'll put me on a blacklist and I'd never get another job in any bank in New York State, Pennsylvania, New England.
You'd get compensation.
If I keep my mouth shut.
That's the way it is, young lady. *We could even make trouble with your visa.*
And of course you'd apologize.
Only in the moment. Now.

Say it, Mr. de Rosny. Just so I know.
Try to prove I was here in your office, Mrs. Cresspahl. Just try to prove it
to anyone!

– I will not refuse to do anything that's necessary to carry out my assignment: Employee Cresspahl says, stiff and polite. She's annoyed with
herself—she let down her guard for a single moment and now, in the empty
space, there's trust. She's scared but not of the right thing.

– That's the kind of courage I admire: de Rosny says, turns, shoulders
open the door, leaves it ajar, and is gone. He was never here.

In the remaining hours, Mrs. Cresspahl does her work as if every last
bit of it had to be finished by five p.m. today. She can recalculate the LIBOR
(London InterBank Offered Rate) again. She can convert it into Czech
crowns a third time. She finishes with only two minutes to spare for the
memo to the head of personnel: Dorrius Restaurant, Amsterdam, The
Netherlands, has one exit on N. Z. Voorburgwal, two on Spuistraat (N. Z.
= Nieuwezijds = New Side; there hasn't been an Old Side for about a
hundred and fifty years): Sincerely Yours, G. C. When the evening heat
assaults her on the street, she realizes she also feels a sharp edge of fear.
That's what it's like when you're trying to forget something. Why is more
and worse being expected of her than of all the people around her, who are
cautiously approaching Grand Central Station and scared of nothing on
this first of July 1968 but a sudden burst of sweat, the nun with the beggar's
plate on her knees between the doors of the east entrance, the ragged old
woman with her swollen legs asleep on the steps of the Graybar Building
with a tattered paper bag held tight in her hand. It's not fear she feels, it's
worse: it's like a farewell. Saying goodbye to New York.

July 2, 1968 Tuesday

The American military in Vietnam is battling the press, telling the flat-out
lie that reporters' access to the news in wartime is as rapid and complete
as reporters could possibly want. And the newspapers apparently believe
it. Last week John Carroll from *The Baltimore Sun* went to Khesanh and
saw with his own eyes how marines were breaking runways into separate

steel plates and dynamiting their own bunkers. Since he assumed that enemy troops in advance positions could make similar observations, he sent the news home. The general from the Press Department confiscated Mr. Carroll's press pass for an indeterminate time; neither embassy nor military personnel will talk to him, and when he wants to get from one place to another no army vehicle will take him. The army says he is an estimated ninety percent right; apparently the remaining tenth of its opinion suffices for a ban. Maybe the retreat from Khesanh doesn't yet fit with what they're calling three months of ferocious defense

In Hesse, in the Federal Republic of Germany, Dr. Fritz Bauer has died. He was the chief prosecutor of the State of Hesse and one of the few people in office who from the beginning considered the Nazi crimes prosecutable under the law, and prosecuted them. He especially hunted down the murderers who tried to use clean hands as proof of their innocence, having washed away the stains, from Eichmann to a number of concentration camp doctors. Without him the Auschwitz trial from 1963 to 1965 would never have taken place. There are many sentences she thought of writing to Mr. Bauer, the child that I was—none were ever sent. Only sixty-four years old, and now he's dead.

The Gesine Cresspahl of the Soviet occupation zone had started a diary in spring 1947.

It wasn't technically a diary. (And this isn't either, for different reasons: here she's agreed to have a scribe—instead of her, with her permission—write an entry for every day but not of that day.) That one she wrote herself, but she left out whole weeks sometimes. It wasn't because she'd made a New Year's resolution. It was to keep things from being forgotten, that's true, but it was for someone else's sake, not hers. It hardly looked like a book or a notebook. Jakob's mother wouldn't have wanted to touch it; Jakob wouldn't have gotten past the first few lines; she had only a very vague sense of why she wanted to protect it. It lay between now these pages and now those pages of Büchner's *Economic Geography of Mecklenburg-Schwerin*, which is a dissertation fat enough for a dedication to the author's parents, thin enough to be a special issue; you could hardly fit more than a couple of slips of paper between its pages. There was no date on the slip of paper—it had to not look like a diary on second glance either. There were few complete sentences, in that adolescent handwriting, just words in rows, kind of like a badly arranged vocabulary list, many of them crossed out. One was still legible: "jagged." Now and then she forgot what she'd been trying to preserve. We find this word a second time. It bears the recurrent sense that Schoolgirl Cresspahl's face must look jagged when she's talking to grown-ups because that's how she feels on the inside. But what are we to do with an entry like "Ya kolokoychik" or "Packard? Buick?" It's gone. And there were not only Russian words in the list, crossed out or let stand, but also German words disguised in Cyrillic transcription. It has run away, no one will ever catch it. It wasn't much of a diary, and it was meant to be one for Cresspahl. If you write something down for a person then he's bound to come back. A dead person can't read, right?

"Ya kolokoychik" isn't crossed out, so it was nothing to be ashamed of at the time. But if *Ya*, "Yes" in German, *Ja*, could also be "I" in Russian, *Я*, as the Cyrillic letter here suggests, then it might also be a clever abbreviation. What did Jakob (Ja-kob, Я-kob) have to do with *kolokoychik*, a little bell? A sleigh bell, *Schlittenklingel*, maybe? Was that supposed to be a nickname for Anne-Dörte, who still hadn't taken him away (Schleswig-Holstein, *Schlittenklingel*)? No, let's hope not. She wouldn't have wanted to pick a fight, especially by name-calling, with a girl Jakob liked better than her. So was it the diarist herself? Was she the bell that was too small?

"Rips." An entry for black market dealings—ribbed fabric, *Rips*—or tears in that fabric, the English word *rips*? Not pain in her ribs (*Rippen*): her unavoidable daily dealings with Jakob hurt elsewhere. No, "Rips" was Bettina Riepschläger, the acting German instructor at the Bridge School in Gneez, not much older than the students in 7-B but entrusted, right after her own graduation and a two-month teacher-training course, with providing a classical humanistic education. A cheerful girl, never insisting upon professional dignity. We did whatever we wanted in her class; she did too. It often seemed like *she* was talking out of turn. The Cresspahl girl wanted to show her that she had no intention of taking advantage of a certain shared experience they'd had in the lobby of Alma Witte's hotel; what she liked best was just looking at her. Bettina had had her fine pale hair cut fashionably short and tousled; she would comb it with her fingers, coming away with strands of hair an inch or two long. Blond, experience had taught, was Jakob's color. As opposed to darker shades. Today she too will know that this fashion came from the movie based on a Hemingway novel, where the Spanish terrorists chopped off a girl's hair, but that Maria was supposed to be a brunette. Best not to mention to Jakob that cornflower-blue dress, hanging so perfectly, or those beautiful full-grown legs, that carefree bright voice able to switch from a tone of camaraderie to a firm one conveying rebuke yet nonetheless safety. It sometimes happened that Bettina acted her age, which was nineteen. She might say: "*Kinnings...,*" and then we would be, for a little while, children. Lise Wollenberg cried once, she was so afraid that Bettina might take a walk in the yard with someone other than her; Lise was now trying to place her feet the way Miss Riepschläger did. She was from Ludwigslust. She didn't often speak in the roundabout phrases Dr. Kramritz used, the anti-Fascist democratic constitution or the leading role of the party of the working class just came up as though they were self-evident, because they were ready to hand. For this teacher we wrote essays like "My Best Friend." Cresspahl from Jerichow had slipped even more deeply into an unshakable need for secrecy so she didn't want to admit to any best friend, falling back on a dog. There was no dog, it was neither the one from the Kommandatura nor Käthe Klupsch's chow chow, she just made it up, body shape to behavior. She went so far as to claim that this Ajax would stay at the edge of the military pool, unafraid, no matter how much she splashed him as she swam by. For this and many other reasons: he was Schoolgirl Cresspahl's best friend. As a grade she received the question, in diplomatic red handwriting: "A bit sentimental, no?" She was very pleased. She now considered this Bettina one of the most reasonable and rational teachers she'd ever had in her life, and that was something about her she wanted to tell Cresspahl about. Rips.

"Škola." School. This was where our diarist had her concerns, worries even. For there were not many teachers like Bettina, who was "free" after school hours like we were. Teachers like Dr. Kramritz believed they were respected, even venerated, just because it was quiet during their classes; almost no one talked about him. Everyone knew that life in Gneez was very different from his exposition of the Mecklenburg state constitution. He had picked up his stiff knee in precisely the war he now described as the nation's guilt, not his own. But it didn't look right when he pressed his wire-rimmed glasses even more firmly down on the bridge of his nose—he seemed to be taking up arms. His punishments were all permissible under school rules; he enjoyed being obeyed. The refugee children were scared of him. Gesine Cresspahl found the trace of a scar on his nose revolting. Still, he was able to force the class to recite what he wanted them to. This was not the case with Miss Pohl, math and geography, one of the women called "Miss" throughout her whole career even though she was over fifty and not an inch of her body possessed delicate grace. Intensely red-brown hair in a crew cut, jet-black eyes, full cheeks, full chin. Always wearing her one green hunting suit, sometimes with matching hat. We called her breasts "the outwork"—in Mecklenburg the tenant farm at the edge of a manor estate, but she didn't know the term, being a refugee from Silesia. She was mad at the world over her share in the German losses—you could see it behind her even, sullen expression. She didn't care. Once a child had failed to understand an arithmetic problem after the second repetition, that child simply lacked a head for mathematics as far as this lady was concerned and was just given up on, even if she couldn't pass with that D+. (Gesine Cresspahl was seen as possessing a head for geography, due to an essay she'd written on the soil properties and economy of China; this mistake persisted into the following spring.) Mrs. Pohl, Miss Pohl may have practiced her profession like a chosen vocation at some time in the past; now it was just a job, the prerequisite of a residence permit and ration card—she would do everything the job required and no more. Student Cresspahl still believed in escape through learning, but with this kind of teaching, time seemed to trickle away and she often had the feeling that something was being missed. The part of this she wanted to tell Cresspahl about came from her memory of his having helped her once, in 1944, with school. In school. Against school.

"Antif." Now that was one of Jakob's tougher evenings. For Cresspahl's daughter didn't come running to him with trifles—certainly not every trifle, and definitely not running; she might be younger than countesses named Anne-Dörte but she'd long since stopped being a child. Jakob might think she was taking what she deserved from him as the man of the house; the fact was she didn't have anyone else to ask the questions she had learned in school as answers. She had a hard time with the word "anti-Fascism." Fascism was something Italian, after all. Jakob had been handed the same word as her, in his own retraining course; he looked deeply resigned now that he had to set it in motion again behind his broad hard brow. They often used to sit on the steps outside Cresspahl's door, with a view of the boarded-up headquarters, seeing little of the guard marching around or the picture of Stalin in the triumphal arch. Jakob, like Cresspahl, knew how to set his eyes to a faraway look. It struck her once again, unfailingly, that his temples looked so solid, his forehead curving so seamlessly into his skull. Why did he get his hair cut so short, so high on his head, when a few days later it would look like a pelt again. If you like a horse's coat, you.... She also couldn't stop thinking about the slight displacement of the wrinkles in the corners of his eyes—they looked so taut, so alive, like he was conscious of his every movement. She hadn't been listening very closely. Jakob was well into an explanation that the Nazis, with their "National Socialism," had stolen a word from the Socialists, maybe two, and that was why a word like "anti-" couldn't possibly turn up near "Socialism," but there was no reason not to say "anti-Nazism" if she thought people would understand her. – Okay.... No: the Cresspahl child said. It was shocking how suddenly a conversation could be over. She thought that was an ugly word. – A shitty word for a shitty situation: Jakob said. She didn't know where to go from there. She'd known the whole time that he was about to stand up, give a nice stretch above her, and say goodbye down from his great height—smiling, solicitous, like an adult to a child. – *Don' forget bedtime*: he said, his Platt already pretty Mecklenburgish, and before she knew it he was past the walnut trees and on the way to town. She took it badly, she wrote it down in her diary. "Antif."?

"One leg, bike." She'd seen a man who could manage a bike with one leg.

"A. in Gneez." She hadn't been able to let go of her—in dreams Alexandra came back to life, came back (and looked nothing like Hanna Ohlerich, who'd spent weeks sleeping next to her, in the same fever). Alexandra in a foreign country, wearing a head scarf so that two bright arcs stood out above her forehead, said in Ukrainian: Here, Gesine. Hold this little guy for a second. And then Gesine really had Fat Eberhardt Paepcke in her arm, he wasn't dead either, just asleep, and dreaming, like her. (In March a freight train had come through Gneez full of people from Pommern who'd been kicked out by the Poles. Gesine had caught half an hour of the train's stopover and run from car to car, plaguing the tired, dirty people on the straw with her questions about Paepckes from Podejuch. Just like in the dream, she knew that they'd died two years ago in April, and as in a dream she couldn't stop herself, running to the next sliding door, her brain a blur of shame and hope, almost crying, her speech slurry.)

"White bread." Three exclamation points. This was Dr. Schürenberg's stalwart resistance to the Communist occupation. Since officially there was no white bread, he would put it on prescriptions.

"R. P." A little line between the two letters had turned it into the formula for *Requiescat In Pace*. This didn't help lay the incident to rest very much, and it was something she'd actually done, not just something that had happened; the memory of it would come back so sharp and painful that she'd flinch, as if from a pinprick. Jakob's mother tried to talk her into letting that evening go; she would speak so softly, so comfortingly, until the child fell asleep, and the next morning there it still was, unforgotten. How can something that started as clear and cold and clean as the feel of a wet-honed knife turn into fear of guilt?

R. P. had shown up in Cresspahl's kitchen one evening. Gesine came home from the despised dancing class that was so indispensable for her education in finer matters, and by then she had progressed so far in higher etiquette that a sixteen-year-old cavalier was standing outside her door, the boy from the pharmacy, waiting to talk further with her about tango steps and the graduation ball. A stranger was sitting at the table in the kitchen. Since Cresspahl had disappeared there were so few strangers in the house, so rarely visitors; she desperately hoped this might be Cresspahl. That wish was ground to dust by a series of miniscule glimpses, faster than anything can turn into words in the mind. The man's shoulders, averted, were round not from age but from laziness. His whole body was too tall; even from behind she knew he would have a ruddy, healthy-looking face. Also, Cresspahl would surely have stood up at the sound of her footsteps, or turned around, said in Platt: *Look a that*....

She was barefoot at this point—no one had heard her steps on the tiles. Sitting at the table with the stranger were Jakob and his mother, not acting familiar but polite enough, a little uncertain, as if for all their right to be there they still had to justify themselves. The man looked up when she stepped to the table, just casually, seeing nothing there but a child. – Hey there: he said, condescendingly, intrusive with his claim to being family, entirely at ease. – Get out: said Cresspahl's daughter, fourteen years old.

This was weeks ago and she was still trying to convince herself that it hadn't been hate. She'd just looked at him. She'd memorized his face: round skull, Mecklenburg type, a bit meaty. Big eyes, the blue that's supposed to mean honesty and that flickers so rapidly. Full, spoiled lips. So respectable, so well-fed. In a suit of re-dyed army fabric that fit as if custom-tailored. The rubber boots didn't go with the rest of the grandeur, but he probably planned to pick up leather shoes here. He still hadn't stood up. – Out! she screamed. – *You get outta here!*

She'd used the informal pronoun and felt bad about that once he'd left; she hadn't really had the right to speak so familiarly. Then it finally dawned on Jakob that this was her uncle, her mother's brother, Louise Papenbrock's favorite child that she didn't want in Cresspahl's house. Bah, he hadn't even gotten a beating. With a crooked grin and a shrug like someone found out, Robert Papenbrock had ducked out of the kitchen, afraid of a younger man who was simply stronger than him. He'd threatened to burn the house down. That was the one time their visitor had had a little stumble, Jakob saw to that, his face landing on the back door's sharp stone stoop. Then she hadn't even wanted to turn him in to the Kommandatura, plus she was too cowardly to; anyway, the cavalier from dancing class was still standing next to the house. The eldest of the Papenbrock line had moved off slowly, across the fields to the southwest, in a dignified saunter, until Jakob, at her urgent request, threw a rock after him. The high green grass was so like peacetime, the low sunlight so peaceful. The rock didn't hit the target, just the left kidney.

The Abses said yes to everything, until midnight. It took her that long to get her stories from the life of Robert Papenbrock straightened out—from deserting the country in the first World War, all the way across the Atlantic, to the fact that he'd been sitting at this very kitchen table. Her own vehemence tripped her up quite a bit: Cresspahl hadn't immediately said he'd throw him out, the elder bushes had still been there, but there was barbed wire in them, before that he'd sent Lisbeth to court, *that was my fathers wife she was,* speaker for the party, recruited Nazis in America, burned down whole villages, SS Sonderführer in Ukraine, kidnapped Slata and her arrest was his fault, beat Voss to death in Rande with steel bars, no, I need to ask Cresspahl about that! – Yes: Mrs. Abs said. – *Ida done the same thing:* Jakob said. – Yes.

That lasted one whole evening. The next day she woke up with an icy doubt impervious to anything she could think of.

She didn't need to stay afraid of this relative. He didn't set fire to the house. He was in too much of a hurry. That was how he ended up in a Red Army guard post by Dassow Lake and had to swim for several hours with a relatively severe flesh wound in one of his fat legs. In his letter from the other side of the zone border, from Lübeck, he called himself "crippled by gunshots" and testified to the genteel bourgeois breeding of the house of Papenbrock by solemnly adding: So I hereby disinherit you.

Maybe it was the right thing to do. But she'd kept this person from seeing his mother again. True, he hadn't tried to see his mother, he seemed to prefer entering Jerichow through a back door. True. She'd been in the right. There were arguments on the other side too. Whatever Cresspahl would decide about it, she needed to be the first to tell him about it. R. P. R.I.P.

But Cresspahl didn't send word, didn't come, was in "Siberia" or dead. His daughter was well prepared for the man who'd been in prison with him, for the woman to whom he'd shouted to send greetings to a house in Jerichow. It was for them that she always carried with her, in her coat as well as her dress pockets, a sheet of paper and an envelope. She would know when the moment came what the first, the most important thing was to tell him.

July 3, 1968 Wednesday

The Union of Soviet Socialist Republics has returned to the USA the plane that on Sunday it forced to land on the Kuril Islands, along with all the servicemen on board, the soldiers. The White House has somewhat apologized for the navigational error. The great and peace-loving Soviet Union gave the soldiers of imperialism red tins of Russian-made cigarettes as a present, too, before sending the death specialists onward to the Vietnamese. Not even three days later and the 214 killers are already on the front, fighting their allies, the bosom friends of every Soviet citizen.

A skilled and eager Communist would be capable of discussing the art of diplomacy here without missing a beat—how negotiations over reciprocal disarmament have been saved; children in my year who went to my school would have taken that as part of their job. I can't do it. I can force myself to, I can do it intellectually, but I can't in my dream! There I'm an honorary citizen of Sigh-da-mono.

Cydamonoe. The Marie of today refuses to believe it.

The other child, in April 1961 and through the summer, peering apprehensively out from under her bonnet at the city of New York, is who found it. That was a child whose hand in mine tightened into a vise grip when a rumbling line of metal boxes came thundering towards us underground, becoming a rolling prison, with dangerous sliding doors, and only gradually the subway, and hers. Marie was three and a half, four in July; she avoided the litter like everyone else on Broadway. She insisted on dressing for others in dresses, girls' suits; she thought pants, never mind jeans, were to wear in the apartment, and she accepted them, for Riverside Park at least, only when she started to see their advantages, financially. It might have been the New York weather too—the sweat-stifling heat and humidity that even our decorous Auntie Times calls "unspeakable" today, and she's right, and the suggestion of a curse only redounds to her credit!—that Marie was afraid of when she lay in bed at night and anxiously awaited what this incomprehensible city would send into her sleep. But fear is precisely what it now can't possibly have been, not in a Marie who plans to live in New York forever and always! In 1961, she lay in her room, the door ajar, unimaginably small, unbelievably chubby, staring at the "safe place" on the ceiling and talking to herself. Even if it wasn't about pushing away her fear, it was Cydamonoe.

She pronounced it the English way, with a sharp initial *S* sound and swaying, dark-brown vowels; anyone who heard her would take her for American. (Today she would say that someone taking her for an American proves the opposite.)

Anyway, four-year-old Marie knew hardly any graver danger, in dealing with peers, than that of revealing Cydamonoe. – You fly there? David Williams said, that immemorial autumn, truly thunderstruck. He was standing with her in a less crowded corner of the playground, hands behind his back, his face completely frozen with the thought that this foreign child was trying to pull his leg, lead him down the garden path, and everything else he didn't want her to do. A girl too. She nodded so shyly that he turned on a dime from a victim to an expert, superior because male. – Through the window...? he followed up, still ready to devastate her with laughter. Marie trusted him not to snap her secret in two; a person has to say what's on her mind sometime; and anyway it was the truth: I can: she revealed.

David stared at her, eyes wide. He too had various special powers no one knew about but him. He nodded seriously, and said: Aha. Now that was something worth trusting a friend over. David Williams became a friend of the Cresspahls.

Not even Marie's mother learned anything more about Cydamonoe until a certain stormy night when Marie wanted to delay going behind her curtained door as long as she possibly could, and the only means she knew for doing so was telling a story. The words came out of her mouth all rounded with urgency—German, English, however it came out. She didn't look at me, ashamed of her betrayal as she was, and she would have fallen into stony silence mid-sentence if I'd let my face show the slightest doubt. She held her glass of juice in her plump little hands, wanting to drink, unable to stop talking.

Cydamonoe was a place you could get to only by air. The voyage there started the second it got dark in the child's head and she knew her whole body was asleep. The vehicle you flew there in was your head and your body, self-guided, no "Stewardessens" (blending German and English, *stewardesses* and *Stewardessen*). The flight lasted as long as it took to realize you were flying. The landing happened in the exact moment when the sun rose behind the earth in an eager leap, like a friendly dog, and it was day.

Cydamonoe was a colony for children—a Kinder-Garten in the intended meaning of the word, a child's garden. It was a time that compensated the child for the false day, from waking up until going to sleep.

As soon as Marie reached that place, surrounded by water, she breksted. In English she told me that "brekst" is what she did and in Cydamonoe language that's the word for "help yourself."

In Cydamonoe children help themselves, to breakfast or to houses. Anyone who needs a house just takes one that's empty. There was no reason to keep the one you have. And every house is equally nice.

In Cydamonoe the streets were grassy lanes and it was against the law to misuse them. But there were pedal carts, tricycles, and jump machines standing there ready, the same number as there were children. Not a single one less, not ever. The same as with the houses, the shared toys, the ice-cream cones: no child ever did without.

In Cydamonoe there were lots and lots of windmills. Presiding in the main mill were Kanga and her husband Kongo and their son Roo. Other than this Ministry of Agriculture there was almost no government or administration.

Unless you count the guards on the landing field. It's a position of honor, being the guard; every child serves sometimes, in rotation, unless they have a toothache.

The guards look at your passport and calculate whether the number of stamps qualifies the new arrival to be a citizen of the Republic of Cydamonoe.

Then they check the places of departure. It has to be one of these: Rastelkin, Rye, Korkoda, Shremble, Stiple, Roke, Kanover, Rochest, Kribble, Krabble, Idiotland, Ristel, Rastel, Kranedow, Scharry, Rinoty, Exremble, Rimble, Stevel, Stretcher, Sklov, Opay, Orow, Irokrashmonoe, Crestelmonoe, or Wrestelmonoe. There's no way to get to Cydamonoe from anywhere else.

There have to be thirteen vaccinations entered in your passport, along with a pill for every week. For Cydamonoe is the only country in the world that's worth living in.

As burdensome and unfriendly as this passport control is, all the children agree it must be. For Cydamonoe is a republic of children.

The grown-ups don't want to accept that. They're constantly sending spies in the craziest disguises. No, not dwarfs. Just normal grown-ups who think they know everything and that children never notice anything. And they're noticed right away, when they climb up out of the river in the morning and go to sleep sunbathing in the grass. The children immediately turn invisible. But they watch the intruder wander around the whole country, take hold of the rain machine the wrong way, bend the stamps in the post office out of shape. Many and many a time have the children debated whether or not to continue granting these unwanted visitors their hospitality since they only ever misuse it.

When the grown-ups come in a group, some children get so mad that they want to turn visible again. These grown-up groups inevitably adopt the same disguise and unfold their guns and shoot. Then they're done, but the children have had a bad night. Who wants to stand up in the dream meeting and admit: "In my sleep I too was at the Berlin Wall and I fired with the rest"?

They're so clumsy, the grown-ups, that they don't just damage things, they hurt themselves. One of them thought the toy factory was a bank and broke down the door and stole billions of billions of dollars and marks. ($4,000,000,000,000.00.) One smoked in public, threw aside their match, and put out their cigarette in the swimming pool. And all sorts of other things grown-ups can think up.

But then they're arrested, convicted, punishable, and they go to jail! In jail they get nothing but bread and butter and milk! The punishment consists of them having to find the hole to slip out through. No child will tell them where it is. Once they've found it, they're free. All they have to do is swim the three hours across the river surrounding the island.

Because of them, the children often have to misuse the many narrow passages and tunnels as escape routes. It takes so much to repair them, until they're good for playing in again!

Mr. CoffeeCan does that. Yes, there is one grown-up who lives in Cydamonoe. But it's the man in the moon. One morning there he was on the landing field, mute, fat and brown and round like the cans where the coffee lives, which you can see through the lid in his head. He didn't have to undergo the examination, he was given his passport and his shots and he promised to take his pills. He isn't always mute. He knows he needs to hang up a new fire bell every day. There are no fires in Cydamonoe but there are dangerous visitors sometimes.

Mr. CoffeeCan is a handyman. He takes care of everything. True, the children don't let him tackle the really tricky stuff, like the island's propeller. But he knows how to pump out the many swimming pools every day, and he's great at giving the birds haircuts. Stephen the policeboy even let him turn invisible once.

Day begins in Cydamonoe once the "entrance of the Stewardessens" fails to occur. Then comes playing, reading, swimming, feeding the animals in the countryside and the trees, and every afternoon at four thirty the class that every child hates: How to say goodbye. One of the games is called, and is:

Jumping up and down,
Kanga-Roo's around the town!

Because since Kanga has a job she gets time off, and since Roo needs to live with his grown-ups he does too. Kongo never has a day off. How could anyone invent even a game if someone showed up and it was just Kongo! Kongo's flour is usually multicolored, not white.

The children in Cydamonoe are alone, or with friends, however they prefer. Leaving a group because you're sad is not permitted, however. When a child has been alone enough and is done with that, they only need to think of being with the others and they are, quick as a wink, with a soft toot.

You can also summon children who aren't citizens of the Republic, just by thinking of them. If you've left, let's say, a Konstanze or a Manuela back in Europe, you can invite them for a visit. But they won't know they've been to Cydamonoe, and the next morning, when they wake up in Hannover or Düsseldorf, they'll have forgotten it.

And if for some reason something is missing in Cydamonoe, you go to the Wunsch und Wille building. Want and Will. It'll be there.

Marie doesn't know how the other children do it when it's nighttime. And you're not allowed to ask. As for her, she gets into bed with Tigger and his father a second before it gets dark, sleeps for a long time, and wakes up in the morning somewhere she doesn't recognize at all. She has to think for a long time. Then she realizes it's ... New York City.

Back then she admitted it. And don't I still carry with me wherever I go a seven-year-old piece of paper on which the unevenly written letters authorize me explicitly and by name to visit Cydamonoe? – But only come if you don't know what else you can do! she begged me back then, when the thunderstorm was over and she was willing to try once more to go to bed. How short a four-year-old child is, lying there.

And now, for the Marie of 1968, none of this is supposed to be true, just because she's almost eleven. Just because New York is now hers—with every mile of its subway system, all its islands, all its weather, at all times—without a world of Cydamonoe to contrast it with! Because she can meet me at the Seventy-Second Street station for a stroll through Riverside Park, in a meticulously faded T-shirt and artificially aged jeans; because she can both keep an eye on the stairs up from the subway and suggest to the sturdy policemen next to them, with a sidelong look no one could prove against her, that he should think what she thinks: Are you really known as New York's Finest even though you've been caught taking bribes again and again? It used to be that she'd avoid such a massive fellow in uniform, because of his wooden billy club if nothing else; this one turns away from her as if she's wounded him. Is it possible she ever had such fat baby lips, with the words tumbling out so pudgily, as if covered in fuzzy skin? Her hair is almost as white-blond as it'll be in August. No stranger will realize that she's now caught sight of the person she's wanting to find; no one needs to know who she's waiting for. That's between us.

In any case, an honorary citizen of Cydamonoe has the right to occasionally speak in phrases such as "except for the fire bells of Cydamonoe," "according to the laws of C."—but only in code, never in front of witnesses, and no more than twice a year. Why today? Why today without the reprimand of a furrowed brow? Because today is the third of July, and the start of a long weekend, and we wish each other a good one, I her and she me.

July 4, 1968 Thursday

In the third summer after the war, Mecklenburg was safer than the city where we live now.

Yesterday a man in his forties, stocky, black-haired, white undershirt, black pants, dark socks, walked into the women's section of a public lavatory at Eighty-Fifth Street in Central Park and shot a twenty-four-year-old woman, the bullet passing downward out her throat and into her chest, killing her. He then climbed onto the roof and fired in all directions, calm, capricious. It was near the part of Fifth Avenue where people like Jack Kennedy's widow live, and more than a hundred policemen stormed into the peaceful area. One of them says he thinks he shot the killer ten times. Apparently the killer had lived in the Soviet Union, Bulgaria, and Yugoslavia, and come here with a Greek passport; there were pictures of Hitler, Göring, and Goebbels on the walls of his apartment. People on the upper floors of nearby buildings had a bird's-eye view. "The police were absolutely great," said Mrs. David Williams of 1035 Fifth Avenue. "It was as thrilling as anything you could see on television."

Around Jerichow there were mostly thefts, and dogs on chains enjoyed an unforeseen respect. Stealing food, up to ten pounds of flour, was considered a hunger tax; a bottle of liquor gone missing earned curses at the unknown perpetrator; news of neither tended to reach the police: why call in the upholders of the law to take a look around, you might just as well catch a rabbit by sprinkling salt on its tail. (Not much went missing at the

Cresspahls' place—behind the cemetery, so close to the Kommandatura.)
It was seen as a sign of economic recovery when tools or machines were
stolen, to work with. You could carve your house number into the shaft of
the scythe, but what about the blade? And why would Duvenspeck give
up his residence permit in Jerichow when Willi Köpcke came back from
the Soviet camps—the director of the gasworks wasn't running away from
just anywhere, and if Mina Köpcke was not to be seen on Town Street for
quite some time, and then was seen tired and gentle as a lamb, it must have
been some other misdeed that she was getting beaten up for.

The streets were practically safe, aside from the Soviet MPs and various
marauders; a child could take a trip with no need to worry, especially if
she was wearing an extra-big sweater and baggy pants that discreetly recalled
a checked curtain, and was carrying her things in a net bag, so fellow
travelers could see everything inside it, there was no need to grab it. Gesine
Cresspahl got off the bus at the Kiel stop on Fischland and walked north
on Fulge, quickly, away from the corrosive yellow stench of the wood
generator; she'd trusted things three days earlier in Jerichow but not here.
She shamelessly bypassed the mayor's office; a returning native didn't have
to pay the visitor's fee, surely. Past the Baltic Hôtel, at the corner where
Malchen Saatmann's place was, she turned right onto Norderende Road,
as though intending to hire herself out to Niemann the farmer for the
harvest, but she stopped in front of a very red cottage with a cane roof,
surrounded by hedges and wild bushes and lush trees. This was her house
here, and she didn't go inside. But it's why she'd come.

She'd forgotten that Alexander Paepcke had signed the property over
to her father; it was hers only because she and Paepcke's children had come
to feel at home here. The slip of paper on the post revealed that total strangers were living at this smallholding now—no one else in Althagen would
need a nameplate. Only outsiders would be capable of neglecting to pull
all the weeds from the stone embankment around the house. The southwest
corner of the thatched roof was ragged—the rain would get in during the
fall. Memory refused to supply anything.

She would probably have walked farther, on the firm sand between the
thick hedges, to Kaufmanns Corner, to the Ahrenshoop Post Office bus
stop—there was nothing else she was looking for on Fischland; it was
only ancient habit that led her to the cottage where the Paepckes used to

drop off the keys over the winter. She wasn't alone, she just felt that way; she greeted the people out for their early-evening stroll—greeted them first, without fail, not because she was younger but strictly according to the English custom, so that several of the men looked surprised. She gave them the slip. Finally she was standing in front of Ille, and each of them was terribly shocked by the other.

Ille had latched the top half of her door to the wall—a *Snackdœr*; suddenly she was standing so still that she was like a picture in a frame. She saw the child who'd always come with the Paepcke children, but they were dead, she knew that. Ille was easy to recognize—the same pensive face, the freckles even more pronounced, her brittle reddish hair like a man's. She was wearing, in the house, a white head scarf, the way people on Fischland do to mourn the dead; she had married her captain after all, at forty-two. The shock lasted the blink of an eye. Then Ille was the elder again, and said, barely reproachful, barely worried: *Gesine. You've run away.*

Gesine had run away from home, and Ille informed her that a note on the kitchen table in Jerichow wasn't enough for Jakob's mother. She had to go that very day *œwe den pahl*, over the fence and the border from Mecklenburg to Pommern, to the post office, with a letter saying she'd come here to visit relatives. Which was true, that more or less was what she'd had in mind. Ille also clarified that the child would be sleeping under the same roof as her, if she didn't mind. It was a bit strange to want to go to Farmer Niemann for work and bread, just because she'd once been friends with Inge Niemann. Ille herself had things for Gesine to do. It was understood and agreed from the beginning: Gesine was no longer one of the master's children. She was welcome here, and she would have to work for her bed and board.

The things for Gesine to do started the next morning in the garden: there were roots to pull, gooseberries and black currants to pick, beds of soil to break up. Carrying water to the kitchen three times a day; the potatoes she had to peel were counted in buckets, the milk canister she had to have Grete Nagel fill every evening held probably eight quarts. All that was missing was for Ille to let her near the stove. When it was precisely to give Gesine a proper respect for cooking that she'd taken her in. Gesine was allowed to make the cucumber salad, butter the bread. Carry the food to the rooms too.

For Ille had guests, paying visitors from the cities, as in earlier times. Except that a family of refugees was there too, though Ille sent them out into the fields with the farmers; they'd suddenly remembered the work that needed doing on a smallholding, and if these Biedenkopfs from Rostock wanted to stay with Ille over the winter, they'd have to pay in work, not rent. She took money from the temporary guests without a second thought, though. Gesine understood only when she found two piglets one morning in the shed behind the house, which she now had to feed and take care of as well; when a sewing machine was delivered and another time a laundry bucket with almost completely undamaged enamel. What Gesine had been planning to think about on Fischland hardly came into her head even once, she was so busy; she understood the folk wisdom and wanted to tell it to Jakob: her recourse to tangible assets now had a possible goal.

She had her opinion about the guests, too. They were not often friendly. They were people from the British and Soviet Sectors of Berlin; from Leipzig; from the state capital, Schwerin. One of them called himself a painter, though he hadn't been seen painting for two weeks. In the old days, something like that would have been reported to the municipal authorities. The others were a doctor and an East Prussian landscape writer who managed various internal affairs of the state of Mecklenburg from Schwerin and didn't want to say anything more specific about it. They got into lots of arguments and yet stayed together, on the path to the beach, in the water, as though there were something keeping them together above and beyond the room at Ille's. The artists defended themselves against something they called Production. That's what functionaries demanded of them. – Just let us process all this sorrow already! the painter groaned. – You'll see: his colleague in the realm of the Muses proclaimed, vaguely gloomy but trying hard to keep an honest countenance. Gesine saw the gentlemen one more time after that. It's true their bodies weren't exactly plump but their suits, hanging loosely around smaller masses as they might be, were made of enviable, well-looked-after fabric. Their faces were smooth, alert, lively. They didn't look careworn to her. She noticed how intently they dug into Ille's smoked roasts, how wastefully they tackled a chicken thigh with a single, encompassing bite. In her experience, people in mourning had a different way of eating. If the men were trying to process something here in the fresh air and sun and silence, why did they bring their wives along to fight with, why did they spend every evening in their cramped rooms where there was so little space between the beds? (Gesine didn't begrudge their children the vacation, that's how grown-up she felt; she was no longer speaking to the children of the Schweriners, ever since they'd tried to hire her to make their beds.) No, she was being unfair here. If the men were trying to attend to some sorrow, it was probably other people's.

The guests had understood right away the boundaries of where they were wanted and kept out of the garden, the stables, the kitchen, wherever there was work to do. Trapped in their rooms, they never heard any part of the conversation that the locals had on many evenings. Yes, Ille had visitors, like in Paepcke's day, whether they wanted a ladle of water to wash the beach sand out of their mouths or wanted to sit down for something serious, a chitchat or maybe a palaver or even a full-on story. Except that there weren't many men there, and not a few women kept their white head scarves on. No one greeted Gesine as Alexandra Paepcke's cousin—she gradually came to understand that here she was known and remembered because of her father. At the same time, no one asked her about Cresspahl either. They discussed what was happening around Fischland, so Gesine got to know Fischland as a place where things happened differently from the rest of Mecklenburg. Most of the houses had summer visitors like Ille's, pursuing endeavors of the mind. The Cultural League for a Democratic Renewal of Germany had more to say here than the number of votes they'd received in the Mecklenburg election would've led you to suppose. The government of the Soviet zone had set up a playground here for the intellectuals they considered well-behaved, or usable. Life in Hotel Bogeslav was like in the old days, except that people like Seipmüller the banker didn't turn up anymore. Actually, well, they did if they were from the British Sector, or even better, England. – Englishmen? Gesine asked by mistake. But she wasn't rebuked for her forward behavior, why should she be. That's right, Englishmen. The Kurhaus was called the Bogeslav now. They got special allotments "from the reserves," whatever and whosoever those were. Fischland was doled out to the intellectuals of the Soviet zone like medicine—after two weeks they'd have to clear out for the next ones. There were some who'd been swimming here since June, though. One had gotten a building permit, in Ahrenshoop, thank God. As long as they don't start putting up their contrived buildings in Althagen. They went for horse-drawn carriage rides through the Darss. That's right, Gesine, during the harvest. Well, we get ours in whatever happens. Yeah, no one knows what happened to the hunting lodge of Reich Huntsmaster Hermann Göring, they don't let anyone near that place in Darss. Other than that, hardly a single complaint about the Red Army. Clearly they were trying a different tack with this corner of the world. Sure, they were armed when they went in search of Alfred Partikel when he went missing in Lower Darss Woods. Seriously, they wanted to save him. You know, Gesine, the painter. From Ahrenshoop, not in the Cultural League at least. What Gesine picked up about the business dealings of the locals sounded no less extraterritorial. It was like there was no tax office here, no Economic Commission for the Soviet zone, as if the police had no admittance. On Fischland, the category "self-sufficient" seemed to mean pretty much exactly what the word implied, not someone refused ration cards. Are you kidding, ration cards!? Now and then talk turned to the house with the sundial, so near the Shoreline Cliff. When would that crumble into the sea, do you think. With west-facing windows as tall as doors. Even if they board them up in the winter the wind gets into the room and dances with the sand. Something often said: You should do it, Ille. No harm in it. Just do it already, Ille.

After Gesine had fetched the milk, she was free to go wherever she wanted. Memory remained absent, all that came was the touch of a moment of the past that calls itself memory. What she wanted was entry into the whole of past time—the path through the faltering heart into the light of the sun of back then. One time they'd stood next to each other on the Shoreline Cliff and indisputably seen the outlines of Falster and Møn islands; Alexandra had turned slightly and her upper arm had jerked toward Gesine's shoulder, without touching it; the feeling of convergence lay in a capsule of her mind, as if buried, and did not come back to life. One time she walked through the lagoon pastures, up to her ankles in squelching water, wanting to secretly get a glimpse of Paepcke's cottage from the back, without the slightest hope left for anything but that touch of the past. She saw the overgrown hedgerow, the maypole, a corner of the Lagoon Room's window. The steel door with the chicken wire was secured with a padlock and chain. She heard a woman talking the way you talk to babies old enough to take in words. All of that brought lost time back only as a thought:

When we....; the words in her mind didn't come to life. Almost every evening, when fetching the milk, she came near the moment when Grete Nagel had offered her and Alexandra a glass of milk, but fresh from the udder, and the cow was turning her eyes to look at them. Now it was a little harder for her to drink milk. She didn't find anything more than that; and anyway it was probably just because Emma Senkpiel's milk in Jerichow was adulterated. In the evening, when the *Zeesenboots* sailed into the Althagen harbor, the cats splashed through the reeds and waited for their hosts, for their share of the day's catch of fish; cats, in the water! She still didn't hear Alexandra's voice. She tried to find expressive descriptions of Alexandra's voice in that moment; even the idea of it almost escaped her. Outside Farmer Niemann's three-story house there were three laundry lines and four people painting next to one another depicting the scene. It was like back then. It was solid and impenetrable, covering over the thought of Alexandra; all that remained was the knowledge that Alexandra was hidden under there, somewhere. In the evening the light from Malchen Saatmann's back room rested in the bushes. She could think: That evening when we still had to fetch bread from Malchen, Alexander was sitting loftily on the sofa, probably tipsy, and he said to his daughter: Well, child?— as if he didn't recognize her.... Gesine could think it. She could imagine it written down. It wasn't actually there. She was conscious that in this minute of standing still outside Mrs. Saatmann's friendly scattered homey light the wind stood still too, as if curbing its pace. She wondered if one day she would have forgotten this too, if it would someday be preserved only in words.

At last Ille did it. She asked Gesine for a "frightful" favor; it turned out to be merely accompanying her on an errand Gesine mustn't ask questions about. She had to keep silent the whole time. Ille's voice wavered. Gesine would've gladly promised her more if it would have made her feel better. The errand was a visit to an old woman in a cottage in Niehagen. Ille put a basket of eggs down in the vestibule, next to an assistant—the fee. Inside, by candlelight and windows draped against the sunlight, she had to put on the table before the conjurer a photograph of the captain and her wedding ring on a silk thread. The old woman avoided any fuss; her manner seemed to have been learned by watching a doctor. Her gaze was that of a businesswoman delivering something a customer has ordered for an agreed-upon price. An open, secretly covert look. She raised her elbows and crossed one hand over the other. The ring swayed on its thread from a previously invisible finger above the captain's face in the picture. It didn't sway, it hung perfectly still from the beginning. The ring didn't move for five full minutes. Where you count to three hundred in your mind. Then Ille started to cry. Back outside, the assistant, apparently the sister or partner in this enterprise, expressed her condolences absolutely as though to a widow—objectively, reasonably, as if such an outcome had been infallibly expected.

– You too? the assistant asked. Gesine had only promised to keep silent. Now that she'd finished accompanying Ille, she was free to run away.

Back home Ille didn't insist on talking about it. We didn't take offense at each other. We could talk to each other. Five days later or so I went back to Jerichow with my wages.

Fischland is the most beautiful place in the world. I say this as someone who grew up on a northern coast on the Baltic, somewhere else. If you've stood at the topmost point on Fischland, you know the color of the lagoon and the color of the sea, both of them different every day and from each other. The wind leaps up Shoreline Cliff and constantly sweeps across the land. The wind brings the smell of the sea everywhere. There I saw the sun set, many times, and I remember three times, the third one not too well. Now the dirty gold is about to drop into the Hudson.

That's when you knew that I'm not coming back, Gesine.
Yes, Alexandra.
That's when you were done once and for all with wanting to kill yourself.
Yes, Alexandra.
You were still thinking about it.
Yes, Alexandra.
But now you won't ever do it.
No, Alexandra, I won't.
I was just hiding, you know.
I know, Alexandra.

In 1947, during the summer, I was on Fischland. Never again.

July 5, 1968 Friday

Yesterday in Bonn, Fritz Gebhardt von Hahn, of the Department of Jewish Affairs under the Nazi foreign ministry, appeared before the court again, accused of complicity in the death of more than thirty thousand Bulgarian and Greek Jews. The defense called a witness who had also formerly been in a leadership role in the Nazi foreign ministry, wiretapping division.

He gave his first names; his last name, Kiesinger, was already known. Profession: Chancellor of West Germany. Such silver-haired gentlemen enjoy the West Germans' trust. The Social Democrats are in a governing coalition with the likes of him.

When had he joined the Nazi Party? Right away, in 1933. "Not from conviction, but not out of opportunism." What other possible reasons are there? No one asked him that. He claims to have had nothing to do with the party until 1940, other than paying his membership dues. At that point, he was trustworthy enough to supervise the appraisal and interpretation of foreign radio broadcasts. When the enemy stations mentioned the extermination of the Jews, Mr. Kiesinger simply took a skeptical position and omitted the matter from the daily digest for his superiors, and as a result the Nazis remained in the dark about what they were doing. (This was how Mr. von Hahn could fail to find out what was happening to the Jews he was sending on their way.) Similarly, Mr. Kiesinger's colleague von Hahn had never heard the term "final solution" until the end of the war. Only late, and gradually, very slowly, did the disappearance of those who wore the yellow star, and stories from soldiers returning from the fronts, make him think "that something or other wasn't right." That "something very ugly was happening" with the Jews. Officially he knew nothing. Under oath. Leaves the courtroom without handcuffs.

In Soviet Germany, in Mecklenburg, on February 26, 1948, the Soviet Military Administration ordered the end of denazification on and as of April 10. It was said of the guilty that they were under arrest or that the Western occupying powers were giving them shelter. The Americans were in possession of a particularly capacious aegis: Dr. Kramritz taught the fourteen- and fifteen-year-old children in class 8-A. Former National Socialists were now being expressly invited to join in the "democratic and economic reconstruction," provided they "atone by honest work." Not being in jail proved your innocence.

Atonement comes in various forms, of course—how could a child know them all?

The Arado Works in Gneez had now been expropriated in writing. Heinz Röhl had even legally forfeited his Renaissance Cinema, due to miscounted admission tickets when the Soviets released its booty of UFA films for the starving Germans, which was the profit motive, hence aggravating circumstances, not mitigating ones as he was probably used to getting under the republic. And yet there was a business king of Gneez, outside the law just like in the days of Freddy Numero Duo. Emil Knoop, we'd almost forgotten about him! As per the rules he was an ex-Nazi, and he'd come to town with quiet pomp and gentle circumstance and soon exceeded all comparison. I bring you tidings of great joy. He'd had a hard time to begin with, over the reputation from the old days he'd left in his wake. For his father, Johannes (Jonathan) Knoop, had always been considered a prominent businessman and upstanding citizen who could be forgiven such little tics as raising carp and rather gentrified hunting. He'd been doing business as Coal Merchant, Carriage Trade, Import and Export since 1925 (1851). When it came to getting in with the right people in Gneez, his boy Emil had often enough been a problem. Take 1932: it was far from clear to whom a businessman had the moral duty to pledge his allegiance. Johannes was leaning toward the German Nationalist Party. But his boy Emil ran off to Hitler Youth shooting practices with his father's whole gun cabinet. That was a dicey year. An expensive one, too, for now Johannes had to give money to both sides. And even if Emil's political savvy could be said to have been proven by 1935, the fact remained that he hadn't learned much more about his father's business than how to reach into the cash register; his teachers had apparently had to carry him across the high-school finish line. Then it was labor service that was supposed to reform him; he came back from it once he'd gotten a girl pregnant in Rostock. The things it took to make her see that her life as Mrs. Knoop in Gneez would be nothing but torment! He continued to learn from his father how to cut a fine figure in Gneez, with a sports car and silk scarf; this, along with alimony and other settlement money, was too much for the company so he had to enlist in antitank defense in Magdeburg so early that he became a reserve-officer candidate, then went off to the Polish war as a private first class and came back from the Soviet one as a first lieutenant. Not straight back to Gneez. In June 1945, at the Kiel harbor, the British released him into the civilian population since he could prove to their satisfaction that he'd never had anything to do with the NSDAP other than his party dues having been withheld from his officer's salary. During his practicum in the black market in Belgium, during his work in all the occupied countries in Europe (except Italy), it had certainly been better for Emil Knoop to be in the party. Whatever it might have been that kept him apart from his loving family for a little while yet, in a Hamburg office that apparently really looked like a counting house of yore, his sojourn there may have helped give his amateur understanding of business a bit of scientific backbone. In early 1947 he took over Gneez. Shows that people were coming from the West after all! He left the coal trade to his father. His qualifications for the transportation business were obvious, seeing as he'd brought with him a more or less brand-new American truck, the kind you could get enough spare parts for in Mecklenburg. He transported almost nothing within Mecklenburg. He spoke little about what he was doing; pretty much all you could get out of him was that he was assisting the SMA with liquidating various businesses. True, one day he'd said a bit loudly in Café Borwin: I've got to get everything for the Russians, *from tank to horse an saddle, don' know which way is up anymore!* Turns out he did, because one evening when he was arranging a deal in Jerichow's Lübeck Court Hotel a waiter came running up, pale as a sheet, and whispered: Mr. Knoop! Berlin's on the line, Karlshorst headquarters! – Right: Emil said, in his self-satisfied way: *They cant do a thing without me.* Turns out they could, sometimes, and then he'd spend a few days in the basement under the Gneez courthouse. He reformed that place in a matter of days, got hold of the keys of the other cells, had food delivered from town (from Mrs. Panzenhagen— liked her cooking more than his mother's), and acquired a record player with jazz discs from the thirties, which was apparently a bit of a burden for the guards and they let him go after six weeks (with feverish apologies). Johannes Knoop grew ever paler with fear until he was almost transparent. Gneez got a taste of Emil's views on filial devotion: by fall 1947 his parents were living in Hamburg, and not in the Pöseldorf neighborhood either, in fact quite far from Inner Alster Lake—out in the country, you might say. They seem to have written him rather few letters. True, Father ran Emil's old office, it's just Emil seemed to have forgotten it. To each his own busi-

ness methods, whether inherited or acquired. Emil's new office was in
Brussels. And why not, didn't the Soviet zone have a trade agreement with
Belgium? Emil's office in the Soviet Sector of Berlin was called Export and
Import, the one in the British zone was a room in a dentist's office and
didn't seem to need any sign whatsoever. The fact that Emil was often away
from Gneez made it that much easier for legends to spring up around him.
A foreign truck, with a trailer, loading every last particle of wheat from
Papenbrock's and the Red Army's granary and driving off toward Lübeck,
the border crossing—that's not nothing. Soon Emil was respected, almost
liked by the proper sort in Gneez. He could be living like Louis the Last
in Belgium, could he not?, and yet here he was toiling away for Mecklenburg
and the SMA. And did he go around bragging of his business success? No,
he kept wearing the same hat every day, bit greasy by now. Did he not show
Christian compassion, time after time? A Mrs. Bell was living in Gneez,
in a room in her villa in the Berlin Quarter. Lucratively divorced in 1916,
a rich woman who took care of problems over the phone. Now that her
phone had been taken away, she couldn't handle the world. Emil went and
sat her down at his own private phone. Needed a housekeeper anyway. Do
you think Emil was the type to wear gold rings? No, if he had anything to
be happy about (*"like a kid"*) it was more likely that, in addition to his
white ("personal") *propusk* required for any long-distance transport orders
from the Central Transport Authority, including border traffic, he'd been
given another one, the red kind, authorizing travel through the whole
Soviet zone, including border traffic! It was age-old wisdom, wasn't it: Just
let the army haul a ne'er-do-well over the coals and he'll know what's what
for the rest of his life. Y'can see it in his short haircut too. Tight, black,
neat. And Emil never bought a round for everyone at the bar—only paid
for the ones worthy of his love. It was nice to hear him tell stories, not
about business but from his life: how he'd shot down two Viscounts near
Cuxhaven in September '39 and made sure the crews were buried with
military honors. How at the "Vistula estuary bridgehead" he'd discovered
that they'd had a concentration camp by the name of Stutthof there, which
was why he'd painted "Stutthof Remains German!" on his truck. You
know, personal reminiscences. And now they finally knew what the weather'd
been like on May 9, '45, when he'd skippered the crossing of the Baltic to
Kiel: the sea was calm. Why begrudge a lucky stiff?—his interzonal pass

was always in order, he could count on being exempted from local motor pools, the rationing board not only recommended him but attested to the legality of his fuel sources. No one envied him his driver, or his 275 pounds. He had such a calming effect. (Nobody wanted a closer look at his black boxy briefcase: too full of dangerous money.) When he did come a cropper—smuggling horses to Lower Saxony; getting beer kegs of "uranium" confiscated at the border—he would laugh himself silly telling stories about it later. A loyal soul, that's what he was. One time, he came back from the wider world of the steel trade to Gneez, where the potatoes on the state-owned farm weren't out of the ground yet. He promised fifty marks for every basket upended next to the trucks, and that night the trucks were filled to the brim and he threw a party for the workers too. He could use those potatoes. Took the small stuff too. And oh how he cried when Dr. Schürenberg told him about the diseases the schoolchildren were suffering from. Chinese beggar's disease, that's what they had, from eating pigweed? Emil couldn't bear to hear that, needed a triple brandy, quick now. What? suffering from scabies? under Emil's very eyes! Dr. Schürenberg didn't inform him that the word referred to ordinary itches; he painted a picture of the children's vitamin deficiencies. The children kept getting their ankles all banged up from their wooden sandals' sharp edges, never healed, led to inflammations of the lymph vessels, horrible pains in the groin. He'd seen Cresspahl's daughter (– *now thassanother good man!*: Emil roared, in tears) standing at the train station, legs so stiff she could hardly walk it hurt so much. – Cresspahl? said Triple-J, the town's military commander, J. J. Jenudkidse. For they were sitting in the Dom Ofitserov, guests of Triple-J. – I swear it!: Emil cried, sobbing. This was shortly before Christmas 1947. – An orange for every child: Dr. Schürenberg said. For he'd been to university and wanted to wipe out on the spot this unheard-of prestige that a common tradesman apparently enjoyed. – And a salted herring for every laborer!: Emil sobbed. Gneez held its breath for the next couple weeks. Emil could always back out by saying, truthfully enough, that he'd been ten linen closets of sheets to the wind at the time. But it happened, punctually too. The salted herring came. The oranges were handed out in schools and children's homes and hospitals. Triple-J provided the trucks, since this time Emil didn't happen to have any trucks "liquid" (such short notice!), while Emil saw to it that the things were pilfered in sufficient number from Hamburg harbor. Gneez had long since learned to believe in Emil.

That was his way of atoning.

And he was innocent, as proven by the fact that he wasn't in jail—a child could see that. A child saw him wreathed in one halo of glory after another. In March 1948, the Communists established the *National News* for him, dedicated to former members of the NSDAP or other patriotic thinkers, to help him feel at home in their Germany; three weeks later, when their People's Police confiscated all products of the press licensed in the West and shut down their distribution, they continued to allow people like Knoop a discreet subscription to the West Berlin *Daily Mirror* to counteract any hint of feeling not at home, mailed in a sealed envelope of course. When he did take a fall, nine years later, he had to say goodbye to a whole colony of boathouses, a pheasant-breeding facility, and the first canopy swing—called "Hollywood"—in all of Gneez and the district too, but for Cresspahl's daughter it came too late. She could grasp that the Communists had let him help them to rise above the level of commodity circulation, as long as they still had something to learn from him and the Soviet Union; she felt sorry enough for him when he was led off past white-faced government secretaries in his waiting room, but it was too late. She'd had to spend too long being ashamed of having reached into that sack of oranges.

July 6, 1968 Saturday, South Ferry day
is also the day when Auntie Times tells us what her special correspondent Bernard Weinraub wrote her from Saigon, South Vietnam, back under the date of June 27:

"AMERICAN IMPACT ON VIETNAM'S ECONOMY, POLITICS AND CULTURE IS PROFOUND

Ten years ago fewer than 1,000 American servicemen were stationed in Vietnam, and their presence was scarcely noticed.

Today, 530,000 American troops and 12,000 civilians are swarming through this tortured country, and their presence is affecting the very roots of South Vietnamese life.

... Lambrettas and cars. In 30,000 to 40,000 homes and in village squares throughout the country, South Vietnamese families watch in fascination 'The Addams Family,' and 'Perry Mason' on armed forces television. In college classrooms students read John Updike and J. D. Salinger. In coffee shops, young men who work for United States agencies and girls in mini-skirts sip Coca-Cola and complain that the Americans have taken over.

The American presence has also contributed to a tangle of more profound changes that remain, with a war on, contradictory and complex. Students, teachers, Government employes and businessmen insist, for example, that the influx of American soldiers, civilians and dollars is tearing the family apart and creating social havoc.

... 'An impossible situation has been created,' said an American-educated lawyer. 'The poor families come to Saigon from the countryside because of the war. The father has few skills, so he becomes a day laborer or drives a pedicab. Before he was respected by the children. He knew about the farm. He knew about the land. Now he knows nothing.

'The young boys wash cars for the Americans or shine shoes or sell papers or work as pickpockets,' the lawyer went on. 'They may earn 500 or 600 piasters [$5 or $6] a day. Their fathers earn 200 piasters a day. Here is a 10-year-old boy earning three times as much as his father. It is unheard of.'

Beyond the impact of Americans and American dollars, of course, there is the over-all, shattering impact of the war itself. Virtually every young farmer or peasant is forced to join the Government forces or the Vietcong; more than a million people have become refugees; the disruption of farms and villages has led an additional two million to flee to the cities...

... since thousands of families in rural areas are physically moved out of their farms by allied troops to create free-strike zones.

... 'The Vietnamese never wants to leave his village,' said a professor at Saigon University. 'They want to be born there and they want to die there.

'That is not easy for you Americans to understand, since you can move from village to village in your country,' he went on. 'But here it is very painful for a Vietnamese to leave his village, and when they are forced to move they hate you. It is as simple as that—they hate you.'

... Another [American] declared:

'It's easy to blame everything wrong here on the Americans—the Viet-namese love doing it. But, look, this society was damned rotten when we got here and what we're getting now is an exaggeration of the rottenness, the corruption, the national hangups.'

...Ironically the strongest American cultural influence has touched folk singing in the antiwar ballads of the most famous college singer in Vietnam, Trinh Cong Son.

The broadest social—and, by extension, cultural—impact of the Americans has fallen on the powerful middle class, who exclusively ran the Government's bureaucracy, taught in primary schools and colleges and served as lawyers, doctors and businessmen. This socially conscious class, to all indications, had little link to or sympathy for the peasants, or even the army.

American officials say privately that the disruption within this entrenched class is welcome. Middle-class Vietnamese are naturally bitter. Especially at their decline in status.

'A university professor may earn 18,000 piasters a month [$150], while a bar girl can earn 100,000 piasters [$850],' said 58-year-old Ho Huu Tuong, a lower-house representative who was a prominent intellectual in the nineteen forties. 'The intelligentsia are the disinherited, the lost, because of the American impact. We have lost our position.'

'Money has become the idol,' said Mr. Thien, the Information Minister. 'Money, money, money.'

The theme is echoed by poorer Vietnamese—the pedicab drivers, the small businessmen, the maids, the cooks—but for them the problem of status is irrelevant and the flow of American dollars is hardly unwelcome. 'How can I hate the Americans?' asked a grinning woman who sells black-market cigarettes at a stand on Tu Do, in the heart of Saigon. 'They have so much money in their pockets.'

...At the official level, only enormous American assistance—$600-million this fiscal year—keeps Vietnam afloat. The figure is exclusive of American military expenditures of more than $2-billion a month.

...Only 6 per cent of last year's budget was met by direct taxes on income and business profits in comparison with about 80 per cent in the United States.

This results in Government reliance on levies on foodstuffs, tobacco, alcohol, matches and other items that fall with heavy weight on the poor. And, through bribes and bureaucracy, the rich often pay no taxes at all.

... Since 1962, land distribution in South Vietnam has been at a virtual standstill and the bulk of the land remains in the hands of absentee landlords.

... There is a general feeling that Mr. Thieu, Mr. Ky or any other Vietnamese leader would have enormous political difficulties, even if they agreed to every possible reform that the Americans have urged.

For the heart of the Government or 'system' is an unwieldy, Kafkaesque bureaucracy that hampers progress at every turn. And in that area, the American impact has been minimal.

Paperwork, documents, stamps, bored officials, bribes are everywhere. Officials work four-hour days.

'It will take us at least a generation to change the system,' said one of the highest American officials at the United States mission. 'Maybe more than a generation.'

... A South Vietnamese publisher told an American recently: 'You are our guests in this country and Vietnamese have been very friendly to you. Do not outlive our hospitality.'

... 'Smugness of so many of them is appalling,' said a junior American official. 'If we were not at war it would be funny.'

But a student in La Pagode, a coffee shop on Tu Do, observed: 'Americans must fight for us so we can live in peace.'

Had the student volunteered to join the army? 'No, I must study, I am a student,' he replied."
© The New York Times

And who else does Auntie Times want us to get to know today? Lynn Tinkel.

On June 19, Lynn Tinkel, a twenty-two-year-old Bronx schoolteacher, was going somewhere with her friend James Lunenfeld, two years older than she, also a teacher, and was doing so on the INDependent's platform under Fifty-Ninth Street. The hour was late—two thirty in the morning—and she thought: Uhh: the thought came into her mind: I feel like taking a picture of my friend James.

But it is forbidden to take pictures in the New York subway! A wise Transit Authority rule forbids it, without written permission, signed and sealed. This was where Lynn had her idea, James his in turn, and that costs a cool $25 fine or ten days in jail!

Yesterday, Lynn stood before a man in robes, in the Criminal Court at 100 Center Street, presumably Chamber 5a (Traffic Court), and was acquitted. For her, it was the principle of the thing. If she felt like taking a picture of her friend on the subway platform. . . . The judge agreed and let her go in peace.

Now the Transit Authority thinks a closer look at this rule might be in order. For instance, it could explicitly tell photographers they can't use tripods, over which people have been known to trip; or that flashbulbs might blind a train driver or passengers . . . that's what its closer look has yielded so far. Anyway, Lynn is free, and if the air temperature above Broadway was lower than 82 degrees Fahrenheit with a humidity index of 73 percent, would we go down into the subway and take photos of each other question mark?

There's something *The New York Times* has missed.

The sidewalks on Broadway are bordered with steel bandages that make the street corners steep and difficult to manage for people with baby carriages or even the kind of grocery carts that families use to carry home food for the entire week. Today, for the first time, our eye is caught and our soles are soothed by the gentle slopes that the city has sunk into the transition between street and sidewalk, a relief to taxpayers and recognition of its obligations; a down payment: as Marie says, still in a bad mood from the muggy air over the harbor, which made it hard for her to sweat.

Can this be? Something escaping the gaze of *The New York Times*—a change in the style of Broadway's furnishings on the corner of Ninety-Eighth, an aesthetic correction, and sociographical event? Alas, it is we who must make sure to mention it.

July 7, 1968 Sunday

Haven't we been steadfastly insisting that *The New York Times* was an auntie? Wasn't that our very own word?

We can prove it with her performance yesterday—her lecture on the profound impact of the US-American presence on the economy, politics, and culture of the part of Vietnam that this country intends to save from Communism. She's considered, double-checked, and articulated everything:

The South Vietnamese in range of armed forces television gobble up *The Addams Family* as eagerly as they do *Perry Mason*; the students read contemporary classics of New England and Pennsylvania literature; Coca-Cola's in the homes and the homes have been torn apart, as are families, by the unheard-of income structures and the forced separation from farm and house and village; the folk singers sing antiwar songs in American styles; the middle class is bitter at their loss of influence over politics and the ruling bureaucracy, bitter at the new status symbol, money (barmaids earn five times as much as university professors); direct taxes cover only six percent of the state budget; a once independent rice-producing country has to import rice; land reform is at a standstill; the pervasive influence of French and American bureaucracy has ruined the local variety: every consequence of the American war is at least mentioned, not even excluding the religious disputes. Only one blessing of Western civilization, while being another American import, does *The New York Times* pass over in silence: venereal diseases. What an auntie.

We could prove it with her manifestation today. Fully eight hundred lines on the brutality of the American police; severely, clinically, she bends over the sinners and asks what this might be about: because civilian citizens don't say otherwise? because citizens lay fingers on policemen too? because policemen like others' pain? because they're filled head to toe with contempt? because they're scared? stressed? because they're ashamed of their modest education? because the police academy fails to conduct psychiatric examinations? This is followed, to make the rebuke all the more stinging, by the blow that it was a New Jersey policeman who, without observing the legal requirements, bought the forty-year-old Smith & Wesson revolver that he then sold, equally illegally, to a second policeman, and only then did the firearm reach the hands of the man who shot and killed a young woman in the ladies' toilets in Central Park four days ago. She is going to make the policemen of this country behave if it's the last thing she does, this aunt.

A person of such stature should be able to take for granted that only appropriate opinions about her are current, namely these (disregarding of course the ill-bred definitions coming out of Moscow and its surroundings). But this noble simplicity and quiet grandeur is beyond her. Instead, risking aspersions on her self-confidence, she'd rather hedge her bets and disseminate on her own what one is to think of her. We have read, for instance, on an agèd enamel sign in Woodlawn Cemetery that: she is indispensable for intelligent conversation; in the subway, that: without her we cannot keep up with the times, and the tempting consolation that: you don't have to read it all, but it's such a pleasant feeling to know that it's all in there; we have read in bronze and marble that: she is the diary of the world; today, though, it's that: one of the nicest things about *The New York Times* is that you can get it delivered—this with a sketch that shows her in the act of delivery.

And so who do we see there?

An older person, not exactly maidenly, but chaste. An aunt.

A short person. What is it that pushes her head forward—is it gout, or so she can better peer over her pince-nez? Beady jet-black eyes, rectangular glasses. Lips curved up at both corners into a delicate semicircle; nothing remotely like frivolity or a vulgar grin. Controlled friendliness. Not a wrinkle anywhere on her face.

On her head a mountain of thick ringlets, falling over her ears. The evidence of hair curlers is clearly visible.

A chubby person, judging by the round shoulders draped in a black knit wool cape with a few stitches that have come apart, or going by the more and more bulging dress whose lower expanse forms a long narrow bell with the upper. (We'd imagined her as rather more lean.)

The clothes are dignified: a white dress with a geometric pattern and wide ornamental trim down the middle and at the ankle-length hem, although some isolated threads are hanging down loose there. (We were sure she'd be more smartly dressed.)

There she stands, her bulky body stiff and straight, her little feet turned neatly outward in their high-heeled ankle boots. Her limbs may seem gaunt with age, thin and brittle, but her left hand keeps a firm grip on a heavy roll of paper, although her right hand, with a splayed middle finger, rests on the carved handle of a cane, which she doesn't need for support since she's planted it at an angle in front of her, almost coquettishly, unlike what we'd expected. That's how she stands there.

That's how she looks, as shown to us by herself.

Hi, Auntie Times!

July 8, 1968 Monday

For more than a week, apparently, workers at thousands of Soviet factories and farms have been holding rallies, right in the middle of the harvest, and condemning, or so we hear, "anti-Socialist and anti-Soviet elements" in Czechoslovakia. The Prague paper *Young Front* declares itself bewildered. Precisely this, cries the *Truth* from Moscow right back at them, demonstrates that the *Mladá Fronta* journalists are among the "irresponsible." The chairman of the National Assembly of the ČSSR has also received letters from Moscow, Poland, and East Germany. Josef Smrkovský has kept their exact wording to himself; first he has to discuss it with the governing presidium of his Communist Party; still, he has acknowledged receipt by insisting that Czechoslovakia would not tolerate interference by other countries in her internal affairs. "Interference." That's all it is.

In May 1948 Cresspahl lay stark naked in a water trough in Johnny Schlegel's flower garden. Johnny was sitting on the bench next to the trough as idle as if the workday were over. It was early in the morning. The cats had sense enough to avoid the site of this spectacle; the stupid chickens kept their heads down and wondered why they were so often mispecking. Most of the time the chickens were the only ones keeping up a conversation. Every hour or so Johnny would knock on the sill of the open window behind him, and Inge Paap née Schlegel would come out with a bucket of hot water and put it down at the corner of the house, keeping her back to the two men, not once turning to look. Johnny, with his one arm, could not only carry the heavy bucket but handle it so well that the water poured over Cresspahl's body in a gentle rush, only a little spray reaching his head.

Since Johnny was no less flustered than his guest, he had a hard time keeping silent. He didn't care so much about the time—he'd assigned the work to be done on the farm, he wasn't needed there. He must be getting on in years for his mouth to be itching like that. And for now this Cresspahl knew only that his daughter was still living in Jerichow, with the Abses, in their own house. Couldn't he come up with any questions to ask after all those years with the Soviets? Johnny cast dignity to the winds and said, as if making some kind of calculation: Now that must have been a long trip Cresspahl'd just taken, all right.

That was probably a bit too close to sentimental for Cresspahl, and he put Johnny in his place by answering: *Yeah, bout the same as the one from Jerichow to the Damshagen pub.* This was a local story from the old days when people used to take trips only when a ship'd been wrecked on the beach. Fritz Mahler the cobbler and Fritz Reink the blacksmith were supposed to report to the soldiers but took a bye in Grems and annoyed the people there. Then they realized they'd been dummies and really should see the world a bit. Fritz goes right, to Damshagen, a mile from Jerichow; Fritzie keeps left until he, too, gets to Damshagen. They run into each other in the pub, and cry, Fritz! Fritz! Imagine meeting you here halfway round the world! In fact Schlegel's farm was near Damshagen too. Johnny admitted it.

But Cresspahl wasn't trying to snub him. Since both these world travelers had been from Klütz, he admitted in turn that on the long trek here from Wismar he'd been at the north end of Wohlenberg Cove and there, with the west wind blowing, had heard the bells of Klütz. How was it they'd kept their bells in Klütz?

– *They say what they've always said*: Johnny confirmed, suddenly a bit uncomfortable, probably giving a sigh. Cresspahl at once took it personally. Because what the bells of Klütz say is:

> It's true-ue, it's true-ue,
> the 'prentice boy is dead.
> He's lyin in the Piglet Pond,
> the 'prentice boy is dead.
> He never used to steal nor lie
> and never a cheat was he.
> Our Lord God, on high-igh,
> have mer-cy, mer-cy, mer-cy!

and even if it's true that Cresspahl had been that apprentice boy for the past two and a half years, falsely accused, now lying at the bottom of a pond without any prospect for rehabilitation by any Lord God, he wouldn't stand for the slightest expression of pity, let's get that clear. That's why Cresspahl said, a little maliciously, that it sure did stink here in Johnny's yard.

Johnny promptly took a deep breath and let out a roar. For the boy Axel Ohr had been busy behind the barn for an hour already, trying to burn, with some old straw, a pair of men's underpants, a kind of undershirt, and a pair of felt boots along with a black rubber raincoat. So far he had managed only billows of smoke, no fire, and Johnny gave him a hell of an earful, effortlessly spanning the several hundred feet separating them. Now Axel Ohr had to carry the fire, such as it was, on his pitchfork around the corner to where the wind would scatter the smoke. Axel came slinking across the yard, shyly approached the corner of the house, and asked to be allowed to bury the things instead of burning them. The naked man as well as the clothed one just stared at him, in amazement, almost contempt, so that he turned back, shoulders slumped helplessly, and ashamed at having tried to quibble with an order from Johnny. Terrible dictator, Johnny was. Unpredictable too. Axel Ohr wasn't allowed to do any more serious work all day, for instance. Out came Inge with a fresh bucket.

Johnny's sigh had escaped him more because of the generally prevailing circumstances than anything; he felt a bit unjustly punished. So he just said: He didn't have any beer on the farm but he could manage a shot of liquor. That put Cresspahl in his place. His head had actually shrunk down into his shoulders at the memory of the sip he'd had to take earlier, as a proper greeting. – *Or maybe a cigar?* Johnny generously followed up, quite the master of the house making up for a bad odor with a good one. Cresspahl made an indecisive movement with his head, so Johnny left his nobly rolled tobacco on the outermost plank of the bench and stepped away for a moment, to see to things in the kitchen and bring Axel Ohr the kindling, which of course the boy wouldn't have thought of on his own. When he came back the cigar was sitting in more or less the same place, barely wet, but Cresspahl was even paler in the face than before, if that were possible. What was wrong with that man's stomach, he couldn't eat!

Then they poured out the broth and moved the tub, following the sun, which by that time had left the living-room windows. The chickens made a terrible fuss. Now there were three buckets of fresh water by the corner.

Johnny came over with the bench under his arm and mentioned in passing his obligations to Cresspahl. He spoke of Cresspahl's Gesine and her remarkable abilities as a farmworker, in the realm of wheat as well as that of potatoes. He still owed her two sacks of wheat but was planning to send her part of it in the form of smoked meat. What did Cresspahl, as legal guardian, say to that? Cresspahl asked what the date was. Because there'd been such a rush about signing the papers the previous morning in the Schwerin prison, plus he couldn't read the small print too well yet. Johnny left and came back with his schoolteacher glasses on his nose, holding Cresspahl's release papers in his hand, from which he read first the date and then all the rest. The naked man now wanted to take another stab at the cigar. Johnny Schlegel told him about the head of the Cresspahl household, Jakob. He was learning how to couple up freight cars at the Gneez station, but he didn't want to sell his sorrel horse. Maybe Cresspahl could have a word with him about that, man to man. Jakob was a man of the world in other ways, after all, with grown-up love affairs, including one on the farm with a certain Anne-Dörte until she decided she preferred her titled relatives in Schleswig-Holstein. Johnny was perfectly capable of going on to tell quite other tragic love stories that had taken place before his eyes—men are like that. But he had failed to notice—men are like that— Gesine's suffering during Jakob's visits, and Cresspahl would spend several years suspecting Jakob of a certain dislike, in private you might say, of the nobility. Now Johnny produced some lie about a canister of kerosene he was supposedly keeping for Gesine too. They had sworn one or one and a half false oaths before, on the other's behalf, these two; clearly one more wouldn't matter.

Axel Ohr took up position ten paces away and reported successful incineration. He'd washed himself too, to Johnny's lengthy surprise. Axel Ohr wanted to leave now. He was the boy on the farm, wasn't he. Though he had his doubts sometimes about whether what Johnny imposed on him in such a threatening tone were really punishments. This runaway city boy, sixteen years old, really should've realized that he'd been as good as adopted by the Schlegels and had, without really trying, learned practically everything Friedrich Aereboe had put in his book on general agricultural business management, even a bit more. Need to finesse the calculation of total deliverables, just ask Axel! Now he stood there waiting to hear his next repulsive assignment. He was to go meet the noon train at the Jerichow station. – With Jakob's sorrel . . . ? he repeated, blushing, afraid he might have misheard. Thats right, on Jakobs horse. Johnny gave his ears a good thorough washing out while Axel waited for the catch. – M'boy! Johnny said, serious, looming. He could be so horribly High German sometimes. The catch was that Axel had to pick up a girl there, even if just a fifteen-year-old. She'd probably hold on to him on the horse. Axel didn't really know his way around girls too good, though he'd known one for years as Cresspahl's daughter. That's how Johnny was, always spoiling your fun. The boy resentfully went and saddled up.

Now Johnny gave Cresspahl a crash course in what he'd missed since the fall of 1945, from the creation of Soviet joint-stock companies in Germany to the regional elections to the Gneez principal who in May had been sent to jail for two years, for writing recommendation letters for schools in West Berlin: Piepenkopp showed firm character as a student, that kind of thing. Associating with the enemy of peace. Driving young men and women into the clutches of the enemy of world peace! Johnny'd had Richard Maass make him a book of blank pages, some good rapeseed oil it cost him too, and he wrote something in it almost every day. He read some to Cresspahl: about the Communist coup in Prague; the SED wished the Germans would do the same. People like you and me. Jan Masaryk, the Czechoslovak foreign minister, had jumped out the window of his own free will, they said. Cresspahl didn't happen to know anyone around here, or somewhere in Mecklenburg at least, who wanted to jump out a window so things here could go like there? Then Johnny explained what "spare peaks" were. That was the new name for surplus harvest yields after delivering the target quota, which you were free to sell to the Economic Commission at a higher price. Cresspahl was inclined to see this innovation as permission to conduct an agricultural business for profit again. Yes. Well. Theoretically, sure. But since Johnny'd had to say goodbye to patrons like Colonel Golubinin, the PSC had been paying quite a few visits to the farm. People's Supervisory Committee. They would hand around slips of paper about "monitoring production and commodity whereabouts" and then raise the target quota to what they saw fit. What did a post-office guy like Berthold Knever have to do with *Triticum vulgare*, much less *Triticum aestivum*? Now some farmers had to buy back wheat at spare-peak prices so they could sell it at quota prices. Naah—not Johnny. He was running the business with the other people on the farm commune-style, remember? It was precisely these progressive, *youd hafta say* advanced features of Johnny's business organization that were a thorn in the Gneez district attorney's side. *Men live longer than cows an learn somethin new every day.* Cresspahl showed that he'd learned something too by that point, whatever else he'd missed. – *Izzat book well hid?* he asked. Johnny nodded, proud, unconcerned. Five years later that book wasn't well enough hidden after all, and since he had the nerve to pretend it was a novel he didn't get out of jail till 1957. For now he was sitting on a bench next to a naked friend and gently refilling his tub with fresh water.

– *Heres yer big seal in the water!* Johnny Schlegel said as he led Cresspahl's daughter to the trough, which was now covered with two big wooden breakfast boards. This was totally wrong. Cresspahl didn't have a beard, his skull was long and high, and in Mecklenburg a seal was someone who gaily got away with risky pranks. Cresspahl sure hadn't gotten out of his intact. It did fit a little, because of the man's blank gaze from an indeterminate, unknowable distance. – *'E wont bite:* Johnny said, and the Cresspahl child desperately hoped that he wouldn't leave her alone with this person. First she only saw the ears, which looked so wrong next to his thin haggard face. They'd shaved him bald so his stubble looked dirty. The head between the edge of the trough and the start of the first board looked decapitated, especially since his arms were hidden. She didn't know where to look, she felt more ashamed than she'd ever felt, she was about to start crying. By that point Johnny had long since left his own garden.

– *Ive brought you summing:* the stranger said with her father's voice.

Johnny was staging quite the scene with Axel in the hall—it was about Axel having let the sorrel out into the pasture. So thoughtless. It dawned on Axel that he needed to get the sorrel again, and the rubber-tired cart, to take this Cresspahl to Jerichow. The valuable cart, which horses had so much fun with that it drove itself in front. He'd be driving like a young king. Well, a viceroy. Not on the way there. Any man with eyes in his head, if not a girl like Cresspahl's daughter, could see that she'd gotten her father back shattered, truly not a well man—you'd have to drive him at a walk. But Axel Ohr could already picture the rush of the return trip, whip planted picturesquely on his left thigh, road swirling with dust behind him between the choppy waters of the green wheat on the left, the sea on the right. Axel Ohr convinced himself to believe his luck, at least for that day.

You didnt cry, Cresspahl.
'Fonly I coulda cried, Gesine.

July 9, 1968 Tuesday

It's a normal American thing—for that reason alone Mrs. Cresspahl should have seen it coming. But she'd never imagined that de Rosny would expect this from her, even with apologies. The stockholders on the board must have pushed it through: this proceeding as medieval as it is futuristic. De Rosny *did* expect it from his Mrs. Cresspahl and informed her by mere interoffice memo, like she was a cog in a machine and the person renting the machine could request an adjustment, a depth control, whenever he wanted. Only in Westerns do civilized murderers announce what they're doing (you won't be going anywhere tomorrow), while it's the villains who shoot without warning, from ambush. Mrs. Cresspahl is sitting in a soft deep faux-leather chair with her back to an older technician. She can remember only his bluish smock; she forgot his face at once in her rage. She's in a room with no windows anywhere so she feels short of breath. The walls are painted in yellowing ivory as you'd expect in a hospital. A rubber loop is coiled high around her chest, a band interwoven with wires is stretched tight across her right upper arm, she has a metal plate affixed to each wrist. Heartbeat, breathing, blood pressure, skin moisture. It's the polygraph, the lie detector that no one believes in except the police, the military, and the business world. The empathetic voice behind her seems to be putting out bad breath. She has already been answering for a long time, heedlessly, tripped up by the question of whether or not she should lie. The walls are so thick that out of all the noise of New York she can only hear the humming of the fluorescent lights somewhere above her head.

ANSWER	Refuse? When my job depends on it?
QUESTION	Now the rules of this game are that you can only answer Yes or No from now on.
ANSWER	Yes.
QUESTION	Again, your birthday. March 3, 1933, was that right?
ANSWER	Yes.
QUESTION	In Jerichow, Mecklenburg, the Baltic.
ANSWER	Yes.
QUESTION	You said before what you were doing at six thirty last night.
ANSWER	Yes.
QUESTION	You said: "I was on the promenade by the Hudson. Since

the river was so calm, my daughter thought it must be ebb tide."

ANSWER   Yes.

QUESTION   "I looked at the time so I could check the tide table in *The New York Times.*"

ANSWER   Yes.

QUESTION   Did you do that?

ANSWER   No. Being invited into this nice room here made me forget.

QUESTION   Mrs. . . . Cress-pahl. You're getting agitated.

ANSWER   Sorry. No. Yes.

QUESTION   I have questions that I'm required to ask, along with others from the client. I'm not making them up. This is my job. You mean nothing to me as a person, so I have no interest in hurting your feelings, or in—

ANSWER   Yes.

QUESTION   It's also not true that I'm drawing any personal conclusions from your answers. The measuring instruments, oscillating in front of me or tracing out curves on the paper drum, take care of that.

ANSWER   Yes.

QUESTION   It's just a game, for us both.

ANSWER   Yes.

QUESTION   Your nationality is German.

ANSWER   Yes.

QUESTION   West German?

ANSWER   Yes.

QUESTION   East German nationality?

ANSWER   Yes.

QUESTION   West German nationality?

ANSWER   Yes.

QUESTION   Earlier you said, "I have about seven dollars in my wallet."

ANSWER   Yes.

QUESTION   "Maybe eight with the change."

ANSWER   Yes.

QUESTION   You're here because your bank wants to give you a sensitive, confidential assignment.

ANSWER	Yes.
QUESTION	You understand that your bank has to insure itself against risk.
ANSWER	Oh yes. Yes.
QUESTION	Do you feel loyalty to your bank?
ANSWER	No.
QUESTION	Do you mean the bank where you have an account?
ANSWER	Yes.
QUESTION	Do you mean the bank where you work?
ANSWER	Yes.
QUESTION	You came to the United States on April 29, 1961.
ANSWER	No.
QUESTION	On April 28, 1961.
ANSWER	Yes.
QUESTION	With a visa that let you work.
ANSWER	Yes.
QUESTION	Your name is Gesine L. Cresspahl.
ANSWER	Yes.
QUESTION	Do you go by only this name?
ANSWER	Yes.
QUESTION	Have you ever gone by a different name?
ANSWER	Yes.
QUESTION	Was that different name intended to evade an existing law?
ANSWER	Yes.
QUESTION	Multiple laws?
ANSWER	Yes.
QUESTION	Did you believe you were right to break those laws?
ANSWER	Yes.
QUESTION	You are not married.
ANSWER	No.
QUESTION	You have never been married.
ANSWER	No.
QUESTION	You reject the institution of marriage.
ANSWER	Yes.
QUESTION	Will you ever get married?
ANSWER	Yes.

QUESTION   You had a happy childhood.
ANSWER   Yes.
QUESTION   Not always happy.
ANSWER   Yes.
QUESTION   When you think about your biographical background, do
            you think it possible that you are psychologically damaged?
ANSWER   No.
QUESTION   Would you call yourself a stable person?
ANSWER   No.
QUESTION   An unstable person?
ANSWER   No.
QUESTION   You have never been married.
ANSWER   No.
QUESTION   Do you feel guilty toward anyone now alive?
ANSWER   No.
QUESTION   Toward anyone now dead?
ANSWER   Yes.
QUESTION   More than five people?
ANSWER   No.
QUESTION   Five.
ANSWER   No.
QUESTION   Three.
ANSWER   Yes.
QUESTION   You have promised not to talk to anyone about your assign-
            ment.
ANSWER   Yes.
QUESTION   Have you ever broken this promise?
ANSWER   Yes.
QUESTION   Would carrying out your confidential assignment pose any
            risk to you?
ANSWER   No.
QUESTION   Your daughter was born in New York.
ANSWER   No.
QUESTIONS   She was born in Düsseldorf.
ANSWER   Yes.
QUESTION   You have no loyalty to the bank you work for?

ANSWER	No.
QUESTION	Do you have an account at that bank?
ANSWER	Yes.
QUESTION	Do you have an account at another bank as well?
ANSWER	Yes.
QUESTION	You come from a Communist country.
ANSWER	No.
QUESTION	You come from a country that is now located on the other side of the Iron Curtain.
ANSWER	Yes.
QUESTION	In fleeing that country you have suffered losses.
ANSWER	... No.
QUESTION	You regret these losses.
ANSWER	No.
QUESTION	Would you betray the hospitality of the United States?
ANSWER	Yes.
QUESTION	Have you ever betrayed it?
ANSWER	No.
QUESTION	You have never been divorced?
ANSWER	No.
QUESTION	Are you suspicious of the practice of polygraphy?
ANSWER	Yes.
QUESTION	You consider the measurements from the so-called lie detector unreliable?
ANSWER	Yes.
QUESTION	Do you have the rest of the day off?
ANSWER	Yes.
QUESTION	All right, we're done.
ANSWER	No.
QUESTION	Would you prefer to take the sensors off yourself, or would you rather my colleague ...
ANSWER	Yes. No.
QUESTION	You don't have any questions.
ANSWER	No.
QUESTION	Usually, other people, they have questions, you know.
ANSWER	Yes.

QUESTION   They can hardly wait. But the results are still strictly con-
            fidential.
ANSWER   Yes.
QUESTION   In your case, I have permission to tell you your percentage
            of truthfulness. If you asked. A very cultured man, a real
            gentleman—French name, de Rosny...
ANSWER   Yes.
QUESTION   You are ninety percent truthful. That's confidential, of
            course.
ANSWER   No.
QUESTION   Yes. You're young, Mrs. Cresspahl, you still have lots of
            opportunities!

The man in the tunnel of the Ninety-Sixth Street subway station who always demands that the Jews get fucked has an opponent, who always crosses his graffiti out. Today the invitation has been forcefully restored.

And, please, who's writing "YOPA!" on the train cars, posters, electricity meters, and station pillars? What does it mean?

It's only quarter past eleven. The sun is making a cozy cave out of the garage on Ninety-Sixth Street. A policeman is there, questioning two employees, one white and one colored. They're sitting on a bench that's too narrow for two people, asses pressed uncomfortably together. The Negro doesn't look up. He lets the white answer. Only after being explicitly asked does he confirm the other man's statement, his eyes still on the floor: Yes, that's pretty much it, you could say that, mister, sir.

July 10, 1968 Wednesday

Now the Communist Parties of Bulgaria and Hungary have written to Prague too. (Romania is keeping out of it, apparently understanding the principle of noninterference in the exact same sense as the Soviet Union claims it applies with respect to its own affairs.) The letters are similar in content: all charge that the Czechoslovak Central Committee had not been sufficiently firm in dealing with the "revisionists" in its ranks, nor with the "counterrevolutionaries" outside the party, both of which groups were misusing the press, radio, and television to spread the truth about the past as well as the present. But Alexander Dubček, as well as Josef Smrkovský, do not wish to appear before a tribunal of their peers; they are more than happy to talk with individual partners. Meanwhile two Soviet regiments remain in the ČSSR, despite the maneuvers having ended on June 30. There weren't any repair facilities for their vehicles: they explain. They weren't given enough transport space on the railroads: they complain.

The blue workman's overalls Cresspahl borrowed from Johnny Schlegel were definitely clean—Inge had washed them. Cresspahl wore them for only a few hours a day. As if the half-day bath at Johnny's hadn't gotten him clean enough, he would often sit in a tub of water in the kitchen when we were out of the house.

– Well at least you've gotten him back from the Russians. Thank you: Marie says. – Congratulations, too, you deserve it. But this is you telling the story, it's not like you'll have the Red Army bring him back in a Mercedes with a motorcycle escort. Since he was innocent and all.

– He'd been sentenced.

– Release is a sentence.

– He wasn't sure of the exact words, and the numbers had only been read to him. But since there were three of them, it must have been paragraphs 6, 7, and 12 of §58.

– Under Soviet law?

– Soviet law. From 1927, partly.

– He was in England then, Gesine.

– And that's why the British had made him mayor of Jerichow; and maybe he'd betrayed something to the British about the Jerichow airfield before the Soviet commandant K. A. Pontiy arrived in all his glory. Up to three years deprivation of freedom per par. 6, Espionage.

– Paragraph 7?

– Sabotage against Business, Transportation, or Monetary Circulation, including to the benefit of earlier proprietors.

– If there was anyone in postwar Jerichow living like a . . . a movie star, Gesine, it was your man Pontiy.

– K. A. Pontiy hadn't changed his testimony. We tried to find him; by that point he was probably locked up in Krasnogorsk for the same paragraph.

– He really did interfere in Jerichow business.

– But Cresspahl did too. Hadn't he retroactively withdrawn, from the frozen accounts of the estate owners who'd fled, whatever he needed to borrow to pay municipal wages?

– And par. 12 punishes the fact of being locked up by the Soviets.

– No, par. 10 did that. Under par. 10 he faced imprisonment for having told them something about his life: Anti-Soviet Propaganda and Agitation. Under par. 12 he was charged with Failure to Denounce Counterrevolutionary Crimes. Six months minimum sentence.

– Robert Papenbrock.

– Or not reporting the visits from Emil Plath. The secret SPD. Or that he hadn't managed to pull together an official SPD in Jerichow himself, because Alfred Bienmüller thought it was ridiculous.

– But the Soviet commandant had forbidden the forming of political parties!

– Pontiy wasn't a witness in Schwerin. In Schwerin there was someone from the Soviet military police, with a machine gun strapped on him, and three judges in uniform. He could request others, by the way, if he thought these ones were biased.

– Well in that case he got out much too soon! According to just paragraph 6 and 12 he should have stayed in jail until October 1949.

– And if the punishment started on the day the sentence was pronounced it would have been till August 1952.

– You and he were lucky, Gesine.

– It was pure luck. Little Father Stalin abolished the death penalty, the "highest form of social defense," only in June 1947. As a rule, an SMT in Germany handed out twenty-five years in the labor camp. Releases from camps on Soviet-German soil started only in July '48. In August the Schwerin military tribunal sentenced a Rostock man named Gustav Cub and eight others to a total of 185 years in the labor camp for communication with a foreign news agency.

– Why was Cresspahl the exception, Gesine?

– That was his bad luck. It made people suspect him of having been given a little something for denouncing others.

– The people in Jerichow had known him since 1932! Since 1931!

– He hadn't been keeping tabs on the people in Jerichow. Today we think that the Soviets found out something about Cresspahl's news-gathering for the British in the war after all, and wanted to save him for possible use later.

– Since there was a par. 10, how could he ever tell you anything about Schwerin?

– He never did. It was probably eight years later, after I'd long since left Mecklenburg, that Jakob heard a word or two about it. He didn't have anyone else to talk to.

– Now he was scared. I'd have been too. Honest.

– He was sick, Marie. These water cures of his. . . . We had trouble keeping him from going to Town Hall to register that first night, with the official certification explaining his absence. The Cresspahl of the old days would've had the mayor come to him. The mayor now, for a change, was Berthold Knever—he'd risen higher than the postmaster Lichtwark ever did and become tentative and jittery under the burden of his new honor. Knever would've come as if following binding orders, with an uneasy conscience. If anything he was glad that Jakob had held the certificate up to him and asked for a ration card for Cresspahl without the necessary personal verification. Knever stood with his back to Jakob for quite a while, sighing; he was the first person in Jerichow to feel embarrassed at the return of his former superior. You know, when Jakob was telling a story he'd sometimes be overtaken by a laugh in his throat as if adding to his own amusement the pleasure he was giving his listener. It was easy to tell when Jakob was happy about something. Cresspahl was still worried he might have gone against regulations. As if rules were right simply because they'd been defined as what was right.

– Aftereffects of imprisonment.

– You are *not* allowed to read the books on the top shelf!

– I've read about that in *The New York Times*.

– It wasn't so bad that whenever I saw him, wherever he was in the house, he'd be sitting down. Meek and quiet, at Lisbeth's desk, at the kitchen table, on the milk stand. He still twitched when he walked and he hadn't minded letting Johnny and Inge see it, Axel Ohr was allowed to see how he'd gotten off the cart, but he didn't want me to see him like that.

– I would have been proud of him for that. As a daughter.

– His daughter was more nervous, until the limp went away. It was bad that he hadn't let Axel Ohr drive him down Town Street, Stalin Street, to let the citizens of Jerichow have a look—that we'd snuck in from the west on Cemetery Road and that for a while he stayed just a rumor. That he put Jakob off whenever he suggested in passing that they go into town. That sometimes as I sat doing my homework I could feel him looking at me as if he just couldn't get used to my profile softening along this line or that, around the eyes, that my hair was that smooth and straight and yet curled in a tiny wave above the braids. No one had ever stared at me like that.

– Someone has stared at me like that, Gesine. And I know who, too. But he wasn't being Mecklenburgish enough for you?

– I've learned it too now. This job of being a single parent.

– That's what I meant, Gesine. But you'd lost some respect for him?

– Not at all! I was embarrassed, nervous. Didn't talk to him without being asked. I was scared of having taken dancing lessons while he was in the camp, or maybe dead. Not to mention the reception I'd given Robert Papenbrock.

– What grade did he give you?

– Hanna Ohlerich had left very suddenly. Cresspahl didn't seem to care about that. I told him about it again, about what I'd said, I even resorted to lying. He nodded. I was breathing so hard that I had to turn away—he was staring so fixedly at me, in that new way of his. For Robert Papenbrock I had Jakob join me, as a witness, but in his telling Cresspahl's brother-in-law had left the house voluntarily after exchanging a few pleasantries about the weather. When Cresspahl learned the truth, he was almost glad. The dancing lessons: he thanked Mrs. Abs for those. He was on eggshells with Jakob; he seemed to feel he owed Jakob something it'd be hard to repay. As for my uptight behavior toward Brüshaver or Granny Papenbrock, he just abolished it. Brüshaver's mouth practically hung open when Cresspahl's daughter greeted him first, and deferentially. I was vindicated in my battle with Brüshaver over religion, and then I went to confirmation class on my own.

– So you passed.

– By the skin of my teeth. Cresspahl could talk to Jakob much more easily—Jakob was the more skillful doctor. I, on the other hand, brought up Alexander Paepcke's Aunt Françoise, the worthy old lady, who as a Mecklenburg MP had gotten the Althagen house released for her personal use; Cresspahl's daughter was afraid of what was to come, you see, and catching up on the past inevitably meant confronting losses. While Jakob, of course, had kept the pamphlet for the Mecklenburg parliament, first term, and updated it too: the MPs starting on page 64 had been neatly checked off if they still had a right to a seat, while others had had their biographies crossed out or their arrest by the NKVD indicated, their flight to West Berlin, to West Germany, their suicide. That's how Cresspahl learned a little something about the lay of the land he'd been released into.

– You were jealous of Jakob.

– I sat and listened, silently pleased. Anyone who talked like that wasn't planning to leave Jerichow for Schleswig-Holstein.

– But why did you stay! Cresspahl had friends in Hamburg, in England!

– He didn't have his Mecklenburg affairs in any kind of order yet. Of course he'd lost all his accumulated fixed or cash possessions while in service to the Soviets; for my sake he wanted to wait and see whether they'd honor my name in the land registry or confiscate the house too. He wasn't better; he would lock himself into the house for half a day whenever another wife came to visit this miraculous returnee to life from "Neubrandenburg" and asked for news of her son, her husband. Only one of his Hamburg friends had sent word, and that wasn't a friend, it was his old-time party comrade Eduard Tamms who needed a letter of absolution—they weren't done with denazification in Hamburg yet. He would never, ever work up the courage for England. That was where Mr. Smith had been killed in 1940 in a German air raid. No Arthur Salomon was alive there who might have put a word in for him; notification of his death had been sent out by the firm of Burse & Dunaway in 1946. And where else would he have wanted to go besides Richmond? The Richmond Town Hall had been damaged by German bombs. It's true that there was a hydraulic engineer in the British Sector of West Berlin to whom Cresspahl had once sold a dog with an excellent pedigree, and Gesine had run into him the previous summer on Village Road in Ahrenshoop, Cresspahl would be welcome to stay with him for a week. But he was too damaged for that.

– When was Cresspahl better?

– On the day when he managed to write a letter to Mr. Oskar Tannebaum, fur merchant, Stockholm, and thank him for a package. Written in one go. That was near the middle of June 1948.

– Now you all could leave.

– Now the Soviet Military Administration in Germany had shut down rail, car, and foot traffic between its zone and the Western ones.

July 11, 1968 Thursday

Alexander Dubček did call the two thousand Czechoslovak words disruptive, a reason for concern, and was far from subscribing to them; now the *Literaturnaya Gazeta* (place of pub.: Moscow) informs him what we should truly think of these words: If someone calls for public criticism, demonstrations, resolutions, strikes, and boycotts to bring down people who have misused power and caused public harm, this is, in direct language, a provocative, inflammatory program of action. It is counterrevolutionary. We can certainly hear the invitation to conceive of *literaturka* as revolutionary, especially in connection with the misuse of power.

At the end of the 1947–1948 school year the teachers at the Gneez Bridge School all agreed that they needed to keep an eye on Cresspahl, class 8-A-II. Only Miss Riepschläger, in the excusable carelessness of her youth, excluded herself from the others' cares. – Gesine has her father back, let her celebrate till she's blue in the face: Bettina said in her innocence. The older, more experienced pedagogues were perfectly willing to allow this for the first two days, a week at the outside, but it certainly was suspicious, wasn't it, if this transformation from a gloomy to an open, even confiding personality lasted longer than that. Frau Dr. Beese and Frau Dr. Weidling were constantly skirmishing over the psychological theories they had learned at different institutions at different times. Weidling resorted to dictation, which she gave with grammatical snippets, *titbits* (back-translation not out of vanity but for educational purposes). She was unaware that her voice, in the heat of the moment of elegant articulation, got rather bulgy, downright owlish in fact, so apart from five students the word *usually* took various fantastic forms, and those five all happened to be sitting around Cresspahl, although she hadn't been seen whispering. How could such a timid child suddenly put her graduation to high school at risk! Even worse: during the break Gabriel Manfras and Gesine went up to the board and openly (!) wrote what they'd heard—Gesine "usually," fine, and Gabriel "jugewelly," then he crossed her version out. The old Gesine would have pinched her lips, would have turned on her heel, stubborn and subdued. This one came running after Mrs. Weidling, pulling Manfras by the arm (!), and asked in a cheerful, friendly way for the correct spelling. *Now wouldja lookit that.* Dr. Beese asked if Cresspahl had gotten a demerit in the class book. No, there was no proof she had whispered the answer: Weidling replied, demoralized once more when she remembered how Schoolgirl Cresspahl had walked on with her, alone, and asking like an old friend if the Dr. got these titbits from British Broadcasting? She sometimes gave it a listen too. Was it conceivable—concluding a pact of silence with a child? Severity now as much as ever: Beese said dreamily.

Gesine simply felt like she'd woken up. All the dillydallying before a decision was gone, and whatever she did was right. She saw no reason why she shouldn't use a wooden briefcase as a satchel one day; she explained the rolling lid, the three compartments to anyone who asked (but not the secret compartment, or its place of manufacture, or its provenance from the personal effects room of a prison)—she was the daughter of a father who could make such a thing with his own hands, wasn't she? It was only right to share her confidence with Mrs. Weidling, if the teacher was going to reciprocate. (She regretted for rather a long time the sudden disappearance of the titbits from the lesson plan.) Even in Miss Pohl's class, her stalwart efforts and stubborn diligence had turned into willingness, thinking along as if enjoying it, delight at understanding; she kept her cool when Pohl slipped back into her earlier conception of pedagogical Eros and grumpily reproached her with comments like: Yes, Gesine, about time! or the one about two minutes before closing time; what she got for her pains was more likely to be a twinkle in Gesine's eye. Gesine not only had a B+ average in math now, almost all her grades qualified her for high school and she'd get permission because she now had a legally authorized head of household who could sign the application. (Jakob had gone to Jansen and started proceedings to be made legal guardian specifically because of Mrs. Abs's contested signature—now she could throw those papers right into the Gneez moat.) The future had arrived, and she'd been on time to meet it.

She was careful not to overdo it. She was one of the first in her class to show up at the office that Emil Knoop, in his inexhaustible patriotism, had cleared out and made available for the People's Referendum. When she got there Frau Dr. Beese was on duty, and since it was before the noon train it was just the two of them behind the windows that showed them one piece of Stalin Street after the next through crossed hammers on frosted glass. Gesine suddenly decided she could say something to Beese after all. Because constituting Germany as an "indivisible democratic republic" sounded fine to her, especially if there was going to be a "just peace" too, but she'd learned about elections a bit differently in school—not these ballot lists on open display and quizzing children aged fourteen and up about their preferences. She asked if this was another right way to do it. – I know your identity personally: Beese said grimly. She was missing lunch that day. Gesine mentioned being underage. – You just sign right there: Beese hissed, snide but somehow coaxing too, and the child realized that this might be important for her permission to attend high school. So she scrawled her name under German Unity, appeased her teacher with a curtsey, and skipped happily across the fluted tile floor of the enormous lobby onto Stalin's blistering hot white street.

Schoolgirl Cresspahl might have gotten her father back; did it entirely escape her what kind of father he now was? He certainly wasn't in much of a position to work, his earnings wouldn't even cover the school fees; but she acted as if she'd woken up, downright cheerful. The way things were seemed to be just fine with her.

Believe it or not, Cresspahl had been released with more obligations than just to register his new address. He was supposed to set up a wood-working facility with the machines that had been taken from him and manage it as a trustee. Even the telephone, previously seized as part of his business property, was reinstalled for him by technicians from Gneez in the interest of another business—the people's economy—and with the old number too: 209. Except the machines he'd driven into the drying shed of the brickyard in April 1945 weren't there anymore. From the carpenter's bench and disk sander down to the tiniest saws and clamps, they'd disappeared—and from right next to the Kommandatura, too, under the very noses of the Soviet military police, behind two-inch-thick doors and an untouched padlock. The room had been totally cleaned out. The noble Wendennych Twins stood there, nonplussed, with the itemized lists from the Schwerin SMT in hand, disgraced in front of this dispossessed German while a judgment from their very own army courts absolved him of this crime. Since they didn't believe in ghosts, for professional reasons, search teams from the Economic Commission started entering numerous workshops north of the Gneez-Bützow line in late May 1948, finding a dovetail jig in a carpenter's shop in Kröpelin, a crude-oil motor in the maritime boundary slaughterhouse in Wismar (now a people-owned ship-repair yard), and also some purchase agreements whose prehistories had a way of fading into obscurity just before reaching one Major Pontiy, one Lieut. Vassarion—business conducted at night, via handshake, sealed by insufficient written documentation. Cresspahl received furious letters from colleagues who at the time had paid in labor or goods for the equipment the Gneez prosecutor's office was now having hauled off to Jerichow. He seemed happy about the fact that the machines tracked down by mid-June weren't enough to reopen a business with, and he put up not the slightest resistance when the post office came to re-remove his telephone after half the brickworks burned down one humid Sunday morning. The honor of the Red Army blazed again in all its old glory; he'd been saved from having to manage anything. The Wendennych brothers had ordered the tardy fire brigade away from the more brightly burning main gate and into Cresspahl's yard so that it kept his daughter's house safe but was unable to save the future workshop. The prosecutor's office found enough molten metal in the rubble to satisfy them and declined to question Cresspahl after he'd had no choice but to refer them to the local commandants as the responsible parties. And what could he have said to their questions anyway? The commandants, nattily dressed and perfumed, came to see him with impeccable apologies and even accepted coffee, standing rigidly upright, after they had called his attention to the smoke in the air. The *People's Daily* reported the accident as an attack by unscrupulous elements opposed to world peace in the employ of the American imperialists; in Jerichow word went round about Cresspahl's experience with fires going back to November 1938; never again did the Twins pay a personal visit to Cresspahl, just as they consistently kept the Germans at a distance from their own residence and persons.

Gesine didn't mind. For one thing, she'd been in no danger from the fire since she'd been moved for the night from her room to Mrs. Abs's on the other side of the hall. For another thing, she wasn't seriously hoping for a return of the old days when Cresspahl would hoist a desk onto his shoulders, an oak top with two built-in stacks of drawers, and march that awkward monster straight through Jerichow to the exact spot in Dr. Kliefoth's study where what he'd ordered was supposed to be put. This Cresspahl was hardly up to supervising a workshop as a manager. She watched him in the yard earthing up potatoes—the ones that Jerichow's nimble fire brigade hadn't run over or trampled; he held the hoe stiffly, moved slowly, head hanging. There had been a time when he could make an interior door with nothing but an ax. He was here now. She didn't need everything all at once.

They were sitting one morning on the milk stand behind the house. Not only was there no school that day, she could sit next to Cresspahl for as long as she wanted to. Who cares if he didn't notice that the milk stand's uprights were rotting and needed shoring up. In the shade, wet with dew, the oldest cat was standing on stiff legs in the overgrown grass in front of them observing a blackbird chick that had fallen out of its nest, not fully fledged. The cat put down two legs in front of the others, not even bothering to sneak up. The screaming mother blackbird was in such a hurry that she dropped like a stone out of the tree, bouncing up already raising her head against the enemy, offering herself as a sacrifice, prepared to commit suicide. The cat gave her a sidelong look, gray and dispassionate, and stepped toward the chick, undeterred by the mother's shrieking. The cat would take care of the first one and then the second one. Gesine didn't know for sure if in earlier times she'd also have stood up and taken the dumbfounded cat away from its breakfast; now she came back with the predator under her arm, accepting the fact that the animal thought she'd lost her mind. She sat back down next to Cresspahl, keeping hold of the cat, which gradually realized it was being stroked but clung to its suspicion. What strange new customs were these? Then Gesine saw Cresspahl put down the stone he'd been about to throw at the cat himself.

Of all the arts these are the unprofitable ones, bringing in neither bread nor money. In the last week of June, Cresspahl's daughter saw how much trouble people could have with the money they'd set aside. Obediently, eagerly, she recited in school for Herr Dr. Kramritz certain things about the West German currency reform that he didn't believe and that she now felt uncomfortable saying: the surviving leaders of the Fascist war economy, aided and abetted by the leaders of the bourgeois parties and the Social

Democrats, were only interested in saving the rotting, crisis-ridden capitalist system—how stark a contrast with the currency reform in the Soviet
zone. But she was exempt from the chaos raging among the people of
Jerichow and Gneez starting on June 24, as was Cresspahl, and Mrs. Abs,
and Jakob too. In their four savings accounts they had a grand total of two
hundred and twenty-two marks after the devaluation; only Jakob and his
mother had the seventy marks per head that could be exchanged for certificates with glued-on coupons at the post office. But many people owned
greater sums, still worth a tenth of face value through June 27 and rather
risky above five thousand marks, hinting at arms deals or black market
business. Miss Pohl was observed storming up and down Stalin Street in
Gneez past emptied shopwindows; by Saturday she had a genuine antique
porcelain object from which punch might have been ladled were it intact,
and an electric heater beyond repair (trading folks were occasionally moved
to offer electrical appliances, given that the power had been cut off). Many
felt sorry for Leslie Danzmann, who'd tried to pay back Mrs. Lindsetter,
wife of the district court chief justice, the two hundred marks she'd borrowed a week before to buy a pound of butter—the worthy matriarch rejected
her offer and refused to come down to even two thousand marks in paper
money. Upon her humanity being appealed to, Mrs. Lindsetter avenged
herself with the cryptic decision: Yes, well, then there's no help for it, I'll
just see you in court, darling! Gabriel Manfras got a violin for Christmas
from the Sons of Johannes Schmidt Musikhaus—guaranteed and unsell-
able for decades—though he didn't know it yet. Mina Köpcke, alarmingly
inclined to the inner life and the exercise of religion ever since that nasty
fight with her husband over a gasworks manager by the name of Duvenspeck,
extended the range of her sentiments to the arts and acquired for a good
three thousand marks two genuine painted pictures (oil), one an early-
spring birch landscape with an overflowing stream in zigzag diagonals and
the other a stag with its head in a position suggesting embarrassment.
Pennies, five-pfennig pieces, and groschen were hard to come by, since they
retained their face value for the time being; it was seriously said about old
Mrs. Papenbrock that she'd rounded her bread prices *down*. The truth is
that she baked less than the minimum daily quota during these days and
Miss Senkpiel offered the rounding off—upward. Mrs. Papenbrock over-
came her disdain of her son-in-law for once and went to Cresspahl for

advice, because the balances in all of her accounts had been canceled the day before the proclamation of Order No. 111 of the SMA of Germany, and the sheepish gentlemen at the government bank hadn't cared to tell her why. Cresspahl assured her, though he didn't really believe it himself, that the Soviets confiscated assets only if the defendants were still alive, and spared her his opinion that she shouldn't even dream of Albert's release. Not that she failed to conveniently forget her offer to lend him the sum he needed to make up his per capita quota; with a gracefully raised double chin she turned around, almost exactly on the spot, and didn't shake his hand, content with the disappointment she'd predicted but for which she could never have found the right words. (This was the first time she'd been in the house since 1943.) Sunday had come and gone and money was still pursuing the Jerichowers with its useless offers; they were left to flop like fish on dry land. Everyone in the house felt bad for Jakob's mother, because the housing that Jakob had refused to consider after the war was now having its equity devalued only fivefold, which meant that the Abses would've had to make payments only until 1955, not 1966, for the property Mrs. Abs wanted merely so as not to have to welcome her husband back empty-handed. She knew she couldn't manage such a property—it was remembering Wilhelm Abs, his uncertain life on or under the earth of a Soviet camp, that she could bear only while sitting alone in her room, praying with unseeing eyes, unhelped by her tears. On Monday Cresspahl received two small packages in the mail containing paper money, payment for bills from 1943 and 1944, but he was not allowed to pay the thirty marks he had been short of his per capita quota after the deadline; Berthold Knever, now back behind the counter at the post office, found that the days passed a little more quickly during the currency reform, occasionally letting him think about something other than his troubles and exert a little authority over Cresspahl with a snippy tone, now no longer a dusky old parrot but one dusted with gray. Then Jakob turned up and gave him trouble aplenty; Jakob didn't shout at the mayor, he only had to look at him with his brooding, puzzled gaze and he got Cresspahl's certificates at once, with the coupons, without a receipt. Emil Knoop, unaware of any more pressing troubles, once again made sure he got the cut he felt he was entitled to, despite it taking a few private visits to the Soviet neighborhood in Gneez; his calculations, sweeping all before them, told him that the soldiers and noncoms must have spent almost all of their month's pay by this point, and the officers and employees of the Military Administration their biweekly salaries likewise, so, charitably, he planned to go in with them on their unrestricted exchange quotas for a mere 5, 4, or 3.5 percent fee. He came to regret his audition with the commandant brothers in Jerichow as a misstep, for when they threw him out onto the street he could expect only a denunciation, which meant a loss, of time if nothing else. Perspiring, a little on the overweight side by this point, he stood in the sun outside Cresspahl's house, again forgoing a visit to his "paternal role model." What did he have to be worried about? But nowhere and never in Jerichow or Gneez did those Western enemies of peace with their suitcases full of old currency turn up, and it was their evil machinations that supposedly justified the whole ass over teakettle in the first place. Cresspahl's daughter was spared all this. She didn't have to participate in the hubbub. They had nothing. They had nothing! In your mind, that can feel like a brisk, cheering wind.

Meanwhile, it wasn't only Mrs. Weidling and Mrs. Beese who were focused on the Western Sectors of Berlin, to which the SMAG was just then cutting off both rail and water connections—whose population they were no longer prepared to supply with potatoes or milk or electricity or medicine; there was a lot of talk about World War III and a little about the prospect that the Soviets might finally try to set up a trade with at least the British: West Berlin for the parts of Mecklenburg the British had gotten to first. The Cresspahl child was seen going to the Renaissance Cinema during these days, twice, for eight marks fifty each time, but hardly in that subdued and intimidated state so familiar—not to say consoling!—to a teacher's eye. She didn't even bite her lip anymore when she had no answer to a pedagogically well-founded question. She was granted promotion to high school, but what deplorable inconstancy of spirit this schoolgirl was remembered as having!

– And that, if you please, was the dividing of East and West Germany, Gesine! Marie says. It's not that she's homesick for one Germany. No, in the middle of West End Avenue, outside the entrance to the Mediterranean Swimming Club, what she cared about were the infamous Communists in Germany. – Now you couldn't get mad at the Soviets anymore! she says.

— It was the Western Allies who started it with currency conversion, you know.

— War was around the corner!

— In early July the Soviet authorities ordered the deployment of German troops under the new name KVP, the Barracked People's Police.

— Well, you had permission to go to high school.

— War was something I thought I could handle, Marie. I'd already been through one. No one had taken Mecklenburg away from me. I had gotten something else too.

— Did it last, Gesine? Did it last?

— Until September. When I came back from Johnny Schlegel's wheat.

— You see, Gesine?

— You mean, that it didn't last?

— Yes. Or are you trying to teach me the lesson that happiness lasts?

July 12, 1968 Friday

Freitag. Friday. Thirty-nine days to go. Not even six weeks.

Read the business section, Gesine! It's nine oh three—the workday has started. Consider the state of the pound sterling. Daydream about the Old Lady of Threadneedle Street, not *The New York Times*!

There's statistics too. The annual tally of major crimes has risen hereabouts, and those are only the reported ones. Car thefts are listed as plus 64.3 percent, robberies at plus 59.7 percent, murders were reported 20.3 percent more, rape sagged 6 percent. Yesterday a man in a black hat and dark glasses walked into the Woodbury branch of the Chemical Bank on Jericho Turnpike carrying a small vial of acid. . . .

The Communist Party of the Soviet Union responds yet again, with the voice of its *Truth*, to the two thousand Czechoslovakian words. As though anyone'd asked them. They claim to have no quarrel with the true objectives of the new crowd in Prague; Novotný may have committed errors and may have shortcomings, but like this, with "subversive activities from right-wing and anti-socialist forces," it is not pleased. The new crowd are trying, in *Pravda*'s view, "to blacken" their sister Communist Party "and discredit" it. That's happened before, too, they say—twelve years ago, in

Hungary. Is it not the case that the party *has* squandered some of its credit? Is it true that the party has kept its hands clean since 1948, innocent and pure as the driven snow for all these years?

Whatever Employee Cresspahl does, August 20 will come. She may go to the Atlantic shore again, open the windows another thirty times, buy Marie her fall and winter things, go to bed with D. E. whenever she feels like it—she will use another two tapes "for when you're dead," Marie needs to get her crayfish soup, maybe one more dream will stay with her past the point of waking up; she will be thoroughly and completely caught in the illusion of being alive. The truth is that she's sliding on the slippery ice of time toward the appointment de Rosny has made for her with Obchodný Banka. If she's allowed to go by boat she'll leave New York on August 12, by plane it'll be August 19. She has to start on Wednesday in Prague. There'll be someone to meet her at the airport. *Pravda* mentions Hungary. That sounds like tanks, doesn't it. What if they go in by air?

It is almost silent in Cresspahl's office. The telephone has been asleep since work started. The sound of Henri Gelliston's adding machine occasionally sloshes through the door. From immeasurably far below comes the yowl of a truck, now gossamer-thin. Alarm system damaged. Pedestrians will be approaching the source of the noise with apprehension, leaving it behind with indifference. Up here someone is writing a private letter—and you're going to regret it.

Dear Professor, it says, I hope you don't mind my writing to you, a friend gave me your address, and since I don't trust New York psychoanalysis, because of the proverbial label of headshrinker if nothing else, and since I'm aware that any diagnosis at a distance is necessarily a misdiagnosis, so don't even bother, she would still really like to know if she should consider herself psychologically disturbed, since she is facing a change in her life circumstances for professional reasons, all-encompassing enough to prompt her to draw up a will and take precautions in case her psychological condition proves dangerous, life story attached, what a lot you're handing over to someone else!

The handwriting alone. You're making large unbroken round shapes with long sharp descenders—what someone once called "tulip writing." If you look closer, you'll see that the letters may be fluid in their middle sections but the loops often aren't entirely completed according to specifications: hence, "open." The upstrokes as well as downstrokes are impoverished (simplified), especially the latter are little more than vertical slashes. Still, if one does think in terms of tulips, these are short ones, standing upright. It's a pronounced handwriting (not spoken pronunciation of course: distinct, inked, marked). What will someone else see in it, though? And what will he make of the fact that you're using black ink?

"... as for absurd actions in my life I'm only aware of the usual ones, including my reaction to the death of the man who was the father of my daughter. Fundamentally I think of myself as normal. The exception: I hear voices.

... don't know when it started. I assume: in my thirty-second year but I don't remember a particular reason it would have started. I don't want to. But it takes me back (sometimes almost completely) into past situations and I talk to the people from back then as I did back then. It takes place in my head without my directing it. Dead people, too, talk to me as if they're in the present. For instance criticizing me about how I'm raising my daughter (b. 1957). The dead don't persecute me—we can usually reach some kind of common ground in these imagined conversations. But are they imagined? Are they illusions? I also talk to dead people I know only by sight, who spoke only enough words to the child me when they were alive as were needed to say hello or give me some candy. Now they draw me into situations I wasn't there for, which I in no way could have grasped with an eight-year-old's or fourteen-year-old's mind. In other words, I hear myself speaking not only from the subjectively real (past) position but also from the position of a thirty-five-year-old subject today. Occasionally, when I hear them, my situation from back then as a fourteen-year-old child changes into that of the interlocutor of today, which I could hardly have occupied then. Many of these imaginary conversations (which seem real to me) are generated from insignificant triggers: a tone of voice, a characteristic emphasis, a hoarseness, an English word with the same roots as the Mecklenburg one. These scraps are enough to create the presence in my consciousness of a person from the past, their speech, and thus circumstances from long before I was born, such as March 1920 on my grandfather's leased estate when my mother was a child. I can hear my mother and the other people in the room not merely as an eavesdropper but with the knowledge that it all was intended for me—everything that, by the end of the imagined (?) scene, proves to have been bequeathed by the people of the past to me, the me of today.

With living people, present or absent, this tendency (?) of my consciousness can also be misused, I mean as a special ability. For example, I can reconstitute my daughter's thoughts from muscular particulars, even if she's not saying anything, and then respond to them (in my mind), even during our worst fights, although I have no proof that the 'transmission' reaches her. As a result, the child is rarely safe from me—she's kept under almost total surveillance. My only excuse is that I do this involuntarily.

It's not only with the child—in everyday conversations, in the office, on the subway, with coworkers or strangers, a second strand runs alongside whatever is actually said, in which the unsaid becomes perceptible, I mean what the other person doesn't say or just thinks. The volume of this second, imagined strand sometimes pushes to the periphery of my attention what I'm actually hearing in the moment, but it never totally drowns it out. Again I feel suspicious of this word 'imagination' here, because even though I absolutely don't count on the authenticity of what I hear only in my mind, it does often enough turn out to be correct, to be something I knew. It's possible that I'm foisting this second acoustic strand onto the person speaking just to give my own opinion an advantage, to corroborate myself—this doesn't seem likely, since I sometimes 'hear' the most horrible things from people whose sympathy I'm always desperate for. I do concede that as a general rule such sympathy may always contain its own negation, but I cannot concretely apply this rule to friends or even acquaintances.

It doesn't cause problems. The second audio reel doesn't paralyze the first, especially not when talking to anyone where there might be professional consequences if I opened myself up to criticism. When I try to tell my daughter about her grandfathers in Mecklenburg and Pommern, it sometimes happens that the interruptions of the dead make me pause, but no longer than the triangle a thorn might rip in a dress. (Or else the child, especially considerate for her not-yet-eleven years, conceals her shock and fear at these moments, allowing herself no physical, gestural reaction.) Such automatic interpositions of conversation do bring about a slightly distracted state, but I can get out of that state at will, considerably faster if the child calls me (but not when a car horn honks outside the window or something like that)—but when she does it's instant, immediate.

Is this a mental illness? Should I adjust my professional obligations accordingly? Does the child need to be protected from me?"

"They talk to me." You snitched.
You! Wherve you been?
Were you waiting?
Well, you dead are usually . . . .
Pretty chatty?
Usually there.
We've been busy.
Tell me.
We have nothing to say.
You never once told me: Here we all are! *And now no one even wants to talk to me.*
What business of ours is the future?
What . . . . (This isn't for me, Marie asked it:) What . . . lasts?
We do.

July 13, 1968 Saturday, South Ferry day

Dear Anita *Red Pigtails,*

First off, hello. Since you asked, I am writing to you yet again about our dealings with the man we call D. E., who paid you a visit the day before yesterday as Mr. Erichson, fringed asters in hand, just as we'd told him to.

If this is a life together, then it's one involving a certain distance: he on the flatter land beyond the Hudson, we on Riverside in New York City; a life together at intervals, each visiting the other for a day and a half at a time. Visits make for plenty of goodbyes, though, and entertaining hellos. Still, he's cautious and avoids springing surprises on us; even after we've made plans he'll call from the airport to check that we still want to see him after ten whole days. We reply that we're looking forward to it, and to news too. Because when this guy goes on a trip, he comes back having found something.

You're thinking: presents. Those too; and we've liked almost everything D. E.'s brought back from his trips. For Marie there was the ingenious revolving sphere showing the temperature in Fahrenheit and Celsius, the air pressure in millibars and millimeters, and the relative humidity too— she's been keeping a record of her observations since June and doesn't need *The New York Times* for her weather. Only during the first year with him did we suspect him of trying to get into our good graces with filthy lucre; now we have, both of us, come to know and like his overly casual, worried look as he tries to assure himself that he's thought about us accurately enough during his absence. (Since after all one of us assesses the air in the American manner, the other one stuck in her European habits.) Presents.

We're more interested in the other things. The moment of pleasure when the car from the air force of this country, dressed in civvies, drops him off outside our short yellow stump of a building exactly when he said it would, within five minutes. (He champions a kind of axiom whereby a person can manufacture punctuality. This doubly amuses us: first, because he manages to do it; second, that we're allowed to make fun of him for it.) What we've been waiting for is the phase right after the hug and the handshake, which I initiate by inviting, practically begging him: Tell us, tell us! And Marie has already clapped her hands and spoken in Mecklenburg Platt and shouted: *You tell such good lies!*

News. Where he was. What he's seen, what's happened to him. For instance, the Irishman in London whom the city government has stuck in the ground, alongside a lever in an elevator in the Underground, singing in his eternal night of a *Johnny, I hardly knew ye,* too slow but believably mournful, with pauses in which he inserts warnings to his middle-class cargo to please stand clear of the sliding doors. In D. E.'s report he's right here with us, with his curly mustache and undersized bass voice—we can hear him and want to go see him. Or the furious old hag in Berlin who screeched at him to leave the country for the peaks of the Urals because he was crossing a totally empty street in her country at a red light, the way one does in America, and he did look a little like a student, with his long hair. (Are people really like that in West Berlin, Anita?) We also believe his insatiability for news from us, about school, about the city. Did we put one over on Sister Magdalena with our skills in the *imparfait* of *connaître,* so that against her will and nature she had to write in the book the letter that points upward? What's new with Mrs. Agnolo, what did Eileen O'Brady tell us, has James Shuldiner been hounding us again with his pronouncements on the narrow benches at Gustafsson's? And then too: the dress you were wearing, the vegetables Anita has growing on her balcony, do you still see us next to the pot in which a certain Anita is boiling up displeasure at American policies in Southeast Asia? From the top, back to front, stem to stern, no ulterior motives. As though each of us, in our various locations, had lived a bit for the other, stored it up, and brought it back, in the interest of reciprocal delight.

You'll say that that's how things are only between people who. . . .

Yes. (There's one exception. We do leave one thing out. Just as I wish he worked for somebody else, he'd be happy to see me not take on an assignment that's looming before me. [Version for the mail censors.] It's not much help to know that he's sworn an oath, or for that matter that my obligation too comes from without, rather than being a project of my own devising the way it's supposed to work in the fairy tale of an unalienated life. We have to settle this with each other by listening right up to the border where advice would turn into instruction. We manage. Is there any reason for me to say out loud that civilian flights from Europe arrive in the evening, not the morning? He knows that I know. He could recite exactly what I don't like about these trips and I'd have to agree on the spot and confirm it and sign it too.)

So, I admit to having reservations. But I can't think of one that makes me unwilling to trust him.

He was in London (aside from the other business) to go to Moorfields Eye Hospital and complain about the fringed veils that, to his eye, streetlights have lately been wearing. At our breakfast table he threw a napkin over his shoulder as a white coat and turned himself into a British specialist and aristocrat, lisping with senile glee and salaried compassion as he tells us: It is to be feared, Mr. Erichson, sir, that this condition is a sign of advancing age. . . .

I can hear you say: If someone goes and admits to a strike against him, a physical ailment no less, instead of sticking to his strong suits. . . .

That's the way it is, Anita. He's not afraid to trust us with anything. We all laughed.

Here we have someone who refuses to try to change us. True, he'd be glad to abolish in our case this country's rule that employees get only two weeks' vacation in a whole year and not a single day for housekeeping; D. E.

would offer me machines that clean the laundry and dry it and put it on the table crisply ironed. But since this household does get by with the communal device in the basement of number 243, and moreover wants to see in person the fish and fruit it's spending its money on, D. E. can have only one of us this Saturday. When the other of us then suggests that he take the measure once more, by ferry, of all the water between the island of Manhattan and that of the Staaten General, she can take his careful nod as deliberate assent, no mere favor.

You see, Anita: I let him have the child. (With one limitation: only once were they allowed to fly on the plane without me—a superstition of mine. Which he respects.) The child goes with him. If Marie is inviting him then maybe she wants a chance to discuss with a man what seems incomprehensible and irrational about her mother; and I don't mind, I think she should, I'm not afraid. Their latest shared routine is one where the first person says (confident, despondent, pleading): *God knows.* And the other (gloating, or reassuring, or giving information, or saying "next, please"): *But he won't tell.* Optional addendum (portentously): *"Will he??"*

With him, you'd be playing this game too after a while. (It was Marie who brought this funny business home with her, from her strict religious school.) Here's what he had to say about you: Yeah, she's someone I'd go steal a horse with.

Marie has been known to forget the condition that she call home every two hours from wherever she is in the Greater New York area. When she's with D. E. the ring of the phone comes tinkling in on the dot, cf. axiom above. (Whatever could you be thinking, Anita? That they don't have pay phones on the harbor ferries?)

In the basement Mr. Shaks (many thanks for your postage stamps!) insisted on helping with the old-fashioned washing machine, and on a conversation. We were well equipped for one of those, between the terrible humidity in the air and, especially, Mrs. Bouton. What, you've never heard of Thelma Bouton? Works at a jewelry store on Forty-Second Street, corner of Fifth Avenue. Man comes in yesterday morning with a shoe box, locks the door behind him. She asks what he wants. He shows her his bread knife. Armed beggary. She whacks him over the head with her broom. Man, did the guy beat it! The whole time I was nervous, fidgety. When I got back to the apartment I knew why. It's no weather to be wearing jackets with pockets, D. E. left the house in a shirt and pants, and there, abandoned on the table, were two pipes, a tobacco pouch, and the poking implement. I truly felt sorry for him.

Now, Anita, you're thinking: That's the way a person feels only about someone they....

Yes. And when I crossed Broadway with my shopping cart (a "granny cart" they call it here), I missed him. For at the end of my rounds I stopped by Charlie's Good Eats to reward myself with an iced tea, and there I read what *The New York Times* had to say today about the difference between kosher caviar (from fish with scales) and caviar from lumpfish (merely spiny skin, not allowed). Third book of Moses, 11:9 and 10. Just to make sure I never forget what kind of city this is that we're trying to make our way in. As a further reminder, my gaze slips from the edge of the paper to the man sitting next to me, someone I know by sight. An old man, a looker-away-er, a stepper-aside-er, always holding his neck as if it's just been hit. One of the people they.... I thought: *A victim.* Unfortunately there is also the term: *to victimize.* His stare from the corner practically sliced off a piece of me, his attention drawn to my hand, to the *Times*, to my nose, what do I know; I promptly stood up from the stool and put on a show of suddenly not feeling well, for Charlie's hospitality's benefit. That was how things were, how desperately I wished I had someone with me walking down the steep street. Ninety-Sixth near us, you know, can look deserted on a hot early afternoon, with the only living thing left the TV set broadcasting the movements of tennis players from some basement.

At home I caught the first phone call. Marie had a win on points to report. The South Ferry, heading south, has Governors Island to port, and Marie was informing D. E. about the dirty rotten US Navy there.

ERICHSON (baffled): I thought it was just the Coast Guard stationed there.

CRESSPAHL (Socratically): And who does that gang report to?

ERICHSON (confident): The navy, and the president. But only in wartime.

CRESSPAHL (gently, not rubbing it in): Think about it. Vietnam. US Navy. Ships. Ship guns.

ERICHSON (embarrassed): This round goes to you, madam.

Second phone call: Marie has taken this gentleman—quite elderly, after all, almost forty; secretly afflicted with the time difference between Berlin and this Eastern Seaboard—she's taken this exhausted man along a pedestrian path away from the ferry terminal down Bay Street. Riverside Drive in the shade is 75 degrees Fahrenheit; there it must be almost ninety. The proposition is an honor, Marie rarely suggests it to me; will he know to appreciate it? Bay Street is a three-hour-long strip of dust with the brackish smell of the water between the piers and the warehouses wafting over it, lined with weather-beaten wooden structures—sheds, gas stations, decaying industry, and the little shacks promising beer in snaky blue or red neon. If you ask me, she's looking for an America that existed when my father was young. But it's true, when there's a wind there it comes in strong after a long sweep across the bay, and in the hazy distance there's a hint of the towers of the bridge over the Verrazano Narrows, a span of almost 4,300 feet, growing larger as you look.

Sir Doctor, in a walk with you / There's honor and instruction too: Marie sounds almost giddy in her latest location report. What happened was that D. E., near Stapleton, requested his companion make a short detour, just up Chestnut, and she granted him that privilege, since he'd invented some professional reasons for it. What they found there, though, on the corner of Tompkins Avenue, was the house in which Giuseppe Garibaldi waited from 1851 to 1853 for the chance to return to the Italian revolution, working for the time being as a candlemaker and famous only because of his housemate Antonio Meucci, who claimed to have invented the telephone before Alexander Graham Bell, a device like the one by means of which Marie casts a line of words across to the island of Manhattan. The only Garibaldi she'd known until then was the one poised in Washington Square in his *verdigris*...what's that in German? his green patina, with his saber firmly sheathed in its scabbard; Marie hasn't even been told that he draws and raises it every time a virgin walks past his feet; now you figure out how many times a day that'd be, Anita.

(In a city like this one, Anita, I've had to tell the ten-year-old child what else men want from women, as a precaution against one of them trying to force Marie to. She looked at me, glowering, disbelieving; held off asking questions until I was done, and then, with a kind of outrage, wanted me to confirm: You and D. E., you guys...you guys too? She didn't have the word for the deed; I'm planning to keep it from her for eight more years. Now how am I going to do that in New York City.) I got this far in my letter and

The earth had turned enough toward the sun that it received the false stains and colors and veils, beaming with poison, that show us each day the planet's end; at six thirty I received a dinner invitation. Can you guess what I asked in return when I accepted? That's right. What dress I should wear.

Now, Anita, you'll say: That's what you do for someone you want to. . . .

You got it. I was to wear the "yellow-and-blue raw silk" one, and I was to go find them so deep in old Brooklyn that I needed to search the city map and the subway map too. Way down in the BMT zone, let me tell you. There I found the two of them with Chinese people, in what was more like a private lounge than a restaurant, and D. E. seemed to have known them quite a bit longer than a day or two. (Since I keep various secrets to myself, how can I deny him his?) And as always happens when he's the host, the proprietors fuss around with *"che bella signorina," "carina,"* all with exclamation marks, this time in Chinese of course, if you'd care to translate it for yourself. And I received a hand on my hand, and a hand on my cheek, because what was I wearing over my "yellow-and-blue raw silk" dress? A men's jacket from Dublin with a tie folded in the breast pocket. And what lost items did I have with me in my briefcase? I'm sure you've already guessed, my sympathetic friend of the house.

You're saying: When a man, I mean, if he sees that kind of thing. . . .

And hears, Anita. Here's how it went:

– We chickened out. We took the bus from South Beach to Bay Ridge.

– Great weather for ironing.

– You'd rather be roaming around the desolate wasteland of Staten Island.

– Do you know what a fig tree on Staten Island shows? You're probably thinking: the time of year.

– On Ninety-Sixth and Broadway? At Charlie's? But he lives up in the Hundreds.

– Chopsticks for me. Are you gonna try to use chopsticks?

– Did the Germans . . . take care of him?

– It was a German woman.

– People live there who remember Italian grandparents!

– He's just hanging on more than living. Used to be German.

– *God knows why.*

– *But he won't tell, will he?*

– His name's de Catt.

– Tell us, tell us!

– *You tell such good lies.*

All the while the proprietors were sitting at the next table doing the same as we were. Passing a bowl or a spoon to someone—they or we, it made no difference. We felt at home there. A ten-year-old boy was standing watch over us through the crack of the kitchen door, with military severity, making sure that we treated his parents with the proper respect. Marie wanted to talk to him, but alas he let his dignity keep him from noticing her existence. D. E. would've loved to stay with the Chinese late into the night (if only to get the boy to join us at the table), but we invoked Mrs. Erichson so that he'd recall, along with his filial obligations, the mail sitting in New Jersey waiting to eat up his time. We did it out of concern for him. And when we said goodbye, outside the three garages under our building on Riverside Drive, one of the mechanics, the middle one, Ron the blabbermouth, let slip to D. E. that he could drive his car anywhere now, not to worry, it'd make it to San Francisco and, hell, kill two birds with one stone, Tokyo—for it seems that a lady came by the garage that afternoon and reminded them specially of the needed servicing and checkup. That's right. This very lady right here with the gentleman, if he wasn't mistaken, yes that seemed to be the one.

But the one who laughed last was D. E., heading west in his swanky Bentley. A silent laugh alone in the night. Because he knows what time I get into bed and what's waiting for me under the sheets. It is Král's *Guidebook Through the Čechoslovak Republic*, 1928. So that I can find my around there now, if the mood ever strikes me, duly noted, Anita. I'd get by with the help of J. Král, associate professor of geography at Charles University, Prague, because D. E. arranged it for me.

Dear Anita. That's how things are with us. Less than more than different between what I wanted at fifteen before I knew better. I'm thirty-five though.

July 14, 1968 Sunday

Auntie Times provides an editorial for anyone who can't avoid taking a trip abroad. Remember the neediest!

"Flowery July.

May is violets and June is roses, but offhand we don't think of July as a floral month at all. But it is, and perhaps we tend to forget because there are so many roadside blossoms.

The mints come to blossom now, from inconspicuous bugle-weed to royal bee balm that is such a lure for hummingbirds and bumblebees. Jewel-weed opens its pouchy yellow flowers and the spotted species is a favorite nectary for hummingbirds momentarily sated with bergamot. Hawkweed flourishes in unkempt pastures, deep orange and pale yellow, and black-eyed Susans add vivid accents to every patch of daisies.

Tall spires of great mullein open little yellow blossoms a few at a time, deliberate in bloom as they are in growth. Butter-and-eggs, the little wild snapdragons, are deep orange and clear yellow, and their big cousins, the turtle-heads, open grotesque mouths, white and pink and cream-pale yellow. The deep blue of harebells and great lobelia fade to lavender in tiny spiked lobelia and Indian tobacco.

July is so full of blossoms that the days can't hold them all. Evening primroses have to wait for late afternoon to open their brilliant yellow flowers."

© The New York Times

In memory, July of 1948, that summer, is Schoolgirl Cresspahl's last vacation, even though she did go to work in Johnny Schlegel's fields, which were parceled into giant rooms by hedges of hazel and hornbeam, blackthorn and hawthorn, dog rose, elder, and brambleberry. As we plowed at 250 feet above sea level, the rows of thorn blossoms tumbled down to the Baltic like waterfalls, later joined by the unambiguous black of the elderberries, the red of the roseships, the blue-black of blackthorn and brambleberry. It was a joyless vacation, for she was supposed to leave—leave Cresspahl and Jakob and Jerichow and Mecklenburg—but was supposed to like it. Could she live alone: that was what she was brooding on as she lay atop a cartload and looked down at the shining Lübeck Bay, over the hedgerows at the spires and chimneys of the city behind the haze of exhaust from Schlutup furnace works, at the boxy white dice-like buildings of Travemünde, at the contours of the Holstein coast to the north, the barber-poled lighthouse on the corner of Dahmeshöved, at the British zone, the West, the other side. She was anxious and happy to let Johnny distract her with his lecturing voice rising up from the depths—the *Lobelia inflata* in the pond in the yard also thrived on the Mississippi, was officinal, and its real name was Indian tobacco. He was trying to whet my appetite so that I'd say: Yes, send me away from you all.

Johnny was embarrassed around me too, as were almost all the adults on the farm. His cooperative now had a stud stallion and in late July a mare had been brought for mating, and Cresspahl's daughter had watched, unnoticed by Johnny, who would surely have diverted her attention away from the proceedings. That night, when he thought I was off at the children's home, I heard him raging like he wanted to rip the nose off Axel Ohr's face; but Axel had an alibi, at the children's home. "The child! How could you let the child!" But it didn't do me any harm at all. I did think it was too bad that people treated the two horses like such animals. Before the mare's hind legs staggered under the stallion's leap she turned her head to us for a moment, as if asking us if she could leave. And I'd have wanted to leave the two animals with each other, instead of immediately leading the distraught timid mare away. Now I was supposed to be forbidden to look. Even a year ago no one had cared when I reported that one of the black pied cattle was in heat. Now I was a child. But supposed to make a decision like an adult.

– But you're a big girl now: they said encouragingly. And I was! And I only laughed at Hanna's package from Neustadt, which included along with the tea and tobacco not a single piece of girl's clothing, though it did have a shirt that fit Jakob like it was tailored. Because I thought I knew how love worked better than her now, ever since I'd seen the engagement notice from Anne-Dörte in Holstein standing on the radio, done in style, on card stock, with a count's crown. My heart was pounding in my throat as I asked Inge Schlegel why the card hadn't been forwarded to Jakob. – She's gonna have to write to him by hand: she said, turning away, and that was good, because blood had surged into my face. So that was why Jakob didn't come even once that summer to the farm where Anne-Dörte had been. Thus love was a misfortune. The one you want isn't enough for you, the one who should come prefers to stay away, and anyone who's seen the course of it calls it cause for mourning. As for me, I was supposed to do without Jakob completely. And on top of that, I was prevented from telling anyone my secret.

It was because of the threat of war. Here too I wasn't a child, when they came to me with talk of the Soviet blockade against the Western Berlin sectors and the assurance that the divided Allies were in conflict elsewhere too about the final distribution of their war booty, just look at the Greek civil war, Gesine! There's the Bulgarian and Albanian attacks, the Truman Doctrine, *containment*—it's you who need to splain that to us, Gesine. And the Soviet Union doesn't have any atom bombs, get that through your head, Gesine. But she refused to see why she in particular should be taken out of it just because she could be. And there were so many times that she heard, in a grown-up tone of voice, unspoken: A child can hardly be expected to understand that; then she balked.

There were moments when I was convinced. One July morning we were standing on a hill behind the Countess Woods, Johnny with a watch in his hand, because it was going to happen at six o'clock sharp. The Red Army had posted notices asking the Jerichowers to open all their windows, including the ones facing south, and that applied to Rande too; Johnny's farm was behind a high furrow in the land, protected from the shock wave. We were about 250 feet above sea level and we could see Wohlenberg Cove, behind which the St. Mary's Church spire hinted how deeply Wismar Bay penetrated into the mainland; the spire at the end of Kirchsee on Poel Island was clearly visible; behind it the land rose up in arches of forested domes and hills into the pure brisk sunlight. All this I was supposed to give up. Since we'd lost sight of Jerichow, I thought, at a heartbeat after six, that it wasn't going to happen, then the first blast went off. The force of the succeeding explosions may have fooled me but I was sure that the earth had shaken and would knock us off our feet at the next blast. But everyone thought they'd felt the tremors. The first cloud of smoke appeared in the long silence—a cauliflower trailing a stem as it rose into the sky. As the whitish mushroom started upending its edges, the next one rose alongside it, and by the time the first had been gouged by the sea wind, there were four. It was in the middle of the harvest but that afternoon Johnny took me with him to what had once been Mariengabe Airfield. It was fenced off with a hundred-meter buffer, but even from a distance we could tell that the whole facility was gone, the buildings flattened, the runways chains of holes. It wouldn't be easy to rebuild that.

And it wasn't rebuilt—German forced laborers chopped it up by hand, the pieces were picked up and driven off, and Johnny showed me: the airfield had been located too close to the "future front line," the border between the Soviet and Western zones; it would have been in artillery range. And now that the British were starting to supply West Berlin by air, why would the Soviets leave them such a superb emergency landing place? Then it was me who was clever, and I countered with how popular the Soviets could have made themselves among the refugees if they'd given them the barracks as living space. He had an easy time disposing of that one: if they'd risked angering the Germans over it, just think how compelling their military reasons must have been! No, seriously, the Russian is seriously underestimated when it comes to tactics, even more so about strategy. I tried one more time with the Border Police Department that the Soviets had set up in June. For Johnny that was one more piece of evidence in his favor. "The Russian" was preparing for a war: he was arming his German allies. I should get out of here.

And things would be different than they were in "the villa." This was the vacation home that back in the Kaiser's time a Hamburg real-estate agent had had built on the cliff behind Schlegel's copse of trees—a shrunken miniature castle with too many windows and an actual tower. It had been allocated to the Protestant Homeland Mission as a children's home, which Cresspahl's daughter used to visit, for Axel Ohr's sake, so he could come too without it looking like he was in love with a certain Elisabeth from Güstrow, he, Axel Ohr! The children had a strict time of it there. What the churchly caregiver ladies demanded in terms of proper behavior at the table and at recess was enough to totally spoil anyone's appetite and the fun. Though anyone sick was treated with a certain tenderness. Almost every day these children ate soup made from pigweed, with noodles added, but it agreed with them, and by the end of those four weeks almost all had gained weight. Earlier Johnny had augmented their fare with groats and meat, as his business dealings and delivery targets allowed; the new lady in charge of the home had taken offense at a "blasphemous" remark of Johnny's, and Johnny had taken offense at that in turn. That's how Johnny was—if someone talked nonsense at him they were dead to him, whether or not children got hurt in the process. (Anyway, they'd be getting CARE packages, his conscience was clear.) Many of these children hadn't ever been to look at the sea, and on the last day of their stay they collected beach sand for the mothers who wanted to be able to scour again. And all this constant praying and the devotional hours! Johnny admitted it: There would probably be religion and religious practices to spare in England. But if I clenched my teeth, pulled myself together, was a big girl....

I sometimes pictured myself in an English boarding school. It was in the countryside, far from any train station so I'd be caught in time if I tried to escape. The whole day divided up with no recourse; one hour of free time. I could only imagine the teachers as unforgiving ladies, so sparing with praise or recognition, in word or look, that I wouldn't get any. I would never be alone—in the dorms, in the giant dining halls, in my free time— and would always be alone. In England, too, food was rationed, but even if the Brits had closed Cresspahl's account at the Richmond Bank of Surrey they would still allow a *ration card* for his daughter. Enough for pocket money. Waiting for the post. School uniform. Permission to leave for the day. Hours and half hours punctuated by the tolling of the church bell: chiming the foreignness through the sleepless night. Practicing the "th" over and over in front of the mirror, tongue between the teeth! then forgetting the tongue between the teeth. The bustle of *cricket* on a blazing field of grass, and me in the middle as the German child, the Fascist child, she deserves it, never getting visitors, in her third year already.

– Were your reasons good enough for Cresspahl?

– He never let me get as far as my reasons. After a whole summer. He looked at me and nodded, and I was scared. Now I wished I had another day to think it over after all.

– It would've been better for you: Marie says, this fearless child who howls with homesickness on her first night of summer camp. Look at her, coolly lying on the grass in this hot humid garden; look how she hides her fear in a squint of her eyes.

– It would've been better for Cresspahl. So now I'd done him wrong, and I'd been a coward.

– I'm a coward too, Gesine. I don't like being without you either. Just because I think you care about me.

July 15, 1968 Monday

The Soviet Union, via *Pravda*, gives us the truth: how puzzled it is by the West's "morbid interest" in its war games in the North Atlantic. It complains about NATO reconnaissance planes in the exercise area and the presence of a British destroyer. Therefore, anyone who couldn't care less what Soviet warships are doing there with their Polish and East German pact mates must be healthy.

The Soviets have halted the withdrawal of their troops from Czechoslovakia. Since yesterday they've been meeting in Warsaw with their Polish, East German, Hungarian, and Bulgarian friends, about and without the ČSSR, and now that the official organ of the press has stated that "a decided rebuff to the forces of reaction and imperialist maneuvers" in that country "is of vital interest," de Rosny might as well give up. On the contrary, though, he sticks with Tito, according to whom no one in the Soviet Union could possibly be so "shortsighted" as to use force against the Czechs and Slovaks. De Rosny is a Titoist.

We were all required to be very mad at Tito. Immediately upon our official matriculation at Fritz Reuter High School this was presented to us as one of our main occupations, and that fall we often marched through Gneez to City Hall in a column of four hundred students, with banners on which we demanded Tito's overthrow, maybe adding a musical number about Spain's heaven that spreads its brightest stars above our trenches. There was no mention of the cold in that song, but now I get cold when I think of the word *Spain*. We had to stand in the cold for a long time until the market square was filled with columns of demonstrators (the ones from the Panzenhagen Sawmill were always late) and the three people on the City Hall balcony could begin their speeches. Whenever one was finished, we shouted our grievances against Tito in chorus, and I would have been glad to be as enthusiastic as Lise Wollenberg, who just that morning in Contemporary Studies had given me a wink while reciting Comrade Stalin's five criticisms of Tito, one of which (the false priority of agriculture) I'd had to whisper to her. Since she was my friend.

That's what she called me. When two girls have spent whole years of schooldays on the train for an hour, and walking to the station too, they'll eventually either ride in the same compartment on good terms or in separate ones on bad. The Cresspahl girl didn't have the courage for an open feud at that point. She and Wollenberg had been almost the only ones to find themselves reunited in the waiting room that ninth grade turned out to be, and Lise was many teachers' favorite—blond as she was, shyly girlish as she knew how to look at dangerous moments, jokily confidential when sucking up was called for. Cresspahl would have found it hard to say exactly what bothered her about Wollenberg. In the end, she secretly thought that this Yugoslav might know the economic situation in his own country more precisely than the wise Leader of Peoples in the far-off Kremlin, but still she called him the Marshal of Traitors on demand—we all lied, to please our elders. Lise exaggerated it, maybe, in the way she looked around her, a tolerant smile on her gentle lips, as though trying to tell us, tempt us: It won't hurt our grades . . . it's just a joke . . . we're just tricking Kramritz . . . it doesn't really matter. . . .

The mistake was sealed when we picked a desk together in 9-A-II. That keeps you together even when you're pursuing other interests. She remained at my side while the boys in the upper grades checked out us girls in ninth grade for our suitability, taking our willingness for granted. Breaks between classes were like a marketplace. But one time it was just me, alone, who was asked to step aside with messieurs Sieboldt and Gollantz, eleventh grade, wearing long pants already. These gentlemen wanted to know what the people in Jerichow thought about blowing up the barracks and potential refugee housing. I had barely drawn breath, blushing with the honor I'd received, when Lise started gushing: Oh, the clouds from the explosions were like parachutes rising up from the ground, now she had a better sense of what atomic bombs must be like . . . word for word what *I* had told *her*. Sieboldt and Gollantz left at once. Lise answered my protest by saying they'd been asking her, and anyway, what difference did a word make? Gollantz did take me aside one more time, alone; he wanted to talk about the election of a class representative for the student government, headed by Sieboldt. Unfortunately I told Lise. She was only annoyed that the gentlemen hadn't approached her. She consoled herself in that grown-up way she sometimes had: Ah, well, they graduate two years before we do, where would that've left us. (Us.)

She probably realized how pretty it looked when she tossed her long blond curls next to another girl trying to keep her dark braids still, and so Wollenberg stuck with Cresspahl when she got invited to go for a walk or to the movies; she accepted for both of us. Up came Gabriel Manfras, stranded in 9-A-I; up came Pius Pagenkopf, Dieter Lockenvitz ... and she'd already sworn that we were inseparable so I had to tag along like a chaperone. Sometimes I looked at her from the side when a bright scene was projected on-screen—hordes of horsemen thundering across the steppe to retrieve stupid Zukhra for noble Takhir—and she was cheering for the extras at the top of her lungs along with everyone else around us, the same as for the extras in *Kolberg* in April 1945, portraying the Final Germany Victory. She could get so carried away. She lived entirely in the present moment. At the performance of *Noah's Flood* by Ernst Barlach, I felt lots of people staring at us and at Lise's rapt intensity, so pensive, so poignant; during the intermission she could hardly control herself, she was giggling so hard over Mrs. Lindsetter, wife of the district court chief justice, who had fallen asleep and whose wheezing during the performance had not impressed Lise one bit.

With the boys she acted sarcastic and snippy to the point of total indecipherability. They had to talk seriously with the third party, me; even Manfras, who never talked much, suddenly had quite a lot to say about interior end moraines as exemplified by Gneez Lake. With almost every one of these boys I managed to beat a retreat under some plausible pretext. The next day Gabriel Manfras was even more introspective than usual. Pius Pagenkopf, tall, dark, and the oldest in the class, kept his head bent low over his notebooks for days after his time alone with Lise, so that he'd be sure to avoid catching sight of her. Lockenvitz, the shy, lanky, glasses-wearing top of the class, slumped to Cs in several subjects after declaring himself to Lise. And in early November, when new personal IDs were to be issued to everyone over fifteen, all three of these boys, separately, took me aside in secret and asked me to sneak a spare print when I went to Stellmann's with Lise. I told her. She laughed, deep in her throat, amused; she giggled getting herself ready for the occasion. A lot of sweet encouragement found its way into that passport photo. She gave me one, which I let Pius have. But one time Lockenvitz dropped something from his wallet— it was a passport photo of Lise Wollenberg, and before her very eyes he slipped it into his jacket at just the place where his heart lived and worked; she burst out laughing, flinging her head high like a colt. Manfras was said to have her standing on his dresser at home in 8 x 10 format, and not an enlargement of the passport photo either. One day, Pius Pagenkopf, walking by the first row, took Lise's ID picture out of his shirt pocket, tore it up, and threw the scraps onto her desk. She smiled quite happily and later asked him if he wanted another one. What was I supposed to say when she told me she acted that way because the boys were "so silly"? Neither Pagenkopf nor Lockenvitz was silly; no one would ever say Gabriel was.

We all wanted Pius as our class representative, and he would have been chosen if only Lise had kept her mouth shut about a kind of boy who was more serious, able to defend us in storm and tempest; Pius furrowed his dark eyebrows, like someone with a toothache, and crossed the name Pagenkopf off the list. Lise was by no means left speechless and started nagging Lockenvitz. He resisted for a while—he was a refugee and would have a hard time of it with the locals—but he put his name up for her sake and was elected on the third ballot. He would have to atone for that for a long time, because in December, when student self-government was banned, the members of the Free German Youth (FDJ) chose him as the head of our class group—he'd been our representative, after all. We'd get a day off and he'd have to go to meetings of the Central School Group Authority (ZSGL), where he found himself reunited with Sieboldt and Gollantz. We didn't unfold the notes he sent Lise during class, he was huffy enough already; he saw her laugh out loud as if overjoyed, but he got embarrassed, so we were mad at him. Once she sent a piece of paper to him—there was nothing written on it. Lockenvitz was being silly, he let his wistful gaze rest on me for a while (and he owned a passport picture of me. I'd given exactly one print away, to Lise). She arranged it so that a passage in our 1949 Class Day newspaper affirmed that Lockenvitz, friend to youth, loved em all, he didn't care, / loved all women, dark or fair.

"Us." She and I were supposed to put our names down together for the Society for the Study of Soviet Culture, which later become the German-Soviet Friendship Society. Dr. Kramritz had mentioned the benefits and advantages of "societal activities"; this was one of the less taxing ones. There was no doubt that Mr. Wollenberg had advised his daughter to join—he wanted to secure other flanks besides the one facing the LDPD; Cresspahl, who really could have used the extra protection, advised his not to. As a well-nigh British schoolchild, I was on the British side anyway and cursed them soundly when they crashed a Berlin Airlift plane near us and had to go to the Schönberg hospital. To make Lise, all by herself, step up to a desk with a stranger sitting behind it—I thought it couldn't happen to a better person. I'd gone with her as far as the door just to humor her.

But Jakob didn't think it was a good idea to let this Lise know about my aversion to Soviet culture, my profound dislike of it; he turned his head slowly back and forth. His categorical headshake. I grasped the damage I'd done only after he suggested: Keep on her good side.

For Jakob, I forced myself to thank Lise when she gave me a dress, now that she was getting more fashionable ones from the new government stores. Anyway, Jakob's mother was glad to see me dressed properly under my black coat; Cresspahl, like Jakob, looked me in the face or would notice the slightest scratch on my hand but worn collars were somehow invisible to them. That Lise was trying to spruce me up like a shabby backdrop really was too much, but I was spared an open breach because after the Christmas break Heinz Wollenberg at last decided it was beneath a businessman's dignity to send his daughter on the cold and dirty train twice a day; for people like Wollenberg the Gneez housing office could find a room for Lise at "a relative's." Besides, the ration cards had by that point been declared valid only at their place of issue; in Gneez there was often sugar or fire starters when there weren't any in Jerichow; Lise could bring some home on the weekends.

Now that we had different routes to school, I had to sit somewhere else in the classroom. When we saw each other only during the schoolday, I could march a few rows behind her and watch her from afar. There she was, swinging her legs in the air and zealously belting out the FDJ songs: "You HAVE a goal in si-ight / that GUIDES you through the world! ....."; there she was, hopping around merrily shouting the slogan against the Greek government, or the celebrations of Mao's victory in Suzhou, or the songs of hate toward that renegade Tito. We had grown apart.

She had a goal in sight; today she's a tax adviser in the Sauerland, West Germany. That dress from her, green organza with large polka dots, would have looked good on me on that Class Day, or for birthdays—but I only tried it on.

July 16, 1968 Tuesday

The worst part is that the bosses do it without warning. And then someone's standing exposed at the podium in the staff cafeteria, under the eyes of four hundred people, maybe in a suit that clashes with the yellow walls, but they have to keep quiet and act like they've completely risen to the dignity of the occasion. The ceremony is ridiculous but in the moment it does take your breath away—everyone acting reverent, following the lead of the CEO standing stiff as a board across from the person, trying to seem taller than he really is, and disgorging a speech of praise so tensely that the victim feels spat upon. This is one of the occasions de Rosny has set up especially for the titular head of the company so that he can feel like he's doing something. An unlucky victim may find herself on that day dressed to match the criss-crossed American flags on display behind the CEO; and some people have even made the mistake of wearing sandals.

Anyone whose number has come up would love to have slipped out for a haircut during lunch, but it takes you by surprise. It can happen on any workday of the year, so you half forget about it; this is why we have to submit our vacation requests six weeks in advance, though. Anyway, if you reflect on how ardent your work for this bank is, why would you be afraid of such a distinction. On top of that, participation in the event is considered voluntary, so some of the victims go just to show how devoted they are to the firm. All employees have to neatly initial a form to attest their atten-dance at the morning's events; anyone who dares can be free and out on the street by four. Employee Cresspahl has a sense of what's waiting for her outside—the cars are standing on Third Avenue with their hoods open because the engine coolant is boiling; how she'd love to get through the muggy heat of this afternoon in a less crowded train car, before rush hour. But no, she has a visitor.

– Give it up, de Rosny, sir: she says. It has turned into a game between her and her boss, ever since he's recently started making use of her and her office "for tea." He demonstrates the growth of the Czechoslovakian loan to her; today she's refuted him with the Warsaw communiqué announcing a severe letter to the leadership of the ČSSR from their comrades in the struggle. And where are these "aggressive imperialist forces" with their "subversive actions" going to go if not hell in a handbasket, assuming the central committee in Prague decides to show a little backbone before the thrones of brothers instead of bowing meekly? Now they're wanting to rewrite the terms of the Warsaw Pact to give every member country its turn as the supreme commander and put a stop to the political misuse of the alliance. That's got to be the end of the line, a bridge too far for the Soviets. De Rosny tilts his head at this and narrows his eyes in a way expressing doubt, as though he knew something more reliable than that, but in so doing he notices his wristwatch. – Should we go downstairs again? he says, urgent like a schoolboy suggesting they cut school. – Take another look at the big production?

He's allowed to call it that—he invented it. Employee Cresspahl is well and truly annoyed at the loss of a whole hour of time, but she doesn't want to give him any leverage by being impolite; she's already been led past all the possible escape routes (stairs, ladies' rooms) and is now sitting in the second row, in front of the podium, cut off from the aisle by de Rosny, who has one leg bent over the other at an angle as sharp as a stork's. Surrounded by his young men, Carmody and Gelliston, he can carry on a perfectly uninhibited conversation with his "young student." She feels the assembled gazes of the staff on her and remembers the other names people in the bank refer to her by; in sudden fury she decides that de Rosny's white double mane is a wig, or at least dyed bluish to match his eyes. De Rosny is pontificating. "We" are not aggressive, "we" are not subversive, "we" are going to teach "our" West German friends to hold their tongues so that "we" and "our" friends in England, in Denmark, won't get mad at a bungled deal. And what does Mrs. Cresspahl think about the Communists in Romania? They've come out against interference in Czechoslovak matters, haven't they, just like Tito? She's almost grateful when the dribble of music falls silent, making him do the same. The chairman is already standing on his platform and has cleared his throat several times. De Rosny feels compelled to whisper to his "young friend": Next time we'll use a curtain for this production!

The performance begins with an oration by the titular president. Mrs. Cresspahl has seen him so many times since the ceremony in which poor Gwendolyn Bates got a silver slap in the face for her excess zeal, and still she can't keep enough of R. W. T. Wutheridge in her mind for her to remember him, even as a still picture. "Rustic" they like to call him. But he must be one of those meek peasants, humble, awkward, following in his ancestors' footsteps, so fearful does he appear to her; his tailored suit looks too short on his little old body; seventy years have taken some of this blue-cheeked man's hair but have given him no dignity in return. The program: First he gives a speech to his own taste. Back then it was the team spirit and what America wants from us; this time it's the same thing, plus he wishes us well. Then the candidates are called up, they mount the carpet-covered wooden box and have to listen to a description of their services eye-to-eye with the Most Senior Spokesman. These speeches are written in de Rosny's office, though, which is why the openings always seethe with distinctions:

It is truly difficult to find the right words . . .

Let the presentation of this award set a precedent in every respect . . .

Not a single member of this firm, to my knowledge, has . . .

It must have been twenty-five years ago that . . .

One is unusually young; or she's already helped conquer Arizona, "her shield on her back, without laying it aside"; or his family has been working in the banking business for three generations. That's how Mr. Kennicott II is dispatched, another forgettable one. Now he performs an endless series of small bows, since "he will always be among the victors," in the personnel department of all places, while the laudatio's last sentence informs him that "he will be leaving us next year"; here de Rosny's sidelong look is meant to remind his "young assistant" of something, was it the white pumps in a desk drawer? is he trying to make amends? Now it's a young black woman's turn, whom we've often noticed in the elevator—her large eyes full of desperation and forgiveness, her motherly demeanor toward the pink-skinned men—now she is identified as Blandine Roy and praised for her accomplishments in the mail room; we recall the serious problems there've been, only in the interoffice mail, and so here they're honoring none other than a token black woman; we are all relieved along with her when she's allowed to climb back down from the stage and disappear into her seat. After her, Amanda Williams's name is called, giving her a nasty shock and prompting an angry look at Naomi sitting next to her. Because the aspirant is supposed to remain unsuspecting, and that means the bosses use an officemate or friend to tail the victim all day and make sure that they show up to the celebratory occasion. Now Amanda, before all our eyes, has to hear herself called lightning-sharp, but modest, and her candor makes the firm trust her commitment all the more. Suddenly Amanda looks awkward in her thin, washable dress, a yellow flower pattern that matches the walls; in her embarrassment she reaches her arm out to the CEO, so that he has to step over to shake her hand; but for the first time the whole auditorium claps, everyone is happy for her, and as Amanda returns to Naomi's side she is already giving her a forgiving smile, realizing what these five hundred dollars will be useful for, given her pregnancy. The next name announced is a new one, never before pronounced like that in this building, with a North German articulation: Mrs. Ge'sine Cress'pahl!

– Trick number 18!: Mrs. Cresspahl tells her daughter in the lobby of one of the fancy old movie theaters on Broadway, where they've taken refuge from the muggy blasts of heat on the street. They cared more about the air conditioning than either of the movies anyway, but Mrs. Cresspahl has a hard time thinking about anything but her public exhibition; she is almost unhappy with Marie's indifferent answers. Unfortunately, Marie is anything but outraged.

– What do you expect from de Rosny: she says.

– He pulled a fast one on me!

– To be dragged along somewhere by de Rosny his very own self is really like the English court. Dubbed a knight or something.

– And when I was standing up there he raised his miserable paper cup of his miserable tea to me like he was toasting!

– He was happy for you, Gesine.

– Until now people knew my name if they needed to know it, or if I told them. Now the whole staff knows it. And the speech is going to show up on everyone's desk on Friday, from the in-house print shop!

– Gesine, I don't like getting prizes in school either, but I need them. I'm standing all alone in the cathedral and wish I could run away.

– But you're trapped, by people and folding chairs, and the confinement makes you anxious.

– Right. Because folding chairs are handy for throwing.

– And for beating a person with.

– All you have to do is stand up straight for a while and keep your belly sucked in—

– Right.

– And breathe deeply and think about anything but your hair, which maybe isn't tied properly, and the next breath you take will make it come loose—

– I managed not to raise my hand to feel it!

– Then there's the president's medal and a check for more than eight hundred dollars.

– But everything they said about me was a lie!

– For you to hide behind.

– "Her studies at European and American universities." Two semesters in Saxony and a little economics at Columbia!

– De Rosny needs an educated assistant for his business, right?

– "Her origins in the Communist sphere have contributed decisively..."

– I was there for that, Gesine. They did.

– "to our ability to abandon our passive position in the Eastern European credit business."

– That was the official announcement. Now it's happening. We're on our way to Prague.

– And then I couldn't get away from the cold buffet afterward either, you know. Champagne and zakuski.

– You'd have expected an apology from me.

– Sowwy, Marie.

– Still, everyone could see that your suit's from Rome. It must have looked great on you there too.

– *Thank you very much.*

– Is that thing genuine silver?

– It is. We'll give it to the old lady out on Ninety-Seventh Street, begging. On the theater steps, I mean.

– D. E. should get that medal.

– He won't like the five-line symbol on it any more than I do.

– Still, you're engaged, Gesine.

– What do you mean I'm engaged?

– You've agreed to marry him. You need to give him something.

– You're right.

– Silver can be melted down.

– Yes.

– Then D. E. will get a silver ring from you.

– Yes.

July 17, 1968 Wednesday

Since Cresspahl's dumb Gesine balked at life in England, he had to take steps to help her get through one in the Mecklenburg of twenty years ago. As was right and proper, he asked his guild master for an interview. So quickly, so readily did Willi Böttcher agree to come to Jerichow for a visit that we could only think he was trying to keep the former prisoner out of his house, out of sight of the people of Gneez. He came on a Sunday, in a black suit, not sweating in the September heat, and sat down hesitantly, preferring to discuss the weather for a while. His good-natured devious face looked crumpled. When I came in with coffee and he humbly asked me to stay—a fifteen-year-old schoolgirl—I knew: he wants to confess something, and for that he needs someone Cresspahl won't use rough language in front of.

– Heinrich: he said heavily, and sighed. What was the good of pleading for nice weather now?

Cresspahl had asked him here to discuss his professional prospects as a tradesman, but if Willi had something on his mind then sure they could talk about that first.

Then it was Gesine Böttcher turned to, called on as witness; her visits to his workshop should let what he had such a hard time bringing out go without saying. But Gesine had watched him at work because she didn't have a father; all she saw was a lot of business. Revenue.

– Never mind revenue!: Böttcher suddenly cursed, as though it were bad luck and trouble too. It was back when—

he looked at me, I passed the look along to Cresspahl, and he gave Böttcher a nod, sparing him from having to say: when they'd nabbed Cresspahl—

that Böttcher's firm had had to keep its head above water with its share of the confiscated furniture that the Red Army kept stored there, as reparations, and then decided it would rather barter back to the locals (for material assets); that and the mechanical production of wood cubes for producing automobile gas had been their bread and butter. Their butter, to be precise. He couldn't exactly count on the reputation that stretched all the way into Brandenburg, which he'd earned with his bedroom sets and other standardized furniture—he stayed with mass production. Through early 1947 it was the watchtowers that the Soviets were ordering for their new prison camps; he'd delivered some all the way to the Polish border. *Ptichniki.* It was easy work, since the Soviets didn't need to see designs first—both parties had a pretty clear picture of what these towers should look like. Since it was good honest Mecklenburg work, it came at a price; every roof was done with beveled siding, for instance, solid enough to last a lifetime. They were worth 900 marks apiece but had to be billed at 2,400, the money had to be divided up so many ways. Of course the Soviets knew that Böttcher had to get his share of the profit and they got this price through the pricing authorities, the finance office, the Gneez commandant. Gesine had seen one.

His look was so pleading. For a moment, as if in a dream, I was sure I'd seen a watchtower in Böttcher's workshop, complete with guard and Kalashnikov. Then, as if waking from a nightmare, I remembered the tower I'd crawled under in the Countess Woods, and nothing could happen to me there because I was with Jakob. It was Cresspahl who'd had to live beneath such towers.

You wouldna built them things for the Russians, Cresspahl? Honest?
Not if they were keepin you locked up, Böttcher. Honest.

The two of them had a drink to this article of Böttcher's production—one schnapps. The bottle stayed standing between them, a monument to the part Böttcher had played in Cresspahl's imprisonment. But it was settled; he sat on a bit more of his chair than the edge, and eventually leaned back. It was true—to his chagrin, he was minting money. His workers were happy about the incoming orders; he let them have the scraps for home heating before they stole them, and continued to negotiate on their behalf for night-work bonus pay, ration cards for heavy labor too. Then came the picket fences for Heringsdorf and other penny-ante stuff; in 1947 he undertook the interiors for the Russian ships in the Wismar and Rostock dockyards. They are still bravely plying the seas, his cabins and berths—shoddy work's not in Willi's repertoire!—but he'd added a hundred-percent surcharge to cover wastage. (Thirty to fifty percent would have been reasonable.) Under these circumstances a complete child's bedroom for the director authorizing billings was handled with a handshake, not an invoice. Then, when the time came to enlarge the dockyard buildings to handle ship provisions, especially the "bazaars," he ran into temporary difficulties, not knowing his way around hustling food supplies as well as his various other areas of expertise. Then Emil Knoop returned to Gneez and helped him out in his hour of need.

What followed was the kind of aria to Emil Knoop's ability to draw profits out of thin air, one that Cresspahl's child could have joined in on. It did make her mad to recall the 1946–47 Hunger Winter when milk and honey were flowing on Böttcher's table. But what did it profit Böttcher, really, that he drove a Mercedes, that the Soviet guards at the free port of Stralsund raised the barrier because his sad frazzled face was ID enough, what good did all that high living with canned goods from Denmark do him? For one thing, he constantly had one foot in jail (– *Ive made my peace with that*: said Willi, gloomily, but still as if somehow looking forward to it). For another, the meetings with the Soviet gentlemen always ended up so terribly booze-soaked. In Stralsund a waiter felt for him and always served him water instead of Richtenberger kümmel (– *You c'n have the money fer it*: said Willi, dolefully—a dignified man with bitter religious disappointments in his past). He couldn't bribe all the waiters on the Mecklenburg coast, though, so it happened once that when stopping to take a leak between Rostock and Gneez he slipped and fell down a steep embankment and his Soviet business partners forgetfully drove off without him, in his Mercedes. All night on the wet ground. No. All of Gneez knew it as well as Cresspahl: Willi Böttcher didn't know how to drink. Not his forte. Lay in bed half a week afterward, every time. And then the wife! *The old lady! The ol' bat!*

All true. Böttcher's got his row to hoe: Cresspahl said, being friendly. His daughter was livid at Böttcher's geniality, but grown-ups were incomprehensible. Now we've told each other some stories, let's bury the hatchet. As if Cresspahl had told stories about Fünfeichen!

But for every line of Böttcher's business, Emil Knoop held an end of it in his hand; if Knoop balked, something went south. Willi had made some wall paneling for the Gneez Kommandatura. The invoice was approved by the pricing authorities, the finance office—Triple-J probably would've paid it by Whitsunday 1948 but there was a deputy sitting in his chair, behind him the 40" x 40" Goethe from the Gneez high school, refusing to pay at all. Willi went to the waiting room outside Emil Knoop's office so early that he was second in line. Emil was about to leave on a trip to Oostende; he had just enough time to give him a little information on his way out the door: the deputy commandant had managed to get only a sewing machine with a damaged base at a furniture distribution but was interested in a young lady on Rosengarten Street and wanted to give her a token of his affection. Willi Böttcher cast his mind back to medieval techniques and made the deputy a new sewing machine base with all the care an aspirant gives his journeyman's piece, complete with inlaid centimeter ruler and other intarsia. So then the deputy paid for the two hundred square feet of wainscoting, had Böttcher sign for it, swept the money off the table back into the cashbox, pointedly locked it, pulled a new receipt out of his drawer, requested a second signature, and handed over the money... By evening the negotiations had moved to Böttcher's shop, where the deputy sat on the planer with him, only slightly drunk, rattling off words of wisdom: You Germans, you think we're all dumb... (Oh, no, Mr. Deputy! Please! How could you even *think*...?) We're better cheaters than you, though.

Cresspahl looked long and hard at his guild master, whose word had once been law in the craft and the bookkeeping of their trade all around Gneez and who now had to make a double entry of every receipt if he didn't want to be hauled off to jail by the tax investigators. He decided to try another angle. He asked where Emil's power and glory had its limits. – *Nowhere nohow!* Willi declared glumly. Although their conversation once again managed to steer clear of the painful topic of Cresspahl's absence, it still sounded for all the world as if he, Böttcher, were complaining to his younger colleague. The latest about Emil Knoop was the saluting practice he'd conducted with a Soviet guard outside the green fence around Barbara Street in Gneez, in full view of German passersby, Soviet military personnel, even the commandant, J. J. Jenudkidse, who looked expertly on from the comfort of his private villa's upper floor. Emil (Emile) corrected the amenable Red Army man's hand position, pushed and shoved at the man's feet, and was saluted by the Soviet ever more briskly, almost up to the old Greater German standards—crowing vigorously, he rooted out aesthetic errors: No! Like that! Look: Chock! Chockchock! Chock! until the present-arms was solid and Emil, with a salute of his own, strode past the guard to his meeting with Triple-J. Nothing happened without Knoop.

The people who said Knoop must have a twin may've been right. Because how could he be on trial in Hanover over a mislaid delivery of blue basalt and at the same time cutting a deal in Jerichow about demolishing the brickworks at the town's expense? Seriously. *You cant catch that guy.* He's off to Moscow, and not with a delegation, alone! As a guest of honor!

I think its time to catch im.

Hes got enough double receipts at the finance office, mine 're sheepdroppings fer him!

Willi—what if he had to help you?

Don' take it the wrong way, Cresspahl. Youve been away a long time.

He has a friend, doesn he?

Hes got lots a friends.

One friend: Klaus. Your boy Klaus.

Jå, Klaas. We think about im all the time. The old lady won' stop weepin and wailin. If hes still with the Russians, is he dead? Is he still alive there? If it wasn for him Id throw in the towel.

Then think of him!

Cresspahl, you're not . . .

Hes got a friend in Gneez whos in good with the Russians and now hes goin for a visit . . .

Emil! Emil Knoop!

If he cant get his friend out a Moscow—

Cresspahl I wont ever forget this. Come and see me, day or night, youll have whatever you want. Whatever you ask for, Hinrich!

If he cant pull it off then hes useless. Then hes through in Gneez.

Ive done nothing to deserve this from you. I wont ever forget it.

I'd rather you forgot it right now.

What?

You dont know nothin, you keep your trap shut, Willi.

This was the kind of operation Cresspahl was capable of by that time. His daughter took it as a sign of recovery, it was fine with her. He was casually picking a fight with the business tycoon of the district, and she was happy to do her part with comments about an Emil Knoop without the power or the glory to get his friend back from the Russians, until Mrs.

Lindsetter, the judge's wife, started talking and Dr. Schürenberg's wife and Mrs. Bell and all the rest of the ladies in their ladiness. The Knoop firm delivered a batch of Finnish timber to Cresspahl, from which he built a workshop behind his house—a large room on stilts at a right angle to Lisbeth's bedroom—and when the Schwerin State Museum inquired into whether he did restoration work it was Knoop who'd in all innocence written him a letter. Then the people from the antiques shop started coming by. Cresspahl had realized the fate of fine handicrafts in Mecklenburg but he thought he'd do well enough to live out his time there. It was his last retreat. From then on he only ever worked alone.

Emil Knoop never discovered who had dared to defy him; he'd written that letter in Schwerin out of sheer goodwill. He carried out the search for Klaus Böttcher in the sporting spirit we were used to from him. True, he did come back from Moscow alone. It was around Christmas when I saw a ragged young man on Station Street, dazed, staring at the people forming a line three persons wide, shivering in the cold, because the Renaissance Cinema was showing the Soviet war booty *Die Fledermaus*, with actors who'd been accessories to Fascism, as he had probably learned by then as well as we had. I didn't know how to explain this to him as I took him to his parents, and I had to see a man of almost thirty cry before I understood why Böttcher had been so desperate to have a good reputation with the Soviets, even when it hurt a fellow guildsman, and what had moved Cresspahl to such a forgiving stance, and I apologized to my father, deeply; as they say when they're ashamed: from the heart.

Still nothing but hints from "reliable sources," no indication of what the letter sent to Czechoslovakia from its allies actually said.

July 18, 1968 Thursday

The New York Times has read the letter to Czechoslovakia from the Warsaw comrades, and informs us that it included the following demands:

"Decisive action against right-wing or other anti-Socialist forces." Okay, that's fine. Agreed.

"Party control of the press, radio, and television." Because they'd made "groundless" charges that Soviet troops in the ČSSR represented a threat to the nation's sovereignty. Well, if they don't represent a threat, then agreed. But let them tell the people what they see.

"We do not appear before you as spokesmen of yesterday who would like to hamper you in rectifying your mistakes and shortcomings, including violations of Socialist legality." If that stays true, then agreed.

The New School taught us to rank one another according to our respective fathers. Just as Schoolgirl Cresspahl was a tradesman's daughter, Pius Pagenkopf was appended to a father with a leadership role in the Socialist Unity Party of Germany and high office in the Mecklenburg state government. Reactionary Middle Class and Progressive Intellectual—how could they share a desk from January 1949 all the way to graduation?

Pius . . . he'd once gotten stuck declining this Latin adjective; he must have preferred that as a nickname to a translation of his last name from Platt into High German (Horsehead). He was also the only Catholic in our grade. Pius . . . if only the mind would do our bidding! Of Jakob I have a sense of his closeness, his voice, his calm movements; of Pius I have only the memory of a photograph. We were nineteen and eighteen, standing before bare April reeds on the shore of Gneez Lake. A tall lean boy with a hard head, shoulders thrown back, annoyed at the camera, in a posture of resistance. He held a lit cigarette like a grown-up. And the snapshot tries to convince me that Pius's face was always so finished. All I know at the moment about the younger girl next to him, with the braids, is that her father wanted to forbid her from smoking, because she is concealing her burning tobacco product in a cupped hand. We look like a well-functioning married couple; we knew each other quite a bit better than our fathers cared to notice.

When ninth grade started, Pius was for me too almost nothing but Mr. Pagenkopf's son. Head of the Gneez finance office and a Socialist, he'd been removed in April 1933 and had to augment his 75 percent retirement pension in the freight department at the railroad station (preventive custody during Mussolini's visit to Mecklenburg). In 1945, the people of Gneez decided to see it as only fair when the British made him interpreter for their city commandant; they held it against him that he became mayor under the Soviets, and the Social Democrats in particular found him suspect for his speeches in favor of unification with the Communists, all the more so now that he was helping the Soviet administration in the district capital. Since 1945, the Pagenkopfs, on paper a family of three, again resided in a four-room apartment—cause for resentment in an over-crowded, occupied city; moreover, Pius's father showed his face in Gneez so rarely that even his son's girlfriend knew him only from pictures of speakers' podiums, or newspaper articles on the New Face of the Party or the Yugoslavian conspiracy. Of his nighttime Bohemianism in Schwerin, it was taken as fact that he had his pick of attractive women there, younger and wittier in conversation than Mrs. Pagenkopf, a farmer's daughter with an elementary-school education—he had to sneak her onto the "In." list, authorizing ration cards for the intelligentsia. With a father like this, Pius would obviously raise his hand at once in the FDJ constituent assembly; with a father like that behind him, he could simply wave aside his election to various FDJ offices as just another "societal activity"—Comrade Pagen-kopf took care of his son to that extent. It came as a surprise to no one when Pius, after the new TO government stores opened, was wearing a fresh sports shirt every three days, a hundred marks each, and leather shoes, two hundred and ten for a pair of those; he kept up bourgeois appearances, he did. The son of such a father could permit himself walks with the daughter of a tradesman (bourgeois), but paying visits to a Heinrich Cress-pahl's daughter was pushing it, and she was not a little shocked to see him at the door in December 1948, on Sunday, at coffee time. Then she thought she saw through his excuse.

They were under threat of a quiz in math class. If someone has a weak heart when it comes to math, surely he can go looking for a classmate—even if she lives in distant Jerichow. Now here he stands, a plausible smile of recognition in the corners of his mouth, nervousness in his eyes, because someone might get the idea that he'd been wandering around Jerichow Market Square just because, or else, say, trying to run into Lise Wollenberg, and not because he couldn't figure out where Brickworks Road was (straight, then right at St. Peter's Church). – *Dobri den'*, Gesine: he says cautiously, almost pleadingly. Turns out she can speak Russian too: – *Kak djela, gospodin*, she asks; she brings him into Cresspahl's room, *sadites'*; next comes *na razvod*, to work!, so that he'll finally believe she's believed him. Her feeling here was less compassionate, more urgent, the way seeing someone's wound demands a bandage. There was nervousness too, though, and with it the thought: Oh my distant homeland! which was sung in

Russian, *Shiroka strana moya rodnaya*, but meant in translation: Well this is a fine mess we're in, and it may get dicey.

But Pius did nothing halfway. When the geometry tutorial was over, the question was stuck in my throat and Pius answered it. We came to an understanding about our fathers—the younger man who served the Soviets and the older whom the Soviet had had in their clutches; both men had made it possible for us to do this, each in his own way. Cresspahl merely remarked that he hoped Pagenkopf Senior wasn't sticking anyone's head in the lion's mouth but his own. Now all that was missing were tiny scraps of paper and Mrs. Habelschwerdt's community spirit.

Ol' Habelschwerdt, nicknamed *Hobel* (the wood planer), had graduated high school in Breslau twenty-one years before and snagged a senior schoolteacher to marry; unfortunately, with him missing "in the East" and her stuck with half-grown children, she'd gone to teacher training school surrounded by all sorts of young things. She taught us mathematics, chemistry, and physics. The boys in the class rated her as genuinely "acceptable" ("good enough for a new husband"); her legs were a solid A-minus given that she was forty; she'd acquired her nickname for her excessively harsh reprimands, overstraining her tiny voice. As a relative and now surviving dependant of a politically compromised person (NSDAP), she tried maybe a little too anxiously to guarantee at least one ("bourgeois") son's admission to the New School high school, plus she needed to hang on to her teacher's salary—she'd zealously memorized the words of the New Progressive Pedagogy and perhaps understood the meanings a bit less well. And so, a week before Christmas, she whacked the desk with her metal ruler (several times over, as if beating a bad dog) when a handful of paper confetti blew into the aisle from Pius's place; and thus she yelled at him, over all the thirty-nine student heads: You of all people should show some community spirit here!

In an English or American school, "You of all people..." would probably have become her nickname. Eva Matschinsky was admonished like this: You don't just lay your abundance down on the table like that, Eva Maria! You of all people... Habelschwerdt was taken aback by our laughter, having forgotten the youthful abundance of her own bosom; she had just been reminding Eva, and us, that as a barber's daughter (Reactionary Middle Class) she had to make up for her social origins with at least unimpeachable conduct. And Pius, of all people, should come across as entirely agreeable, given his father (Progressive Intelligentsia). But given Mr. Pagenkopf's position, she accepted with a sigh that Pius refused to give her— his teacher!—an apology. I alone knew: it was Zaychik who'd done it.

Pius shared a desk with him, Dagobert Haase (Platt for *Hase*, "rabbit," *zaychik* in Russian). They'd shared it since the start of 9-A-II, because they took the same route to school. Not a friend, a habit. High-spirited, pushy, clever, usable. But Zaychik just wouldn't stop passing notes. Playing Battleship right under Mrs. Habelschwerdt's nose, Pius cured him of that. But when a scrap of paper is passed from the right it's considered an affront against solidarity to shake one's head, and unfortunately this one was addressed to Pius himself (Eva's already wearing a . . . ; Eva has already . . .); Pius had ripped the message into tiny bits and left them on his opened book. The teacher neared, the book was slammed shut, the telltale cloud between the legs of the desk testified to Pius's lack of community spirit. Now it might be that such spirit abandoned Pius when it came to the community of teachers, but if such a sensibility was a virtue, a public virtue, then it was unjust to be told one lacked it because of someone else's offense. Worst of all, Haase Zaychik failed to avail himself of the honor code to which a member of the Free German Youth was bound—he didn't try to clear up the situation. The girl to whom he explained all of this, in a state of multilayered uneasiness, was also unattached.

And so began the first "work collective" in the Fritz Reuter High School in Gneez, two years before such things were officially introduced, and it was scandalous. First of all, classroom seats could be traded when the school year started, never in the middle except on a teacher's orders. Second, a boy or girl left over was to sit alone—if worst came to worst a boy and girl at the same desk might be allowed at the front of the room. But in any case . . . Cresspahl's daughter was almost sixteen and Pius was already seventeen! On top of that, the desk Pius had moved to with me was in the very back corner of the room, hard for a teacher to keep her eye on, and since Pius had offered me the chair next to the window, he also screened me from view down the aisle. The school might be "New"—if you didn't count the building, and the furniture, and most of the teachers—but this was an offense against propriety, letting young people of the opposite sex sit together at the same desk. Unheard of!

"Oh, Angelina, you've got to wait . . ." was sung in our direction before first period the first day after Christmas break; there was a lot of anticipatory giggling around us, because a visit from the principal was expected—Dr. Kliefoth, was held to have old-fashioned ideas, and in fact a corner of his eye did twitch when he caught sight of us, as if a fly had attacked him there. He tested the class his way. He started with Matschinsky, jumped to C when W was up, took some P's, then relaxed against the back of his chair, hands in his lap, initially with a stern sidelong glance from under his beetling brows. The stiff white tuft of hair on his skull was perfectly still, although the heat was by no means on full blast. Pagenkopf and Cresspahl had to translate, in alternating lines, the letter from E. A. Poe's "The Gold-Bug," which, unfortunately, opens "My Dear" and goes on containing phrases that would also be appropriate in a love letter. We had to deal with foggy light from the frosted-glass lamps, we were in no mood to giggle. Lise Wollenberg, whom the slight had made reckless, forced herself to burst out laughing and in return got a mark against her in the record book for disrupting the class (a delicate matter for someone from the bourgeoisie). He gave each of us an A. Kliefoth's position was murky: bourgeois, militarist, but on the other hand Progressive Intelligentsia as principal; after his tacit approval what could the Wood Planer do to us? Luckily for her, she saw the change in the seating plan actually recorded in the principal's handwriting; we saw her sit up with a start at that. Never again would she convict Pius of a lack of community spirit; the following year she even invited us for an afternoon coffee—together.

When the singing and jeering about our new desk started, Pius furrowed his eyebrows as if in pain and his lips grew taut the way they used to when he was standing under the horizontal bar, collecting himself for his leap. This was someone who'd stuck it out through every decision he'd had to make in his life. Since he stared straight ahead so haughtily, as if our intention alone guaranteed our success, I lost my trepidation and knew for certain that everything was going to work out fine. And since we'd apparently nodded at one another after Mrs. Habelschwerdt's sigh like two horses who'd been sharing a harness for a long time, we were considered a couple from that moment on.

Because of our fathers, it stayed a secret for quite some time that the Cresspahl girl went home from school with the Pagenkopf boy and did her homework with him, or that Pius gave up a half hour of sleep to meet Gesine at the milk train from Jerichow. We didn't shove our compact in anyone's face, even each other's. Cresspahl got through it because custom dictated that you had to go with someone; by this point she was afraid to look too closely into how things stood between her and Jakob. And now Pius always had someone he could walk right past Lise Wollenberg with, as if the thing with her passport photo had been settled when he tore it up.

July 19, 1968 Friday

– It's all gonna come down today. (Eagle-Eye Robinson)

  – It's all gonna come down today, Gesine. And don't smoke so much! (Eileen O'Brady)

  – Hope it all comes down today, my gardener made a bet with me. (de Rosny)

  If only it all would come down today—the heat that's hanging over the city, making the mornings pale, the days hazy, the tops of buildings blurry at the edges, standing still in the sun unbearable because the heat from the sidewalk penetrates up through one's soles. Last night the dirt in the air left nothing but a small sweltering hole for the sun. After you've swum eight blocks through the hot liquid air, the artificial climate of the bank hits you like a blow to the heart. If only it all would come down today.

  So what did Czechoslovak Communists' peers in East Germany, Hungary, Poland, and the Soviet Union have to tell them, and what did the presidium of the Central Committee of the Communist Party of the ČSSR reply?

  They say: We've read it, and first off: greetings! But we *have* already addressed your concerns in our May plenary session.

  Yet how could we instantly clear up all the conflicts that have accumulated over the twenty years preceding our January plenary session? If we start with healthy Socialist activities, it's inevitable that some of them will overshoot their marks, whether it be a little heap of anti-Socialist forces or the *fronde* of old dogmatic-sectarians. If we're trying to unify our new line, not even the party itself can remain untouched. Many of us are so accustomed to rule from above that the wishes from below always fall short. We wish to admit these facts, to our own party and to our people. You know that.

But you do have eyes in your head, so how can you possibly claim that our present situation is counterrevolutionary, that we want to give up Socialism, change our foreign policy, break our country loose from you. After everything you've done for us, during the war and in the years since, you mustn't doubt us. That's an insult to us.

We are friends in Socialism. And things can only improve with mutual respect, sovereignty, and international solidarity. We'll try harder. You can count on us.

You mention our relationship with the Federal Republic of Germany. Well, it is our immediate neighbor. And we *were* the last to take definite steps toward the partial regulation of mutual relations, particularly in the economic field. There were other Socialist countries that did so earlier and to a greater extent, without it causing any fears.

We thoroughly respect and protect the interests of the DDR, hand in hand with it. It is our Socialist ally. We do all in our power to strengthen its international position and authority. We said so in January and have done so in all the months since.

What we've promised to you, in agreements and treaties, we will respect. Our commitment to mutual cooperation, peace, and collective security is proved by our new friendship treaties with the Bulgarian and Hungarian People's Republics, and also the prepared treaty with the Rumanian Socialist Republic. (You know why we here bracket out China. And Poland.) No hard feelings!

The staff exercises of your forces on our territory are a concrete proof of our faithful fulfillment of our alliance commitments. We gave you a friendly welcome, we were where you needed us to be. The restlessness and doubts in the minds of our public occurred only after you repeatedly changed the time of your departure. Did we ever say to your face: Get going?

We know this: Give up our leading role and it's all over for Socialist society. For this reason alone we must understand each other on the question of what is required to lead. We depend on the voluntary support of the people. We are not implementing our leading role by ruling from above, but by acting rightly, progressively, socialistically.

Any indication of returning to the old methods of compelling obedience would evoke against us the resistance of the majority of party members, workers, cooperative farmers, and intelligentsia. That is just how we would imperil our political leading role, would threaten the Socialist advantages of the people, how our common front against imperialism would waver. That cannot be our hope.

We have our tactical plan. We've told you what it is.

First. We are going to give the specific people responsible for bringing the party into this unfortunate situation a good talking to. If that's justifiable.

Second. At the fourteenth extraordinary congress of the party we'll take a look at what we've done since January. We will lay down the party line, adopt an attitude to the federation of the Czechs and the Slovaks, approve the new party statute, and elect a new Central Committee with the full authority and confidence of the party and all of society.

Third. Then we'll tackle our internal political questions: the improvement of the socialist National Front, self-government, the actualization of the federal constitutional arrangement, the new elections, and the preparation of a new constitution.

Just now it's darn tough. We're winning, if also suffering drawbacks. But we have the situation in hand. The delegates elected to the congress are a guarantee that the future fate of the party will not be decided by extremist or unreasonable people.

We have clearly rejected the "2,000 Words." They were never dangerous words, but since you got so mad at them we want to tell you loudly and openly, so that all Czechs and Slovaks can hear us and understand: This must not be repeated, for that could anger our Soviet friends, from whom we require not ill will but patience. Nothing of this kind will happen again.

But believe us, it's been easier to do our job since we abolished censorship and restored freedom of expression and of the press. People are no longer whispering behind our backs but expressing themselves openly. For the first time, we know what they think of us.

If we now discuss a certain painful matter with you, but in everyone's hearing, and despite the fact that you have records of it in the files of your secret police already, this is actually an act of politeness and to be taken as information ex officio. The law about the rehabilitation of innocent people who in earlier years were persecuted illegally with the help of the law has been a success. Since it was passed, people are hardly ever even looking in this direction.

In September, immediately after the party congress, we will confirm the permanent existence of the parties of the National Front and pass a law clarifying the legal regulations for the formation and activities of various voluntary organizations, associations, clubs, and all that kind of thing. The enemies of Socialism will show themselves, and we will have the opportunity to effectively face them down.

Dear friends, are you trying to make us look bad in front of our own people? We can hardly return to the days when we could convince them that you weren't butting in when you were butting in. Help us save face. We cannot decide on our own policy anywhere but at our own congress.

So what are we asking you for, then? For time. For two months.

We are ready to talk with you. It was probably just a misunderstanding about the date of that meeting—it happens. But leave us in peace, just for a bit, it's touch and go here. Of course we've always been ready to talk. We will kiss your hand, we will embrace you cheek to cheek, if you'll leave us to act for just a little while yet, dear friends, just two months.

In the name of our common fight against imperialism, for peace, the security of nations, democracy, and Socialism.

Why don't you all say anything! You're still treating me like a child whose fun you don't want to spoil!
Maybe it will *be fun for that child.*
Yeah, maybe!
Gesine, you're forgetting: we have no power over the future.
But you always gave me advice when you were alive, for the future!
Then we could get you back, if we had to.
The fun is over.
Gesine, you don't want us to treat you like a child.

Today it all did come down—it's been four hours and still we're telling one another where we were when it caught us. D. E. claims he was standing on his mother's lawn after lunch, hose in hand, nose raised aquiver, and he put his equipment away because cool dry air from New York was moving past him overhead; he's more than a little proud of his nose, and we will remember him looking self-satisfied like this, exuberantly waving his wine glass around. Employee Cresspahl watched the beginning, neglecting her official duties: the light between the glass skin of the blocky office buildings had darkened and then turned exaggeratedly clear. All the edges sharpened to clarity. Then, at a quarter past four, came the first thunderclap. Marie is convinced she saw the very same bolt of lightning, in the wide cutting of Ninety-Sixth Street sloping down to end in the dark window of the river. She was outside the Good Eats when the first fat drops burst at her feet, and Charlie waved her in—a regular customer—but there was a man pressed against the Broadway side of the front window, lacking the change for a cup of coffee, who surrendered, shoulders slumped, to the rivulets flooding the sidewalk. Just then the rain was pouring torrentially down at the bank's palace, too, and from the thirteenth floor you could hear the cars tires whooshing on the wet asphalt. Just then D. E. had stopped at a streetlight in New Jersey, next to a pedestrian marching along as if in a parade, with a piece of cardboard over his half-bald head and letting the rain blacken his suit all it wanted. Just then Marie saw a Negro dancing across Broadway, a large cardboard box on his shoulders that he heaved up higher again every five steps, never bumping into anyone. Then the fire engine began to wail on Third Avenue. Racing mountain streams were pouring down D. E.'s windshield, but if he's said he'll be somewhere at six then there he will be, at 1800 hours, and we're grateful. On Lexington Avenue, in contrast, the commuters seemed to think it was more important to keep walking than to keep dry; clearly rain engenders less solidarity than snowstorms or heat waves—here in this country of ours. It was now twenty minutes since it had started coming down, and a men's clothing shop had its window sign ready: Umbrellas, On Sale. But Mrs. Cresspahl marched grandly on, under the roof of a folded *New York Times*. The beggar stationed on this side of Grand Central Station, who when on duty shocks people with his bared double leg prostheses, had taken a break and was now leaning against a wall inside the Graybar Building, his pant legs rolled down. When Marie stepped outside she learned a new kind of breathing, which D. E. can now explain to her as due to the plunge of at least ten points in the air humidity. In the subway it was still muggy, only half of the fans were running, the people stood grumpily pressed up against one another even though they had, after all, survived another week in New York. At quarter to seven the rain was so weak that it could only trickle, but still it had swept clear the clump of fog from New Jersey so we could again make out the opposite shore in its semidarkness. Then the thunder trampled back and forth over the Hudson, unable to let the river's water be. Now it's quiet, the asphalt mirror of Riverside Drive shows us the treetops in their close friendship with the sky. A squealing birdcall comes over from the park, like that of an injured young animal. A seagull? Yes, Marie saw it over the tops of our trees—a seagull sawing into the wind, the wind bearing down on our building.

July 20, 1968 Saturday, South Ferry day

At the table lavishly set for breakfast (American version, for D. E.), opposite the festively sunlit park, *The New York Times* came between us—we almost slipped into a fight. Twenty American-made machine guns have been dug up under a bridge between Cheb and Karlovy Vary. In five kit bags (or knapsacks) bearing the date 1968. Plus thirty pistols, with the appropriate ammunition. Near the West German border. And *Pravda*, Moscow, was able to publish the news yesterday morning, before the Czechoslovakian interior ministry could even announce the discovery. To a Professor Erichson, this means it's possible that such caches have been placed across the country, waiting to be found and to thus give the Soviet Union justification for any military invasion: Sudeten German uprisings. According to this expert, airborne troops are most likely. But there's a woman sitting at the table who's planning a trip to that part of the world in a month—she'd prefer to be presented with a slightly brighter picture. Then came Marie's glance, up from below, amazed at this new fashion of someone in our family criticizing a person for expressing their thoughts; both of them stared at me like I was simply overworked, I needed a break. They can have their outing, but during it they will have to listen to the Pagenkopf story: as a warning, as a promise, however they want to take it.

"Can Love Really Be a Sin?" This song, too—famously sung in a low, smoky voice by a Nazi actress and now put back to work, this time by Sovexport, to distract the Germans from their hunger—who do you think got this song sung at them in Gneez's Fritz Reuter High School starting in January 1949? It was sung and drummed and whistled at Cresspahl's daughter and Pius Pagenkopf. We were the Couple.

Lise Wollenberg believed it too. She'd taken as deskmate the niece of Mrs. Lindsetter, wife of the district court chief justice—a delicate blond who, despite her soft flesh, was nicknamed Peter because she'd always worn her hair cut short, since the early days of the Soviet occupation. It looked striking next to Lise's long curls. Wollenberg said about me: yes, well, with a father like that Cresspahl was well advised to suck up to the new regime.

But Mrs. Pagenkopf was not a fine lady with elegant clothes and hairdo and political slogans on her lips; to me she looked bent, stout, and worn-down, dressed as frugally as Jakob's mother. Her shoulders were hunched as though she had a lot of fear left over from the twelve swastika years and new worries too given her husband's "lifestyle" in Schwerin—which was, of course, how the good people of Gneez couldn't help but understand Mr. Pagenkopf's political activities. She was far too shy to let herself be drawn onto the stage at the Renaissance Cinema for the political address after a screening, much less when it was later moved up ahead of the films after people had started heading for the side doors en masse as soon as they saw the words "The End." She did read the front page of the Schwerin *People's Daily* and would have been perfectly able to spell out for her comrades what had happened to the SED since the first party conference in January 1949. (She actually helped us with our So-Sci essays.) The neighbors interpreted her taciturn manner as revenge for the times when the Pagenkopfs were people it was better not to talk to. She talked about me as "*your Gesin,*" in a voice of fond reproach; she rarely talked to me. But since it was me her boy Robert had chosen, she soon found a rhyme: *Röbbertin his Gesin.* Anyway, if she had talked to me I'd have had to shout back. Since her near-deafness had remained incurable, she turned her right ear, not her eyes, to everyone but Pius—who knows if she ever once looked me in the face. It was as if Pius's mother lived in the kitchen; she was visible most of all in the ceaselessly washed windows, the polished floors, the scrupulously assembled sausage sandwiches that Pius carried in from the kitchen with the tea. Yes, there was tea. And butter on the bread, for the Pagenkopfs had three ration cards and would never be short of the fifty-five marks for a pound of margarine from the TO store. The sandwiches were generous.

After 1949 I was never hungry in the East again. To that extent, Lise was right—I was enjoying one of the pleasures connected to the ruling class.

I thought I should keep this Pius away from Jakob (I was after all being unfaithful to Jakob, whether or not he'd been with other girls). Several weeks went by and then I saw Pius talking to him: the tall, elegant boy in a polite pose in front of the stocky guy in his greasy railroad worker's outfit. Jakob's protecting hand was over me every step of the way.

Pius and I were a couple because we'd walk together from our shared desk onto the Street of German-Soviet Friendship to Pagenkopf's place, where we'd do our homework in the "salon." (The maid that Helene Pagenkopf had once been had filled the living room to bursting with flower stands, étagères, spindly little tables, and club chairs, leaving barely enough room to walk around a piano, the contribution from Pagenkopf Sr.) Since we left the house together too, we were a couple.

The teachers soon got used to it. When the beanpole gym teacher couldn't find me, he asked Student Pagenkopf to tell me the practice time. Naturally he'd be accompanying Student Cresspahl to the pool, with her swim things in the basket of his bike. He, like she, joined the SC Trout swimming club because his father had asked him to add more "societal activities" to his schedule. Since each member of a couple has to look out for the other, Pius discovered that children who excelled in a sport were rewarded by a transfer to a special school, where they received more training in their specialty than in practical subjects, and thus after their tournament victories would have to scramble professionally while never catching up to their peers. Cresspahl the front-crawl ace soon saw her times slump to almost normal. There was little that anyone could prove against her, since the other teachers reported steady performance from this student, and the gym beanpole banged his stopwatch as he accused Cresspahl of paying too much attention to Pagenkopf. Still, he did say I could stop coming to his practices, since he didn't like interfering with couples. He must have liked us, as a couple.

KLIEFOTH: What is all this fuss supposed to mean, Mrs. Habelschwerdt! It is precisely at their desk that the two of them are safe with respect to your...valuable concerns!

The world thinks it's cute when the two members of a couple are similar in certain ways, and I became a bit more like Pius by joining the FDJ, just like him. For his father had now seen fit to request a bit more societal activity from "my son's girlfriend" too. He required more than a bit, it turned out—my booklet sporting the yellow-on-blue rising sun soon proved insufficient and I had to get myself the tall narrow one with the black-and-red-and-gold flag waving in front of the Soviet flag, both diagonal flagpoles stuck into a circle. This latter booklet was for the Society for German-Soviet Friendship, and after Cresspahl read the Stalin telegram ("Hitlers come and go...") printed after my name he promptly raised my allowance by fifty pfennigs, "for the next ones." Small wonder that Pius was elected president of our FDJ class chapter at the start of tenth grade, and I his deputy; we held these offices to the end and they were noted in our transcripts.

We biked as a couple to the unofficial bathing spot on the south side of Gneez Lake and swam without the others across to the boathouses Willi Böttcher was in the process of building for the Progressive Intelligentsia; we came swimming back to the rest of the class together, and clearly we'd been talking to each other the whole time. When I happened to be there without him they sometimes still sang that question about whether love might be a sin, but Pius had cured me of my old bashfulness and they learned to ask about him through me. We were, after all, the ones who dried off with the same towel—the couple.

When two people have been a couple for a while, they go to the movies depending on the state of their wallets and the attractions of the film; when two people are far from being a couple, one of them has to pay for the other's ticket and spend ninety minutes laboriously exploring whether they might become one. If only one member of the couple is there, people keep a seat free for the other: next to Pius, "Keep that free for Gesine"; to you as you come in, "Here's your man!" In the FDJ meeting, on the field trip to the theater in Schwerin, on the potato fields during harvest service. When one of the couple is on card-checking duty, Gesine will take Pius's plate with her and bring him his school lunch. A couple has more time than other people; they can save the strolls, at least two afternoon hours, up Stalin Street and back down it, keeping a trembling lookout for the object of their longing: those in a couple already have it.

I should also tell you: Pius was no more Catholic than she was Protestant.

In spring 1950 we signed up together for maintenance duty with the German Railway, because this time old Pagenkopf had requested a more visible societal activity. For three weeks the couple poked around in the scruffy track beds of Gneez station, with shovel and pickax; in the photo you can see "my son's girlfriend" shoveling while Pius, amiably leaning on a handle, looks into Jakob's camera, a knit cap on the back of his head. The reward (the material incentive) was a free train ticket to any destination, but we were unable to take a trip together because Cresspahl needed my pass for a trip to "Berlin" (never referred to as "East"). So Pius went by himself to Dresden, detouring via Wittenberg on the way there for the sake of his father's reputation, returning via West Berlin for my sake, because when one person in a couple goes on a trip he brings back a souvenir for the other. Gesine Cresspahl, 10-A-II, now owns a ballpoint pen.

The last game was *pretty pathetic* but here we have Fritz Reuter High School versus Grevesmühlen, with Pius as center forward again. And look, two minutes before the starting whistle here comes Gesine. Over there, in that empty part of the bleachers, the one with the braids, straightening her long skirt around her legs. The one sitting up straight, so Pius can see her. Why should they wave to each other! he's already seen her. Look, she doesn't clap for him either. Well he already knows. They're a couple after all.

Yes, but can love be a sin?

In the winter the power cutoffs would interrupt us diagramming benzene rings or laying out the societal motivations of Lady Macbeth, and there would often be another hour before the evening train to Jerichow. Then it might happen that Pius would sit down at the piano and play me what he'd learned in eight years (he had diligently practiced Schumann's "Träumerei," and once, on a dusty, languorous summer afternoon, I heard him playing it from the street—he kept his dreams of Lise to himself). Other times it would be perfectly silent behind our dark windows. Early on, Zaychik and his girl Eva Matschinsky burst in on us with the excuse that they'd wanted to bring us candles. They saw Pius go back to the piano and Cresspahl calmly go on smoking—they must have thought we were uncommonly slick, and moreover they'd now lost their pretext for visiting. Pius had told me about his elder sister's death from typhus, I him about Alexandra Paepcke. We could certainly say: We knew things about each other.

One time—I was sixteen—the rail service to Jerichow was canceled and I spent the night at the Pagenkopfs', alone in a room. I didn't wait up for Pius.

Pius would have refused to tell me anything about the modified second line of the song about that girl Angelina who had to wait.

We were careful never to hold each other's hand.

In the summer of 1951, we were out biking and, at Cramon Lake, opposite the village of Drieberg, we stopped for a half-hour swim. While we were changing I was clumsy, he was clumsy, for the span of a breath our feet touched each other.

Just a fling wouldn't have been enough for me, Gesine.
Where no love grows, it's hard for sin to flourish.
Don't say her name, Gesine.
Don't ask me about Jakob.
But we didn't say a word to each other that time, did we!
No, Pius. We swam right across the lake.

Pagenkopf and Cresspahl spent vacation together. They biked to Schönberg, to Rehna. Pius lived at the Cresspahls' for two weeks! They went to the beach together every morning. It's six of one, half a dozen of the other, what they do when they're alone! That's our couple.

"MARIE H. CRESSPAHL   New York, N.Y., July 21, 1968
Dear Anita Red Hair,

It's still my birthday, but I want to write you my thank-you note today since you took the trouble to send me two full pages. Other than that I only got cards—one from Denmark, one from Switzerland, two from London, and the rest from the USA, mostly New York. Thirty-two in total.

I liked that your present can be worn in a blue leather envelope on a ribbon around my neck like a medallion and none of the clever nuns, not even Sister Magdalena, will suspect a watch. Because wearing a watch during class is 'verboten.' People say that here in German when a rule is totally unreasonable. Jewelry is also 'verbotten' (same), but they won't be able to see this under the blouse of the school uniform. Thank you and I'll remember you every time I wear it.

I hope the alarm built into this watch wasn't meant to teach me something. Because I always get up at the same time as Gesine, so that I can see her awake at least once a day. On Tuesday she went straight from the door to her bed and stayed lying there till the next morning. On the other hand, I'm always on time to school and have never once needed to take the 5 bus there. 'Don't take the bus, pay the fare like everyone else.'

To tell you the truth, I'm also writing to you because I have stationery with my name printed on it for the first time. It's a present from D. E. 'Because everyone older than ten needs some.' I turned eleven years old at seven thirty this morning.

I should tell you something about D. E., you probably know him as Erichson. Gesine's going to marry him. In the fall, when we're done with Prague. It's going to be *en petit comité*, with you as our best friend (and a mother-in-law too). As a result Gesine will become a citizen of the USA, and I'll be from a totally different country.

This was my first birthday without a party. I could have easily had ten people over. But it couldn't happen without Francine, the black girl who lived with us for a while until welfare came and got her. We've looked for her everywhere on the Upper West Side and even D. E. found not a trace. Francine would've been the first on my list to invite. Maybe she's dead. But D. E. would find a grave.

Anyway we need to learn how it goes as a trio, so this is the first birthday D. E. did for me. When I had to leave my room I put a blindfold on and went back to my room from memory too because I wanted to see the table only when they were both there. They were supposed to call me and most of all they needed to sing the song they sing in Mecklenburg to wake up the birthday girl or boy: 'I'm happy you were born.' D. E. sang it for me. Then I came in.

The table was set with the damask tablecloth that came to us from Gesine's mother. We normally use it only on New Year's Eve. How did they smuggle flowers into the apartment! But once you get to know D. E. you'll stop being surprised by miracles. Eleven candles, in all four colors, and the one for 1962 had a ring painted around it, 'because years are different from each other, of course.'

Before I'd cracked it myself. 1962 is when he met us. He likes to show you something to think about but then you've got to do the thinking yourself.

Your present was there. You know what, I just now saw the 'HMC' engraved on it. It's probably part of your job to think so carefully about other people, isn't it. Gesine gave me a model of the prewar English Daimler I've been missing for a long time. (Do you think it's dumb to collect things like that?) Jason, Shakespeare, and Eagle-Eye Robinson gave me a deluxe carton of chewing gum, which was very good of them but now they've given away my secret to Gesine. She thinks chewing gum is bad for your teeth. Mrs. Erichson gave me a two-yard-long shawl in the Mecklenburg colors (she's going to be my step-grandmother). From de Rosny, that's Gesine's highest-up boss, a savings account. (Seventy-five dollars.) From D. E. this printed stationery and a look as if butter wouldn't melt in his mouth. Don't trust anyone over forty.

But since he was watching like a hawk I acted like this was the end of it and innocently let them take me out for a walk in Riverside Park. Gesine was wearing the Copenhagen blouse, since he'd come over in a matching blue linen suit. (He still doesn't have a closet here.) So you see, they're arranging everything together.

At first I didn't suspect anything, since it was Sunday, and families often go for walks on Sundays. (Even though I was born on a Sunday.) They were discussing, like people on TV, whether or not there were evergreens in the park. 'You've got to keep your eyes open,' D. E. said, letting me think this was another piece of education in disguise. I did have to listen to how the little white beech on the slope below the retaining wall across from Ninety-Eighth Street was the kind of tree used for the wall of trees in the gardens of Versailles. But if you had kept your eyes open you saw a package next to the trunk, wrapped in colored paper, with ribbons, something even the most respectable person would steal it looked so tempting. Give up. We'll be fumbling around in the dark till the end of time if we try to figure out how he smuggled it there. I was walking behind him the whole way, he can't have thrown it. Give up. It was an ID bracelet, a silver chain with a tag saying my name and:

$$A_2$$
$$\text{cde } cD^uE.$$

For if I need blood from someone. After an accident. This is something a Czechoslovakian doctor can read.

Now you realize that D. E. must have broken into a doctor's office on Park Avenue. At least.

The third of the good things was an electronic calculator at the Memorial Fountain on 100th Street ('To the heroic dead of the Fire Department'). It was sitting there shining, way below the plaque to honor the horses that died 'in the line of duty' too. And you know Gesine, the educational ideas she has—she of all people says I can use it for homework, all four arithmetical operations plus percents. ('To get exponents you'd have to promise me something.') Only at home.

This Erichson was imitating Alexander Paepcke. That's an uncle of Gesine's (dead), he was an expert in things like this. D. E. doesn't want to be too much like a father. And that's why I agree to it.

Then came another thing, but it was the fourth and good things come in threes so it doesn't count. It was an apartment.

You're probably thinking: an apartment for the future married couple, Cresspahl & Erichson. That too. Up by Columbia University, where it looks so much like Paris, a fourteenth floor on Riverside Drive, five rooms, and they walked around in there like people in a bus station who have time to kill before they need to board. They called one of the rooms "the Berlin room." Obviously they'd secretly been here before. I don't know any more than that.

Because there's a door in the apartment and it had a sheet of paper like this one hanging on it, and behind it was mine. An apartment for me, with locks and a bolt, with its own bathroom, walk-in closet, air conditioner, phone, a hundred and thirty feet above Riverside Drive, with a view of the Hudson, the George Washington Bridge, the Palisades Amusement Park, the shore of New Jersey all day. The open space of park drew me in so much I felt like I was falling out the window. Down below, the thick bustle of the treetops along the roads, not as thin as the forest in West Germany when you fly into the Rhein/Main Air Base. Between the trees the number 5 bus came creeping up like a long strong animal. It had a very clean roof. I'll live a bit more alone in that apartment. Before we were two plus one. In the new apartment, he's one of the Two, I'm the One. New math. Group theory.

At night when he paces back and forth here talking, she runs along after him, just to make sure she doesn't miss any of his *statements*.

But she also lays into him. The Soviet Army has now signed the letter to the Czechs and Slovaks too. D. E. brings up airborne troops, she says he mustn't. It goes by fast, they often lose me: 'Not after Hungary!' Erichson: 'For most Americans the last war was in the Pacific...' Now you're supposed to think about Vietnam. But she's denying 'objectively comparable functions of power' and he's already ready and waiting with the concept of crowds.

It seems this apartment has another room with three windows facing the river. Now I hear them negotiating which one of them will get it—they both want the other one to take it. After their six years of practice it can't help but go well, can it?

Dear Anita, are you coming to see us in Prague or have you made yourself unwelcome in the ČSSR too with your travel agency? If they're rebuilding your Friedenau post office now, and you're losing your PO box, you'll have to shut up shop, won't you. You're hard to find in a PO box but in a four-room apartment with a phone the lights will give you away. (I'm sorry you lost your studio.)

There were relatives living in Friedenau until 1943, the Niebuhrs, also dead. We've just gotten a letter album from them, with photos, Gesine wanted to look through them alone. When she came back I thought she'd been crying. But does she let anything show?

My favorite dream about Friedenau is the market, because you can buy fish there and rhubarb and butter in bulk, not just sweaters and suits like sometimes at Fourteenth Street here. But how come the fishwife still asks after me?

When you come to New York I'll take you to Park Avenue, where it becomes a poor neighborhood (I'm only allowed to go to Harlem with a grown-up), and I'll show you La Marqueta with the Caribbean fruits, from habichuela blanca to ají dulce. The Puerto Ricans brought this market with them, and their neighborhood is called Spanish Harlem.

When you come for the wedding we'll only need to go swimming in the Hotel Marseilles. You can stay with me. Be my guest.

M.

P.S.
But my name will still be what you see on the top left corner of this sheet of paper and on the letters on the watch you gave me."

July 22, 1968 Monday

So what is it that threatens to end civilized life on earth? More than any-thing else, the bomb that produces heat through nuclear reactions: says one of the people who invented it, and he would now like to see the Soviet Union come to terms with this country, in this realm as in other hygienic regards. So industrious, scientists' regrets are.

Another expert, this one renowned in mathematics and philosophy, sounds antsy. The Soviet prime minister needs to assure Lord Bertrand Russell and the world that the Red Army renounces all use of military force in the ČSSR. Just so we know what's coming. Always these uncertain-ties about the future.

In fact the Soviets concluded their war games in Czechoslovakia three weeks ago and still they have their troops in the country. Their army news-paper reports from Moscow what they're doing there. They're looking for sacks of American weapons, and they've found another three.

From the late summer of 1948 on, the widower, the proud old bachelor Cresspahl was surrounded by three women. One you know; the second, a fifteen-year-old, you can guess; the third will surprise you. The first always wore an item of black clothing, a collar or scarf or something, mourning in advance, unfortunately; the second was often referred to behind her back as a hussy; and then there was the third, paying visits like back in the old days—Mrs. Brüshaver, the pastor's wife. Plucky of mouth, glasses stuck up on her head at an awkward angle, a careless part in her now-dull ash-blond hair, this is how she came over, careful not to seem to be looking around like a stranger. But her old path, between the Creutzes' greenhouses and the masters' villa, was now a Soviet restricted zone, off limits, so she had to come openly, down Brickworks Road from Town Street, a coat over her apron for decorum's sake, easy and relaxed from her first visit. But Cresspahl was pleased that she saw him busy in the kitchen with his daughter and Mrs. Abs, as if safe in a family, and dismissively asked her what they might do for her.

She started in as only a woman can, snatching something out of thin air; in her scattershot way she hit on how men were always bustling about and making a fuss and in general just you know. This was hard to contradict, and she tacked on, as it were reasonably, an invitation for Cresspahl to come by the pastorage and take a look at a window that was letting in rain, making puddles on Aggie's waxed floor. She thereby reminded us that we used to know her as Agatha, and reminded Cresspahl that his job used to be fine woodworking and carpentry in general. She had her opening. Now we had to mind our manners, and since in her pride Gesine Cresspahl forgot them, Mrs. Abs offered the guest a chair and a tin mug of coffee made of roasted rye. She immediately praised it. Because if a certain husband, hers in fact, hadn't taken her wifely advice then she'd now be drinking unhealthy imported coffee from a porcelain cup on a white tablecloth in Schwerin, as wife of the minister responsible for church matters in the state of Mecklenburg(-Vorpommern). In brief, Aggie was bustling and fussing and just-you-knowing as if the last time she'd dropped by was the day before yesterday and not ten years ago. Cresspahl kept his eyes on the stove into which he was putting more wood, maybe to warm the room a bit for her, and still he let himself be tempted into a question. – *Right?*: she said, the way only a woman who grew up somewhere between Grabow and Wismar can say it. The ministry post was something the Communists in the government had dreamed up as a reward for Brüshaver, whom they planned to introduce as a comrade from Sachsenhausen and Dachau. But they themselves *had written a "P" in front of that*, upset the apple cart, by mentioning their fellow soldier Brüshaver to their secret police K-5 a little too often, just because he kept bringing up, again and again, the matter of certain members of his congregation who'd disappeared and were staying wherever they were at the pleasure of the Soviet friends. (At this, someone in Cresspahl's kitchen felt her ears turn red with shame. She'd been refusing to greet the pastor on the street because she thought he'd betrayed her father.) And just as with the secular authorities, Brüshaver's stubbornness had made a hash of it with the religious ones, all because he'd had to refuse church rites to head senior detective Herbert Vick of the criminal police at his funeral. – Vick?: Cresspahl asked, dumbfounded, and not at the death. – Vick!: Aggie cried, quoting: "Because I am a faithful National Socialist!" Now the ten years between them were over and gone; now they were talking together again. The democratic civil administration of Mecklenburg had wanted to use Herbert Vick's arts, at least the criminological kind, for educational purposes too, at K-5 in the Neubrandenburg zone, and had hoped to repay his service with a Christian final benediction, as if the whole thing were just for show. Brüshaver, though, felt professionally obliged to consider, as a German and an anti-Fascist Christian, how this honored keeper of the peace had abstained from religious service and communion throughout his life; Jerichow as place of baptism scarcely mattered. So the Volkspolizei had had to find a pastor in Gneez to do the final honors, and Brüshaver was summoned to the state superintendency for a gentle warning. The Mecklenburg State Church was hoping to avoid a collision course; they'd told him so in writing, Brüshaver could frame it, just like his official certificate as "Fighter against Fascism" (category 4), if there were any frames to be had, and speaking of which, she'd dropped by today to discuss something about a window frame... Not a word about the Cresspahls, or the Abses, failing to attend her husband's sermons; not a word about Gesine's haughtiness. Thank you for that, *Fru Pastor Brüshaver.*

The next morning, Cresspahl cleaned one of his carpenter's rules, oiled the hinges, put it in his pocket, and really and truly walked partway into town, among other people, for the first time since October three years ago, since May of this one. Went out on a job.

It was a window ledge (*window breast*) on the upper floor of the pastorage. Aggie showed Cresspahl how she'd been bracing herself while polishing the window and the heel of her hand had gone right through what looked like perfectly intact enamel paint into the rotten wood, more than an inch, and she wasn't kidding. It turned out you could scrape off two thirds of the sill with your bare fingers. Aggie wanted an explanation, since the window had been repaired as recently as 1944. A master craftsman knows how to watch his words and refrain from appraising someone else's workmanship. In 1944 it had been Pastor Wallschläger—that shining light, annunciator of Nordic preeminence—reigning here. If someone had it in for him, all he needed to do was use the softest wood, black poplar it looked like, and make one or two channels in it with a spike or screwdriver, cover it all up with some paint, and leave Jerichow in good time. The rain, driven hence by the west and sea winds, will separate the ledge from the board (*window sill*) within a year, stealthily wash out the mortar, and before long leave nothing to keep frame and masonry together but the interior wallpaper. By that time it's too late to repair it—we're dealing with a total loss, which'll take more than ten pounds of tobacco on the black market to fix. – *I'll have to make a botch of it:* Cresspahl said soothingly, in English, since he had to get accustomed to his profession again gradually, and he didn't want to translate it, because it meant two things: to mess it up, to cobble it together. – Emergency first-aid for the winter: he promised, and Aggie was calmed, because he measured the window as if it might be saved. His keeping the sabotage from her is what I consider the second step in Cresspahl's return to life with people, instead of, as required, against them.

Now *you* try to find some cement in Jerichow or Gneez, just a paper cone full!, to slap over the masonry and bandage the rest of the ledge with, in exchange for the reformed currency of East Germany and some cheap words. You'd be more likely to run across a full sack of wheat. Then there's the problem of finding a hunk of beech or Cornish oak, 20" x 6" x 3", and let's not even mention the sodium silicate solution or synthetic resin to waterproof it with. If that's what you're looking for you've got to make your way around, offer at least conversation, and then when you come to inspect the wound in the wall with its makeshift covering you'll see Pastor Brüshaver standing in the garden, bent over the flowerbeds he's spading but still looking up as if he knew you. Conversation topics in that situation might include the days when the pastor had to make an appointment to talk to Mayor Cresspahl in Town Hall about a permit to hold an assembly (religious service). Or: that it's May again and here we have a new constitution, whose Article 44 sanctions religious instruction in secular schools, except maybe in Jerichow, where Brüshaver finds his charges waiting outside a looked door on School Street and the district commissioner conducts himself during the pleadings as though the Evangelical Church were a dispensable social group for an upright Communist and its Jerichow pastor more of a burdensome supplicant than a comrade in anti-Fascism. Potatoes need loose soil, Pastor. Hoe em before the sprouts show. When they get four inches high, hoe them again and pile them, pile em again when the plants are as big as your hand, *it'll do your waistline loads of good.* And then Brüshaver, with all his Greek and Latin, had to ask what this meant, and Cresspahl informed him: *Juss thins people say.*

Being neighbors. Teasing. Aggie Brüshaver now brought the ration cards over to the house, Street Representative for South Jerichow as she was ("since someone had to do it, and from me they'll get only the receipts, no character references"). When Cresspahl tried to refuse the vegetable fat and bacon Aggie had diverted for him from the Swedish Aid, he heard back that she was acting out of a sense of medical need, not charity, and a sixty-one-year-old patient needed to follow a state-registered nurse's orders. She'd noticed how my father held his head and before long I came upon her massaging his shoulder and neck muscles, and felt jealous, because he'd never asked his daughter to do that. – *Surely I'm closest to hand now*: Aggie said when he thanked her, and she gave him a pat to tell him to put his shirt back on. One time Jakob was with us for the weekend and she came in and fussed and bustled and lectured him as if reading him the riot act, or Leviticus. Jakob had gone to St. Peter's for Easter 1949, for the sermon on the resurrection, and she accused him of having sat there with his arms crossed till the end, even if in the back pew. – Like you were considering an offer!: she shouted, and after a while Jakob nodded, as if admitting it. And because I can still hear her, it gives me another chance to see him. Brüshaver had been getting along without teeth for three years now—they'd knocked them out of him in Sachsenhausen; finally Aggie talked him out of his suspicion of "German doctors" and he turned up with yellowish plastic structures in his mouth, chewing and chewing like someone when something tastes bad. – Say *"sixpence"*: my father told him, and Brüshaver would attempt the English word, and they went on babbling away at each other in made-up words like two little boys. I once saw Jakob's mother looking at them, her lips stretched so tight it seemed they had to hurt—she was attempting a furtive smile. When Jakob's mother wanted to speak severely to Aggie, she called her *"young Fru!"* They had gotten to the point of confidences in the hospital. And if some forgave me out of Christian duty, others had to only, let's say, for reasons of residence—because I lived and belonged there.

For the Gesine Cresspahl of 1948 wanted only to tolerate her neighbors. First of all, she was now a student at the academic high school and had settled the matter of God for herself, in a way she considered entirely original; second, she could soothe her unbelief simply enough, by recalling the prayer that a Lutheran chaplain of the US Air Force had offered up for the crew of the plane about to drop the first atomic bomb on populated territory; she credited Protestant theology with enough tactical and strategic judgment to realize that a conventional destruction of the city of Hiroshima would have sufficed, given the state of war as of August 6, 1945, 9:15 p.m. (Washington time). Student Cresspahl was well aware of why the New State in its New Era tended to schedule its parades, conventions, and

work details to coincide with religious holidays; she felt she was superfluous in this duel, believed she was taking neither side by keeping silent about
how the cigar butt had ended up in the schoolroom, which was the justification and excuse for shutting out the church: the boy Ludwig Methfessel was severely reprimanded and told to obey his new teachers' every word.
Anything else would've meant being a tattletale. And anyway, what did
she care about the church!

The heathen girl, she cannot live in peace / If other heathens do not let
her be. Look at Jakob, carrying a rain-soaked cat into the house and holding the dripping bundle up by the nape of its neck before dropping it with
the report: Wet as Jonah! and only then does he notice Cresspahl's Gesine
sitting there and he lets his glance slip right off her, idly, as if she didn't
know about biblical whales anyway. Hear the proverbs Heinrich Cresspahl
comes out with that summer, English and Protestant at once: *Don't preach
to the converted! Don't mock the afflicted!* and Gesine has to translate them
for him into current German, as if she were too uncultured for Luther's.
Jakob's mother lets him tease her for her Old Lutheran peculiarities since
that at least gives her the rare chance to discuss religious matters, but this
fall she goes for the first time to Brüshaver's church, takes communion
from him. Finally, in October, the daughter of Johann Heinrich Cresspahl,
b. 1933, well known to the authorities already, appears in the pastor's house
of St. Peter's Church in Jerichow to request for a second time, in person,
permission to take confirmation class. Enjoying already the blessings of
her elders' permission and agreement. So eager to please, this child.

In the warmer season Pastor Brüshaver had gone for walks with his
charges, holding lessons in a clearing in the Countess Woods; there were
not enough of them to keep warm under the oversized dome of the church.
He tried to borrow a living room for this one hour a week on Saturday
afternoons, trying the Quades, trying the Maasses (strictly avoiding Cresspahl's house); the good citizens complained about all the dirt the fifteen-
year-old children would track onto their sacred floors. Right after the war,
Mrs. Methfessel had been pleased to refer to the "community of destiny"
in which Brüshaver and her husband had found themselves; now she was
no match for her bullheaded boy, Ludwig, practicing with his soccer ball
right outside the parlor just when the pastor was holding his classes. Mrs.
Albert Papenbrock had the biggest hall in Jerichow—and the firmest faith

in the Evangelical Church, to hear her tell it; she was afraid to stir up the displeasure of Albert's wardens by having hopefuls for church membership in the house. She wrung her hands with scruples and hesitations, she lamented in a slight whine: people were always expecting more from her than from anyone else. . . . Brüshaver reserved the back room of the Lübeck Court, now a rathskeller. The tenant, Lindemann, let it be known that gatherings had to be registered and authorized, just like club meetings. The Jerichow mayor's office prohibited the use of secular premises for religious propaganda. (This was the one after Bienmüller: Schettlicht, the bright-eyed agnostic from Saxony.) Brüshaver thought he could see Red Army policy behind this; he hesitated to test out his theory at the Jerichow Kommandatura; how could he have known that the Wendennych Twins would have bit Comrade Schettlicht's head off! Eventually Jakob lost patience and the German Railway shunted a workshop car onto Papenbrock's now governmental siding, with benches, as if set up for a meeting, and a stove, for which the gasworks donated a wheelbarrow full of coal; because wherever Jakob worked with people they were always willing to do him a favor, as he was for them, the way friends do. In this train car, under the light of barn lanterns, Cresspahl's daughter stuck it out till Christmastime.

She tried to play the humble child, eager to repent through hard work; she was also prepared to accept as only fair that she got little praise for rattling off the main elements of the sacrament of baptism. Baptism is not just plain water, obviously. But she had to force herself to sit still and she avoided looking at Brüshaver's face too much. It seemed to be stuck in a perpetual smile, but it was just strained muscles, torn tendons that pulled the corners of his mouth into a grimace, froze his crow's feet into the involuntary semblance of a grin. He also acted like the pinky of his right hand had always stuck out from his palm like that, the stiff hook at the end of a sweep of pain pulling his shoulder down. When he lifted his book with his index and ring finger before pushing his thumb onto it, as though by accident, his hand looked artificial, sinister. He didn't realize he groaned every time he used his lower arm—that's the kind of thing it hurts to look at. Religious instruction takes the form of a catechism; there was no refuge from Brüshaver's damaged voice, which sounded like there was something unpleasantly sandy in his throat, being turned around and around, every syllable another wound to the sensitive tissue there. Gesine obsessively told herself that these were what he'd brought back from six years in Oranienburg and near Weimar, to be counterbalanced against an official certificate that by now his comrades at the town hall, the Gneez district school commission, the district council authorities raised their hands in front of as though shooing something away. But she couldn't keep perfect control over herself, and it was certainly against her will when she heard herself say, through a drone in her ears as if she were talking underwater: she knew the part about the doctrine of ubiquity by heart and could recite it at will but couldn't bring herself to believe in it.

She said it and ran so blindly to the train car door that she almost toppled down the high step onto the platform and ran down wet cold Station Street into the dim abyss of Market Square, hid in the broken lightless telephone booth, racked by wheezing sobs, afraid of the twilight when everyone would see her.

Cresspahl remembered the winter of 1944 when she'd sought out that same booth to hide from school and the authorities; he came to rescue her before dinner even. He led her off like a child, one arm around her shoulder, and the route they took spared her the light on at home and the look from Jakob's mother, with her dark eyes, enlarged by her glasses; the journey took them into the marsh where only rabbits and foxes could hear that the bodily presence of Christ in the communion wafer seemed like cannibalism, and they didn't care. This was the last time he held her and walked her somewhere like a father; she retained one of his efforts to console her, the one that absolved her: *You gave him a chance.* You tried, Gesine.

The next afternoon she saw Mrs. Brüshaver come into the yard and disappeared lightning-fast into the Frenchmen's room, which Jakob's mother, in her proper way, had cleared out for us to use as a dining room. In her hiding place, Gesine tried as fast as she could to think up various arguments against this emissary of the church—weapons in case she was discovered: Aggie had stopped instructing children in the Christian faith as early as 1937. Did she doubt what her husband proclaimed as articles of faith? She told Cresspahl to have himself hung upside down in front of an x-ray to get at the roots of the pains in his neck while she let her husband walk around with a case of Dupuytren's contracture, knots of tissue creating a thick cord in the palm of the hand, and a surgeon could take care of that; she was a nurse but turned her back on her husband's troubles with this government too, and went off to Jerichow's hospital leaving him to deal with all the paperwork of the parish too; are these the precepts for a Christian marriage, then, Aggie?

Aggie's response came through the closed door. She was in the hall with my father, thought no one else was listening, and asked him, despondently, as if asking for forgiveness for herself: What if the child's right, Cresspahl?

The sun hung in the western mist, already a quarter turned away from the earth; its low rays filled the room with a thick, blood-colored light. It was the first time I'd ever been in such a menacing red haze.

In March Cresspahl installed a new window ledge in the parsonage, handmade from a rail tie so soaked in carbolineum that dewdrops would sit on its surface without seeping in or running off. Meanwhile the Brüshavers had found a three-foot-wide section of crumbling wall, running alongside the chimney from the attic to the ground floor, bequeathed by enemies of the Mecklenburg State Church in 1944 with a few chisel blows to the copper flange. This was part of what Brüshaver had inherited. The pastor of Jerichow lived in a house that was falling apart.

The Sunday after Palm Sunday, 1949, there was a christening at the Brüshavers'. Aggie ("everything just grows like that with me") had had another child, a boy, Alex.

Those who challenge the omnipresence of Christ are neither worthy of confirmation nor equal to the duties of a godparent, it goes without saying, and Cresspahl's daughter wasn't jealous when she heard that, along with Jakob's mother, another child from confirmation class had been chosen to watch over Alexander Brüshaver's Christian conduct—a girl from former East Prussia who could not only recite the doctrine of ubiquity but believe it. Gantlik's daughter is who it was. Her name was Anita.

– Bit heavy on the church stuff, Marie?
– Did your pastor lose his hair too?
– Brüshaver without his biretta was a sight you did not want to see. The remains of a wound were still visible on his temple—a reddish indentation the size of a walnut.
– What was the Old Lutheran Church?
– Idiosyncrasies about justification, atonement, the trinity. If you ask me, a dispute about the right of association.

– Jakob's mother gave it up for you?

– Only children, who think they're the center of the world, believe things like that. No, she could only make it to the Old Lutherans in Gneez or Wismar once a month. She wanted to be able to go to church every Sunday.

– Were you being honest when you ran away and fell off the side step of the train car?

– Maybe I was being arrogant with my idea. Anyway it serves me to this day.

– Since you all had to lie everywhere, you took your own truth out on Brüshaver. Admit it.

– I admit it, Marie. And I wanted it to finally be over.

– You were much too young, Gesine. How's a child supposed to decide whether she believes or not. I'll get confirmed when I know for sure—maybe when I'm eighteen.

July 23, 1968 Tuesday

Enter Anita.

Not a "little Anna"—a big tall girl with strong shoulders like a boy, practically athletic from the work in the fields she'd had to do in the village of Wehrlich for nothing but food and a straw-sack pallet under a dripping thatched roof, because she was no local child, she was displaced, with almost no property to protect her, no mother, and a father who left her in servitude to the farmers and kept his pay from the Jerichow police for himself, apparently wishing ruin and death on his daughter. That's how things looked, and when the child came to town for religious services and confirmation classes, one and a half hours' walk and barefoot, she went right past her father with a calm, indifferent look, no anger. How could such a child—with no guardian, no support—escape from day labor to the state capital of Gneez, to an academic high school, to an apartment in the most desirable neighborhood, by the town moat, in a three-story building with running water coming out of the walls and light out of the ceiling?

When she first entered ninth grade the rumors had preceded her and gave her a nasty welcome: "the Russians" had helped her out. That was true insofar as the gentlemen commandants of Jerichow, the Wendennych

Twins, when they wanted to tour the country as conquerors from the Red Land, took a detour through Wehrlich and had Anita, a fifteen-year-old child, sit with them so she could translate what these Germans in Mecklenburg were trying to say. That was fair to the extent that the Comrades Wendennych compensated her for her services as though she were one of their own: with a purchase coupon for a bicycle, a Swedish import no less, the crown jewel of the government store on Stalin Street in Gneez; the citizens of Gneez called this the first bike in Mecklenburg that "the Russians" paid cash for; they called Anita "the Russians' sweetheart" while they were at it. As a result, Anita could bike to Fritz Reuter High School punctually on September 1, 1948—one and a half hours every morning, one and a half hours back to Wehrlich, over unpaved country roads, into the rain and the west wind of that cold wet fall. She only had to lock the bike—it was safe from damage because even though dealings with "the Russians" hardly constituted a recommendation, crossing "the Russians" was a bad idea. A bicycle with white tires, TRELLEBORG stamped on the tire rims. It's true that the Wendennych gentlemen also asked her how she was doing and were scandalized at her habit of doing homework in the former municipal library, now run by the Cultural League (for a D. R. of G.), since she had no home and her slave driver of a host—he doesn't need a name—might at any moment send her away from her books to go clean out a pigsty; Jerichow's Kommandatura arranged with Gneez's to get her a change-of-residence permit and have her assigned to Frau Dr. Weidling's living room—out of turn, a favor. A dangerous one, only worsening her reputation, even though Dr. Weidling had been hauled in by the *Kontrrazvedka* that November because of her carefree travels through German-occupied country with a man in a black uniform, not because she meant to leave Anita Gantlik a whole apartment to herself. But that's what people said. And we were there the first time Anita was called on in class by Baroness von Mikolaitis, who was allowed, as an act of mercy, to sell her Baltic origins to us in the form of Russian lessons; Anita humbly stood up, suggested a curtsy, and gave the jittery older lady a longish answer. Its length was about all we could understand of it, even after our three years of instruction in Russian; it sounded a bit like: The Russian word for "train station," ma'am, *voskal*, is derived from the amusement park near London's Vauxhall station, much like the park that Czar Alexander II Nikolayevich built in his city of Pavlovsk, *rayon* Voronezh. Anyway the word *"voskal"* definitely came up. The baroness was not used to such fluent, unforced, natural speaking from us, and not up to following it either; in pure self-defense she found fault with the way Anita pronounced her *o*'s. Anita had made them sound dry, not elongated as in our Mecklenburgish. She thanked the baroness for her guidance, in Russian. The following week she raised her hand and told Mikolaitis that she'd pronounced her *o* for some *native speakers* (said in Russian, not English!) and they'd given it their seal of approval as standard Moscow pronunciation. If she sounded helpless, pleading, it wasn't an act—she was asking her instructor for a decision. The end of the story was that Mikolaitis invited Anita to take private lessons, hoping to learn a more natural Russian herself. A Solomonic move; in fact she was a coward; in general we found little worth emulating in adults. It was incontrovertible, though, that the loudspeaker above the blackboard would crackle three or four times a week and the voice of Elise Bock, school secretary now as before, would come through it: Gantlik to the principal's office. Anita said goodbye to her German or biology teacher with a slight sigh, curtsied per regulations, and packed up her notebooks as though saying goodbye forever. Two periods later, sometimes after three o'clock, she'd be back at her seat—having translated for Mr. Jenudkidse in City Hall; since Slata was gone. A modest girl. Walked into the school in her well-worn black suit as if joining a solemn rite. Spoke softly, eyes downcast. She probably thought that wearing her long dark-brown hair in braided loops around her head was the fashion in Gneez. A wide, squat forehead behind which there was a lot of worrying that fall. She was clumsy, too— borrowing notes for the classes she missed from none other than our top student, Dieter Lockenvitz. His hair stood up straight and white with distraction; under the pressure of his cogitations he failed to notice that this girl would have liked very much to sit down at his desk for a minute and have him point out various of his lines and formulas, especially for her, so that for once he'd notice her. When Lockenvitz would stand up at the board and try to force his way through to an algebraic victory—for in math his wheat bloomed half-choked with wheatgrass—her wide-open eyes would be fixed on him, visibly hoping for him, longing to help him; I trembled a little for her, she would've been a tasty morsel for Lise Wollenberg to gulp down. But only Pius and I saw the hopes and dreams going to waste. If she was ever happy that winter, it was when she'd forced her father to register her as a resident in Gneez and then skedaddle by return train—for the first time she was alone in a room, behind ice-cold glass, with a view of the fog and the freezing tops of the linden trees, in a foreign land, but on her own.

You know, Gesine, Gantlik wasn't my real name.

Was he your stepfather?

I wish, Gesine! Unitam! *If only he'd been a stranger with no rights over me.*

"Anita," is that a fake name too?

My mother saw a movie with a Spanish scene, heard a 1933 hit song. "Juanita." I forgive her.

But not your father.

Maybe when he's dead.

Our gentle Anita, thirsting for vengeance.

We were living on the Memel, where it's called the Neman, with a good Polish name that Gantlik's the stump of. The Germans came and offered us blue IDs—German People's Census Group One, for Persons of German Nationality with "Proven" Active Participation in the National Struggle— because of a grandfather from Westphalia. My bonehead father ups and joins the German Swastika Party because he likes seeing German tanks flatten Polish villages. Support for the Germans, and all of us along for the ride: mother, brothers and sisters. Gantlik.

Without a German passport the Germans could've easily conscripted him to work in Old Germany, Anita. Without his family. You all had ration cards, you were allowed to go to school.

A German school.

A school. You were allowed to go to the movies.

The City Mouse and the Country Mouse. *Or* Hitler Youth Quex.

And your mother could go to cafés with you, to restaurants, could shop in the stores.

And my father, as a citizen of the Reich under his German pseudonym, was compensated for the farm, was given a new one near Elbing. When the Red Army caught up to us in January 1945, we could show them in writing that we were Germans. My mother, my brothers and sisters, we buried them in an open field. My father, the German, he couldn't take care of an eleven-year-old child.

You pray, Anita. There's a request in there, about forgiving.

I do forgive. The three Russians who took me one after the other, all the Russians lock stock and barrel.

But never your father.

You mean Gantlik. Not till the day he dies. This was his war. He did it.

And then you were curious about the Russians. The kind of people who could take revenge on an eleven-year-old girl.

I was, Gesine. Still am today.

Do you know what we used to say when Triple-J summoned you out of the classroom? "Anita's off to give blood." Because it always had to be you. Because you came back so exhausted.

It was Pius who said that.

Pius was a good man.

I should say so. I didn't used to tell anyone about the Neman, the Memel, because I was scared you'd all call me Volksdeutsch *behind my back. Or "foreign war-booty girl."*

Student Gantlik rid herself of her father when she was able to trace, via the Red Cross, a sister of her mother's—a widow with two children, starving in the Ruhr District, to whom the words "Gneez" and "Mecklenburg" sounded like dinners with meat again. On paper this aunt became the head of Anita's household by the town moat, with Anita's pay the mainstay of the household budget; no sooner was the Western zone cut off from the Soviet one than she started whining about the sacrifice she was making for her niece, living in a region whose money bought less of everything, from butter to wristwatches, complacently forgetting that Anita had given her a roof over her head, that Anita's fees filled the common coffer, that it was Anita who was raising her aunt's two sons, around eleven years old. Her father still came up when we had to recite our genealogy to the school in order to be eligible for educational stipends (twenty-two to thirty-two marks). – My father's a worker: Anita said in as East Prussian an accent as she could manage—and wrote. Later the questionnaires became more nitpicky and general information was no longer allowed. – My father knocks rust off the Warnow shipyards in Rostock: Anita testified.

Did we profess to each other that friendship was our destiny? We most certainly did not. Anita borrowed neither paper nor pencil from the Cresspahl/Pagenkopf collective; she was also suspicious of such playacting of marriage among high-school students, or else maybe wanted to show respect for it by keeping her distance. In was Pius who, while walking past her desk, put down his extensive set of compass instruments for her, because all she had for geometry homework was a homemade protractor with no degree scale; once again Pius was trying to rub Lise Wollenberg's nose in something, plus it was hard for him to look on while someone was struggling. When Anita returned the things the next day, she thanked him with a giant sigh but ignored Student Cresspahl sitting next to him. While I was worried she would take any word from me as condescension, she was wanting not to impose. For she felt like an outsider, an undesirable, an intruder, a refugee. On a school trip, 9-A-II met a charcoal-maker building a pile and Kramritz the humanities scholar translated the sooty-skinned wanderer's Czechified comments into scientific fluency; Anita started explaining, in a voice squeaky with agitation, this work she herself had had to do as a child. Schoolgirl Cresspahl was eager to learn how you made charcoal for flatirons; Anita's voice grew softer, stammered, then ceased.

Anita, the outsider, found a patch of meadow with a path through the reeds on the south shore of Gneez Lake and thought she could be alone there; how startled she was when students from all four ninth-grade classes turned up in her habitual swimming spot, still off the beaten track in April. She covered up with her towel at once, embarrassed because she was well along in terms of developing a bust; long slim thighs and firm calves remained visible. – Nice legs: Pius said as we swam across the lake to the boathouses. – FEISTY legs: I corrected him; I'd learned that once and for all. When we got back we found her besieged by young men from tenth grade wanting to borrow her towel, complimenting her wavy, copious hair, offering her cigarettes—the usual male courtship rituals. In her confusion Anita said something dismissive in a shaky voice about how dumb people were who learned all about the structure of the human lung in school and then went and spoiled it by inhaling tobacco smoke. We—Pius and I— looked around for Lockenvitz, even though we knew he wasn't there, he was at a ZSGL session; the person who was, however, clearly visible on the edge of the group of swimmers with a cigarette between her fingers was the Cress girl, Cress on a Pole, *Röbbertin his Gesin.* What else can a person do in such a situation but proudly squint into the May sun and take a long slow draw of her cigarette—from Dresden, twelve pfennigs apiece you know, genuine imitation Lucky Strikes?

That was rude of me, Gesine; I didn't mean it.
And how could I tell you in front of all the boys there that Pius had once held your godchild at his breast—six-month-old Alex—and told me about the refreshing air that babies exhale?
Like fresh uncut silk crepe.
A breath I thought I might still have. If I wanted to keep Pius from hungering for it, I had to start smoking.
If I'd known I was causing you pain, Gesine!

That was one rapprochement; it wandered off into the reeds of Gneez Lake and was lost forever. What could Anita be expected to see but more contempt? At the same time we felt deeply sorry for each other. She for me because I'd troubled the pastor of Jerichow with a show of sincerity; the concerned and pitying sidelong look she gave me, which I could merely feel in the dim light of the confirmation car, I remember it to this day. I for her because she understood absolutely all the assignments in our science classes (math: A; chemistry: B+; biology: A) and yet the bottom line of all her equations was inevitably a God present in the molecule, the atom, the sparrows he makes fall to the ground by shooting them off the roof with nuclear weapons. Anita, authorized for Gneez, took it upon herself to travel every Sunday to St. Peter's Church in Jerichow, just because the dean in Gneez Cathedral supported the Mecklenburg pastor Schwartze (Ludwigslust) and denounced his very own bishop, Dibelius (West Berlin), as a warmonger and "instrument of American aggression," as "Atom Dibelius"; Dibelius had spoken of the administration of the Soviet occupation zone and its K-5 as a "government construct," and of the

> violence
> overstepping all lawful bounds,
> inner lack of authenticity, and
> hostility to the Gospel of Christ;

Brüshaver, on the other hand, wanted to try his luck again with Martin

Niemöller, now on the council of the Evangelical Church in Germany, signatory of the Stuttgart Declaration of Guilt, and author of the proposition that every occupying power should withdraw from the remains of Germany and keep the peace through the UN. That was why Anita was missing every Sunday when we raked the city parks in our blue shirts or dug up a third of the schoolyard for a Michurin garden; she went to see Brüshaver in her little black dress, probably dropped in on the Kommandatura to see the Wendennyches too because unlike us she was never was reprimanded for unauthorized absences. By then her name was Anita the Red, because swimming under the sun of the spring of 1949 had bleached her hair and let a reddish note shine through.

> *And I had a godchild in Jerichow, Gesine.*
> *And you took communion in Jerichow.*
> *Once every six months. Most times I wasn't worthy to.*
> *Because of evil thoughts? Tell me, Anita.*
> *Due to envious thoughts, Gesine.*

Anita could have stayed as a child of the house with the Brüshavers, but she was afraid of seeming to intrude, afraid above all of pity. Plus Aggie was just a nurse, whatever her degrees; Anita needed someone bound by a doctor's oath to keep her secret. If she'd trusted me I'd have come with Jakob's mother on the spot. That aunt from the British occupation zone let Anita do all the housework, naturally including the laundry, and they shared a bathroom but she didn't have the sense to ask a sixteen-year-old about her cycle. Everyone else Anita saw in the world were men. She went to the Gneez public health clinic, corner of Railroad Street and Town Moat, hoping the machine there might process her and let her come out the other side still anonymous. The bit about the machine was true enough. Behind those frosted-glass windows bordered with peacetime vines she learned about the gonorrhœ cervicitis that the Red Army had given her when she was eleven. She had almost *fayassn*, as they say in East Prussia—forgotten that act of revenge, thanks to constant efforts not to think about it.

Anita would later describe the quarantine barracks in Schwerin, to which she was whisked off with an infectious-disease certificate, as a camp. She was locked in with young and older ladies who'd acquired such internal complaints voluntarily, sometimes for money. Anita remembered the head doctor as a harsh, prudish woman—a bitch, "a Naziess" whom she could easily picture with a swastika on her smock. Anita was snarled at like she was guilty, or because a different guilt had come to light. The woman, with her medical expertise, accused Anita of dillydallying, but Anita had been detained in Poland when the children around Jerichow were being officially ordered to report for VD examinations (signed H. Cresspahl, Mayor), and the course of the infection was almost entirely lacking in visible symptoms, except for moderate discharge. The finding was that the infection had advanced to the cavum uteri, with endometritis specifica as the result to date. They congratulated Anita on having gotten away without pain; – Stop making such a fuss!

They used the formal, adult second-person with her because she'd been advanced into tenth grade; the radiation treatment and the sulfonamide drug that stained the urine red seemed risky to her. She escaped from the facility and made her way east, through forests and down footpaths, in the night. But there was one person who wanted her back—Triple-J in Gneez. Uniformed men in his service and pay were waiting from the Countess Woods to down in the "gray area" for just such a girl, creeping along by herself, unarmed, and claiming to be Russian. Alone in the jeep with a child who refused to give him information in his language or any other, he thought of a drinking buddy, Dr. Schürenberg, and gave him a bad scare by knocking on his door at midnight. Schürenberg at that time still had the right to place selected patients in the city hospital under his own care; it was he who finally notified the principal's office of the high school. And who was the third man with whom these two had sung and caroused in the Dom Ofitserov? None other than Emil Knoop, the man with the heart of gold ("by weight, Yuri, by weight!"), who brought the antibiotic, penicillin, back from Brussels and Bremershaven. Here one man was doing his job, and anyway he was sworn to help and to keep secrets in confidence; the second man was being diplomatic, since Comrade Jenudkidse could hear the wind of an East German state blowing across the fields of Stalin's foreign policy, and if the Soviet Military Administration was about to withdraw step by step from Gneez City Hall then a generous gesture would go over well. The third man, Emil, was not the sort to worry about laws and regulations describing such imports as a contamination of the anti-Fascist

German People's Movement with drugs of Anglo-American imperialism, not over a mere refugee girl (never mind that penicillin was being manufactured in the southern part of the Soviet Zone by a copycat people-owned pharma firm for the use of the higher echelons of the party and security force). You could learn a lot from Knoop—all of it illegal, unfortunately.

Anita spent the whole summer vacation of 1949 lying in bed, at first for just four days, because of the four injections she was getting, and then on orders of the referring physician, for malnutrition; we traveled by water, traveled to the Black Forest, passed beneath Anita's windows, and forgot her. The Twins of Jerichow, the Wendennych commandants, turned up at Anita's bedside in visiting hours to give her sweets and a volume of poetry by Aleksandr Blok. Triple-J appeared with his entourage, bringing red carnations, and decided to interpret the word "cystitis" on Anita's fever chart as tactfully as the Pagenkopf/Cresspahl students, who'd been sent—no, delegated—by their FDJ unit to call on Anita at the start of the school year. She looked disbelievingly at us, wide-eyed, not recognizing us right away—that's how permanently prepared she was to be alone, to stay alone.

Did praying help you, Anita?
It did help, moshno.
What did you think about?
I puzzled over the three boys in Red Army uniforms, one of whom was carrying gonococcus. Burning sensation when urinating, purulent discharge from the urethra—a man notices that, even during a war. So he knew what he was giving me.
And what did you read, Anita?
The kinds of things you read up on at sixteen when you've been told you have pyosalpinx, curable and infertility, permanent. That you'll never be able to have children. Mayakovsky. Nado
      vyrvat'
           radost'
                  u gryadushchikh dney.
V etoy zhizni
          pomeret'
              ne trudno.

Anita stayed alone when she came to terms with the fact that if she went east she might reach the Havel River at best but never the Neman. She spent a school year staying by herself in the 10-A-II classroom while we had gym. If only she'd trusted Aggie Brüshaver. But she saw her as someone whom Christian marriage obliged to tell her husband, a man, everything.

"Anita the Red": that stayed with her. Because she still went and helped Colonel Jenudkidse with the German language, now in the Barbara Quarter, behind the green fence taller than a man's height. What were we supposed to think if not that she'd taken the Red Army's side? While the deputy president of the 10-A-II FDJ group had a terrible time unloading at least three copies of *Young World* journal among her fellow students, Anita used issues of the Red Army's *Krasnaya Zvezda* in Contemporary Studies class, even if it was from a subscription she shared with Triple-J. Her windy aunt now complained that Anita had recently started locking a certain room in the Weidling apartment behind her, both when she left and when she was there, merely because she was worried that the healthily boisterous lads, Gernot and Otfried, might damage her record player, and what was Anita listening to anyway, behind her locked door, allegedly without company? Tchaikovsky, every time. And the Red Army station, Radio Volga—the signal came in weakly from the Potsdam area. Insatiable was her curiosity about the Red Army of the Russian Workers and Farmers.

What she'd have to say to the latest news from the ČSSR would no doubt make sense to me. The Czechoslovak Communist Party leadership has rejected a meeting with their Soviet comrades and their followers in the latter's territory, accepted one in their own. As though it wasn't going to be a friendly match.

For the ČCP to make them rearrange their travel plans really is adding insult to injury. Why would they ever forgive that?

And they're wanting to send troops to the Bohemian border with West Germany.

Do you hear what you're saying? They want to send troops!

In Poland, three miles north of Czechoslovakia, they've driven up half a dozen army trucks with extra-high aerials, secured by two regiments of combat troops.

Gesine, if I were the Red Army I'd station myself in the Olza River valley

*too. It's the easiest place, there are mountains all around. And what does an
army need when it's going somewhere?*

A communications center.

You're learning, Gesine.

"Red Anita," too—this out of ethnographic error and prejudice. For
while Anita continued to contribute more than her share to her aunt's
household budget (to keep her aunt in the household and herself with a
right to the apartment), she did keep a little something to herself for purposes that were... should we say private? Yes, if that means: secret. First
of all, she had to pay back Emil Knoop for the cost of her medication, at
a rate of six to eight East marks per every last one from the "West" (– only
death comes for free: Emil said in his jovial way, not noticing how she
started at the word). Finally, acting as a businessman, he gave her work to
do helping with his correspondence with the Soviet Armed Forces in
Germany, where Jenudkidse's help failed to reach. Her credit with Knoop
she left untouched, even when she had to fool her hunger with oats and
sugar roasted together with no fat. Then she would take Madame Helene
Rawehn, fine apparel, Gneez Market Square, utterly aback with fabrics of
pure wool and raw silk and terrify the young men of Fritz Reuter High
School with grown-up tailored suits, with tight skirts a hand's breadth
above the knee, with sweaters of a kind worn this year in France or Denmark and due in Mecklenburg sometime around 1955 if they were lucky.
Next to Anita, Habelschwerdt looked shabby and threadbare; but how do
you ban a student's appearance that's *comme il faut*, if a little too elegant?
It's to encourage and awaken Dieter Lockenvitz, we thought at first; except
he was precisely who she avoided. But she came to the class parties, accepted
invitations from twelfth graders and eleventh graders too; she didn't dance.
A gentleman who escorted this lady home would find himself heading
home with thanks but no handshake. Anita received requests for much
more than her towel; asked if she'd go for a walk at night around Gneez
Lake she asked the young men their intentions so openly that they had no
choice but to recognize as an imposition what they'd wanted to keep floating in the air above the promenade as a lovely dream. – What for? Anita
asked, unmoved, businesslike, and raising her head with a slight jerk, lips
pursed, clearly well aware of why and wherefore. She wore her blouses but-

toned all the way up, with a thin velvet ribbon in a double bow; "Bitter Rice" was sometimes shouted after her anyway, alluding to another Italian film notorious for very different reasons. The Anita from before had worn knee socks; cured Anita made use of stockings, nylon, seamless.

"Red Pigtails." She'd had her hair cut while still in the hospital. A short, close-fitting plumage, crisscrossing her forehead in well-judged fashion, was all that remained of her braids. Fiete Semmelweis Jr. had left two tiny stray strands at the nape of her neck that stuck out startlingly red under the outer brown, shifting against and over each other every time Anita turned her head even a little.

July 24, 1968 Wednesday

On Sunday we watched an old man being taken from the bus stop bench across from our windows into a Knickerbocker ambulance—a bum in rags and a long beard, recognizable from the two shopping bags that contain his worldly possessions. He seemed to be about to cause trouble so two boys in blue made him get a move on. Since yesterday he's been back on the bench; he may live there. In return for giving back to society, needless to say, he entertains the waiting passengers: Eh, ma'am: he says: it was just that I ran into a syringe (points to his calf). So I had the police call me an ambulance.

His next sentence betrays the fact that he thinks he's in Alabama, and he wishes us a pleasant river voyage on the Manhattan and Bronx Transit Authority bus. They've shaved him a little, by force it looks like; he's a little cleaned up. He could use a shepherd and keeper besides the police department.

Anita, as a godmother.

Jakob's mother gave the baby Alexander Brüshaver a sterling silver food pusher; – *from Cresspahl an is daughter*: she said, for completeness sake. Anita would've given a lot for the matching spoon; she stood by the cradle empty-handed, clenched her teeth, looked furious. Brüshaver thanked them both for their prayers; Anita didn't yet venture to see any of her prayers as producing a result.

Easter 1950 was looming and with it a first birthday; Anita put a

Scandinavian bicycle up for sale, 600 km on the tires but well cared for, in good-as-new condition. Pius offered her eight hundred marks, cash in hand; the next day she asked him to a parley, in private, as if it were a matter of life and death. Lockenvitz had bid up the price: Pius told us, and we looked at each other in disbelief, from under furrowed brows. Lockenvitz may have an A in Latin and another in English, but he didn't have any money. Anita put down on the Brüshavers' table, as if it were nothing, a silver napkin ring with DEUT4:40 – A. B. engraved on it. Mayest thou prolong thy days upon the earth.

1951. Anita had turned into the kind of person who needed to learn to knit for this child. A two-meter-long scarf.

In 1952 was our Abitur; Anita made a wall hanging for Alex, without paying much attention, because while tying the knots she also had to memorize that force causes a change in a body's momentum m over time, following the equation $F = dm/dt$ (according to Isaac Newton). Until he was ten Alex fell asleep to a color rendition of IL FAUT *travailler* – TOUJOURS TRAVAILLER. The only formula she trusted, at that point.

In West Berlin Anita lived in a grimy building two blocks from Karl Marx Street in Neukölln, on a rear courtyard, with Mrs. Machate. Look at that, Anita has learned how to hug. The room was so cramped that there was just enough space between the bed and the wardrobe to prop up an ironing board for the guest to sleep on. First we confessed that each of us had done all right in the past four years. Once it occurred to me that the Brüshavers might have named their last child in memory of a former neighbor, I had to spend until morning telling Anita about Alexander Paepcke, in death a comfortingly good man. (Because Anita wanted to trade and sleep on the ironing board, and I refused, we woke up midmorning and lay in the one bed.)

On Anita's shelf in Mrs. Machate's kitchen I saw artificial honey and margarine; she gave me good butter and expensive smoked fish to take with me back to Alex. She rode the streetcar with me to Baumschulenweg, as if she still had papers for the East; friendship was one thing, intrusive questions another. One of her errands in the "democratic" sector must have been to get the messenger through the pocket search of democratic customs officers. So that Alex would get his needs met.

Anita was relentless with the child. Until he was eleven he got an orange from her every fourth day—never candy or chocolate. An electric tooth-brush when he was six.

In 1955 other children in Jerichow might have a schoolbag; Alex Brüshaver was equipped for his educational institution with a solid fountain pen. – Ballpoint pens have ruined all our handwriting: Anita said in her forth-right way.

In the fall, Anita began her letters to Alex *Your father Brüshaver is dead*. In the letters she had to avoid causing any trouble with the officials who opened and read and wrote reports to the authorities on them; even so, I wished they'd been kept.

Anita had worked out a basic diet for Alex's monthly packages, but she always thought of something she'd forgotten, something like band-aids. – Boys like to run around and they get scrapes!: she said, disgusted and angry at her prior forgetfulness.

And, inevitably with Anita, a children's illustrated Bible. Since what Alex was learning via the printed word were texts from the people-owned People's Knowledge Textbook Publishers:

Today the Young Pioneers are all on the meadow.

All are wearing the blue scarf.

"Be prepared!" some shout.

"Always prepared!" the others answer.

She owned a tasteful frame with a removable back for photographs of Alex. In 1956 she was definitely strapped for cash, with just enough to move near the university, but expensive enlargements of the Jerichow snapshots were a necessity. Once I noticed that there was no recent picture. Anita turned away. The photo showed Alex making the Young Pioneers greeting, with the famous triangle of scarf around the neck, hand to forehead, palm out, fingers clawed heavenward, promising his support to the oppressed of all the continents of the earth. How I had to beg to be allowed to see that one!

When Jakob had died and the funeral had happened, Anita the god-mother treated me harshly. She thought my presence at the cemetery would have helped me. Since she was talking over an open phone line from West Berlin to Düsseldorf, she spoke vaguely. As if a doctoral student in Slavic Studies knew ways to sneak into Mecklenburg.

– There are factions in the Red Army too: she said.

Anita connected to a Soviet military mission? Carrying messages? She didn't invite any questions.

In 1956 Anita already possessed a passport from the Republic of France, and it finally occurred to her: A boy needs a pocketknife with thirty-two attachments.

What a boy of eight could really use is a bicycle. So it was a good thing that the Gift Service GmbH, Genex, headquartered in Switzerland, was founded in 1957. Payment in Western currencies, deliveries in East German goods, but punctually, within the space of a month. Anita could even decide whether Alex should ride to the Baltic on a blue or silver painted frame, with or without a gearshift. (She avoided giving him unambiguously Western devices. Alex should grow up without the envy of other children, without warnings from schoolteachers.)

She suppressed any missionary impulses. She worked hard to forgive her classmate Cresspahl for leaving the Evangelical Church almost as soon as she'd found a paying job "in the West"; she even forgave her her argument that the Church has it so good uncontested under capitalism that it doesn't need a tax to help it out. Anita confidently expected that the child Marie would be given a Christian baptism; if she was upset and disappointed, it was for our sake.

In 1959 Alex Brüshaver was safely doing the right thing in school. He came in first in an essay contest and won a toy: a battery-operated tank, in olive battle color, that could roll on its treads and swing its cannon to face the class enemy at the same time. To strengthen Alex's will to defend the homeland. You'd think a child would love such items of mechanical art. Anita wasn't sure, and asked. He sent her a postcard with a picture of the East German custodian on one side, and on the other he'd dedicated the following to her:

> What use is it to dream of peace?
> Who defends the young state?
> The doves themselves need armor,
> That's why I am a soldier.

In his next mailing the thing itself arrived, in wrapping paper and olive-green ribbons. For years to come, Alex stood up every morning in school to hoist the flag and recite the slogans, the Song of Rebuilding included. "Youth, awake and rise up! Build up, build up, build up!"

In 1960, Mrs. Brüshaver was kicked out of the Jerichow pastorage but was given two rooms near the Rose Garden in Gneez. Anita took two weeks off to travel to Mecklenburg with paint, to help set up a widow's apartment, to spend fourteen days with Alex. (Whenever Anita considered a legal regulation unreasonable, she got around it without a second thought. Anarchism? Stubbornness? Mischief?)

Before we moved to New York there was a vacation Anita invited us to spend in West Berlin. For self-interested reasons, she insisted. She'd been going out with an émigré from the lands of Karelia for years, and now he wanted it in writing that they belonged to each other, and she wanted another woman to check him out first. Sometimes a godmother needs a godmother of her own. I had to swear to her twice before she entrusted me too with the explanation of why she would never in her life have a child besides Mrs. Brüshaver's in Mecklenburg. She'd told her boyfriend—he wants to be known as "the old man," nothing else—in their first year; she still wasn't sure if he was truly willing to forgo reproduction. The old man and I—he passed the test, we came back from a daylong walk through the Berlin woods near Schulzendorf, Anita was sitting with Marie in the Old Tavern garden in Dahlem. Marie was startled, the wind or she had knocked over a full glass. Anita was explaining the course of events to her. – *Le vent*: she said: *vous comprenez?* – *Le vent*: Marie said: *vous* . . .

The other matron of honor was Mrs. Brüshaver, – *because I'm closest to hand now*: the gallant lady felt. But the truly closest was Alex, twelve years old, in his confirmation suit and tie. So Anita had two children at her wedding. Protestant, of course, what else.

Anita watched the children, who were bored by the ceremonial meal, passing the time with pen-and-paper games. Anita wrestled down her prejudice and cried out: They're both good children!

For many years Marie thought of Berlin as a city flooded with breezes and sunlight, where you go to get married.

After the authorities in East Berlin built a wall through Berlin to keep their citizens from continuing to vote with their feet, Anita is said to have used a bar on Henriettaplatz as a travel agency that helped people cross the borders of the other Germany. She denies it. The bartender on Henriettaplatz had a different name, she says; that bartender was just twenty-four, had problems with her relatives . . . When Anita wants to she can easily look four years younger, even today. And she doesn't care much about names when they're printed on official paper, we know that.

Whoever it might have been, I took trips for Anita after I lost my job in New York. I tried out passports in transit from Prague to Warnemünde, from Trelleborg to Vienna. During these trips my name was often that of the people about to take these trips, and I pleaded an age that wasn't my real age too, just as Anita requested.

By 1962 the East Berlin philosophers had convinced themselves that cybernetics was a science and a tool, not an instrument of capitalist exploitation; Alex had long since been the owner of a beginner's computer-science handbook. Likewise books that state who actually invented the telephone. For reference.

At fourteen Alex was conceited. Couldn't pass a shop window in Gneez without checking his reflection. Making sure the dark lock was curled on the right corner of his brow. Anita was worried. – Who'd he get that from?: she asked (in letters to New York).

She sent him the American gold miners' pants with the studded pockets when he asked for them. Then, since she happened to know his size, she had a khaki-colored linen suit made for him. Anita won that round.

At sixteen Alex started smoking. After 1962 a citizen of the GDR could purchase Western tobacco products at domestic stores, the Intershops, assuming he or she could put West German marks or American dollars on the counter in such establishments. Anita sent her godchild no cash. Cf. Gneez Lake, "Lucky Strikes" from Bulgaria or was it Dresden?

In 1966 Alex was seventeen and signed his name "Alexander." He sent a photo from a trip to Poland, from which a round-headed Mecklenburger looked out at us from under curly tousled hair, with soft lips, but somber. His broad shoulders, wet from swimming, were like Anita's. Still, it bothered her that this photo might have been taken by a girl. – He's still just a child!: she cried.

The next year he was eighteen, of age under East German law, and for his birthday he was informed of two things. First, that as the son of a pastor he would not be permitted to study at the university (mathematics). Second, that he was invited to fulfill his military service requirement in the defense and protection of his Socialist fatherland. Anita had predicted the first; she was prepared for the second.

If Anita were the missionary type, she would have managed to convince him to work harder in Russian. She accepted his merely satisfactory grades in this language, if with a sigh. The hiking trips to Poland, he'd thought of those without her too. She may have been waiting for him to say he wanted to go to "where you got married" again; she didn't let herself try to talk him into it.

So how would Alex ever get the crazy idea into his head that Anita could take him by the hand and out of the country to wherever he wanted to go? He's a do-it-yourselfer, and he lets himself get caught in the Stettin harbor in the proven act of trying to leave a Socialist fatherland behind at his own discretion. Alex is sentenced to three years in a prison in Saxony. He's allowed to write to Gneez from there. Anita is left empty-handed.

And what does Anita write to tell us, as though she had no troubles of her own? She invites Marie to live in West Berlin for as long as I'm working in Czechoslovakia; she promises to keep a perfectly regular household—with no trips. Anita with no trips. She asks Marie to visit, so she can work on her own English.

As if she, too, has agreed to present me with the ČSSR as a country you don't take a child to. You send the child to a godmother.

July 25, 1968 Thursday

To dissuade Soviet troops from any thought of crossing the Czechoslovakian border to defend it, Prague television is showing the vigilant tanks, dogs, and barbed wire fences that they have there already. The West German government has decided to move the maneuvers they'd planned for Grafenwöhr and Hohenfels, near this border, to the area near Münsingen and to a mountain ridge known as the Heuberg, in the state of Baden-Württemberg, some 100 to 150 miles away. So that the Red Army can withdraw, to its homeland, eastward, with one less thing to worry about.

Dr. Julius Kliefoth was removed from his office as principal of Fritz Reuter High School before the end of the 1949–50 school year. His students had to get through the change without an official justification; were they supposed to think Kliefoth had shown "conduct unbecoming a teacher"?

Stubborn, that's what Kliefoth was. In 1947, summoned before the school board to accept a food parcel he'd been allotted so that at least the head of a civil service office would be properly provisioned amid the ravenous children, he refused any special treatment; apparently he was sufficiently taken aback to utter the word "corruption." A year later, in March 1949, the German Ministry of People's Education officially approached him and ordered, at the behest of the Soviet Military Administration, an increase in his salary and purchase coupons above and beyond his ration card, as well as preferential credit in case he wanted to build a house of his own. This was meant to keep people like him from going forth and building a log cabin in the Western occupation zones. Kliefoth would have loved a two-week visit to England. When reminded of his rank in the school administration, and how inappropriate it was to be subletting an apartment on Field Road in Jerichow, he declined to move into an apartment of his own on Cathedral Square in Gneez; he took the milk train to work, often didn't return home until evening, on the bare wood of the unheated compartments, and considered himself lucky when he'd managed to buy kerosene for his lamp. Now the Mecklenburg Ministry of People's Education lacked a lever with which they could remind him of favors received. *Kliefoth was a tough ol Murrjahn but in the end 'e had ta give in.*

The Mecklenburg Interior Ministry was disappointed with Kliefoth as well. He was ordered to report to Gneez City Hall on May 15 and 16, 1949, where they were holding the vote on the Third German People's Congress. It was a historic session in its exemplary eschewal of the word "election" or "choice," *Wahl,* boiling things down to a single alternative. The question was simply whether the eligible voter were for peace or against peace—whichever one you want, really. A Yes would install in power a Unity list of candidates from the existing parties, en masse, so that anyone's displeasure at, say, the Communists, over, say, their strangulation of West Berlin would also lessen the mandate of the Free German Youth; or a preference for the party of the Soviet Union, perhaps because it had let food and work materials back into that city for the past three days, would equally unintentionally advance the cause of the Cultural League (for the R. of a D. G.). Kliefoth was a civil servant; he failed, in his innocence, to realize that the authorities wanted to take advantage of the civil trust he enjoyed— things were surely aboveboard if *our Julius* was supervising them. Educated man and all, had ta respect him. Now he obeyed in all rigor, feeling bound by a formal, official assignment. On the first day, his polling place was run like a classroom. He looked at the voters like examination candidates, welcomed the uncomfortable ones with encouraging murmurs, obligingly spoke Platt. In *this* location Gneez voters, either presenting a valid ID or known to him personally, would step up to the urn on their own, the police having no other right than to escort non-local individuals out onto the street. Kliefoth leaned his head back to look at each person stepping up to his table, instead of merely raising his eyes—an effort growing slower and slower toward evening. If he looked stern it was because he hadn't been able to smoke—the dignity of the proceedings forbade it. He was the very picture of a civil servant carrying out an assignment the government had given him.

On the morning of the 16th, instructions arrived from Schwerin—a "Blitz Telegram: Rush To Desk," signed Warnke, Interior Minister. According to these instructions, Kliefoth was to declare ballots found unmarked in the urn as valid; the large preprinted YES was sufficient. If there was writing on a ballot, it would count as one of the desired votes, except where the text showed signs of a "democracy-hostile" disposition, whatever that was. By dint of these numerical chicaneries, Peace plus the Unity list found as much assent in Mecklenburg as 68.4 out of a hundred—888,395 people— but 410,838 people had managed their ballots in such a way that their NO was immune to metamorphosis. The presiding officer's signature was missing from the Gneez Electoral Commission report; Kliefoth had given himself a leave, for "philological reasons." For the historical files he had to revise this to a "sudden onset of medical weakness"; how could a belligerent and party-loyal minister like W. be expected to approve of a civil servant who took almost a whole Monday off on his own insubordinate say-so?

Fired because of his past: was Lise Wollenberg's opinion, stated with her well-known propensity to gloat. But when the Soviets, in their Decree No. 35, declared that "denazification" was complete in the Soviet Occupation Zone as of April 10, 1948, Kliefoth had not had to interpret his life story before the special court even once (unlike Heinz Wollenberg); Kliefoth had slipped away from Berlin's Hitler party as early as 1932, to the rural pastures of Jerichow, and since the start of the war he'd kept tucked away from it in the army. Of course the Red Army wanted in writing what had been ordered in the Demyansk Pocket under Hitler's supreme command

and his, Kliefoth's, responsibility as captain on the staff of the Second Army Corps, everything up to and including his final rank of lieutenant colonel, but the Soviet Military Administration must have deemed it satisfactory. For in 1945 they left him free with an honorable discharge, and in May 1948 they recommended him to their German Administration of the Interior as an instructor of tactics in the training academies of the newly formed German People's Police, the Volkspolizei, offering Kliefoth the temptation of two salaries, civil and military, and a doubled pension; he excused himself with a medical certificate that he was missing eight teeth, and everyone knew a soldier needed a full set of thirty-two to bring to the army's table. They'd offered him back pay from the army, too, retroactive to May 1945. Of course you'd be a bit mad at anyone refusing such munificence.

It was also said that he'd allowed his grip on the reins to get loose—we know who took the reins out of his hands. For that fall of 1949 was a season of meetings in the Fritz Reuter High School. Emerging from the Third People's Congress (which Kliefoth had indeed rubbed the wrong way) had come a German People's Council, and thence a People's Chamber, which on October 7 declared the territory of the Soviet Occupied Zone to be a German Democratic Republic and the inhabitants therein to be members of said state, with a constitution, a government, and for the time being the traditional eagle on black/red/gold stripes, all to be celebrated with solemn yet festive rites in the assembly hall, which lasted either two class periods or an entire morning. For each of these, Kliefoth asked one of "the younger gentlemen" to do him the favor of presenting to the assembled youth how these events between Mecklenburg and Saxony looked in the context of other circumstances in the world, how they advanced or hindered them, with particular attention to China; Kliefoth seemed to be asleep behind the red-draped table on the podium, his narrow skull with its tuft of white hair tilted forward, hand on chin; in fact he was calculating how much of the prescribed curriculum was being lost in the time these performances took up, and watching the afternoon, too, disappear in teacher conferences on curricular renovations, meetings he had to vouch for in person to the Mecklenburg Board of People's Education. When he eventually stood up to bring the ceremony to a close, his shoulders were bent, he seemed bowed down with the cares of his office, and the claws of the Picasso dove of peace painted behind him seemed to have him by the neck—he who had once been able to speak in a tone of confident authority, looking forward to his return to work. – In this spirit . . . : Kliefoth loyally said; true, he did sound exhausted.

Kliefoth had come a cropper over the new national anthem: proclaimed individuals such as Mrs. Lindsetter, solely to pride themselves on their musical understanding. For this additional requisite of a state—a song—had been integrated into the lesson plans of the Fritz Reuter High School for November. In 2/4 time, in a simple three-verse symmetry, it accompanied the rhymed resolve of a plural subject, a We, to rise once more from the ruins and turn to face the future, along with that of a singular subject, "you," to serve a "united German fatherland," "so that" (last couplet) the sun might shine across this land, "beautiful as ne'er before." Each grade rehearsed this pretentious good-natured piece under Joachim Buck (Julie Westphal was elsewhere, in Güstrow, studying for her job as a New Teacher). "Handsome Joachim," shining of tonsure, swirling of hair thereround, lips playing incantatorily, was adept in the preparation of state occasions, having been thanked for adorning official proclamations both in the Weimar Republic and under Reich Governor Hildebrandt (see *Mecklenburg Monthly Bulletin*, 1926–1938); he gave his respective all to the present authorities as well, hurled invisible weights in the palm of his hand from way down low up to the coffered ceiling of the school auditorium, conjured his singing underage throng with an elderly rowing motion of the arms that sometimes made him look like he was pushing a medicine ball, and nodded punctually from the neck when the last note had rung out—this was how he rehearsed the lower grades. He thought he owed the twelfth graders, facing their Abitur, a more substantial scientific underpinning, a "musical history of ideas" as it were, so he opened his instruction in the new state melody with a practice waltz from *The Theoretical-Practical Piano Tutor: A Systematic Course* by the musical pedagogue Karl Zuschneid (1854–1926), a 3/4 number that sounded like a model for the admittedly less jumpy anthem. Joachim turned his amply shining eyes upon his students, so that they might notice the blindly gliding fingers at the end of his long arm. With a variation of Zuschneid's rhythm he slipped into an impudent tune that, like the preceding, seemed related, by descent and by family resemblance, to the subject of the lesson, and proceeded to inform the class that this was a song from a 1936 film, *Water for Canitoga*, sung by Hans Albers and René Deltgen to a tune by Peter Kreuder (1905):

Good-bye, Johnny,	(Newly risen)
Good-bye, Johnny,	(from the ru-ins)
we were really great together.	(to the future turned we stand.)
But, ala-as,	(Let us serve your)
But, ala-as,	(good weal truly,)

now those days are gone forever (Germany our fatherland etc.); naive handsome Joachim, simply retaining and recognizing a melodic line he may have picked up during his studies, or at the Renaissance Cinema in Gneez thirteen years ago. Still, the criminal police, D Squad (successor to K-5), accused him as early as February of having imputed a borrowing, a plagiarism, a theft to the composers of the latest version of the anthem; still, his pretrial custody turned up correspondence neither with Peter Kreuder (Argentina) nor with Hanns Eisler (Berlin/GDR). Since handsome Joachim was willing to concede a passive knowledge of the constitution, from his reading of reports, he talked his way into Article 6, "Incitement to Boycott" and Related Offenses, and as a result Buck saw the light of day again in 1952, in Lüneberg, in the West, somewhat disappointed by the state of musical scholarship there, which dismissed the origins of the East German anthem as a bagatelle rather than anything newsworthy, still, surrounded once more by a community of followers thanks to his secular performances of "Oh Eternity, You Word of Thunder" or "The Heavens Declare"; a loss for Gneez, to hear Mrs. Lindsetter tell it. And Kliefoth? Principal Kliefoth received an official reprimand. Almost entirely lacking in musical culture himself, during the official faculty meeting he had simply smirked at the curious fact which the newly founded State Security Service, the Stasi, had unmasked as an attack against the establishment of democracy. – *What nonsense:* Kliefoth replied in his measured way, when the district school board accused him of not having denounced handsome Joachim on the spot, as he should have. The two gentlemen had been in former times, 1944, confederates—they had shared an academic semester; at that point the oaken chair was heavily shifted and out was cried: *Principiis obsta!* (Ovid). Kliefoth preferred Juvenal and cried out: *Maxima debetur puero reverentia!*, by which he meant not just twelfth grade but all the students he was responsible for. His adversary was dismissed even sooner than Kliefoth was, but not before ensuring a comment in Kliefoth's file.

The end of the professional line for Kliefoth came: it was furthermore said: with the academic subject of Iosif V. Stalin (b. 1879); others were sure: it was Christmas 1949.

1949 minus 1879 equals the biblical, magical age of seventy for the distant Generalissimo, and just as the people of the new nation, the East German republic, sent "the Soviet Union's Genius Helmsman," "the best friend to the German People" close to thirty freight cars of presents, along the rail lines that still remained (adding shamefaced apologies for the delay in supplying a planetarium for Stalin's own city), so too did the students of the Fritz Reuter High School, Gneez (Meckl.), make their offerings under the Loerbrocks portrait of the honoree (members of the festival committee: Sieboldt and Gollantz; responsible for the contribution of class 10-A-II: Lockenvitz). Julie Westphal—eye sockets clenched in rigid zeal, brow curtained with bangs of stone, bosom quivering in her jacket of mannish cut, this *Olsch* on the wrong side of fifty—had had her conducting skills freshened up in Güstrow by that point; under her baton, a female choir of ninth and tenth graders performed the birthday boy's favorite song, which, with its desperate longing for the grave of a lost love, Suliko, intoned by sixteen-year-old girls' voices, was apt to cast a pall over the proceedings; following Julie's choreography, the eleventh-grade students, dressed in regulation blue shirts and blouses, stepped solemnly forward and back, raising and swinging their flags; in Julie's mandated tempo and meter, the graduating seniors called in chorus what the younger audience responded to in chorus as a vow to the Architect of Socialism, the Lenin of Our Time, the Teacher of Vigilance in Confronting the Agents of the Enemies of the People, and whatever other personal descriptions Burly Sieboldt had gleaned from the daily press of Stalin's party in Germany. Cathedral Cantor J. Buck—handsome Joachim—on guest piano supplied the P. Tchaikovskian stylings, stiffly, vivifyingly armed with neither premonition nor warning. Final number: the new anthem. Principal Kliefoth was present as master of ceremonies, grayish green bowtie in his worn collar as usual, wearing the baggier of his everyday knickerbocker suits, his thin lips performing a dry chewing motion and the discomfort of a man abstaining from smoking out of respect for the occasion. Mission accomplished.

That was December 21. For the 24th, Kliefoth had authorized 10-A-II to give another festive performance. That was thanks to Anita. This foreign child, from "East Prussia," hadn't been satisfied with the information we'd given her about the man for whom the school was named—what she'd been told about his writings had been couched in the phrases and circumlocutions Mecklenburg children used to brush one another off. As a result of her shy inquiries, we rehearsed the description of the Christmas celebration in Chapter Seven of Fritz Reuter's Plattdeutsch monument *Ut mine Stromtid* (*Seed-Time and Harvest*, 3 vols., 1864) and performed it for our parents as a narrative with staged episodes. For what parents we had. Normally Anita would've had to pay for her suggestion by appearing on stage in person, but we were sufficiently embarrassed to cast Student Cresspahl, alas, in the role of Fru Pastor Behrendsen. In the words of the poet: *Everything about her was round,—arms and hands and fingers, head and cheeks and lips*; Cresspahl wound blankets around her hips and stooped and pretended to be forty and did her hair up in a bun—Anita was upset. Anita had invited the Brüshavers and thought Aggie would take offense at this embodiment of a pastor's wife scurrying *like quicksilver* round the Christmas tree and perpetually asserting that *surely she's closest to hand*. But Aggie laughed along with the rest of the audience, and clapped—*a good woman, she was*. Burly Sieboldt took a turn as Pastor Behrens, and Lise was *Lowise*, and *Rika with er loud voice* was played by Schäning Drittfeld who fainted on us right after the last *Julklapp* Christmas gift. There was no shortage of village youths—Fru Pastor had real pfeffernuesse and apples to hand out. We'd cut the part of melancholy Franz in favor of Jürn the coachman: Pius was Jürn, and the commentator, and had the last word with his *drive through the village, the songs coming from the poor little laborers' shacks, and up in the heavens God had lit up his great Christmas tree with a thousand shining lamps, and the world lay stretched out beneath like a Christmas table, which winter had spread with a cloth of whitest snow, that spring, summer, and autumn might cover it with Christmas gifts.*

That Dr. Kliefoth thanked the participants and wished them and the audience a merry "Christmas holiday" was the straw that broke the camel's back. Because he could have stopped us. He'd had on his desk for at least a week the directive permitting winter school celebrations only for the Generalissimo, or else for the Soli-boy, whoever that was. Kliefoth was likewise informed that the official designation of this break in the school's operations was henceforth "the winter holidays"; and that is what it has been called in Gneez and Mecklenburg to this day.

It meant "the Solidarity Child," Fru Cresspahl.

With a nightshirt, a lit tallow candle in hand, like the Darmol ad?

Or the Coal Thief caricature. But I must say, that part about the camel's back is an Anglicism, Fru Cresspahl.

All right: Which drop made the barrel run over? How did we lose you?

They could take their pick of reasons. Safety violation: no firefighter on the stage.

There was a bucket of water and a bucket of sand, Mr. Kliefoth—we'd thought of that.

But was there anyone wearing a helmet, axe in hand?

There was no medical team either.

Right! And whatever was wrong with Christiane Drittfeld? I remember her as a buxom lass, rosy-cheeked even. No, stout.

She was about to go away with her parents over New Year's, to the West. The need to keep silent, the secret goodbyes, were probably too much for her.

Moreover, you had the wrong author.

Fritz Reuter had given his name to the school! I say this in a dignified tone.

The wrong text.

Written in 1862, in Neubrandenburg, Nigen Bramborg!

In which books are also distributed to children, at the end.

"Writing books and slates and primers and…"

"And catechisms," *Fru Cresspahl! Utilization of a democratic-pedagogical venue for Christian purposes, that's what that was called. Propaganda, it was!*

"Quosque tandem!"

"Videant consules" *is what I said.*

But you weren't fired until the following April.

That was when the fat really hit the fire. There was sposed to be an essay writtn everywhere cross Mecklenburg, "What My Teacher Has Told Me About Stalin," and none came in from my school.

A kind of pedagogical public referendum.

Not in my school.

Plus it would've been better if you'd gotten a few less letters from your friends at English universities.

Or joined the National Democratic Party, where they'd gathered all the known Nazis in one place, and the riffraff from the army. That would've helped for a while.

So who's right, Lindsetter? Or bringing in Stalin? Or Christmas?

You figger it out. They could use my age too.

Dr. Kliefoth was a full year away from retirement age in 1950.

But you know who was called a Murrjahn, and was one too.

The last time Gesine Cresspahl saw her principal in the school was when he substituted for one of his "younger gentlemen" and taught a class in the map room. He had trouble handling the long poles wound with big heavy sheets. A thin line of spittle was on his lips after a Latin class with the seniors. He recognized her right away when it was her turn and she asked for the physical geography of South China, but he looked at her as if her eager greeting came as a surprise. Alert, cheerful eyes in steep-sloped sockets, tucked into thick wrinkles—an owlish look. And because Kliefoth disappeared in the middle of the school year, without an assembly to thank him and say goodbye, it was too late for a torchlight procession in his honor the first time he resigned, and later such a gesture was seen to be "inopportune," a translation for a simpler word. Because it would have meant a twelve-mile trip for his students, from Gneez to Jerichow, where Kliefoth was spending his premature retirement alone with Mr. Juvenal, Mr. Cicero, Mr. Seneca. And the stories going round about his ample pension also soothed a sixteen-year-old conscience. But Student Cresspahl was now on her guard in Jerichow, her own town! She avoided the path to the garden plots where Kliefoth was cultivating thirty rods of land with potatoes and tomatoes and onions and carrots the way he'd learned to as a child in Malchow am See. As if she wasn't so sure he would fill her hands with berries.

Friday July 26, 1968

When a Czech general suggests rotating the command of Warsaw Pact troops so that it's assigned to a state other than the Soviet one for a change,

Moscow snorts and accuses him of having divulged military secrets. In Prague the ruling presidium of the CP of the ČSSR gets cold feet, removes Lieut. Gen. Václav Prchlík from his high party post, and sends him back to the army. The Soviet air defense command announced "exercises," operation "Sky Shield," extending into regions near the border with Czechoslovakia, and now the Polish Communists, too, venture to criticize their Czech brothers for lacking the will to fight against the "forces of reaction" threatening them. The Associated Press adds a photo—a camouflaged Soviet truck on East German soil, a hundred yards from the border at Cínovec; a half-recognizable wheel looks about as tall as the two Red Army soldiers next to it.

A prosecutor in Frankfurt am Main has sought a life sentence for Fritz von Hahn, for the 11,343 Jews from Bulgarian-occupied Greek territories that he sent to Treblinka, for the 20,000 Jews from Salonika that he sent to the gas in Auschwitz. He'll get his sentence next month, maybe.

Employee Cresspahl plans to write a letter today. At five to nine she steps in front of Mrs. Lazar's fortresslike desk and tries to give her a smile; she may be here straight through to evening with this work she's assigned herself. She does it with the door open, without first taking out the colored ribbon and typing on white paper with a carbon underneath. She does it *with company equipment, on company time*—that's how reckless she is now. Because anyone who comes in, Henri Gelliston or another of the vice president's young men, will see a page of writing in a foreign language, not addressed to an allied firm, suggesting private business.

Salutation.

Missing. Could endanger the recipient. Because of the name, or the code name. He has renounced the usual adjective himself, although we'd much rather have begun with *Dear...* Unfortunately it would be something of a lie.

(Dear) (J. B.—cut); we can't do that. The salutation in German would say that we like and respect you, and also expect the same in return. And who is it who's prevented us from saying that? You have, by lying to us. The salutation sticks in our throat. The tongue in the throat, you remember. We speak to you with dissembled voice—no, not even to you, just in your direction. We give no address, neither Rövertannen in Güstrow, nor Christinenfeld in Klütz, nor Markkleeberg Ost in Leipzig (alter all the names!).

We don't want to make it any easier for them to look up your notorious registration card with the People's Police by giving a building number on any Street of Peace/of German-Soviet Friendship or even a Stalin one now renamed half after a mysterious Dr. Frankfurter and half after Marxandengels. Anonymouses of the world, unite!

We're saying *du* to you, the informal pronoun, to make it clear how we used to address each other; we're talking to you as if to an unknown cat, with shimmering fur or unkempt, it makes no difference, and needing our care or our contempt for letting herself go like that.

We're talking to you as a "we," to give you the excuse of the unfathomability of a group, and conversely so that you can presume for the time being, and write in your report, that one is speaking for others with whom he/she has taken your side, to ensure that you are trusted and the very mention of your name respected. Take your pick and you'll figure it out— also what you've destroyed.

In deference to your anxieties, you will find this in your mailbox but not brought and previously inspected/photocopied/registered/indexed by the German Post Office of your country, since we intend to pay only for conveyance and delivery, by no means for technology or personnel costs in Location 12. That is why you might receive this between bedsheets that a people-owned business, Lilywhite, or a Workers' Cooperative Union, Progress Laundry, returns to you. Or when opening a book you've requested to borrow. Or unexpectedly crinkling in your jacket pocket. Some way that it'll end up right in your hand, and yours alone.

So that it'll be well and truly concealed whether and that you have ever been an in-law/friend/sublettor with or of anyone named Gesine Cresspahl (cut this), a person still thinking of you from beyond your borders. So that you could be a nominal aunt of ours. A seminar leader, female; a teammate, male, whom we always had to greet with a balled fist or the cry of "Friendship!" Anyone from among that innumerable company of members of the Socialist community of humankind—we're quoting here. A man in a gray flannel suit (cut).

You should always be in a position to state for the record that this must have been addressed to someone else, you've never in your life been the author's Roman or countryman. Whether you're male or female, bearded or uncurtained—we say nothing. Nor about the business/laboratory/institute in the German Democratic Republic in which you so laudably ply your trade/science/ability/habits, albeit without glorious honor and recognition from your national government, but still so that certain of your patrons/sponsors/coworkers/pen pals deem it appropriate and worthwhile to honor the round number or some other number of your birthday with a collective reminiscence/tribute/festschrift.

It's no secret how these German-style festschrifts go: the jubilarian is supposedly never and reliably always asked whom he'd like to see included and who would be embarrassing, who an unattainable honor, who a scandal; in your case: whether you could make your peace with a publisher and place of publication abroad, where those honoring you can do so without harmful or awkward consequences for your honorable person. Far be it from us to reveal whether the editors here have found a publisher in Finland or France, Sweden or Switzerland; all we have to say about the place of publication is that it should be in a country on a large body of water between two oceans. Or three. Nicer typesetting, presumably. But printed in a British colony? Gibraltar? Hong Kong? *Our lips are sealed.* And let it be a private joke, among the like-minded, for your sake.

So we were deaf in one ear, while happily hearing perfectly well in the other, when the editors approached someone to open the string of pearls of expert dedications and obeisances with a biographical squib, which many years of contact and inclinations thereto made that someone capable of; and also at whose request: yours. *For your comfort and safety* I double-checked, twice, in writing: yes, you asked them to ask me. It was clear in any case—who else could have given them my address, my apartment, down to the phone number, if not you. I (= we) had to take it as an assignment from you. Confirmed and attested in black on white. Here we had a place to begin, it seems.

We are, as you well know, subjected to five eight-hour days a week of work; I can tell you in confidence that it's more than that. Still, there's always the weekends. It's true, we could have foisted the job off onto a Comrade Writer we have handy, in fact totally in our hands; but since you suggested me, it had to stay with me, between us. My English, as you might well imagine—the stipulated language—unspools passably enough in professional matters, when it comes to *assets and liabilities* and credit lines resulting therefrom, but never in my life have I attempted belletristic prose with it. And that's what's needed to put down on paper a person's life, what can be known and presumed, what's been seen and heard. Don't you think? For other people to read as well, and recognize you there, for their amusement and instruction? I admit it, humiliating though it is: I needed two dictionaries on my desk. As though my English would disappear on the spot if I tried to use it to say how someone was (might have been) in school, how he looks biting into a Thuringian bratwurst (a cold boiled egg), how he gets through a storm at sea (a summons from the secret police / the East German Stasi), whether he can sleep easy or should take to his heels immediately. I started by moving around you like a tailor (male or female), trying to find out what's under the fabric and how my own might sit on your shoulders and limbs. I also tried to look at you like a young girl/boy with a crush on the special way you purse your lips, move the muscles around your eyes, place your legs. How you clear your throat, how you . . . I thought, as you know, about your parents. There was one thing about which I kept absolute and perfect silence. I praised what I liked, wove what bothered me into a stitchery of teasing. My thoughts hurt the whole time, I was working so hard; by the end I could sometimes feel your presence, as if you were now there. Fourteen and a half pages, two thousand characters each, and off to the main post office at eleven at night to send it off to the editor with the next airmail.

Then silence, and the date of the occasion came and went. Finally the explanation that you'd had my document smuggled over the border to you, in pants pockets, matchboxes, what do I know, so that you could read what I in particular had to say about you. What'n honor (but: "festschrift" and "jubilarian," qqv.). After another while, the information that you'd recognized yourself, actually both of us, in the piece and, while admitting to a certain diffidence, were happy to accept the portrait as on the whole accurate, knowing what I'd left out of it out of friendship.

Well all right then. 'Slong as you're happy. No problem. I waited for requests for changes. Again like a tailor.

But none came. Instead, the message that there's no possible way to publish our piece, because it's known that we're so-and-so.

You could've known that when you asked us, doncha think?

Obviously we'll withdraw the piece. True, we do have a contract (payment: zero); but we won't insist on it. Why should we stand in your way if you've got a hankering to become a factory manager/a Meritorious Doctor of the Republic/a coach of the national team/no-previous-criminal-record? with regard to your art/technique/physical ability to travel to the NonSocialistEconomicSphere, the West? On the contrary, we would like to see your knowledge or skills presented in Helsinki and Leningrad, Pasadena and Mexico City, by none other than yourself.

Without our needing to be there in person, of course.

You have stipulated a festschrift in the field of endocrinology/forestry/molecular biology/mathematics/art history/heating engineering—purged of the piece of life that you had in common with us.

Which makes us think that here, like there, you are transferring the needs of your government into your own person—exigencies of a kind that you simply impute to the GDR in an interpretation that is all too obsequious and far-fetched.

For if we do run into today's emissaries and guardians of your national government, they'll likely hold it against us that we left without asking the law, whose answer to such questions we knew in advance to be No and which punished even the asking with prison. And yet the machine guns remain unraised before us; the GDR says Good day and Have a nice trip; it provides room and board if we're willing to pay in our NonSocialist money, while keeping the non-NonSocialist money that should be ours locked up safe in its very own State Bank. Auf Wiedersehen, it says that too.

Possibly it's keeping in mind the useful services we might be able to render it after our farewell, namely mentioning it as a foreign (*ausländisch, outlandish*) state, as it is required to be for reasons of recognition (details under a three-letter abbreviation; direct mail to the editors). That would be one of our deeds worthy of gratitude.

You took up our time. Which is fine—I've liked a lot of people in my life. But you misused it, since you knew it would be in vain and for nothing; you *wasted* our time.

We understand the limitations you're operating under; but we're sure that you've brought a good part of them on yourself. Still, since you say so, all right: you can get only from us, via a private mailing address, a thousand little things of everyday life that your national custodian and his successors keep from you, from academic books to toilet paper. You're perfectly happy walking around in your country wearing a jacket made from fabric you've had us send you, a transistor radio at your ear that we sent you on your request. But it's impossible for you to admit to any contact with us professionally, publicly, or in official correspondence—even the proximity of our name would harm your career/cadre dossier/biography/reputation. We understand that. We in no way intend to keep you from perceiving your human rights.

Last night it was relayed to us, as indisputable sight and sound: you are walking around in your country with our memories of you, the eulogy you've swindled out of us so that you could hear it while you were still alive, the things we've preserved about you and considered valuable. We hear: you're reading it to friends, always in an intimate circle, as a plea for pity for your bad situation, in which you're unable, for reasons of state, to have such nice things about you printed.

Since last night we've been walking bent double, inwardly, we're so embarrassed. So ashamed.

We'd like to take back what we wrote for you, trusting you.

Elli Wagenführ. (Change the name. But how could Somebody Orother replace Elli Wagenführ?)

We told you about her, and that was not right. How she used to slip out of Peter Wulff's kitchen, plates in both hands, – Coming through!: she'd cry: *Hot and greasy!*, and the market-day clientele would declare that something hot would suit them nicely, even in the middle of the summer, and make remarks about her fat. Undid her apron strings. Looked forward to getting a slap. I'm sorry. I take it back. (Change the name. Pub in Jena.)

And the gorse. We walked past the gorse, the German broom, it was in full bloom; I couldn't help but express my pleasure in its blue and yellow. – Gorse? you asked: *Ginster*, like the guy who wrote the novel written by himself? You got our gorse; we contest your ownership of it.

And that we ever thought we had no need to take further precautions, and we could send you the collocation, a piece of the old homeland, a view of the Baltic: *blue as blue can be.* We're confiscating that back.

And that I expected my father to put up with you, when he had to say yes because he was trying to console me. If I was bringing him a stranger, I was vouching for that person too, was I not? So that he'd watch you as if you deserved his politeness, maybe offer you his hand, as a guest. How can I make that never have happened. I'm ashamed of it.

*If I have to choose between betraying my friend and betraying my country,
I hope I shall have the guts to betray my country.* —E. M. Forster

You all gotta look at it dialectically, doncha. Well, then, be glad.

And don't worry. We'll deny knowing you. We've never known you.
Will that help you out? No, you've had nothing to do with us. We
don't care two figs about you. Will this assurance help you/give you a
promotion/get you a lease on your apartment? Is your national variety of
self-understanding, your *identity*, relieved of any possible offense? We're
strangers. Always have been. How could we sign off in the end if we'd ever
been your acquaintances/coworkers/roommates. To other people, we say
Bye or *Take care* or *Mind where you're going*, sometimes by request *À Dieu*.
To you we say Enough and Never and Finis.

(Send a clean copy as a photocopy to be forwarded. Pretend to be covering a signature here.)

Today *The New York Times* wants us to feel sympathy for a housewife
(who herself prefers that her name not be mentioned). She comes into
Manhattan from Long Island to do some shopping. Suddenly, hey, she
decides why not meet her husband for lunch? Tries the phone booth on
the southwest corner of Sixty-Second and Madison. Her dime comes back
out—no dial tone. She marches twelve blocks north up Madison, trying
seven more public phones; the eighth doesn't even have a dial. She's three
dimes poorer now.

But the phone in the bank obeys for once. Sam sends a warm ham sandwich straight up from the basement at her request, with tea, brought by a
messenger, who as requested puts the paper bag down on the chair next to
the door without a word. He understood the dime she'd left there likewise.

Things are going reasonably well in international communication too.
Around when we're finishing our clean copy we get a call from the Stafford
Hotel, London, will we accept the charges? Of course. And there at the
other end of line, at an hour when the English should be asleep, is de Rosny,
a vice president, checking up in person.

– Working hard as always, my dear Mrs. Cresspahl? de Rosny pronounces.
He is imitating an Englishman. No, he announces to a colleague: Just look
how well trained my people are!

– But of course: Employee Cresspahl replies from New York, shamelessly.

– Desk still full then? de Rosny says, exaggerating the Etonian voice.

– Almost empty. Just finishing up now. Sir.

– Before the big trip, eh?

Which we'd have preferred to forget.

– Do I know this . . . person? Marie wants to know back on Riverside Drive. If she were older than her proud eleven, you would have to call her look solicitous. Is her mother ultimately hurting herself? True, she's sitting there making the heraldic Mecklenburg ox-head—both fists on her temples. Isn't her mother plucking out something that offends her, and in the end it's a bit of her eye?

– I forget the year. You were eight and a half. We were visiting . . . a Socialist country, planning to meet Anita, and instead we ran into this person and were glad that he was . . . at least able to take trips in an . . . easterly direction.

– This was the person you sang in public with, right?

– The wine was strong that night, Marie.

– "Marble Breaks and Iron Bends"?

– You were so ashamed of your mother.

– I was jealous. Just bursting into song whenever you're in the mood— that takes courage.

– *Which you did solely to keep New York clean.*

– "But our lo-ove will ne-ver end"?

– That's what he used to think, once, in 1955.

– So this is the person you—

– Careful now!

– also went places with before my time?

– We plead innocent, Your Honor.

– And why is Socialism bad in privately printed matter from the Non-Socialist Economic Sphere?

– Because its custodian has an unfortunate predilection for archives.

– Who delivers mail like this for you? Anita? Günter Niebuhr?

– I'm afraid we can't answer that, Your Honor.

– That's how you kick people out of your life?

– That's how I send them off, and wish them bon voyage.

– You want me to learn that.

– I want you to know. And since when does our apartment smell of roast cauliflower in the early evening, with the windows open? Were you cooking? The breadcrumbs are out, there's parmesan in the air.

– I . . . It's a secret, Gesine. I'll tell you tomorrow.

– I'm much too tired to eat anyway. Is it all right with you if I go to bed now? If you let me sleep till ten tomorrow morning?

– Sleep as late you want, Gesine.

July 27, 1968 Saturday

Woken by the silence: it was roomy, it contained birdsong. All through the night sleep knew that the alarm clock was muzzled, and wake-up time it set for when the cars are deployed on Riverside Drive, the first children taken to the park. The dream showed a wood thrush, showcased a red-breasted thrush, went as far as to offer a tanager—all discarded. For all these are busy by this time of year remodeling their nests, raising their progeny. The one singing here was a wren, a *Zaunkönig*—king of the fence. A cheerful little monarch perched on the park's chain-link, beyond the hot still road, in the warmed shadows of the magnificent *hickories* . . . the walnut trees, present in the dream as an oil print in Pagenkopf's hallway. I woke myself up.

Quarter to ten; greeted by a staging of breakfast: tea waiting on the hot plate, two places set, two eggs waiting under their little caps; only the napkins are still empty of rolls. *The New York Times* is there, and what's not there is Marie or even a note from her. The young lady is out for a mysterious morning walk.

Edward G. Ash Jr. of Willingboro, NJ, US Army, and David A. Person of Tonawanda, NY, US Navy firefighter, are reported as killed in Vietnam.

The British Communists are avoiding any hint of reproach of their great Soviet brothers, but they nonetheless stand there and find it just swell how the Czechoslovak party is tackling "the wrong of the past," insisting on Socialist democracy, and what do they serve for dessert? "Only the Czech people and their Communist party can decide how to deal with their internal problems." These number 32,562 people in Great Britain (not counting abstentions).

Antonio (Tony Ducks) Corallo, of the Mafia, got what was coming to him in the Federal Court on Foley Square. For attempted bribery of a Water Department official: three years in prison. But the maximum sentence would have been five years and a $10,000 fine. Now, assuming good behavior...

Yesterday a thirty-four-year-old man from Astoria (we almost lived there), Vladimir Vorlicek, walked into the gun department of Abercrombie & Fitch, bought shotgun shells for $5.50, surreptitiously loaded a shotgun—apparently such things are just lying around unsecured there—and shot himself in the head. He had arrived within the past year as a refugee, from Czechoslovakia. He would have made one more.

– Good morning, Marie! Look what we have here—such a beautiful child! Out visiting friends? What an elegant dress you have on, blue and white stripes, perfect with your blond braids, and silk ribbons on your bare shoulders too! Perfectly gellegant!

– Good morning, Gesine.

– Is something troubling you, young lady?

– Obviously.

– But today's not a day when anyone should feel troubled! It's the weekend, the sun is out, we could go right to the South Ferry, just say the word, Marie!

– It's that... Sometimes you like hard-boiled eggs for breakfast, Gesine. When they've been left to cool overnight.

– I do indeed! But I don't need any today.

– I wanted to make you some last night, but when they'd been on the stove for a while I started reading, then went off to my room with my nose in the book. There was a bang, and I thought of Eagle-Eye Robinson's old jalopy and its busted muffler. When I finally noticed the smell, the saucepan on the gas was black and warped and the eggs had exploded all over. Up to the ceiling.

– You sure did a good job cleaning up.

– *Danke.*

– German's the language of the day, then?

– Okay.

– In that case you need to call it a *Stielkasserolle*, a handle-pot, even if the people here somehow imagine it's a pan. Oh, sorry! Sowwy.

– Here you go. The closest…handle-pot I could find on Broadway. Aluminum too. With my own money.

– The old one was old, we should've thrown it out a long time ago. Amortized for four years. Tell me, classmate, are you in the mood for a quick lesson on amortization law? The keeper of the household budget deliberates, approves, and authorizes the expenditure.

– Make it halfsies.

– Half and half! Done! So now smile! I'm the one to blame, with my sense of smell! Roast cauliflower!

– I fear, Madame, that this, Mrs. Cresspahl, is a sign of advancing age.

– Is today a South Ferry day, Marie?

– I'd rather have *brunch*. The tape recorder is saddled up, toast's on its way, and a lemon for the tea.

– Supposing, *posito*, we had a guest with us from the ignorant *Wildernis*—from, let's say, Düsseldorf: how would we translate that for him?

– *Breakfast and lunch in einem.* A big…midday breakfast. *Gabelfrühstück!* Breakfast with a fork!

– Instead of fish with a spoon and scrambled eggs with tongs.

– What do you charge for an hour of German lessons?

– An hour of "Contemporary Studies," you mean. I'll take one *insalata di pomodori e cipolle. Puoi condirla?*

– *Coming right up! Coming right up!*

– Contemporary Studies: that was a New Subject, insofar as the Nazis would've called it "Ideological *Weltanschauung* Inculcation," and also insofar as there would be a new instructor at the Fritz Reuter High School teaching it to class 10-A-II in 1949–50. Her name was Selbich—not much older than twenty, we'd heard, and the principal pro tem. Teaching this kind of subject would be seen as quite useful probation if she was out to get her promotion made permanent.

– Selbich…Selbich…

– Principal replacing Dr. Kliefoth.

– Oh boy. His successor was an outsider, and young, and female. That's not easy.

– And that is precisely why the seventeen-year-olds decided to give her the benefit of the doubt: it must have been the dignity of her office that kept the new principal from shutting the classroom door behind her herself, and give the nod for the task to the lowest in the room, Mrs. Lindsetter's niece, Monika ("Peter"). We were perfectly ready to make allowances for her teetering along as if her feet hurt (– Not like any woman alive: Pius whispered), standing up stiff and straight as a commanding officer reviewing soldiers on parade, and surely she couldn't keep her grown-out blond hair from hanging down so stringily unless she brushed it for half an hour every morning. The students of 10-A-II rise to their feet and stare at the new Contemporary Studies teacher's shirt. For she was wearing, with a brown skirt, the blue FDJ shirt, complete with epaulettes and an emblem on the sleeve. At this point Kliefoth would have made a hand gesture to release us, sure of having the whole class's attention; this person inspected us at length before saying: Sit down! And since when do I like quince jam?

– Since D. E. sent us some from Lenzburg, Switzerland, Gesine.

– All right, I'll let that go. Less edified (than I by this jam) was 10-A-II by this instructor's first question. She asked in a sharp voice: why were we all, without exception, in civilian garb rather than sporting the proud blue shirt of the Free German Youth? Pius looked at me as if wanting some kind of cue or advice. I gave my head a little twitch, meaning: Go for it! By this point our quick precise silent communication system ran practically perfectly, eluding the pedagogue's eye or at least not being provable. I knew Pius would needle her, and now that I'd recognized her I was hoping she'd join in our game. Pius raised his hand, received a stiff nod, stood up, and said in exaggerated Mecklenburgish: The blue shirt, our garment o' honor it is, ma'am. It's only on festive occasions we'd wear that. Lise Wollenberg made a similar false move, which she too would've known better than to try if she hadn't recognized this Mrs. Selbich. She blurted, unasked, without standing up to speak, familiarly, quoting from the dress regulations: *Plus a course a girl don' often have a black dress to wear every day now* (her eyes clearly on Madame Principal's brown-clad hips). But Bettina had changed more than her name—she'd lost her sense of humor, and spoke differently, in a hard voice, as if wanting to threaten us, as if we were dirt—

– Bettina Riepschläger?! It was her?

– Bettina Riepschläger, married name Selbich, divorced name Selbich too. She demanded "Silence!" in a voice as imperious as it was clumsy, and also demanded to know who the 10-A-II FDJ class president was. That was

Pius again, and while she made every effort to intimidate us by announcing that shameful conditions had been permitted to spread unchecked in our class, our whole basic attitude was in need of serious reassessment—

– Were you "a bunch of pigs"?

– she was derailed by Pius's lengthy explanation of the enormous sums of money we'd paid at the district office for a mere one shirt each, which we certainly wore for rallies, street marches, and year-end meetings, but which was too good even for potato harvest work details,

Our blue shirts black with the sweat of toil . . .

and as for the girls in our class, every last one had had complaints about the ungainly footwear that went with the uniform. – I reserve the right to return to this matter again: this new Bettina announced, as if about to hand out punishments. The old Bettina would've made it back safe to shore with a smile, telling us we must think of every moment as a festive occasion. It all could've still turned out fine.

– The things a teacher training course can do to a person!

– And a failed marriage too. And having applied to be a party member. And who knows what else.

– Had she . . .

– She'd thrown in the towel. Upset the apple cart. And this was the first time Pius shook his head when I told him something: that in middle school she'd been friendly, fun, someone you could trust, someone you studied hard for just to make her happy. Pius made a face as if now he had to start all over again if he wanted to get me; his brow was furrowed with concern, even.

– But I bet Lise Wollenberg showed up to Selbich's Contemporary Studies class the next day in a blue FDJ shirt.

– Black skirt, too. Civilian shoes though. It didn't take long before it was all tripping off Lise's tongue: that the employers in capitalist West Germany are atremble at the sight of the freedoms that the workers have won in the German Democratic Republic and will someday bring with them to the West.

– Kliefoth had had to make predictions like that too.

– A Julius Kliefoth says whatever he feels like saying. He'd translated cognitive therapy into his own terms and decided that teachers should put at children's disposal whatever the contemporary moment actually contains. If Austria gets a peace treaty all for itself, or Indonesia independence, he would in the first case assign an essay on economic geography, in the second expect us to know at least the country's population. When the Bulgarian politician Traicho Kostov admitted to planning to assassinate Dimitrov and join his country to Yugoslavia, then denied both charges, and then was executed anyway in December 1949, Kliefoth passed that information on to us as news. He held press conferences with us; we were allowed to be like reporters and ask him: Is it true that...? (that England has diplomatically recognized China? We could have set him up so many times; the thought of his astonished reaction, those drawn smacking lips, was enough to dissuade us. We had an agreement with him.) From the newspaper principle he transitioned to the newspapers he'd actually been allowed to subscribe to before the war—three months each one, from various French *départements* and English *counties* in turn. How beneficial this practice was for fluency in a foreign language, he said; how it nourished one's awareness of contemporary events. (Sitting in front of him were children getting a vague sense of what he had learned to do without, children who already knew that possessing a West German paper meant censure in school, while showing it to anyone else meant jail.) When Zaychik insisted on wanting to learn a foreign word for *Düsenjäger*, Dr. Kliefoth wrote to his academic friends in St. Andrews or Birmingham; he defined *jet* to us as best he could in technical terms as the *Düse*, and we learned that a *fighter* was a battle plane, a weapon at the ready. We could hear in his voice the staff officer well acquainted with airplanes from the eastern front when he added: Frightful thing, that.

– Did Bettina believe the things she wanted to hear back from you in Contemporary Studies?

– I hope so, for her sake. How terrible for her if she didn't! If that was part of her burden, she must have seen in our silence the mocking sympathy we felt for Dieter Lockenvitz when he stood up by the map stand in the front corner and had to report tidings of joy with respect to the imminent demise of the West German economic system, as a result of more than two million unemployed. He writhed, shuffled his feet, tried to hold tight to the map stand, and Bettina critiqued: The concept is correct in itself but you're getting stuck in it; you're twisting it around like you're trying to look at a ball from all sides!

– Look at that. She's trying to make the sale.

– This was one last remaining bit of the earlier Bettina, wanting to win over a boy not much younger than she was: Come on, we're not so different, you and me, we can come to some kind of agreement . . . It's just that Bettina had developed some blind spots. She had no sense that her students might possibly be agonizing over the news from January 1 that ration cards had been abolished in the territory allegedly facing such imminent economic demise. No eyes to see that he was avoiding the gaze of the pair of students in the southeast corner of the classroom, because only recently he'd debated with them whether the much-lauded collective labor contract of May 1950, with its mandated acceptance of centralized planning, wasn't actually a total abnegation of worker's rights, and whether a woman gutting fish in the people-owned business FishCan really was in a position to comprehend her individual share in the ownership of the factory or at least of her labor. Bettina should have realized that Student Lockenvitz's recitation was stumbling over his own thoughts.

– And the fact that you all were lying like an American president—minor detail, right?

– Since when is school an institution we trust with anything more than the prescribed curriculum? I'm sure that when it comes to your Sister Magdalena, too, you know in advance who's going to win any argument.

– I just wish you'd won *once*.

– I did. By the length of a bathing suit.

– Tell me! *You tell such good lies!*

– "Now comes the time of victories": the nation's custodian had said in April, but coal sometimes failed to turn up for the evening train to Jerichow, where my swimsuit for the Baltic was. If I woke up in the morning at the Pagenkopfs', I would head out with my bathing suit for Gneez Lake and swim a few hundred meters there, usually with Pius, who would've preferred to sleep longer but who forced himself to be the good chaperone. When we didn't have time to detour to Helene Pagenkopf's laundry line on the way back, we'd take the wet things to school. It was May, the windows were open, they'd be dry by fourth period on the sill in the sun. Keeping my face turned to the teacher, I would sometimes stick my hand out the window and feel the fabric, which smelled of fresh water.

– And Selbich had it in for you.

– Maybe, since the sight of me reminded her of a time and a situation when things were going better for her. When she caught me with my forearm on the window ledge, she yelled at me and said all sorts of infuriated things about people who fondle swimsuits; she got tangled for a minute in the fact that when a person is changing into a bathing suit he or she is naked for a moment... and this while someone is standing here telling you about the personality of Comrade Stalin, the wise leader and guarantor of the world peace bloc!

– Telling "you" with a plural? Who were "you" besides you?

– She meant Pius and me. Even though the Gneez swimming area had separate changing rooms available and mandatory. Pius was already halfway out of his chair.

– What a sight! Big strapping boy decks helpless New Teacher!

– He'd have been sorry, that's for sure. I held his jacket tight with my right hand and moved my lips as if telling him something. If he understood it, it was the word "Kliefoth." For in 1939 Kliefoth had resigned from his teaching post because he'd pulled an eighth grader back from thin ice but the boy was in uniform and started proceedings: You, sir, have insulted the honor of the Führer's coat. Bettina, too, was wearing her heraldic blue that day, and assaulting it might have cost Pius his graduation. Instead of him, Schoolgirl Cresspahl rose, leaving Pius with all his thwarted manhood behind, and walked up to Bettina Selbich, perfectly calm, without any permission to do so. Selbich started to panic and shouted: Sit down! and eventually, in the informal form: Stop, Gesine!

– It was like she suddenly recognized you again.

– If being in tenth grade has any advantages, one is that pupils are to be addressed with adult, formal pronouns—but I could let that go. The other one is that teachers aren't allowed to grab or touch you.

– Oh to be in tenth grade!

– I stopped right in front of her, one girl facing another, and looked at her as obligingly as I knew how—like this, look—

– That's your nicest one, Gesine.

– and pursed my lips a little and showed her the tiniest bit of the tip of my tongue.

– No one else saw it.

– It was nothing she could ever prove. She alone had understood what I was telling her there, one woman to another; she was shaking in her blue shirt as I turned and walked out the door. She was shrieking, this Bettina was.

– A tenth grader could let that go.

– And could march, wrapped in all her dignity, straight to the principal's office where she asks Elise Bock for a piece of paper and an envelope, accepting Elise's invitation for a cup of coffee. Rumor later turned that into: FDJ-member Cresspahl wrote to the FDJ ZSGL

– What on earth is that?

– to the Free German Youth's Central School-Group Authority and filed a complaint against FDJ-member Bettina Selbich, Principal (pro tem). The truth is that I hid in the map room, so now Bettina also had to worry that I'd run out onto the street; punctually at the start of the next class I was standing behind my desk. Pius smiled the way Jakob sometimes did: relieved, just a hint in the corners of his eyes, up from under his brows.

– He was grateful.

– No, but he forgave me for having ruined his chivalry. We were scared. The principal's office had a cabinet full of radio equipment and a microphone, she could issue an order through the loudspeaker in our classroom that I come to her office. That would not have been good.

– But not a peep.

– On the other hand, the rumor I mentioned started going around, peeping with all its might. It said Mrs. Selbich had slapped Cresspahl's daughter in the face so hard that the girl had to see a dentist. It insisted that after Student Cresspahl left the room, class 10-A-II started acting up—she had friends and allies, of course—so that Mrs. Selbich felt the need to put her chair on the front desk and climb this tower with the aid of a second chair to keep the class under surveillance from above, putting on quite a show of the Riepschläger calves and thighs in the process. (Unfortunately for Bettina, rumor wasn't exaggerating in this case; Pius swore that had actually happened.) The alleged complaint miraculously turned into charges of mistreating a student, filed at the city's DA office: it was said that Mrs. Selbich had tried to strip Cresspahl's daughter; Pius and I refused to comment. But in town I was often and ardently greeted, the way I imagine beautiful princesses passing through town used to be in the old days; news of the spunky schoolgirl defying the throne of the principal had already reached Jerichow, too. I went to get our milk at Emma Senkpiel's and she took my can to the back room and brought it back heavier than usual. Twelve people watched me weigh the free extra weight in my hand, all looking like gleeful co-conspirators. So it cost a few marks extra. Back home Jakob's mother found a dozen eggs in the milk; during the ten-day ration periods in May, we redeemed our egg coupons for margarine.

– You're lying, Gesine. Those are my eggs that exploded!

– And thank you very much, otherwise I would've forgotten about Senkpiel's.

– Now for the complaint.

– Burly Sieboldt caught up to us the next day at the swimming place off the beaten track; he used to just come up to me publicly in the schoolyard. He had an air of secrecy, of something circumspect. Talked to everyone there until he had me alone and could take me aside. As Chapter Secretary of the FDJ ZSGL, he had nothing but praise for my having Elise Bock's sheet of paper in my breast pocket, blank, and the envelope, unaddressed; – *now thatsa matter for my mothers own son*: he said, every inch the functionary in charge, clearly having premeditated what he wanted to do, and not telling me. He acted like an unexpected task had suddenly appeared in the middle of his neatly organized schedule, an impossible but rewarding mission. He was known as Burly because he had something bull-like about him—*Bullen* not *pigs*, remember; anyone who didn't know him and unexpectedly found themselves in Sieboldt's paddock would feel menaced, but I was *Cresspahl sin Gesin* to him. He liked keeping it vague, and he knew his reputation.

– Gesine, is this going to be another water-butt story?

– Don't worry. All that happened was that Granny Rehse, whom Bettina Selbich in her new magnificence had hired as a cleaning lady, gave notice; now Bettina had to clean her own apartment on Cathedral Court. The landlord gave notice, too; Bettina won that suit but the general tone on the stairs in the building was quite different now. A garbage can might be left somewhere in the dark hall, for instance, and Bettina might take a little spill.

– You're all so mean.

– I agree. And Jakob, two hours away at the Güstrow Locomotive Engineers School, had by then been friends with Jöche for a long time; Jöche liked being Jakob's lieutenant. Bettina ran into a patch of bad luck traveling by train. The conductors always checked her ticket much more suspiciously than the other passengers', who then tended to move away from her. The railroad police would walk through the whole train not paying attention to anyone, and then pounce on Bettina, check her ID— only hers, openly suspicious. How could they know by sight someone who'd moved there from far-off Ludwigslust! Bettina got careless; she misplaced her ticket somewhere between Schwerin and Gneez. Questioning at the Gneez main station, a report filed. How did the passenger present herself? Distracted. Sufficient grounds to consider her capable of the offense (subreption of conveyance services)? Premeditation is suspected.

– The main station . . .

– Yes indeed. Connection to Jerichow.

– She had no way of knowing that a railroad employee was a registered resident with the Cresspahls in Jerichow!

– That thread of Ariadne was unwound for her by someone else. Someone who had something bulky about him.

– Oh my distant homeland!

– The Chapter Secretary at Fritz Reuter High School had certain questions from the FDJ head office that he needed to discuss with the principal, also an FDJ-member. Overburdened as he was by his duties in office, as well as preparing for his finals, he could only manage appointments in the late evening hours. He was observed in Cathedral Court during the night several times.

– Oh my distant homeland!

– We had an ally on the faculty too: the beanpole gym teacher. He never failed to wave us over when he saw his former star swimming with Pius (we were The Couple). And so we heard that someone had suggested at the grading conference that Colleague Selbich give Student Cresspahl a higher grade than her usual "Good" in Conduct this year. She apparently sat there stiff as a board. But in fact this student had not been caught in the slightest breach of school rules all year. She finished tenth grade with a grade in Conduct of: Very Good.

– And once bitten, twice shy?

– Mrs. Selbich ignored the back right-hand desk in 10-A-II whenever she could. She had to spend three weeks, too, on a page in the class book which she'd had to replace by hand, having written something reckless on the original page before coming to her senses and tearing it up in front of the class.

– I'd have felt sorry for her by now.

– Me too. She even started combing her hair in class, unconsciously I'm sure—the Riepschlägers hadn't raised their Bettina like that. Two years earlier she'd have never allowed that, neither from us nor from herself. She usually noticed the wide-toothed comb in her hand only after she'd passed it through her hair—not especially helping her hair either, by the way.

– You and your bathing suit and Comrade Stalin.

– Now hanging—the suit, not the comrade—with Loerbrocks the painter. He'd been made our janitor. And there it was for all to see at the edge of the schoolyard. The Cresspahl Monument. Bettina probably wished it was back on the window ledge outside 10-A-II.

– Make it up to her!

– We were obedient. She expounded the decline of capitalism in general (miners' strike in the USA) and particular (a month of every West German's salary goes to pay for the military occupation); we repeated this back on demand and refrained from asking how much per capita the East German worker paid for the Soviet occupation. The rise, in contrast, of Socialism: the pact between Stalin and Mao, a $330 million development credit. If anyone wanted to hear why such sums were calculated in dollars, that desire was duly suppressed. While Bettina combed her hair. Zaychik interpreted the liberation of India as the fall of the British Empire; the sound of the British airplanes helping to break the blockade of Berlin still rang in our ears. Gabriel Manfras spoke at length about the Soviet gift of work standards, numbers of work units, time norms—flush with quiet enthusiasm, it seemed. Bettina Selbich praised the vigilance of the Socialist battalions, the trial of ten priests in Czechoslovakia for treason and espionage in April 1950, sentences up to life in prison; Anita recalled the troubles that had befallen Pastor Brüshaver on account of Herbert Vick's bequest, obeyed Bettina, and regurgitated what Bettina wanted; Bettina kept combing, head to one side, with tugging motions. Triumph of the World Peace Movement! The British have had to stop their bombing of Helgoland. We sat before her in the hot June light, the scent of the linden blossoms wafting in; rather inattentive, since the only thing we could learn in this class was a way of behaving. Bettina confirmed the younger Seneca yet again: *Non vitae, sed scholae discimus.* We learn not for life, but for school. One student, at least, was definitely daydreaming about a time when trips to the vicinity of Helgoland would be permitted once more. In any case, this New Teacher had ruined any chance she had to ask about our obedience, our patience. Like we would tell her anything. We were exaggeratedly polite and deferential in her classes, you could hear a pin drop—half a pin drop; her class put us to sleep. That was the first time I hoped I would never become a teacher anywhere they were trained and transformed from Bettina Riepschlägers to B. Selbichs. After three such classes at most I would have crawled out of the classroom in tears, without argument or discussion. She kept at it, though. Now you say what you wish for, Marie.

– I wish you could sleep as late as you want and need to, every night. *Yours, truly.*

July 28, 1968 Sunday, South Ferry day, even though it's the second-to-last day to edit Karsch's book. Are we really cocky enough to smuggle the proofs into the office disguised as work? Written words are getting the upper hand here. J. B. since June; for almost a year, the days that the other friend of our youth, Comrade Writer, has wanted to write up. We'll be so happy when there's an end to all this un-published writing.

The New York Times brings us my dream from yesterday morning.

And says that the East German Communists are again spreading what they call the fact that "life may appear quiet and normal in the streets of Prague these days," but it's a facade—apparently they know all about fa-cades—and behind this one is "a creeping counterrevolution." "The coun-terrevolutionary tactics employed in Czechoslovakia are more refined than they were in Hungary." And the blows against the rectification of this country, how refined will they be?

Down with Bettina! that's what Marie wants. But the teacher and act-ing principal only stumbled in the summer of 1950, though repeatedly; she might have fallen.

We tried. As 10-A-II's teacher, Bettina let Pius register our candidates for the trip to the FDJ's Whitsunday rally in Berlin but insisted on exam-ining them herself, primarily with respect to the added condition that they keep their distance from the Western sectors of the city. She accepted Pius of course—he was our class president, after all, and son of the meritorious Comrade Pagenkopf in the district capital, where via the Department of Popular Education he could spit in the soup of an unprotected New Teacher whenever he wanted. The deputy class president, Cresspahl, claimed home-work as her reason for not wanting to go, would you believe it. She didn't bring up her father's warning. In early May they were still saying "Free German Youth to Storm Berlin!" and Heinrich Cresspahl considered the lessons that Gesine had brought home from her New School. According to which the West had thoughtlessly picked up right where the Weimar Republic had gone off the rails; he remembered policemen in shakos attack-ing demonstrators with billy clubs, or shooting, and didn't want to have his child "storming" Berlin or anywhere else, nor did he want his daughter returned to him all beaten up. He practically begged her, promising her a solo trip to "Berlin" over the summer to make up for it. Gesine reserved the right to refuse that trip too; she always willingly submitted to her father's concerns; so eager to please, this child. (And because it was still a comfort to Cresspahl when someone listened to him, paid attention to him.) She didn't tell him the real reason, of course: It might happen that Jakob re-membered his filial duty on Whitsunday and paid a visit to Cresspahl's house. Gesine thought to await this eventuality in a deck chair by the milk rack behind the house, pretending, for Jakob, to be reading for school.

So Student Cresspahl was absent. Gabriel Manfras declared, in a guarded way: Everywhere we go we must show how sincerely we stand for peace; Bettina believed him (as did we). Lise wanted to take the opportunity to go shopping in West Berlin and made no bones about it, neither to us nor to Gabriel, who was disconcerted to hear her parrot what he'd just said, cheerfully, not quite exactly. Anita was smart; she talked her way out of the trip with interpreting duties for Triple-J and Emil Knoop. In fact, she wanted to make some money at Emil's adding machine. Student Marschinsky had every right to feel tricked. She'd wanted to go so that she could be with Zaychik over the holiday too (Dagobert Haase was dreaming of going to see the West Berlin car show but pretended he was curious about the new construction in the "democratic" sector); now Eva awkwardly hemmed and hawed. Dieter Lockenvitz took the same line as Zaychik, if rather more finely drawn: he spoke of the limited autonomy of the superstructure, i.e., new Berlin architecture as an expression of national form. Since he did so with a straight face, and citations, moreover, from the works of J. V. Stalin on Marxist linguistics, what could Selbich do to him? (He'd never been to Berlin: we thought.) Eva got her permission, maybe because Selbich felt a need to ingratiate herself with 10-A-II. Where the earlier Bettina would have smiled and heightened Eva's anticipation, today's Bettina said dismissively, contemptuously: Ah well. You don't have the consciousness.

(Such pronouncements—unconscious students in 10-A-II!—were by that point the topic of avid questions on the part of those who had no pedagogical dealings with Selbich. Even Julie Westphal, who after all was no spring chicken, always liked hearing the story retold of how her younger colleague and superior had presided over the class from her vertically extended desk.)

Pius took the trip with more than the required accessories (blue shirt, toilet kit, fighting spirit). (He was traveling as the Pagenkopf/Cresspahl collective's representative.) And so Gesine had paid a visit to Horst Stellmann's on Stalin Street in Jerichow, asking him for an "instant" camera. – Eyes to the wood: Stellmann said, in the old soldier's phrase, slightly pulling down the skin under his left eye with his finger; – Eyes peeled: Gesine responded, always willing to go along with the games a grown-up wanted to play. Stellmann dug up a Leica from his rearmost drawer, truly moved by the thought of how accommodating he was willing to be with Cresspahl's daughter. But she wanted something less conspicuous, something that could pass the new luggage inspection at Nauen or Oranienburg without raising any suspicion of black-market dealings with West Berlin. Horst eventually brought out a humbler bellows camera, three hundred marks deposit instead of two thousand, which you could raise to the eye and then tuck away in nothing flat. How startled he was to catch a glimpse

of Cresspahl's daughter on Town Road in Jerichow on Whitsunday, nowhere near any surveillance activities in Berlin.

Pius came back on the Tuesday after Whitsunday, reporting train delays
that suggested a certain indifference on the part of railwaymen when it
came to transporting young human freight in the interests of peace. Ac-
commodations in a business school in Berlin-Heinersdorf, on straw; fistfights
with students from Saxony over nighttime thefts; a five-hour shuffling march
to the platform holding the country's custodian and the head of the FDJ.
Honecker was his name, not yet thirty-eight at that point, and he weighed
the takeover of West Berlin against the bloodied heads of his Young
Comrades. As compensation, he offered up something bizarre about potato
bugs. Berlin residents annoyed at the blue-shirted visitors getting free rides
on city transportation. Zaychik and Eva had made it to the expo at the
radio tower. Dieter Lockenvitz set out for the Congress of Young Fighters
for Peace, at Landsberg Avenue station on the ring road, with opening
remarks by the poet Stephan Hermlin; he later said he'd gotten lost, and
remained missing, untraceable. Pius knew what Gesine was waiting for but
droned on and on; by then the two of us liked to tease each other, like a
married couple. Finally she swallowed her pride and asked: Did you get her?

Pius had her, in his box. The youthful, still confident principal, in charge
of the delegation from Fritz Reuter High School, Gneez—how could he
lose sight of her! She made it easy by falling into a helpless panic at the shy
earnestness with which Burly Sieboldt, in Berlin too, tugged at her blue
blouse, as though he wanted to reveal his admiration to both her and an
audience. She was dazed, letting Pius follow her as if under a cloak of invisibility, until he eventually surprised her on Palace Street, Berlin-Steglitz,
American Sector, West Berlin. Outside a shoe store—she was still just a
young thing, Bettina was. When she saw Pius, camera raised, it must have
dawned on her with a stab of anguish that she could not accuse a single
student from Gneez of a peace-betraying excursion to West Berlin as long
as one of them possessed a photograph showing the principal and FDJ-
member succumbing to the temptations of capitalism on the level of commodity circulation. Which is why she tried to take his camera away. But
Pius had strong hands, from gymnastics on the high bar; he also asked her,
familiarly, if she wanted it to unload it for West marks. Wouldn' advise
that, Comrade. Since the West mark is about to collapse and all. (So that

she could see at least some of what she extolled in her lessons as an economic law of nature had stuck with him.)

Better safe than sorry. To be safe, Pius sent word apologizing to the head of the Gneez youth delegation (sunstroke; and through Axel Ohr, so that Bettinikin would suspect Student Cresspahl might be involved); he went home on a different rail line from the one on which the railwaymen were shunting the school transport back to Gneez. Horst Stellmann was simply delighted by the secrecy with which he was asked to develop the film; grown-ups are like that—letting themselves get distracted by the Western shop sign and not noticing the person under it. And that was where the Pagenkopf/Cresspahl work collective let it stand in the campaign against Bettina Selbich; but she couldn't know that. She defied our blank looks with a pride through which we could see a quaking terror. (Her gray eyebrows were a little mismatched; how I'd once enjoyed looking at them.) Were we unfair to her? Maybe. Until the end of the first week after Whitsunday—*may*be, Marie.

Marie is eager to hear if Bettina managed to keep it together instead of hightailing it out of Gneez. Moving somewhere she wouldn't have to deal every day with students who had her in their power and pocket. Out of shame, if nothing else. There's no way to solve this riddle, Marie, here in the murky aggrieved haze of Staten Island, with a view of the Verrazano Bridge's west pier. Selbich hardly seemed up to defiance and the strength required for a move. Unless she'd decided, under that unevenly cut blond hair of hers, that the photographic evidence might just as well catch up to her in Zwickau, at the other end of the country. Would we have been so cruel? We might, if we had to be.

End-of-year grades in Contemporary Studies: for Pagenkopf, B; for Cresspahl likewise, "Good."

– The look she gave me in Steglitz: Pius told me, about that scene on the corner of Palace and Muthesius Streets between the policewoman, caught in the act, and the thief, magnanimous: it was like what she wanted most of all was to bite me! Tssss! Like a snake. (Sometimes Pius acted younger than me.)

It was just the two of us, tucked under the shoreline cliff west of Rande, muffled by the roar of the Baltic. True, one of us expanded on the description until we got to venom, snake-poison—but just between us. It must have been through osmosis that Bettina S. soon got a new nickname, first in our class, then throughout the school, and that this is how she is still remembered: "blond poison," the German phrase for a blond bombshell. Selbich, The Blond Poison. TBP. After summer vacation in 1950, Julie Westphal told her about this sobriquet she'd acquired, pretending to do it out of pity. Luckily, the phrase's author slipped through her fingers; our Blond Poison must have thought to the end that it was a malicious invention, not by accident.

Whatever nicknames might say about a person's behavior, Pius was safe thanks to his family and his apparently telling Bettina what she wanted to hear in a tone that was even more devout than was strictly required. Gesine had no nickname. Marie had one only in nursery school, in 1961–62 ("our lil' kraut"). And it is this young lady, the most steadfast of the children in the Cresspahl line though in no way the bravest, who asks a favor once we're past the Verrazano Bridge. The trip to Czechoslovakia looms. Could we maybe test the waters in the restaurant on the East Side, where the people speak and act Czech?

– Perfect! That's why you're wearing a dress instead of pants! That's just what I have a checkbook in my bag for! Let's go to your detested Svatého Václava!

– On Riverside Drive I still thought we wouldn't. Now I think I need it.

It turns out Jakob reconsidered the visit he owed his mother (in Cresspahl's house). He sent a photographic version of himself, taken privately, in postcard format. It showed a long swimming pier with a lifeguard's station and Island Lake in Güstrow with boats in the water. Jakob sent his regards from a training course that had been unexpectedly extended. When he did lie, it was only to spare others' feelings. A training course has breaks. In breaks you can take a girl out on a boat ride. And that was why Gesine Cresspahl had stuck out the Whitsunday sun in Jerichow, in her dress for special occasions, from the West—all she got for it was sunburned knees.

July 29, 1968 Monday, Dirty Monday
To be fair, if you look at it objectively, we do leave our apartment in the lurch when one of us goes to the corner of West End Avenue where the

summer camp's orange bus is waiting and the other one lets the subway whisk her from the Upper West Side to Midtown and the desolation of work; we leave our twenty-seven hundred cubic feet of inhabitable space floating in the wasteland of Manhattan's architecture, unprotected, miles away, and that in a city where a dignified bum tries to steal Marie's grocery cart while she's watching through a window. Where, sitting on a bench by the river with Mrs. Ferwalter, we keep a wary hand on our brown paper package that contains nothing but laundry, at some cost to our intelligibility in the conversation. Where philanthropists passing through town count their cash outside in broad daylight, within reach of greedy observers, and a Mrs. Cresspahl grabs the wallet of this trusting man of the world, this Anselm Kristlein, and holds it tight at her side and only then apologizes for overfamiliar behavior. The fact is, we deserve punishment.

And we've expected it. The statistical average of two murders a day in the five boroughs of New York suggests a daily quantity of additional crimes as well. Ever since our Mrs. Seydlitz, trusting the sharp eyes of the doorman who watches over the elevator doors in her building, nonetheless found herself facing a seventeen-year-old boy's knife—his fear more dangerous than his weapon—we were disappointed, we shuddered slightly, at the fact that this course of probable everyday events had continued to pass us by. Now, after seven years here, it was our turn. Time to put behind us what the city administration's criminal science bureau has specified, just for us, as the degree to which hitherto unrealized events are possible. So that we'll be safe till the next iteration of what we're owed.

We enjoyed the bliss of the commonplace until Marie came home today to find a door with a dangling lock, which made her stop and listen and retreat downstairs; until Mrs. Cresspahl poked the lamely hanging piece of woodwork with a (gloved) finger and immediately noticed two crooked cracks in one of her storm windows. Marie has come to the point where she can laugh at the slow-motion gesture with which her mother raised both hands to her hair, and actually the hairdo was in almost as perfect shape as it had been when she'd left Mr. Boccaletti's beauty salon. The apartment was trashed.

We know what to do, we kept our fingerprints to ourselves for the time being and went down to the basement to use shamefaced Jason's phone. But does the NYPD know what to do?

New York Police Department: How do you know they came through the window?

Citizen Cresspahl: Because the window's broken.

NYPD: You have children?

C.C.: One.

NYPD: Well then.

C.C.: Are you planning to send someone over, or would you rather we just chitchat for a while?

NYPD: When did you move in?

C.C.: May 1961.

NYPD: And when are you moving out?

C.C.: Is there any chance that the law enforcement branch of government might want to see the scene of the crime in person?

NYPD: You can fix the window yourself.

C.C.: Then I guess I'll turn around and ask a private agency.

NYPD: Hey! Listen you, now calm down.

By the time a boy in blue from New York's Finest appeared, stranded in the doorframe, we could work out for ourselves what had happened before we arrived. The time was missing—the alarm clock stolen. But in some minute or another after 8:25 a.m., someone entered an empty lobby on Riverside Drive. At 243 Riverside Drive, to be exact, where there's always supposed to be someone watching out for our money, either Eagle-Eye Robinson or Esmeralda. A glance to the left of the elevator, at the open door to the stairwell, which according to fire regulations is to be kept closed at all times. How often we've daydreamed of taking a razor and cutting the thread tying the door to the heating pipe! Someone in a hurry, someone who doesn't belong here, settles for the next floor—apartment 204. Since the elevator is in motion right next to it, he has to manage with a few stabbing strikes around the clever stupid lock, with a mighty blow that rips out the chain anchored to the frame (by four two-inch screws). He sees from the keyhole that the people here can lock the door from the outside; if anything moves inside then they're home. Silence. In he goes. Puts the brass cylinder back where it was, more or less, so as not to be noticeable. What does he see?

Salvation Army furniture on hardwood floors (no rug), casually laid out, as if no one here ever had to turn their back on each other. Luxury?

Yes, two windows facing the western light of Riverside Drive, the woodsy park, the distant glittering of the river. Waste of effort. Better to scram.

But no, maybe he's thirsty, and there's a friendly refrigerator just waiting for him, to the left of the door. If someone gets mad because what he wants isn't there for him—a cold beer—he'll pull out one shelf after another, everything bangs gently onto the tiles, mixing the tomato paste, mustard, milk, and liverwurst. From that point on he leaves traces, our visitor.

Along the back wall of the middle room there's a structure of wood and glass—perfectly natural that the green curtain might scare a person. There's a key in the lock, but how could anyone know that, a few blows here and there does the job too. Books. More books. Still, people keep money in books, between the pages, he's heard that. The empty books anger him and he swipes them off the shelves by the row, including those that are too old for such treatment. *Outline of the History of Mecklenburg*, by Paschen Heinrich Hane, second preacher in Gadebusch, printed 1804, unlisted in ADB, NDB, Brunet, Kraesse, Cat. Schles.-Holst. State Bibl.—the fragile leather spine on that one breaks; likewise *Everyman's History of Mecklenburg, in Letters*, Printed in Neubrandenburg by C. G. Korb, Printer to the Grand Duke, 1791, motto: Moribus et hospitalitate nulla gens honestior aut benignior potuit inveniri. Yeah, right! Stomp.

The secretary that the Dane left us glances over with its many drawers, all with locks, better we just break it open, the glassed hutch too. Ha, some loot! A folder with *Taxes* written on it. Still, taxes have to do with money. Overwhelmed with the presence of mere information, he'll fling that across the room into the slimy sauce of edibles and broken glass.

To the right he sees curtained glass doors, they give way under a light kick revealing a room with a fleece carpet, a child's painting *al fresco* on the white wall, a table with a typewriter. All right then! We'll take that.

The tenant has sent her child down to the lobby, under the super's protection, to wait for the NYPD. The tenant herself is waiting in, as close as possible to the middle of, the room. Before her calm eyes the front door opens, rustling in the breeze, a finger reaches in. She says to the hand: *Marie, je t'en prie!* but the body part belongs to a different person, a man, who shows his confused, half-polite face and stutters. Must've made a stupid mistake, sorry, he'll just try the stairway door next to this one. All while taking slow backward steps from the woman. She watches him knock next door, until a second man, invisible behind the wall, comes up in the stairway and tells his friend, as if they were alone: Good idea to take care of the super. Both stumble off, abashed but relaxed before the unarmed female, only starting to run when they get to the super's floor, and they burst out the last door onto Ninety-Sixth Street into a cop car, which traps them in the corner of the sidewalk with the bridge underpass, because Citizen Cresspahl is shouting something excitedly, in Italian: *Al ladro! Al ladro! Fermateli!*

Then Marie has finally followed her out and for the first time ever she sees handcuffs being used for real. (All things considered, it feels like something performed for her, a fairy tale—all going off without a hitch.)

Admittedly, these two men don't have anything on them, and the policemen were only trying to do a (clearly hysterical) lady a favor, but after they'd traipsed around all the addresses the gentlemen supplied and found no place of residence anywhere, after one had tried to slip away from them into a subway station packed with rush-hour traffic, the team of patrolmen, one after the other, called up Citizen Cresspahl asking for forgiveness and thanking her—her assistance had given them some points in the precinct bosses' tally; the suspects were junkies, too. – You did the right thing, ma'am! Calling us right away, that takes care of it.

Meanwhile the man with the powder had come and he was dusting the shards of window on the floor with his little brush; with Marie watching him so closely as he worked, he'd rather have taken the whole window with him. His partner had found marks from the crowbar on the bottom frame, and, on the hooks attached to the outside wall that the window washers use for their belt, a belt for window washers, and, on the sidewalk below the window, a bucket with wash rags inside that had fallen over.

Do we insist on filing a complaint, which would only make more work for the NYPD? We ask for a police report.

Missing: One portable typewriter with European keyboard. One shortwave radio, on which we listen to the water levels in the ČSSR every night. A tape recorder, including the tape from Saturday (gone: one Blond Poison), in fact all the cassettes that would have been gathered and sent to a bank vault in Düsseldorf the day after tomorrow. One document folder with private correspondence and nothing but some loose change, not even a foreign passport. Such a hurry he was in, no? (Except that our visitor found the time to fill the toilet bowl almost to the rim with his indigestibilia.) And? One leather bag from Switzerland, big, with stamped initials. For carrying stuff away with, first, before repacking, y'see? Your initials, if you don't mind, on the double.

Once we can touch the telephone again, the young lady from the phone company tries to make a fuss about our disavowal of any long-distance calls that might have been placed from this number since this morning, whether to Eugene, Oregon, or Yokohama, Japan. What's that, you want official confirmation? Please remain on the line. *Ne quittez pas!* Here's a representative of the Twenty-Third Precinct.

It was still light out, we'd cleaned up the broken things and shard-filled sludge, laid out the mistreated books on spread nets like wounded birds; in came Jason, looking somber. He had pulled himself together, out of the shame of this having happened to us under his watch, above his very head! for he'd been in the building all day. With him came Eagle-Eye Robinson, bashfully feeling the crispy furrows of his hair with his fingertips—he should have been keeping watch. Together they measured the shattered door and spent till midnight putting in a similar one, admittedly numbered 1201 but freshly cloaked in steel, with an undamaged lock and a chain latch attached to the wall with rivets. Since such installations make noise (i.e., so that tenants next door might remain unaware that we're treated like favorite children), they invited us downstairs to the super's office, to watch TV, some ice tea for the younger of the ladies.

We both decided we'd rather take a walk. Passed from the shady Hudson, through the catacomb tunnel under the Henry Hudson Expressway, to the Eighties on Riverside Drive and back. Maybe we were looking for Marjorie. (If, Mrs. Cresspahl, the city of New York has ever done you harm or made you suffer...) It was too late at night. She was nowhere to be seen.

July 30, 1968 Tuesday

The Soviet Politburo, largely unlocatable since Saturday, emerged yesterday morning, nine men strong, in fifteen green sleeping cars that a red, yellow and green diesel engine pulled across the damp wheat fields in Czechoslovak territory from Chop, a Soviet border town, into Cierna, led by the party chief, Leonid I. Brezhnev, who was greeted at the brick station by Alexander Dubček and fifteen of his advisers. Kisses? Embraces? None. A three-and-a-half-hour meeting, then each delegation ate on their own in their own train.

No communiqué unless we fish one out of *Pravda*, which informs the hosts, scout's honor, that: the Soviet Union supplies their country with virtually all its petroleum, four-fifths of its iron-ore imports (border cross- ing point: Chop/Cierna), 63 percent of its synthetic rubber, and 42 percent of its nonferrous metals. Soviet prices are also more advantageous to Czecho- slovakia than ones in the Western markets, where favoritism and dis- criminatory trade practices are rife.

Unless we bend our ear to the NY *Times.* This energetic lady, with her hypnotic compulsion to research every angle, opines: a Soviet invasion of Czechoslovakia would be a disaster for the French Communists. But she also concludes, on the evidence that the Soviet government has banned its own journalists from traveling to Czechoslovakia, that its own propaganda is a fabrication. But what if the Soviets only wanted to protect their re- porters—a valuable cadre—from a future where people visiting Prague might have one or another hair on their head harmed?

On the first day of school after the Whitsunday trip, those who returned were given their welcome, along with those who'd stayed home to pen a love poem to Comrade Stalin, or to TBP, or to a girl he'd noticed sun- bathing as he peeped through the gaps in a gooseberry hedge. At first many failed to notice the welcome. Gneez, like Jerichow, was covered with post- ers—why would they notice the DIN A5 sheets plastered on the glass in the main entrance of the Fritz Reuter High School and in rows at eye level around the walls of the building? They showed members of the Free Ger- man Youth, in formation, the color blue all too recognizable as well as the question to the FDJ'ers: What are you marching for? The desired answer came so automatically that Pius hadn't bothered to keep reading and had forgotten all about the handbills by the start of second period; Gesine too. Equations with two unknown variables, with three, can challenge the free German youthful brain, distracting it.

Then, right into the middle of the math problems being rehearsed under Mrs. Gollnow, burst Bettina's voice from the loudspeaker—hoarse, despondent, desperate, brittlely harsh. All students are to remain in their classrooms, ignoring any bells. Teachers currently in the room are in charge.

It was evening, a late-May twilight, before the last students were let out onto the street. The criminal police (D Squad) started their questioning with the seniors, so six hours passed before 10-A-II's turn. At first Mrs. Gollnow conducted class as usual, finishing the day's planned lesson; then she offered extra one-on-one tutoring to anyone who wanted it; eventually she started telling what she called "tales" from her life. What it was like at Leipzig University; her correspondence with the writer Joachim de Catt, who went by the pseudonym Hinterhand. The windows were wide open; there was plenty of air; around noon the 10-A-II classroom started to feel like a prison. A merry one, for a little while. For Dr. Gollnow—who to universal gratitude decoded her first initial for us: Erdmuthe—would rather let us see her as an ingenious person than do without out of pride any longer: she was a smoker, and admitted it. Referendum: permission to smoke in the confines of a room meant for educational purposes. Inventory: all available tobacco products. Communist distribution: to each according to his need, not his merit. Still, by around two o'clock the filterless Turf cigarettes

<u>Th</u>ousands <u>U</u>nder <u>R</u>ussian <u>F</u>lags.
Thousands,
I tell you.

as well as the hit-or-miss imitation Americans were gone, and secret terror was creeping up to our throats, since Gollnow had banned all speculation about the quarantine. Something must be going on out there that affected the whole student body. Was Gneez in flames?

At around three o'clock, a doggedly uncommunicative Loerbrocks, guarded by a civilian unconnected to the school, handed out rolls from the cafeteria: dry bread with no water or soup; before long it hurt to swallow it. The silent guessing, the confused (sometimes scornful) questioning looks, the helpless shrugs; it soon got hard to keep up one's confidence. Anyone who needed to go to the bathroom could give two knocks on the classroom door; they would be let out, but accompanied by a male or female officer, who refused to say anything. In 10-A-II they started calling students by seating position, not alphabetically (did the school office have a copy of the seating chart?). So Gantlik came before Cresspahl, Wollenberg before Pagenkopf, and no one came back. Cresspahl was the last person waiting with Gollnow, who had run out of anecdotes and whispered something about Good luck!, as if this student might be in particular need of it. A burning, hungry look had come into Dr. E. Gollnow's eyes.

Gesine did have good luck. In the hall she saw the single raincoat abandoned among the countless empty hooks and she slipped it on as if it were hers. She felt paper in a pocket; while waiting outside the principal's office she was even able to read some of what was written there in block letters. Elise Bock's job was guard and watchman; she gave the student a soothing look and had already snatched the scrap away when the incoming call rang the bell of her phone. Shadows of trees behind Elise's back.

That was neatly done, Anita. Thank you, thank you, thank you.

The cops first covered 10-A-II as a whole, with TBP smack bang in the middle of it. But you're the target.

I went numb racking my brain trying to figure out why.

They wanted to know if you were mad at the state. Over the shitty deal the founders thereof gave your father. Fünfeichen and all that.

Always direct and to the point, our Anita.

Since I was in a hurry. Also if you'd skipped the Germany Rally so you could secretly go to West Berlin—

Where I don't know anyone except a German shepherd.

—and collect handbills showing free German young people marching under and behind barbed wire.

So that's what I get for serving in the FDJ.

They don't give a rat's ass about that; if anything it's a strike against you, Gesine.

Which is why you hid behind block letters.

Keep guessing, but later. Right now they're after your head. They want to know if you've got someone with the railroads.

A student stepped into the principal's office, the interrogation room, with head lowered, braids feeling heavy; she barely lifted her head to look at FDJ Comrade Selbich, who was staring at her from behind her desk, fists clenched, and who jerked her head toward where the visitors were. A set of upholstered chairs, confiscated from the Bruchmüllers; on one a Mecklenburg man with the badge of the Unity Party on his lapel, almost too tired to take the trouble to be crafty; next to him a young man Bettina's age, who would have plunged Lise Wollenberg into a fit of jealousy if he picked another lady instead of her—a gentleman. Fabric of elegant cut on his chest, knees showing off the creases of his freshly ironed pants. A stern, mocking look which said: Don't worry, we'll get you too. The student said: My name is Gesine Cresspahl, 10-A-II, born on . . .

– *There are serious matters, ver-r-ry serious matters* that we have to discuss with you . . . : this upright citizen began, in a mix of Platt and High German—the nice uncle who doesn't like punishing anyone, unless it be deserved, or needed. An upraised palm stopped him in his tracks, like a well-trained animal: – . . . to discuss with *you:* he said again, using the formal pronoun: *We wancha to see right off that we're treatin you with all due respect. Tenth grade, all that horseshit.* Now, you probably know where Hans-and-Sophie-Scholl Street is in Schweri-en?

If that's all you want to know, Mr. . . . (no name given to fill the pause). From the main train station in Schwerin you take a right onto Wismar Street, in other words south toward Stalin Street, continue to St. Mary Square, now called Lenin Square, where the Dom Ofitserov is, and, to the east, the arcade to the palace, known and loved across the country. Past that, Kaiser Wilhelm Street, nowadays the Street of National Unity, branches off to the right, still heading south, and leads to Count Schack Street, going right and left. That's the shortest way, I think. Count Schack Street, every young Mecklenburger knows that address—that's where you go dancing, at the Tivoli! There are only twelve numbered buildings on that street; the municipal health insurance building used to be there, part of Mecklenburg State Insurance, and Pastor Niklot Beste lived at 5C, he was a member of the High Consistory after the war, state bishop of the Evangelical-Lutheran Mecklenburg State Church after 1947. Count Schack Street is part of the original Schwerin suburbs. Adolf Friedrich von Schack, born in 1815 in Brüsewitz just outside Schwerin, member of the Munich School of poets starting in 1855, made a count by the Kaiser in 1876, died in Rome (Italy), 1894. His epic poem *Lothar* . . .

How happy, I! Oh childhood bliss,
The golden days of life's sweet dawn!
A light we in our blindness miss,
Last glimpse of infinity shimm'ring on,
It shines upon thee yet!

Those who cherish this opus know all about his street, whatever name it now bears. From the left, eastern half, you can look down toward Castle Lake. In New Mecklenburg, this part was renamed for the Scholl siblings.

– Shut UP, Gesine! Shut up already! She's making fun of you, Comrade, this brat, this . . . bitch!: Bettina Selbich shrieked, raising and shaking her fist so that her blue shirt seemed to flutter all over. The local interrogator's partner was up in a bound, sending a whiff of fruit over to the accused, who sat there looking as meek and contrite as could be. This stranger busied himself about his comrade. Your nerves, my dear lady. It's been a long hard day, a blow to our World Peace Movement, please calm down, perhaps out in the waiting room if you'd rather . . .

Thenceforth it proceeded as if tea were laid out on the low table with the crocheted doily, as if the lady being held there were constantly being offered cakes, a glass of sherry if she wanted. So, the student knew about the Scholl siblings? Yes, they were students during the time of the Nazis, Hans and Sophie, executed in February 1943 at ages twenty-three and twenty-two in Berlin-Plötzensee for having distributed leaflets at Munich University. – Excellent!: came the grade from the Sovietnik, glancing at his German trainee as though encouraging him to learn these dates too, though not with much confidence he would. – And we: he said, with a touch of delight, with clear amusement: We are from the M.f.S. on Hans-and-Sophie-Scholl Street in Schwerin. We are looking into the leaflets that arrived last night at the Gneez station and were handed over to a total of four distributors, one of whom patched up your high school. Perhaps it was you, Miss Cresspahl? Would you like that?

What followed was a back-and-forth of verbal blows, today I'd say: a squash game; but one with my skin at stake. (– Skin is always on the outside: a friend likes to say.) The only thing that made it easier was the fact that the tempo stayed the same, furious as it was, racing past the Mecklenburg minion as Achilles did the tortoise, thus numerous times, because an infinite series does converge on a finite sum, both in mathematics and out; a microphone from (the people-owned business) RadioTech had been placed, as a precaution, on the extended leaf of the cabinet:

And may I ask what M.f.S. stands for? *Ministerium für Staatssicherheit*, the State Security Service. Thank you very much. Don't mention it, happy to help. Was the founding of the M.f.S. somehow skipped in Contemporary Studies? It was, as far as I can recall. The historic date of the law of February 8, 1950? Maybe because of the excitement over the Peace Rally trip to Berlin. Name of instructor responsible for the omission? The Bl— Bettina Selbich. Incidentally, we already know everything, FDJ Comrade Cresspahl, all we need is confirmation from you. / So, she claims as an alibi that she arrived in Gneez on the milk train, after the school had already been wrapped in paper inimical to the state? Since the freewheel on her bicycle is broken and you can't get a replacement for money or coupons. There's a little device to separate a driven wave from a driving one, trademark Torpedo, ready and waiting for Miss Cresspahl, you can get it at any bike shop in West Berlin. Denial of having made any shopping trips to West Berlin. But FDJ-member Pagenkopf seems to have no problem paying visits to that den of iniquity. Pagenkopf is well aware what he owes to his father's position in the leadership of the Mecklenburg State Unity Party. And to himself? The FDJ class president does have a proper consciousness, yes. / Occasional overnight stays with the Pagenkopfs in Gneez due to arguments with her father? Not at all, he knows and agrees to it. Political agreement too? My father tries to understand the nature of contemporary events. With Miss Cresspahl instructing him? My father is not a talkative man, and also too weakened for extended conversations. Grandmother in the LDPD? Not an illegal party. Grandfather in custody with our Soviet friends? The proceedings are up in the air. A brother-in-law of Cresspahl's in the West, working for a ministry? Not on speaking terms with the family. Cresspahl himself imprisoned, most recently in Fünfeichen? My father describes it as a verification; trust is good, control is better, as LENIN says. Excellent, and now here is a quotation from STALIN! "Never in world history has there been a party as powerful as our Communist Party—and there never will be." Your grade in Contemporary Studies, Miss Cresspahl? B. Well, we'll have to discuss that with our colleague Mrs. Selbich. / Please, what was your first thought when you saw these handbills! Visual advertising defeats its purpose if it irritates the viewer. You are criticizing the use of visual advertising, such as why smooth paper is available for it but only wood-fiber stock for school notebooks? Or that there is more fabric available for propaganda banners than consumer textiles? Oh, no, nothing like that; just that the fliers were keeping the light out of the front staircase. Why do you say "fliers" rather than "posters"? Because of the size of the paper. And now your second thought, if I may ask. The form of address. "Young friend!" No, it said "FDJ'er." Like biker, gameplayer. To Mecklenburg ears it could sound somewhat childish, or maybe South German. The Red Biker bike messengers in Munich? No—modes of locomotion or athletics should be kept separate from the discriminating name of a youth organization which . . . Worth considering, I might pass that along to my superior. All right, quick now, Comrade J. V. Stalin's birthday? December 21, 1879, New Style, in Gori, near Tiflis, Georgia. Why "in Rome (Italy)"? Because there's a Rome near Parchim, Mecklenburg, about four hundred souls, Mr. Inspector. / The advancing darkness invites us to respect proper form concerning two gentlemen and a lady alone in an interrogation. (– Hee-hee: bleated the Mecklenburg colleague.) Might we have a light turned on? At your service. Thank you. Look friendly, now, we are bringing in another witness. The principal? No need, she can mind the phone. My first interrogation—how different the dream is from the reality! Hello again, Mrs. Elise Bock; you, Selbich, get us some coffee, quick now. / Student Gantlik. Member of FDJ class chapter; employee of the local Red Army commandant. Student Lockenvitz says he got lost in Berlin. A new, strange city. Student Lockenvitz's social origins? Something about farming in Prussian Pommern. This young friend's attitude towards the government's decision to hand his homeland over to the Poles? To the People's Poland: is how Lockenvitz puts it. Jakob Abs, officially registered as living with Cresspahl, Brickworks Road, Jerichow, as a courier of leaflets from West Berlin? Of posters to paste up. Travels by rail on a free pass. After graduating with honors from the Locomotive Engineers School in Güstrow he registered for a course in Elements of Materialist Dialectics. The third tenet of this doctrine? The transformation of quantitative changes into qualitative changes. Railwayman Abs's private life? Handball. His plans for the future? He's a grown man, why would he discuss things like that with a seventeen-year-old girl! / Student Cresspahl comes to class in a white blouse. Blue shirt only for festive occasions. Turns up at school in a petticoat, dragging in the fashions of a declining empire. Completely incorrect: a petticoat is a woman's underskirt. I hereby regret falsely accusing this FDJ friend of coming to class in an underskirt. In fact it was, out of vanity, a full, lightly starched skirt, made following illustrations in the democratic press. Student Gantlik has been found guilty of Protestant leanings. Well she is extremely interested in Max Planck; the physics here is way above Student Cresspahl's head. Planck, the one stamped on the back of a West German two-mark coin? I've never in my life had a piece of Western currency in my hand; never seen it; no hide, no hair. Any liking on the part of Colleague Selbich for senior-year student Sieboldt? Only hearsay; it does look like she's in love. Is it mutual? The principal was too young to have any influence on Abitur final grades. The principal seems to have it out for a certain some-one. If only I knew why. Hypothetically, just between you and me? For myself. Psychology, is that it? and now, quickly, to your third thought upon seeing these criminal postings on the wall of the school, showing young friends in the FDJ behind barbed wire. Barbed wire? I never saw that.

Here Student Cresspahl paused, for the first and only time. She was saying something true, for once, but she felt uncertain. What arises, what happens, when consciousness suddenly formulates a perception it had shrugged off nine hours earlier? An afterimage? On the anonymous scrap of paper in the coat pocket, "barbed wire" had been just a pair of words; now the twisted lines with their braided-in barbs were a mental image, and underlying them was the tone of voice from the evening's broadcast of the BBC: *barbed wire*, in English. How, from the miserable feeling of tedium last night at yet another wave of posters, could the resolve arise to testify to barbed wire, as strong as if it had been taken in the morning?

– After intensive self-examination: Student Cresspahl began to confess, but then stopped.

She remembered Kurt Müller. "Kutschi," chairman of the Communist Youth League in Germany in 1931. Sentenced in 1934 to six years in prison for "Preparation for Treason," then moved to Sachsenhausen concentration camp. After the elimination of Hitler's battalions, state chairman of the Communist Party, Lower Saxony; deputy chair of the national party, 1948; member of the West German Parliament, 1949. Under the protection of parliamentary immunity, paid an official visit to the German Sovietnik

Republic, and was reported as "missing" on March 22, 1950. Two months later, the M.f.S. had confessed and admitted that same date as the date of Kutschi Müller's arrest. He was sitting behind bars and wires on this very evening; if the members of the FDJ were marching for anything, it was, in fact, for this reinforced wire.

She remembered a boy in 10-A-I arrested over a pop song. Tipsy at a class party, he had altered the dreamy image in the first line of a sentimental number: "When, by Capri, the red sun sinks into the sea." Instead of "sun" he'd sung "fleet"—to be flip, and probably feeling sure that his position as president of his FDJ class chapter was bulletproof protection. Paulie Möllendorf it was, and his fast talk in front of the court had probably hurt him more than helped. Four years in prison.

She remembered Axel Ohr. Axel, though eighteen, wanted to go to the Germany Rally of Free Youth too, his luggage seeming a bundle of newspapers; he had almost seven pounds of electrolytic copper inside it, which he was planning to sell in the forbidden half of Berlin, to buy baling twine for Johnny Schlegel's agricultural commune. Johnny got off unscathed because Axel had dreamed up this contribution to the work in the silent chambers of his own mind; Axel was threatened with the maximum punishment, five years in prison. True, there was a law against exporting nonferrous metals, but that didn't help bring in the harvest. Axel was in pretrial detention in the basement, a dungeon surrounded by wire with barbs. When the New Free Youth went marching in their blue shirts, it was also for that.

Young Friend Cresspahl repeated, after lengthy consideration: she had noticed no barbed wire. Asked what the FDJ were marching for, she gave the desired answer. She was admonished to inspect any visual advertising in future with greater attentiveness (she'd claimed morning sleepiness), in the interests of dialectically utilizing the perniciousness she herself had invoked. And keep your ears open too, got it? – *Vas slushayu*, yes sir: Student Cresspahl said, which went over well with the interrogator although it was also something of a bitter pill since he was equally proud of his nationality and of his skill in concealing it. With a sudden laugh like that of someone annoyed at himself, he answered with sudden unexpected rudeness: *Da svidanya*. Until next time. That's a promise.

Outside the gate of the educational institution almost every student

Cresspahl had ever exchanged a word with or shared a smile with stood waiting. About seventy of them were there to make sure this child would be returning to their midst. People shouted "Hurrah!" the way brave young princesses used to be cheered in the old days. There was singing.

Lise Wollenberg had gone home.

And Student Gantlik, just visible on the bridge over the city moat, made off in a hurry as soon as she'd seen enough. She continued to consider it unwise for the time being to reveal even the scrap of a connection, a bond, between herself and Student Cresspahl. Yes you do talk like that, Anita.

We almost unanimously felt that Bettina must have thrown herself at the investigators from Schwerin while bullying and threatening the students under her as though we were dangerous vermin, lepers, contagious, keep your distance! (and again, though, like she wanted to bite us). Maybe we stepped aside a bit too eagerly when she came marching up with the two gentlemen in their leather coats. She was drooping now; we heard her lamenting, as she said goodbye: And it had to happen in my school, of all places, Mr. Inspector!

She now turned violently on us, ordering us to get water and scrub brushes from the janitor's and get the rest of the handbills off the school walls. (The school's front door—two large slabs of oak, prewar manufacture, from 1910—had been taken off its hinges and hauled off by the Gneez police.) And so the young dandy from Hans-and-Sophie-Scholl Street, Schwerin, was once more forced out of his black cherry–colored car, polished to a mirrorlike sheen (from the people-owned firm Eisenacher Motor Works, EMW, not a Bavarian BMW), to reprimand Comrade Selbich and keep the crowd of suspected culprits from further studying even the remaining small print as they scratched away at it.

And he singled out Student Cresspahl again for a parting word. He planted himself in front of the young lady in a comradely pose, in his made-to-measure easy-to-clean suit, and informed her: his name was Lehmann. (I would recognize him to this day, from a harelip too hastily repaired. But let him languish in boredom in Leningrad or Prague; why should I bother him.) – A name to remember: he added, revealing himself as one of the ruling powers of this New Mecklenburg.

Now after this did Bettinikin still manage to make the leap from principal pro tem to principal?

Anyone worried about that will of course set out on the long summer vacation of 1950 with a heavy heart, unsettled, practically troubled, with little prickles like a swarm of ants all over their brain as they fall asleep.

– Three times you could have nailed her during the interrogation: Marie says; she's complaining.

– First of all, Bettina did get her knuckles rapped. Plus we had promised each other: only in an emergency.

– If that wasn't an emergency then tell me what is!

– *Coming right up!*

July 31, 1968 Wednesday

The New York Times wants to show us a helicopter from which four crates are dangling, with supplies for Marine outposts near the Demilitarized Zone in Vietnam. A photo that looks like propaganda; no news value whatsoever.

In Kosice, the gentlemen from the Kremlin and those from the Hradshin are keeping the topic under discussion at the Junction Club in Cierna to themselves. The ones from Moscow are reported to have stomped out at 10:30 last night, looking rather angry, and boarded their green train. In order to have something, anything to report, Auntie *Times* describes the Czechoslovakian train cars as, unlike their Soviet counterparts, painted blue.

Pravda, the press organ of Soviet Truth, reprints the East German understanding of quiet, normal life on the streets of Prague these days, along with their conjectures about what's going on behind the facades. As evidence. It also puts out, in photographic facsimile, a letter from ninety-eight workers at Auto-Praha asking the Soviet troops to linger in the country.

And a New York City councilman has spent a week living in East Harlem, posing as a writer; now he says he knows about life there. He saw no rats, but said he didn't think rats could stand that building on 119th Street between Park and Lexington.

Personnel changes during the first half of the 1950–51 school year in Gneez, Mecklenburg:

First, to open the new term, a stiff-legged man (blue shirt) climbed the podium to the lectern facing the assembled students and introduced himself as the new principal, with all the powers and privileges pertaining thereto, and with the enameled badge (SED) showing clasped hands (KPD, SPD) on his lapel: Dr. Eduard Kramritz. He pressed his wire-framed (now gold-plated-wire-framed) glasses into the sores on his nose and announced: Some of you already know me. Applause. The rest will get to know me— soon. Applause.

Of course Bettina Selbich was innocent in the matter of the posted query to the members of the FDJ about why they were marching. But at an institute of secondary learning conducted with all due vigilance such questions never come up in the first place, do you follow that, Comrade? In addition, the district school board had received two letters, from the typewriter of the councilman, since replaced, and from the hand of Dr. Julius Kliefoth, both evincing knowledge of Latin, remarking on the moral maturity required in anyone called upon to thoughtfully supervise the course of education in young student souls (by this they meant us; Kramritz being made principal must have come as an embarrassing surprise to them). The Unity Party, meanwhile, showed a certain generosity in not rejecting Bettina altogether; it extended her waiting period as a candidate for membership by a full year.

Changes in the teaching staff: Dr. Gollnow is retiring, two years past the mandatory date. In her place we have Eberhard Martens—soldierly bearing, blond crew-cut, "the Evil Eye." Student-teacher in German, fulfilling his internship with the members of what is now class 11-A-II: Mathias Weserich, MA in language and literature, Leipzig University: another limper, somewhat more flexible at the knees, whose greeting took the form of a bow from the neck, his mouth pulled open to almost a rectangle full of unnaturally white teeth. Colleague Selbich's new assignment: instructor in German, and also Contemporary Studies. Applause.

Student Gantlik (alone) and Students Pagenkopf and Cresspahl (together) had paid a visit to Erdmuthe Gollnow at the start of the summer. Tight bun, friendly gaze down into cups of apple blossom tea, grandfather clock, dresser with knick-knacks, sofa with curved wooden arms. Anita had been stymied by the niceties of visiting; it was from Anita's two schoolmates that Mrs. Gollnow later heard that Anita too had meant to ask her to seize the day when the keys to the principal's office were dangled in her presence. The old lady sighed, and sighed again, and thanked them for the trust they placed in her, and said she was too weak. (In terms of health she was in better shape than Alma Witte.) – Ah, yes!: she croaked in a bouncy voice: Ah to be sixty again!

As the assembled faculty stepped humbly over to the right side of the podium, the Central School-Group Authority of the Free German Youth (FDJ ZSGL!) clambered up and took their places behind the red-draped tables, a wall of cloth. (That, Marie, was to keep any undignified leg movements from diminishing the devotion of the Young Friends on the auditorium floor.) Beneath the talons of Picasso's bristling dove, Sieboldt and Gollantz surrendered their offices, thereby entering the Rostock University groups. The secretary and treasurer resigned, pleading overwork in view of their coming Abitur. Elected as new secretary to organize the school group, by a vote of 288 to 23: Dieter Lockenvitz, 11-A-II. As president, with 220 votes and numerous abstentions: Gabriel Manfras, 11-A-II. Young Friend Manfras, step forward!

We'd never have thought that Gabriel had it in him to give a speech! Yet what a ringing voice this taciturn child suddenly launched from his throat. Maybe he was making up for the silence he kept from first period to last, from class visits to the theater to end-of-year parties; our old idea that he was shy was now instantly forgotten. The meeting now proceeds to the election of the presidium. Nominations please. Dr. Kramritz, as friend and partner of the FDJ school group. Acclamation. The beanpole gym teacher, because he rakes us over the coals politically too. Good-humored laughter. The members of the ZSGL, of course. I propose as first member of the honorary presidium Comrade Josef Vissarionovich Stalin, a shining example to us all for his mighty labors for peace; his daily efforts for the improvement of the proletarian capital; the opening of the Great Northern Seaway; the draining of the swamps of Colchis; not least as thanks and reward for his completion of that work of genius on Marxism and questions of linguistics. Frenzied applause, breaking off suddenly. The president of the People's Republic of Poland, Bolesłav Bierut, in honor of the peaceful encounter of our two peoples at the Oder and Neisse Rivers. Comrade Mao, liberator of the People's Republic of China and partner of Comrade Stalin. The writer Thomas Mann, in memory of his late brother Heinrich, recipient of the Goethe-bicentennial National Prize, who displayed in his journey to Weimar the realism that shines forth from every buttonhole of his writings! The author of the work *The Socialist Sixth of the World*, a theologian ostracized in his own land, Hewlett Johnson, the "Red Dean" of Canterbury! The cheering, standing audience is requested to go easy on the bleachers. Now Young Friend Manfras has the floor, to present an appraisal of the prospects for world peace, and also in Gneez.

Gabriel looked strangely at us, gripped the front of the lectern with his right hand, propped the knuckles of his left against the bottom edge in back, looked down at his manuscript, and was ready to give a speech. (The boy standing there had been given advance warning that he would be nominated and elected; he had a lecture all prepared.) Young Comrade Manfras began, appropriately, with the date: September First, the Day of Peace, we too pledge that. The criminal invasion by North American troops and their South Korean mercenaries into the northern republic, whose leader we all. Well might the West Germans groaning under the yoke of capitalism fear the coming war—they are buying droves of sailboats to flee in, hoarding gas, standing in long lines outside the South American consulates; we, on the other hand, enjoy safety and security under the newly elected general secretary of the newly founded central committee of the Unity Party, W. Ulbricht, and the disgraceful use of the nickname *Sachwalter*, "Custodian," for Walter U. can only reflect pitifully on anyone with a German dictionary at his. The Party's vigilance, as demonstrated in the unmasking of leading comrades Kreikemeyer and company, co-conspirators of the American agent provocateur Noel H. Field and his disgusting three-way marriage; this vigilance we too shall. The imminent collapse of the British Empire at the side of the USA can only. The hateful interview of the West German chancellor with the organ of high capitalism, *The New York Times*, showing only his contempt for humanity; his proposal for the quick reestablishment of a German military force will inevitably lead to. We adjourn this meeting with the song: "We are the Young Van-Guard / of the Pro-le-ta-ri-at!"

In Gabriel Manfras's whirlwind world tour, he had woven in the obscure German word *Diversion* more than once, and at first those among us who knew some Latin thought: What an old-fashioned fellow. But when he added into the mix the people with the paste brushes who had been so interested in the goal the FDJ was marching for, and called them American diversants, the grammatical connection was at last broken for his listeners; only after the song could we find out from Anita that there is indeed a Soviet word, *diversiya*, meaning in no way a distracting maneuver but rather an attack. From the side? No, a frontal assault, or all around actually: Anita said, embarrassed. If only she'd finally realized that we'd long been impressed with her work for Triple-J, as jobs go!

As for Gabriel Manfras, we now had a pretty good idea how he'd spent his summer.

Dr. Kramritz, too, had undergone a course designed to hone him to a fine political edge, during which he had kind of misplaced his family. Lost sight of his wife. And so propositioned his colleague Bettina Selbich, who by then was sporting a tight-fitting blouse, non-blue, and a charmingly humble manner. In case of divorce, so he'd know where to turn for refuge. Rumors wanted to supply a slap in the face at this point; an eyewitness, Klaus Böttcher, had seen a couple in tears on the wooded path winding its way around the Smœkbarg. But now Bettina's landlord won his eviction case; she could find a single room only in the Danish Quarter; she was commended by her party group for moving closer to the working class; she was scared of Wieme Wohl. And who should move into the full apartment on Cathedral Court, three rooms with kitchen basement bathroom and a view across the parish meadows down to the rows of poplars on the shore of Gneez Lake, but the reconciled Kramritz family. "Protecting the cadre of specialists," it's called. If you want to protect your cadre, choose wisely.

The news of Thomas Mann's signature on the Stockholm Appeal—calling for a ban on nuclear weapons irrespective of whose—had consoled us about our own. A year later we were ashamed.

This "document" was not new to me . . . as part of a photomontage purporting to show me in the act of signing the Stockholm Appeal in Paris in the spring of 1950. I am shown on this occasion wearing a suit that I did wear in summer 1949, but did not bring to Europe in 1950. The black tie I had tragic cause to wear in mourning in May 1949 is visible in the photograph too. How this came to pass is something I am neither able to discover nor interested in. What I do know, and what

I have said, truthfully, is that I did not sign my name to the Stockholm Appeal. © Katja Mann

Kreikemeyer and company, that meant German Communists in French exile, imprisoned, Kreikemeyer helped to escape in 1942 by Field, the American Unitarian, then leader of the illegal German Communist Party in Marseilles. Seven years later, Willi Kreikemeyer was installed as the head of the German Reich Railway, Jakob's topmost boss. In May 1949 he'd gone out on a limb for his party when the West Berlin railwaymen went on strike for payment of their wages in the currency of the city where they worked and bought their bread. On May 5, Willi K. promised them payment in West marks, then retracted his commitment. One dead in clashes with the police, and several wounded, were added to the weight he bore on his shoulders for the party. On May 28 he promised up to 60 percent payment in West marks, and: refraining from any reprisals. In late June, to keep his party from losing face, he broke his word again and fired 380 railway workers without notice or transfer to locations in the East German Republic whose very currency they'd scoffed at. Willi Kreikemeyer, member of a party and adherent of its constitution that claimed to respect professions of religious faith, promised the Jehovah's Witnesses twelve special trains to take them to a congress in Berlin, that was July 1949, he took their money and then canceled the trains—all for his party. Now that party has been accusing him, since late August, of having passed addresses to the American OSS. Jakob went around dejected in the summer of 1949; a loyal member of the FDJ will of course recite such things on the evenings of his training course; if I'd interrupted, he would have asked me: And what kind of school do you go to, Gesine?

Once the Carola Neher club was done with her, I commissioned from D. E. Willi Kreikemeyer's life story; all three scholars with all their expertise in registers and sources and cross-references could find no lifespan for him extending past August 1950.

As for the West German chancellor, Bettina Selbich clued us in to the illuminating similarity between his name and that of the President of Columbia University, commander since 1950 of the armed forces of the North Atlantic Treaty Organization. Eisenhower, Adenower. Contemporary Studies.

As for the North American president, we were supposed to ridicule Harry S. Truman because he fraudulently used his middle initial to claim American dignity when in fact the S stood for itself, not a whole name; there was also Truman's former job selling neckties and suchlike menswear, which we were to invoke as proof of his inferiority. Contemporary Studies.

The first time the East German Republic observed Activist Day was October 13, 1950, and Elise Bock was awarded the title "Activist of Merit" and a tidy sum of money. One last greeting from Triple-J, who was now free to return home. The administration of Gneez had been turned over to the Unity Party; his successor was a military commander who moved out of the city into the woods around the Smœkbarg.

On August 15, the government of the East German Republic (a person, too) requested some kind of convoluted operation involving ballots having to do with the People's Chamber and the state, district, and municipal administration. It counted 99 percent yes votes, and another 0.7 percent on top of that.

The Waldheim trials started in the summer of 1950 and on November 4 it was time to start the executions. Cresspahl wore no crape for the man he might have remembered as his father-in-law. The Cresspahl child still felt sympathy for Albert Papenbrock, because there had been a time when she hadn't been allowed to take candy from anyone; he sat sadly under the sun umbrellas at the outdoor tables of the Lübeck Court in Jerichow, forced to consume a whole large ice cream by himself. Gesine Cresspahl wasn't brave enough to show up to Mrs. Selbich's class with mourning crape on her sleeve; by that point Selbich was quick to apply to Principal Kramritz for demerits. Thomas Mann's family suppressed his letter to the custodian in the collection of letters published for the time being; in fact he did write the *Sachwalter* in July.

Some ten trials took place within an hour. No defense attorneys were allowed, no witnesses for the defense allowed to testify. In handcuffs, though almost none were accused of real crimes, the accused—the men and women found guilty before the trial—were brought before the court, which, by the book, pronounced prison terms of fifteen, eighteen, twenty-five years, even for life. [...] Mr. President! Perhaps you are unaware of the horror, the revulsion, often fake but often deeply felt, that these trials with their death sentences—and they are all death sentences—have called forth on this side of the globe; how conducive they are to ill will and how destructive of goodwill. An act of mercy, as sweeping and summary as the mass sentencing in Waldheim has all too clearly been, would be such a blessed gesture, serving the cause of reconciliation and hope for détente—an act of peace. / Use your power . . . ! © Katja Mann

But the custodian needed his power to set up judiciary performances of the sort his wise leader and teacher Stalin had showed him in Bulgaria, Hungary, Czechoslovakia. Why should he restore the honor of a few useful dead when only fifty-one thousand among the living in his country found the courage to mark their ballots with a No—only as many people as lived in Gneez, plus Jerichow.

Klaus Böttcher was sitting in his dad's kitchen, cooling his feet in soapy water. In comes his wife, Britte, and she says: Hey, there're three men here, *all in black suits, they want something from you.* Klaus is out the window, dangles from the sill high above the shop yard, drops down, and takes off, barefoot, over the fence, the moat, the city walls, and keeps going, in the direction of West Berlin. In Krakow am See he has to go to ground at a carpenter colleague's, his bare feet are bleeding so badly. Britte can read her husband's mind and gets a call put through to Krakow. – Y'can come back, Klaus, they're all from the college, they wanted to go in together orderin a boathouse from you, dummy!: said fond Britte. When asked about the consciousness of guilt his behavior suggested, Klaus would always repeat, embarrassed anew each time: *Hows the hare supposed to prove hes not a fox?*

In December 1950, Jakob's mother applied for an interzonal travel permit. This was the piece of paper that would officially authorize a trip from Jerichow to Bochum, West Germany. If she'd been correctly informed, there was a remnant of Wilhelm Abs's family living there. The Abses would write to one another at very most in the event of a death, or a birth, two weeks late; she was old, of course, and wanted to get as close as she could to the news she feared. Jakob made time to go back and forth among the various offices and authorities; Cresspahl's daughter lacked the kinship necessary to help. So it took until January before Mrs. Abs had collected:

a police registration certificate,

police certification of a clean criminal record,

a handwritten autobiographical statement (fourth draft),

proof of the political or economic reason for the trip (here Cresspahl and Jakob invented an inheritance for her in the Ruhr district, and Dr. Werner Jansen, attorney by trade in Gneez, conjured up on his typewriter when his staff was out of the office a district court's affidavit of delivery with a West German dateline),

a statement from the Unity Party endorsing the trip (which Mrs. Brüshaver got through via the CDU office for V.o.F. [Victims of Fascism] in Schwerin),

a statement from the Gneez tax office confirming the absence of any outstanding tax liabilities;

and then all she had to do is get everything translated into Russian. Lotte Pagels took twenty-eight marks for that, with all its Krijgerstamian mistakes. Anita, you would've done it as a favor, admit it! But since Anita was avoiding eye contact with Student Cresspahl, how could the name Abs mean anything to her? And how useful she could have been as an interpreter with the Sovietnik in Gneez City Hall whose job it was to "advise" the city administration in the sovereign German republic. It probably wasn't too much to expect for Gesine to make an effort and approach Anita with the request; Gesine was against the trip, Mrs. Abs seemed to be preparing for it very carefully, sometimes people take a trip and don't come back; she used shyness as another excuse. If the application came back denied it would be her fault.

Aggie, into December, was busy doing what a govt. exam.'d lic.'d reg.'d nurse considers her job. She hid behind Dr. Schürenberg, district medical examiner; Dr. Schürenberg summoned Cresspahl, examined him plausibly enough, and wrote out a certificate attesting him unfit to work.

In 1950, for the first time since 1937, New Year's Eve was celebrated in the Cresspahl house. There was no carp, but Jakob brought crayfish. It's true that crayfish are best in the months without a letter *r*: in the opinion of Hedwig Dorn, in *The Housewife's Helper*, an opinion shared by Frieda Ihlefeld; still, one doesn't have to take it so literally, if one doesn't want to, even Ihlefeld seems to regard it as a kind of folklore. For the first time we in Cresspahl's house were something like a family. Gesine watched from afar as Jakob's mother scrubbed the live creatures with a birch brush in cold water, then brought them to their death in boiling; while the church-goers in the family were out at services, Gesine stood by the pot, eyes on the clock and the paper with the recipe, and she ladled off the floating fat, added wood to the fire, let it cool, scooped out the red roe butter; distracted, though, because Jakob at the window spent a half hour showing her how a young man of twenty-two shaves for a nighttime celebration. Maybe the New Year's carp was missing—the fun was there. Cresspahl wrote the final lines in his last account books. Four people confessed their resolutions for the coming year; four times Jakob poured Richtenberger aquavit into Gesine's glass.

Jesu, let me gladly end it, / This my freshly entered year. / Thy strong hands' upholding lend it, / Ward off peril and its fear. / Lastly, in Thy mantle furled, / I shall gladly quit this world.

Oh now dont be leavin us just yet, Fru Abs.

Ive had it. These engines, these wornout tracks, let the devil ride em. Godet Niejår, *Gesine!*

Happy New Year everyone.

You're asking—

For what's different here in New York in the state of New York. You know that this is one of the places to which West Berlin newspaper publishers send tiny porcelain bells to families one of whose members has been killed trying to kill members of other families on the other side of the world in Vietnam. For one difference.

Well, take yellow. Here yellow is in different places. I mean the whole color family—genuine yellow or as near to yellow as ocher or canaries or anything else in the zone between red and green, not only *any of the colors normally seen when the portion of the physical spectrum of wavelengths 571.5 to 578.5 millimicrons specif. 574.5 millimicrons is employed as a stimulus*: as Webster says, but, you know, yellow. Here yellow is in different places.

Not only in eggs, Mongols, jaundice, sponges, butterflies, marsh-marigolds. I've never seen as much yellow as here.

Here someone jealous, envious, cowardly, melancholy, treacherous, a deserter, or someone like Brutus (because he was not an honorable man) may be called yellow. Yellow people here are contemptible; the tabloids here are the yellow press, like the yellow *Bildzeitung* in Germany; there are yellow oaks and yellow perch.

Underbidders are yellow dogs, who sign yellow-dog contracts, which means they agree not to join any union but a yellow one.

Someone yellowing here is throwing his weight around.

The language here believes that certain natives in the southwestern part of the country have yellow bellies, yellow like sulfur.

You see yellow lines on one-way avenues, with yellow writing reserving a car's width for certain vehicles only.

Two yellow lines divide the two-way avenues.

One yellow line divides the two-lane side streets.

Yellow in broadly applied lines marks off the pedestrian areas in intersections.

Yellow are the casings of the traffic lights unable to speak words, capable only of round disks of color.

On yellow rectangles the authorities warn drivers of curves or children ahead and recommend certain speeds.

Yellow signs surround men at road construction work, and they say: Danger.

The barricades, planks on four angled legs that police place around buildings gutted by fire or use to keep the curious away from festive first-nights or parades, are yellow, sometimes with a touch of orange but the yellow remains unvanquished.

The edges of long-distance railroad platforms are painted yellow.

Yellow has a national quality—think of the only yellow platform edge in all of West Berlin: at the US Army station in Lichterfelde.

The platform edges in the subways are yellow; the railings are painted yellow; the platforms under the passenger's feet say Stand Clear, in yellow.

In subway stations the first step of a staircase and the step before a landing and the vertical edge of the last step are smeared yellow, sometimes the whole landing too.

The curbs in front of fire hydrants and bus stops are yellow: No Parking. Yellow is the color of the entranceways to garages, yellow the curbstones.

Post office steps are marked with yellow dots.

Gold, admittedly, but still yellow because not quite as red as gold, are the numbers and names and logos painted on the glass doors of buildings and stores and bars.

Official suggestions, too, such as: You are advised against coming any closer, or: Don't even think about smoking on public transportation, or: Please note that this car's name is 7493.

In the revolving doors of official buildings you find little arrows on yellow stickers. More and more the old street signs are being replaced with yellow ones.

Gravely the heads of famous ladies look down at you from the upper edge of an edifice that announces in yellow and gold: I am the Metropolitan Museum; I'm free of charge; I am very rarely closed.

Yellow wherever you look.

Yellow are the light fixtures in the windows of Western Union.

Western Union is a telegram service. What President Johnson keeps saying is: Great Society.

Yellow: Johnson commented two years ago about the dress of a wife of a Philippine visitor of state: yellow's my favorite color too. Actually: she confided later: My favorite color is pink.

Yellow are the raincoats of the workmen crawling under the street and looking for holes in the gas pipes.

The air here is yellow when it's suffocating.

Yellow circulars are carried around here, I pass you a note on yellow scratch paper, and many ballpoint pens, disguised as pencils, are yellow. Sometimes even orange juice.

Becoming tarnished in accord with nature is surely what the brass on the outside doors of genteel hotels, apartment buildings, banks would prefer to do; their baseboards, doorknobs, peepholes, handles, the surfaces of their noble locks are scrubbed yellow; their hydrants, mostly twinned, are shined yellow. The massive shingles of the exorbitant doctors are polished yellow, to a line of sheer gold, only the rational mind still considers it brass.

And golden triangles on the glass doors of fancy buildings are there to keep you from bumping into them.

Yellow are the envelopes known as manila. Yellow Pages are what they here call what you know as a business telephone directory.

The butter is suspiciously yellow.

Whereas it might get serious here, much like on the other side of the world, the signs indicating shelters against radioactive fallout are yellow. Prophetically placed therein are the three triangles above the little circle in which, in yellow, the number of persons who can here be saved is supposed to be stated but regularly isn't, as if it were something unknown.

Yellow are the Broadway Maintenance trucks that wash and sweep the streets, that carry away trash and/or cars that need to be towed. Yellow are the cars of many taxi fleets. Yellow are the symbols, products, packaging, and delivery vans of numerous enterprises and institutes.

But why? That they do not know.

Yellow is a color that attracts attention: they say. But why it does so, no one knows.

Maybe because a nephew of the country's first president owned an ocher factory?

Yellow is yellow: the answer runs.

And those who tell you that are authorities. It's true and I admit it: the authority says: Even if it was my favorite daughter who called me yellow I'd give her a good smack. But I feel that we, and by we I mean our whole nation: We can thank our lucky stars that we can at least kill these peasants in Viet Nam or whatever it's called there for reasons other than that their skin is yellow. The only people who can understand our reasons are those who belong, and who know: What Yellow Means. End of quote.

You have to admit, finally, that nobody in New York or any other city in this country is killed because of his yellow skin. In the first place, there are darker shades in the mix. Second, this is a free country. You need to see things in a yellower light!

—for it.

August 2, 1968 Friday

The *Times* would have so loved to report that the Soviet and Czechoslovakian delegations sat down and broke bread together. But she, too, was merely given the communiqué mentioning something about an atmosphere of complete frankness, sincerity, and mutual understanding. They're planning to meet again tomorrow in Bratislava, but this time with the leaders from Poland, East Germany, Hungary, and Bulgaria. Will they throw a wrench into whatever the Soviet Union may have signed at the Cierna railroad junction?

And how was the weather in July? *The New York Times* has worked it out and tells us: Unseasonably hot. We must've had a miserable time of things around July 16. A Tuesday. We could've done without a half of it. *Don't wish your life away.*

Anyone who remembers German class in grade 11-A-II in Gneez in 1950–51 will of necessity cry: Schach! Schach!

The teacher was Mr. Weserich, a student teacher from Thuringia, and the Cresspahl/Pagenkopf collective had already gotten to know him slightly toward the end of the previous summer. They'd seen him on a bench outside the dressing rooms at Gneez Lake—it was early, he thought he was alone, and he was adjusting the screws on an aluminum structure at his left knee, which was where his leg ended. His mouth formed another square; he looked like he was in pain. We were horror-struck.

But it was he who opened by apologizing. – Well that's that: he calmly said once he'd pushed himself up into a standing position. – For Führer and Reich; I believed it too: he added, leaving the rest to us, trusting fully to our diplomatic skills. As a result he already had a reputation when demoted Principal Selbich introduced him to us, in her sour way. – We will be reading *Schach von Wuthenow* by Theodor Fontane: he said, announcing his intentions as clear as daylight. How we would have quaked in our shoes if we'd understood what he meant.

We had German four days a week. Weserich told us about the century of Fontane's life, starting on May 5, 1789, with Count Mirabeau, deputy of the Third Estate; he was perfectly open in laying out his traps but we failed to see them. He told us about Fontane's childhood years, his time in England and France; read to us from letters to his family, *car tel est notre plaisir*, as the king and Fontane's father used to say. Neat, clear High German, drawn from his mind while his gaze was elsewhere. On September 11 he had the effrontery to ask us our first impressions after reading the work by Th. Fontane mentioned at the start of the semester. Out of the blue, one week to the next, with shining eyes full of anticipation!

Anita raised her hand—she was willing to sacrifice herself. He ignored her hand but smiled at her, and her alone. The rest of us, numbering about thirty, were permitted to remonstrate that there was only one single copy of this work in the Culture League library; that only novels like *Effi Briest* were on our shelves at home; we tried to talk him out of his plan. The upshot was that he complimented us, praised our resourcefulness, and promised to repeat his question on September 18. – We'll be seeing one another quite a lot this year: he promised.

To keep him favorably disposed to us, we each contributed a thirtieth of what Elise Bock charged to type out a hundred and thirty printed pages; Pius procured the mimeograph stencils on a visit to the FDJ district office. (– Thou shalt not muzzle the ox when he treadeth out the corn: he admitted, but only in his collective work group.) Before the pages could be run off, though, Anita had to swing from City Hall a certification of harmlessness and authorization to reproduce a text. On the 18th, there we were with our bundles of rough spotty paper, and Zaychik the rabbit was already looking forward to what he was about to say.

– *Issan old story*: Zaychik said: You bed 'em, you wed 'em!

The visitor thanked him for this instruction in Mecklenburg folk wisdom. And he was right—what had spoken from Zaychik's mouth was the spirit of the Gneez townsman-farmers (and the banished nobility); he didn't even realize the speculation he was inviting about his parents' marriage, or about his own dealings with Eva Matschinsky. She shrank in her seat, blushing.

Dagobert Haase stood there, naive and slightly chubby in body, grumbling and defiant in manner like someone who follows instructions but doesn't have to. And he said: It's about a hunnerd an fifty years ago. A cavalry captain has a girlfriend that maybe he wants to marry. Suddenly he falls for her daughter, twenty years younger, but because people're crackin jokes about the pockmarks in her face he wants to duck the consequences. The king orders him to marry, and he does, but he shoots himself after lunch. He leaves his name and the child to her.

Zaychik obligingly turned half around to let us see in his face what he thought. Ain't that always the way?

Mr. Weserich thanked him for the plot summary. Might Haase be prepared to answer an additional question?

Zaychik let his head fall forward—the silent sufferer. Upon request, he named the main character (same as the title), the daughter (someone named Victoire), the mother's maiden name . . . (not sure about that).

The address of the von Carayon family? this German teacher asked the room, past Zaychik, explicitly to spare him, and when Student Cresspahl could only give Berlin, we were permitted to return to the opening of the story and begin again:

"In Frau von Carayon's salon on Behrenstrasse in Berlin, a few friends had gathered on the customary evening . . ."

We were then informed that people of rank at that time . . . but it wouldn't be worth the trouble, presumably, to ask what the year might be?

– 1806: Anita suggested, and then had to say why. – Because the characters are talking about the Battle of the Three Emperors at Austerlitz as something that just happened, and that was in December 1805, on the 2nd.

. . . at that time chose their addresses with great care. Where they lived expressed their self-regard and was held up to others. Therefore—alas!—he had no choice but to inform us that Behrenstrasse runs parallel to and one block south of Unter den Linden; the von Carayons were blessed with a house on the corner of Charlotten Street, a short walk from the Opera, the Lustgarten, the Palace. Behr Street is named after the heraldic bear of Berlin—this opinion is widespread, but the truth is that the street honors the engineer Johann Heinrich Behr, to whom Berlin owes French Street and, as of 1701, Jerusalem Street and Leipzig Street as well. Well known to every tried and true Berliner and now to every member of class 11-A-II, from personal experience, at least since September 11, if from a different source. Moreover, were we to consider that the author of this tale surely eschewed any mere coincidence, why would he mention an architect from the turn of the seventeenth to eighteenth century in the very first line? Perhaps to infuse the past era of the story with a hint of an even older past? Make sense? And are any of us now inclined to turn to the subtitle? "A Story from the Time of the Gensdarmes Regiment"? In response to the resulting determined, stony silence, a young student-teacher spent the rest of the class expatiating on the origins of the name of this regiment of cuirassiers, bearing swords instead of lances in the cavalry of Charles IV of France. A nod to the author's French background, perhaps? *Gens d'armes, au Moyen Age, soldats, cavaliers du roi?* Since our session, full of fascinating moments for which he was in our debt, was now drawing to a close, he ventured to request that by Wednesday we at least try to *read* the first two pages.

Class 11-A-II needed almost three weeks for the first six pages of the novella, and no matter how much you stared at Mr. Weserich for wasting all this time he refused to lose any sleep over it. We started to look forward to his outbursts of cheerful despair, when the perfectly clear words "in England and the union states" actually failed to call forth in our minds a picture of the United States of America, or to ensure that we learned more about the origins of the von Bülow gentleman, Adam Heinrich Dietrich v. B., than that he'd been arrested for his writing. Could it truly be the case that there was only one single encyclopedia in the whole city of Gneez, loaned out to someone else for the next several years?

No one could accuse Weserich of pettiness. We were inclined to work with him; we were equipped to handle the Latin quotations, thanks to Kliefoth, and now and then even translated one ourselves (*hic haeret*). After a while Weserich realized that, though a knowledge of Latin might be helpful in the learning of French, it could by no means replace instruction in the latter. This surprised him; he didn't want to admit it; was this reason to challenge the intellectual fathers of the Educational Reform Law who had replaced French with Russian? Thenceforth he had us present to him utterances in Fontane's second language for translation into German—always at least three at a time, please, on that he must insist. – How the time is running away from us! he'd cry, and this was late October, and we were on chapter two. So we looked things up in the dictionary, things such as *embonpoint, nonchalance*, the realm in which a gourmet excelled and the one in which a gourmand; we asked old people if they'd ever seen that kind of sinumbra lamp (an oil lamp on a pedestal, casting very little shadow). When Mathias Weserich was happy with our knowledge, to the point of putting on a show of surprise and disbelief, it was meant to be fun for us and so we did him that favor.

Two weeks of class on the riddle: Why did Fontane give titles to his chapters here, unlike in *Under the Pear Tree* only three years earlier, or *Count Petöfy* one year after *Schach*? What is a title. It is placed at the top (but why are paintings signed at the bottom or the side?); it indicates what is to follow. It's a courtesy to the reader, who at the end of a chapter is invited to take a breath and then know in advance where the voyage is going—to Sala Tarone, to Tempelhof, or Wuthenow. Yes, and is it supposed to whet our appetite? Such writers do exist, but we are dealing with Fontane here. A title is a milestone along the path: Wanderer, after twelve miles you will be in Jerichow. A sign at the edge of town—when a stranger reads "Gneez" it doesn't tell him very much at first, but once he's entered that city he knows where he is. A title as a warning. As an ornament, accompanying the old-time fashions of Berlin in 1806. Perhaps. The question remains: What is a title?

We had something of a mishap regarding the Sala Tarone Italian Wine and Fine Food Store on Charlottenstrasse. The gentlemen have to squeeze their way through rows of barrels and the cellarman enjoins caution: – There are all kinds of tacks and nails here: he says. *Pinnen und Nägel.* There was a boy in our class named Nagel. We could have acted like adults; the next day, his name was Pinne Nagel, Tacknail. He took it well. Underneath, he was glad that he now had something of his own, a nickname. From then on he'd say, about tricky math problems or cramped quarters: There are all kinds of tacks and nails here. He survived eleventh grade, Pinne Nagel. Today he's a jaw surgeon in Flensburg.

But what precisely is a *Pinne*, our Mr. Weserich begged someone to inform him. He understood the difference between a *Pinne* and a *Nagel* only after we'd connected the dots of the Little Erna story for him, with piety and tact: Lil' Erna's Grandpa's lyin' in his coffin and her mom wants to make him look just like he used to when he was alive but she can't get the beret to stay on his bald head, she fumbles and fumbles and then finally Mr. Piety-and-Tact comes by and she tells him the problem and he says Give me a minute I'll take care of it and when she comes back it's right there on Grandpa's head just perfect and she says How'd you do that? and he says Carpet tacks! It was the same with the Plattdeutsch during Schach's visit home: Weserich truly acted like it was all Greek to him. We translated why the old goat was always butting Momma Kreepsch where she hurt—in writing, since he asked us to. One time he came to us with reproaches: We'd kept a word from him. Right at the beginning, as early as the fourth chapter. We were crushed and promised to make it up to him. It was about Aunt Marguerite, "who spoke with a pruned mouth the Berlin dialect of her day, which almost exclusively used the dative case"—this without quotation marks around the offending term. We'd acted like everyone knew what this meant! That was the word, then, and he asked us to show him what it meant, and he stood in front of one schoolgirl after another (we'd convinced him that only girls pruned) and watched her protruding mobile lips, then thanked her. We responded in kind, gathering up our skirts at our side, which were below the knee in those days. *We curtsied.*

We were already in Wuthenow, page 122 of our transcript, chapter 14; we'd had enough of Schach (the person, after he'd spoiled the boat ride on the lake for us with his lachrymose shirking, not the book), when Weserich invited us to expound (with no notes!) on how we'd made this Schach's acquaintance. A forty-five-minute debriefing, right to the bell. It turned out that the weeks and weeks frittered away at the start of the year had paid off: we found the last line of the first paragraph where he is mentioned as absent, and nameless. The gentlemen there—von Bülow, his publisher Sander, von Alvensleben—are conversing with their hostesses, the Carayon ladies. Von Bülow is looking to start an argument. He quotes his man Mirabeau's comment about Frederick the Great's celebrated state as a fruit that's already rotten before it's ripe. In the sermon, he gives himself airs, as if by chance, with the maxim: *nomen et omen.* Not the *est* we learned in school, but *et*—name *and* destiny, bringing them into closer and more pregnant proximity and significance. After von Bülow's emphatic pronouncement that "Europe could have stood a bit more of the harem and seraglio business without any serious harm," whose name is announced midsentence? Cavalry Captain von Schach, the Shah between two women; his adversary is there already and will have the last word to the end. Fontane and the science of names. Fontane and the art of introducing a character.

A list of characters: Josephine, Victoire, Schach, Aunt Marguerite, the king, his much-bemoaned queen, Prince Louis, General Köckritz, the Tempelhof innkeeper...

A list of places, settings: The Carayons' salon, the tavern with the tacks and nails, the carriage ride, the (invented) church in Tempelhof, the villa on the Spree at Moabit across from the western *lisière* of the Tiergarten (our consultation of reference works should by now have led us to a place where we might find the reason for this word choice), the parade in Tempelhof, the bedside scene, Wuthenow am See, Paretz Palace and its park, death on Wilhelmstrasse. Make sense? A vote, in writing, anonymous, of favorite locations. The lake came in first—we were again mostly from Mecklenburg by this point; the students from the Memel (the Neman) or Silesia had to accept it. Pius showed me that he'd voted for Paretz. Student Cresspahl's favorite image was of the swans that came swimming up from Charlottenburg Park in a long line.

Another ugly incident: Schach is going on and on about the prince, his gracious lord, whom he loves *de tout mon cœur*: he tells Victoire. But, he says, with all his adventures in love and war the prince is "a light that burns with a robber." Again we'd tried to slip a word past our German teacher! He was left standing there completely unaware of what a "robber" on a light might be in this Northern Germany of ours! We agree that we have earned our punishment and request an ample measure of it, as schoolchildren used to be made to say. A robber is a light with a wick that gives off a very sooty smoke—that "steals" the candle wax away. When candles were still made of wax . . .

Anita saved herself the trouble of the curtsy we'd all adopted as a way to tease Mathias Weserich. She had the chance; she outsmarted herself. It was common practice in our class to turn to the back left corner of the room whenever it was Dieter Lockenvitz's turn to speak; Anita, too, liked watching him talk. If the talk was rebellious, her eyebrows rose in concern. There were certain details of a story from the time of the Gensdarmes Regiment that displeased Student Lockenvitz. In the fourth chapter and the Tempelhof churchyard, hazel and dog rose bushes grew so lushly that they formed a thick hedge, "notwithstanding the leaves weren't out yet." A student would get a red mark for that "notwithstanding." In the chapter called "Le choix du Schach," it said, "After arrangements like these one parted"—was this a misprint? or something wrong with the grammar? What annoyed (i.e., *ärger*'ed, and by now we could think *aigrir*'ed too) this student most was Fontane's habit of giving words of direct discourse in both the subjunctive and quotation marks; Weserich interjected questions to keep the boy's spirits up, although he regularly conceded the points anyway. But students were now officially required to form collective work pairs, one stronger student and one weaker, and Anita, who could have put herself in a position to observe this Lockenvitz for hours, and from close up, too, instead chose a girl, Peter (Monika), who was weak in chemistry and math.

When Weserich interrupted his aimless drifting among us to stop and stand by Lise Wollenberg's desk, we would see the phrase come to life: she was "hanging on his lips." She was, and she wouldn't have taken it particularly amiss if he'd solemnly ushered her out of the classroom and offered her his hand and his heart. But Weserich must have had some experience with girls like this who throw back their head when they laugh, whinnying like a colt; it was only in the seventh month of our collaboration on a man from the Regiment Gensdarmes that he gave her a speech, for her alone.

– My dear Miss Wollenberg! he said.

– You are looking at my mouth, as though something were missing there. You mention the color of my teeth at a volume that cannot but reach me. I now have the honor of confiding to you that no hair grows around my mouth because the skin there is transplanted. My teeth have an unnatural appearance because they were made in a factory. Do you have any other questions? Would you care to tell me where, in this story about a cavalry captain, von Schach—you remember him—where you suppose the person telling it is?

– Nooo: Lise said, straining for insolence. We felt sorry for her, the big blond child caught in the act of trying to be frivolous with a grown-up ("and with true horror maketh sport"). But we didn't hold Weserich's counterattack against him, after all the embarrassment Lise had caused his colleague H.-G. Knick.

Something different for a change. Who is the narrator? How does he conduct himself in performing this activity? Was he present at all the events that have taken place? Would those involved have wanted that, or allowed it? When are they outside the range of his observations? when they're writing letters. Once the letters are written, the narrator tells us what they say. What does he refrain from telling us? Why do we learn of the stolen hour of love only from the use, twice, of the informal second-person pronoun *du*? Good taste, or tact, or a well-developed ability to cope with life? Lockenvitz, let me give you a striking term for your collection, one which will bear you aloft on its wings to your final exams and beyond: the authorial narrative situation.

He knew where the ice was thin, our Mr. Weserich, and kept off it. Von Bülow, staff captain but also political essayist, admits, in the quoted subjunctive that so vexed Student Lockenvitz, to an abhorrence of pubs in which he felt "police spies and waiters were strangling him." There were pubs like that in Gneez; birthday parties had long since ceased to be thrown outside the house. Here Mathias Weserich could play innocent—he was from Thuringia. In his first appearance with Schach, von Bülow mentions the indissoluble marriage between church and state; Weserich could casually remind us to always stay in the temporal frame of the story. When Victoire writes her friend Lisette a letter that mentions "your new Masurian homeland," he knew that he had before him a child who had lost his own home in that part of the world; the discussion turned on the claims Victoire felt entitled to make from life, as revealed by this letter; how could the teacher suspect that Anita, too, felt herself to be a person "restricted to no more than her lawful share of happiness." He probably didn't even notice the silence that greeted his mention of a "Möllendorf" infantry regiment.

If we take the variety and energy of the relationships between the characters to be the mainspring of the narrative, then what happens if we place Aunt Marguerite at the center?

As the New School curriculum expected of Mr. Weserich, he paid due attention to the social critical element. Two classes worth of discussion of the concept of honor, the attitude towards it; dishonorable actions. Make sense? A passing ideological government inspector could sit in on our class without anything to worry about, or any need to question us in Weserich's absence—no harm would come to his career as a result. Fontane had supplied the novella with salt on which the Regiment Gensdarmes organized a summer sleigh ride on Unter den Linden; when asked what the lords intended to do with the soiled but expensive condiment afterwards, the nobility, in full consciousness of their omnipotence, replied: As long as it doesn't rain. It'll still be good enough *pour les domestiques.*

– *Et pour la canaille*: someone says; for the people, known as the mob. Weserich impressed upon us that the idea had come from the youngest cornet; we thought we knew everything we needed to know about seventeen-year-olds.

Time passed. The Israelites went out into the land. Marlene Timm, inevitably nicknamed "Tiny Tim" despite her average height, received official permission to go visit relatives (aunts) in Denmark—this was much marveled at, she was merely a guest among us; Axel Ohr was taken care of, five years' hard labor; Jakob hadn't been given the chance to drive more than a couple of engines, it's true, and was transferred to signal stations between Gneez and Ludwigslust for disciplinary reasons, meanwhile earning credits at the Transportation Technical College in Dresden, which might as well have accepted him as a full-time student; in March, Jakob's mother was refused permission to travel to West Germany; Heinrich Cresspahl, Brickworks Road, Jerichow, had his pension reduced when he'd faithfully reported his income from repairing chests and *sideboards*; his daughter actually did go to West Berlin to get him whittling knives, the kind with retractable blades; Oskar Tannebaum sent a *"petticoat"* from Paddington, which according to Cresspahl was a railroad station in London; in November of 1950, in the city hall of Richmond, Cresspahl's intended home town, the second version of Picasso's dove of peace was on view; the Americans got a punch on the nose in Korea; the seasons took their course; and still we were reading *Schach*. Schach!

We had discovered that he remained invisible throughout the hundred and thirty pages; intentionally, we were willing to assume for Fontane's benefit. Almost everyone called him "handsome"; therefore vain: opines Josephine de Carayon. Von Bülow mocks him as His Majesty, Captain von Schach. Victoire sees "something of the solemnity of a church councilman about him." He is occasionally knowable through his actions: when he poses as the conscience of his regiment and then denies it; when he gives a needlessly nasty report about Victoire at the prince's; when he cravenly hides from his mamma on the stairs and from his duty in Wuthenow; in short, behaves in such a way that Josephine de Carayon is moved to weigh her own family against his made-up Obotrite nobility. All of us thought his chickening out was obvious and inexplicable; Anita had the last word. She stuttered at first, stumbled over a word; we took it to be nervousness, common enough among seventeen-year-olds. – Getting her pr-pr-pregnant: Anita said: she could accept that. What were we to think it was but an ordinary linguistic mishap? Anita could pursue a train of thought while speaking as resolutely as if she were alone. – But to not even try (and to need to be ordered by his king, and by his queen) to be a good person!

It had slipped out of her involuntarily, unwillingly; she braced herself for our laughter over this old-fashioned term. We were embarrassed for her; we were proud of her. Who knows, if it had been Eva Matschinsky we might have laughed; because it was Anita we all stared straight ahead, I even saw some nods of agreement; and no one outside of that class ever heard Anita say what her conception of a person's honor was.

– The Gensdarmes Regiment was also abolished two years later in the army reforms: Zaychik said, to break the silence. He had learned to eat crow, our Dagobert with his *ol' story*.

A full hour's deliberation on the *beauté du diable, coquette, triviale, celeste,* and fifth and finally the *beauté, qui inspire seul du vrai sentiment.* (The only girl embarrassed by this: Lise.) On who Berlin's Alexanderplatz was named after, and what a member of the nobility can do with a pock-marked girl once his prince and gracious lord has transfigured her for him so that he can see a *beauté du diable* in her.

And does von Bülow's pronouncement at the end reflect the author's judgment? He's just a blockhead. (Would the class please be so kind as to enlighten its teacher about "blockheads"?) Because of his logic-chopping. We've had this already: the omniscient narrator. Here it was Lise Wollenberg who found an argument for why we had to consider von Bülow as separate from his creator: because of the finest white clothes, "something at which Bülow in no way excelled."

We are nearing the end. We know because Weserich, with a ceremonial air, takes us back to the beginning: the title. We were categorically prohibited from consulting Fontane's letters (– Declarations of intent say nothing about the work itself); he quoted one to us, the letter from November 5, 1882, which explores various possible titles for the novella: "*1806; Outside Jena; Et dissipate sunt; Numbered, Weighed, and Given Away; Before the End (Fall, Downfall)*." What could class 11-A-II in April of 1951 adduce to Mr. Weserich as reasons for the final choice of title?

– Because a person's name is always the most honest declaration: Lockenvitz (he got that from Th. Mann).

– Because the others almost all imply a judgment, forestalling the reader's own. Fontane wants his readers to decide for themselves!: Weserich now taught us, and now we were to start in on the delight and pleasure of reading a novella by Th. Fontane about the year 1806 again, afresh.

But we ruined it for ourselves. It was Lockenvitz who blew it. We were responsible too. Lockenvitz, now a member of the Pagenkopf/Cresspahl collective, asked us in passing if we thought Mr. Weserich himself would pass a test. It's true, we gave him permission; we predicted only that this student would complain about Fontane again—the first sentence, for instance, the hiccup that the present participle there could give rise to.

What Lockenvitz presented, though, right after the Easter lambs, was a journal from the half-capital, in a colorful jacket band—called *Form*, or maybe *Sinn*, in any case East German national culture's emissary to the rest of the world. In it (vol. 2, pp. 44–93), the reigning expert on Socialist literary theory wrote, about Fontane's *Schach von Wuthenow*, that the novella was a "lucky accident." The critique of Prussian culture it contained was "unintentional," was "unconscious," Georg Lukács wrote.

Lockenvitz had requested permission to read this out loud toward the end of class time, to spare Mr. Weserich any possible embarrassment in front of the students. Weserich listened, his mouth forming a rectangle, as though listening to a terrible pain. He thanked his student, asked to borrow the valuable printed journal, and stalked out of the room on his one leg. (Whenever the stump of the other *aigrir*'ed him he'd always recited the start of the poem about the knee that wanders lonely through the world / It's just a knee, no more.)

He was out for a week. Student teachers do sometimes need to travel on professional business, just like other teachers: thought 11-A-II. The one who came back, though, loathed us.

Schach was canceled. For the rest of May and June he rushed through Fontane's novel *Frau Jenny Treibel*; we had two weeks left over at the end of the school year. He still listened to what we said when we interrupted his speaking with our own; he nodded, as if at something he'd expected. He refused to allow any of what he called "jokes." The stove was out, the egg was broken, the dish was eaten.

Lockenvitz was ashamed, sheepish, crushed. Whether or not he'd actually hoped for a duel between a high-school class in Mecklenburg and a grand dialectician, it had all gone wrong. He tried, he asked for permission to add something about Count Mirabeau, after whom Victoire de Carayon called herself Mirabelle: evidence had been found after this French revolutionary's death that payments had been made to him from the French royal exchequer; the removal of the besmirched ashes from the Panthéon surely must have been known in 1806? – Your Herwegh's like that too: Weserich said drily and dismissively. (Herwegh receives somewhat merciless treatment at Treibel's hospitable table.) – Acts all grand at the head of the 1849 worker's rebellion in Baden, but when things went wrong he fled across the French border, disguised as a day laborer!

The informal pronoun—*your* Herwegh—didn't gratify Lockenvitz, it choked him. This child of conflict and dissent, we saw him gulp. He lowered his eyes. He sat down without a word.

Lockenvitz wrote a twenty-page essay about *Schach von Wuthenow*, without asking for help and without being asked to write it at all, and mailed it to Weserich the German instructor during the summer; only years later could he again feel proud of having discovered that Fontane never grants Schach a first name—a custom of the nobility, to be sure, but also a comment on the person. Our Weserich resumed his studies at the University of Leipzig; he didn't have time to correspond with a schoolboy in Mecklenburg. Mathias Weserich's dissertation on *Schach von Wuthenow* was printed in Göttingen, across the border.

We knew he was using us the way a biologist uses guinea pigs, and we weren't mad. We'd also raced against him swimming, 100 meters, by stopwatch, not cheating him by swimming slower on purpose. It was clear from his shirts that he didn't have a woman to look after them. And maybe grown-ups were like that: after they've been shot in the mouth once, they take steps to avoid a second bullet. He'd owned one single suit (gray summer fabric) that he wore every day with a handkerchief in the breast pocket and a tie—as if he owed us respectable attire. And he had taught us how to read.

August 3, 1968 Saturday

The New York Times still has not been able to prove that Leonid Brezhnev and Alexander Dubček had lunch together, but thanks to the time difference across the Atlantic she can at least tell us this much: This morning the two men embraced at the Bratislava train station. The way Auntie hears it, Brezhnev's feeling friendly, having received written appeals from the leaders of three Communist parties: the Yugoslavian, the Italian, and the French.

But the way the East German leaders are threatening the Czechs and Slovaks with lip-smacking references to the Soviet Union's overwhelming military might—we have to look away.

Helicopters are again allowed to fly to the city's airports from the tower above Grand Central Station. A Douglas Commercial, type 8 has crashed near Milan—fifteen dead. We're flying soon too.

Charlie in his Good Eats Diner, after two hours of frying and cooking, certainly doesn't look like he's been playing genteel leisure sports. Would they let you into a club with such messy, unevenly cut blond (yellow) hair? His customers wear their shirts untucked, loud lumberjack plaid, a bit stained too. This morning the men were razzing one another about their golf handicaps, though, and not as a joke.

This is something about America we'll miss: Marie ordered a patty on a bun with onion, and what does Charlie shout back toward the hot grill? – *Burger takes slice! Do it special for my special lady, now!* and Marie looks down, blushing, as she should. And proud, because she belongs.

A special message in the entrance down into the subway:

$\sqrt{\text{RADICAL}}$
is a state of mind.

And, as if no one would ever burgle an apartment whose inhabitants were two hours by car out of town, we spent today, from morning to early afternoon, at Jones Beach, thanks to the Blumenroths since this state park is accessible only to people with cars. Mr. Blumenroth, burned red under his thin frizzy hair, may have given the Cresspahl household a new catch-phrase: *There's a reason for everything!*

He expressed this harebrained wisdom after deciding that his supervision of Pamela's games on and under her inflatable raft was sufficient. After she'd drifted some seventy feet out to sea, Mrs. Cresspahl went with him to the rescue. (Once, in the Baltic, she swam for three hours chasing a ball, out of stubbornness. The ball put wave after wave between itself and her before drifting off toward Denmark.) Pamela took a long time to come to terms with the confiscation of her plaything as a grown-up measure; her father spent a long time looking stupefied with reasonableness, he'd endured such a fright. Only after a while did he start up again with the sidelong glances meant to remind us of our meetings at the Hotel Marseilles bar; Mrs. Blumenroth had her hands full with the job of overlooking her husband's goings-on. To keep him from saying it, she said it herself: That's a bust you can be proud of, Mrs. Cresspahl.

– Thanks very much: she replied, in the American way of accepting, not denying, a compliment, which this time she found tiresome for a change.

What do we know about Mrs. Blumenroth?

Born in 1929. "I'm from the Carpathians." Yes, the Germans came and got her. She wasn't allowed to take anything with her. Except her clothes.

Arrival in New York: 1947. Marriage: 1948. Fear of having been made infertile. Pamela: 1957.

A harsh Hungarian accent in her tinny voice. She knows that her voice was softer and gentler as a child, hence her preference for whispering.

She admits to one flaw: an inability to lie, unless she consciously intends to, which hasn't yet happened.

Her black hair is maybe dyed. Cut very short, in heart-shaped curls; one sharp point drapes her brow. A face with few wrinkles, its expression more fearful than approachable. When she wants to laugh, what comes out is invariably: Ha!

"*I'm fussy, nervous.*" A younger parent would be more patient with children.

One time, she almost laughed. Her husband had put together a new bed and now the guest was to test it, sit on it. Mrs. Cresspahl's verdict: Quality merchandise. Mrs. Blumenroth: Ha! Ha!

Unusually tidy home. Everything always put away promptly.

What she found hard to take after the war was how a woman from a good background, with a sense of what's proper, could slip so easily into a false, uncertain position.

Stubbornly working hard to keep a well-groomed appearance; always afraid that the roof is going to fall in.

"At my age, my back can't help hurting."

She would take in a German child as a foster daughter.

And now Pamela, a possible companion for Marie's later life.

She stands with her chest flung out, her head thrown back atop its short neck. Opens her mouth wide—everything is pulled back and down, as if her head had grown straight out of her rib cage. Her whole face laughs. Marie beams when she sees her friend.

Marie carries out plans, pursues things; gets excited. Pamela behaves like a second child. A "girl" in the European sense.

She'll turn into a practical, nice woman. Not especially intelligent, but unshakably proper. We want to see it all. We want to go to Pamela's wedding.

On the beach there were a lot of head shapes and physiognomies like those of people in Germany, as one often sees on the streets of New York—doppelgangers, especially of the poet Günter Eich, sit in great number on the benches and at shop counters and bars. You never run across an Ingeborg Bachmann. But there are also people whom you're glad to find are false alarms—certain stately blonds, for instance. Memory awaits an illuminating flash of similarity with Mathias Weserich, with Wm. Brewster (in his younger years).

In the afternoon, at the playground in Riverside Park, various members of the public are relaxing; someone who recognizes Mr. Anselm Kristlein there will have been fooled for a while before realizing it's him. Maybe because she knows he's in town. In secret, incognito—but if that's how he wants it, he shouldn't have called Ginny Carpenter. She called him back that night, at his hotel on Central Park South; Kristlein always avails himself of the most expensive option, since cheap purchases have cost him dearly before. Ginny told the story giggling with delight at his cautious questions over the phone: – Yes . . . ? Always wary over the phone. One knows so many ladies in this city, one might turn around and want something from him. Better not to name any names for the time being. The *tête-à-tête*, the *souper à deux* with the wife of reserve officer Carpenter—the usual for Anselm. Ginny's words. He's had himself examined at the Mayo Clinic: he says. Golden words. He's come to New York to collect donations for antiwar events in Europe; this nimble gentleman invites Ginny to come advise him while shopping on Fifth and Madison Avenues. He inquires circuitously, casually into any recent pregnancies that might have emerged in Ginny's circle; when she tells him one, he flicks the fingers of one hand as if burned. Mrs. Carpenter has promised him a check from her husband's hand—he doesn't have an American bank account to deposit it into. What is someone like Anselm Kristlein looking for on Manhattan's West Side, in this neighborhood whose shabbiness Ginny so complains of? He couldn't be looking for her?

Anselm Kristlein in our park was recognizable from the insistent looks he was casting over the top of the real estate section of the London *Times* at a young woman sitting two benches away and keeping an eye on a three-year-old girl's path from the sandboxes to the fountains; he could barely tear his gaze away from her bright red blouse of rough material, the reddish hair sitting on her neck, wound up in a knot with apparent casualness and consummate skill, from her dry but unwrinkled brow, lightly freckled, from her lips, from her monstrously blue sunglasses that shielded this face from him. So that's what he likes? Then he better do something.

What with trying so hard to disguise his looks to the side with glances at his paper, he's let the child he's here with run away. Maybe it's Drea. We saw him dash around almost desperately in search of this child, from one playground structure to the next, back and forth, and he was already halfway up the stairs to Riverside Drive when he succeeded in getting what he would have denied he was looking for: a wave from the woman.

She raised her hand and swung her outstretched arm until he saw her and she could point to his child at a corner of the fence, drinking from the water fountain; she had already walked over and said something to the child and returned to her place before he was standing at the fountain.

Holding his child's hand, he walked over to the woman and explained: *She did not understand you. She does not speak English.* The woman nodded. Her own child was sitting under her arm; she moved her arm gently. She made sure she had something to occupy herself with. In her other hand she held her magazine, waiting; both she and her child looked patiently at the man and his child.

We've seen him suaver than that. He stood with the soles of his feet stuck fast to the concrete ground. He'd started a conversation and wanted to extend it. – *Thank you:* he said, instead of asking to borrow the magazine. The woman said Hmm, twice, with such finality that he finally let his child drag him away.

Later I saw him on his bench staring helplessly at the woman as she went past him to the ice cream man, who had just parked his cart on the park path; I passed right into his line of sight but he had eyes only for the woman's firm petite ass.

Later he was with his child at the swings, two places away from the woman with hers, and sometimes he missed a push busy as he was storing up for the weeks to come the memory of how she let the box with her child hit her raised hands and then with a firm little push, only slightly visible in her beautiful bare feet, sent it back up into the air.

He was still there when everyone left for dinner; when I sat down by the window at around nine, I could still see, through a gap in the leaves, the young gentleman standing in his stylish wool shirt, looking up, with jutting chin; and if he'd recognized me a few hours earlier—

(but Mrs. Cresspahl wears her sunglasses in front of her eyes, or in her dress pocket, never pushed up on her head. The oils in her hair can leave traces on the lenses, which would then look like dirt to anyone standing behind you)

—I'd have been able to, maybe even would have wanted to, tell him he'd be waiting in vain till next Saturday, and so, in his desperate need to take the sunglasses off this woman too, just once, would he dare to tell her what happened to come to his mind?

Mrs. Cresspahl was tempted to go out to the street, make herself known, invite Mr. Kristlein up for a nighttime glass of something, one for the road. But she realized in time that he was waiting for someone else, wanting to get to someone else. He'll definitely make the attempt; we can leave him to it.

And to flick his fingers like that, in such a year.

August 4, 1968 Sunday, South Ferry day

– Gesine! You were up past midnight listening to the record of the variations for that student Goldberg. The quodlibet twice!

– Sowwy. There was a party in the apartment upstairs. I wanted my own noise.

– Got you! You thought I was picking a fight! The music gave me sweet dreams.

– Marie, I want to make a bet with you: We're not going to have any
fights with each other until October. Starting in October.

– I bet I'll win!

The joint communiqué out of Bratislava from the Soviet Union and its
charges: twist and turn it however you want, all it says is what they've
been saying all along, from the victories scored by Socialism to the West
German thirst for revenge. It closes with a mild affirmation of national
self-determination from all signatories, without mentioning Czechoslovakia. The Soviets promise to withdraw their last sixteen thousand soldiers.
Censorship is still abolished. Freedom of assembly and association remains
in place. One single concession: the leadership in Prague has asked newspaper editors to refrain from printing articles with opinions that might
sadden their allies. Articles with facts seem to be allowed.

On the second to last day of October, part of the trial of Sieboldt and
Gollantz was held in the auditorium of the Fritz Reuter High School in
Gneez. Principal Kramritz had been instructed to put a sheet of paper on
Elise Bock's desk; those who wished to testify had to print their names
and sign it. They all received postage-paid postcards, machine-numbered,
with letterhead but no text: their invitations. But if they turned up outside
the auditorium on Monday afternoon with nothing but their FDJ membership booklet, the two uniformed women at the check-in table promptly
turned them away. The women wanted to see each student's "PID," the
new personal ID—maybe because they were suspicious of the administrative approach apparently in style in the youth chapter headquarters (mim-
eographing stencils and paper gone missing!). Also, police-issued documents
are harder to forge and easier to trace. Then anyone who showed up in a
lumberjack instead of a blue shirt was turned away by Bettina Selbich: for
"insufficient consciousness." That meant, in the end, that there weren't
many students in the assembly hall; it was largely minders from out of town.

– A shirt in October?

– Student Cresspahl had bought a blue one two sizes too big for her so
she could wear a sweater underneath. Pius pretended not to notice. Lockenvitz froze.

– I wish I knew what you think about him!

– Work it out for yourself.

– A "*lumberjack*"?

– See? You don't know Canadian!

– Do too. A woodcutter. *Every man jack.*

– In the fall of 1950 it came into fashion to wear jackets of lightly ribbed crepe, with wide collars, a zipper you'd leave open, and inside and outside zippered pockets. The way the woodcutters supposedly dressed in Canada.

– That's called a *lumber jacket*!

– We didn't know Canadian either.

– Like the Indian headbands here?

– What those jackets meant was: the wearer comes from people with Western money; he likes Canada.

– But Pius had one.

– *Elementary, my dear Watson.*

– Like blue jeans these days in Budapest? And East Germany?

– What do I care! Where people obey a custodian who's jeered at and whistled at outside City Hall in Bratislava!

– Gesine, you said: not till after October.

In memory the auditorium is an oak-dark room, lined with paneling six feet high, filled with benches as sturdy as in a church, topped with a coffered wooden ceiling. At the moment it was a great hall for displaying the colors of flags, in which the FDJ didn't come off too well—there were twice as many of the Unity Party's reds, sometimes with the clasped hands, sometimes not, as well as the black, red, and gold of the national flag adorned with the symbols of the peasants (ring of grain opening upward) and the workers (hammer). (Contemporary Studies with Selbich: We are proud to leave the eagle, that circling vulture of bankruptcy, to the reactionary forces in West Germany!) On the front wall, above the red-draped table for the judges, was Picasso's dove of peace, second version. The décor made it clear that this was an official gathering, not that of a club or some other group. Manfras and Lockenvitz, the highest-ranking functionaries, were sitting on the 11-A-II bench most compliantly for the occasion. Silence, as in a funeral hall, viewing the coffin. Once the blue of the People's Police completely surrounded the school building, the armored transport vehicle from Rostock drove up to the gates. An armed company escorted the accused up the six turns in the stairs to the auditorium. We heard the clicks from the open doorway and we knew: their handcuffs were just then being taken off. Sieboldt and Gollantz presented straight, almost rigid backs and a deliberately relaxed gait as they were led to the podium and took their seats between four constables. Two boys, nineteen and twenty years old, dressed in their dead fathers' Sunday suits. Imperturbable faces avoiding the least sign of greeting, even one they could've managed unnoticed with the corners of their mouths or their eyelashes. But they were looking, very carefully too, to see who'd come to bid them goodbye. Then the presiding judge realized his mistake and ordered them to look to the side. This judge was a chatty man, helpless, fussy as an aunt: How *could* you, but that's *terr*ible, this depravity at such a young age—that's how he talked. The prosecutor was likewise hampered by a bourgeois upbringing; he had a penchant for nasty insinuations which he offered as delicate irony. About the defense attorney, not one word—except that he too was wearing the state party's button on his lapel. They'd brought along their own lackey, who called them the Honorable Court for our benefit. It was cold in the auditorium. From the high windows came the pale glowing light that exists only in October.

– Now Burly Sieboldt will be able to tell you all what was on those fliers!

– Student Cresspahl had come to see Gollantz and him one more time. The way you go to see someone you're never going to see again.

– To pay your last respects?

– When you're seventeen you can feel that way. But we did know the verdict in advance. Little Father Stalin had reintroduced the death penalty on January 13—the highest measure of social protection—but for these two it'd only be twenty-five years. The usual.

– For a few fliers.

– And Pius had proven to me once and for all that we were friends. Because of his father, the Pagenkopfs were thought to agree with the custodian's government, and they of all people got something slipped through their mail slot. One time in June, Pius waited for me to ask him for the table of logarithms, and what I found between the pages might have been left there by accident. So when he handed the picture with the barbed wire and printed words over to Section D, fulfilling his obligations as a vigilant friend of peace, he'd be able to swear with a clean conscience that he hadn't shown it to anyone. When I finished reading it, a look hung in the air between us of the kind you experience maybe three times in your life, at most, if you're lucky.

– You dried off with the same towel! You slept under the same roof! But you only trusted each other once you could get him sent to prison?

– From that moment on I had another brother.

Ex-Students Sieboldt and Gollantz were accused of private and conspiratorial visits to West Berlin. The East Office of the West German SPD was located there, the Investigating Committee of Free Jurists was housed there, the Task Force Against Inhumanity was operating there. East German courts had proven that these groups had blown up a bridge, had set fire to a barn. Jakob, on the other hand, had told stories—and I believed him—of a railcar found in Rostock with forged freight papers, diverted from Saxony, the butter in it now not going to the people of Leipzig, assuming it was still edible at all. But Sieboldt and Gollantz had no interest in taking out other people's anti-Communism on *their* friends and neighbors and relatives, for instance by disrupting the distribution of food any more than the East German authorities had managed to do by themselves just fine; they'd gone to West Berlin with an idea of their own. So much the worse: concluded the court. They'd accepted from one of these groups, which were all registered with the West Berlin district courts, a picture of young people marching in a column behind reinforced wires, but had done so on the condition that their own text be added to it. So much the worse: concluded the court. The defendants were merely forced to admit the shameful infamy of these printed remarks, while at least two students had them more or less memorized: That the slogans about Peace and the Struggle for Peace were just euphemisms for the securing of what the Soviets had acquired in Central and Eastern Europe; since the Soviet Union, too, now possessed (by theft) the atomic bomb, it had started preparing an offensive, by manpower reinforcements and additional arming of the Volkspolizei, by propaganda among the members of the FDJ to join this

army-in-disguise, by appointing one of its leading officers to the Volkspolizei's central administration; what are you marching for, members of the
FDJ? That was what Students Sieboldt and Gollantz had worked out.
Aggravating circumstance: Verbal disparagement of the World Peace Movement. Namely by claiming that Picasso's dove of peace had appeared in
French newspapers armed with a hammer and sickle. The English apparently described it as *"the dove that goes bang,"* now would you mind translating for us this outrageous insult to the striving for world peace? *Die
Taube kommt mitm Knall* but a little less casual. My stars, where ever did
you hear such a thing?

– Gesine, you daredevil!
– I was a little scared when it came up. But Burly Sieboldt said, unhurried: Oh, it's in the air; and he directed his gaze to the air over Student
Cresspahl's head, but toward where the balcony around the assembly hall,
blocked off for the day, was filled with armed men.
– What if he'd suspected you! Just the idea that you had betrayed him
and he'd have brought you down with him!
– Things were carefully set up to deal with such matters in that German
democratic country. If Cresspahl's daughter tells her classmate Sieboldt
what she's heard on BBC radio, he is required to report her. If Sieboldt
seems happy to hear something worth knowing from his classmate's mouth,
she is required to report him. But Sieboldt's family would have disowned
him forever if he'd denounced someone. That's what denunciation meant.
Cresspahl would've never spoken to or looked at his daughter again if she'd
been praised for the arrest of a neighbor's child.
– To hear you tell it, it's all pretty easy. But someone denounced them.
– Everyone knew that Gollantz was practically engaged to a girl from
his senior class, one Lisette von Probandt. They were "the Couple" in their
year; the children in ninth grade just watched them ... the same way the
former ninth graders had watched Pius and me. Now if you put a girl
under arrest and give her the third degree ...
– So Sieboldt had something to blame Gollantz for.
– Meanwhile the Honorable Court tried to get Gollantz to admit that
Sieboldt had led him astray. Gollantz stood his ground so that he'd be
given exactly as many years as his friend.

– That darn Statue of Liberty, do you see how her arm is drooping? They're going to close it off to visitors any day now, it's not safe.

– *Elementary, my dear Mary.*

The accused were repeatedly told to express greater contrition. For they seemed quite content when they were shouted at, threatened, and cursed, as if they'd have been disappointed more than anything if they weren't. As if they were expecting it. And the children in their blue shirts sitting before them could tell what the accused considered reason enough to be happy, reason enough to feel the meager serenity that stiffened their backs in the face of twenty-five years of forced labor for sabotage:

> attempted continuation
> of reactionary student self-governance,
> a vestige
> of the pseudodemocratic inheritance
> of the Weimar Republic,
> by means of
> obtaining under false pretenses
> high
> and highest
> ranks
> of the Central School-Group Authority
> of the Free German Youth;

for espionage:

> scouting out
> the vulnerable flank
> of the Peace Movement
> of the Republic;

for terrorism: since they truly had undertaken to spread a view in Gneez and its high school different from the view that the ministry of the interior (which they insisted on calling the ministry of war) expected;

for illegal association (Sieboldt with Gollantz). Then Mr. Kramritz stood up and thundered about the "Abiturs obtained under false pretenses"— in fact they had gained acceptance to the university by working hard in the subjects being tested. Then one Bettina Selbich took the floor, stammering, recalling nighttime visits from FDJ officeholder Sieboldt; if her victim had chosen to speak, he would surely have said: The cavalier takes his pleasure and holds his tongue. He spared her, and if it was hard for him, it was after all how he wanted to think of himself later. Manfras, too, spoke up, with a "position statement" of the kind that the new tradition of democratic justice called for; his indignation, his voice trembling with rage, were perfectly understandable to the defendants, and to us too. For it was just when the FDJ school group had been about to mail off its protest against the murderous incursion of US troops into the peaceful land of Korea that they'd set him up. Disgraced him. Wounded his political conscience.

– Now of the circa eight million people earning their living in the vicinity of this ferry the *John F. Kennedy*, surely one or two of them remember that it was the other way around?

– We knew it too. Because when we were ordered to a schoolwide assembly at noon on June 26, Bettina's efforts at the lectern were aimed at making everything the imperialists' fault. That was one piece of edification. To demand we approve lies by acclamation, vote yes to untruths, was a mockery and a game to any child who knew how to use a radio. And who had been chosen, outside the auditorium door, to suggest the wording? Who came back with a mosaic flawlessly assembled from the costume jewelry of newspaper language? Sieboldt and Gollantz. And whom did they thank for his resolute editorial assistance, whose skill with words did they extol for the succession of FDJ leadership in the Gneez high school? Gabriel Manfras. They'd chosen him to ascend the Town Hall balcony that afternoon and read in passionate tones to the people marching on the square below a text that seemed unobjectionable to him; now it turned out he'd been manipulated into cooperating with a falsehood, rewarded for his political work with the taint of doubting the cause of peace. He had a right to be mad about that; the defendants could respect that.

– In conclusion.

– Sieboldt and Gollantz thanked the court for its efforts, again denied any consciousness of wrongdoing, each for himself, and voiced one final qualm: Maybe it would have been more appropriate under the circumstances if they'd been allowed to witness the afternoon's proceedings wearing the garb of honor of the Free German Youth?

– No! I could never do that.

– Maybe you could, Marie. Some people do when whatever they have is behind them and they're looking at twenty-five years in the slammer. Never to take a ferry across New York Harbor. Losing your girl. Never once to wake up except from the clang of a blow on an iron bar. To know that your only baggage will be your memories from age nineteen and twenty.

– If I were Lisette von Probandt and had a memory, I'd hate life.

– The twenty-five years turned into just five, at which point a West German chancellor visited the Soviet Union. Sieboldt and Gollantz were handed over with the rest of the prisoners of war; they studied law together in Bonn and Heidelberg and were accepted into the Foreign Ministry in 1962. Soon there'll be an embassy where we can go visit them.

– So the Soviets educated two civil servants for the West Germans.

– That's called cadre development! And Lisette had her seven years of waiting. She married Gollantz, and Sieboldt is their child's godfather.

– I could never forgive someone that way.

– You could, Marie. You will. You'll learn.

(Sunday, too, is South Ferry day when Marie says it is.)

August 5, 1968 Monday

On ČSSR television, Alexander Dubček announced: The conference in Bratislava had given the country new scope for its liberalization, it "fulfilled our expectations" (not: all of our). He was apparently trying to hide his party's satisfaction.

Yesterday in Florida, as was only proper for a Sunday, a man with a girl about two years old hired a Cessna 182, to sightsee over the area: he said. Then he pulled out a revolver; the plane had to fly to Cuba.

Yesterday a Convair 580 collided with a small private plane over southeastern Wisconsin and proceeded to land with the crushed wreck of the smaller plane, and its three dead bodies, embedded in it.

We're flying soon too.

Student Lockenvitz.

(Because you want me to, Marie. Only what I *know*.)

In the spring of 1950 we invited him to join the work collective of Young Friends Pagenkopf and Cresspahl.

For selfish reasons. We wanted to learn from this tall, lanky, starved boy how he could think in Latin. – Eundem Germaniae sinum proximi Oceano Cimbri tenent, parva nunc citivas, sed gloria ingens: he said casually when the subject of the Obotrite nobility came up.

Social background, father's profession: Farmer. On a 1949 questionnaire: Agronomist. In 1950: Director of Municipal Gardens, Parks, and Cemetery Plantings in (*don't worry, I won't say the city's name. Besides, you always pronounced it the Polish way. Anita was the only one who could understand it, if even she did*) of one of the larger communities in what is today the People's Poland. Bourgeois.

Political background, parents' party membership before 1945: None. Before 1933: German National People's Party. Imperialist. His father had kept his distance from the Nazis—Lockenvitz insisted on that. So how did he explain that he spent fifth grade in a NaPolIn? He said his father was given a choice in 1944: being drafted into the army or professing his faith in the Hitler state some other way. Heavy financial burden, the fees for a National-Political Educational Institution. But these places were unlike the Hitler Youth Ordensburgs in their lesser emphasis on physical ability. Take his glasses. The metal frame sent rusty trickles down his nose in hot weather.

And then why did the Soviets take his father away, if he was in neither the army nor the party? In February 1947 he was "last seen lying dead on his bunk." (A witness statement; his mother was hoping for a pension. The pension was denied, provisionally in 1947, definitively in 1949, cf. husband's previous social position. Application for educational stipends for Student Lockenvitz: Approved.) On the questionnaire in Contemporary Studies, Lockenvitz said: My father had an argument with the owner of our house; he was falsely denounced. Once he could trust us, he confided, asking us to tell no one else: That was when the Soviet Kommandatura was in our house.

Arrival in Gneez: Age eleven. They'd decided to try to defend that city in the East, so his father had sent the family with the relocating German Army in the direction of the western front; the city is now rubble. Mother's occupation since 1945: Garden worker. Son's class: Proletarian? No: Wage workers.

First apartment in Gneez: Across from the cemetery, with Mr. Budniak, the gravedigger, in a single room. Since 1949: Two rooms near the dairy. Starting in March 1951: An apartment converted from barracks in the Barbara Quarter, once the Soviets had left (and demolished a third of the barracks). In the plaster on the top of the barracks' facade were the outlines of the German eagle and the circle he'd been sitting on, the circle for the swastika.

An only child. Peasant relatives in father's birthplace, Dassow am See, where he spent his holidays, paid in kind for his help in the harvest. 1948 to 1949: twenty hours a week working in a bicycle repair shop on Street of German-Soviet Friendship; he needed the money for books. (The city library closed at five thirty, but you can read until midnight.) Starting in 1950: express messenger for the district of Gneez, German Postal Service, which was why Anita had forced him to take that Swedish bicycle; (without him realizing, absentminded as he was, that at the price she gave him it was practically a gift). He was paid twenty cents per tariff kilometer; bonus if it was raining: fifteen cents. Whether or not it had been raining was decided by Berthold Knever. One time a woman in Old Demwies had been waiting so anxiously for her letter with the red sticker and the address crossed out in red—her pass for the West—that she gave him an egg. But he spent a lot of the afternoons in the sorting room just waiting for an express delivery to make; and doing his homework.

A sensitive child. With a name like that! Nickname (bestowed by Lise Wollenberg): Dietikin. And Lockenvitz, when your hair is actually in *Locken*—blond unruly waves—with a *Vitz* or *Fitz*, a tangled patch, at the back! He lowered his head and pressed his lips together, as if deciding to take action; but cf. here GOETHE:

> For a person's name is not like a coat, which merely hangs about him and may, perchance, be safely twitched and pulled; it is a perfectly fitting garment, which has grown over and over him like his very skin, and at which one cannot rake and scrape without wounding the man himself. (*Dichtung und Wahrheit*, Pt. 2, Book Ten)

Such a child, if he had his way, would have such books in his house ready to consult at all times.

An afflicted child. During all the many moves, a framed photograph of his father, an enlarged driver's license picture with the staples clearly visible, was more important to him than all the furniture put together. Mrs.

Lockenvitz, however, was just thirty-five when her husband "was seen" for the last time; all she took from him was the mission to get the boy to the gates of a university. (His father had a degree in agronomy.) That was why, after Carnival in 1949, there was a photo in the window of Mallenbrandt Pharmacy with a story to tell about the festivities: a young woman with her breasts squeezed together by her bodice. A child who feels ashamed. A sixteen-year-old beaten by his mother because after a man had spent the night he'd taken his father's picture off the wall and hidden it; because he made his mother feel ashamed. At one point, when electrical devices were in short supply, Lockenvitz had mounted over his window a bell from a sleigh left behind in the east, with a cord of sack string coated in pitch hanging down, he was so eager for visitors; now he unscrewed the bell, ignored knocks on the door.

A young man who knows how to enter a room that contains a lady, how to manage his knife and fork now that Mrs. Pagenkopf sometimes brings a third plate in from the kitchen for him. Who insists on the good manners of thanking her for every snack, with a servant's bow from the neck; who declines to accept another sandwich—just to be polite—he would stay hungry for a long time. Until we could convince him that there were none of the "eavesdroppers who never hear anything good" at our house. It took a long time.

Because it hurt him to tell a lie. When his school demanded it, so much the worse for the school, as far as he was concerned; he did his best to let the teacher in charge know how he felt too. Bettina Selbich watched him nervously as he recited the seven commandments of the Stockholm Appeal:

I vow to
stop railroad trains,
unload no military cargo,
withhold fuel from such vehicles,
disarm mercenaries,
refuse to all my children or spouse to serve with the country's
armed forces,
withhold food supplies from my government,
refuse to work at a telephone switchboard or for a transportation
system—
to prevent a new war.

Bettina felt she should say something about his speech. He'd set all kinds of traps for her before; she tried once again and asked him where he'd gotten that text. Anita said, to no one in particular, in a respectful voice: It was in *Pravda*, first week of July.

(We thought she was trying to protect you. Or was it that she used to slip sheets of paper with transcriptions from her Russian reading into your notebook?)

With us he took a cautious approach. But then Zaychik and Eva came over—memorizing nitrites and nitrates had gotten boring—and shot a questioning glance at Pius's POB RTT radiogramophone, and when Pius as the host gave his nod, they shut the windows but turned the knob straight to Radio in the American Sector. RIAS broadcast a hit parade on Fridays—Zaychik was delighted to hear Billy Buhlan singing:

Yoop-de-doo—

You can't slam your head through a wall!

Yoop-de-doo—

This should have reassured Lockenvitz. For Bettina had informed us in Contemporary Studies that listening to Western stations was forbidden, explaining: Musicians who use their offerings for opportunistic reasons to adorn Mr. Adenower's road to war will forever be void of the humanism that might let them interpret the immortal symphonies of Mozart and Beethoven!

Lockenvitz waited until it was just the three of us; remarked: This text from West Berlin does call forth a sociological analysis, does it not? The other side must need to pacify the population, lure them away from making any demands. Lockenvitz was talking to the two of them the same way he'd heard them talk in school. Pius looked at me, brow furrowed; I shrugged as if baffled. We were all acting like diplomats! Pius tried again. So, what kind of music did Lockenvitz like?

Lockenvitz did rather like "boogie-woogie."

This was American jazz from the early years, recently promoted, by government decree, from the music of imperialist-decadent exploiter to progressive insofar as it had developed from the work songs of an age of openly practiced slavery. This boy went in for conversations by the book.

Then the East German government brought about what it had promised to its youth at the Germany Rally. On June 23, it communicated the following warning to its allied governments: American terror planes had dropped large quantities of potato-bugs over the territory in its control, in an effort to harm Socialist agriculture. In late September, the students of 11-A-II started pacing off the furrows of the potato fields around Gneez, heads bowed, seeking out *Doryphora decemlineata*. Now *If yer wearin butter on yer head you shouldn go out in the sun*—they were all embarrassed at a state power expecting them to believe this nonsense about agroterrorism and prove their belief by joyous action in the field. You would need a whole book of its own, Comrade Writer, to describe those afternoons, lasting so infinitely long, the earth turning east toward the sun so infinitely slowly.

And Lockenvitz showed his true colors to us, at least as the son of an agronomist; thunderstruck by the memory, he cried: Ha! Those crafty imperialists! The potato bug hibernates two handspans deep in the soil and appears as soon as the temperature exceeds fifty degrees. Early May, in other words. Now when is the Germany Rally to take place? End of May. So the bugs arrive on schedule, the females dutifully lay their eggs in batches of twenty to eighty, about eight hundred per bug in total, the larvae hatch after seven days, and they need another fifty days after pupation until they're ready. In July! Not on June 23. Not by Whitsunday. *Boys n girls!* If we have potato bugs here in Mecklenburg, they must be descended from the ones that were first sighted in southwest Germany in 1937! They're thriving here because the land-reform policies cut down all the hedgerows, and in those hedges there were nests, and in those nests there were birds that exterminated this pest! And because pheasant breeding went out with the nobility's estates!

– We: he'd said to the two of us. We'd done it.

Now he'd do it to entertain us, too, for instance when he pontificated to Bettina S., carefully exaggerating, losing himself as if unwittingly in the labyrinths of thoughts: These six-legged emissaries of American invasion. But our land is armed and ready. We have the pheasant, do we not. Small game that lives in bushy terrain, also in cabbage patches. Eats caterpillars and worms and beetles, pests in general! A bird that's easy to hunt since it's not a good flier. But what people hunt is the greater foe—the fox. Hence the pheasant's proliferation. Historical research can trace the economic brutality of the American aggressors back to the *Lend-Lease Act* of 1941. Under the pretense of aiding the heroically struggling Soviet Union with food and weapons, they smuggled in 117 different kinds of insect species and weed seeds!

Baffled Bettina was about to go put another A next to his name in the book, but just to be safe she asked a follow-up question. These facts from the war years were entirely new to her, and since she intended to bring them up at an agitprop meeting in the state capital . . . might she ask Student Lockenvitz where he had come upon them?

– Of course: he said: In the *Literaturnaya Gazeta*.

(And wouldn't you know it, Bettina went and asked the school's Russian teacher if this was an émigré journal.)

The student body of the Fritz Reuter High School, four hundred people, found a total of seventeen stray potato bugs; nine of them were ladybugs. Lockenvitz wanted to do what a friend should, and asked us: Did we also know that there was a watch list posted on the distribution shelves of the German Post Office, and that pretty much every day a couple of letters would go spend the night with the Stasi (the State Security Police)?

Now *this* Lockenvitz was someone we could ask about his meeting with Hermlin, the poet, on Landsberg Avenue. Lockenvitz had squirmed his way around a lie: On a streetcar for Grünau he'd gone astray and ended up in Schmöckwitz, was invited into a house there for discussions about art in Mecklenburg, about Barlach the sculptor; tea, red wine. Lockenvitz borrowed a pair of shoes from Pius; his own had been waiting to be repaired for four weeks. He told us his thoughts without holding anything back: Our Socialist accomplishments all presuppose someone they've been taken from, someone who's now standing in the corner and sulking. What's been holding up our American shoe-resoling plants?

This Lockenvitz of ours was who we picked when 11-A-II suddenly had to delegate someone for an FDJ training course in Dobbertin, near Goldberg. At first, when we saw Manfras vote against absenting himself from home and curriculum, when Lise Wollenberg used her vote to avenge herself for being neglected and punish Lockenvitz in general for having ancestors from somewhere else, we kept our hands down. Then Pius, with the powers vested in him as head of the school-group authority, asked: What did the candidate himself think about taking such a trip. – Any organizational secretary for the ZSGL must constantly strive to extend his or her understanding of theory: he answered, like someone agreeing to sacrifice himself for us. Second round of voting: Unanimous—as was in fashion.

In November 1950, he left; in January, we had him back. It went badly. Start to finish: a flop, a mis-hit.

Literally. The start: In November the Ministry of State Security picked up Mrs. Lockenvitz's brother in the Wismar shipyards; charges of sabotage and espionage. Mrs. Lockenvitz tried to hit her son who was off to practice getting into the mental universe of such a ministry. He grabbed her wrists and said, as if conducting a medical evaluation, that she seemed to be hysterical; distracted by curiosity, she asked him what the symptoms of this illness were and didn't like his answers. Now he was off in another town and mustn't even think of going back to Gneez and the apartment in the Barbara Quarter.

He never told us exactly how it ended in Dobbertin. It must have been something like an instructor wanting to hear more about the third principle of dialectics—that could easily lead to a bad grade and a "Badge for Superior Knowledge" in bronze instead of gold.

For his first question to Bettikin had been: If quantity necessarily changes its nature as it increases and is transformed into a qualitative difference, how does that work when you're comparing Turgenev's brain to an elephant's?

(LOCKENVITZ, from before his course in Dobbertin: Children should be spared this. In 1946, when I went to answer the doorbell in Budniak's house, there were two people standing there asking about Mrs. Scharrel. Mrs. Scharrel lived on the second floor and was a black-marketeer, professionally. Mrs. Scharrel: Just tell 'em I'm on my way to Wissmar! That was hard for me, but you do what grown-ups tell you, right? The first time, you forget—if you're lucky. In 1948 the catechist asked us: Who had never told a lie in their life. I raised my hand, because no one else wanted to. And presto! I'd traded up from one lie to two. Now the process is running fine, from a technical point of view. But children should be spared.

The child Lockenvitz, in 1949, after having worked his way through the

Old Testament for a second time, requested an audience with the cathedral preacher of Gneez and gave him a well-organized explanation for why he would henceforth not be coming to the meetings of the congregational youth group. We bring this up to remove any doubt about the fifteen-year-old we're dealing with here.)

He was stubborn. Introverted. Teasing Bettinikin had lost its appeal. His grades slipped in Latin. He lost weight—in memory he is sitting lost in obsessive reflections behind his cheap glasses, wearing a blue shirt that hangs on him in folds. Then came January 12, 1951, when an eighteen-year-old high-school student was sentenced to death in Dresden for "Incitement to Boycott" and for the attempted murder (with a pocketknife) of a People's Policeman; in Gneez, the regular police went into the Renaissance Cinema, not even in disguise, to find out once and for all who was murmuring or laughing whenever the custodian appeared in image and sound, speaking his southern German dialect. Sachwalter Walter considered the sentence appropriate, both before and after it was reduced to fifteen years in prison. This provoked Pagenkopf's female partner in the work collective to thoughtlessly comment: If it's really true that this statesman is such a thorn in the Americans' side, why haven't they bumped him off yet? It's been three years!

Luckily for all of us, she did this outdoors, one evening on the Gneez ice rink. So Lockenvitz could do a few figure eights alone for a few minutes, then curve back into our circle and show us how he'd now learned to think. The ice was gray in the evening darkness, you had to keep your eyes fixed on the track. Sometimes there was the sound of a blade grating; the night surrounding us and Lockenvitz's hard, even, almost adult voice kept getting bigger and bigger:

– It used to be that when the commanding prince fell in open battle, this damaged the troops' morale. Today it would only lead to needing to close ranks. The result is always uncertain; the successor may be even more aggressive. You have to guess what strategy he has in mind, whereas before, you knew what you were dealing with. Any individual is surely expendable, even if they hold power; unless he has charisma, and the abilities that go with it, which is rarely the case. Not counting our dear friends in Moscow, needless to say. Conclusion: The machine is running and it will keep on running. Second: Even now, war is not a *free-for-all* with no rules, where every side is allowed to do whatever it can. People in the highest circles invoke such rules or norms precisely because they are occasionally (secretly) broken. One such tacit norm rules out murdering the opposing leader, other than in open battle. If such excellent rules were rashly, consciously violated, then trust in the validity of all the agreements that limit behavior would wither. The consequence might be a counterstrike with nerve gas against the capital of the offending state. Conclusion: Fear of negative effects rebounding on the perpetrator of a major violation of norms. And that's why everything stays the way it is.

– Grammarian: he'd said a year earlier when the current 11-A-IIs had been asked to state their choice of profession. – What do you want to be now, Youth Friend Lockenvitz? A historian?

– A Latin teacher: Lockenvitz said grimly.

That was the January when, in Western Germany, the Allied High Commission met with the chancellor, his assistant, and two generals at the Hotel Petersberg to discuss whether Germans should once again be rearmed.

That was the January when the East German Volkspolizei sent recruiters into high schools, wearing blue shirts under their uniform jackets, to talk to the boys of 11-A-II, one Youth Friend to another. They promised training in devices that rolled, swam, and flew. Lockenvitz made an appointment with Dr. Schürenberg, specified to the minute; in the hall of the villa on what they called Quack Lane in Gneez, he performed twelve knee-bends, repeating the exercise in front of the doctor's desk; he was given a piece of paper certifying "vegetative dystonia."

To make the school administration believe it too, he applied for exemption from gym class. From then on he would leave the schoolhouse when the Phys. Ed. beanpole hounded us onto the pommel horse or spun us around the high bar; he'd go for walks by himself. At handball or soccer games he would crouch behind the goal, elbows propped on his knees, chin on his folded hands, watching, coming back down to earth when a girl asked him what the score was.

At the start of the 1951–52 school year, nominated for a second term as organization secretary, he declined the candidacy, giving as his reason:

Academic demands. (Still, there wasn't that much he had to do: convene us for marches, campaigns against bandit potato-bugs, and assemblies; report once a month to the central council of the FDJ, on preprinted questionnaires, that we had done this or that in the cause of peace, and that so-and-so many members of the school's chapter had subscribed, for money, to the organization's newspaper, *Young World*.) He was a solid A student in Latin, English, German, and Contemporary Studies, with Bs in the other classes, except for a C in chemistry, which really rankled.

For Christmas of 1951 he found a bag hanging on his mother's door, filled with pfeffernuesse, walnuts, a pad of ink-proof linen-stock paper, and a pair of knitted gloves not made by a machine. It was a freshly washed gym bag, with a drawstring, the kind girls used. Lockenvitz came to see and thank Gesine Cresspahl.

She was dissatisfied with herself, for not having had the idea first; she assured him she was innocent.

(If only you knew that it was from Annette Dühr, 10-A-II. She was so good-looking, so pretty with her hazel eyes, dark-brown braids, a face that invited trust. Later she became a stewardess for the East German Lufthansa; she was allowed to go through training with Pan American, and when she got back her picture was on the cover of Berliner Neuen Illustrierten. *She liked you, she wanted you to like her. You could have found her so easily—all you needed to do was walk back and forth across the schoolyard with her gym bag visible in your hand. Annette reached out to you, in secret but still; she had every right to think you were conceited for having other things on your mind besides girls. But it would have been better for you if you'd wanted to find her.)*

Lockenvitz would now come join our work collective at the appointed times and leave as soon as the math or chemistry homework was done. Pius asked me, once and only once, to pose the question of how Lockenvitz imagined these tasks fitting with a woman's talents; I refused, I was scared of Lockenvitz's mother and had no desire to hear her say he was in unrequited love with anyone. Lockenvitz probably meant it as an apology for his guarded manner, as a gift, when he brought us a note explaining what was keeping him aloof from us:

People insert between events and the free apprehension of those
events a number of concepts and aims, then demand that what
happens conform to them.

We urged him to fob this off on Selbich as evidence of the nature of the
field of contemporary studies under an imperialist regime, especially since
she would never in her life figure out who'd written it (G. W. F. Hegel,
1802). He shook the locks from his brow with an exasperated laugh—as
though he were done playing games with Bettinikin.

Pius and I kept our mouths strictly shut when we saw him one November afternoon coming out of the building where Bettina S. had been rewarded
for her loyal endurance with an apartment.

We were mad at Zaychik for half a year. He wanted to start a correspondence with some socialistically inclined English girls, along with a schoolmate. Lockenvitz did him the favor, even wrote something to Wolverhampton
for the sake of peace and the mail censors. Then he found out that Zaychik
had included in the envelope, by way of introduction, a photograph of Pius
instead, because he thought Pius was more attractive to a young girl's eye
(in fact the girls of 11-A-II considered Pius merely "striking," while Lockenvitz was "our handsome young man"). Hopefully it did him some good
to hear that we took his side in such a momentous thing.

Lockenvitz was the first person in our school to wear plastic-framed
glasses, which he could prove he had bought on Stalin Street. (Opticians
were a protected species all across Mecklenburg, safe from in-depth tax
audits; they allowed themselves practically metropolitan window displays—
almost never was an optician brought before the court in Mecklenburg.)

He owned no Canadian-style jacket.

During vacations we each went our own fine way—Pius, Cresspahl's
daughter, and Lockenvitz too.

He had been careless about one factor in his calculations, if indeed they
were calculations. Vegetative dystonia doesn't exactly go with long-distance
bicycle riding.

He rode like a healthy person, twenty-five miles an hour was nothing.
He could've been in Jerichow in half an hour! But he took his two-wheeled
trips in the other direction on weekends. We could only hope that no one
would notice.

Matthew 16:26. Yeah. Shit.

My dear Marie, this is everything I *think* I know about Dieter Lockenvitz.

August 6, 1968 Tuesday

If we want to get through today in one go, we'll need numbers.

I.

A New Yorker who has their apartment broken into can wait till they're blue and yellow in the face for the insurance payment to come, but if they've paid their premiums into a plan that de Rosny has dreamed up, they can send in a list of missing items on Tuesday, certified by the Twenty-Third Precinct, and get a cashier's check in the mail precisely one week later—good money, legal tender from Manhattan to Leningrad.

Just as de Rosny's bank wants its cut from the insurance underwriters for the people he calls "my colleagues," so too an in-house travel agency should make its profit from the money that these colleagues can afford to put into vacations. And anyone who enters this room on the eighteenth floor without the financial institution's five-line symbol above her heart, without a nametag, in a white linen suit like a passerby off the street, will have it pointed out to her that this business is not open to the public.

– I am aware of that: Mrs. Cresspahl replies, content. Here for once she is not known as "our" German, "our" Dane. The girl behind the counter with a beehive of blond hair keeps her lips tightly pressed; her morning is not going well. We wish we could show her the cartoon from the latest *New Yorker* that we kept for D. E.'s amusement: Under a sign that says SERVICE WITH A SMILE stands a butcher in an apron, handing a customer the bag with her purchases; he looks a little baffled, questioning, serious. The lady shoots her nose into the air with irritation; her mouth is creased with indignation. The caption below says what she's asking: *Well?* (Where's that smile?)

Here things go very differently from the usual sales transactions—we're asked questions, short and snippy: Bank ID? Social security number? Department? Supervisor's extension?

Employee vs. Employee. We're going to whip this girl into shape though.

There are mornings when we too find it hard to force that grimace of fake friendliness onto our face, but it's from the explicit demands of people like her that we learned to. We'll show her the lay of the land, particularly the path that leads to the telephone of the ostensibly admired Mr. de Rosny, without speaking his name. And here you have it, a once-in-a-lifetime opportunity, step right up, free of charge: the chance to see an employee's face ring the changes from shamefaced to scared to meek to submissive, and finally to heartfelt. – *I am ever so sorry, ma'am! My apologies—!*

Now we both felt a little ashamed and settled down into a perfectly normal discussion of how you can cancel a reservation for two to Frankfurt/ Main on the evening of August 19, plus a car rental, the convertible in which we'd planned to drive to the border crossing at Waidhaus in the Upper Palatinate Mountains, hello there Czechs and soldiers! The date and time can stay the same but we now want to fly on Scandinavian Airlines, Pan American is fine too if you can arrive in København in the morning. That's how our friend Anita wants it; you probably don't know her. There must be a hotel on the beach somewhere near Kastrup Airport, where people can check in early in the morning and stay until, say, early afternoon. To catch up on our sleep, you ask? Yes, that's just what we were thinking; now we understand each other, don't we. If the hotel dining room is usually crowded we would also like a reservation for a table for four. Even though we are only two travelers? That's right, thank you for being so thoughtful. The thing is: we don't want to share the table. Then a reservation for a flight to Ruzyně at around four p.m. Really, even an American travel agency should know the names of the airports in Communist countries! Ruzyně, in Prague. Prag. Praha. We'd have to stop in Schönefeld, outside of Berlin? Passing through East Berlin doesn't especially bother us. And now what about that car rental, have we forgotten? The circumstances have changed, we don't think we'll be able to manage that. Impossible, but thanks anyway, *as the actress said to the bishop.* What's that, you want to send a telegram to a Communist country so that at eight p.m. on the 20th there'll be a car waiting for us from the people *who try harder*? The same way you're trying? You know what, we are going to send you a postcard. Do we have our visa? We do. International driver's license? Yup. The bill goes to the bank? It does. Linen too hot to wear when it's 75° out? You'd be amazed how cool it keeps you. Try Bloomingdales. No, thank *you!*

II.

A good hour before the Fifth Avenue department stores are overrun with people on their lunch breaks, Mrs. Cresspahl is to be found as a customer in a luggage department. It was supposed to have been Abercrombie & Fitch but someone from Czechoslovakia shot himself there on Friday the week before last. We would have recognized the door as the elevator went past. About this store, we'd say: It's maybe 3 percent cheaper here.

Is it the linen suit, the crocodile leather handbag, the footwear from Switzerland? Can you tell from her hairdo that a Signor Boccaletti has taken this customer into his care? Whatever the reason, the manager approaches to serve this client in person. So much for the commission for the younger salesladies. Good morning, she wishes us; gorgeous weather, she calls the shining dirt outside the windows; what can she do for us, she asks.

Hello too. We'd like two large suitcases, here's the size. They should look as shabby as possible, please.

What? You want low-quality merchandise in a store like this?

Like they're made from a worn-out carpet. But solid, and each with two wraparound straps, and locks that even at first sight can clearly be opened with bare hands.

I think I'm beginning to see what you mean.

These might be all right. But only if this distinguished establishment also carries two aluminum shells that can fit perfectly into them.

I see I see!

That's what we want. We've seen how a gentleman by the name of Professor Erichson prepares for his travels, and we liked it. We're adopting this D. E.'s practices, you might say.

When the customer requests delivery to Riverside Drive, a less respectable address, the full-figured woman betrays a certain hesitation at the sight of the checkbook we've opened. Decision time, my good woman. We look her right in the eye; she's facing the choice between more than two hundred dollars in revenue and not trusting us. The bank that the check is drawn on is two blocks away. If the lady decides she wants to call that bank, we'll have to allow it. She has the right to request our employer's address; the right to ask Mrs. Lazar if we're creditworthy; we could be mired knee-deep in suspicion of fraud. At this precise moment in our negotiations, she decides to smile. Is it dramaturgically justified? It clearly is, because now she tells us: I can see it in your face, you'd rather break a leg than cheat an old woman! Believe me, I can judge people . . . ,

And since it's true, we would, we give her a good look when she comes marching into the store's restaurant—every inch the supervisor who can set her own lunch breaks, but then turning into a kind and friendly woman, somewhat harried, telling us about her insomnia, no pills help. Her name is Mrs. Collins, she lives in Astoria, Queens. What a coincidence! There was something else she wanted to say: it was a week ago today that a man came into the store, in one of those South American hats, he bought suitcases like you, Mrs. Cresspahl. You understand, forty years helping people choose suitcases, you wouldn't believe what . . . I certainly do believe it. Six hundred dollars, paid in cash. And the next day he came back, asked for me especially, said he liked the service he'd been given . . . Not as much as I did, Mrs. Collins! And introduced himself as the impresario of a ballet troupe—such people do exist! Of course they do. He wanted a present for every ballerina, a reward, a bonus, I don't know; came to $2,000 altogether. That's a sale you like to make! You're perfectly happy to accept a credit card! We don't carry more than three tens around on the streets of New York either, Mrs. Collins. And the next day it bounced. A stolen card. A two-thousand-dollar loss! We don't like to have to go to the management either. There, you see, Mrs. Cresspahl? I just wanted to tell you that after we gave each other that look before, will you forgive me?

III.

The New York Times has taken a look into people's wallets in New York and northeastern New Jersey. A factory worker in that area, assuming an average hourly wage of $3.02, has to slave away for one hour and forty-four minutes for a rib steak in a restaurant.

The Bratislava conference has swept into the mists all the daily fare that's been coming from the Moscow press—the suspected counterrevolution, anti-Communist plots, etc. What does *Pravda* suggest? That none but the imperialist "enemies of Socialism" are to blame for the fact that such a debate has arisen at all.

At LaGuardia Airport they've opened a STOL runway—Short Take-Off and Landing. Want to bet D. E.'s going to take us for a look at the thing next Saturday?

IV.

When Mrs. Collins came running back into the restaurant, she had a message. Would we be so kind as to call New York, such-and-such number? Thanks, Mrs. Collins.

But actually Employee Cresspahl was angry. She hadn't told anyone at the bank where she was going to buy luggage this Tuesday morning; for a moment she had the intolerable idea that someone was following her. *That she might be under surveillance!*

There's a remedy for that. What are all the things the Czech word *hrozný* means? Terrible, horrible, frightful, appalling, dreadful, gruesome, harrowing. And what personal name does *hrozný* remind you of? *Hrozná doba*, time of terror. *Hrozná bída*, unspeakable misery. *Hrozná zima*, terrible cold. *Hrozná počasí*, frightful weather.

By the time she gets to *to jsou plané hrozby*, "they're only warning shots," she can think calmly again and arrive at the idea that someone might have gone into her office and looked at the desk calendar. It's written right there: the time, the name of the store. And what is this time, in which she is out and about? It is within the span of time she has rented to the bank. And what was she doing in said time? Buying luggage for a trip that the bank is sending her on, a trip she'll moreover be compensated for. That's what Anita would say. You see how docile a person gets once they've become an employee, Anita.

V.

The address was "good," a nice place in the Thirties on Park Avenue, a lawyer's office. We first met Mr. Josephberg at one of Countess Albert Seydlitz's parties—a man you can go off into a corner and speak German with, about Kurt Tucholsky, one of his former clients in Germany; about Tilla Durieux, who alas kept marrying men other than Mr. Josephberg. "For the actor posterity weaves no wreaths": these husbands were clearly the exceptions. Then D. E. heard me mention his name and gave us another connection to him: this man, ennobled by emigration at the very beginning, February 1933, is D. E.'s lawyer. And now he's ours. Anyone D. E. trusts, we trust.

– *Is it ready?*: Mrs. Cresspahl asks from a phone booth in the Grand Central post office, should she come right away? – *Mr. Josephberg urgently requests your presence*: his secretary confirms, formally, as if she's forgotten all my appearances with Marie in her waiting room. Or is it supposed to be sarcastic? Because of course you need to be there in person to sign something? It's a quick hop on the subway running under Lexington Avenue. And it's a happy occasion. After Anita told me about an American school in the south part of West Berlin, we've added an addendum to the Cresspahl will.

Anyone taking a trip should leave behind a last will and testament. I hereby bequeath everything I own to my daughter Marie Cresspahl, born July 21, 1957, in Düsseldorf, the daughter of railway inspector Jakob Wilhelm Joachim Abs. The life insurance policy number is. Marie is requested to keep until her twenty-fifth birthday all the Mecklenburg books with a date of printing before 1952. The child is to be brought up by Mrs. Efraim Blumenroth.

That was right, and it was wrong. Mrs. Blumenroth lives on Riverside Drive, so Marie could keep her school, her homeland; children will survive with the Blumenroths, even if they lack a mother of Jewish descent. How could I dream that Anita would be prepared to do without trips, for Marie! So now we've worked it out this way: A lady in Berlin-Friedenau, tried and found true for twenty years, will be responsible for bringing up the child; the child's legal guardian, however, will be D. E., who is required to go to Berlin in person four times a year and check whether everything is being arranged properly for the child. That's what I was going to sign, and I was glad it was ready.

VI.

– How are you feeling today, Mrs. Cresspahl?

– Fine, thanks, Mr. Josephberg.

– Heart? Circulation?

– I had no idea you were taking up medicine, Doctor! Yes, I'm all right. Maybe a little tired from work.

– Please forgive me for not being able to talk to you today the same way I've so enjoyed in our earlier conversations.

– Let's get it over with, Doctor. Is someone suing me?

– It's worse than that, Mrs. Cresspahl. Please forgive an old man for making a personal remark, based on what he feels he knows about your life.

– All right.

– This is going to be the worst thing you'll have heard since your father passed away.

– All right!

– The last will and testament of Dr. Dietrich Erichson states that you are to be the first person notified in the event of his death.

– He's dead.

– He died in a plane crash near Helsinki-Vantaa Airport, Finland. On Saturday. At eight a.m.

– What kind of plane was it.

– A Cessna.

– He's licensed to fly a Cessna!

– Both Finnish and American police have identified him beyond a doubt.

– People are incinerated in plane crashes.

– Indeed. The doctors estimate that Mr. Erichson may have lived for five minutes after the impact. Without regaining consciousness of his situation.

– Consciousness of being smashed to bits and on fire!

– Yes. Forgive me, Mrs. Cresspahl.

– This is the kind of thing that *The New York Times* would report.

– The government that employed the deceased voiced a wish to have the news suppressed.

– How do they identify someone who's been incinerated?

– From the teeth.

– Why couldn't it be a bullet in the chest? An injection? A stabbing!

– Clearly the deceased had been instructed to leave a copy of his dental records where it would be readily available.

– Why am I hearing about this only today.

– Because the American board of inquiry had to fly from Washington to Helsinki.

– That's ten hours!

– Because the gentlemen in question preferred to release the news of his death only today.

– A photograph!

– There are no photographs of the site of the accident.

– There are official photographs, taken by the board of inquiry.

– If you make a formal request, I can contact the authorities responsible and . . .

– Now I believe it.

– Mr. Erichson left everything to you, Mrs. Cresspahl. His mother has the right to live in the house until she passes away. Aside from the real estate and monetary assets, there are various copyrights—

– No.

– If you'd prefer it, I can inform Mrs. Erichson.

– No.

– My deepest sympathies, Mrs. Cresspahl. Please be assured that anything you need in the coming weeks—

– Could you ask Mrs. Gottlieb to walk me to my office? Without telling her what . . . what you've just told me?

VII.

The office—the only place in New York where you can be alone, behind a locked door. When someone dies, whatever you do or were doing turns into a reproach; playing in the water and flirting at Jones Beach. In a storm Jakob's mother used to set a lit candle on the table and pray. We were in such a hurry when we were hunting through Minneapolis that we assumed the edge of the wall frayed by the broad noonday light, the surface of light beyond it, was the famous river and we didn't look closer. And that was fine, because we were definitely going to take a trip to Finland together next year. He wanted to fly over the Alps with us; we had a date in Rome. According to Protestant belief, God can see what's written on airplanes. The aggressive honking of horns on the streets of Manhattan—how could we ever have felt homesick for sounds that just come from rudeness. Also, the planes rising along a diagonal offend an eye accustomed to order, to the perpendicular. A child is sitting comfortably on the floor, leaning a shoulder against the wall, raising and lowering something while making two connected sounds, almost like a melody. A rhythm in which a tired body unwillingly feels itself as nothing but a firing of nerves in the brain, with a feeling of complete despair, keening helplessly with those two sounds each pulling the other behind it. A heavy pendulum, blocked in its swing just before it snaps, the pauses lengthening ever so indiscernibly slightly.

In my day it took eight hours to fly to New York. Sometimes, when I arrived in Hamburg from Copenhagen on summer afternoons, the blocked light in the passport room felt like home. When I like something, *D. E.'s glad.* Guh-ZEE-neh! people say, with a pleading tone in the second syllable, like they're trying to trap me with the name; D. E. does it differently, I like hearing him. *Big Maries dead, lil Maries a-waitin for D. E.* He said "*My daughter*"; once. – *Gimme another, Mr. Pharmacist, he said. An she did.* And the white ball, like a cherry bomb, dangerously heading straight for a closed eye, cheating the gaze, making the brain echo, but sometimes nice, like birds flying, white midsize birds, maybe seagulls. There are people who don't mind flying only because the situation includes the possibility of an unexpected crash, yes look out and that's it your life's over, and so the moment, like arguably every other moment, contains a demand that you organize and settle your personal affairs once and for all, including your death. Those who adopt such an attitude cite philosophical reasons. D. E. was flying to Athens, way down below a tiny little patch of prepared ground amid a boundless body of water, – Will we hit the target? I can see what they mean about helicopters; we'd want to at least hear our own crash. Comes back from a trip and suddenly knows, on top of everything else, about the Gothic origins of the churches of Prague buried under the Jesuit Baroque. He was definitely there. Took a look around as a favor to me. "Jan Hus and the Symbolic Function of the Chalice for the Utraquists." Imagining: being on a flight over JFK and never leaving the airport; the child that I was. *I expect to die very soon; would you permit me to make arrangements that would keep you cared for? At least on behalf of the child?* Lying down, seeing the white sky lagging behind, swept by the dry branches of the treetops. You're bad at suffering, D. E.! You turn everything into cause and responsibility and pay what you owe accordingly, then forget people. – Why should I suffer, Gesine? A bus has a long breath. Airplanes grind the air, don't they? Today I'm the cat waiting for the host who'll disappear someday—scabby, tunneled through with pus, limping, blind in one eye. DOES THE AIR OVER MANHATTAN MAKE YOU UNHAPPY? IT MAKES US TWICE AS UNHAPPY. A year ago the old dial tone in the telephone gave up the ghost—since April 1967 there's been a bell-like, purring, plump tone after the 9. The variations for Goldberg on Saturday night, they were already D. E.'s dirge.

VIII.

– Please free the line, Mrs. Cresspahl. We have an international person-to-person call for you.

  – This is a test. This is a test.

  – Anita! You're calling me at the bank, you know.

  – There's something we need to talk about. It'd be too risky with Marie around.

  – Indicative, Anita. It *is* too risky.

  – Helsinki airport, indicative?

  – So I'm told.

  – Was it yours?

  – If I can believe it, it was mine.

  – Do you want me to go to Helsinki?

  – There are no remains.

  – But there is a death.

  – Anita, he had a piece of paper on him whenever he traveled that said in the four major world languages: To be cremated at the place or location of death with no music speeches flowers or any religious or other service *whatsoever*. You know, so he wouldn't put me to any unnecessary trouble when he died.

  – Tell me what I can do.

  – Come to Prague in two weeks. My vacation.

  – *Ty znayesh'.*

  – Tell me what to do.

  – Does Marie know?

  – When I tell her it'll destroy her.

  – Let me think about it until tomorrow morning. Can you hold out till then?

IX.

– Well, Mrs. Erickssen!

  – Evening, Wes.

  – How's Mr. Erickssen?

  – He's fine. Away, I'm afraid. But fine.

  – What can I do for you, Mrs. Erickssen?

  – A drink.

– Most certainly. But what kind of drink, that is the question.

– Something to pick me up, Wes.

– Mrs. Erickssen, with all due respect: could it be that you need something different to pick you up?

– Anything.

– I'll get you a taxi, Mrs. Erickssen.

X.

Waiting at Riverside Drive, of course, is airmail from Finland. A map of Meklenburg Ducatus, Auctore Ioanne Blaeuw excudit, excusably a bit naive in its geography, with Muritz Lacus blithely combined with Calpin Lacus, but Fleesen Lake still awaits discovery; a friendly yellow griffon appears on the coat of arms instead of the Mecklenburg *oxhead*. Still, there's no doubt about the Mare Balticum: two jaunty galleons sail the sea and right by the brightly colored gold-rimmed windrose above the Bay of Wismar you can read what in truth it really should be called: Oost Zee. Above to the right you can picture Finland.

If you put on your makeup until Marie gets home and then sit looking out the window the whole time—maybe you can get through it.

We're in time, just barely. On WRVR, 106.7 on your radio dial, "Just Jazz" is starting. D. E. asked us to tape it for him. How could we forget.

August 7, 1968 Wednesday

It's done. We've deceived Marie.

The child sleeps through the night while at two a.m. her mother goes shopping on Broadway; there was everything—hashish, heroin, hits, but no sleeping pills. This too has been known to happen: instead of helping make breakfast, the mother stays hidden behind closed doors, Marie saying goodbye in a cheerful voice: *Walk, don't run! A fall is no fun!*

Eagle-Eye Robinson steps out of the elevator with a letter in his hand— airmail, special delivery, stamps from Suomi. The text begins: Dear Ilona! Then the "Ilona" was crossed out and replaced with: Gesine. Oh, your jokes, D. E.

At the bank, the room for the young gods Wendell, Milo, and Gelliston has been cleared out, down to the floorboards. In Cresspahl's office, the furniture has been stacked into a tower and covered with a tarp. The telephone, complete with its connection box, has disappeared.

– We sent you a telegram: the girls in de Rosny's lobby claim. – Here's the carbon!

Dear Mrs. Cresspahl due to damaged cables your section of the sixteenth floor is closed stop we will inform you as soon as you can return to work stop this will not count against your vacation time stop *have a good time*

Employee Cresspahl requests an appointment with Mr. de Rosny. On the spot. At once!

It's her own fault. She should've realized that the telephone exchange keeps a list of all international calls. Has to keep a list. Someone heard Anita and me, a second person translated it, a third person put us in their files, a fourth person explained us to three more people at a meeting. *Hrozebný, hrozivý, hrozící!* Threatening, menacing, impending! *Hrozím se toho,* it terrifies me! *Hrozba trestem,* threat of punishment!

De Rosny sends word that he is very busy at the moment. During her stubborn two-hour wait, Employee Cresspahl realizes that, all the same, her lapse of discretion has resulted in a thoughtful gesture. De Rosny has invested in this employee. It truly would be a little loss for him if she broke down. A machine is overloaded so he turns it off for a while. *Dům hrozí sesutím,* and we hope it does! The house is threatening to collapse!

Before lunchtime, de Rosny coughs up an appointment: Monday, August 19, at nine a.m.

Hrozný?, python! *Hrozitánský,* monster!

– My best regards to the vice president: Employee Cresspahl says. She can see that he's gone to a lot of trouble. At least six movers hauling desks at the crack of dawn. If it's a game, she'll play along. She won't set foot in this building before August 19! *Hrozná doba.*

We need to apologize to Wes. Wes sells alcoholic drinks. Drunks disgust him. Mrs. Cresspahl may have looked that way yesterday.

– Wes, I just want to say, about—
– *My dear Mrs. Erickssen!* Don't mention it! All bartenders hand out medicine; you needed a taxi, you needed to go to bed, I could see that with the naked eye!

– Send me the bill, doctor.

– I'll send it to the professor, Erickssen. *A sweet man.* The kind of husband a woman can only dream of.

– Goodbye, Wes. *Thank you kindly.*

– Allow me the honor, Mrs. Erickssen.

– In the middle of the day? Unaccompanied by a man?

– Today I am the man accompanying you, Mrs. Erickssen.

D. E. spent parts of his life here—parts he liked. We were together here. This is the best place to reread the letter from Finland.

Even on rereading it's news of a trip. Finnish neutrality. The Port of Helsinki. What professional business brought D. E. there?

Eventually "Ilona" sticks out—not a woman, an abbreviation, a hint at a code. With just a pencil from Wes and the back of an Irish betting slip it's tricky business. A machine would crack it in five minutes but Mrs. Cresspahl spends two hours deciphering D. E.'s ILoNa.

D. E. has been to Prague many times. (But never with a passport that had my name in it, Gesine.) So the best thing for us to do at passport control in Ruzyně Airport is act like we have all the time in the world, since the young men behind the bulletproof glass are going to read our documents the way other people read poetry. D. E. recommends that we keep a car while we're there—it's a hassle to take the 22 to the Czernin Palace, the Foreign Ministry, especially when the streetcar bangs into the loose rails in the city center or is driven downhill in Mediterranean style.

– Does he always write such tricky letters?: Wes says, refilling his friend Erickssen's wife's glass after half an hour. And does she want to take Erickssen's ticket for Ireland now? It's ready for him.

Once at the Czernin Palace, D. E. recommends a wine bar called u Loretu, with outdoor tables. Diagonally across from a café where an uncle will inquire, in a doctorly manner, into the condition of our shoes, at which point he will adjust Marie's sandals and repair at most a torn strap. He will offer us wine as if we were in Italy.

The best thing to do, then, would be to find an apartment on Paris Street in Prague. After the opening of the ČSSR to capitalist tourism in 1963, our money will make us welcome. We should be careful of young men who come talk to us without looking at us—they just want our foreign currency.

So we might be an irresistible object of interest to craftsmen, but as for turning up any paint, Gesine, a faucet, a windowpane—God help you. You'll probably take frequent trips to Frankfurt, on a commuter flight that rarely runs. If you need onions, for instance. But if we know you, you'll have friends in a village somewhere within a month, Gesine. And all the better to eat you with in Frankfurt, Gesine. *À dieu, yours, truly*—

– Give my regards to Professor Ericksen!: Wes requests when I get up to leave, and he walks alongside Mrs. Cresspahl behind his forty-foot-long bar until she gets to the door, feeling the awed looks of the remaining gentlemen on her back. A guest of honor, that lady. Food and drinks on the house. Wife of an aerospace engineer or something.

Mrs. Cresspahl goes for a walk, all the way to the Upper West Side. On Forty-Second Street she passes a shop selling *Der Spiegel*, but she'd rather stay true to the old man on Ninety-Sixth Street. – I've kept it aside for you for a long time, sister!: he says. "That just as when you were alive / the clocks still run, the bells still ring..."

Waiting at Riverside Drive is de Rosny's telegram, signed by Kennicott II; starting at seven o'clock, Radio WKCR will be bringing us "Jazz and the Avant-Garde," with pieces by Eaton, Monk, Tristano, and Taylor, we'll tape them for D. E. There are some illnesses where music is life-threatening.

– Mrs. Cresspahl, Berlin is on the line.

– Gesine! Say something! Let me hear your voice!

– Your school friend Cresspahl speaking.

– Say the date, the day of the week!

– Anita, why are you crying.

– Say something!

– Wednesday. August 7th.

– It's really you.

– Unfortunately.

– I've been calling all day, every hour, and the exchange keeps saying: This line has been disconnected.

– Construction in the bank.

– I was shaking in my shoes!

– I'm not like my mother, Anita. As long as I have a child I need to take care of, I'll try to live. I don't have a husband I can leave the child to either.

– Promise.

– Yes. I promise. Now your advice please.

– Are you still going to Prague, with Marie?

– If it's up to me.

– It'll destroy her, like you said. At first I was in favor. But there's no coffin for her to look at.

– And she'll hold it against me for ten years that I waited a single day to tell her.

– Try. In Prague, after the 20th, I'll help you. Do you give me permission to go to Helsinki?

– If I knew why. Nothing's there.

– That's what I want to see for myself.

– But only tell me about it when I ask you. Not until Prague.

– *Ty znayesh'*, Gesine. What else are you doing today?

– What's a double widow who couldn't go to either funeral supposed to do? I'm listening to music.

– That's poison, Gesine!

The person scratching at the door is our Eagle-Eye Robinson, with two large, expensively wrapped packages and the business card, the warm greetings, the home address of Mrs. Collins, Astoria, Queens. Yesterday morning I was still alive. And there's Marie behind Mr. Robinson—enthusiastically looking forward to unwrapping the suitcases. Now the lying starts.

– Why are you wearing sunglasses *indoors*, Gesine? "*Indoors*"...

– "*Im Hause.*" There're workmen in the bank. I banged my eye.

– Did you go to Dr. Rydz?

– No, another doctor. I'm supposed to rest my eyes like this for three days.

– Does it hurt?

– Yes. He gave me pills too.

– I was wondering... But are you tired?

– Go ahead and ask. I'm just slow.

– Is today going to be a normal evening?

– Should we do something different?

– I'll cook, even though it's your turn. It just dawned on me that something else must have been going on during that August of 1951 when Cresspahl wanted you out of the way in Wendisch Burg.

– In July the Stasi searched Cresspahl's house. The pretext was that he'd started making a lot of money from his work, more than his pension. The truth was that this state couldn't get it into its head that it could wrong a person a second time, and a third time, and this Cresspahl would still try to follow the law. But your something else had started earlier.

– Is it anything to do with Jakob?

– With Jakob too. Because it's reciprocal: the same way I've liked a lot of people, one or two have liked me.

– I know one person, who's flying on Scandinavian—

– On Finnair.

– and looking forward to seeing you.

– And to seeing you. You're even prettier than I am.

– Gesine! The Papenbrock hair!

– Widow Papenbrock was feeling crabby about the Cresspahls. When the state power, after Albert's death, confiscated the mansion in town, the warehouse too, the *ol lady* waited for us to invite her to move in. Cresspahl wouldn't risk his little finger for that. And it would have meant the Church taking over the house. She left for Lüneberg, where there was still some of Albert's real estate. We took her to the Hamburg line since we were hoping this would be our last goodbye. She didn't wish me especially well, but she still said, despite herself: At least you got our hair.

– And your lovely breasts, nice and high.

– Marie! What a thing to notice! Anyway, my breasts were just hypothetical among the young men of 1950. None had seen them bare.

– They wanted to.

– About that I was unaccommodating. Which damaged my reputation, because whenever someone dreamed up an affair with me and it didn't happen, he just made one up and spread the story around anyway.

– It's like weeds.

– They never stop growing. One of these boys was a literary type; he slipped a piece of paper with a quote on it into my bag, something like: "Not that Gesine had turned into a highly sensitive woman of delicate feeling all at once. She remained the way she was. Self-confident and timid, voracious and cowardly, longing for all 'the higher and finer things in life' that were starting to be shown in the cinematograph theaters." It took me forever to figure that one out! It was a Gesine in a novel.

– I'm sorry to hear that.

– Go look at our cookbooks—there's one from 1901, published by Appleton and Company in New York, *European and American Cuisine*, and written by the proprietress and president of Brooklyn Cooking College, now what was her name?

– Gesine Lemcke. I don't like that.

– You have the same name as other children too.

– I wish no one but you had your name.

– The reason I was given it was that once upon a time Cresspahl wanted to run away, across land and sea, with Gesine Redebrecht from Malchow. You got yours from Jakob's mother.

– One part of it's true. You were self-confident. Are.

– That's easy when Jakob's watching over you like a little sister.

– No kisses after dance class?

– I was waiting when it came to that too.

– Are you trying to teach me some kind of lesson here?

– You want me to tell you stories. I also had admirers who were satisfied when I vaguely knew they existed. One was my classmate for almost four years. In 1951 he wrote on the blackboard: "'Effi Briest,' a very pretty name I feel because it has so many 'e's and 'i's—those are the two fine, delicate vowels." Theodor Fontane.

– You knew who that was.

– And since I withheld what he wanted from him too, I think I'll at least not tell you his name. Actually I should start being vague with names in general from now on. When Cresspahl hustl—arranged some Danish business for Knoop, Gesine was invited aboard a boat, a yacht in Wismar harbor, for the toast. We don't want to cause trouble for the guy over his unpatriotic dealings with Communist Germany; but I'm grateful to him for a cruise to Denmark.

– Past the East German coast guard.

– They didn't have a wall floating in the water yet, in 1950. A Danish sailor can do anything, and will even smuggle a girl on board. As long as Cresspahl knew about it, and as long as everything stayed proper between the young lady and the older gentleman (around thirty), no kisses on the cheek, I was happy to learn navigation.

– Gesine, you were on vacation in Denmark when you were seventeen! That's why you showed me Bornholm!

– It wasn't a good idea to talk about it, though. What a Mecklenburg sailor can do, and does, is talk in his cups—the devil take him. So here was another story involving me, it was pure dumb luck that the police didn't get wind of it.

– There was the boy who lived upstairs from the Jerichow pharmacy.

– No name for him either. But I had a hard time getting him to realize that if he has a crush on someone who sees herself as long since taken, that's his business. They sometimes act like they have a right to you, boys do.

– Self-confident.

– Sometimes a bit too much. I liked to go dancing, because it meant I got to move—

– And because people like to do what they're good at.

– not because of the hands on my back. When two boys locked horns over me, I let them settle it between themselves—pretended not to notice. I wasn't anyone's property! But now here's another story about Cresspahl's daughter. Sometimes people mix up their own desires with other people's, you know. The truth is: I never led anyone on. I could never stand those anguished looks.

– There were the overnight stays at the Pagenkopfs'.

– And Lockenvitz sometimes came to Jerichow, when he could still show friendship, and stayed until morning. There were nights I was under the same roof as three men.

– Pagenkopf, Lockenvitz, Cresspahl . . .

– And Jakob. You're right, he's in a different category. But it was Jakob who tried to defend my good name in Jerichow on Town—on Stalin Street. All I know is that he came home bloodied; the next morning I was put on a train to far-off southeast Mecklenburg, to visit the Niebuhrs. How shocked Klaus was to see me handle the H-Jolle dinghy like a man! Luckily for me, he'd already gotten together with the girl from the teacher-Babendererdes, Ingrid. The other Ingrid, you're thinking of Ingrid Bøtersen. Four weeks with them on Wendisch Burg's Upper Lake and Town Lake before Cresspahl sent word. I found out right away what everyone in Cresspahl's house was trying to keep from me: Jakob had spent eighteen days in the basement under the Gneez district court for assault and battery.

– I had a boy who got into fights for me too once.

– Do you like how it feels?

– When someone insults me I'd rather take care of it myself.

– See? And now Jakob had something that would stay on his criminal record for several years.

– Did he do that a lot, get into fights?

– Don't worry, Marie. We both learned our lesson that time. I stopped going dancing except at school events. I would have to say that my conduct with men, since 1951, has been practically unimpeachable.

– Is that "pruning," what you're doing now?

– That is pruning. Someone once offered me a private lounge car! A West German Railways one!

– What, like Hitler had? You're lying, Gesine!

– Hitler didn't come from money. He just stole from the state. No, believe it: a real live millionaire brought me up to the mountaintop, showed me the treasures of the world, and said: All this is yours. The mountain was Platform Three at the Düsseldorf train station and the AllThisIsYours was a thing in which Hitler might have taken his fits for a spin. A kind of converted sleeping car.

– You and a millionaire!

– If you're a prosperous citizen of the USA on good terms with your government, there's nothing to keep you from stopping by the woods around Mönchengladbach and checking out how your army is working to defend Western Europe.

– And instead your eye is caught by a secretary with the Papenbrock hair, sitting prim and proper at her desk, knows her way around a typewriter too, has a gellegant Jersey wool sweater on, so you offer her—with her superiors' permission, of course—a modest railcar that you're forced to ride through West Germany since the rails are in such bad shape in the US.

– Envy is an unbecoming quality in a bank, Marie. That's a message from de Rosny *himself.*

– I'd've liked to see it.

– What's to see? A cramped four-room apartment, cabinets like on a sailboat, train phone, telex.

– Paintings on the wall. Framed. And seven guest rooms.

– One guest room—mostly occupied by the valet, who also does the cooking when the boss hosts a dinner. Other than that: a double bed. After six months gallivanting around that would've been the price.

– Would he have married you?

– I could've counted on a severance package after two years. He's still riding the rails from Munich to Hamburg every day, or maybe Hamburg to Munich. On special occasions they'll pull him through the Ruhr instead of the usual into Frankfurt and back out of Frankfurt. From Wunstorf they can couple him to the express to Regensburg. He forgave me, by the way.

– Can I ask about Taormina?

– I liked traveling with him; you could really talk to him at the table. He also seemed to grasp that I do what I decide to do, not what my hormones or glands tell me to. He made way too much of an overnight trip to Taormina, in separate rooms.

– And then came the man you'd been waiting for the whole time.

– Then came Jakob.

– You were . . . twenty-three.

– And a half. Now since you're talking about handsomely placed breasts, I should probably warn you that it's considered a bit ridiculous nowadays for a woman to wait so long. I'm sure you don't want people laughing at your mother.

– Please, dear lady, I ask you. Everything we tell each other is in strictest confidence! And would you be so kind as to make yourself at home, though I am retiring to bed. You can play the variations for Goldberg as late as you want, and the quodlibet twice.

I've never read a newspaper at midnight before. In East Germany, the press and the TV have suddenly stopped hurling their trash at the Czechoslovakians. They do suppress that the custodian was booed in Bratislava, even told *Damoi!* go home! The official report is: "Passers-by waved and called out friendly greetings again and again."

Last night a radar system for the flight paths around New York failed.

Planes circled in the air above JFK for more than a hundred minutes, unable to land.

We're flying soon too. And actually we've read the paper after midnight plenty of times! On Eastern European time. After we've come home.

– *What kind of a caller are you? Can't you dial the number for the time first?*

– Sorry, Gesine. It's just me. Anita.

– Okay.

– I was off by an hour with the time difference. Are you—

– I'm okay, as they say here; in German it'd be different. At the moment, the worst thing is that D. E. knew about Jakob. Knew that Jakob was the only man I wanted to live with, to have near me. Men do like to be the one and only, and if possible the first.

– Maybe he wasn't stupid. Maybe he was what your friend Anita calls a good person.

– He was. But that he knew—

– He was very happy he got to spend six years with you. Put that on the balance sheet too.

– Anita, I need you to keep telling me things like that. For a while yet.

– *Ty znayesh'.*

August 8, 1968 Thursday

Delivering a death announcement.

The buses threatened on D. E.'s stretch of road to New Jersey are now running: the whole lower deck is higher than the driver's seat; no smoking. The windows are tinted so dark blue that the landscape is barely visible. And so, memories. – *Oh, you can't buy memories!*: Esther once said. *And you can't get rid of them either.*

The bus comes out of the tunnel south of Hoboken. That's where, years ago, D. E. took the child and me to an apple-juice shop at the marina where the men were eating mussels from stoneware bowls and tossing the shells into the sawdust on the floor. Marie was studying him seriously, her friend and host. Back then she was still a child who might take a candy from a lady stranger on a bus but would then, after she ate it, hand back the wrapper—*to keep our city clean*. She was so delighted when he demonstrated the flick of the wrist she could use to send her shells whacking into the wood paneling. – Chock!: D. E. said. I guess he did have fun with us.

South Newark. He invited us to Newark with a topography: On Sunday mornings Newark consists of a church respectable citizens emerge from with calm expressions on their faces. Also worth mentioning is a statue behind the station, immortalizing in white and treacly fashion the first and to date only American citizen to have been sainted: Frances Xavier Cabrini. The main street is called Broad Street, located four hundred steps away, comporting itself like the local idea of *downtown!* (sing that word)— the setting for a parade caricaturing Polish peasant costumes. It's called the PATH, as you probably know. Van Cortlandt Straat, then left. *Yours, truly, D. E.*

We went there to meet D. E. in rattling icy weather, under the Hudson, to a scabby landscape piled high with never-decomposing garbage at the edge of a putrescent river. D. E. had his Polish parade to show us in Newark, with its dark-skinned participants marching like clockwork; then a cellar in which you could eat pea soup with pieces of ham à la Mecklenburg. Herr Professor Dr. Erichson was so happy when we ordered seconds! He was amused to see that a mother knows the precise moment when a frozen child's nose will start to run once she's inside and warm; Marie trustingly stuck out her face right into the napkin being held at the ready. D. E. enjoyed being with us, there's that too.

It's a surly Mrs. Erichson who opens one wing of the double door to D. E.'s stately farmhouse. Her expression is stiff, smooth white hair is stiffly sticking out from under her black riding cap. Jacket, pants, boots, and bow at the collar of her blouse are black. She's already had one visit today, from a pair of gentlemen in sports jackets who pulled something out of their pockets on a chain and quickly tucked it away again, as if they'd actually showed it to her. They wanted to take a look at D. E.'s study, maybe rummage around a bit too; she showed them the door. Now she's in a bad mood, and a little anxious. In a foreign country you need to show deference to people sent by the authorities, don't you think, Gesine?

She's relieved to hear that she'd acted within her rights. Reluctantly, because she was just about to go out riding, she brings the second visiting party of the day across the hall, opens the kitchen door, marvels at but allows the visitor to lead her into the living room instead and seat her safely in an armchair so that she won't fall at the moment of the news that her only son, the focus and pride of her old life, has allegedly and by hearsay met his death in northeast Europe, in a plane he's known how to fly for four years. She sits there as if waiting for an execution. Then comes the blow, and the slump of the head and the sagging of the body to make it look smaller. Then, all in Platt:

– Dyou believe it, Gesine?

– Im supposed to. I have to.

– Burned up n buried n now theres nothin?

– Thats how he wanted it.

– Now you can jus stick me in tha ground too.

– Youre gonna live a long time yet. You were off to go ridin somewhere n put the fear a God into that horse. You need to take care a his business.

– But I got a letter from im, written on Sunday!

– Postmarked.

– Written, see?

– I see it. But its your sons lawyer, sayin—

– Dyou have an inheritance certificate with you, Gesine?

– Lets not have any a that.

– You won' kick an ol woman outta her house.

– You can stay here forever.

– Are you pregnant, Gesine?

– Nope.

– Dyou wish you were?

– How could I bring up another child without im.

– Littl Marie. Hows she holdin up?

– Ive been afraid to—

– Can you come stay with me?

– We need to go to Prague.

– But he just died.

– He wouldve wanted it that way: first you do what you need to do.

– Jå. Thats how he is. An once youre done with Prague?

– Marie has to go to school. You should come stay in New York.

– Thats so far away from im. What, youre leavin?

– The taxis waiting outside. I have to catch the bus. Maries waitin at home. You can come with.

– No. Im gonna go for a ride.

In Spring 1951, Robert Pius Pagenkopf enlisted with the Armed People's Police at the Aero-Club in Cottbus. He was the only one of the three hundred and seventy high-school students at that time to do so; a lot of students were leaving school after eleventh grade then, since many parents felt that that was the equivalent of diplomas from the old days when there'd been a one-year military service requirement. These young people decided to go to the West, most not realizing that compulsory military service was awaiting them there with open arms. Pius went for the other side. Since we'd only been acting like a married couple, he made the decision by himself.

I wantd to be alone, Gesine.

Pius, if I was bothering you—

Stop it, Gesine. You were the girl for me.

Pius, Id—

Its fine. It's just that, later, I always compared other girls to you. That wasn't good for me. Marriage is hard, Gesine.

Y'left me sittin alone at our desk.

You would have gone your own way after graduation, without me. I could tell we'd be separated, I wanted to break it off myself.

To be alone.

All this peace struggle shit, Gesine. They were right you know, Sieboldt and Gollantz.

Like there's no political reeducation in the army!

There it's service, Gesine. In the army my superior has to be able to believe what I tell him, and no member of the force can doubt that I believe it. There're no more winks, stiff smiles conveying and commending your lies in one. There I can think whatever I want and no one has to hear it.

That means you'd never have another friend, Pius.

I thought I still had you, Gesine. We'd managed to create that.

And what did you plan to do if there was a war?

Then I'd be where they pushed the button. In the end, what I did with the plane would be up to me—I'm in command, I decide.

Pius's first enlistment was for three whole years; a cold glory hung in the air around our desk with plenty of room left over for Student Cresspahl as she sat through the last year of school in 12-A-II, alone, in a much smaller room on the fourth floor—one of fifteen students, alone at her desk, with a window view of the cathedral and the courtyard. We tried to talk Pius into staying through the Abitur. Even his father, the functionary of merit in the party administration in Schwerin, was scared, notwithstanding the significant boost to his reputation this new "societal activity" on his son's part would give him. You can lose a son that way. Helene Pagenkopf stuck to weeping for weeks; when Pius took the woman in his arms and stroked her shoulders, you could see how big he'd grown. Six feet tall, plus another couple inches. When we said things about the advantages of a terminal certification of knowledge in the sciences and humanities, he smiled at us for still believing in such things. As if the science of equine dental anatomy, say, would be of any use in later life. Whatever physics he'd need in the coming years, the air force would take care of teaching him. Student Lockenvitz was jealous of Young Friend Pagenkopf for the tactical savvy of his plan, not so much for the course of action itself, which was not an option for him anyway, given his eyesight. And yet he too would talk to Pius, encouraging him to consider the value of a Latin proficiency certificate, recognized by universities around the world; then Pius looked stern, keeping his dark eyebrows rigid, apparently feeling pestered.

Pius's decision was such a rare jewel in the crown of the New School's educational aims that he could easily have slacked off for the rest of the year and still received final grades that matched his standing in January. But being lax and being Pius were two very different things. Pius stuck to the syllabus and thereby kept Student Cresspahl in the habit of schoolwork—the form that learning is meant to take in one's youth. The thing is, he knew what his future held, which gave him a perspective far wider than that of school. In a ninth-grade class in 1951, the FDJ had a competition for selling their newspaper, *Young World*; it was won by a resourceful fellow who deposited his whole bundle with Abel the fishmonger on Street of National Unity, which cost him some money but saved him from having to pester passersby. It was the talk of the day at school. Pius just shrugged. Made you feel like a kid next to him. In 11-A-I there was a boy named Eckart Pingel who avowed in Contemporary Studies: In the Soviet Union they also have the biggest pigs! That was going to take him down a notch in class; Bettina Selbich put in a request for disciplinary proceedings. The thing is, Ol' Pingel wasn't just any father, he was the foreman at the Panzenhagen sawmill—proletariat nobility. Word started going around the working men of Gneez that Pingel's Eckart was getting thrown out of school just for telling the truth. That was why he was allowed to talk his way out of trouble at the teacher's conference, invoking recent Soviet advances in breeding the common domestic pig. Bettina threw the excuse right back at his head; he could recite from the textbook his class had unearthed for him (his school class). Now it's true, Eckart Pingel avoided mentioning his scientific findings too often, but everyone knew it about him and he wore it as a badge of honor that he'd hit on it first. Pius laughed too, but just by snorting some air through his nose; it came across as rather disparaging. His belonging among us, as one of us, fell from him layer by layer like an onion; he looked at us as if from a great distance. He was almost grown-up. There were evenings he spent in the Danish Quarter—without telling his mother, but without making a secret of it either. Afterwards his body would smell different, and to his silent, eyebrow-raising surprise, his friend Cresspahl started expanding her morning toilette routine to include perfume. Pius also went to bars frequented by the railwaymen of Gneez, including the Linden Pub, where the women conductors sometimes danced on the tables. For the assembly to conclude the 1950–51 school year, Gabriel Manfras proposed that the FDJ school group "delegate" Youth Comrade Pagenkopf from its ranks for service in the Armed Police; Pius looked at him so hard and so long that Manfras, who in no way had the guts for such service, finally turned red in the face for once. Pius was "bidden farewell" by the students and faculty.

He went to Cottbus for military basic training, was accepted as a fighter pilot, promoted to PFC and then corporal; he signed one letter as a "cornet." Mrs. Selbich remained part of the life of 12-A-II, as homeroom teacher, and suggested to Student Cresspahl that she read to the class from his letters, so as to share the edification of Pagenkopf's patriotic example. Cresspahl was tempted. For the letters discussed how mail censorship was handled "in our outfit": the recruit had to hand in his private letters in the guardroom, unsealed. That makes a person careful about what he puts down. Another thing the recruit has to learn: that the Comrade NCOs read the contents of incoming letters aloud to one another with gusto and commentary—not so good when they're written by a woman who's not his mother. When it is his mother, that can turn out badly too, for instance if she writes that she's worried about her "child," who has now been un-masked as a momma's boy. – To hear the old-timers tell it, it's worse here than in the army: Pius told us in writing; he sent his news via civilian mail, contrary to regulations. Gesine would've loved to make all this public in class, as a model case of Stalinist vigilance. But she had the feeling Bet-tinikin would snatch the letter out of her hand the moment she brought it to school; it contained, among other things, forms of address like the Russian word for "little sister" (Pius was a year and a half older than her). She denied that they were corresponding.

Gesine had an awkward time with her own letters to Cottbus. First, she had to avoid calling him what she was used to calling him, because she didn't want to hang a nickname around his neck, especially with the extra weight that'd be added in the barracks—but for her he was "Pius"; he was "Robert" and "Rœbbing" for his mother. Second, how could she tell him in a letter that would be read by others that three "bourgeois" people from Gneez had been sent to take a course in Socialist orientation; of course they all distrusted one another; but as soon as they walked into their room in Schwerin the first one covered the keyhole, the second one blocked the window with his back, and they both gave the third one advice as he scoured the room for the microphones; they came back to Gneez after four weeks in total harmony, sworn friends, and were appointed revenue officer, dairy manager, and head of personnel at Panzenhagen. A whole new network of relationships (though well known in its essentials) was forming throughout the city—it sometimes no longer mattered that X had known Y for some twenty-odd years: now how could she write that without blowing his political credentials for forever and a day? That's why she was relieved when he asked again what'll happen to Abel the fishmonger in England: He'll turn into *Able*, so he'll change his shop sign to "Ebel," so then people will call him *Eeble*, and then he'll, and so forth. Glad, too. For she took this to mean that he was being taught English again, and in case of emergency might be able to transfer into civil aviation. The whole Pingel family had left in a westerly direction after Eckart's "early graduation," clearly not happy with the school—that was another item not suitable for correspondence. What she liked best was when Pius came to visit and went for walks with her around Gneez Lake and had brought her a present. Because Cresspahl was once again feeling up to exertions of paternal force and had privately threatened the tobacconists from Jerichow to Gneez if they ever sold his daughter something she might smoke. So Pius turned up with cigarettes from China, brand name Temple of Great Joy (men in Pius's squadron could volunteer for duty in that People's Republic). There's a photo from this visit—our only photograph.

In 1953, Gesine Cresspahl took up residence in the state of Hesse, West Germany, and was worried that she might have lost Pius, too, in the move. She had every reason to think that Pius had learned to disapprove of such freedom of movement; and surely he wasn't allowed to correspond with residents of enemy countries. But the old friendship was rust-free! Pius now sent his letters home to "My dears." Gesine was included among his dears, otherwise Helene Pagenkopf would much rather have kept writings from her son's hand than dutifully forwarded them to *Röbbertin sin Gesin*. In 1954 Pius extended his term of duty and became a professional officer, a lieutenant by Christmas, and Gesine complained to her Robertino (having finally brought herself around to that form of address) about how hard it was to get by with her English in an American-occupied province. By then Pius had his Himalayan cattle firmly under control—the Yak-18 for training, the Yak-11 for doing—and was allowed to come back from the Soviet Union; stationed in Drewitz: squad leader (acting). Gesine sent the elderly Mrs. Pagenkopf a tiny electric shaver that a young man might use; Pius was now flying MiG-15's—in formation, but one time on his own, which was why he was transferred to be in charge of parachutist training in 1955. Gesine thought this was a demotion and that Pius had been grounded, or *gegroundet*, as it was called in the hybrid language spoken where she was working now. That can happen to a person for health reasons or as punishment. So she was happy to hear that he was uninjured; he had taken his fighter on a joyride under the autobahn bridge that crosses Zern Lake west of Potsdam. Eventually his regiment forgave him: First Lieutenant, Merseburg.

In January of 1956, the custodian of East Germany admitted that he was training young people to fly for reasons other than their own enjoyment of the pastime; those "clubs" of the Armed People's Police were now part of a National People's Army, NPA. As if a People weren't National already. Six months later the air force of the Red Army, now known as the "Soviet" Army, started asking around among its underlings in the GDR: any pilots available? They should be ones whose flying ability had stood out to a marked extent. Comrade Pagenkopf, for this predicate had now been granted him, had his file card pulled from the registration offices of Gneez and elsewhere; his personal data was now entered into "the most desirable passport in the world": the one with the emblem of the Soviet Union. Gesine didn't send out many notices of the birth of a healthy baby girl in July 1957; Pius gave the child a doll inside a doll inside a doll, with instructions for use: In this country they call the smallest, innermost one, which can't be opened, the soul. Major Pagenkopf started another round of basic training: on MiG-21A, 21B, and 21C's, to prepare to tackle the MiG-21D, an all-weather interceptor (known to NATO as: "Fishbed"). Gesine was undergoing a rigorous training course too, at a bank in Düsseldorf; Pius was busy with an Su-7 ("Fitter"), a heavy fighter-bomber suitable for nuclear assignments. In photographs he is always standing alone now, a young man in a tailored suit meant to look British; his look is haughty, distant; to a junior lieutenant he is a model, to an East German officer a person commanding respect. Because the air force of the GDR is under the air defense of the Soviet Union; the former was given no "Fishbeds." Pius as bearer of state secrets; he gave out as his view that the Caucasus resembled Grunewald less than Göring had contended—an air marshal from the old days; Gesine could now understand that this meant he too was being taught the history of the war, and must by now be up to the Battle of Stalingrad. Gesine was dispatched to the USA to study advanced tricks in the replication of borrowed money; Pius, undaunted, asked "My dears" about Marie's latest adventures in American English. When supersonic jet fighters boomed over West Berlin to scare the population, they were piloted by people other than Pius—he was a test pilot, a valuable commodity, a protected cadre. Medical exams every month; rest cures in the sanatoriums reserved for cabinet ministers and up. And unreachable. Anita, with all her skill in traveling, spent a long time looking for him in the Soviet Union and never once saw him alive. He now could pronounce his *o*'s like a Muscovite. Gesine was out on her ear from her first job in Brooklyn; Pius was testing whether any modifications were needed to the Su-9 ("Fishpot"), a fighter plane with a top speed of Mach 2, not given to the NPA. Maybe that's why he didn't visit his homeland. After he'd come home, rumor had it that in 1962 he'd shown up at his mother's place one night at midnight. After President Kennedy was assassinated, Pius wrote a letter meant to console a Gesine in New York City. For form's sake, dismissively, he mentioned to "my dears" a short marriage to a Masha (a Marie). He was alone, and always would be. Did he find himself in his work? His last job was on a Tu-28, a long-range ultrasonic fighter; he commanded a machine that was a hundred feet long, wingspan sixty-five feet. Colonel Pagenkopf. Want to bet that the Russians said the *k* in his name more like a *g*? And since he had earned the affection of the Soviets for his services improving their airborne weaponry, in December 1964 they sent a welded casket back to Gneez, Mecklenburg, instead of burying him onsite. It would have taken industrial-grade machinery to open it. Almost thirty-three years old, Pius lived to be.

(We would like to thank Herr Professor Dr. Erichson for the technical descriptions above. He procured this information on trips over the course of more than two years, in discussions with confidants in both the US and West German air forces [among whom we are especially requested not to single out one Mr. B.], all at times when he would have no doubt preferred to relax and drink a glass of, let's say, tea. Thank you, D. E.)

For information about Pius's funeral ceremonies we would like to thank our school friend Anita Gantlik. With her collection of documents, she, a Protestant, traveled to Gneez, to the Catholic service that his Socialist parents had agreed on. According to her, then, the delivery of the matter to be transformed was announced by two tolls of a bell. There was mention of our brother (formerly: our servant) Robert Pagenkopf. He was given the "viaticum" he had long done without. For them, too, there was a "This is My body, this My blood." Pius's mother stepped forward to take Holy Communion; the elder Pagenkopf stood stiff as a post, conscious of his guilt. Then it was said: We are beginning the Catholic rite of burial. We knew that already. First sight of the coffin in the chapel. Lots of kneeling. Joyful anticipation of Pius's union with God. "Angels will usher him into Paradise." Parting at the grave, with incense.

No military presence. The coffin without a flag of the Red Army or the NPA. A brass plate on the coffin with his full name. His address for eternity.

Among the mourners I noticed. The wreath ribbons read. This Gesine from New York could surely have come up with something more appropriate than *Ræbbing sin Gesin*. Oh, it can be a dative in Platt? "To Robbie from Gesine," not "Robbie's Gesine"? *You dont say*. An elaborate Mecklenburg lunch, conversation with the priest.

Delivering two death announcements.

As for our work, we're right there in *The New York Times*, page 1, column 3: Czechoslovakia wants $400 million to $500 million in hard-currency loans to buy industrial equipment. De Rosny: At your service!

A sad and upset child is waiting on Riverside Drive, wanting to commiserate: A telegram came, and unfortunately I opened it. It's from D. E. in Finland. He's had an accident. Forgets to put his address, the scatterbrain! Now we can't write back! Signed: Eritzen.

Now that is Anita's handwriting. Make sure you give it its due, Comrade Writer!

Handwriting of Student Gantlik comma Anita: No deformations; excellent; especially in telegrams.

– And is your eye feeling better, Gesine?

August 9, 1968 *Friday*

We'd learned it once and for all—the way to get to LaGuardia Airport is to take the West Side line to Times Square, the Flushing line to Forty-Second Street at Third Avenue, the airport shuttle to Long Island. Amid all the rubble of abandoned factories, the private houses built too small, the actual garbage, the cemeteries living on after their death—in the middle of all this an airport shows what's possible, with a glass semicircular two-story building of enormous halls for the processing of waiting, with generous coffeehouses and stores (containing nothing but products of a folklore gone to seed), with marble and other genuine stone, with clean floors and no muzak and a Mayor Fiorello LaGuardia incompletely hewn from a block of granite, as an artwork that has its place here. From the upper level you can look out at the air traffic; it's quite elegant how the count-less planes use the space around the two ramps, quickly, in orderly fashion, rolling up to the gates and deigning to receive a little help at departure from the small bullish (yellow) tractors, until they can safely unleash their strength. The airfield's location on the water makes it easier to see in all this merely a well-established, reasonable sport when the beasts start racing—slow, controlled—until they lift their nose, retract the nose wheel, gracefully rise up into and over the dirt while augmenting it with their viscid exhaust. We stand there for a few minutes and then another plane aims at the run-way from the north, seems to spread its wings, sits politely, gingerly down; it will come taxiing right up like a polite taxi. That's the one meant for us.

And who are the Cresspahls this morning? Merely travel companions, or an escort, a guard detail, for Annie and her children, the capitulating remnants of the Killainen family?

When Annie called us last night, she categorically refused to come over to the Cresspahl apartment. We had to go find her (because you're my friend, Gesine) in a hotel at Lincoln Center, where included in the cost of the night's room is the youth of the building, its proximity to the workshops of art, the wall-to-wall carpeting, hygienically sealed toilets, interchange-able furniture, leather intimacy your hand sticks to. Annie wanted to show us that she's brought money with her—a kind of independence. From a friend. We were going to go to a restaurant, two adults with four children in total, until Marie offered to supervise as F. F. Junior, Francis R., and Annina S. Fleury tried the room service. Thanks, Marie.

Annie née Killainen insisted on the restaurant, a velvety cave hollowed out of East Midtown, lit by blood-colored candles (how striking that one woman there looks, the one with the sunglasses), tended by supercilious waiters whose snooty French you could rip off their faces with a single complete sentence in that language. Annie orders, Annie lays her purse on the edge of the table—she's paying; what she has in mind is putting on a show of security.

It turned out to be not so easy for her to play the carefree lady with three kids in a Finnish small town, who'd run away from her American husband, the Romance Language specialist F. F. Fleury, over an argument about Vietnam. Especially since the specialist in question did, as promised, get himself sent to southeast Asia by a Boston newspaper and has since confessed and reported the error of his ways, to Annie too, in patient, shamefaced articles; in fact, the paper fired him over his coverage of the body bags that an American helicopter team brings along as a precaution on its missions against the enemy that the emissaries of Western culture refer to as "goons"—his coverage of the filling and transport of these bloodtight bags. Pleading letters. But if Annie needs someone at her side for her return to her husband, that seems like a warning sign: Cresspahl wants to suggest. And in so doing she would eat once more the bitter bread of responsibility, she would offer herself up as the scapegoat for future rifts in the Fleury marriage; she refrains. F. F. Fleury, he's really humbled now, bowing and scraping with remorse, scraping hard?

Annie nods, a bit ashamed of herself, forces herself to be honest and admits: *En jaksa enää.*

She can't do it anymore—life without a husband is too much for her. So what else can we do? We call the Mohawks and reserve six seats in a very small plane that hangs low from its wings—it calls itself a Vista Jet even though it has visible propellers (maybe it has hidden turbines) and it rises stubbornly into the air at always the same steep angle. Annie's two elder children stick to their defiance, their exaggerated obedience; Francis R. Knock-knees Fleury is three now and looks down at the unfamiliar landscape completely confused—a hilly country of thick woods in which highways, gas stations, and bulk-purchase stores have heedlessly cleared openings. Admittedly there was also something Norwegian about it, with the white and red painted slate, scattered hamlets or isolated jewelry boxes located high on hilltops with barely visible roads leading to them. We'll be flying somewhere soon too. Anyone sitting under the wings can see a leg being extended until all the joints are straight enough for it to stand. The airport doesn't seem built for bigger planes—it consists of just one narrow wooden barrack. The lone aircraft marshaller walks up to the taxiing Mohawk until it obeys him and comes to a stop. Then he puts down the brake chocks, takes off his earmuffs, and fetches the cart for the luggage that the passengers are allowed to retrieve under the open sky, as if theft were very rarely a concern in Vermont. The Cresspahls turn away from Mrs. Fleury right away; they want to confirm their reservations for the next flight to New York/LaGuardia; they feel they don't need to witness the scene where Annie sinks sobbing onto the chest of her lawfully wedded husband—a limp overgrown child with her tailored suit askew. The Cress-pahls, too, must have their hands shaken, he insists on that; in silence, as if someone's died.

Then a drive down Main Street, past the stores with their adamantly understated airs. The bakery calls itself Bakery and poshly disdains to advertise Super-8 bread or suchlike big-city substitutes for the real thing; the other rural stores show similar restraint. Then a walk. The proximity, the presence of the university causes the glass doors of the shops to bear requests such as: No bare feet. The clothes look respectable; buyers can as a rule leave the souvenirs alone without disgrace; the windows seem washed daily. The hotel on the corner is wrapped in a porch on which new swing chairs in traditional style are resting all alone with their boredom. Annie's future world. The house, built by a *gentleman farmer* around 1840, out of stone, and with an oxblood-colored barn added, at first sight sheltered by old maples and bushes but at second hearing revealed to be closely sur-rounded by neighbors in prefab houses and the streets they drive wildly down. The inside badly cleaned, violently straightened up—Annie's future life. The hotel sent lunch; the guest is offered a slice of toast by the chas-tened, dejected couple. Here Mrs. Cresspahl said, without believing it, the line from Martje Flohr's toast that one says in such situations, ever after etc. How happy Mrs. Cresspahl is, how relieved Marie, late that afternoon when they get back to the airport and the dispatcher looks at them like familiar faces! He'd already tinkled the brass cowbell once, which here announced a takeoff.

The New York Times is handed out. Marie busies herself with Svetlana Stalina Alliluyevna and her latest howling. She wants to tell the world: she's planning to buy a car, the best there is in America! she has thrown her Soviet passport, the most desirable in the world, into the fire!

But they really have pondered and planned it, the East Germans. In mid-July they ordered a partial mobilization of the 650,000 men in the National People's Army reserve for an invasion of Czechoslovakia. Three weeks ago it almost happened.

This was an excursion. And how can we take one to Mecklenburg? Anita does it for us.

She went there on Ascension Day / in the very merry month of May, and from her train window she observed with concern the stones clearly visible amid the low growth, how they'd grown since 1964, some of them now larger than children's heads, *hardheads*. She thought back to the times when the day laborers would have been out with buckets collecting them, the farmers behind them even madder. The estate owners used to take care, since fields without stones saved machines from damage. Apparently there was no slot for clearing the end moraine in the work units of the AyPeeSees. Agricultural Production Cooperatives, that is.

When an Anita wants to partake in the Gneez station restaurant, then it may well say right there on the door that it's closed but a waitress will see that the waiting room, with its loud group of construction workers over their beer and schnapps, is no place for such a lady; she'll open up early. Neat and tidy fresh tablecloths. Flowered wallpaper, chairs upholstered in plastic, bamboo stands holding leafy plants, next to current newspapers on awkward racks; delicate tulip-shaped lights (electr.) on the walls. Then an Anita will wrinkle her nose, as if something smelled sour. The waitress will notice and immediately apologize for the just ten grams of butter for the bread roll—if the customer orders another roll she's allowed to set out ten more grams. Today: this young citizen of Gneez says: used to be a holiday, now theyve taken that away.

We don't permit ourselves any provocations.

Service to Jerichow is canceled due to work on the line: it says in the ticket window, which only opens twenty minutes before the train is due to depart. Behind it sits a public official—about sixty, punctilious uniform, white shirt and tie; on the phone. Passenger at the wrong window: better teach her a lesson. After ten minutes he honors her silent waiting and tells her the departure times for the railway replacement bus. Anita takes a taxi to Jerichow. It's an exception, she feels, that nowadays all you have to do to catch a cab is walk out of the Gneez mail train station, and in forty minutes one appears.

The driver's a disappointment, a Mecklenburger, a yakker. So, the lady's visiting relatives I suppose? But Anita saw a horse waiting indulgently for his farmer who was standing on the corner, *chatting away*; that's just how people are. There are actually people out picking where the road crosses the rails; maybe they're maintaining the line to Jerichow. The new construction in Gneez: factories in exposed concrete, barracks as temporary storage for fuel, fertilizer, farm machines. The industrialization of the north. Communal Administrative Association (Casket Warehouse—Woodworkers).

Windmills with no sails, wooded sections, a thirty-foot rise and the first glimpse of the gray line under the sky: the sea. This used to be Anita's route to school; she speaks of "your" Mecklenburg. She had to spend five years there.

Because of the stones, she asked. They must break the harvest equipment, no? – Auh: the man said: we jus' set the combine t' two feet!

He was eager to hear her address in Jerichow so that he'd have something to report. Then Anita—he'd already noticed something foreign in her accent—held out a box with some *papyrossi* sticking out, filterless, the way only the Russians smoke them daily. Now there was silence. – To the train station: Anita said.

At that very place she was met by a weather-beaten plywood sign on the monument to the fallen: Learn, Ye Who Have Been Warned. To the Victims of the Imperialist Wars.

Jerichow's Town, Ad.-Hitler-, Stalin-, Street of Peace.

Buildings in various conditions. Some of the mostly one-story buildings have been cleaned recently, with wider windows added, some new doors. Others, if they bear the mark "CHA"—Communal Housing Administration, the sign of ownership by the state—may have bare stone showing, uncovered and gnawed by decades of sea wind, and outside window frames scoured gray by the rain. Dangerous-looking bulges in the timber framing. The finest paintwork on the interiors, though; flowerpots; irreproachable, tightly drawn curtains made of Dederon, the miracle synthetic fabric of the East.

Blessed are those who withdraw / From the world without hate... (Goethe)

An antenna on almost every roof, for receiving TV signals, pointing in a westerly direction.

What felt weird to Anita: the scarcity of visual advertising. About eight flags along Town Street. Empty mounts on almost every front door.

The Karstadt department store was Magnet. (Because it attracts, Gesine— "Karstadt: Quality Attracts.") A table saw could be sold only to someone with an Essential Non-Private Purchaser ID. Electronics reserved for repair work. Schuko plugs and sockets only upon presenting a Specialist Worker Letter. Refrigerators were free.

A private business was selling radishes, turnips, apples. Potatoes. They were out of tomatoes. Outside butcher Klein's shop window there was a line of people equipped as though planning to stay there until closing time.

There are no picture postcards of Jerichow.

How startled Anita was to be greeted on the street, by an old woman in a headscarf and nylon coat! From that point on she said to anyone who looked five years older than her: *H'lo.*

There is no building on Jerichow's Town Street with the inscription: Do what's right and fear no man! nor a building with a carved, green-painted hedgehog on both wings of its double door! unless maybe it was next to the collection point for used glass. That was where there was one knocked out of the row and down into the cellar, an extracted tooth.

Peacefully alongside each other: boxes with announcements under glass, this one public, that one private:

It's up to you, your word and your deed. The Military Police Cabinet is open from to. Youths and maidens, live and act like the revolutionaries of today! Fanfare Corps rehearsals starting now.

German Shepherd Breeders Club invites you. Rabbit Breeders Club, Pigeon Breeders Club. A trophy is being awarded for the first time—who will be the proud winner? We'll find out in August! The shooting competition will be held on.

The display case outside the evangelical parsonage contains an illustration of the naked man that the Soviet Union donated on November 4, 1959, as a gift and monument for United Nations Plaza in New York. A work by Yevgeny Vuchetich; pendant piece at the Tretyakov Gallery, Moscow. The male nude has bent a sword so far that it looks like a plowshare at the other end; hammer held out in his right hand. WE SHALL BEAT OUR SWORDS INTO PLOWSHARES (Isaiah 2:4). Nation shall not lift up sword against nation, neither shall they learn war any more!

The roof of St. Peter's Church is half dismantled, the other half already covered in new bricks, biting red but that'll fade in the sea wind. The construction scaffolding, the ladders look long unused, unclimbed; the piles of rubble at their feet have dwindled. As happens every couple of centuries.

At the cemetery office, they shake the hands of even out-of-town visitors. It's called Department of Landscape Gardening, Funerary Facilities Branch. Although the graves of the house of Cresspahl would be hard to miss. They've smudged the letters of your father's gravestone by removing the rust. The planting looks as if the state had to pay the municipality for the selection: lily of the valley. Your mother's cross is falling apart: the cast iron is flaking, you can stick two fingers right through it. Jakob's slab is standing upright like a price tag; the 1964 rosebush is growing nicely. Your place is still empty, Gesine.

The house on Brickworks Road—your house—has been divided. The smaller half belongs to the People's Solidarity Veterans Club, closed unfortunately. The other half may turn into a kindergarten later. So far there's only a future kindergarten: Off-Limits to Children Not Attending This Kindergarten; Parents Are Responsible for Their Children. Much later. It's so dilapidated tradesmen would need weeks to fix it. The roof covered in Eternit. That doesn't bother any storks.

On the Bäk, Anita talked over the fence with older people, complimented the hyacinths. Yah, the roots on em are from the West! In some front yards are car tires, painted white and filled with earth, as flower bowls—a new Mecklenburg folk custom? Teams of horses pulling panel wagons; sullen boys on dirty tractors.

On the Bäk, a group of children, eight years old, in civilian shirts, shouting in chorus: We demand that the Volkspolizei be permitted to search this house! The inhabitant of that house standing there with a laugh on her face, agreeing. Kids, righ'? Most of the children are wearing genuine blue jeans and have Bowie knives too.

An RFT column (large loudspeaker) outside Emma Senkpiel's store; silent for now. In Emma's store Anita was given, against regulations, a glass of milk. Gesine, there's no one in Jerichow who'd recognize you.

The phone booth on Market Square has been repaired. You can tell because the pavement around it went missing during the repairs. Now the door opens onto the street instead of the sidewalk. When the Gneez Taxi Cooperative then refuses to send a car to Jerichow in good faith, as an indefensible burden on the People's national economy, a person can really feel stranded in Jerichow, abandoned on Öland Island. The railway replacement bus was scheduled for much later, five o'clock; the conductors certainly don't take the timetable too literally (helpful warning from a policeman in a green uniform).

Anita crossed the street to the former Wollenberg store; speaking insolent Mecklenburgish, she procured herself a bicycle. She had to walk it on the main street, due to the cobblestones and the scandal it would have been to ride it in her short skirt. Then she rode the twelve miles south in an easy hour, attacked again and again by a plane painted red/white/red, which was supposed to be scattering fertilizer this afternoon. The pilot may have been enjoying Anita's bobbing skirt.

What Anita felt was lacking, in a northern region like this: a sign with a basket of eggs painted on it, and a hand with a pointing finger: "1000 ft." People with portable tables on the streets, offering "Eel, fresh from the smoker"; raspberries, strawberries, picked by old women in gardens close by.

In the woods west of Gneez, on the Lübeck–Rostock road (ferry connection to Denmark), she came across the Happy Transit Hotel. Formerly an excursion destination, now a solid two-story building standing there aglow in its white scratch coat of plaster, reflecting in its golden-tinged windows the woods and Anita on her bicycle; in the back, a row of bungalows made of prefab components, every little cabin equipped with a TV antenna.

The man behind the reception desk thought she must have gotten lost; he nodded imperiously over to the placard across from the photographic depiction of the nation's custodian: Payment accepted here in foreign currency: marks, pounds, dollars, French francs. That was fine with Anita—her question was: Why did the Unity Party insist on parity between the German currencies?

With West German people in transit sitting all around her, Anita ate grilled eel off fine china with silver cutlery, drank a Chablis from a crystal glass. Let the girl who's learned everything the college of hotel management for the obtaining of foreign currencies had to teach her explain the procedures: Now that you've finally finished your meal, it's time for me to clear away your bread basket! that's how I learned it! In the middle of northwest Mecklenburg, Anita was waited on for dollars.

There is no Joachim de Catt Street in Gneez.

As for the name "Street of National Unity," you can still make out traces of Unity. Other than that it's named for the first President of the German Democratic Republic and it still leads to Schwerin.

Also in Gneez, no lines outside the drinking establishments (in the City of Gneez Hotel, a line outside the former manager's office, where Western detergent and chocolate and liqueurs are swept off the counter in exchange for Western currency, double-quick). But, Gesine: your Mecklenburg now does its drinking early in the day. The restaurant in the main train station was still closed, the waiting room packed with beer drinkers. Isolated conversations: Ten thousand tiles put on, half of em loose; only a blockhead'd talk about that. – But therere folks who'll talk bout it.

There they accepted the country's legal tender from Anita again; piqued. There it had been a long time since any customer had asked for a tea with lemon, though it was on offer, according to the menu. (You could see the calculation. The complaints book was lying out on the counter.) Then the tea came too. Everyone looked at the stranger accusingly. A beer's what you have at around five o'clock, that's a given!

The banknotes showed Humboldt on the fives, Goethe on the twenties, Karl Heinrich Marx on the hundreds.

On the rails, in front of the two streaky windows, a heavy diesel train of Soviet make was wearing down the foundation. There was still the word "Deutsche" on the mark coins, but it had already disappeared from the pfennigs.

All of Anita's attempts to get rid of the bicycle ended in awkward failure. None of the men had so many hundreds of marks on him while out for a beer. They watched with confused forebodings as Anita clambered up with the conveyance into a first-class compartment on the express to Neustrelitz. For fifty-five miles the conductor argued with her over the obvious fact that storing such means of transportation in the luggage net of an express train is not allowed, verbotten! When she transferred to Berlin, she left the bike behind, locked to a public bike rack. In the forests west of Neustrelitz the Red Army is sleeping and drilling like peas in a pod; there, before long, they'll be drawing lots for the prize of a men's bike of East German manufacture. In case there are factions in the Soviet Army, and Anita sends them letters with bike lock keys in them.

That was on Ascension Day. The military restricted zone, the gently rolling countryside, it shone in the distance. (—ANITA.)

August 10, 1968 Saturday

Yesterday a derelict known only as Red climbed to the top of the mast of the old lightship at Fulton Street. He wanted to talk to Mayor Lindsay. *The New York Times* shows us, in three photos, how he fell to his death; she tells us the kind of film she used, the shutter speed. Instructions for us?

A British passenger plane crashed yesterday in Bavaria. Forty-eight people on board, all dead. We're flying soon too.

In Hitler's schools we were warned against the stunted shadow of the man in the plutocrat's hat: "The Enemy Is Listening." In the New School we learned to warn one another: An FDJ Friend Is Listening.

At first we were suspicious of the loudspeakers in every classroom, since they seemed to simply replace the hand-carried notes that had done fine communicating school announcements until 1950. Maybe the devices contained equipment that transmitted sounds in the other direction. That might work to monitor a teacher; we didn't think it'd be able to pick out one student's voice from the thirty in a conversation during break. You'd need a person for that.

In the hour of the study of contemporary events, we'd been taught about the criminality inherent in Hitler's language, for example in the word *Untermensch*, "subhuman." During the break after that class, Zaychik, amused at the memory, carelessly remarked: *If I've ever in my life seen a one a those it was Fiete Hildebrandt.* He meant former farm night watchman—"after-hours agricultural surveillance monitor"—Friedrich Hildebrandt, appointed by Adolf Hitler as gauleiter and Reich governor over the good state of Mecklenburg; Pius approvingly mentioned that Hildebrandt had been shot in 1945, in an open field near Wismar; Cresspahl denied it: he'd been sentenced to death in 1947 by an American military court and executed in 1948 in Landsberg am Lech, Bavaria. She'd heard that from her father, who kept an ear out for the postwar life paths of peacocks of that sort. As recently as five years ago, the mere name Hildebrandt had been a daily threat to him—Wallschläger, that shining beacon of the church, had included this special commissioner for the defense of the Reich in his prayers in church in 1945. At the June 1950 teacher's conference, it came up that 10-A-II showed a regrettable interest in information that the state media rightly withheld from the East German people as being unhealthy; showed, in fact, a treasonous concern for the fate of criminals. We looked around at our classmates; who among them was listening in on us and passing our casual chitchat along to the authorities?

Which of them had brought himself to deliver Teacher Habelschwerdt to the knife (disciplinary transfer), by furtively quoting her stupid comment about community spirit? True, something called "community spirit" had been one stated pedagogical goal in Hitler's schools, but anyone who'd spent years needing to recite this surely might misspeak the words once. Was Mrs. Habelschwerdt now squandering her gifts for the natural sciences as an arithmetic teacher at Niklot Elementary School because of one of us, someone we went swimming with, maybe even shook hands with sometimes?

Gabriel Manfras was the last person we thought of. First of all, how could we believe that the First Chairman of the FDJ school group would waste time and effort filing reports? Then, we felt protective toward him, which made it hard to see him properly. Gabriel Manfras was afflicted with a mother who used to thunder at him, even five years after the war: Our Führer will return and he will judge you! Gabriel Manfras was haunted with the memory of the crowd lining the road among whom he, too, quivering with enthusiasm, had waved and shouted "Heil!" when Hitler's man in Mecklenburg had staged a rally including a drive through Gneez. Of course he'd want to get distance from that; and so we accepted the repellent seriousness with which he now professed another brand of Socialism. We smiled only a little when he told us about his triumphs as a "People's Correspondent," when an article in *The Schwerin People's Daily* was signed "gms"—a report on a skating or skiing competition, say, where the US team had won, a fact that "gms" neglected to mention though he did say that the Soviet Union had finished in an honorable second place.

Student Cresspahl could still recall the elementary-school days in Jerichow when she'd wanted this quiet, darkly brooding boy with the razor-sharp center-part to finally notice her. Once, as a joke, for her own amusement, she told a story about Soviet Darwinism without paying attention to whether Gabriel Manfras was in hearing range: Michurin, the Soviet man of science, is giving a lecture about insects. He shows his listeners a flea standing on his right hand, orders the flea to jump to his left, and the flea does it, repeatedly. Then the professor pulls the flea's legs off and orders it over and over to jump; the insect refuses to comply. Here, the professor announced, we have scientific proof that amputating a flea's legs causes deafness . . . Gesine Cresspahl laughed—delighted by the twisted logic, enjoying having others laugh with her. She should have paid closer attention to the labored, contemptuous smile that Manfras was forcing onto his face.

Student Lockenvitz was no doubt making a subtle grammatical point and nothing more when he applied his linguistic stethoscope to the chest of the word *Volkspolizei*, trying to diagnose a possessive or accusative genitive. The German People's Police—who was the possessor, who the direct object? Policing by the people or of the people? It was pure semantics for him when he translated *res publica* as "affair of the people" and detected the tautology in the term "People's Republic." Even the question of why this label was granted to China and Poland but not, for the time being, to a "People's Republic of Germany"—even that would be used against him, later. Thanks to Manfras.

A book was going around school on hidden paths: *I Chose Freedom*, the work of a defector from the Soviet Purchasing Commission in Washington, DC. It told of compulsory spying on colleagues, institutional falsifications in industrial manufacturing, brutality during state police interrogations, concentration camps and forced-labor colonies in the Soviet Union. This Victor Kravchenko had had to sue a French Communist newspaper for slander, after it had called him a lying agitator in the pay of the Americans; a Paris court found that his evidence was true and convincing. When Burly Sieboldt loaned the book in confidence to Cresspahl's daughter, he simply trusted she'd know who she could pass it along to; Lockenvitz found it badly written, or at least badly translated into German, at which point Pius decided not to read it, he just wanted it summarized. Up came Gabriel Manfras with a trusting look, and he nudged the conversation to the topic of the enemy's arguments, that it was necessary to know them before, and were they not to be found in a book by the name of? Gesine denied any knowledge of such a book—among other reasons, because it might do painful damage to Gabriel's idea of the Soviet Union, where the heart of man beats so free in *shirokaya natura*. She thought the book's contents could bring about a fight with Gabriel, in which his feelings would be hurt; she wanted to spare the boy.

On the market square of Gneez, the new one, a loudspeaker on a pillar droned on and on all the livelong day, from morning, when the sleepy workers emerged from their trains, till night, when they'd earned their rest. The plaintive cry rang out: We don't want to die for the dollar! – That's fine: Pius said, brooding: but why is all the business at the Leipzig Fair conducted on a dollar basis? Manfras rushed that question to Instructor Selbich. But Pius was almost a soldier, rallying to the defense of the republic, he was not an easy target. So she pretended that "someone" in II-A-II had asked her that question, and expounded to the class the temporarily unavoidable exigencies of the world market—not having an easy time of it, and pressed by Student Lockenvitz's invocations of Socialist autarky. As far as the Pagenkopf & Co. collective was concerned, he'd been caught red-handed—the spy, the informer, Manfras unmasked as someone ready to do whatever dirty work the Unity Party wanted. From now on we could protect ourselves, but how could we warn the others? Writing something in block letters on the board would have gotten us a house visit from men in uniform or, worse, not in uniform. We made do with surreptitious nudges in the ribs or casually clearing our throat when someone among us started candidly holding forth about a foreign general and marshal with troops stationed in Mecklenburg. A covert nod in Manfras's direction as he sat there, head lowered, pretending to do his math—we avoided even that.

Hünemörder came back to Jerichow and Gneez from the Lüneburg Region in the West, true to his vow never to return until Friedrich Jansen and Friedrich Hildebrandt and all their trash had been smoked out of Mecklenburg. He'd brought with him a few pounds of nails and tacks, thinking to open a hardware store in Gneez; with his solid business sense he had it all figured out, he just needed a saleslady. He couldn't believe it when he heard that Leslie Danzmann was available. Danzmann, the fine lady? That's right. After losing her job at the housing office she'd done so again at the people-owned business FishCan; repeatedly accused of embezzlement and unlawful appropriation of eels etc. and prevented from giving evidence in her own defense, she had finally, in her pride, given notice. She'd applied to the Schwerin CDU, helped once again by her past reputation; was allowed to help out reporting on legal matters in *The New Union*; was saved for a while from the fright it gave her to be offered under-the-table merchandise as a preferred customer—from the butcher, at the dairy—goods that hardly came up in the sales patter but made themselves known in the final total price. Her column, "Courtroom Glimpses," made her name known for a while in almost all the cities and towns of Mecklenburg, but then what was written in the files about her past life caught up with her again. Leslie Danzmann was available, any hourly wage would be fine. Grateful, she dispatched with friendly homespun phrases the lines of buyers pushing up against Hünemörder's mostly empty shop window. After two hours of commercial activity the People's Police was informed, showed up in pairs, and led Leslie off, her wrist cuffed to Hünemörder's. No one knew what Hünemörder got for his attempt to sabotage the people's economy via individual distribution of quota-regulated commercial goods, because that was handed down in the capital; Emil Knoop, through whom this supply line should probably have run, had just set sail for Belgium (by this point Knoop had barges crossing the border for him). Leslie Danzmann was held in the basement under the Gneez district court for a few days, not knowing what she was charged with, kept busy cleaning the cells and passageways. She says she was released the moment she'd finished straightening up the detention areas. This was the latest piece of social instruction Danzmann had received, but what improvement in her social consciousness would it bring her?: the Cresspahl girl asked, in a circle of friends, noticing too late Manfras's encouraging face as he walked up to them.

Bettinikin was furious. The brooch on her blue shirt quivered. (– Where the brooch sits is out in front: this saying, too, had been brought to her notice.) But she had to let it go with a vague threat against those whose sympathy for persons of the Reactionary Middle Class... Student Cresspahl gave a deliberate smile. She, like Bettina, knew about a certain photograph showing the teacher wistfully confronting the middle class.

The potato-bug uprising brought matters to a head. Class 12-A-II had been ordered out to the fields for the purpose of learning to distinguish between Coccinellidae or *Rodolia cardinalis* and *Leptinotarsa decemlineata*. Three students were missing. Whether they'd planned it or were just being absentminded, Students Gantlik and Cresspahl decided they'd rather take a stroll around the Smœkbarg, maybe because they could be sure that the rest of the class was out of town. Zaychik said he'd had to load coal into his auntie's cellar. All three were summoned in writing to justify their actions before the teacher's conference. There, Instructor Selbich confronted Student Haase with the fact that, after storing the briquettes—an act defensible in the interests of the people's economy—he had found the leisure to patronize the Renaissance Cinema. Instead of leaping onto his bicycle and hurrying to join the potato-bug inspectors! While we waited in the classroom for our *consilium abeundi*, Zaychik told us who'd screwed him over: outside the movie house he'd run into Manfras, excused for political service. (A photograph exists of this bench of public penance: Zaychik stands with his coat collar looped around the hook of the map stand, neck skewed sideways, arms slack, as if being painfully hanged.) A contrite and repentant Anita was saved by her contract with the Soviets. A contrite and repentant Cresspahl had a guardian angel circling overhead who had taken a picture of Bettina in West Berlin. Zaychik was credited with the fact that at least the work of filmic art he'd chosen to view was *The Council of the Gods* (East Germany, 1950, not shown in West Germany), thus informing himself about the imperialist conspiracy linking IG Farben, Adolf Hitler, and Standard Oil, so he got off with a severely worded reprimand, thanking the faculty for their lenience.

Anita took it upon herself to notify the party in question. Student Gantlik did not ordinarily go up to Student Manfras's desk during a break as if she had something important to tell him; the class fell silent and everyone saw the furious twitching of the two reddish spikes of hair at her neck, heard her voice ringing with passionate intensity: Anyone who takes the things we tell each other in private, family matters, personal business, and hauls it to the principal's office, brings it up before the Party, is... he's...

What was the worst condemnation Anita could come up with? He was... a bad person.

Gabriel kept his face blank, his head still, tried to look as if he was listening closely, even nodded once or twice like someone willing to endure even this for the higher political cause.

Since then, we've had reason to think of him when anyone mentions *Les Lettres Françaises*, or slander in matters whose truth has been established. This in turn brings before our eyes his appearance at the rally at the end of the 1951–52 school year, where, standing behind the presidium's red table, he contemplatively sang along in chorus the words that had been handed down to us since July 1950 as both statement of fact and confession of faith:

> The Party, the Party, is always in the right!
> Comrades, Comrades, it is always with you . . .
> The Party's given us everything—
> The sun, the wind, it gives for free.
> Born from the Party is life itself.
> What we are, we are through Thee!

We are definitely familiar with what a court in East Germany has determined about people like you: the term "informer," the court found, is not an insult but a job description. Since after all a building monitor's duties include supplying the political leadership with information about the population.

You'd better believe we remember you. It was you who turned our class 10-A-II into a place of intimidation. It is thanks to you that school, from eleventh grade on, was one long fearfest. Hope you're happy.

For the Party *has* given you almost everything—the sun, the wind, and never a headwind either. It started by accepting you as a candidate in 1951. It continued by promising you a slot at Humboldt University in Berlin a year in advance. It showed its trust in Young Friend, later Comrade, Manfras by permitting him to complement his Marxist studies with visits to, stays at the *British Centre* in West Berlin. It imposed one restriction, which we find fair enough: Since his father was a smallholder, not a farmworker, he is deficient in proletariat aristocracy and thus still excluded from the meetings near the Werder Market, Berlin, every Tuesday, in which decisions are made about East German policies, foreign and domestic. And thus Comrade Manfras tries all the more zealously to expound these decisions to others; Anita sees him on TV sometimes, for a few seconds. For this he is rewarded in abundance—for free, like the song says. He can walk into the State Bank and help himself to whatever he needs from the foreign currency drawers, for unrestricted trips to the lands of his enemy. His English is apparently international now, with a British tinge. A villa on Müggelsee, a car, cadre protection, shopping privileges in West Berlin—it's all there. His one dream, though, is to be accepted into the diplomatic service. But there's a built-in barrier, practically insuperable if you notice it only in your thirty sixth year. In his articles reporting on the high society of his country (consisting of the likes of him), the telephones always ring "madly," even though each of these devices can be counted on only to do what its electrical current makes it do. He has issues with participles and will hardly earn an honorary doctorate for descriptions of people like: "The coffee-making, rose-breeding minister's wife..." But maybe we're wrong and he'll end up an embassy counselor someday. Hopefully somewhere other than Prague.

– Two questions: Marie says.
– Motion granted, your honor.
– At one point you gave Pius the rank of general.
– It's been three and a half years since he... But when I think about him as if he'd stayed alive, he'd be a general by now, major general at least.
– On the other paw, you think you have this Bettina Selbich under control.
– You're saying she could slip out of our grasp at the drop of a hat?
– You're in a catch-22. You guys took her picture doing some forbidden window-shopping in West Berlin—
– But?
– The guy with his eye to the viewfinder was there too—if it ever came to producing the evidence.
– Lucky you've only told me this now!

Back home on Riverside Drive the daily telegram from Helsinki is waiting. Today it says: Patient temporarily unable to drive. Signed: Eritzen.

August 11, 1968 Sunday

In Vietnam yesterday, near Tabat, over the Ashau valley, a US fighter bomber of type F-100 Super Sabre went into a dive and fired rockets and guns at American troops. Eight dead, fifty wounded.

Over West Virginia, a twin-engine Piedmont Airlines plane tried to make an instrument approach to Charleston's airport, 982 feet above sea level. Crashed and burned just short of the runway. Out of the thirty-seven people aboard, all but five lost their lives. We're flying soon too.

Before we do, Marie wants a children's party, as long as it's not called a goodbye party. It's just cause they're my best friends: Pamela, Edmondo, Michelle and Paul, Steven, Annie, Kathy, Ivan, . . . and Rebecca Ferwalter, which is why we've made plans to meet Rebecca's mother on a bench in the park to negotiate kosher items on the menu.

She watches us approach, clearly not wanting to be there, her bare, too-fat arms buttressing her on either side; she is trying to look pleased. Mrs. Ferwalter is back from the part of the Catskills she calls "Fleishman." Rebecca found a boy there named Milton Deutsch, called Moishele (Moses). Moses Deutsch loves Rebecca very much and hits her; Rebecca cries it out with her mother then goes back over to Milton as soon as she catches sight of him from afar. Mrs. Ferwalter says, vows in fury: Never again will she pick a place Milton Deutsch might be!

Park-bench conversation.

Will the Nazi Party come to power in Germany?

Most people in Germany don't want that.

What's their platform?

Changing the borders, to start with.

Do the Americans have the right to get involved?

If the government in Washington wants to do it, it'll do it.

My dear Mrs. Cresspahl, please leave it to me. I'll bring Passover cookies, they're colorful, thick frosting, children like them at parties, they taste like marzipan. The last time we baked them at home was in '44. Our village was part of Hungary then. Transports had been coming through since 1941, and people were being rounded up in the country. In May 1944 they took everybody. I had a Catholic passport, religion Catholic. The Germans took one look at me and arrested me. The Hungarians and the Germans, they were made for each other. They were all soldiers. Sorry, what are Swabians?

People living in a southern German province called Swabia, we thought.

Were the Swabians more for Hitler than the rest?

The rest were too.

These were Danube Swabians.

(Transylvanian Saxons?

No. Those were anti, you know.)

We were taken to Auschwitz. I was there eight months. Most were sent straight to the **crematorium**. A lot of the **wardens** are still running around, you'd be amazed to see where. The same way you and me are sitting here talking right now I once talked to Mengele.

I was **selected** for the **depot** to do **distribution**. In the kitchen two girls carried baskets behind me. I divided up the margarine and dropped it in the pots. The girls immediately fished the margarine out and tossed it into buckets of water to harden it. There was a good woman there, my **boss**, her name was **Frau** Stiebitz. She looked the other way.

Can we put that aside?

– Do it but watch out.

Mrs. Ferwalter now explains what a block is, with parallel vertical hand movements marking straight lines: The buildings there were like this. There were girls in one block, thirteen years old. After hours she would bring buckets of soup there. One time she was stopped on the way by a Jewish **Kapo**: You're stealing, you pig.

– And you pay for yours?

The Jewish **Kapo** threatened to report her and the next morning, after standing for hours, she was in fact called forward and accused of resisting a **Kapo** and theft. **Frau** Gräser, the head of the women's camp, said: You're going to be shot. Call a **guard** over.

Frau Gräser had fallen for a girl, and made this girl her right hand. Frances was her name. Frances said: But everybody does it. If you really like me, do me a favor, let her live. She's good in the kitchen you know.

The sentence was commuted to one hour's kneeling on sharp gravel while holding two stones in raised hands. It took many weeks before her knees were back in their normal shape.

Frau Stiebitz didn't say a word during all this. You have to understand. That's how it was in 1944: the Germans were *fed up* (this in English).

When we got there, there was nothing. Then they planted some trees, like for a park. The ones who were still alive had turned into *Tiere* by then (*animals*, not *beasts*).

When we got to Auschwitz we were **deloused** ("you know, some kind of disinfection") and had our heads shaved. The hair grew back, of course, and **Frau** Stiebitz liked to say: Oh how pretty. It was, too. Yes, the **selection** was like a beauty contest. **Frau** Gräser, too, she said once: You could be a beauty queen.

As part of my **punishment** they shaved a road through my hair that had grown back. I went and had the rest cut off too. Twenty-one years old I was.

We worked in two shifts. The day shift was all right. It was bad in the night shift. There were seven crematoriums going in our corner. At the end of the night shift the sky was as red as fire. I heard people screaming: *"Help, help!"* (this in English).

You'll understand, Mrs. Cresspahl. You're a **woman**.

From Auschwitz we were taken west to an ammo factory, maybe in Germany. I saw a sign: Geh-len-au. It was a small camp, to hold the French.

We saw the English parachutists jumping. We were herded to the station and locked into boxcars. The people who lived in that town were looting the stores. Just half an hour more and the English would've been there, but the train pulled out. We were taken to Mauthausen. I was **liberated** in Mauthausen.

In 1945 **Frau** Stiebitz went into hiding in Austria. The prisoners got clothes for her and an American pass (she drew a very long rectangle in the air with two fingers) so she could get back to Germany.

The first couple days after the **liberation** (May 9) we lived on a farm. Good food, real milk, red apples from last year (this in a housewifely tone). But we were scared, there were SS hiding on the farm next door. They could come right out and start all over again. One **warden** in Mauthausen had fifteen-year-old girls brought in to him every night.

The Jewish **Kapo** who'd caught her with the potatoes, she saw her after the war in an office building in Tel Aviv, Israel. I'm going to turn her in. Then a friend advises her: Why do you want to tackle all that? running around to the court, testimony, signatures. I let it go.

In Israel then, everything was rationed and people were leaving the city to go foraging in the country. This very **Kapo** comes into a kitchen through the back door and shouts something. The farmer sitting in the front room, she'd been a prisoner in Auschwitz, recognizes the voice and screams. Everyone runs out onto the street, catches the **Kapo** as she's running away. She got a year in jail.

Another girl was brought to court in Israel from my home village, she was terrible to everyone except me. She'd been made **Kapo** in Auschwitz. Back then you'd be let go if as many witnesses testified for you as against you. I went up and spoke for her. She's an old friend, she's a bad person.

But God punished her. She married a man who didn't treat her right; she's divorced.

The really bad thing was: that the Germans forced the Jews to kill each other. Shove relatives into the fire still alive.

(Rebecca has tripped and fallen while running:) *"My child, I have waited for you so long, eighteen years!"*

(Rebecca gets a sandwich roll to make her feel better; there's fish an inch thick between the bread halves:) You see! (Since Rebecca is constantly being stuffed with food she's a little fat, despite her petite frame.) If only my child would eat like yours!

We left the ČSR legally, with passports. We could take all our **belongings** with us. 1948. It took eight or ten days to get to Tel Aviv.

My brother got black-market sugar on the black market; it was rationed. Six months in jail: The sentence was due to start the next Monday. He had no desire to wait till then and went to Bratislava, over the border to Vienna. The police showed up on Monday. And so with the help of the Almighty we're now in New York.

So it's agreed, yes, the cookies for the children's party I will bring, Mrs. Cresspahl?

August 12, 1968 Monday

The New York Times wants to prepare its readers in advance for an anniversary: seven years ago tomorrow, the custodian of East Germany cut off his part of Berlin from the Western Allies' sectors with a wall, to prevent his citizens from leaving and those of West Berlin from visiting. Exceptions were permitted: if there is a death in the family; if the legal retirement age has been reached. "When I had my birthday I felt happy": a woman from the **democratic** Berlin writes to her daughter in the other one: "getting older. Now it is only five years until I can embrace you." The wall is manned with two East German brigades and three training regiments, totaling about 14,000 soldiers.

On October 7, 1951, the East German national holiday, some select households in Gneez, Mecklenburg, as well as two in Jerichow, received identical anonymous letters for the first time. The envelopes and sheets of DIN A5 paper were blotchy, pulpy, bulgy, easily torn, like the paper the government agencies used for their communications; the text was always written on the same typewriter, with the *e*'s and *n*'s unfailingly misaligned. Someone who, like Cresspahl's daughter, copied these missives out by hand before turning them over to the German People's Police as testimony to her Stalinist watchfulness received piece by piece a preliminary list of the workings of justice in Mecklenburg since 1945.

(The sender presupposed that his readers were familiar with the fact that Z might stand for *Zuchthaus*, "jail." He counted on their hunch that the series of letters SMT stood for "Soviet Military Tribunal," LDT for the "Long-Distance Tribunal" passing judgment from Moscow. He also relied on the supposition that a literate individual in Mecklenburg could easily picture from ZAL a *ZwangsArbeitsLager*, a "forced-labor camp," and understand by "verh." not *verheiratet*, "married," but *verhaftet*, "arrested." Clearly he was in a hurry, or else rarely had access to the ramshackle typewriter in question:)

1945

Prof. Tartarin-Tarnheyden, JD, from Rostock, b. 1882, verh. Nov. 20 1945; sentenced by SMT to 10 yrs. ZAL.

Prof. Dr. Ernst Lübcke, b. 1890, scientist, detained by Soviet officers on Sept. 8 1946; taken to the Soviet Union, disappeared.

Fred Leddin, b. 1925, chemistry student, verh. Sept. 27 1947; sentenced by SMT to 25 years ZAL.

Hans-Joachim Simon, science student, verh. on September 27, 1947; disappeared.

Herbert Schönborn, b. 1927, stud. jur., verh. Mar. 2 1948; sentenced by MVD (*Ministerstvo Vnutrennikh Del'*, the Soviet Ministry of Internal Affairs) special court to 25 years ZAL.

Erich-Otto Paepke, b. 1927, med. stud., verh. Mar. 8 1948; sentenced by SMT Schwerin to 25 yrs. ZAL.

Gerd-Manfred Ahrenholz, b. 1926, chemistry student, verh. Jun. 23 1948; sentenced by SMT to 25 yrs. ZAL.

Hans Lücht, b. 1926, med. stud., verh. Aug. 15 1947; sentenced by SMT Schwerin on Apr. 30 1948 to 25 yrs. ZAL.

Joachim Reincke, b. 1927, med. stud., verh. 1948; sentenced by SMT Schwerin to 25 yrs. ZAL.

Hermann Jansen, b. 1910, Catholic student minister for Rostock, verh. 1948; sentenced by SMT Schwerin to 25 yrs. ZAL.

Wolfgang Hildebrandt, b. 1924, stud. jur., verh. Apr. 3 1949; sentenced by SMT Schwerin to 25 yrs. ZAL.

Rudolf Haaker, b. 1921, stud. jur., verh. in Apr. 1949; sentenced by LDT to 25 yrs. ZAL.

Gerhard Schultz, b. 1921, stud. jur., verh. May 6 1949; sentenced by MVD special court to ten years ZAL.

Hildegard Näther, b. 1923, ed. stud., verh. Oct. 8 1948; sentenced by SMT Schwerin on June 9 1949 to 25 yrs. ZAL.

Jürgen Rubach, b. 1920, ed. stud., verh. Feb. 8 1949; sentenced by SMT Schwerin on June 9 1949 to 25 yrs. ZAL.

Ulrich Haase, b. 1928, lib. arts stud., verh. Sept. 22 1949; sentenced by SMT Schwerin to 25 yrs. ZAL.

Alexandra Wiese, b. 1923, applicant to University of Rostock, verh. Oct. 18 1949; sentenced by SMT Schwerin in April 1950 to 25 years ZAL.

Ingrid Broecker, b. 1925, Art History stud., verh. Oct. 31 1949; sentenced by SMT Schwerin to 15 yrs. ZAL.

On Dec. 17, 1949, an SMT in Schwerin sentenced eight defendants, including two women, to up to twenty-five years ZAL.

Jürgen Broecker, b. 1927, applicant to University of Rostock, verh. Oct. 21 1949; sentenced by SMT Schwerin on Jan. 27 1950 to 25 yrs. ZAL.

On Feb. 17 1950, a Schwerin SMT sentenced one Helmut Hiller and eight others for alleged communications with the SPD's East Office to a total of three hundred and seventy five years ZAL.

On Apr. 16, 1950, a Schwerin SMT sentenced high-school students
Wolfgang Strauß
Eduard Lindhammer
Dieter Schopen
Winfried Wagner
Senf
Klein

Olaf Strauß
Sahlow
Haase
Ohland
Erika Blutschun
Karl-August Schantien

to a total of 300 yrs. ZAL.

The president of the Mecklenburg state youth council of the Liberal Democratic Party, Hans-Jürgen Jennerjahn, was sentenced in the same trial.

Horst-Karl Pinnow, b. 1919, med. stud., verh. Apr. 2 1949; sentenced by Soviet LDT in May 1950 to 25 years ZAL.

Susanne Dethloff, b. 1929, applicant to U of Rostock, verh. May 4 1949; sentenced by Soviet LDT in May 1950 to 10 years ZAL.

Günter Mittag, b. 1930, med. stud., verh. early June 1950; sentenced by SMT, term unknown.

On Jun. 18, 1950, Hermann Priester, teacher, from Rostock, was sentenced to ten years Z; in the Torgau penal institution, Volkspolizei Constable Gustav Werner, known as "Iron Gustav," beat him so badly that he suffered a broken thigh bone. When he was unable to stand up, the VP constable screamed he was a faker and stomped on him, breaking his pelvic bone. Hermann Priester died of aftereffects in late June.

Gerhard Koch, b. 1924, med. stud., verh. July 13 1950; disappeared.

On Jul. 15, 1950, the district court in Güstrow in the Hotel Zachow ibidem sentenced nine leading employees of the credit union cooperative to a total of eighty-four years Z. Among them Arthur Hermes, b. 1875. Hans Hoffmann, JD, because he had tried to transfer the assets of the farmers' self-help association from Mecklenburg to Göttingen. (Two tanker ships, five tank railcars.) "Unfortunately, he succeeded." Prof. Hans Lehmitz, b. 1903, natural sci., member of the Unity Party: fifteen yrs. Z.

On Jul. 18, 1950, the district court in Greifswald sentenced additional members of the cooperative to Z.

Friedrich-Franz Wiese, b. 1929, chemistry student, member of the LPD university committee, verh. Oct. 18 1949; sentenced by SMT Schwerin on Jul. 20 1950 to twenty-five years ZAL, by SMT Berlin-Lichtenberg on Nov. 23 1950 to death.

Arno Esch, b. 1928, stud. jur., LPD Mecklenburg executive committee member, verh. by Soviet security officers in the night of Oct. 18–19 1949 upon leaving the Rostock branch office. Opponent of the death penalty. "I have more in common with a liberal Chinese than with a German Communist." "In that case I have established that we do not have the freedom to make decisions here. Please enter that into the record." Sentenced to death on Jul. 20 1950 by SMT Schwerin per §58 Par. 2 of the RSFR (= Russian Soviet Federative Socialist Republic) penal code: Preparation to Commit Armed Rebellion. Mocked during pretrial custody for his pacifist position. The death penalty was reinstated after his arrest, only when he'd long been in prison. Executed in the Soviet Union on June 24 1951.

Elsbeth Wraske, b. 1925, English stud., verh. Apr. 11 1950; sentenced by SMT Schwerin on July 28 1950 to twenty yrs. ZAL.

On Aug. 8 1950, SMT Schwerin sentenced Paul Schwarz and Gerhard Schneider, both members of Jehovah's Witnesses and therefore both previously in Hitler's concentration camps; sentenced on Aug. 1950 to 25 yrs. ZAL each for "Anti-Soviet Activities."

Siegfried Winter, b. 1927, ed. stud. and most famous handball player in Rostock, verh. Aug. 16 1949; sentenced by SMT Schwerin on Aug. 27 1950 to 25 yrs. ZAL.

Karl-Heinz Lindenberg, b. 1924, med. stud., verh. Sept. 16 1950; sentenced by Greifswald district court on Oct. 21 1951 to fifteen years ZAL.

On Sept. 28, 1950, the Schwerin district court sentenced high-school student Enno Henk and seven others, charged with distributing pamphlets, to up to fifteen years Z.

Alfred Loup, b. 1923, ed. stud., verh. July 3 1950; sentenced by SMT Schwerin on Oct. 31 1950 to 25 yrs. ZAL.

Gerhard Popp, b. 1924, med. stud and chairman of the U of Rostock CDU chapter, verh. Jul. 12 1950; sentenced by SMT Schwerin on Oct. 31 1950 to 25 yrs. ZAL.

Roland Bude, b. 1926, Slavic stud., FDJ school group leader, Rostock, verh. Jul. 13 1950; sentenced by SMT Schwerin on Oct. 31 1950 to two successive 25 yrs. ZAL.

Lothar Prenk, b. 1924, ed. stud., verh. March 24 1950; sentenced by SMT Schwerin on Dec. 9 1950 to 25 yrs. ZAL.

Hans-Joachim Klett, b. 1923, med. stud., verh. March 23 1950; sentenced by SMT Schwerin on Dec. 12 1950 to 25 yrs. ZAL.

On Dec. 18, 1950, a Schwerin SMT sentenced fourteen former Volkspolizei officers to death for "anti-Soviet agitation and forming illegal groups."

On Apr. 27, 1950, the Schwerin district court sentenced a defendant named Horst Paschen to life in prison for "agitation for boycott in conjunction with the murder of a coast guard."

Joachim Liedke, b. 1930, stud. jur., verh. in June 1951; sentenced to five years Z.

Gerhard Schönbeck, b. 1927, philosophy student, verh. Sept. 6, 1950; sentenced by Güstrow district court on Aug. 22, 1951, to eight years Z.

Franz Ball, b. 1927, classics student, verh. Jan. 18, 1951; sentenced by Greifswald district court on Aug. 22, 1951 to ten years Z.

Hartwig Bernitt, b. 1927, biology student, verh. June 29, 1951; sentenced by SMT Schwerin on Dec. 5 1951 to 25 yrs. Z.

Karl-Alfred Gedowski, ed. stud., b. 1927, verh. June 26, 1951; sentenced by SMT Schwerin on Dec. 6 1951 to death.

In the same trial:

Brunhilde Albrecht, b. 1928, ed. stud., verh. June 29, 1951; fifteen years ZAL.

Otto Mehl, b. 1929, student of agriculture, verh. June 29, 1951; 25 yrs. ZAL.

Gerald Joram, b. 1930, med. stud., verh. June 29, 1951; 25 yrs. ZAL.

Alfred Gerlach, b. 1929, med. stud., verh. June 29, 1951; death.

Above the entrance to the Soviet Military Tribunal (SMT) courtroom in Schwerin were posted the words: JUDGMENT SHALL RETURN UNTO RIGHTEOUSNESS. On the dais was a court of three officers. Present in the room, besides the accused: an interpreter, guards, and larger-than-life-sized portraits of Stalin & Mao. Accusations: Contact with Berlin Free University; production and circulation of leaflets; possession and circulation of antidemocratic literature. Verdicts justified under §58 of the Russian Soviet Federative Socialist Republic's penal code, Paragraph 6: Espionage; Paragraph 10: Anti-Soviet Propaganda; Paragraph 11: Formation of Illegal Groups; Paragraph 12: Failure to Report Counterrevolutionary Criminal Activity. Karl-Alfred Gedowski (qv.), in his closing statement: To decide in favor of one ideological worldview, one must also know the other.

Gerhard Dunker, b. 1929, physics student, verh. Dec. 24, 1951; disappeared...

The author of these thoughtful missives may have been circumspect, mailing the letters with different postmarks from Stralsund, Rostock, Schwerin, Malchin, Neubrandenburg; he gave himself away with his selection. He was apparently indifferent to the fact that Peter Wulff had been accused of having, in the years 1946 to 1948, cheated the state (which didn't exist before 1949) out of a total of 8,643 marks of income tax, business tax, and sales tax, and whereas he was found in May 1950 to have long refused to pay the 8,500-mark fine as per a settlement arrangement with the Gneez tax office, he was sentenced in July as per §396 of the tax code to a seven-thousand mark fine and three months in jail—Wulff belonged in his annals. Nor did the author seem to care about economic policies, e.g., that farmer Utpathel, in Old Demwies, went to jail for two years over failing to deliver his quotas of meat, milk, wool, and oilseeds; this despite pleading his age of seventy-three years, the poor quality of the seeds supplied by the state, the loss of his entire herd to the Red Army in 1945, and the cattle plague of 1947; the local court in Gneez conceded these "objective difficulties" with the caveat that, as a progressive farmer, he should have mortgaged his business and procured cattle on credit to fulfill his obligations to the state and the people; for Destructive Activity Against Large-Sized Farm (104 acres), confiscation of property; for Economic Criminality per Ec.Pen.Reg. §1 Par. 1 Subpar. 1, two (2) years in prison. Z. Now Georg Utpathel's farm sat uncultivated, abandoned to cannibalization by the neighbors—apparently a bagatelle for someone more interested in legal proceedings against high-school students, someone who deemed only purely political, ideological penalties worth communicating; that's how they'll catch him, and his copyists too: Jakob said, and he took Cresspahl's daughter's notes away, supposedly to discuss them with his friend Peter Zahn. Her pages were thus kept safe with an unknown third party in the railroad union headquarters in Gneez, who would send Cresspahl's daughter her property after Jakob's death, in an envelope with a Dutch postmark.

In the meantime, the nameless court reporter (who never used a mailbox in Gneez) kept his involuntary subscribers up to date on the treatment of hotel and tavern owners on the Mecklenburg Baltic coast taking place under the codename Operation Rosa—just for variety. Maybe he was trying to avoid monotony, and that was why he also slipped into the string of personal stories this comment from the Soviet News Agency, TASS, about the death penalty: It bears a profoundly humanistic character, in that... Then he returned to his focus on high schoolers, telling us about Burly Sieboldt's transfer from Neubrandenburg penitentiary to an unknown location, and his preoccupation with university students in Mecklenburg, as if he was planning to apply for admission: in Rostock, the State Security Service, the Stasi, had pocketed the "People's House" across from the university, for instance, and built cells in the basement and on two floors, and the interrogators threatened to apply Hitler's infamous *Sippenhaft*—punishing the prisoner's whole family—and indulged in beating suspects when the mood struck. For instance. Or, again, he'd direct his attention to the future that Mecklenburg's university students faced, explaining to his recipients the origin of the name of "Bützow-Dreibergen" prison—from the three hills (*Drei Bergen*) on the southwest corner of Bützow Lake, whose shores the facility was meant to be built on; he told us about the first head of the facility after 1945: the journeyman locksmith Harry Frank from Bützow, who passed himself off as a privy councilor until he had to hang himself in a cell in June 1949; told us about the goon squads named after Volkspolizei Lieutenant Oskar Böttcher that rampaged through the overcrowded prison. This information reached us in an objective, dispassionate tone; only once did the compiler give way to anger, ending one report with an appeal: Mecklenburgers! All we're known for now are the turnips our political prisoners get as feed—"Mecklenburg pineapples." Is that what we want?

After the Christmas—the winter—break, the following students were arrested in Gneez and around Jerichow: Gantlik, Dühr, Cresspahl; evading capture: Alfred Uplegger, then in 10-A-II. The men in their leather coats arrived at his farm just when he was busy chopping wood with a long-handled ax. *Hows the hare supposed to prove hes not a fox*: he deliberated, and hit back. With assault and battery against the state, he had suddenly committed a real crime, he could see that on his own; he took to his heels for West Berlin. One student had been in jail since the start of vacation: Lockenvitz.

On January 3, 1952, Jakob paid a call to the Volkspolizei district headquarters in Gneez to ask the whereabouts of Cresspahl's daughter; he could afford to speak calmly since he was noted in their files as a violent man. Since even a man in a blue uniform doesn't especially like meeting such a character when he's angry, for instance on a dark night on a lonely path between garden plots, the people at headquarters gave him a reasonable response: they would've clued him in a long time ago if they knew anything; *you know your Johnny, Jakob!* Jakob took a leave from work and settled in for a long wait in the lobby of the villa in the Composer's Quarter where the local State Security sorted out short-term deliveries in the basements until they were ready to be transferred to Hans-and-Sophie-Scholl Street, Schwerin. Two of our gentlemen promptly opened the door for him, meticulously went over his documents with him—union ID, Free German Youth ID, police ID, Society for German-Soviet Friendship ID, social security ID, German Reich Railway ID—and then he could begin. Rueful and sympathetic of mien, they advised him to go by Volkspolizei district HQ, the agency responsible for Missing Person cases; in this building, the name Cresspahl was unknown even by hearsay. – That's what we keep telling you, Mr. Abs!

The door to the waiting room was ajar, and Cresspahl's daughter could hear Jakob clearly until he left, disgruntled, a citizen who'd come to look into something and found his own personal credentials examined instead. Student Cresspahl was standing on the hardwood floor for her second day, three hours at a time, strictly ordered not to move. The interrogators wished the suspect to keep her gaze fixed straight ahead on a nail driven into the wall four inches above average eye level, on which, in a gilded frame, hung a colorized photograph of Marshal Stalin. Unprompted speaking was frowned upon in this building; speaking when requested to do so by the gentlemen was recommended in the strongest possible terms. The whole time Jakob was standing in the lobby, it was hard for Prisoner Cresspahl to breathe, due to the gloved paw being held over her mouth. When the front door closed behind Jakob with a sighing, satisfied smack, it started again: Raise your head! Arms out! Palms level! Writing exercises were scheduled for the end of each three-hour shift: repeating her life story, followed by discussions of any variations from the version written the day before. Jakob's appearance had given the interrogation personnel a new weapon. How to respond to the question of whether high-school student Cresspahl was involved in a sexual relationship with this railwayman? This was followed by more stationary gymnastics, a good fit with the suspect's annoyance at this idiot Gesine Cresspahl, who, on a dim Wednesday morning in January, had boarded the milk train to Gneez and sat down in a compartment by herself, making it possible for her to be loaded with hardly any fuss into the back seat of an EMW at Wehrlich station. And now for a short appraisal

of the criminal activities

of the enemies

of Socialism;

we've even convicted the second-in-command of Czechoslovakia, you know, that Rudolf Slánský; now, if you don't mind, Young Friend Cresspahl! Raise your head! Arms out!

She got herself just one slap in the face, toward the end of the ten-day inquiry—she'd fainted. On the night of January 12, when she came back to Cresspahl's house, she got a hug from Jakob as if he knew what he was doing, as if he'd made a habit of that with her.

That was a Saturday. The next day, at lunchtime, Anita came from church to see us—another first. We both started talking at the same time: Hey, I've got something to tell you! (Just between you and me.)

Guard duty in the villa that had once been Dr. Grimm's had been so carefully arranged that neither of them had had any idea that the other was housed on the other side of the wall, being fed bowls of Mecklenburg pineapple, sleeping under filthy blankets and the smell of many different sweats. They agreed about who they were afraid they owed this stay and treatment to—the interrogations had primarily poked around the origins, statements, and proclivities of "our handsome young man," Lockenvitz. We were offended, our sense of manly toughness disappointed. We appreciated that he might want to buy time on the backs and palms of three unwitting girls; still, disappointing. Until Jakob played Solomon for us and said: Heaven protect him from such complaining women! Did we think we'd ever get a husband at this rate? Just think about what they'd have to do to someone before he'd let a girl get hurt!

Anita liked it at my father's house. There was Cresspahl, who squared his shoulders for her when he said hello and looked her in the eyes as he thanked her for coming over. *There was an ol woman* who said grace before the meal. There was a young man who pulled out a chair for her, served her food, waited on her with talk and stories, and you could get a straight answer out of him too.

We recognized our third co-conspirator in a gym class where we were combined with 11-A-II. Annette Dühr was walking stiffly—she'd probably had to stand with straightened knees longer. She'd been seen leaving something at Lockenvitz's apartment door; they hadn't believed her as much as they did us. The glass face of her watch had been broken. She had blue welts on her back, from the beatings. She was missing a tooth. She avoided our eyes, pleadingly; she didn't want to be part of a group like this.

One girl felt left out: Lise had been hidden in Maass the bookbinder's attic as soon as two 12-A-II students went missing. Mrs. Maass would have taken her out to the Countess Woods in the night, to a waiting car, the moment the Stasi seemed to be coming for her, and driven her to safety in West Berlin; all *for the cat, for the birds*, for nothing. Like she had nothing to offer, this useless Lise Wollenberg.

By that time nobody would say a word to or take a slice of bread from Gabriel. His own school class pressuring him, the Dühr family imploring him to get the Central School-Group Authority to intervene to help the missing girl, he had declared: such requests were signs of a regrettable lack of confidence in the Socialist state. – Our security forces know what they're doing—no more than what's necessary. You don't ask questions. You help them!

Maybe Manfras was insulted by the indifference the girls had shown him since the summer of 1951; we would strike a yearning pose and sing right to his face, until he inevitably blushed, the current hit: Don't look at me that waaaaay / you know I can never saaaay / (no to you).

Someone else came from Cottbus, with medicine: Pius, ordered to Gneez to give a statement. He brought Temples of Golden Joy and a rebuke: we had never actually seen a denunciation against us in Lockenvitz's hand, or with his signature. The investigators had proceeded on the assumption that the perpetrator must have roped in accomplices. And who would willingly type up what a young man asked them to? Girls, that's who. – And you of all people, Gesine! He took special care to protect you!

(I deserved that. After Easter vacation of 1951, henceforth to be referred to as spring vacation, Dieter Lockenvitz left the Pagenkopf & Co. work collective. Just stopped coming, with no explanation. Asked in class whether there'd been a fight, he said he was in love with Gesine Cresspahl, he couldn't stand the hours spent watching the favors enjoyed by his rival,

Pius. Since then Pius and I had tapped our fingers to our foreheads in
public, calling him crazy, but we let him have his way. He'd worked it out
so that no one could attest to any dealings between Student Cresspahl and
him—or a single one of his mistakes—in more than eight months.)

Lockenvitz's trial was held on the morning of May 15, 1952, in the district
court; though the transcript was to state that it was a public trial, no public was present in the courtroom. Students Gantlik and Cresspahl had
made provisions by committing the criminal act of successful bribery of
court employee Nomenscio Sednondico; this N. S. alerted class 12-A-II via
Elise Bock so punctually that a riotous assembly of young citizens in proud
blue shirts had gathered in the courthouse even before the start of the
proceedings; shouts were heard: Friendship prevails, friendship prevails!
and: We are the defendant's school class! Among the importunate throng
was Colleague B. Selbich, who'd had to leave school with her subjects to
smother their open rebellion as much as possible; the fact is, we owed it to
her officious cowardice that we were able to see him one last time—former
high-school student Lockenvitz.

The Stasi had visibly done to him what his newssheets accused them of.
They could have hidden some of it behind a pair of glasses replacing the
ones they'd broken, if they hadn't been so cheap. As it was, he was brought
in with his face bare, seemingly blind, stumbling; he slumped in the dock,
hanging onto the chair as if even this was beyond his strength. He held his
head in a listening pose; he avoided looking at us. Since his upper front
teeth were elsewhere, he had trouble articulating certain syllables.

Witness statement from MANFRAS: The defendant's work in the ZGSL
was, in practical terms, sabotage.

(Whatever work there was to do in the Free German Youth organization, Lockenvitz had done it; Gabriel's role was to give the annual addresses,
his overview appraisals of the state of the world. Now he accused himself
of lacking the vigilance that Great Comrade Stalin always...)

Witness statement from WESTPHAL: Dieter Lockenvitz assisted in the
Culture League's library starting in 1948, organizing, cataloging, and placing orders for the collection; he is familiar with the premises. How could
I suspect him of leaving a window open so he could climb in at night and
use the typewriter?

Witness statement from LOCKENVITZ (MRS.): My son is a secretive child. He can't have gotten that from me or his father.

Witness statement from SELBICH: Missing. (Afternoon walks in the Rose Garden, Gneez.)

The prosecutor, during his training for the People's Court, must have skipped his German classes. Wild grammatical flailing. Somersaulting voice while mispronouncing the foreign words.

The defendant's attempt to obtain a diploma underhandedly. (His Abitur would have been the kind you see once a decade [except for chemistry]. He was meant for an era when people were rewarded according to their abilities.)

The defendant's monstrous ambition (am-BITZ-ee-own) to make public the judgments of the court kept under seal by the criminal chambers of the sovereign republic in the interests of the state! Collection of Subversive Information.

Terrorism. (Since he'd also sent his correspondence to the district court judges in New Mecklenburg, to affect and intimidate them if possible.)

Motion to have the defendant's mother in the courtroom arrested, for suspected complicity. (Gerda Lockenvitz, b. 1909, garden worker; sentenced to 2 yrs. Z. for Neglect of Child-Rearing Obligations and Active Collaboration.)

The implement used in committing the crime—one (1) bicycle, Swedish (foreign!) manufacture—is hereby confiscated for the use of the state.

(No comment whatsoever was made about how a child not even originally from the country could have gained access to secret files and records of closed trials. The detailed information in the reports about June 18 and July 20, 1950, and December 6, 1951, were just asking for a cross-examination. Yet the court acted as if no one not sitting on the bench knew a thing about the details of Lockenvitz's one-sided correspondence; perhaps this meant that he was still trying to protect his sources.)

Question: Do you admit that you are an enemy of the first workers' and peasants' state to exist on German soil?

Answer: I admit to an unambiguous German and Anglo-Saxon genitive. I admit to proclaiming the law in the public square in Germany.

Fifteen years in prison. And since the Soviets had decided not to take an interest in this lone-wolf criminal, he was spared a trip on the Blue Express to Moscow—a coupled-on prison car disguised as a vehicle of the German mail service. He also forfeited the privilege of learning to mine coal in Vorkuta or cut trees in Taischet. He also missed the Soviet amnesty of 1954, which annulled the verdicts of military tribunals. Since he'd been convicted by a German court, he served two-thirds of his sentence.

In September, the interrupted correspondence resumed:

Gerhard Dunker, b. 1929, physics student, verh. Dec. 24, 1951; sentenced by Güstrow district court on June 17 1952 to eight years Z...

In the beginning, 12-A-II knew where Lockenvitz had been taken: to Bützow. Two students in that class were allowed to choose a job for him, since he'd also told them which companies placed orders for convict labor:

People-Owned Business Rostock Shipping Combine,
P.O.B. Güstrow Garment Works,
P.O.B. Cadastral Unit, Schwerin,
P.O.B. (Combine) WiBa Wittenberg Basketwork Manufacture,
P.O.B. High-Voltage Installations, Rostock,
Wiehr & Schacht, Bützow;

they had some idea of his daily menu and were able to calculate from his reports an hourly wage of ninety-four cents, which left him at the end of the month, after the deductions for tax and social security and imprisonment costs, with fifteen marks, just enough for two pounds of butter and four jars of jam; they knew the maximum allowable contents of the packages they were sometimes permitted to send him as a reward for good conduct:

500 grams of fat,
250 g cheese,
250 g bacon,
500 g sausage,
500 g sugar,

and, up to the maximum total package weight of 3 kg: fruit, onions, and store-bought cookies in their original packaging;

Anita could bring herself to send such a package only once, and it was returned; the sender was required to be living in Lockenvitz's jurisdiction and be related to him.

Thanks to his spywork, we were able to picture him with a one-inch crew cut, in hand-me-down Volkspolizei overalls, saluting the constable by doffing his cap and averting his gaze to six feet in front of and three feet behind this dignitary as he strode past, assuming a military posture, marching in formation, sleeping (never alone) next to a shit bucket. We left him alone.

Were we expecting his final statement to include an apology for our ten-day detention and questioning, or what? If Pius was to be believed, Lockenvitz probably thought no one had been arrested but him. Jakob said: *Thass somethin you gotta learn: bein stuck in the slammer.*

Starting in the summer of 1952, after those responsible for administering East German justice had disciplined Lockenvitz, they began to have their doubts about whether the secret arrest and incommunicado imprisonment of fellow citizens were sufficiently daunting to those remaining on the outside thus far. Maybe it was this high-school student's publicity campaign that helped inspire the criminal courts to start publishing their verdicts in the provincial newspapers. Let people read the deterrents in black and white.

Or was it simply disturbing to watch an eighteen-year-old boy sacrifice his future—from which he had every right to expect admission to university and, with luck, a profession of his choice—for the truth, whatever kind of truth, a proven fact or not? Remembering Lockenvitz sets our thoughts aflutter slightly. Birds starting up in the dark.

We got word from Gneez that his mother had returned there as soon as she'd served her two years. She tried to wait in Gneez for her son; however, the cathedral preacher whom Anita had gone all the way to Jerichow to avoid took the trouble to thunder down from the pulpit against her, using words that the Bible offers for the casting out of the undeserving. They say she's waiting in Bavaria somewhere.

Starting in 1962 we could have made inquiries about Lockenvitz. But his schoolmate Cresspahl decided she'd rather wait and see whether Anita would take back or tone down her threat from 1952: If I ever run into him in the subway and he offers me a seat, I'll stay standing!

The fact is, we sold Lockenvitz down the river. To give Anita the last word: We are guilty before him.

August 13, 1968 Tuesday

The New York Times on her front page shows us how an East German delegation in Karlovy Vary is greeted by a Czechoslovakian one: without Russian-style embraces and kisses. The onlookers cheered for Alexander Dubček; they bestowed a silence on Comrade Ulbricht, and later the two crews ate at separate tables. In her three-column history of the East German custodian's life, the World's Chronicler mentions a 1957 exchange of words between "Walter Ernst Karl" Ulbricht and one Comrade Gerhard Ziller. The former's subordinate: While we were in concentration camps, you were making speeches in Russia; you have always been safe. The latter's superior: I will never forget what you've said here; we'll discuss the matter later. Subordinate: (goes home and shoots himself). We wrote a tall question mark in the margin next to this story, since we want to ask someone for information to assuage our doubts—until memory, once again present, reports for duty at the place where said person now finds himself.

(Yesterday's telegram from Helsinki: UNABLE TO WRITE – ERITZION.)

Employee Cresspahl has now promised her daughter that she can do whatever she wants through next Tuesday; Marie has hesitantly renounced the military swimming drills in her summer camp. Yesterday they went to Chicago; because the flight takes more than an hour. (Because unfamiliar men keep calling the Cresspahl telephone in New York acting familiar, with urgent questions to ask about a certain Missing Person; also because one has neglected to report that person's possible demise.) Marie liked that the passengers on this airborne commuter line simply take a number and pay the stewardess on board, who is equipped with a money pouch at her belly like a train conductor. In Chicago we took the rattling trains on the Loop downtown. We looked for the hotel where we stayed in 1962, like a princess and infanta; torn down. In Marina City's round towers on the Chicago River, we toured a model apartment as if we were planning to move in; there was a gentleman in the elevator in an Italian jacket, winking confidentially. Marie thought that's how it goes when a lady gets a proposition; he was definitely from a different society. And, so that the telephone behind the locked door of the Cresspahl apartment can spend the day ringing into the empty air, today is perfect for an excursion out to Rockaway Peninsula in the Atlantic, taking more than an hour to get to by subway—the only stretch where you have to pay a second token.

Here we have a child about to take a trip in seven days that she is not looking forward to—the country is too foreign; she wishes she could talk it over with someone but he is unreachable at the moment on the Gulf of Bothnia in the Baltic. So it's time to give her something, a foretaste, long saved up to be used in case of emergency. Does Marie know that Jakob, in the fall of 1955, wrote a letter from Olmütz, Olomouc, where he was learning the operational techniques of dispatching at the *hl. n.*, located at railway kilometer 253 from Prague?

In Brooklyn the train to the beaches of Rockaway is crowded already. All of the Negroes among the passengers are going farther than Forty-Fourth Street; the white-sand beach, to Sixtieth Street, is indeed covered with none but the pink-skinned, lying in pairs on their blankets. The men are holding their hands still on the girls' backs; it looks quite unimaginative. On the subway, a young black man has nudged his napping girlfriend in the ribs, tipping her head onto his shoulder; while she puts on a show of comfortably snuggling up to him, he gives himself compensation for his goodness by feeling her upper thigh.

– Jakob used to work where we're going? Will we go see it?

We'll go see it, in ten days, if that's okay with her. We'll look for a family, Feliks and Tonya, with two daughters who'll have left home by now—they'll know who we are when we say Jakob's name. Jakob lived *en famille* there; he told the story of how the days began: in the morning there was only a big blue-black window in watercolor, with a pot-bellied lamp in front, on a peaceful white tablecloth, trying to put a plump dent in the darkness outside. At that table, with the guest from Mecklenburg, was the gentleman of the house, still drowsy but acquainted with the work of the day and certain to master it. For now he waits with concealed amusement to see which of his daughters will be first. On this morning of Jakob's letter, it was the younger, just seven years old, who fetched plates and silverware for five from the cupboards and set the table, all with a tense, worried look about her, perhaps meant to express: Yes, what would you do without me! Then the mother sits down with her tea and coffee pots, four people are already eating when the elder daughter comes to the table, sluggishly half-asleep but in a rush, handed a piece of bread while she's standing, eating while she walks, everyone's sympathetic awareness that she has a quiz in school today guarding her back, and not just any quiz: Russian. By now the wind was going at the darkness of the sky with a grater, making long pale slashes start to appear. These people liked to talk. About the farmer expostulating to his cackling chicken: Now they wouldn't getcha for those eighteen heller a yours! (that was the price of an egg, approximately: eighteen heller, eighteen cents). Or: Lookit how that redbreast's puffing up his feathers on the wall, it must be zero degrees outside. Hope the jay comes. Nest robbers have it hard too; a whole swarm of blackbirds just flew at him. Blackbirds? That's right, "black-birds." By now the left, northeast half of the sky is almost entirely cleared, the right half dissolved into streaks, so they *were* clouds; now the light comes leaping in. North wind. Wear your hat today, it'll be cold. Then they all said Bye, or Adieu, and everyone's day began at last; Jakob went to the train station.

– Jakob couldn't speak Czech!

If Jakob wanted to get along with the people from the Czech railroad he would have to spare them his Mecklenburg Russian. What Jakob quoted in his letter: *Protože nádraži je velmi daleko.* (Because the station's far away.)

Ne, jejich manželky jsou Češky. (No, careful! Their wives are Czech.) *Ještě dělám chyby.* (I still make mistakes.)

– The things you can do, Gesine.

But there was a boy standing at the window for Jakob every morning, four years old, waiting for his friend:

– I see you.

– *So do I.*

– *Well, see you later.*

– *Will do.*

And he knew his way around station talk, among Czechs:

– I can beat you, doesn't matter you're tall!

– Go ahead.

– Cause I'm short, I can run fast.

Feliks: black goatee above a perpetually white shirt collar; bald circle surrounded by hair. Tonya: A kind look from behind awkward glasses, despite her worries; hair in a bun.

What surprised them both: that such a young man, just twenty-seven, was so good at living alone! She ironed his shirts.

North Moravia district, Marie. On the Morava. I'm sure you'll be getting to that in school *fore long:* the Punctation of Olmütz. Around seventy thousand people. An archbishopric. A St. Wenceslaus Cathedral. The biggest pipe organ in Moravia in the St. Maurice Church. Church of the Virgin Mary Visitation on Holy Hill! The Olomouc language island!

– That sounds like lots of lonely walks.

Feliks the railroad man took his colleague Jakob along when he went out for a beer. The family took him to Prague, three hours by express train, and led him from the corner of Kaprova and Maislova ulice to Dušni ulice, Mikulášska, Celetná ulice, to the Old Town Hall, the Fishmarket, the Kinský Palace, the Karolinum, the Assicurazioni Generali building, the Workers' Accident Insurance Institute building, to Bílkova ulice, to Dlouhá třída: so that he could take pictures there, as a good friend in West Germany had asked him to. Since she was unable to visit Czechoslovakia herself at the moment. Since then she'd had a standing invitation. That night they went back to Olomouc and found a wrecked apartment.

– Some people must've taken a trip there from Riverside Drive, New York, and broken in!

They'd forgotten about the cat and not left the basement window or back door open for her to slip out of. The cat, however, knew as one of her work obligations that she must relieve herself only outdoors; she felt a pressure in her body, and in her distress she jumped from china cabinet to sewing machine, from the egg basket into the molasses barrel. How sheepish she was when they came back, her human employees. How cruel she thought it was for them to punish her with a laugh and a warm bath. She had problems enough with the son, the affectionate blond boy, useless for hunting birds and mice, too lazy. To be unmasked like that, before the younger generation!

Not at all like dogs: Jakob wrote. With them, scratching is more of a symbolic act. But cats want to bury what sticks unpleasantly in their noses. You need to fence off a flower garden from a cat—and try finding wire here!

– And so Gesine sent some chicken wire from West Germany.

To thank them for the information, she did. By that time Tonya and Feliks trusted the colleague from Mecklenburg, despite his having been raised to follow Luther and being therefore destined for Hell; they told Archbishop Josef Beran about him. On June 7, 1948, Prime Minister

Gottwald signed the new constitution because the president for life, Eduard Beneš, had refused, and he asked the archbishop to accompany him in a thanksgiving service. A year later, though, the archbishop of Prague was prevented from preaching, in August he was robbed of his rights and his ability to leave the house, and in March 1951 he was banned from Prague. As for the titular bishop of Olomouc, on December 2, 1950, he was put away for twenty-five years. In Communism there are governments where you never know.

And to make sure that our colleague Jakob returned to his homeland knowing all about Olomouc, the railway workers entrusted him with the story that the city was most recently famous for. This was the perfume-box plot, and no one was supposed to know about it. The bombs came to Prague in wooden boxes marked "Perfume," one meant for the leader of President Beneš's National Socialist Party, Peter Zenkl, one for the Minister of Justice, Prokop Drtina, and one for Foreign Minister Jan Masaryk. The general secretary of the Communists announced in a public meeting that Peter Zenkl's people themselves had sent them. Now there was a carpenter near Olomouc, named Jan Kopka, concerned by the party's manhunt since he'd made the boxes himself and knew their intended use too. He went to confess, was accused of lying by the chief of the party police, and had to sign a statement saying so. There were still democrats in the Ministry of Justice and they rearrested Kopka, searched his carpentry shop, and found machine guns, hand grenades, ammunition. Kopka, as a Communist, wanted to share and share alike and named a fellow comrade, a railwayman named Oplustil; a much bigger arsenal was found at his home, which he must have gotten from the Olomouc Party Secretariat, and when Oplustil seemed reluctant to hide the guns, he was warned: you could be crushed between two cars, or fall off a train, without anybody ever knowing how it happened. The person telling him this, Communist Deputy J. Juri-Sosnar, had made the perfume-box bombs himself and was caught because they had the same serial number as explosives from the Olomouc depot, and now who'd been the one to tell *him* to do it? One Alexej Čepička. Klement Gottwald's son-in-law. So the case never came to trial, and you'll already have heard about the situation with the archbishop, Jakob. And now who jumped out of a third-story window the following February? Former Minister of Justice Drtina. And for what did he spend the next five years and three months in prison when he didn't die? For false accusations of attempted assassination. That's what we're known for here in Olomouc, Jakob.

Jakob, in Cresspahl's English household, had gotten used to tea, and there it was ready and waiting on the warmer at Tonya and Feliks's (all that was missing was the juice of a fresh lemon; and the tea lights). A young man abroad, you have to take care of him, don't you, and Tonya took an extra trip to Brno where there had been lemons the day before yesterday. Feliks built some tea lights.

Tonya was embarrassed about her figure; Feliks didn't mind it.

A love affair under her supervision, she didn't begrudge him that, despite the pain. But being lied to (betrayed), that went against her self-respect. A person's got to keep her self-respect.

Jakob learned from Feliks that in the Middle Ages sneezing was thought to be a sign of the plague, hence the good wishes. What do your Italians say about that, Gesine.

Each of them thought, about the other: if they do it, it's for the best.

– So you knew back then what he wanted to discuss with you, Gesine?

Now Marie wants to know why she's never seen a letter from Jakob in Moravia. Because it's safe in Düsseldorf. Will Gesine Cresspahl swear to her daughter that this letter exists? She will, she does, hand on heart. (And even if it was lying under oath, I'd do it again.)

But the child is looking out at a beach in America. Next to beachgoers at leisure, there is work being done—a backhoe with its snout full is creeping on treads toward the point of a jetty, shaking its load into the net of a crane that's making its own space to stand that much longer. Along the broad boardwalk, "colored" workmen are tearing the foundations of rotted bungalows out of the ground with crowbars, piling the slabs up neatly. May makes everything anew, as they say—the permanent season of speculation.

Behind the boardwalk, crooked weather-beaten collapsing wooden shacks that one can rent as temporary apartments or summer houses, even if the owners' phone numbers are bleached away, peeled off. One of the handwritten blurbs: *All the bungalow people can kiss my dick.* In the shimmering sky, airplanes towing advertisements. YOU LOOK SUNBURNED. COOL IT OFF WITH ... Stands selling meat products that may as well be factory-made. Tin cans of twenty-seven different drinkable liquids. Marie trusts the ice cream she can buy here; not the kind you get abroad.

Coming back on the wooden beach path, she gets a splinter in her foot by the second step, but keeps stoically still as she's learned to do in camp, savoring her multicolor ice cream while her mother tears open her skin with the point of a scissors. But the splinter breaks apart into several pieces. A plump, quickly spherical drop of blood appears under the scissors. Again we have a limping child.

When the beach narrows, the housing projects approach the water, the ones where the people live who want to be called Negroes—people with formal manners, looking friendly. Four seventeen-year-olds are trying to carry a fifth into the water, because a school of sharks was sighted off the coast last Saturday. In the abandoned shop windows are the advertising insignia of the "whites." A grandfather with three children and their fishing rods to play with; he's left his own at home. A region capable of lush vegetation, going to ruin under the industrial garbage. A single-story wasteland all around (as a writer once said). Amid the hurrahing of a crowded subway platform, one of the women is reading a book: *The Loneliness of the Individual in Modern American Society*, it says on the cover, in German. Marie saw it, she laughs. Sighing, brave, she says: Still, if we could only stay.

August 14, 1968 Wednesday

Two men entered Union Dime Savings Bank at Park Avenue and Fiftieth Street at about 9:05 a.m. yesterday, dressed neither especially well nor especially badly ("about what a police lieutenant would wear," in the police's estimation); one was armed with a pistol, the other with a machete or meat cleaver. When they were back out on the street with $4,400, bank employees behind them shouted "Thief! Thief!" and no taxi would take the fare, during the morning rush hour and everything, and they spent the rest of the morning at the Seventeenth Precinct station. (One had just been released from Sing Sing in June, where he'd been serving time for additional episodes practicing the art of bank robbery.)

The custodian of East Germany left Karlovy Vary so incensed at the refusal of his Czechoslovak colleagues to muzzle the press that he had his own press refuse to say where he'd been for twenty-seven hours.

Citizens of Czechoslovakia have given forty pounds of gold and the equivalent of nearly $20 million to a fund to strengthen their Communist Party; the party, though, would rather they shortened their frequent breaks for coffee or beer; cut waste; worked harder. One worker, in a letter to *Prace*, the labor newspaper, asks why. When young workers have to wait for ten years to get an apartment, and still have to pay 40,000 crowns ($2,500). We need new machinery in our factories! And something like the feeling that work pays!

Permission to leave high school—a diploma, a certificate of readiness, the Abitur: Student Cresspahl acquired it several times.

Once from her teachers, in the form each saw fit to give it.

From her Latin teacher, a hunchbacked, timorous old man who overlooked with a show of absentmindedness the fact that his favorite disciple in grammar, the famulus Lockenvitz, had left the class apparently never to return, while Miss Gantlik and Miss Cresspahl had been absent for ten days without the required excuse notes from their parents. He gave himself away by not calling on them until February, when they'd presumably caught up on what they'd missed. He flinched a little if anyone mentioned, in regard to his Marcus Tullius Cicero, that this orator against state corruption might have dipped into the till to satisfy his own need for ready cash, or, worse, if anyone brought up the fact that it was Christian missions to Western Europe that had been responsible for the spread of Latin; he'd already gotten burned once, and badly, by history: disciplinary transfer out of Schwerin. He would have had a heart attack and fluttered away on the spot if a class delegation, appealing to his well-proven moral sense, had requested instruction on how to react to the unfortunate custom of one student memorizing and reporting what the other students casually said during tours of gasworks and breweries. All he longed for was to reach retirement, leisure time in which he could compose his deeply personal monograph on the Schelf Church in Schwerin. Anyone who stood their ground with him on the ablative absolute received an A as a final grade: in gratitude for considerate treatment.

In English, Hans-Gerhard Knick gave the graduating Cresspahl girl an

A. He had learned this language with the help of LPs and believed he could speak it after he'd gone to the World Festival of School and College Students in Berlin in 1951, while still in short pants, and a group of socialistically inclined British girls had responded indulgently to his efforts at playing the translator. When Cresspahl, having carefully read T. Dreiser's *Sister Carrie*, slipped into conversation the word *conductor* instead of *guard* for a *Schaffner*, Knick at first tried to correct her, then quickly gave up on her. She also enjoyed a certain amount of protection given that she was planning to go to university and study a subject he himself could have used a review in; and another certain amount from something Lockenvitz had bequeathed to her in the FDJ: he'd known Mrs. Knick in their lost homeland, as a well-to-do bourgeois, not a daughter of the Workers and Peasants as befit the wife of a language instructor who hoped to be accepted as a candidate for the Unity Party.

There was a B in Russian on G. Cresspahl's final transcript, mainly because of her taking part in a plot to help a young teacher named von Bülow learn the language well enough to teach it. This von Bülow was already scared, due to her noble ancestry; the psychological tips she'd been offered in her training courses had thoroughly confounded her, since they had so little to do with the actual behavior of 12-A-II students in Mecklenburg. Instruction in Russian was therefore administered by Anita. Which was a sacrifice. For there on the lesson plan was Stalin's essay "On Dialectical and Historical Materialism," teeming with "Furthermore... Therefore... Therefore perhaps... Thus ends... Thus transforms... Thus must... Furthermore...," followed by the same author's discussion of "Marxism and Questions of Linguistics." *Vas slushayu.* None of us could have bought a pair of nail scissors in Kiev or Minsk with any of that. This Eva von Bülow left for Hamburg at the end of the 1951–52 school year and is still there, an interpreter in the West German/Soviet steel and shipbuilding business.

In Music a B from Julie Westphal. Because the Cresspahl girl had been happy to remain among the second altos—gaining some extra free time when the first-string school choir had to rehearse for their summer tour of the Baltic resorts, followed by time for unsupervised vacations. Also because Candidate Manfras had informed this Westphal that the Cresspahl girl once described one of her, Westphal's, teacherly opinions as "nonsense":

this being in reference to Julie's verdict that the song "The Moon Has Arisen" should vanish from the musical repertory of a democracy due to the plea therein that our sick neighbor too should sleep peacefully: solicitude that undermined the ideological vigilance of the class-conscious member of society, since the neighbor might well be an enemy of the people in disguise, whom it would be criminal to let sleep in peace. Third, because, while the Cresspahl girl had listened to and recited back Mrs. Westphal's lectures about the cosmopolitan reactionary nationalists and enemies of the Soviet Union such as Paderewski, Toscanini, Stravinsky, and other composers and musicians, she had then asked her teacher for a demonstration of these scandalous traits in the works of the condemned musicians—just a few bars on the piano, Mrs. Westphal, to give us an idea.

In chemistry and biology, an A from a little old man, weak and womanish (an "Auntie") like the Latin teacher but fat, almost spherical. It was from him that we were given, in tenth grade, the block of instruction meant to explain to children the sexual needs and abilities of the human being; that was when this drooler, a lady-killer in his own mind, had thrown a sop to his thwarted libido by reciting to the boys, with a wink, forefinger quivering erect near his eye, the line from Goethe—"The thought alone will lift Him"—followed by the poem:

When you're aware
Of Him hanging there,
So loose,
So big
In your trouser leg...
You've a dirty mind!
And I like your kind
("Heinrich Heine")

(Now where would a girl in 10-A-II know that from, where would she have heard it? Guess! Your best answer would be: osmosis.) He was still bustling around in front of us, getting all excited about examples of "e-vo-lution" in nature; in 1952 he offered his students the myth that bananas caused infantile paralysis, the same canard he'd offered the children of 1937, another period in which you couldn't buy bananas. The students in chemistry and biology had their doubts that this teacher, given that he'd been trained at Heidelberg University, actually did revere Stalin's favorite son the Soviet biologist Trofim Denisovich Lysenko; still we dutifully recited to him that whether plants passed on acquired characteristics depended entirely on environmental conditions. The fact that they did this was the sum total of our knowledge in this field, which was why Anita, on a tour of a seed-growing and hybridization farm, went up to the man in charge with a question about Michurin and his pupil Lysenko. This man was a chaired professor, holder of multiple doctorates both earned and honorary, winner of the National Prize, who had decided it was more important to stay in his field of experimental study than to worry about the temporary circumstance of the New State appropriating his results. Anita speaks to such a man in a modest, respectful tone that he can't help but notice. Maybe he had a backlog of anger stored up from a meeting in Rostock or a session of the academy, but furious, stern as a privy councilor, he laid it out for her and her alone that somatic detours might cause a fixing of genetic properties perhaps once in 106 million years—otherwise the theory of the evolutionary progression of life would collapse. You won't find any Lysenkoist cultivation here, young lady! We were standing nearby, saw her downcast eyes and flushed face. At moments like that we missed them—Pagenkopf, Lockenvitz; they would have taken measures, each in their own way, to keep a girl in their class from being hurt. Fortunately, Comrade Professor himself realized in time that it was Anita's school that should be ashamed of itself, not Anita; he put his arm around her shoulder and took her on a little stroll, to tell her a thing or two about productivity appraisal and seed-grain certification, as well as the fact that in a small country agriculture can't afford to take chances with arbitrary measures in genetics. We stood around our school biology expert in a group, ignored his embarrassed babbling, and hoped that Anita would be brought back to us consoled. – Hail Moscow and Lysenko! Student Gantlik said (when no Youth Comrade Manfras was nearby either): that afternoon she renounced a career she'd been aspiring to.

Both Gantlik and Cresspahl got A's in math and physics, from Eberhard Martens, nicknamed "the Evil Eye" because he had kept from his days as an NCO a searching, hypnotic gaze ever on the lookout for criminal activity. The kind of teacher who sticks to his syllabus long after it should have dawned on him that only three of his students had grasped the concept of value assignment rules (not functions, because "the essential content of the concept of a function is the fact of assigning a certain value, by virtue of which certain objects may be defined as belonging to others, not the dependence of the magnitude assigned"). He was bashful with us, trying to solve the riddle of our stiff courtesy. We had heard him tell smugly confiding stories, in a broad Mecklenburg accent: *I hardly ever sweat, the marches in Russia got me out a that habit; the others were always drinkin; theres just one sitcha-ation when I sweat*...We'd also heard him tell Special Instructor H.-G. Knick, man-to-man, about a certain noteworthy encounter on the streets of Warsaw in 1942: *Someone comes up to me, bats her eyelashes till I notice that her breasts are outta phase with her walk, so I put the make on her. Turns out the little monster'd crosslaced rubber bands from her garters to her bra, would ya believe it*...Technically racial desecration, I spose. "The Evil Eye" tried to leave East Germany in 1954 but baggage check at the border found what looked like private photos of Heinrich Himmler and the SS general who'd ordered the Warsaw Ghetto leveled and the survivors sent to their deaths—two years in jail. We kept up our obedience to this teacher through graduation.

We could have relaxed a bit more around our German and Contemporary Studies instructor, but as a rule we preferred not to. Because in 1952's ninth grade there was a girl named Kress, half of Cresspahl, and when asked who Comrade Stalin was she offered the guess that he was President of the Soviet Union. – Sit down! F!: our little Bettina screeched, and in the same breath: Your whole family's under suspicion as far as I'm concerned! Since Bettinikin had never seen this Kress before and knew nothing about her family either, a different girl in 12-A-II knew just which student she really had it in for.

Serious of mien, we recited in German class stanzas from "The Cultivation of Millet," a poem that the contemporary writer Bertolt Brecht had published the previous year:

20
Joseph Stalin spoke of millet.
To Michurin's pupils he spoke of dung
        and dry wind.
And the Soviet people's great Harvest Leader
Called the millet an unmanageable child.

21

But she, the moody daughter of the steppes,
Was not the accused as they interrogated her.
In Lysenko's greenhouse in faraway Moscow
She testified to what helps her, what disturbs her.

Her thoughts possibly dwelling on a different house, also far away, where
a student named Lockenvitz was being interrogated about what was bothering him, Anita interpreted for Mrs. Selbich the poetic goals of these lines,
namely, providing a scientific foundation for the Marxist concept of social
development—mankind's being shaped not only by his social milieu but
also by the inheritance of virtues acquired therefrom (and she included
the difference between this environmental theory and those of Marx's
contemporaries, while strictly avoiding the term *sociology*, at the time still
outlawed as an expression of imperialist pseudoscience).

Moreover, "The Cultivation of Millet" had been adorned with a musical setting, which could be sung with a lengthening of the final "a" in each
line:

1

Tchaganak Berziyev, the nomaaaad,
Son of the free desert in the land of Kazakhstaaaan . . .

and how was Bettinikin to take this if not as a somewhat childish excess
of enthusiasm within the framework of the curriculum?

In Frau Selbich's class we studied another work by the same author,
"The Herrnburg Report," a poetic recollection of how the West German
police at the border crossing of Herrnburg had treated West Germans
returning from the All-German Rally of 1950. The Schleswig-Holstein
interior ministry had ordered these young people to submit their personal
information and place of employment for registration, and that they be
given medical exams because they had slept on straw; they fought back
with fists and stones, bivouacked in the open for a night and a half, then
eventually gave in and held out their IDs to be stamped "Processed" or
"Valid." For Brecht the poet, this turned into their having "planted" the
flag of the Free German Youth on the roof of the Lübeck main train sta-

tion, and having been victorious; he also passed the following verdict on two party chairmen in the Federal Republic:

> Schumacher, Shoemaker, your shoe doesn't fit,
> There's no way Germany can walk in it.
> Adenauer, Adenauer, show us your hand,
> For thirty silver pieces you have sold out our land.

This news item in musical form was sung at the Third World Youth Festival of the FDJ in Berlin, and the socialistically inclined English girls there, surrounding our H.-G. Knick in his knee pants, might well have thought that what he translated for them was *awful*:

> Germans taking Germans into custody,
> Just 'cause they've gone from Germany to Germany...
> Roadblocks and fencing,
> Why even try?
> Look at us dancing
> Merrily on by.

We were crazy enough to suggest a performance of this choral work at Fritz Reuter High School in Gneez (Herrnburg being just a stone's throw away, after all), thereby delighting Bettina S. (at her pedagogical success). Julie Westphal put a stop to that; she had an inkling of our puzzlement at a poet who could be outraged at West German police measures by virtue of being largely immune to East German ones. But the school had achieved its true pedagogical purpose. By only presenting Brecht's hackwork to us, which had earned him the National Prize (a hundred thousand marks), the school kept us away from his *One Hundred Poems*, which came onto the market that same year, 1951—we had every reason to think they were equally maggoty.

Anyone willing to part with a used copy of Bertolt Brecht's *One Hundred Poems*, in any condition, preferably with dust jacket, is hereby requested to name their price to Mrs. Gesine Cresspahl, Address: . . . , c/o Státní Banka Československá, Prague 1.

Bettina worked hard denouncing cosmopolitan enemies of the people.

What she knew about Rainer Maria Rilke was that he was a lyric poet alien to the people; Stefan George she called a stylite. But what to say about Jean-Paul Sartre? The Cresspahl girl submitted that this individual had published a book named *L'Être et le néant*, aka *Being and Nothingness*, in Paris in 1943, under the Nazi-German occupation—enough for an A. Oh, how we missed Lockenvitz!

He'd still been with us on our class trip to see Ernst Barlach's works; he'd worn a suit to Güstrow, while Cresspahl wore her Sunday best because her father had suggested that this was proper when visiting a dead man. The Mecklenburgers, always under the leadership of Fiete Hildebrandt, had so plagued and tormented Barlach that he'd died in 1938, in Rostock, but he'd wanted to be buried in Ratzeburg, in the West. Here, before the hovering Angel in the Güstrow Cathedral, before *The Doubter*, the young woman from the terrible year of 1937, we listened to Bettina's interpretive mush and then went back a second time to contemplate the sculptures in silence. (Lise Wollenberg managed to pin the nickname "Fettered Witch" on her former friend Cresspahl, due to an alleged resemblance *en face* to the statue in question; these days Lise was occasionally stared at, by boys, as if she were out of her mind.) It was with a set of reproductions of the "Frieze of the Listeners" that Gesine Cresspahl moved to Hesse, to the Rhineland, to Berlin, and to Riverside Drive in New York City.

That trip had been in September 1951; in December, an exhibition of Barlach's works opened in the German Academy of Arts in Berlin, NW 7; the following January, an instructor in German and Contemporary Studies used the SED's newspaper, *Neues Deutschland* (*New Germany*), to teach us

What are the circumstances in which we construct the genitive as "des neuen Deutschland"?

Why do we here say "an issue of des Neuen Deutschlands"?

what Bettinikin had misinformed us about four months earlier. The SED had dispatched its official art expert to the Academy—one Girnus, well-versed in the practices of Formalism so inimical to the people—and Girnus was willing to concede that the Nazis had treated Barlach as someone inimical to their sort. But Barlach had been defending a lost position;

Barlach had been, in essence, a retrograde artist. Taking no inspiration from the 1906 Russian Revolution. Wrapping a world of "the barefoot" in a halo of sanctity. What, in contrast, had Stalin said about this world of barefoot pilgrims in his opus *Anarchism or Socialism*? He had responded to it by saying: The truth is, rather, that . . . Barlach's orientation toward a decaying social stratum had barred his access to the great progressive current of the German people, per Girnus. Insulated him from it. That was the whole secret of the growing isolation he had chosen for himself.

We dutifully wrote an essay for German class about said whole secret, scrupulously distinguishing between what a certain N. Orlov had written in the newspaper of the occupying power, the *Tägliche Rundschau*

Daily Review*! Latest issue!*
Faily review, no one'll miss you!

and certain ideas of the sculptor Ernst Barlach (now promoted to the status of Formalist) about the connection between the three-dimensional world of ideas and "more solid ideas of the material involved: stone, metal, wood, firm matter." We lied like troopers; we were working toward our final exams.

Ever since their visit to Barlach's lakeside house on Inselsee in Güstrow, the students Gantlik and Cresspahl had shared an agreement, a secret. Both of them had turned away from the art-critical tour-guiding on offer from their instructor, Selbich, and found themselves on the ridge of Heather Hill, at the top of a slope well known to the children of Güstrow as a sledding place but which also opened onto a sweeping view of the island in Inselsee and the gently rising land beyond the water, dotted with backdrops of trees and roofs, radiant since the sun had just managed to scatter some dark rainclouds—may this sight be before me in the hour of my

We don't give a damn if you think it's a bit much, Comrade Writer! You write that down! We can still cancel this whole book of yours—today if we want to. The plans we've made for our death shouldn't be beyond you.

dying. We told each other our private thoughts about people's essential need for the landscape they grew up in, learned about life in. We told each other how much we liked each other. For the rest of the school year we were still considered two people, strangers to each other, but in fact we were joined in friendship.

Anita almost cost herself a diploma. She was a member of the Free German Youth and so she was expected to come out in favor of the resolution of the Fourth FDJ Parliament of May 29, 1952, stating that serving in the Barracked Volkspolizei was an honorable duty for all members. She, Anita, who had sworn only two years earlier that she would refuse any job, even just in a telegraph office, that was involved in any war effort, was now picked to march like the Leipzig FDJ girls with their rifles slung across their backs, the boys carrying theirs shouldered. A future was being prepared for Anita in which she too could acquire the FDJ sharpshooting badge, twenty-one rings in three shots for First Class. Anita sat in the class chapter meeting with her head lowered, neck tendons red and taut, stubbornly silent. Who knows if she was still even listening when Gabriel Manfras spoke up in a threatening way about a balance between academic achievement and the political consciousness required as an accessory to any assault on the citadel of scholarship.

Student Cresspahl, presiding over the meeting, suddenly said, sounding very upset: I could slap myself! Here we are discussing the Stockholm Appeal and military service and not even noticing that Anita is sick. You're not feeling well, are you, Anita? Go straight home. A vote on student Gantlik's indisposition. For. Against. Abstentions: None.

And so School Group Fritz Reuter, Gneez, could telegraph a unanimous endorsement of militarization to the FDJ central office in Berlin—unanimous approvals were in fashion. And Anita moved to West Berlin as soon as she had the piece of paper with her academic achievements in hand.

Suitcases were prohibited on trains to East Berlin stations—this was meant to hinder citizens from fleeing the country. Anita deposited a suitcase at a station south of Teltow.

She pinned the following onto her clothes for the trip: her Large Sports Badge, her Small Sports Badge, her Insignia of the Society for German-Soviet Friendship, her FDJ Insignia, her badge "For Correct Knowledge" (silver), and a membership badge for the German Socialist Unity Party that she'd been deft enough to pilfer from a Contemporary Studies teacher; she suffered under the cool, disparaging looks of the other passengers, especially since she also forced herself to shout "Friendship!" as a greeting to anyone in uniform. On her second day in West Berlin she left the Auto Hotel where a certain Mr. Cresspahl had put in a good word for her and took the train back across the national border to fetch her luggage, medals and insignia on her breast. The luggage wasn't there. She put up a fight, as befit someone wearing all those party insignia ("The party seminar starts tomorrow, and here I am without a towel!"), and succeeded in getting her suitcase sent to East Station, against regulations ("You'll be hearing from me whether it actually gets there, I promise you!"); she tried to transfer to a westbound tram. On the stairs leading to the platform for trains to Spandau, she saw a table across the way with Red Army soldiers. She dashed in comradely fashion over to the Russians. They were happy for the diversion and flirted with their German ally; considerate, watchful, they interrupted their conversation by crying: Run, Comrade, your train's coming. Across the border her hardware attracted attention; she brought her left hand toward her shoulder several times, scratched a little through her overcoat, slipped one medal after another into the palm of her hand, and let go of it in her coat pocket.

Had there been any other funny business during the Abitur exams? Of course. There's one legend about English texts hidden in a rotten bench in the assembly hall—but here we should, in all fairness, fall silent, since most of those involved (implicated) are still alive, and living where they acquired their certifications.

My first Abitur had been my last encounter with Lockenvitz, on May 15, 1952.

My second was dated June 25, and was accompanied by the general remarks:

G. C. has been a conscientious, reliable student, who did her work thoroughly and independently. Her initiative has been a model for her classmates.

Societal activities:

G. C. has been a member of FDJ since 9/10/1949. She has performed good organizational work and consistently striven, successfully, to gain greater understanding in questions of ideological worldview.

Certificate #: Zc 208-25 3 52 5961-D/V/4/59-FZ 501.

There it was again: that banned word *worldview*. Mrs. Habelschwerdt had to pay for that misspeaking. New School, old words—you try to figure that one out, if you have to, or want to.

My third Abitur took place in Jerichow.

In the final days of June, Cresspahl's daughter was biking home from a swim in the Baltic on the Rande country road at the strange time of about five o'clock, just when the retired senior secondary-school instructors in English and Latin stop working in the garden plots behind New Cemetery and head home to brew their tea, a habit acquired during their years at the universities of London and Birmingham. There he was, an old man in a torn shirt walking with rake and hoe over his shoulder, and his former student Cresspahl said hello as shyly as she felt. He replied just as he had two years ago, and pretended to be appalled when the child seemed about to dismount and accompany him part of the way. He wouldn't hear of it; he begged the young lady to forgive his unseemly attire.

To be quite sure she would no longer have to see it, he sent her up ahead into town with precise instructions about the croissants and crumb cakes and "Americans" she should buy in the former Papenbrock bakery. By the time she arrived at his two-room apartment on Jerichow's market square, Kliefoth had shaved and put on a black suit; he was standing at the door like the young lady's most obedient servant. It was the guest herself who then had to eat all the pastries, every last crumb, while making a confession that covered two years of school. He sat upright at the table, his gaze steady. He was quite at ease, you could see it from the way he held his cigar away in the air, benevolently observing her. The student herself was uncertain of a good outcome.

– *Iam scies, patrem tuum mercedes perdidisses*: Kliefoth eventually said, challengingly.

"You will soon know that your father has gotten nothing for his tuition money." What they've taught you in that school, Miss Cresspahl, is poor equipment indeed for a life of study and learning.

Cresspahl's daughter spent only half the summer vacation of 1952 by the sea; every weekday, she had to go to Kliefoth's apartment with a bag of pastries right after lunch and receive instruction by means of a book which included this maxim: *It may be fairly said that English is among the easiest languages to speak badly, but the most difficult to use well* (Prof. C. L. WRENN, Oxford University: *The English Language*, 1949, p. 49).

And when she left for university she was given, as a present, Gustav Kirchner's *The Ten Main Verbs of the English Language: In British and American Forms* (Halle/Saale: 1952), a reliable tool with which she would eventually move to the other side of the world.

For as long as she still came back home to Mecklenburg, the student Cresspahl continued to visit this teacher. And every time, she had to eat pastries in his presence, because that was one of his notions about young ladies.

He gets an update from us by letter every year, and as many as seven more, if we feel like it.

Student Cresspahl once asked him, in passing, what life was like for a ten-year-old child in 1898 in Malchow am See, Mecklenburg; he sent her thirty pages in a handwriting like embroidery:

"I myself might have been the ten-year-old country lad of '98, but we city boys kept our distance from these *post numerando* coeval 'country Moritzes' (local corruption of 'local militias'). In M. the average pediatrician would chuckle in amusement because the teacher always went around in '*Mähl-spich*' (shirtfront and high stiff collar) while the townsmen and tradesmen put on theirs, '*Kreditspitzen*,' only for important walks through town—heard in passing and relayed without comment: '*Didja hear, Heinrich? Fritz A. gotanother assfull this morning.*' Now how did our ten-year-old get from the countryside to the city? Via bicycle, then still called velocipede, Plattd. *Vilitzipeh*, I know of only one case and only in dry weather. Out of all the estate boys only a coachman's son and the district governor's walked with me, the latter having already covered the three miles from his estate on foot. Residents of lakeside municipalities (Petersdorf, Göhren, Nossentin) came to the city (on Sundays) mainly by rowboat. To be cont'd. 9/20/63. Kl."

All because I was curious how my father might have grown up. But what does Kliefoth have to complain about—he can devote a whole week to Robert Burns's poems when he wants, and sometimes even discovers one he'd forgotten.

We send him, via Anita, the cigars and tobacco that are his due according to his need and his merit (the same way Brecht wanted to supply a fresh rose every day, in East Germany, for the poet Oscar Wilde); as a result, his letters invariably begin: Admonishing finger raised at the spoiling of a useless old man . . .

He signs his letters with a teacher's siglum, as though grading a paper.

He starts them with the words: Dear honored lady and friend Miss Cresspahl.

If only we deserved them.

My third Abitur: that one counts.

August 15, 1968 Thursday

At JFK N PODGORNI, a ticket agent, or at any rate someone required to wear a nametag to that effect on his uniformed chest, so he must be used to outlandish incidents, and maybe he's been working for this same airline for six years: anyway, this morning he looks doubtfully at two ladies named Cresspahl wishing to travel to California with no luggage apart from whatever they have in their coat pockets, possibly including a firearm; if it were up to him he'd have frisked them both. Life's dealt you lemons, Mr. Podgorni; good day, sir.

What makes us want to go to San Francisco for the day? We want to fly in over the bay with the Golden Gate. Marie should see the giant wheel that pulls the cables hauling cable cars up over the city's hills. The boxy Spanish-style houses on the hills, shining white in the earth's vegetation burnt brown. Maybe at the main post office we'll run into the same beggar who thanked us for a quarter there six years ago by informing us: *You're a real lady, that's for sure.* We'll need a window seat at Fisherman's Wharf. And why are we allowed to do this? Because Marie expects a return flight to New York City at nine p.m. or thereabouts. Because we want to reacclimate ourselves to long-distance flights. And why do we want to do this? Because there are strangers' voices arriving over the phone lines in New York, Italian as well as American, asking about one Professor Erichson. Because a telegram from Helsinki could arrive there at any moment, informing us that someone is unable to speak. Would the two ladies with the name starting with C. please be the first to board the aircraft? We would like to welcome the C. sisters on board our 707 for this morning's flight to San Francisco.

– To get used to goodbyes: the younger of the traveling C.'s guesses after the climb during which she surveyed her earthly belongings, namely the island of Manhattan and the two-story orange ships in the harbor. – I'm never going to leave my home for good!

– Easy for you to say, with so many institutions of higher learning there, and the likes of Columbia right around the corner.

– Gesine, do you think I should go to college?

– If you want to learn how to see all the sides and corners of things, and how they fit together with other things, or even just how to look at a thought and arrange all its interconnections simultaneously in your head. If you want to train your mind until it takes over everything you think and remember and want to forget. If you want to become more sensitive to pain. If you plan to work with your head.

– And if all you'd ever learned in life was how to milk cows or boil potatoes for pigs?

– Then lying would be just as bad, and guilt, and responsibility toward other people. But your memory would be less sharp—life would be easier, I think. Like Benn says, "To be stupid and have a job / that's . . ."—sounds good to me. There's no one else in the world I'd admit it to, Marie.

– If you'd stayed in Jerichow you would've gotten married in St. Peter's, three marks for the wedding decorations, four marks for choir and organ music, without the painful singing.

– The grain of truth in that is that I'd like to be buried there. If you can get the town to open up the old cemetery one more time. It doesn't need to be my own grave; Jakob's is fine with me.

– Because the earth never passes away.

– Right. Because I'm superstitious. Official statement from the earth of today, thirty thousand feet over Chicago.

– You'll have to give that to Dr. Josephberg in writing. Because if we crash, we'll die together.

– I hope so.

– D. E. will take care of it for us.

– D. E. can cook, D. E. can bake / and the day after tomorrow / the child he'll take. *And there will be / an end of me.*

– *Of him,* Gesine. Rumpelstiltskin.

– Saying goodbye in 1952 was like the first time, in 1944. Cresspahl took his daughter to the front door, leaned against the frame, said his last words to her. *Make sure ya wear yer scarf.* As if I was only going to Gustav

Adolf Middle School in Gneez, not Martin Luther University in Halle, on the Saale River. *Just tha he was smokin like a littl man bakes.*

– But my grandfather was tall!

– *The littl man*—in Mecklenburg, that meant the poor man. He heats his stove with brushwood, which "smokes like a chimney." The richer people used beech logs, which give off a fine, even smoke.

– Ah, when someone's about to lose something.

– He chain-smokes.

– Now tell me your dowry.

– My dowry was a rented room in Halle, on the moat, five minutes walk to the Saale—Jakob had arranged that for me. They sure do get around, those railwaymen. A wooden chest with a compass-rose carved on the lid was delivered there: Herr Heinrich Cresspahl, Master Carpenter (ret.), Jerichow had equipped his daughter for a life on the Saale with a winter suit, two new summer dresses (Rawehn, Fine Apparel, Gneez Market). Dr. Julius Kliefoth had contributed: FEHR, *English Literature of the Nineteenth and Twentieth Centuries: With an Introduction to English Early-Romanticism*; KELLER and FEHR, *English Literature from the Renaissance to the Enlightenment*; WÜLKER, *A History of English Literature from the Earliest Times to the Present*; the *Columbia Encyclopedia* of 1950; a MURET-SANDERS bilingual dictionary from 1933. From Jakob's mother: a bible, with an inscription on the flyleaf: 1947, acquired for a hare; God Bless G. C. away from home. There was also a bank account at the postal check office, Halle/Saale.

– That's pretty bold, having your scholarship money delivered by the state.

– No scholarship money for me—I was from the Reactionary Middle Class.

– But your father paid taxes! And you'd served the state's youth group with flying colors!

– For Cresspahl, the state was someone he didn't have a contract with, but it had power over his labor. He didn't want any help with his daughter's tuition or expenses from them. Sent her 150 marks a month, thirty less than children with proletariat pedigrees could pick up from the dean of student affairs, 8–9 University Place.

– That would've made me mad.

– I was fine, Marie. I could buy butter.

– Mad at the government, I mean.

– Please step back from the platform edge! At a moment's notice I could lose the offerings from the Department of English Language and Literature (6), fall semester, September 22 through December 19, 1952:

History of American English;

Modern English Syntax, with seminar;

English Conversation Practice;

Hist. of Eng. Lit. under Industrial and Monopoly Capitalism, with seminar;

Hist. of Am. Lit. under Imperialism;

and to get all that, Lib. Arts Stud. Cresspahl showed up bright-eyed and bushy-tailed to the mandatory classes in Russian, pedagogy, and political economy; wrote up neat and tidy in social sciences that Trotsky, in his vanity, had once offered to die for the Revolution as long as three million party members watched him do it. When the Communist Party of France gave the university a banner showing Picasso's dove of peace (third version), this student voiced no objection, she clapped along with everyone else at the ceremony—and even if she'd been enrolled in biology, she wouldn't have said that doves are nasty creatures that destroy one another's nests and that any house they choose as a nesting site is soon sorry.

– Such a quiet child. That must've stood out.

– The Cresspahl child had learned from her friends Pagenkopf and Lockenvitz. If she had to walk a tightrope, she'd make sure there was a net underneath. When asked for one of the most important sentences in American literature, she obediently recited what J. Lincoln Steffens (1866 to 1936) had said about his visits to the Soviet Union:

I have been over into the future, and it works;

and if you also knew and could produce on request that the English called a *Kommode* a *chest of drawers*, not a *commode*, you were in good shape. She'd learned her other insurance policy from Pius: societal activities. At Martin Luther University it was enough at first to sign up for a swim class in lifesaving. She swam fifty meters underwater in heavy clothes and with a weighted backpack, turning to come up for air; how could anyone spying on her guess that this was to make up for the disgusting shower on Moat Street that she could use only once a week? A student like her, who needs to squeeze in an additional fifteen hours a week just for English, has no time to hold office with the young German free. And if she's offered one, then she's seven steps ahead now that she has an upper-level swimming certificate to show them—she spends two hours a week going to a club that the interior ministry founded in August 1952 to teach young people telegraphy and marksmanship.

– No, you're lying, Gesine!

– Pius Pagenkopf's decision-making power as commander of an armed aircraft was now to be his friend's, too, with the help of a small-caliber rifle. She thought she'd deliberate at her leisure over who she would finally aim the gun at and pull the trigger.

– You don't even have a gun license, Gesine!

– Since when do I need a piece of paper to shoot?

– You battle-ready amphibian, you!

– Envy, *my dear Mary*, is not an attractive quality—even for a bank. *Although bankers have human feelings, too.*

– I give up. I believe you.

– You're welcome. Service with a smile.

– Now something about Saxony.

– I'll tell you about three or four people in Halle. The first two considered themselves a couple and charged twenty-five marks for a furnished room in the second-best neighborhood. The woman worked for the manager of a People-Owned Business and had strayed just a titch out of her marriage into getting to know her boss better. His mood was how her day went. One time she came home and proudly reported having straightened Comrade Director's tie in the nick of time before a meeting. That wasn't how I'd pictured things in a People-Owned Business; by now I have a feeling I know what an East German executive secretary had to do to get ahead in those days. The man who was merely her lawfully wedded husband felt forgotten, neglected; he developed a habit of knocking on the door of his female sublettor, at night when possible, to discuss wives who don't understand, wives who go off to meetings and conferences past midnight. Student Cresspahl left the slopes of the Reilsberg before the second month was up and moved to a place near St. Gertrude's Cemetery in Halle. The sign on the head of streetcar No. 1 gave its destination as "Happy Future" (a street name); the house by the stop was impoverished, with one bathroom for four parties on a landing between the floors. The people living there were suspicious of the newcomer, partly because she was awkward with the local variety of German, partly because her clothes looked as if she could afford more than they could with their ration cards or coupons. The landlady made an effort—she needed the twenty marks. She washed the window, swept out the mansard that Anita recognized from a single description as "Schiller's death chamber." On January mornings the water in the lavoir was frozen. That was when I vowed to myself that if I ever had a child—

– *Thank you ever so kindly.*

– . . . that child would grow up in a room of his or her own, not sublet, with hot running water and a shower.

– I'm so happy to have you as a mother. I'll miss you so.

– *A tua disposizione, Fanta Giro.* Now should we order some champagne from this miserable airline?

– Live a little, they always say. I want my steak well done. *If you please.*

– The fourth person in Halle was of the Gabriel Manfras variety.

– Snooping out attitudes and opinions.

– My file had been transferred from the district headquarters in Gneez by then, and just as Faust wanted to learn what held the world together in its innermost core, so too did the university's party chapter want to learn Student Cresspahl's. Any lingering effects, perchance, from her father's stay in Fünfeichen concentration camp? or the failed house search last summer? The boy pretended to be a suitor, followed me around, acted surprised to happen upon his classmate at eleven at night on Peißnitz Island between the "natural" Saale and the "shipping" Saale, and oops, he'd given himself away by waiting on the Bridge of Friendship. He soon gave himself away for real, letting slip things about Gneez and Jerichow that an ordinary person living outside of Mecklenburg would hardly know. His victim acted innocent, though, and with plausible pauses and hesitations told him the stories that were no doubt already in her file and that he'd been briefed on. He was a fan of the dialectical principle that any fact, even the abolition of the name Nightingale Island, must be seen in the light of *cui bono*

– We've had that! I know that one: "for whose benefit?"!

– so that "your fact" has now been transformed, or extinguished. He also wanted to make out. He'd probably managed to sweet-talk his way into a girl's bed once. The way men go on about my breasts—praising them as if I had anything to do with it! As if I could take them off and put them on!

– Not to mention the prettiest legs on the whole number 5 bus north of Seventy-Second Street.

– *Grazie tanto*, you American. I like it better when people look me in the face; that wasn't easy for our little stool pigeon. He thought he was on his way to a complimentary fling; I kept him around to go places with me like a big dog, and it cost him, or rather the ministry's "reptile fund," quite a chunk of money. I wouldn't go with him to the dance hall on Thälmann Square—the Tusculum, free admission, free feeling-up—but he could make things up to me with an invitation to the Golden Rose on Rannisch Street or old Café Zorn on Leipzig Street, now renamed after Klement Gottwald for geographic reasons. He might have thought he was in the home stretch when I watched his slim wrists gracefully twisting and turning as he spoke, which he clearly was well aware of as one of his good points. He tried to get his future lover drunk and trip her up with a more incriminating fact than that she'd also have liked to study Romance Languages; by the time she admitted, with reservations, that she considered a double major to be a "bourgeois remnant," Grün's Wine Cellar at the city hall had gotten the price of two bottles of Beaujolais out of him and the girl was still sober. She'd graduated from Cresspahl's school, which taught that a slug of Richtenberg aquavit was medicine; she'd celebrated New Year's Eve with Jakob at the Linden Pub in Gneez, where the unit of measure was a double shot of vodka—and she wasn't going to tell a young agent in Saxony that she'd smacked the cap off a Red Army soldier's head that same night, supposedly by mistake, but intentionally, as a sign of discontent with his outfit's post in the Countess Woods, *izvinite, pozhaluysta!* When my second semester started, I was especially precious to this young man, having come back from mysterious Mecklenburg still on the fence about when to become his—then I ended our little game of spying via propositioning.

– Too bad. I was kind of enjoying that. Still, he doesn't deserve a name.

– Let him go to . . . Really Existing Socialism! And he got there with an invitation to Frau von Carayon's salon on Behren Street, aka Ludwig Wucherer Street in Halle, where older students behind splendid late-nineteenth-century facades discussed aspects of Diamat—Dialectical Materialism —that left them unfulfilled. Maybe Jean-Paul Sartre's investigation into nothingness and being, *Das Sein und das Nichts*, Hamburg, 1952. Undergraduate Cresspahl knew these men from sharing study tables at the university library; they said hello when they saw her, with a certain scornful acknowledgment, and now she was out to get them. For the snooper's sake, she started objecting to the rule that a female guest was welcome in these gatherings only when a male one vouched for her loyalty and discretion; now he had another reason to admire her, as a pioneering fighter for women's emancipation. Now she got scared and called in reinforcements.

– I know that one! In Platt, from you: *My big brother, he's got nails on is shoes.*

– Jakob showed up in the city of Halle on the Saale in a German Reich Railway Sunday uniform, a star or two on his epaulettes, and patiently took *his lil sister* around from one student hangout to the next until she found her handler and pointed him out. While I put on an untroubled smile, Jakob went over to him and played a few bars; on Sunday morning, when we strolled to Pottel & Broskowsky on Orphanage Ring, a middle-class restaurant and wine bar with neat clean tablecloths and silver cutlery, the snitch stared right past us—his expense account wouldn't cover that. It was probably dawning on him that his victim wasn't as defenseless as he thought; this dish was spicier than he'd be able to finish. He no longer aspired to scale my upper arms in darkened projection rooms. The smile was stiff on his face. Lib. Arts Stud. Cresspahl could act like she'd forgotten him.

– What I wouldn't give to know what Jakob told him!

– I'm afraid I was curious too, unfortunately...

– It's not curiosity, it's just that I always want to know everything.

– Marie, your father always felt that a man does what he knows he needs to do and makes sure he gets it done, but he didn't feel the need to tell a young woman about it.

– Even if she's grown up with him, twice, like a sister.

– What do you think he said?

– "I have a criminal record, sir. Grievous bodily harm."

– Such big guns for a two-bit kid? When I asked Jakob what he'd said, he remembered what it was and smiled—but he was smiling at me too, with a slight note of warning, as if wanting to keep me from unbecoming behavior. With Jakob I was always the younger one. He decided to celebrate with a morning at Pottel & Broskowsky, Cresspahl's Gesine all to himself

—she should conduct a privatissimum on one Professor Ertzenberger and how amusing he found the pronunciation of a certain first-semester student from Mecklenburg. Professor Ertzenberger had left for a university in western Germany after January 12, when Great Comrade Stalin discovered, brought to light, and crushed a conspiracy of Jewish doctors in his very own city of Moscow. After colleagues in the halls of a university in Halle stopped speaking to him.

– I'd leave a country like that too. What I wouldn't give to know why Jakob stayed!

– You and me both. Maybe it was because he'd promised to work for the German Reich Railway—someone had to do it.

– But you were already thinking about leaving the East.

– That's what you think because you know what happened later. There were so many things that started the process, I remember only the first one: I told Jakob and he nodded, even though we were sitting under a roof with no holes, tended by gentlemen in long white aprons under their tail-coats, duck on our plates and wine in a bucket of ice. He asked me to think it over for three months.

– Think what over? Whether to leave Halle on the Saale?

– That part was easy—by the time I left I'd known that for six months. I knew which spires and towers were people's favorites there; that they think a little square called Reileck is the best in the world; I'd learned to understand their language. But I avoided walks that went by Robert Franz Ring (they like Rings there instead of Streets), because the Saxony-Anhalt Ministerium für Staatssicherheit was located there. Penitentiary Halle I —the "Red Ox"—was at 20 Church Gate. I now knew that right around the corner from Grün's Wine Cellar was Halle II prison; unfortunately I had places I needed to go on Short Stein Street between the polyclinic and the main post office. How would you feel slinking to the Paulus Quarter to stick an unsigned note under the door of an apartment on Ludwig Wucherer Street that says that someone wants to have confidential discus-sions of existentialism and can smile and smile and be a snitch!

– So they didn't need you there, and you left. We're over Omaha, Nebraska.

– Also, since May 1952 there was reason to think that the custodian, Sachwalter Walter, might close the borders. That was when the Stasi took over guarding the border. They drew a patrol strip ten meters wide along the demarcation line, plus a third-of-a-mile no-mans'-land, *plus* a three-mile restricted zone, from which they resettled anyone they knew to be unreliable: merchants, innkeepers, craftsmen, major farmers. You know, the ones the government had attacked with taxes and fines, making itself unpopular. The trap was shut right then.

– Volunteer soldiers like that must realize they'll have to move in on their neighbors?

– A kid who's grown up in the countryside, seeing backbreaking work all around him, usually for other people, with no hope of getting anything for himself—the recruiters for the Armed Police just promise him a decent uniform, better food than the farmhands get, light duty, and financial support for a whole long life and he's more than happy to sign up. An apprentice in the city, tired of endless grinding and scraping, maybe tired of work altogether, signs up for a fixed term because then he too gets a ration card with more coupons and a housing permit. (Conscience doesn't stand a chance against material incentives —ANITA.) Anyway, an experienced head of state will know to deploy his Thuringian recruits in Saxony, the Saxon ones in Mecklenburg. By the way, no more state of Mecklenburg.

– What? You're kidding me, Gesine.

– There was a Law for the Further Democratization of the Structure and Function of Government Institutions in the States of the GDR—July 23, 1952. You were only allowed to say "Mecklenburg" in a linguistic or anthropological sense. Otherwise it was now three regions: Rostock, Schwerin, and New Brandenburg; the state parliament and state government were transferred there. They picked up a piece of West Prignitz in the south, and Uckermark in the east. But since the law abolishing the states referred to the states, the regional legislatures kept electing representatives to the state senates until 1958, who had to keep showing up and declaring that they had no objections to the law of summer 1952.

– Are you sad about the end of the Blue, Yellow, and Red?

– I miss the blue, because Rostock's golden griffin looked so good against it. I miss the red and gold, for Schwerin. The red of the tongue in the black buffalo head for the Wendish lands. Another piece of one's origins wiped out.

– And you left Mecklenburg because the workers and peasants later rose up against the government of the workers and peasants.

– These stirring words, Marie!

– That's what they teach us in school.

– American schools tell you that as the first and most important thing to know about Socialism so that you'll ignore the Negro uprisings from Watts to Newark!

– Gesine, you said not till October.

– Sowwy. The Gesine Cresspahl of back then didn't know a single worker well.

– Excuse me, there was *one*.

– Two, actually; because of one mistake. In May 1953, Lib. Arts Stud. Cresspahl was actually short of money, and had forgotten to get a free train ticket from Jakob, and wanted to discuss something with Anita. To save some money she took the train just to Schkeuditz and then stood on the autobahn cloverleaf between Leipzig and Halle, book bag under her left arm, right arm raised and waving. That lasted one and a half hours. Most of the drivers in the West German cars flicked their brights, which meant "Sorry!" because picking up passengers in the transit zone could get them in trouble with the People's Police. Round flashes of lightning, brighter than the morning sun. The people who eventually did stop for a demoralized undergraduate were two beefy guys moving furniture from Saxon Vogtland for some POB; they were pleased with the company and kept their guest quiet by repeatedly trading stories featuring ladies waiting at night by the side of the road prepared to remunerate their free ride in various positions on the bench behind the driver, at which point he almost steered the unwieldy truck into a ditch from sheer anticipation. On Frankfurter Allee in Berlin, which had been rebuilt in honor of Great Comrade Stalin, they turned on the girl they had, until she forked over twenty marks, more than the train would've cost. Good-natured threats of being prepared to get rough.

– How sleazy.

– Only fair, if you ask me: a lesson on the community of interests between workers in the transportation industries and students between Halle and Leipzig. It's true that that was the very year when a compass, representing "technical intelligentsia," was added to the hammer and ring of grain on the East German national emblem; that wouldn't have stopped the two

Vogtland guys from being just as ready to kidnap and extort money out of an engineering student. Anyway, we were—

– "We"?

– Anita and her Mecklenburg friend were constantly amazed at what the workers in East Germany put up with: changes to the collective labor contract in January 1953, namely the addition of "Socialist content," which meant raising the work norms, which to wage earners meant a slow decline in the amount of food they could buy for their money. The custodian wanted to take back the higher wages he'd decreed the previous summer; excess purchasing power gave him a hard time, since he'd opposed things like the primacy of consumer-goods industries on "scientific" grounds and now had too few shoes and pots to put on the market; because the party is not a human being, the party is always right.

– You knew Eckart Pingel's father in Gneez.

– Ol' Pingel would have greeted Undergraduate Cresspahl with a quick wink, meaning the cheerful, amused question: So, Gesine, you here too? He'd have taken his cap off before shaking hands and starting a conversation. If I'd asked him about the engineering work quotas courtesy of the Soviet Union, he'd have sidestepped the question as overly intrusive. Because around then, when Eckart Pingel had practically run away from school ("because he told the truth"), his father saw anyone allowed to go to college in the New State as one of its minions—an ally of the authorities.

– You knew farmers.

– Not many. After the war, the nobility's estates near Jerichow were given away to settlers (except for the von Plessens', to the south, and a much smaller one, formerly the Kleineschultes', on the Baltic; the Red Army kept those two to handle their own supply of meat, flour, butter). (And a third one, the Upper Bülows', taken over in one piece as a people-owned farm under contract with the Wismar city hospitals.) Not many of the people who'd taken over five- to ten-acre plots of land in 1946 were farmworkers from the old days—who understood the business and knew better than to try to make it with less than twenty-five. There was one single village with only peasant farmers, since the fourteenth century. Traffic sprang up there in the black-market days, so the Cresspahl house got some potatoes for the cellar: but it was Jakob who took care of that until 1950, by which time Cresspahl had relearned how to go for walks around the countryside. The Cresspahl child had been going to school in the city of Gneez since 1944, and recently even farther afield. She didn't know any farmers. She'd taken a detour on her bike at Dr. Kliefoth's request, once, through Pötenitz and Old Demwies; she reported back on empty farms abandoned by their settlers when the custodian, after only six years, tried to take his gift back by converting the farms into Agricultural Production Cooperatives. (*Now we know!*) She'd heard unwatered, unmilked cows bellowing in pain; she was cured of the superstition that no Mecklenburg farmer would ever leave a head of cattle without food and supervision for a single night. Didn't know any farmers.

– Georg Utpathel.

– He ended up in the usual way, but at least he'd been in jail a long time; he could make himself feel better, tell himself he'd lost his farm to the law. Wait, I knew one farmer!

– Johnny Schlegel.

– He was one of the exceptions. An educated man, with opinions about how they'd run agricultural communes in the Weimar era. According to one of these opinions, a proletarian working the fields, even if granted (bribed with) a cottage and garden plot and grain allowance, would never consider his labor his own—it only went to maintain and increase the landowner's or leaseholder's property. Under the scourge of Hitler's and Darré's agricultural laws, Schlegel had to work his three hundred acres in the old feudal way; now that they'd lost their war, at home and abroad, he'd handed out his inheritance in ninths to refugees from the lost eastern territories, as long as they were farmers or willing to learn to be. For each of these gifts, nominally loans, he'd entered an invented amount of money in his farm's books and at the land registry; he operated an agricultural commune on his own terms under the protection of his friends in the Red Army. Even in 1951, an inspector from a people-owned land purchasing and incorporation business wouldn't scare him off the road. Then came the East German government's scientific recognition that a Socialist agriculture meant large-scale farms; then came their shock that in 1952 some people on the Baltic near Jerichow had long since been working in a cooperative advanced far past Socialist Type III, in which only the collective use of the land, draft animals, vehicles, and tools was supposed to have been socialistically introduced. At Johnny's farm, household tasks were done in common by all the members too—the food cooked in one kitchen, meals eaten at one table. The fictitious sums of money had now turned into the kind with which Mrs. von Alvensleben could be bought out for her share when her children asked her to join them abroad to fulfill a grandmother's duties; that money came right back when Mrs. Sünderhauf brought her brother over from the West, where he'd had to work underground, mining in the Ruhr. Assessed as farmers with midsized holdings, the members of Johnny's project were required to deliver quotas several times higher than what was due from the settlers and small landholders: eight double centners of wheat per hectare instead of two, seventy-five of potatoes instead of twenty-five, fifty-nine of meat instead of thirty-eight; and still, as late as the end of 1952, they were in good enough shape that Johnny could reply to a worried visitor: like this!

– Gesine! How can you bend your elbow and make a fist in an American airplane?!

– This is an international flight. *Io sono di Ierico.*

– You gave the old man across the aisle such a start! He knows what that gesture means.

– *Vi forstår desværre ikke amerikansk, kære frøken.*

– And now you'll say something like: Envy is an unpleasant trait even in a Socialist administration? *Socialist rulers have human feelings, too?*

– How can you even think such a thing! No, they longed to learn what held Johnny's world together / in its innermost core; the quota experts carried out an in-depth investigation. The 1952 harvest had been so-so, the Schlegel collective had fallen behind on milk; the collection officers magnanimously and per regulations gave him permission to deliver pork instead, and if that meant he was short of his pork quota, he could deliver *that* in beef instead.

– That means he'd get even less milk in his buckets!

– No, he was allowed to keep his pledged cow in his own stall—he just had to pay for it.

– For his own cow?

– At quadruple the price. If he'd actually handed it over for his quota, only the 1941 fixed price would have been credited to him.

– I'd make mistakes in my books, too, with all these twists and turns.

– Johnny's books were perfectly exact and complete. Alas for him. Now the tax inspectors could decode from regular "withdrawals" that Johnny, in fall 1947, had gotten from the von Maltzahns a wedge of land that had been bothering him for fifteen years—a few acres—and he had paid the money for it into their foreign account in Schleswig-Holstein via West Berlin. Private foreign-currency transactions.

– Arrest?

– In February 1953.

– Ah-hah! said the judge. Very bad.

– Excellent: thought the judge. And Otto Sünderhauf had exchanged the money for his share in Frankfurt, where he only had to put down twenty-three Western marks to get one hundred Eastern ones. The criminal exchange rate of the imperialists.

– Supply and demand.

– And thus the defendants were found guilty of being profoundly arrested in capitalist ways of thinking.

– That makes two!

– That made four. After Sünderhauf, Mrs. Bliemeister and Mrs. Lakenmacher were brought in for questioning. It turns out Johnny's collective followed a different plan than the one they'd handed into the authorities in duplicate, triplicate, and more. In that plan, provision was made for the death of young animals.

– Gesine!

– You think it's only babies who die prematurely? A calf can catch cold and die of pneumonia too.

– That's what doctors are for.

– Out of the five veterinarians in Gneez, three had "made their way West" by that point, Dr. Hauschildt in the lead as always. When Johnny factored into his calculations his own knowledge of veterinary medicine and what expert assistance would have cost, a certain amount of lost headcount was to be expected. And the state—the same state the veterinarians were fleeing—turned this into accusing Johnny of slander. Economic criminality. Incitement to Boycott. And when Johnny, in his closing statement, wanted to know why the court was tearing asunder what the *Krasnaya Armiya* had sewn together for him: that was breaking the Law for the Protection of Peace.

– *They threw the book at him.*

– Fifteen years in prison. For the other defendants: eight to twelve. Confiscation of property. By April, Johnny's cooperative had been cleaned out. The members had hightailed it to the refugee camps in West Berlin, with all their children. Inge Schlegel stayed a while longer; she wanted to try to save the house at least, and someone had to take care of Axel Ohr, send him his packages in prison. Now it was clear where Johnny had miscalculated: she needed him there. If a woman alone is trying to keep a large farm in working order, it's going to have sagging doors and holes in the roof after a month. She'd been left with a single horse: *Jakob sin Voss*, the sorrel. Once the horse had been shot, she left. That's a story . . . like the one about little children falling into a rain barrel.

– Well, I have to learn to be brave. Tell me.

– Don't ask, Marie.

– I'm eleven years old already!

– You'll be sorry.

– It's on me.

– Jakob's sorrel was listed in the books as one midsize workhorse. That requires, per year:

  10 double centners of hay,

  16 d.c. straw,

  20 d.c. turnips,

  18 d.c. grain feed,

  and 30 d.c. green fodder,

some of which it can forage from the fields on its own. Now if you figure that a centner of oats cost twenty-five marks in 1953 . . .

– then a horse like that will break Undergraduate Cresspahl's budget.

– The spring semester of 1953 ended on May 9; by that Monday I was visiting Inge Schlegel. She held me by the shoulder when *Jakob sin Voss* was led past us; I followed him into the large fodder-preparation kitchen. The man holding the lead turned around with a goofy grin on his face, like he was inviting me to come watch a show, a surprise. The horse walked cheerfully along, with friendly nods at the guy's encouraging patter. A few ribs were showing; he was totally healthy. His looks said: you did let me go hungry for a while, you humans, but now you're taking care of me again, I'm glad we're back on good terms. When the bolt gun was placed on his forehead, he trustingly closed his eyes; this was a new one from the humans.

After his death, knocked onto his side, his legs jerked violently, every which way, and kept beating against the echoing floorboards. It looked like painful agony; from a scientific point of view it was just residual functioning of the nervous system. The sweet-tempered animal *Jakob sin Voss* had suddenly turned into a disgusting piece of meat wrapped in blond fur; still recognizably him, from the open eyes.

– Gesine! You didn't wait outside the door?

– How could I know that the stranger was a butcher from Gneez! I saw his two assistants with the knife too late.

– The next time I brag about how old I am, Gesine, just put a stop to it then and there. Give me a slap in the face if you have to.

– We are now over Salt Lake City, Utah.

– You'd had enough.

– I still had to watch Elise Bock's bedroom furniture being auctioned off in Gneez—it was People's Property once Elise moved to West Berlin. People crowding and pushing in a narrow, dirty yard outside the open shutters of Elise's windows; a man in a threadbare suit inside, with the Unity Party emblem on his lapel, holding up photographs for the gathered crowd: a chair, the lamps. The bidders, Alfred Fretwust in the lead, hooted their humorous comments like a bunch of kids, or drunks. That was when my leaving started.

– Were you legally adult?

– Under East German law. Cresspahl and Jakob's mother stayed up a whole night with me, listening. I was scaring an old woman. Cresspahl hoped the child would reconsider. He said something about recuperating and feeling better. "A vacation at Anita's."

– And Jakob?

– Jakob gave Undergraduate Cresspahl a free ticket to Halle University, not via Stendal but for the route Gneez–Güstrow–Pritzwalk–Berlin. But the child at border control, without complete papers, under suspicion, liable to end up behind bars! He prevented that. And he'd realized that in June the mornings are bright, the sunlight dances in the woods, the lakes near Krakow and Plau glitter—that was to be her farewell sight. Only when the conductor gave her back her ticket with its brown horizontal stripe and the Reich Railway stamp, like a coworker, did she realize: Jakob had given her a round-trip ticket.

– *Welcome to San Francisco, Gesine!*

And what are the Chinese doing in SF?

Some of them are standing around glumly in a shooting gallery where you aim a BB gun at moving targets. They see a European tourist and her American child exchange words in a foreign language. The lady walks up, takes a rifle, and in ten shots has won an alarm clock, the grand prize. They clap, unenvious, these spectators. That's what the Chinese are doing in S.F.

August 16, 1968 Friday

Trying to find today's *New York Times* in New Orleans is like *chercher une aiguille dans une botte de foin*; a copy turns up like something exotic in a bodega on Canal Street offering mostly products of the foreign press, and is sold with a ten-cent surcharge—air freight. The only news for us: yesterday there was a fire in New York. At shortly past noon a midsized fire stripped bare the Rockaway Parkway elevated subway platform: exactly where we spent Tuesday with Jakob's letter from Olomouc, ČSSR. Marie asked for the page with the photo of the site, despite the resulting increase in the weight of our luggage, in preparation for a discussion of coincidence with D. E.; – for when we're back home.

Marie can't get enough of the Chinese of San Francisco—their sympathetic way of watching the yellow- and black- and pink-skinned people dealing with one another on the sidewalks and in the cable cars, making room for people according to fragility and age, in solidarity. Maybe also because they remind Marie of a Sunday walk in New York in July with D. E., where a dark-skinned fellow citizen was lying on a wall along Riverside Park with his eyes closed, a wall with a fifty-foot drop; asleep and trusting the sun. – That's all we've managed in our city!: concludes a shamed and disappointed child.

What with her delight in the boats of Fisherman's Wharf it's easy to miss a bus, even a taxi, to the San Francisco Airport; she approved our suggestion that we make the trip triangular. When a young lady in the company of an older one marches past a liveried hotel porter with no luggage except a ticking package, the house is honored to put them up for the night: *if* we act like we do this every day, like D. E.!: the child cries, looking forward to seeing him again.

Marie brings up Professor Erichson, who has departed this life in a northeastern part of Europe, once again when she praises her mother for rebooking a plane reservation: the way he's taught us to do it!: she declares. She carefully observes New Orleans for him, hoping he's never been there and she'll be able to tell him that you get out of that airport only in a six-seater limousine whose driver takes his last two passengers, unasked, to a family-run hotel between Canal Street and the Mississippi and drops them off at a narrow staircase with the shout: *Folks*, I'm bringin you some'un! And again a reception clerk was amazed when we actually copied a passport number into the register!

As long as we're irrevocably booked for a return flight to New York tomorrow morning, she's willing to accept a city on the Mississippi. The river does seem yellow to her, dirty; its harbor ferry is a poor substitute for the one in her city. The balconies in the Vieux Carré, the wrought-iron ornamental grilles outside the inner courtyards with magnolia trees inside, long shiny leaves and pinkish white flowers—she looks upon all of that as a quotation from the Europe looming on Tuesday and not a moment too late; she doesn't complain but she does mention the heavy hot humidity, the cool musty odor, – like a cemetery: she now finds it, making Mrs. Cresspahl shudder in anticipation of a discussion of coincidence, since now it will be expanded to include the topic of premonitions. What earned the city points for Marie was a big turn-of-the-century hospital, from which emerged dignified dark-complexioned fellow Americans, looking concerned. The newspapers printed on yellow and lavender paper—she likes that just for the variety. The unused areas in the restaurants are dirty, in her view; only the front halves of the grills are shiny, unlike in New York, where the whole surfaces are polished. Some streets near Canal Street are so poor and rundown that Mrs. Cresspahl, too, wonders how a person gets here—surely not by plane. In a luncheonette, Marie liked the cat longingly eyeing her double-decker sandwich.

On June 9, 1953, the custodian of the East German Republic made a few suggestions to his citizen Gesine Cresspahl, with respect to her possible return into his clutches.

His party, he said, intended to disclaim one of its virtues of the nonhuman type: infallibility. It had, in fact, committed errors. One consequence of which was that numerous persons had left the Republic. This applies to you, Miss Cresspahl!

Since the party had gone so far as to reset the scales to zero with Peter Wulff, as promised—"to zero grams!" as it liked to say in its zeal—it planned to go so far as to allow him to reopen the grocery store adjacent to his pub. It intended to supply him with goods to sell, even. And no need to worry, for now, about the taxes and social security deductions not paid since 1951. An end to repressive measures, Mr. Wulff!

Now as for the others near and dear to you in the Republic, Miss Cresspahl. Ever striving to stay true to our principles, we have converted a cooperative farm on the Baltic near Jerichow to "Devastated" status, so that no receiver would want to touch it with a ten-foot pole, and if Mrs. Sünderhauf, Mr. Leutnant, Mrs. Schurig, Mrs. Winse and all the children—*The Englishmin*, Epi, Jesus, Hen and Chickee, and the others under eighteen—cared to return to Johnny's agricultural endeavor they would get their property back along with aid in the form of credit and inventory. How do you like that, Gesine Cresspahl.

We plan in earnest to send your Georg Utpathel home from custody along with all the other people sentenced to just three years under the Law for the Protection of the People's Property. We would prefer to keep the ones we've convicted of graver crimes, such as Johnny Schlegel, notorious atheist and enemy of the nobility. But maybe not Otto Sünderhauf, let's talk.

The last time you paid a visit to Wendisch Burg you were mad at us for having harassed a girl by the name of E. Rehfelde over her Protestant faith and adherence to the Church; we'd persisted until Klaus Niebuhr and his girlfriend Ingrid Babendererde renounced their graduations too and left the country, obviously thinking that this would preserve their equality under the constitution. Well, Rehfelde is to be readmitted. If Students Niebuhr and Babendererde decide to return to Wendisch Burg, they too will be permitted to make up their final exams. What do you say to that?

And as for you, Lib. Arts Stud. Cresspahl. We made an exception in your case when we let you go to university, but in future this will be our general policy for talented young people from the middle classes. Once we no longer consider that a handicap, Miss Cresspahl, you might even get a scholarship.

Regarding your father, too, would you mind taking into account the following couple of concessions. The additional food cost we imposed in April will be abolished as of June 15—that's this Monday. We will also inform Jerichow City Hall that Mr. Heinrich Cresspahl, Brickworks Road, is again entitled to coupons for rationed articles, effective immediately.

So now tell us what you think, young lady. Just come back—we'll act as if you've just been on vacation. If we have already confiscated any of your belongings, we'll give them back. Or make restitution. Ration cards, German ID—it'll all be yours. Please come, Miss Cresspahl, and bring your friend Anita too!

These were some of the suggestions that the East German custodian's Socialist Unity Party made to Cresspahl's daughter in the event of her return.

You spent the summer months of 1953 in the Grunewald neighborhood of West Berlin, Miss Cresspahl?

As you already know, apparently.

In a mansion in Grunewald?

In a house in ruins from the second floor up.

Would you care to tell us the name of the street?

Forgot it.

The name of your host?

I don't recall.

The circumstances behind your connection to this household?

You know already. A dog named Rex. Or King. Or Voshd, whatever you want to call him.

What can a dog born in 1933 have to do with anything twenty years later?

I saw him again before he died. A stubborn patriarch of a German shepherd, gray-black all over. When he went outside he didn't seem blind. A hundred and twenty-six in human years.

And that was why you were in Berlin no later than 1951 to obtain carpentry tools by the criminal conversion of Western currency?

I was seeing a family friend.

Friends because you shared the presence of a dog in your family photos? Or because of business relations in 1944, 1947, 1949, and 1951?

No comment.
Someone gives you a room and breakfast and a house key and pocket money all because of fond memories of Cresspahl?
Strange but true.
We're supposed to believe that, coming from you?
Take it or leave it.

Anita worked for department stores and ad agencies over the holidays, addressing envelopes, one half West pfennig each, until she found people who would offer her one mark per page for translations from Russian. (Let us refrain from discussing those bastards; we will say: they wanted the work done for the Department of Cultural Cooperation at the French Army headquarters, West Berlin. That'll have to do.) We had a standing arrangement to meet at Nikolassee streetcar station for Wannsee Beach whenever Anita had time. We had to keep our eyes peeled "for the less expensive pastimes"; we were too poor for movies or plays. Again and again, whether we were swimming the Havel from north to south or I was spending the night at Anita's room in Neukölln on Mrs. Machate's ironing board, she would be surprised to hear the latest argument her friend Cresspahl had dreamed up to give her a reasonable path back to Jerichow or Martin Luther University. One time it was that she'd remembered the news that in April all the Jewish doctors Stalin had accused of a plot against the Soviet Union had been released and fully rehabilitated, professionally and civically. Mightn't one draw a line from that straight to an eventual rule of law in the East German republic?

– Tell that to the two who died under torture, Kogan and Etlinger!: Anita said. – Tell it to the Jewish writers who that bloodthirsty killer had shot just last summer!: Anita said.

Stalin had died on March 6: Cresspahl offered.

And how did you feel when the East German newsreels in Halle showed the funerals from Moscow and the East German ceremonies with their lowered flags and inconsolable music?

Cresspahl admitted that the sight had caused in her, too, a creeping nausea.

So the passing of Stalin, which fills all progressive humankind with deepest sorrow, is an especially heavy loss for the German nation? The

Socialist Unity Party will remain forever true to Stalin's victorious teachings? Forever?

That was what they'd promised: Anita's friend admitted.

And now Anita could have said: See? But she didn't give advice; she was helpful, she reviewed the vacillating Cresspahl child's papers and checked them for anything missing, anything invalid. – Technically you'd be safe on a trip to Halle anytime until September 10: she concluded, exhaling deeply—it was practically a sigh. Anita and the freedom of a Christian.

Lib. Arts Stud. Cresspahl spent June 16 on the Havel; on the 17th, as she was going to check with her own eyes the radio reports of an uprising in the Eastern sector of the city, the streetcar she was on, line 88, was stopped at Lützow Street, where it normally crosses Potsdamer Street and runs to Kreuzberg along the border to the Eastern sector—by West Berlin police who were trying in vain to move the curious off to the south, one by one. (She wasn't cocky enough to attempt a streetcar ride into East Berlin itself; the station patrols could easily pack her off to Halle on the Saale sooner than she wanted to go.) And so she experienced the uprising only as news, in words and pictures, and as hearsay from students who made it from Halle into the refugee camps in West Berlin:

Two or three hundred women stood outside Penitentiary II on Stein Street, shouting: Let our husbands out! A column of striking workers from the Buna and Leuna plants who were marching up saw this and stormed the gate, taking the prisoners out of their cells, many of them women and in bad physical shape. The workers cleared out the court building. A female warden waved her pistol around, was beaten up. The Unity Party's headquarters on Willi Lohmann Street, the district headquarters at Stein Gate, the headquarters on the market square: stormed. Volkspolizei were waiting at the gates of the Red Ox, by the Church Gate—guns drawn, safeties off. The crowd pushes open a side door; is fired on from the roof; disperses. Here there were apparently people wounded. The main post office remained in police hands until morning. At around six p.m., about thirty thousand people are gathered on Hallmarkt. The speakers' demands: General strike against the government; loyalty to the Red Army. Discipline. Punishment for hoarding, looting, killing. Dissolving the government. Free elections. Reunification with West Germany. Around seven p.m., Russian tanks come rolling from Obermarkt; cautiously. Joining the pieces of paper that had already come sailing out the windows of the stormed government buildings were copies of a flier signed by the garrison commander and military commandant of the city of Halle (Saale), declaring a state of emergency, banning demonstrations and gatherings, imposing a curfew for the hours between nine p.m. and four a.m., and threatening armed force against any resistance.

There is a photograph of the striking workers, men and women, marching into Halle. It shows about ninety people in all—the women in summer dresses, the men mostly dressed as if for work, in gray or dark overalls or pants and shirts. They are in uneven rows, arms swinging, a few people waving at one another (unaware of the camera). Two people have brought luggage. There are eleven bicycles visible in the picture; why would these people have brought such expensive articles with them if they were planning to cause violence or expecting to suffer it?

On June 21, the Central Committee of the East German Unity Party gave Citizen Cresspahl one additional suggestion, for the event of her return: The uprising in its republic must be understood as merely events that happened. As the work of the American and (West-)German warmongers who, disappointed at the gains of the peace movement in Korea and Italy, wanted to throw the torch of war across the bridgehead of West Berlin . . . discovered by means of bandits with weapons and secret radio transmitters being dropped from foreign aircraft . . . trucks full of weapons on the Leipzig-Berlin autobahn . . .

She got a letter from Gneez saying that workers at the Panzenhagen sawmill had opened the cellars under the district court, shouting: We want our exploiters back! She presumed, in all modesty, to know the workers better, even by sight, than the East German custodian, and know their complaints: the revoked discounts for train tickets, the family fights caused by reduced minimum pension rates, spa treatments now counted against annual vacations, workplaces polluted by informers, the sense of *travailler pour le Roi de Russe* as exemplified by the Unity Party's insistence on a 10 percent increase in work norms the very day before—on the morning of June 16. She would have gone back anyway, if everyone from Gneez to Halle were now allowed to say: We've seen who's in charge in this country—the Soviets. When she did decide to leave, it was hardly because the Americans were the occupiers in charge of that other Germany; it was because she was afraid of being called on in a seminar at the university by the Saale and expected to recite that on a certain date, X, it was not the workers who...

Memory offers—insists—that she arrived at the Berlin-Marienfelde refugee camp. The writer today may not be sure that it was already in operation in July 1953; the mind asserts that it was under construction starting on March 4. In any case, whether in Marienfelde, on Kuno Fischer Street, or on Karolinger Square, she there for the first time met a young man from Wendisch Burg—a skinny boy, bullheaded, with blond hair then, absently trying to strike up an acquaintance on the basis of his connection with the fisherman-Babendererdes and the teacher-Babendererdes as well as the Wendisch Burg Niebuhrs. On a stroll around Dahlem, near the West Berlin university, he observed the local students disdainfully and called them "all these beautiful young people"; she at first thought him conceited about being an upperclassman (physics). She described her amazement that Klaus Niebuhr would give up his school, his residence in Mecklenburg, all for the idea that he should renounce his citizenship to avenge an insult against a girl named Rehfelde. This Erichson (dipl. phys.) liked that; he immediately accused Miss Cresspahl of similar conduct. – For five years you accepted the gap between your thoughts and the things your schools demanded of you; now that the gap has grown just a little bigger than you'd like, you're through. Ever heard of the third principle of dialectics, the transformation of quantity into quality? You can apply it somatically too: he said in response to her excuse that she wasn't feeling well. Hardly a courtship. He let himself be flown out of Berlin before she'd even reached Preliminary Examination I in the refugee emergency admittance process.

The official questioning grew more and more repulsive from one office ("station") to the next. The medical examiner determined she was twenty years old and nothing he had to worry about. Station Two was responsible for determining responsibility. After the referral, the police, and the registration came Station Seven: preliminary examination by the Task Force Against Inhumanity. This group didn't take a liking to Undergraduate Cresspahl, nor did the next—the Investigating Committee of Free Jurists—since she blamed them for their part in the verdict against Sieboldt and Gollantz and moreover made fun of their initiatives, like the one according to which people in the "Soviet Zone" were to proclaim their resistance by boycotting movie theaters on a given Wednesday, and as a result, obviously, everyone rushed to the Renaissance Cinema in Gneez to shore up their political reputation. Here she was given reprimands, bad grades, as she realized once she got to Station 7c, Police Commissioner's Office, Section V (Political Section)—they looked at her like a bad, recalcitrant schoolgirl. For 7d, British Counterintelligence, she'd gotten Anita to brief her about the prison camp in Glowe on the island of Rügen, where around four thousand forced laborers, in exchange for bread and margarine and potato soup, slogged away at a circuit rail line around four runways for bombers and jet fighters, at a naval base for submarines and light surface craft; this was one of the rumors going around Mecklenburg. (Unfortunately for the Soviet strategy. Cresspahl was still mad about the "Red Corners" on public squares, known as Stalin's icon altars; she and Anita agreed that the Soviets had brought in their tanks on the 17th so carefully because they were only carrying reserve troops and equipment for the brutal strike should it be necessary.) Alas, the rumor was known to the British gentleman with the woolly mustache as well; he waved his pipe with regret. The recording secretary, with nine rings too many on her fingers for a woman only twenty-five years old, gazed with preemptive schadenfreude, not fellow feeling, at this girl from Mecklenburg trying to buy support for her refugee ID with such cheap coinage. The next question was about the students at the Fritz Reuter High School in Gneez who'd volunteered for service in the Armed People's Police.

The interrogatee twisted her statement away from that topic to Martin Luther University in Halle, where students in all departments could use small-rifle and radio-unit training by the banks of the Saale as a way to keep their noses clean; she then said she wasn't feeling well; she was sternly admonished to return to resume the examination.

Outside, in an offputtingly undamaged neighborhood of villas and empty sidewalks with only a maid every now and then waking a dog, she was alone with her concern that she had not much helped Prisoner Lockenvitz, and might have harmed NCO Pagenkopf. If this was the price of an official exit to West Germany, she'd rather slip through the bushes when no one was looking.

Anita found it, that path through the bushes. Did her friend Gesine know the lawyer on Lietzenburg Street who'd paid off debts in installments on behalf of Johnny Schlegel?

That was how Gesine Cresspahl came into a permit to move to the state of West Berlin; out of turn, too. She was allowed to register as a permanent resident of the Grunewald district of the city at a regular police precinct, not with Section V. Such a person with such a file has the right to a West Berlin personal ID. With a loan of a hundred and twenty West marks (the ticket alone cost over eighty), she flew in the second-to-last week in July as a private person to Frankfurt/Main, in a Douglas Clipper type 3, at night.

A person can imagine they recognize, under the wings of a DC-10 in transit from New Orleans to New York, while still over the Atlantic, the offshore island, the whitish shelf of land where Mrs. Cresspahl tried to vacation a year before. Marie, looking ahead, not down, sees the island of the Staaten General, Manhattan, Long Island.

– Welcome home, Gesine!

August 17, 1968 Saturday, South Ferry day

Waiting with Eagle-Eye Robinson at Riverside Drive is a single telegram. From Helsinki, of course, with the signature mangled: CANNOT CURRENTLY BE MOVED – ERISINION.

For breakfast, a telegram from Helsinki: NO NEED TO VISIT – ERISINN.

With the regular mail, an official-looking letter postmarked from Germany: from the Psychoanalytical Research Institute, Frankfurt am Main. Not counting the time in transit, the answer took less than a month. A professor taking the trouble to write three and a half pages to a bank employee named Cresspahl, on his private stationery! in his free time!

And he's never even had the pleasure of making our personal acquaintance. (As he says in all sincerity after reading our letter.) He refuses to attempt a long-distance diagnosis, due to insufficient information and too narrow a basis for judgment—nor had she wanted one. But he is willing to say: If I hear the voices of the dead, of people not present, and they answer me, it may be due to the predisposition of the person having this type of experience. Please take from my inferences only what's useful to you. There must be a firm bond between such a person and her past; there's no way she can have put it behind her. She's on the right track when she assumes that we're dealing with aftereffects of wounds, of losses; she is wrong when she thinks that it's about Jakob, or Cresspahl; in fact it started with her mother, who was "de-ranged" out of her place in this world. We're talking about you, Lisbeth née Papenbrock! Alienation, yes; delusion, no. It's just that you haven't dealt with this first rejection by the mother and put behind you (the second rejection, the third rejection). There's no risk of your passing it on hereditarily. There's just one thing that isn't right, Mrs. Cresspahl: your sometimes knowing your child Marie's answer before she says it. That can be a self-serving move, trying to protect the child and, in her, yourself—but for the child such symbiosis will soon turn dangerous, restricting her independence. You yourself described it in your letter as an illegal activity ("kept under surveillance"), and that gave you away, Mrs. Cresspahl.

"You need to have the courage—the considerable courage—to reject defense mechanisms, even though doing so cannot help but feel like negligence, given your life experiences. You would save some time if you chose to avail yourself of a, I know the word is on the tip of your tongue: a "*headshrinker.*" This metaphor really hurts you more than it hurts my American colleagues; it keeps you from making use of a medical service that could help you reach a more appropriate sense of inner security. Why not try it, it's harmless—you can break it off whenever you want. Kind regards, A. M."

What he clearly omitted: any concerns about an inability to work. Based on how I come across in a letter, I am equipped with what I need for a job abroad, in Prague.

"Dear Professor, I am somewhat ashamed to admit that I don't know how to express my . . ." Serves you right, Gesine Cresspahl. You asked him to do something difficult, now rack your brains over a thank-you letter. It'll take you three weeks to write it!

Over breakfast, the news from Bonn in *The New York Times*: the West Germans have thought long and hard about the treaty that they inherited, dated Sept. 29, 1938, when Chamberlain, Daladier, and Mussolini gave Hitler the Sudetenland. Hitherto this treaty had been regarded as "no longer valid." Now the people of the ČSSR might get their way and a signature under the wording: "null from the outset."

After Marshal Tito, it's now the president of Rumania paying a visit to Prague. Nicolae Ceauşescu describes how you do it: a small Communist country can totally accept credits in convertible currency as long as it remains in a military alliance such as the Warsaw Pact. If a delegate from a New York bank turns up in the capital of a small Communist country the day after the day after tomorrow, what's the problem.

– So now Undergraduate Cresspahl at a West German university: Marie requests as soon as she's done supervising the casting-off of the ferry.
– Lib. Arts Stud. G. C. at a University of . . . what did they call universities in West Germany?
– One was named after Johann Wolfgang von Goethe, was located in Frankfurt, and was willing to accept this rising second-year student from Halle on the Saale into the English Department. (And do you know why? Because I'd been enrolled at a university. Anita's Abitur meant nothing in West Berlin—she'd had to retake all her exams.) When I saw the tuition and fees I forgot about that.
– Your father had Western money! A few thousand pounds at the Surrey Bank of Richmond, with interest accrued since 1938!
– I'd left Cresspahl's country, left him, against his will. Just think how much more unreasonable I'll be when you leave me! He also probably thought his assets there had been confiscated as enemy property.
– Your father was trying to punish you.
– That would have meant he was trying to get his daughter back. No, she should have it her own way and live accordingly. As for academia, she'd seen through her illusions.
– Too bad, if you ask me.
– "Dr. Gesine Cresspahl"! Can you imagine?
– "Professor Cresspahl" sounds pretty good.
– Sure, "Prof. Marie Cresspahl"! You become one.
– We'll see, Gesine, won't we.
– And what kind of job can you get with a degree in English?
– Teacher.
– I'd lost all desire for that career at the Socialist high school in Gneez. Standing in front of a class knowing that you're hiding something, that the students think you're lying—no thanks.

– In a free country you could teach what you wanted.

– In grammar, poetic meter, form—sure. But I couldn't analyze the content with the kind of dialectics that made sense to me in 1953! Anyway, all I really wanted was the language.

– So because of your father...

– If I wanted to get that unraveled by a *headshrinker*... a psychoanalyst headhunter, Marie, then we wouldn't be able to take any more trips to New York via Frisco and Louisiana. A translation school was enough for me, and if it happened to be located in a river valley on the left bank of the Rhine, then in the morning mist it would look like Flanders after the battle. There you needed the abilities of Hitler's chief translator at your fingertips no less than you did the proverbs of Solomon. There the students would graduate and leave the nature conservancy park of academic jobs and pensions for life in the wild as working translators. Lots of chip-laden shoulders there. Narrow-gauge academics. Someone pointed out one of them to me who'd been in a translator's squad for Hitler's army, a former actor in Leningrad; no hands. Another one, when in his cups, used to brag about his many seductions; he was why I avoided Russian. Italian, French— yes. At least we learned how to speak; chockchock!: as Emil Knoop would say. Besides, Dr. Kliefoth and two semesters in Halle had hardly been able to fix everything from H.-G. Knick's classes. *Knickei*—a real Grade B egg. He'd sent us off with the information: The use of the passive is very common in English. That was that. Lots of *remedial teaching*.

– Simultaneous translation?

– That's a cinch, I can do that in my sleep. No, consecutive interpreting, at a conference, that's the pinnacle, the real art—translating a forty-five-minute lecture and saying it as if you'd written it yourself. Here is one of my many professional dreams that never came true: being elected a member of the AIIC, the Association Internationale des Interprètes de Con-férences. They only accept you after two hundred days of conference work and if five colleagues vouch for you. For that I would've had to pay for ten semesters on the Rhine, at Schifferstadt, instead of my six minus two for previous experience.

– How did you pay for it, Gesine? You show up there with five marks in your pocket. A dollar and twenty-five cents.

– Probably more like seventy-five cents. Student Cresspahl would've been fine working in the institution's kitchen; but that would have made the rounds among the fifteen hundred students; it wasn't done. So here's your version of the American hardworking-dishwasher story: Student Cresspahl standing behind the counter in a cloakroom in Mannheim at night saying Thank you for every dime someone left on her plate. Visitors from the school included Rhine maidens, heiresses from the great houses of Düsseldorf or South America, who even in their third year still thought it was funny to come out with Germanisms like "*yes, yes*" or "*I have it not necessary*" instead of "I don't need it." They complained to the management: indecorum. At a nightclub the glasses should be washed in public. Next came the night shift in a factory making toys and garden gnomes. And if a lecturer needed something typed or translated, just ask Cresspahl; she charges a bundle but what she turns out is ready to turn in. After that, she was in demand in the northern neighborhood of Frankfurt where the streets are named after writers—from Franz Kafka past Franz Werfel and Stefan Zweig to Platen—and the families of the American occupiers lived. They went out at night and left their children in the care of one Miss Cresspahl, paying her German money; she wanted to learn nursery rhymes and fairy tales from the children, and how you say, in American, "On your mark, get set, go!" In her last semester, when she felt sure of a diploma, it seemed justified to pay her for holding conversation classes.

– You were starving again, Gesine!

– It was my own fault; I needed a typewriter. I went hungry the scientific way, with yogurt and brown bread every two hours; with practice you can do it.

– And two cigarettes a day.

– No more smoking till after 1955.

– And you were homesick for Jerichow, for Gneez.

– I'd seen the 1953 May Day parade in Gneez. Armed People's Police marching past the stage on New Market, swinging their brown-uniformed limbs, wearing expensive boots (and holding tight to their rifle straps, to keep from falling); the comrade from the district office screamed, as if he had a knife to his throat: Today we still say Gee-Dee-Ääh, but next May we will be able to say Uuu-Gee-Dee-Ääh! A belated decoding of Goethe's remark that was on display at purely academic occasions on the front wall of the auditorium:

I HAVE NO FEAR THAT GERMANY WILL NOT SOMEDAY
BECOME ONE; OUR GOOD ROADS AND FUTURE RAILROADS
WILL DO THEIR PART, BUT ABOVE ALL LET IT BE ONE IN
OUR HEARTS...,

center-aligned. This was a declaration of civil war. I was supposed to want
that? Only armed force would bring about a Unified German Democratic
Republic. Student Lockenvitz had already commented on this, quoting
what he'd found in Voltaire about the Holy Roman Empire.

– That it's neither an empire nor Roman nor holy. I've done my homework.

– Homesick! You don't get it at all. At Gneez main station, one Alfred
Fretwust, prison warden under the Greater German Reich, had gotten
lifetime rights to the bicycle stand. So what if he'd turned a pair of soldier's
boots into credit in a Hamburg bank account, even during the war. So
what if he'd been in Bützow a couple times. In the time of the New Economic Policy he'd accepted payments for motorcycles in the Industrial
Products Government Store on Great Comrade Stalin Street—motorcycles
that were never, ever delivered. Now here he was again. When it was still
going well, he rented allotment garden sheds on Grosser Werder—to be
alone, to meet female friends. Never drank more than a shot of liquor an
hour during the day. At home every last plate licked clean as if by a cat;
family life in the kitchen; a stupefying naked Venus over the marital bed.
Insistently played the good middle-class citizen, which others were willing
to believe since he had enough money coming in. An informer. Only when
a drunk drunkenly called him a crook did it come to blows. Now here he
was again. Had to watch over the bike stand at the station. Thirty cents
per bike per day at most. And since he needed his sleep, of course, the wife
with all her pride actually did the work. Alfred Fretwust, prison warden,
free and clear, denazified at first go-round, unpunished—I'm supposed to
feel homesick for him?

– And yet you did go back, to see Jerichow.

– I did go north for a visit once, to the Holstein coast in the West, at
Whitsun, and in the slowly creeping line of day-trippers from the city I
could see the gray sea under an overcast sky, above the shining yellow of
the rapeseed in bloom and the rain-deepened green of the meadows, with
a remarkably straight line of land at the very end; in the evening, in the

harbor, the northernmost stretch of the Mecklenburg coast, blue with white patches, a hand's breadth, and next to it the sea turning inward at *Great Point* and *Lesser Point*, and behind that bay, more or less, was Jerichow. Past the coastal hedge at the edge of the land you could look over the bay, with the west side to the right and across from it, unconnected, the east side under the inky, wind-chased cloudy sky, irregular, with peaks like jutting bluffs, coves like harbors, needle-fine spires like steeples, cracks like lurking guard boats. When I close my eyes I can remember it perfectly. That same that different roaring.

– *When the oak blooms 'fore the ash, / summer rains come hard and fast. Y' know that, Gesine. But when the ash the oak precedes, / summer's warm and dry indeed, like in 1952. This afternoon I saw my big oak trees, they'll be green soon. The ash is standing there deaf and dumb! On May 1, we used to, now y' know I'm older than you Gesine, we used to take off our clogs an socks, there weren't no shoes 'cept on Sundays. We'd go cuttin thistles outta the rye barefoot. Nowadays I'd rather wear gloves. Back then the winter started in October and lasted till February, it did, and snow too! We walked to school on top of the hedgerows and when someone slipped off into the soft snow we were twice as far above him as we were tall. Now winter lasts a lot longer. On First a May the rye should be high enough to hide a crow! Nowadays you can see a mouse runnin through it! No. And we only have one hay harvest. Before, the first one was in early June, the second in early August, you call that the aftermath, we call it the rowen. Who still feeds with hay nowadays. I gotta say, the seasons've all shifted. 'Tsall the atomic bomb's fault. There's no summer anymore. Didja ever think! . . . Yer not sayin anythin, Gesine.*
– *Why do we see so clearly in Mecklenburg?*
– *'Ts cause a the humidity in the air. But the people over there, I mean your father, they got our afternoon's weather this morning.*

The Cresspahl cousin stayed only one night. Being so close when there was nothing I could do—it hurt.
– Nostalgia is a painful virtue, Gesine. *Daughters have human feelings too.*
– *Right.* I too was expendable. When the Maritime and Merchant City of Wismar wants to celebrate its seven-hundred-and-twenty-fifth birthday

in 1954, it can do so just fine without a visitor from Je—, from the Rhineland near the Main. The commemorative publication reaches her because her father sends one: a thick volume on glossy paper with a lot of corrected history, and notices from the government stores praising the New Courses, and the saying, which they call Mecklenburg folk wisdom, that when an old person is left in the lurch by the housing office his grandchildren will always take him in.

– In 1954 you turned...you became an adult, Gesine.

– Twenty-one years old. And Johnny Schlegel's attorney in West Berlin, acting on behalf of Dr. Werner Jansen, attorney at law, Gneez/Meckl., in accord with the last will and testament of Dr. Avenarius Kollmorgen, sent me a sealed package.

– And woe is you if you don't tell me what was in it!

– I'd be happy to.

– You better.

– It was two gold rings. "Upon reaching your majority, my dear Miss Cresspahl, the undersigned is permitted to lay at your feet." "Since, owing to the intervention of untoward circumstances, I myself." "For any marital connection, so long as it be one you have chosen, I offer my devout." There was a way of speaking that went to the grave with Kollmorgen.

– Wedding rings! From the grave!

– They're...for you. Yours.

– Like I'm ever going to get married, Gesine!

– That's what we said about me too. Don't forget.

– So, no plans to return to Jerichow or Halle on the Saale.

– The radio took care of that. "The Soviet Union has invented penicillin." One time an announcer said a song title with a sigh: "'*An* American in Paris'—oh, if only!" So taken with his own agitprop brilliance that he didn't realize the obvious comeback: how desirable it would be to have only *a* single Soviet in the East German republic, on vacation in Ahlbeck by the Baltic. It's as if they hoped to win over the airwaves! As if they thought they could divide the sky.

– Which party did you support in Western Germany, Gesine? You could vote now.

– In 1954 the Social Democrats, at a party congress in Berlin!, declared their willingness "to participate under certain conditions in joint efforts to safeguard peace and defend freedom, including by means of military action."

– Now if I know you, that threw cold water on the Socialists as far as you were concerned.

– Look at that, you do know me. The president of the country was a member of the Free Democratic Party who in 1933 had helped prop up Hitler with the Enabling Act that finished off the Weimar Republic. Now he was telling his citizens about *Vergangenheitsbewältigung*—that they had to overcome or work through the past—and since this wasn't an act of labor or a material object—

– *To accomplish. To master.*

– the only verbs left were "to prevail over," "to subjugate." All while he avoided any public "working through" where his own personal past was concerned. The chancellor, meanwhile, was a Christian Democrat—what kind of expression is that!—and he had a little dog which was allowed to yap "Quite right!" in the Bundestag whenever the chancellor spoke of a "reestablishment of German unity in freedom," for example on the day of the June 17 uprising. Then, with his other hand, he drew his republic into the economic nexus of the European Coal and Steel Community and locked it into a military organization named after the North Atlantic. There was a national song about him, which premiered on May 16, 1950, in Munich.

– If only I wasn't so shy, Gesine.

– So what you're saying is that you're embarrassed for your mother on a half-empty ferry where you don't know a single tourist.

– Okay. If it's a sing-along I'll take the second part.

– *On your mark. Get set. GO!* "Oh my Papa / was a most amazing clown / Oh my papa / was a gray-ayt ahtist! / Oh my papa / was so splendid to look at …"

– Defamatory to the state! Punishable by law.

– It definitely was in East Germany. In the West, anyone who sang it with tears of devotion wouldn't know who they were praying for.

– Gesine. This was supposed to be your home country!

– Student Cresspahl tried to make it so, starting when she moved to Düsseldorf and had a job and was living in a furnished room near the Flingern North post office, with a widow who was the treasurer of her local Communist group and crabby about a tenant who'd left her party comrades in East Germany behind; no visits from men allowed. The disinherited child wasn't looking for any men anyway—she divided her evenings between the central pool on Green Street and the state library on Grabbe Square, where people were considerate toward a patron who wanted to see newspapers from the past, year by year, one after the other. Catching up on the time she'd missed since 1929. Reading, reading; like after an insidious disease. She thought of Düsseldorf as the end of her travels; tried to get used to the smooth, joined facades of the row houses. Kept change at the ready on November 10, for the children carrying lanterns for St. Martin; wished she weren't in town the next day, when the carnival started. Avoided the cartwheelers. Read up valiantly on Jan Wellem and Karl Immermann; started a collection, with the guidebook *Welcome to Your New Home*, with *Düsseldorf at the Turn of the Century*. Walked to Kaiserswerth; found a hint of Jerichow—a shed for unharnessing painted oxblood-red in a dilapidated garden behind an inn. In a pub, when she saw a master craftsman's certificate with a swastika in the official seal, she furtively stuck a postage stamp over it, but then again the stamp still showed the head of the man who'd betrayed his state and was now head of state in this country here.

D'you see that guy telling off the waiter? Runs a photo shop now. If we'd won the war he'd 'a been sitting pretty. Brought down sixty-four tanks, he did. One time he got ten with fourteen shells, broke open a whole flank. Knight's Cross, they gave 'im some land in Bohemia too. He just let 'em get closer and closer, using the ones he'd already taken down as cover. His turret gunner panicked—said it wasn't courage, he was just nuts. Nice guy, not conceited at all. You're so quiet, Miss Cresspahl, is something wrong?

I can't get a bite down with this kind of talk, even if I were hungry. Thanks for inviting me out. I have to go now.

Düsseldorf was a home once the name Cresspahl had a separate phone and a door to her own apartment she could lock. The allied British and American militaries, on whose behalf an employee in the woods outside Mönchengladbach was negotiating with local German officials over the assessment of and compensation for damages from maneuvers, wanted her safely housed and easily reachable. A simple converted attic—one big room with a small bedroom and kitchen, all the windows looking out at the sky. Düsseldorf-Bilk, that was my neighborhood, in pincers of rail noise from the streetcar lines and the tracks to Krefeld and Cologne. Near Old St. Mary's; every day a view of the memorial plaque to "THE BILK OBSERVA-TORY, DESTROYED ON THE NIGHT OF JUNE 11 TO 12, 1943"; center-aligned. In a building with brows over the windows and two balconies—truly like raised eyebrows. There were little parks, refreshment stands, you could stroll to the South Cemetery; a few blocks north was the city pool on Konkordia Street. Anything that was missing in the apartment when Jakob came to visit Düsseldorf he plastered on, screwed in, glued up, varnished over. For Jakob I splurged on a yellow silk blouse with a loosely hanging collar and long ribbons, even though I knew it was wasted on him—he looks me in the face.

– But before that you visited him in Jerichow!

– Who told you? . . . There's someone who's told stories about me, that I was on an official trip to Berlin and I broke the law on the East German stretch of the line and got off the train and snuck through the woods toward Jerichow. Well, since it's you, I'll admit it. It didn't work out well. I got myself into a situation that Jakob had been trying to protect me from. One Mr. Rohlfs, who wanted to talk to me about Jakob; he already had me in his files, from Gneez to Berlin-Grunewald to Mönchengladbach. I can't believe how completely we all trusted Jakob!

– How did my father like Düsseldorf, the West?

– He couldn't care less. He wanted to know if I was getting my eight hours of sleep every night; he walked me to my bus to work every day; he asked when was the last time I'd been to a dentist. He brought me a shawl from Mecklenburg! When I got home to Bilk, by Old St. Mary's, Jakob had roasted me sausages à la Jerichow—a man who can cook with blood and flour, raisins, marjoram, thyme, and apple slices, just so his Gesine can eat a meal like she remembers from back home! After he'd familiarized himself with the fine-food shops on Count Adolf Street in Düsseldorf there was no sign of envy. Okay, so the ten kinds of bread day in and day out, he wished that they had those in his country too, or rather the coun-try he'd come for a visit from. When we walked past a construction site and saw bricks being unloaded as gently as porcelain, wrapped in thick paper, tied six times over, he sighed. And yes, he grumbled about the railway in the Western republic running express trains with just one engineer. Or because the trains would start suddenly, smoothly, without warning. He was just visiting, there to see Cresspahl's daughter. There were some things he thought were funny. The jolly ol' lady who'd gotten fat sitting behind the cinema's ticket counter taking one last walk up and down the aisle before the feature presentation, with an atomizer, numbing the guests with bursts of scent. Humphrey Bogart in *The Desperate Hours* on a day like any other. The words people said to the tune of the North German Radio call sign: "Is the rá-dyo páid fór?" How two kids fought: A Persian lambskin coat's just sheep; You're a sheep, my mother has one. He was bothered, though he didn't show it except by a shudder in the shoulders, when he saw in an ad a character actor expelled from the East, turning a phone conversation into a chance to use and recommend an electric shaver, for filthy lucre. When Jakob recognized something in me that he knew from before, a smile would crinkle the corners of his eyes—like when I paid the bill without asking him at the Park Hotel on Cornelius Square in Düsseldorf, just as I had at Pottel & Broskowsky on Orphanage Ring in Halle; he was in my city, he was my guest.

– He could have stayed.

– The things we discussed for the following year, and the years to come through 1983—arrangements in the invisible, plans for a future—now they're all just stories like the ones where small children fall into a rain barrel; it hangs by the thread of a minute whether someone will come and save them.

– You know the drill, Gesine. Say it.

– He goes back east, across the Elbe; in the morning mist he crosses a railyard he's been in charge of for two years and a shunting train gets him; he dies under the knife. Cresspahl arranged the funeral. Only told Mrs. Abs and his daughter after Jakob was in the ground. That was good for one of the women, bad for the other. The first one missed her chance to kill herself—she wanted to tidy everything up first, put her house in order. That's how life arranges things so people will live. Later, by the time someone came along to prevent me from killing myself, I'd almost forgotten about it.

– Who can stop you from doing anything, Gesine!

– It was a very strong person. When I stuck my finger into her palm, she made a fist; she could dangle three feet in the air, holding on tight. A contented person, constantly sleeping, waking up with soft guttural sounds. Four weeks later, she looked at me like she trusted me. By the third month she knew my voice; returned the smile of a Communist widow in Flingern North. In October 1957, she listened to me, signaling agreement with her voice. On St. Martin's Day she turned her head toward where my voice was coming from. By Christmas she was looking in the same direction with both eyes. In the new year she starts to talk, going in for the usual: yeah, yeah, my, my; she looks sweetly, but distantly, at her grandmother. In February she laughed when a bottle fell over, even though it was hers. She's proud of her toys; she knows they're hers. In April she crawled under my apron when Cresspahl came into the room. In May she tried to stand on her own. In June she knew the way to the South Cemetery, to the Hofgarten; she threw toys out of bed to make her mother get them back. In July she could crawl up steps, stand up for a moment or two, knew her name.

– It almost sounds like you liked me.

– When it came to you, the difference between good and bad had been wiped out—that's why in North German mothers call their children: my heartbeat. *They're so dumb, these mothers, they've got their kid on their hip an they're shouting Where are you my little chickadee, where are you?!* We lived in a symbiosis, if you'd care to go look up that word; it's something we'll soon be putting a stop to. You got sick if I was even a little upset.

– You know the drill, Gesine. Say it only if you want to.

– In September, when we walked past our house with the raised eyebrows, the instruments were sharpened, the patient prepped. A trailer was on the curb, a yellow sign on the front fence. The next day wreckers knocked out the house's teeth; they carefully carried the doors and windows off to the side, the reusable material. Then they sawed through the house's bones, broke its spine, cut it apart from its neighbor—the neighbor played deaf. A red-and-white poster appears on all the doors next to the victim. At eleven a.m. the house suffers a blast wound and collapses into a heap, a pile so small you could hardly believe it. Beams are still sticking out, the remains of balcony railings. The dust tastes like an air war. Two Caterpillar power shovels pull up to clear the rubble, two conveyor belts. The cast-iron fence stays intact almost to the very end, until a single smash of the shovel breaks it and sweeps it away. A young tree gets tangled up in all this; a blow to the

roots and it's gone. The bared walls of the adjacent buildings look so unprotected, with their three sealed door openings, that they seem to be
shivering in the sun. Up in the shimmering air, that's where I lived with
Jakob.

– And so what did I get sick with?

– A fever. Almost 106°, the medicine couldn't fight it. You were unconscious for two days. When you woke up, there was Cresspahl again at your
bedside, watching his heir.

– You were in line ahead of me though.

– Jakob's child—she had priority. For a Marie, daughter of Jakob,
Cresspahl even broke the law. According to East German law, people were
to be arrested and sentenced if, in their letters abroad, Location 12 found
any complaints about the wisdom of the custodian—imagine what the law
threatened for private transactions in foreign currencies! But instead of
notifying the Gneez tax office or the East German post office about his
account at the Surrey Bank of Richmond, Cresspahl went to see a lawyer
on Lietzenburg Street in West Berlin, Inge Schlegel was another client,
and he drafted for him a letter in English. A postcard came to Jerichow
with Easter wishes from Anita; version for the censor; translation: a bank
is relieved to report from Richmond, England, *bankers have human feelings
too, believe you me!*, that one *Mr. Cresspahl* will admit to all those pounds
sterling that have been saved up and accruing compound interest since
1939, unfrozen three years ago and now at the disposal of former enemy
aliens. Cresspahl, almost sixty-nine years old, boarded a plane for the first
time in his life to bring a bank statement to Düsseldorf. That was half of
it. From Düsseldorf, Cresspahl traveled to that office in the forest outside
Mönchengladbach and made himself known by means of that *half penny*,
minted 1940, on the front was a jaunty galleon and on the back was
GEORGIVS VI and as many letters of DEI GRATIA OMNIUM REX ET
FIDEI DEFENSOR as the coin had room for. Faith and loyalty were given
their reward; Cresspahl received his thirty shillings. That was the other
half. Cresspahl, citizen of East Germany, in a will drawn up in Düsseldorf,
packed two big piles of pounds sterling into a box made of rods of the law
that neither you nor I can break into; if needed a legal guardian with tes-
tamentary authority could.

– So who is my legal guardian, besides you?

– Just me for now I'm afraid.

– I want it to be your Erichson.

– He... he has enough problems at the moment; would Anita be all right?

– Maybe, after I've talked it over with D. E.; maybe. Was I hostile to my grandfather?

– At first his black overcoat from 1932 scared you; but then you liked the velvet lapels. Before long you thought it was funny to copy us; you'd sit down across from us, cross your legs, fold your hands, and look resigned, head hanging like you were sad. Cresspahl was upset that how he looked had saddened a child; he held out his hand to you, a big hard carpenter's claw, and you punched it with your cat-paw fist. You went to sleep without fear when he told you stories about once upon a time when the devil was still a young lad who had to go fetch kümmel for his grandmother.

– And my own grandmother? Who I'm named after?

– Mrs. Abs was now afraid of a Jerichow where someone like Mr. Rohlfs with a Stasi badge might take her aside and start asking questions about one Gesine Cresspahl—she stayed in Hanover. We invited her to come live in Düsseldorf; she only came for visits. So by day you were brought up in a kindergarten, not by a grandmother. She would look at you, Jakob's child, and the tears would come to her eyes. She was worried her grief might be bad for you. Wanted to live alone and die alone. She was buried behind the palace in Hanover.

– Why don't I remember?

– Because it was kept from you.

– Why did Cresspahl go back to Jerichow? He could have stayed with us.

– *When it comes to dying we're all masters and apprentices.* He wanted to take care of that alone. Just not be a burden to anyone, even his own daughter. He kept his promise: he took Joche and Muschi Altmann into the two rooms that had been managed by the German Reich Railway for Jakob. There was no danger

Fer me to be sittin here dead and none to see me

ol' people can see farthest ahead.

– Am I going to be a rich woman when I turn twenty-one?

– It'll be enough for five years of college.

– Still, Gesine. You could've used it when you needed it.

– It would have been three times more than I needed. Anyway, he did give me something from it: for the child. A child who'd been thrown back into sublet rooms because commerce in the West German city centers was smashing to bits anything the bombs had left standing; how could a grandfather stand to see that! He furnished a garden apartment on Lohaus Dike—for the child. Paid the rent for a year, so that her mother could start another course of study, this time for banking—for the child.

– He should've given you a car.

– I paid for that myself, once you'd learned to talk; I was happier about it that way. From a big dealer who advertised his chariots with the sign of a hand (secondhand). You had to have a car. Hard for you to understand today.

– We took trips to Denmark.

– You spoke Italian as a small child, and French.

– But never went to England. For your father.

– I would tell you what stopped me, if I knew.

– The trips to London with D. E. cured you?

– *Thanks, Doc.*

– Now there's something I have to say to you. Something serious. Düsseldorf had become your city, like Berlin for Anita.

– And like the Niebuhrs feel about Stuttgart.

– When you want a treat, you go eat in the Düsseldorf Central Station restaurant. When a bridge is dedicated in Düsseldorf and named after a president of the federal republic, you grumble about the old man and go see it. It's your bridge. Heinrich Heine's praise of Düsseldorf—you couldn't agree more. You're ashamed for this city when it disavows that same Heine. And suddenly you're up and off to America with a defenseless child under your arm! Gesine!

– It wasn't Gesine, it was Employee Cresspahl. When a bank "on friendly terms with us" offered her two years of advanced training in Brooklyn, New York, she had to act thrilled and grateful. Deference pays—maybe she wouldn't be fired quite so soon. For propriety's sake she demurred just a little; secretly she was relieved.

– You've let me believe to this day that New York was my decision!

– It was your plan, at least the general outline. Crédit Lyonnais or some firm in Milan would've been all the same to me. I wanted to get out of that country for a while. In 1959, in Cologne—just around the corner—a synagogue had been defaced with swastikas and slogans: GERMANS WANT JEWS OUT. Dora Semig had put in an application concerning her husband and they ordered him to report to the Hamburg municipal court by September 2, 1960; if he failed to do so he would be declared dead. That was one thing.

– That would've been enough for me.

– The other thing was the career of a certain West German politician. This is going to be boring, Marie.

– Well, just so I can never say you haven't told me, on board a South Ferry in fact, in New York Harbor, afternoon, direction Manhattan.

– All right, grin and bear it. As a young man he was in the Nazi student organization. When he was twenty-two he applied to their Motor Corps, fulfilling the prerequisite: politically reliable and prepared to burrow ever deeper into the National Socialist mindset. In the war he was an "Officer for Militaristically Inspired Leadership" at an antiaircraft school in Bavaria; prerequisite: National Socialist activism. After the war he said he was in the resistance; he was in charge of the denazification proceedings in Schongau, where he was the district commissioner. At a public gathering in 1949, he shouted: "Anyone still willing to take gun in hand, let his hand wither!" Starting in 1957 he denied he ever said that. By then he was the West German Minister of Defense. In April 1957, when eighteen scientists from Göttingen University warned against equipping the German Army with nuclear weapons, he called one of them an "ivory-tower professor"; he himself is a high-school graduate. In the capital's press club he described the Professor of Physics and Nobel Prize Winner Otto Hahn as "an old fool who can't hold back tears and can't sleep at night when he thinks about Hiroshima." In June 1957, fifteen recruits drowned in the Iller at a training exercise that they hadn't been properly prepared for; the minister responsible, rather than resigning, celebrated his wedding the next day, ordering up a platoon of MPs—practically wartime-strength, with steel helmets and white leather gear—as an escort. Didn't go to the ceremony for the victims. That same year, he came out with this pronouncement: he was not a conscientious objector, but nevertheless was no coward. The following year, he provided the West German republic with a national hero: On April 29, 1958, a traffic cop named Siegfried Hahlbohm was on duty at an intersection outside the federal chancellery in Bonn when the minister's vehicle of state crossed it, ignoring the policeman's hand signal and forcing a streetcar to brake abruptly. Hahlbohm reported the minister's driver (who already had five previous offenses) for four traffic violations and two criminal infractions: Causing a Traffic Hazard. The minister vows to remove this officer from the intersection; when his efforts become public, he calls it "a betrayal of state secrets." In October 1959 there was a meeting of "organized bearers of the Knight's Cross" in Regensburg; the minister sends along three army officers with salutes and music and his regards. In 1961 he smeared a political opponent, who'd had to emigrate during the war, by saying: "But there is one question we can surely ask of you: What did *you* do during the twelve years on the outside? The same way people ask us: What did you do during the twelve years on the inside?" I read that when I was already in New York, relieved to be out of Mr. Minister's reach. The next year, he provides his officers with a "full dress suit" featuring an ornamental lanyard, known in Hitler's time as a "monkey swing"; he prescribes for the other ranks a belt with a buckle that says: Unity and Law and Freedom. After that, he tried to destroy—with denunciations, with lies—a West German news magazine whose editors had conscientiously investigated his financial dealings and official conduct. He knowingly lies to the West German Bundestag: "This was not revenge on my part. I had nothing to do with the whole affair. In the truest sense of the word: not one thing!" After that, he had to step down from the government for a bit; in 1966 a West German government again found him good enough to be a Minister of Finance. He can't get a hunting license without shenanigans and dirty tricks. He wants to be chancellor of West Germany with his finger on the nuclear button; what they say about him in the Bundestag is that: Anyone who talks like the Federal Minister of Defense would shoot, too.

  – That's just rude, Gesine.
  – If I were ever tempted to feel homesick for West German politics, I'd just hang up a picture of him.
  – He doesn't get a name?
  – He deserves the name he's made for himself.

– And so now we're in March 1961, on our way to NYC. New, York, City!

– Since Employee Cresspahl showed herself to be duly compliant, she got four weeks' vacation first. We spent it in Berlin with Anita.

– Where you have to watch what you say! If you try to buy a superlong sausage, they'll ask you if you're feeding a big family. I was so proud of my mother when she shot back: Nope, I'm founding a hermitage! Berlin, city of airplanes.

– Airplanes above the rattling skylight. Fitting into the gaps left by ruins, skimming roofs, adding to the church tower, skyscraper, rain. In parks, stadiums, gardens, on streets and balconies, everywhere there were planes looking down, veering off, sending in others. Invisibly high but far-seeing, the jet fighters of the Red Army, the Beautiful Army, the *Krasnaya Armiya* squeezed through the sound barrier and threw off that punching, booming, breath-stopping blast of sound. When we took off for Paris, we saw Anita down on her abandoned balcony, waving.

– And now, all aboard the *France*, for New York!

– Still, I know a certain child who for a long time could draw how the furniture was arranged by the garden windows in Düsseldorf. Who was almost in tears when she thought back to a birthday party where everyone sang in chorus: Now you are three! Now you are three!

– But I turned four in New York. We've finally gotten to what I remember. *Welcome home!*

August 18, 1968 Sunday

Cresspahl's daughter was living in New York when Cresspahl died in the fall of 1962. America is too far away for me to imagine. *Sevenny-four years's long enough.*

He tried to fall asleep on his back. He wanted to be found close enough to morning; he wanted to spare them any trouble with a stiff corpse that hadn't lain down in bed the way it would lie in the coffin. They used to break bones in such cases, before. But he turned to the side, even if only his head, as he went to sleep. In the morning, as the night thinned out in his brain, his head turned his nose straight up. He already felt himself being carried out, tipped over slightly in the narrow door to the room, then finally out in the cool winter sunlight striped by the bare hedgerows. The jolting on the pavement sent gentle waves of blood surging up behind his brow as he heard Prüss the medical officer say: In cases like this it's hard to say how long you have to live.

This morning the sleeping daughter once again saw herself stand up, swing hand over hand out the window and onto Riverside Drive, down the green-patinaed pier of the bridge to the street below. Following doctor's orders she was wearing only a coat over her nightgown. Pulled the car door shut behind her, quiet as a thief; let the wheels roll eastward to the entrance to the passageway under Broadway that in waking hours the subway crosses. By now she was escorted by black-lacquered carriages—trapped. The trip went as if on rails; all she had to do was press the dead man's switch. When she arrived under the cemeteries she found a circular, concrete-lined cave hollowed out for her and divided by hospital doors. Behind the first of these doors was the clothes closet; she was supposed to change here for the operation. The doors reappeared along the inner arc of the hallway; these were labeled Heart, Lungs, Kidneys, Blood. At the last door she was handed a small package: the remains of the autopsy.

Let's start the day over.

At five a.m., the radio station WNBC plays popular works by Mozart and Haydn. At six, WNYC follows with Brahms's *Requiem* and Schubert.

A weekend day. No work. Marie wants to throw a children's party, to say goodbye.

August 19, 1968 Monday

The New York Times, number 40,385.

News from Bogotá, Jerusalem, Iraq, Cairo, La Paz, Peking, Biafra, London. Who would question its comprehensiveness? Yesterday morning, gunshots were fired at a Long Island Rail Road commuter train; one young man dead, another wounded.

Pravda has hinted at what it wants readers in Moscow to accept as the truth: If workers in Prague have beseeched the Soviet troops to stay longer in their country, that is because they are being subjected to "moral terror." On every Prague street corner there are agitators and gathering demonstrators, all "subversive activities by anti-Socialist forces." Just to clarify things, yes?

About the chancellor of West Germany, that mild-mannered usherette the *Times* today sees fit to report that: he went boating on Starnberg Lake and saved a dachshund from drowning.

In South Vietnam, northern forces and their guerrilla allies attacked in nineteen places. American forces, under machine-gun fire, allegedly lost only ten men, ascribing five hundred casualties to the other side. These round numbers.

Tonight at six, radio station WNRV brings us "Just Jazz" with Ed Beach. We'd wanted to record it, but we've already missed it.

When we were on our way to the U.S. of A., it'd been just five years in April since a staff sergeant of the marines (one beer and three shots of booze in his belly) had led a party of inexperienced recruits into the tidal wetlands of South Carolina where six were drowned. MPs stood guard over the flag-draped coffins as if the men had died for their country.

That's why Marie, just last year, thought we had a duty to buy every single record by Pete Seeger: because he'd sung about the incident: "But the big fool said to push on!"

When we got here America had fewer than a thousand advisers in South Vietnam. The new president, J. F. Kennedy, increased their number to three thousand in 1961, ten thousand in 1962. Always these round numbers. In 1964 the commanding officers of the destroyers *Maddox* and *Turner Joy* claimed to have come under fire from the coast of North Vietnam while in the Gulf of Tonkin; they could report no damage; in August the new president, Lyndon B. Johnson, was given free hand by Congress. The Marines landed in 1965, without a declaration of war but bringing the number of Americans in Vietnam to a hundred and forty-eight thousand. Local guerrillas killed eight Americans on February 7, 1965; the bombing of North Vietnam began and, starting in April 1966, was carried out by eight-engine B-52 bombers. The Soviets didn't move. 1967 saw the start of the chemical defoliation of Vietnam's forests. All the better to bomb you with. One air force general whom the Americans number among their allies calls Adolf Hitler his political role model. After the Communists' Tet Offensive in March 1968, an American president acknowledged his mistakes; LBJ announced he would not run for reelection. His successor might be Nixon, a Tricky Dickie, nix on him; he announced as his 1968 slogan that instead of negotiating for an American defeat we should be negotiating "how we can push even harder for a victory." The awareness of being implicated, not far from guilt, that weighed on our shoulders through the dirty Algerian War of the French, 1954 to 1962, is back—it's just a different war this time.

What was the first piece of foreign policy the USA offered its guests the Cresspahls? They'd only been here two weeks when troops, with President Kennedy's approval, attacked Cuba's Bay of Pigs.

That summer, the party that is always right walled in the city of Berlin and put up a fence around its citizens. The initial fear: had there been deaths. – None on the first day: Anita said into the phone: maybe in the next few years.

In December, Employee Cresspahl, dragged at high-speed under Manhattan and the East River for two half-hours a day, lost her job in Brooklyn. She had happened to be walking by the branch's information counter and tried to be nice and help an elderly customer—a woman who was trying to look American and who spoke with a German accent. Saxony. East.

German bonds issued in dollars? We do have those.
Could it be something from Saxony?
We have municipal bonds from Dresden and Leipzig, from 1925 and 1926, each paying 7 percent, maturing in 1945 and 1947.
I got a tip that you can get those for a song.
You have been informed correctly, ma'am. That's because they're excluded from the 1952 London Agreement on German External Debts. It's by no means certain when they might be guaranteed.
So you'd advise me against it, Miss . . . Crespel?
Whoever gave you that tip is not exactly your friend, ma'am.

The reproof from management: Miss Cresspahl, we pay you to *sell* securities! Here's your notice. If you're so good at giving investment advice, go open your own broker's office, don't screw us out of a commission!

Starting in January, the unemployed Miss Cresspahl, with a four-year-old child as an adviser, blew through her savings traveling from the Atlantic Coast to the brown beaches of Oregon and had no one to discuss her troubles with but the talking road:

Stay on the Sidewalk
Prepare to Stop
Slow Traffic: Keep Right
Be Patient: Passing Lane Just Ahead
Center Lane for Left Turns Only
No Passing
No Parking
CORVALLIS, pop. 38,400
Please Drive Carefully (We Need Everybody)
This Lane for Passing Only
Railroad Crossing
R x R
NO XING
Falling Rocks
Trucks Entering
Right Lane Must Exit
Soft Shoulder
Thank You
Thank You

and she often felt like the pigtailed girl on the sign who's leading a smaller child by the hand across an implied road with zebra stripes. Children, children!

Then Anita turned up with her illegal propositions. Anita paid the expenses. Gesine was a tourist with an American passport, in Prague, asking the way to Wilson station, long since renamed Střed. A tourist with French papers trying to exchange Czech crowns at Berlin-East station.

Now that our widely revered Vice President de Rosny has entrusted his subordinate Cresspahl with the transfer of a few million into the Czechoslovakian national budget, he's admitted to her why he gave her a job despite her prior record: because she admitted her offense. Or because of the nature of it.

A job in data entry. Nobody heard one word more from this "coworker" than was necessary to be polite. Employed and under observation since 1962. Found suitable in 1967.

In 1962 one Prof. Dr. Dr. D. Erichson found us and proposed marriage after he'd gotten to know Marie; was given, for the time being, the name D. E. because Marie liked the tiny hiccup between the American D and E sounds. Dee-ee. Later she realized she'd meant: Dear Erichson.

In 1963 I was still from somewhere else. Capable of a laugh when I saw an office building, steel and glass and concrete, and its name was inscribed on it in lavish aluminum and that name was U.S. Plywood Building. And if my translation of a gold phrase on a green delivery van was correct, it said: Theatrical Moves—Our Specialty. My throat still tickling with laughter, I stepped into an elevator with thirteen men and saw them all doff their hats. Such things happen in the beginning—or what I thought of as the beginning.

I felt secure: I'd been to the Social Security Administration. Down on Broadway, between restaurants and stores, a startlingly businesslike entrance with two brass door handles. On the second floor a room as large as a baseball diamond, with no partitions. Closest to the elevators, little groups of chairs to wait on. Then a desk, ceaselessly asking via posted notice: May I help you? On a pillar, the photograph of the president, framed in black as if he were dead; matted under the photo in the same frame, the signature that the Soviet prime minister respects. Along the wall, writing surfaces as narrow as the ones in German post offices. The file card wanted to know the name the applicant "goes by," as well as the one acquired at birth. I hereby declare under oath that I have never applied for a *social security number* before. Necessity is the mother of deception.

When the old-fashioned printed card came from Jerichow, Meckl., in the fall of 1962, I lingered in the bar of the Hotel Marseilles. The ladies there were all in tweed and adorned with the accessories recommended on the women's pages of the news magazines, but they were waiting for the husbands who paid for that lifestyle, while I was waiting for Marie and paying for myself. The men were smiling. One, with his glasses pushed up on his nasal cartilage, busy with the paper, with the stock market pages, like it was a Book of the Times—this absentminded professor asked about George.

– They nabbed him in Brooklyn.

– But he lives in the Bronx.

– For knowing all sorts of inside information about the "weather." What'll it be?

– The same. Nah, probably not. Something similar.

– What I gave you?

– You're the better doctor.

– Here's your Ballantine's. Came here all the way from New Jersey.

That was like a permission to watch other people living, even if it seemed impossible to go on with one's own life. Then a parched-looking beanpole stepped up to the bar with frantic gestures and needed to know:

– Where can I get some water!?

– If you can't find it anywhere else, then right here. Sir.

– Gimme a glass of water.

– Free of charge: Mr. McIntyre said, indicating with a private pursing of the lips that there are some rude dirty dogs too old to learn new tricks. McIntyre, shaking the last drops from a bottle into a customer's glass like a sacrifice, a gift, a holy offering. McIntyre, whom they'd recently unexpectedly sent to an island, dressed in easily visible clothes, so that he couldn't tell stories from behind the shelter of a bar for a while—things that only the FBI claims the right to know.

In 1963, D. E. for the first time ventured to suggest: that I try to enjoy life. I went along. And I found it hard to break the habit of Mr. McIntyre's company. These were conversations that were worth it: McIntyre took on a teacher's responsibilities, always with an apology, and told me how English words were pronounced in America, that here a "public holiday" meant a legal one and a "proposition" was just a suggestion, not, as in England, a suggestion and a deal and a case and a consideration and an alternative and a plan and a sentence and a declaration. All this among taciturn men who'd likewise found the day's events unsatisfactory and who expressed their wishes so monosyllabically that Mr. McIntyre assumed an air of mock defensiveness. One of them, annoyed by the ice cube in his glass, dropped it into McIntyre's hand like a tip; he said: Just what I've always wanted. And I told myself that I was enjoying life, because in ten minutes the kindergarten bus was due to arrive and the bellboy would announce Marie's name and she'd walk into the bar, looking at us with a serious and friendly look like Jakob, but speaking a natural American English that by this point a certain someone would ask Marie to produce for her. Then we would walk hand in hand down the sloping street to Riverside Park, and I thought that just being alive was enough.

In 1964 the business of being homesick for New York while still in New York started. The sounds alone: they insisted that I admit it, I felt alive. Even though the big red fire engines were heading into danger, after all, rushing by as if already too late amid the throng of cars down below them idling in place; even though the firemen's helmets and coats, black and striped with yellow, were still stained from the old days when misfortune had been unpreventable and fires were like the plague; even though the mighty wail of the siren, lurching back and forth every second, and the animalistic roar of the horn resounded with the old fear; even though the expert at the back of all that efficient technology steered the overlong vehicle out of its spot so casually that it seemed like he'd accept an accident with a sportsmanly shrug.

In July 1964 a policeman, more than six feet tall and over 220 pounds, shot and killed a skinny black kid who, with some others, had been harassing a pink-skinned fellow American by throwing bottles and trashcan lids. The people of Harlem fought for four days and three nights, with cocktails à la Molotov, bricks, looting, and arson, against New York's boys in blue with their riot gear, billy clubs, guns, and tear gas. For weeks afterward, a German woman carried her passport around the city with her to prove she was a foreigner.

In 1965, in March, the American military started dropping incendiary bombs over Vietnam. Napalm.

In a bank in New York City, a foreign-language secretary's office was supplied with a removable plastic nameplate outside the door on the left, and it said: MRS. CRESSPAHL.

On November 9 at 5:28 p.m., when the lights went out in the northeastern United States, the residents of New York City were concerned. One woman from abroad, who had tried to worm her way into a new homeland's favor by studying its history, brought up August 1959, when electric power had gone out for thirteen hours in the area between the Hudson and East Rivers from 74th to 110th Street—this was part of the history of the Upper West Side, her neighborhood. She recalled June 1961: on the hottest day of the year the subways had stopped, elevators left hanging. Everyone has their own special story about the blackout of 1965: since Mrs. Cresspahl had managed to take the bank's emergency staircase down to the street and make her way from midtown to Riverside Drive on foot but was still expected to contribute a story, she described the conductor of the Wolverine Express diesel train in Grand Central Terminal who'd talked her into buying a sleeper ticket to Detroit for the night. She nods when someone explains the blackout as a computer failure in a key position in the network controlling the Niagara power plant; she emits grunts of skeptical assent when someone persists in suspecting a military exercise preparing for the coming civil war. She doesn't need to know everything; it's enough for her to have realized that night that she was alive. She returned to the candlelit windows overlooking the park, to Marie's silhouette, as to a home.

It was getting harder to say goodbye, even if those goodbyes led to vacations in Denmark, in Italy. One evening in 1966, in the Copter Club on the roof of the skyscraper that Pan Am has planted on Grand Central's shoulders, I was stunned by the quantity of haze through which a whirring-winged craft was to carry us to the airfield now called JFK. The lake in Central Park was a paler rag pickling in pallid brine. Two office slabs stood sentry, presumptuously clear and black and white, before the towerscape of buildings draped in fog. Park Avenue was visible up to Ninety-Sixth Street, you could see where the streetlights bordering the center strip stop, where the trains of the New Haven and Grand Central lines come up out of the tunnels. Trains would be safe on such a foggy day. The south brow of the Newsweek Building insistently proclaims in red: 77°; 7:27 p.m. By this time the helicopters were taking off every fifteen minutes, their flight numbers corresponding to the departure times. The rolling boil of the copter blades came out of nothing and after a while vanished back into nothing. Marie asked to look at our tickets, checking for the reservation back to the place we were about to leave.

In 1966 a man named James Shuldiner, thirty-one, tax adviser, first tried to strike up a conversation with a lady from Germany—in a smoky little restaurant, at a red-and-white checked tablecloth, in a cramped little pocket behind the passage between the drink bar and the food counter. *Everybody here lives on the verge of crime. And one crime leads to the next.* Once: he lectured: a society fosters hostile energy instead of transforming it (*police brutality, glorification of transgressions, violence against small nations*), murders like the ones in Chicago every day are only to be expected. (The next murder of the year was about to take place in Austin.) – On the other hand, these killings are setting a record it'll be hard to break! For a long time his Mrs. Cresspahl tried to keep secret from him that since 1961 she, too, had considered herself a student of New York City. Mr. Shuldiner felt she'd given him advice when he married a Jewish girl disgusted by the work nurses had to do in Switzerland. Now she's cooped up with her unclean skin in a sparkling clean apartment on Broadway with a grand piano and a guitar. Marie, to be polite, accepted a graham cracker from the skinny and arrogant Mrs. Shuldiner, who then snidely asked her if she was starved at home. James looked abashed, felt shame, regret. He gave us sidelong glances meant to solicit shared responsibility; we pretended we didn't see them.

Everyone in New York has their taxi-driver story; Mrs. Cresspahl has two on tap. The first driver, after admitting to her his Jewish descent, which she'd already gleaned from the ID card showing his face and license number, then told her he'd contracted a form of impotence from sexual intercourse with a German girl. Can't get erect, you understand what I'm saying, lady. Would you be willing to give me the only treatment on earth that might help?

The second was taking her to St. Luke's Hospital with Marie—a child who had something wrong with her knee, a 104° fever, terrible pain in the joint; in her distress she begged for help in German. As the mother carried her child up the hospital steps, trying in vain to cradle the hanging head in her elbow since the girl's braids were so close to trailing on the dirty sidewalk, the driver shouted after her: I hope your kid dies, you German pig!

In 1967, same as every year, a foreigner has to present her visa at the government office at the bottom of Broadway where they register resident aliens; every year the men there ask her what moves her to stay in NYC when she could also be living and making money *in that wonderful country, Germany*. They look incredulous, baffled, when the applicant informs them that if she had the choice between New York City, Düsseldorf, and Frankfurt, she would pick New York, but she wouldn't know what to decide between Düsseldorf and København. The compliment she was trying to pay the officers' homeland remained undetected. Since then she has taken to vaguely bringing up the exchange rate between "deutschmarks" and dollars; this gives her an air of prosperity and speeds up the process of renewing her permit. The expressions they'd have on their faces if she invoked a certain poet as her sworn witness, and sand-gray, the color of New York lions!

In 1968 we decided not to follow the law according to which we're supposed to take things slow and wait for events to take their course, await the gradual progress of history before dark-skinned people can live in friendship with pink-skinned neighbors: we plucked a girl named Francine out of a melee of stabbings, an ambulance, police. This little person with wide-set eyes sometimes appears in fuzzy morning dreams, tilting her head and weaving her stiff stubborn braids, and she says, both mocking and longing: "Yes ma'am, Yes ma'am"; when she leaves, she places a white kerchief fringed with lace over her dark gaze and dark head—the color of mourning. She may have died; she is lost.

In 1968, at the start of our eighth year here, I heard two dark-skinned men talking about me at the Ninety-Seventh Street bus stop. I wasn't trying to eavesdrop. When I eventually did start trying, and failing, to tell if it was English or Spanish they were speaking, I realized how far I was from the dream that I would ever understand this foreign language.

In 1968 came what for now is the last message from D. E., who liked the way we lived. That agreement about a birthday apartment for Marie on upper Riverside Drive will stay unsigned. D. E. had word sent that he's gone, an airplane has carried him off, to his death.

The air-freight ticket agents give us some backtalk. Two big suitcases, another one like a wardrobe, for Prague—a Communist country, whaddaya think yer doing, lady? The lists, the permits? – We're not diplomatic personnel, sir. The bill is going to a midtown bank. Do you see that green piece of printed paper under my hand? the hand I'd be happy to pick up if you want? So the shipment will be waiting for me at Ruzyně Airport tomorrow evening, yes? – Absolutely. Since it's for a lady like yourself. Have a good trip!

– You wouldn't be giving up your apartment, Mrs. Cresspahl?

– What crazy ideas you have, Mr. Robinson (Eagle-Eye).

– It's just, a boyfriend who takes his girlfriend . . . Someone saw you looking at apartments in Morningside Heights.

– Just visiting someone, Mr. Robinson. You can hear from the telephone ringing that we're planning to stay on Riverside Drive.

– My apologies, Mrs. Cresspahl. And you can be sure: no one else is going to break into this apartment!

– We'll see you a little later this year.

– Understood. Yes indeed, Mrs. Cresspahl.

– This is the operator.

– We haven't placed a call.

– You have recently called abroad several times, Berlin . . .

– Helsinki once.

– We're afraid there's a steep bill on its way.

– It'll get paid. That's no reason to disconnect our line.

– We were wondering if maybe it would be easier for you if you paid in installments, Mrs. Cresspahl?

– With customer service like yours, we'll definitely be staying with you.

– Our pleasure, Mrs. Cresspahl.

We arrive by subway under Times Square at the wrong time. Thick columns of people surge toward us out of the shuttles from Grand Central, diverted onto the three different staircases by the traffic police. – *All the way down. All the way down.* The authorities are acting paternalistic today. As soon as they see us, they clear the middle lane. – *Make room for the lady! Make room for the child!*

In Grand Central Terminal the streams of people flow through one another, formed of such well-aligned and coordinated movements that everyone is out of everyone else's way two steps in advance and gets where they're going faster than if they'd been trying to hurry. Three escalators run down from the Pan American extension—motionless terraces of people detach themselves with a jolt as they make the transition onto the walking surface, as if on ice. Straight lines swerve deliberately off toward the next destination—left and right to the commuter trains, a soft left to Lexington Avenue and the Lexington Avenue subways, a soft right to Madison Avenue and the hotels, straight ahead to Forty-Second and the tiny information rotunda. People flow in from Lexington Avenue through the double doors on countless thousands of feet, swim off beneath the low four-leaved domes, are replenished from the exits of the Graybar Building, rush dense and uncrowded at us beneath the barrel vault with the starry sky in gold, seemingly incised there. Under this high canopy we go in the wrong direction.

Waiting around the corner are the airport buses, elephantine bumble-bees. The tinted windows pull a curtain of shadow before the city. The ride will pass between the cemeteries, to a terrain where bushes and lawns are trying to turn an industrial zone into a park. We will wait till the very end; wait for the loudspeaker announcement that calls us back to New York. Until they say that this is the last and final call for passengers to board the airplane. *Passagererne bedes begive sig til udgang. Begeben Sie sich zum Ausgang. Please proceed to the gate now.*

August 20, 1968 Tuesday. Last and final. In a beach hotel on the Danish coast, across from Sweden. In a dining room for families: wicker furniture, linen tablecloths. In the garden, behind the bushes leading to the promenade. On the beach. From noon until four.

An eleven-year-old child, her voice soft with exhaustion, weary. A lady, around thirty-five, coming downstairs behind Marie, in happy anticipation because she'd been called to reception. Anita had promised Prague; Anita is more than capable of already being here to welcome us in Klampenborg.

The porter, the driver, the waitress; hotel staff.

– Thank you for waking us up on time. *De har vist mig en stor teneste.*

– *Ingen årsag!* There's a gentleman wishing to see you as soon you're ready.

The gentleman is out on the patio—shrunken but standing straight by force of will, dressed in formal black and white, with snow-white hair—arms raised, he delights in the welcome. A raven, trying to hide how moved he is.

– No! No! (This is what older people from Mecklenburg do.)

– Herr Kliefoth. Marie, say hello to my instructor in English and proper manners.

– *I'm very pleased to meet you, Dr. Kliefoth. My mother has told me stories about you.*

– I think it would be a good idea to avoid German. This country was occupied by the Germans once.

– *D'accord, mine leewe Fru Cresspahl.* I am here illegally as it is. Your friend Anita, she puts an eighty-two-year-old man on the train to Lübeck, sends an ID to Lübeck that will let him travel on to Copenhagen, and the Jerichow police *never know a thing.* But the name in the passport is Kliefoth, it's my picture—I could keep it, just like this.

Seen from the front Kliefoth's head is narrow; in profile, forgotten depths are visible once again. At the table he rests his head in his hands, making his glasses slip up a little higher, their top rim over his eyebrows. Now the dark pupils are exactly in the center.

– That you took all this trouble, Fru Cresspahl. A stopover in Copenhagen for the sake of a useless old man.

– We have Anita to thank for that. She didn't like the idea of our changing planes in Frankfurt. We do whatever Anita tells us to do.

– She booked me a room here for ten days. If it's all right with me!

– *Shes a good person, that Anita; we think so too.*

– Please. A lot of the time all that's missing are the onions. The same goes for what used to be called tropical fruit. It's only when one runs across an advertisement for a fish-smoking plant in a magazine from 1928, mentioning thousands of tons of smoked eel—*you start to wonder. Theres no smoked eel in Jerichow or Gneez.* No, the reason I'm looking forward to our meal is for company's sake; it'll *give us a chance to talk.*

– *Hvad ønsker herskabet?*

– Pickled herring. Mackerel in tomato sauce. Smoked eel with scrambled eggs—go ahead and laugh! And which wine ... *hvilken vin vil De anbefale os til det?*

– It's six thirty in the morning for us, Herr Kliefoth. In our school we're ranked by numbers. I'm number four in my class. What was my mother like in school?

– It is due more than anything to my being the oldest of the survivors. I have to go to the cemetery when I want to talk to anyone.

His eyes close with exhaustion. Reaching under the temples of his glasses he massages his own with the thumb and index finger of the same hand. The skin around his eyes is gray, heavily wrinkled, unmoving. Sitting there like a dead man—until he wakes himself up with those clambering fingers.

– What was said at my father's grave, Herr Kliefoth?

– Hokum. So I threw a wrench in it. *I wrote a P in front a it.* Now what would have happened if you hadn't liked the wine?

– I would have sent it back. I learned that from a person who...

– Now what makes you think of that, of all things! Jakob came to see me five times during the year after you left when he could no longer keep an eye on you. Came to read your letters, wanted to know what was going on at interpreters' school. Your father was a dependable, caring man, my dear young Miss Cresspahl.

– Herr Kliefoth, I'm only eleven. Please, call me Marie.

– Your mother, Marie, was about five foot four in May 1953. She wore her grayish black hair in a bob. Broad shoulders, narrow hips. When she was in Jerichow she liked to wear pants that would allow her bare legs to tan. Dark eyebrows, wary glances, thin lips—careful preparation for her adult face.

– What's it called in Jerichow when there's no wind like this?

– "Fine ladies' sailing weather," Fru Cresspahl. Present company excepted, of course.

A voice of jagged hoarseness, booming bass when relaxed.

– Herr Kliefoth, I dream about it sometimes. I'm on a Polish ship. It stops over in Liverpool then docks here in Copenhagen. Arrival in Rostock on the Old Channel, views through the Doberan Woods, Wismar or Gneez station. Or, if I'm not allowed Jerichow, Wendisch Burg. At worst Neustrelitz, Waren, Malchin, where no one knows us, where I can make enough money for an apartment with a view of a lake, a little dock for a boat, winter mornings on the ice, shadows of reeds, a fire in the stove... but Rohlfs is dead or never made it to major with his unconventional ways. We're only allowed to travel through Mecklenburg in transit; if we stop at a hotel it's under supervision; there's no way to choose where we want to stay.

– If only a person like myself might be a rich man someday, Fru Cresspahl. *I say this truly!*

The old man's pants are pulled up to his nipples. His threadbare clothing has been shortened every so often. We thought of cigars, of tobacco— we forgot about fabric for a suit.

– I've bequeathed my furniture to a museum in Rostock. If you were related to me, Fru Cresspahl, you could have gotten the table and the wardrobe—they are presents from your father, after all. I have an agreement with my landlord. In the event of my death he will keep the remaining furniture, but he has to arrange for my removal.

Kliefoth kneads his hands, thinking. The pain narrows his pupils.

– I cut myself once and put my foot in Jakob's hand while standing on the other foot. He looked at it, then let the foot slide down in the same rhythm as my hand on his shoulder; the movement passed through my whole body with no pain. I think that happens to someone only once in their life.

– *Må jeg bede om Deres pas? De er nok med Deres underskrift, resten ordner jeg.*

– *De er meget elskværdig.* You're very kind. *Hvor meget bliver det ialt? Det er til Dem.*

– My wife had a problem with her . . .

– I've had to tell Marie the essentials, Mr. Kliefoth.

– with her nursery. A woman like that has children flocking around her apron, in the kitchen, in the garden. Fundamentally there is only one thing we know about life: that whatever is subject to the law of becoming must perish according to that same law. I certainly shall, don't worry about that. My Latin has become wobbly; my memory is barely adequate these days. I can only be grateful to destiny for treating me so mercifully. And I thank you, my dear Fru Cresspahl. You've helped it.

– Herr Kliefoth, may you live as long you want to.

– Your father granted me the honor of his friendship. One of his opinions went like this: History is a rough draft.

– As for how we've been doing, we've written it down, up to starting our job in Prague—1,652 pages. We'd like to give them to you, if you don't mind. All that's left to add is the two-hour flight south. What could happen to us on a Československé aerolinie plane, ČSA, operating internationally under the letters O and K? We have a confirmed reservation, OK? We'll call you tonight from Prague.

– *Will you take good care of my friend, who is your mother and Mrs. Cresspahl?*

– I will, Herr Kliefoth, I promise. My mother and I, we're good friends.

As we walked by the sea we ended up in the water. Clattering gravel around our ankles. We held one another's hands: a child, a man on his way to the place where the dead are, and she, the child that I was.

[January 29, 1968, New York, NY–
April 17, 1983, Sheerness, Kent]

Translator's Acknowledgments

MY ENORMOUS thanks to Astrid Köhler and Robert Gillett, Patrick Wright, and Holger Helbig for giving so generously of their time and expertise in reviewing much of this translation; to the organizations listed on the copyright page; and to the many editors and copy editors at NYRB Classics. All remaining errors and stubborn decisions are, of course, my own. I would also like to acknowledge the earlier, partial translation by Leila Vennewitz (Parts 1–3) and Walter Arndt (Part 4) of a heavily abridged version of the original, published as *Anniversaries: From the Life of Gesine Cresspahl* in 1975 (Part 1 and half of Part 2) and 1987 (the rest of Part 2 through Part 4). I referred to it often and borrowed some of their many inspired solutions to difficult passages.